The Dead Witness

The Dead Witness

A Connoisseur's Collection of Victorian Detective Stories

Edited by Michael Sims

Walker & Company
NEW YORK

Published by Walker Publishing Company, Inc., New York
A Division of Bloomsbury Publishing

ISBN: 978-0-8027-7918-2

Typeset by Westchester Book Group
Printed in the U.S.A.

To the other four of the Five Investigators (circa 1970):
my brother, David Sims
and my cousins J. R. Yow, Greg Norris, and Ken Norris

Contents

Here is my lens. You know my methods.

—Sherlock Holmes

✳

Introduction: Prophets Looking Backward

by Michael Sims

WHEN I UNWRAPPED THE books, I found a whole new world. I was fifteen at Christmas 1973, when I received as a gift from my mother a book I had specially requested—had, in fact, insisted upon. It was William S. Baring-Gould's two fat, beautiful volumes of *The Annotated Sherlock Holmes*. When the oversize books arrived in the mail, the postman had to honk his car horn because he couldn't fit the package into our big mailbox out by the gravel road. The mailbox was my connection to the world. We lived in rural eastern Tennessee, without a car or a telephone, but somewhere I had learned about mail-order book clubs and read about these books—and decided that I must have them.

That Christmas night I sat up almost until dawn, savoring details about hansom cabs and dark lanterns and why Dr. Roylott's snake in "The Adventure of the Speckled Band" could not have been a snake. These volumes taught me that in every work of literature you can find an entire cosmos of history and biography. Victorian England unfolded out of Baring-Gould's pages like a pop-up book and later blossomed into my love for crime writers such as Arthur Conan Doyle, Grant Allen, and Catherine Louisa Pirkis, as well as their colleagues in the larger world of literature— Lewis Carroll and George Eliot, Charles Dickens and Robert Louis Stevenson. I found a window into history, which formerly I had considered opaque. I found escape from the confusions of adolescence. And I reveled in the kind of writing that William Dean Howells once disparaged as "a complicated plot, spiced with perils, surprises, and suspenses."

I kept exploring the field of Victorian detective stories, and the result, almost four decades after I opened *The Annotated Sherlock Holmes*, is *The Dead Witness*. Aiming to represent the vigor and charm of the Victorian detective story at its best, this anthology features works that were originally published between 1837 and 1915: numerous short stories, a couple of novel excerpts, a magazine profile, a newspaper article, and the transcript of a coroner's inquest. Investigators hail from England, Scotland, Australia, Canada, France, and the United States. You will find female and male detectives, police officers and private investigators, a Canadian half-native backwoods detective, a blind man, and a teenage boy—characters ranging the moral spectrum from Father Brown to Jack the Ripper.

IN THE LONG VIEW of history, detectives are a recent phenomenon. Crime is not. As archaeologists often demonstrate, deception, theft, and violence haunted society even before we left caves or invented agriculture. Consequently, because our imagination is as natural as our penchant for brutality, crime has flourished as a cultural theme from *Antigone* to *Law & Order*.

Many people think that Sherlock Holmes was among the earliest detectives in literature. In *The Dead Witness*, however, he doesn't appear chronologically until about halfway through, because he had numerous ancestors. Among the legion of villains and heroes in world literature are a handful of fascinating proto-detectives who waxed Sherlockian long before Loveday Brooke and November Joe and the other characters you will meet in this book. These figures insist upon the importance of justice and evidence in criminal cases—rather than accusation and torture—or demonstrate a rational approach to problem solving. They pay attention and theorize about what they observe. While the stories in this volume are adventurous, suspenseful, and sometimes amusing, the detectives in them behave in many ways like scientists, luxuriating in the act of reasoning while benefiting from its practical results.

The biblical Daniel seems to have been the first fictional detective. Aside from his roles as interpreter of dreams, tamer of lions, killer of dragons, and spouter of visions and prophecies, Daniel participates in a couple of thorny criminal cases. First he solves the earliest locked-room mystery on record, which is also an exposé of the follies of idol worship. King Cyrus the Persian asks Daniel, "Why do you not worship Bel?" and Daniel replies cheekily that he worships a living god, not an idol. Cyrus points out that every night Bel consumes a vast amount of wine and food, not to mention forty sheep, and must therefore be quite authentic. Daniel laughs and says, "Do not be deceived, O King; for this is but clay inside and brass outside, and it never ate or drank anything." Furious, Cyrus orders his priests to prove Bel's reality or die. They depart, telling the king to lay out the usual daily god food himself. The next morning it's gone, and Cyrus prepares to execute Daniel for blasphemy.

In the kind of scene that would later become standard in detective stories, Daniel stands among suspects and accusers and unravels the true story. In doing so he provides the reconfiguring of the narrative—the reshuffling of what the reader *thought* had happened into what *actually* happened—that is one of the great aesthetic pleasures of detective stories. The night before, Daniel had secretly covered the stone floor with a fine layer of ash. As the king and priests stand before him, he points down at the floor and explains. His ploy has recorded the nocturnal scurries of the villains, the footprints of the priests and their families, who have entered the sanctum through a secret entrance under a table. Cyrus executes them instead and applauds Daniel.

Another Daniel story, the sad, apocryphal tale of Susanna and the Elders, opens with the miscreants and their victim, like an episode of *Columbo*. Two judges lust after Susanna, the beautiful, young wife of a prominent elder named Joakim. Each hides in the palace garden, hoping to meet the nubile maiden secretly. Right on cue, Susanna decides to bathe in the pool—a scene that later provided endless opportunities for artists to portray female nudity with an ecclesiastical stamp of approval. The voyeuristic judges rush out and threaten to accuse her of adultery with another if she doesn't secretly commit it with them. "I am completely trapped," Susanna moans. "If I yield, it will be my death; if I refuse, I cannot escape your power." Yet she bravely refuses to submit. Instead she screams. But the men shout as well and run to open the garden gates, and as people rush in, the judges begin their glib lies, claiming to have witnessed Susanna fornicating. Predictably, she is condemned to die.

Daniel now provides the first courtroom reversal. He interviews the two alleged witnesses separately, finding that one claims Susanna was fornicating under a mastic tree, while the other says it was a holm tree. Clearly one is lying, because the mastic (pistachio) is much smaller, a mere shrub overshadowed by the evergreen holm. One tree could not be mistaken for the other. Thus Daniel is the first known literary figure to use physical evidence in a criminal case and also the first to cross-examine witnesses for discrepancies in their testimony.

More than two millennia passed before the next major proto-detective appeared in literature. In the 1740s, the French satirist and philosopher Voltaire published *Zadig, or, The Book of Fate*, a volume that was to prove influential in the history of literature, science, and fictional detectives. The title character is a Babylonian philosopher, but the vanity and injustice mocked by Voltaire are derived mostly from the author's daily life in eighteenth-century Europe. Like Candide, poor Zadig suffers a roller coaster of misfortunes, in a wildly adventurous story replete with love, war, politics, and philosophy. At one point even his devotion to science and observation gets him into trouble.

Zadig is walking outdoors when a royal eunuch runs up and demands, "Young man, have you seen the queen's dog?"

"A bitch, I think, not a dog," replies Zadig with the smugness of many detectives to come. "A very small spaniel who has lately had puppies; she limps with the left foreleg, and has very long ears."

Of course the eunuch wants to know which way the dog has gone, but Zadig insists he hasn't seen it and goes on his way. Then a horseman runs up and asks Zadig if he has seen the king's missing horse. Zadig replies, "A first-rate galloper, small-hoofed, five feet high; tail three feet and a half long; cheek pieces of the bit of twenty-three-karat gold; shoes silver?" The huntsman naturally exclaims, "Which way did he go?" but again Zadig explains that he hasn't even glimpsed the animal. Not surprisingly, he is hauled before the royal court and condemned to a labor camp. Then the dog and the horse are found. The court reluctantly nullifies its verdict but fines Zadig for lying.

Only then does Zadig explain himself. With the encyclopedic gaze of a textbook detective, he had seen a small dog's paw prints in the sand, showing faint streaks between them wherever the sand rose, indicating that it was a female with the pendant teats of a bitch with pups. Other brushings of the sand alongside the front-paw prints hinted that she had long ears, and a fainter imprint of one paw suggested lameness. Zadig also noticed the equidistant horseshoe tracks of a trained galloper and marks upon stone that told him its shoes were silver. He could discern where its tail had brushed to three and a half feet on each side in a narrow alley, and leaves had been knocked down from a height of five feet. The horse's gold bit had left marks on a stone. Like his descendant writers in the detective story genre, Voltaire did not hesitate to stack the deck on behalf of his protagonist.

NINE YEARS BEFORE VOLTAIRE died in 1778, Jean Léopold Nicolas Frédéric Cuvier was born in France. He would become one of the great zoologists, remembered now as Baron Cuvier. Surprisingly, he demonstrated that extinction had occurred—contrary to the static perfection of ecclesiastical nature—yet actively opposed the evolutionary ideas of Lamarck and others. Nowadays we honor him mostly for his pioneer work in comparative anatomy. Especially relevant to detective stories is Cuvier's theory of the correlation between various parts of animals—his realization that, because of their predictable interrelation, a single bone can tell an experienced scientist a great deal about the structure and behavior of the animal that once possessed it. This idea became the cornerstone of paleontology, and such similarities were part of what Darwin later reinterpreted as evidence of kinship.

"Today," wrote Cuvier in the early 1800s, "someone who sees the print of a cloven hoof can conclude that the animal which left the print was a ruminative one, and this conclusion is as certain as any that can be made in physics or moral philosophy." Then he evokes Voltaire's contribution to his thinking about scientific detective work: "This single track therefore tells the observer about the kind of teeth, the kind of jaws, the haunches, the shoulder, and the pelvis of the animal which has passed: it is more certain evidence than all of Zadig's clues." He was not speaking only of what would evolve into forensics. He was demonstrating that scientific work of this kind is a detecting process—observation, research, the pursuit of clues, the rejection of false clues, the weighing of evidence, its presentation before a critical group of peers—and by implication that detective work is a kind of science.

In 1841, inspired by Cuvier, Edgar Allan Poe had C. Auguste Dupin, his detective in the first full-fledged detective story, "The Murders in the Rue Morgue," seek enlightenment in a work of science. From this genesis story in the field, the detective is presented as a genius with a gift—not a professional, not really trained, but somehow far more astute than anyone else who might be looking into this mystery. Poe created the melancholy, erudite, nighttime-loving, eccentric Dupin out of Romantic Byronic types. In some ways Dupin is first cousin to Victor Frankenstein, but Poe added various interesting traits that would later show up in Conan Doyle. In the story, he hands a science volume to the narrator and says, "Read now this passage from Cuvier." (The story appears in this anthology; telling more about it would be unfair, in case you have the good fortune to have never read it before.) Dupin consults the great zoologist in part because they have similar methods—the construction of a full scene from a few pieces.

Most scholars proclaim "The Murders in the Rue Morgue" to be the first official detective story in the genre—the first account built around the investigative technique employed in deciphering clues and solving a crime. Yet, although it fully deserves its fame, it was preceded by an earlier tale, "The Secret Cell," published by William E. Burton in 1837, the year that Victoria became queen. In this action-packed story, the adventures of a detective identified only as L— include investigative legwork, disguises, and the trailing of suspects, all told with a lively sense of adventure and a good ear for dialogue. Prior to its inclusion in *The Dead Witness*, Burton's story has never been reprinted since its first appearance.

Curiously, a scientist gave a poetic name to what detectives such as Dupin do. In 1880, renowned biologist and educator Thomas H. Huxley (famously nicknamed "Darwin's bulldog" for his willingness to tackle any opponent of evolutionary science) carefully analyzed Voltaire's hero in an essay entitled "On the Method of Zadig," which bore the intriguing subtitle "Retrospective Prophecy as a Function of Science." Huxley argued that "the term prophecy as much applies to outspeaking as to foretelling." He went on to make parallels relevant to detective stories: "The foreteller asserts that, at some future time, a properly situated observer will witness certain events; the clairvoyant declares that, at this present time, certain things are to be witnessed a thousand miles away; the retrospective prophet (would that there were such a word as 'backteller'!) affirms that, so many hours or years ago, such and such things were to be seen." Huxley elegantly explained why such evidence-based observation was a threat to authoritarian regimes, in Voltaire's imaginary Babylon as well as in Huxley's everyday Victorian England.

SEVEN YEARS LATER, ARTHUR Conan Doyle published his first novel about Sherlock Holmes. *A Study in Scarlet* is a detective story wrapped around an adventure story; Holmes and Watson disappear for the central half of the book. But first we witness their initial meeting and their moving in together as roommates. It is a legendary moment in crime fiction. In the setting that has become even more a part of popular culture than Huck Finn's raft or Ahab's ship, the sitting room at Baker Street provided a stage for exhibitions of brainpower. Sherlock Holmes is a Romantic figure but also a modern one—the hero as thinker and observer, the man of action as man of science. "This agency stands flat-footed upon the ground," he declares later, "and there it must remain. The world is big enough for us. No ghosts need apply." Conan Doyle himself never quite committed to this extent, and the loss of his son and other loved ones lured him permanently into the darkened parlors of quack spiritualists. But his most famous creation remained adamant. Sherlock Holmes was interested in evidence and would find it through his own hybrid of observation and reasoning. Like scientists, who require experience in the field as well as familiarity with their specialized literature, Holmes is both a noticing machine and a walking archive of criminology. "It reminds me of the circumstances attendant upon the death of Van Jansen, in Utrecht, in the year '34," he says as he examines a corpse. When Inspector Gregson admits that he doesn't know the case, Holmes says, "There is nothing new under the sun. It has all been done before."

One morning early on, Watson mocks an anonymous magazine article entitled "The Book of Life," the author of which makes grand claims for the value of inferences from minute observation in deciphering the lives of others:

From a drop of water, a logician could infer the possibility of an Atlantic or a Niagara without having seen or heard of one or the other . . . Like all other arts, the Science of Deduction and Analysis is one which can only be acquired by long and patient study . . . By a man's finger-nails, by his coat-sleeve, by his boots, by his trouser-knees, by the callosities of his forefinger and thumb, by his expression, by his shirt-cuffs—by each of these things a man's calling is plainly revealed.

"What ineffable twaddle!" exclaims Watson. In reply, Holmes explains that he himself wrote the article, that he has "a turn both for observation and for deduction," one of his rare understatements. Later Holmes explicitly compares himself to an eminent naturalist. "As Cuvier could correctly describe a whole animal by the contemplation of a single bone," Holmes pontificates, "so the observer who has thoroughly understood one link in a series of incidents should be able to accurately state all the other ones, both before and after. We have not yet grasped the results which the reason alone can attain to."

Holmes's comparison between detective work and natural science was even more relevant than it seems. A man of science inspired the very creation of Sherlock Holmes. As a young Scottish medical student, Arthur Conan Doyle studied in Edinburgh under Dr. Joseph Bell and later worked as Bell's outpatient clerk at the Royal Infirmary. A colorful teacher with a quick eye for diagnosis, Bell taught classes that were as memorable as plays. Once a sunburned man walked into the examining room and Bell remarked confidently, "You are a soldier, a non-commissioned officer, and you have served in Bermuda." Then Bell explained his reasoning to the students around them: "He came into our room without taking his hat off, as he would go into an orderly room." Therefore he was a recently discharged soldier who had not yet learned civilian ways. "A slight authoritative air, combined with his age, shows he was an NCO. A slight rash on the forehead tells me he was in Bermuda, and subject to a certain rash known only there."

Decades later, Conan Doyle would recount anecdotes about Bell and add simply, "So I got the idea for Sherlock Holmes."

When Holmes and Watson first meet, Holmes says casually, "You have been in Afghanistan, I perceive." Later, after Watson challenges his confident assertions about observation, Holmes explains: "From long habit the train of thoughts ran so swiftly through my mind, that I arrived at the conclusion without being conscious of intermediate steps. There were such steps, however. The train of reasoning ran, 'Here is a gentleman of a medical type, but with the air of a military man. Clearly an army doctor, then. He has just come from the tropics, for his face is dark, and that is not the natural tint of his skin, for his wrists are fair. He has undergone hardship and sickness, as his haggard face says clearly. His left arm has been injured. He holds it in a stiff and unnatural manner. Where in the tropics could an English army doctor have seen much hardship and got his arm wounded? Clearly in Afghanistan.' The whole train of thought did not occupy a second."

As you will see in the pages ahead, in comparing the debuts of Auguste Dupin and Sherlock Holmes, Conan Doyle clearly borrowed a great many ideas from Poe—a brilliant but eccentric mastermind who mocks the official police, a narrator who serves as dogsbody and admiring sidekick, even the use of newspapers to lure suspects. Conan Doyle admired Poe, but he made Holmes dismissive of his literary predecessor when Watson remarks, "You remind me of Edgar Allan Poe's Dupin."

"No doubt you think you are complimenting me," replies Holmes, lighting his pipe thoughtfully. "Now, in my opinion, Dupin was a very inferior fellow. That trick of his of breaking in on his friends' thoughts with an apropos remark after a quarter of an hour's silence is really very showy and superficial. He had some analytical genius, no doubt; but he was by no means such a phenomenon as Poe appeared to imagine."

Soon Watson is thinking, "This fellow may be very clever, but he is certainly very conceited."

NOT ALL EARLY DETECTIVE stories featured a brilliant eccentric. Many protagonists were not only not geniuses but not even real detectives—perhaps an innocent victim of a conspiracy or someone otherwise caught up in a crime. This was the approach taken, for example, by English radical William Godwin (now remembered as much for being the husband of feminist Mary Wollstonecraft and the father of Mary Shelley, author of *Frankenstein*), in his 1794 novel *Things as They Are; or, The Adventures of Caleb Williams*. Edward Bulwer-Lytton took the same approach in his 1828 novel *Pelham; or, The Adventures of a Gentleman*. Legal shenanigans, atmospheric settings, menacing strangers, obscure clues, misleading circumstantial evidence—all the elements were there, minus only the unifying presence of a series detective as protagonist. Often, however, the stories were wrapped in a Gothic fog that distracted from the case and kept the books from reading like what we would think of as a detective story. Other writers came near the detective story—the German fabulist E. T. A. Hoffmann, for example, in "Mademoiselle de Scudéri"—but never quite crossed the Rubicon.

Other stories purported to be the memoirs of real-life investigators. In 1811 Frenchman Eugène François Vidocq, a criminal turned policeman, founded the Brigade de la Sûreté, a civil police and detective bureau, and two years later Napoléon Bonaparte turned it into a national police force. Vidocq's legendary adventures—going undercover in various colorful disguises, pursuing miscreants through slums, training agents who had also risen from criminal origins—appeared in his ghostwritten memoirs in 1828. Vidocq's secret-police activities and sometimes violent methods resulted in scandal, a reorganization of the Sûreté, and ultimately his own resignation. In 1833 he founded the first known private detective agency, which also provided security officers. Meanwhile the books about him had inspired authors such as Honoré de Balzac and Victor Hugo, both of whom wrote often about criminal activities, and would later serve as models for Émile Gaboriau in France and Anna Katharine Green in the United States.

While the notion of the detective as a kind of Romantic-era scientist was evolving in the popular press, real-life detective work—which originally bore little resemblance to its fictional representation—was progressing as well. In 1829, eight years before Victoria became queen, Sir Robert Peel succeeded in getting parliamentary approval for his proposed Metropolitan Police Act. He argued that a guarantee of arrest was a stronger crime preventive than severity of punishment should arrest ever actually occur. The new law created a metropolitan police force to supplant the corrupt and inefficient network of parish constables, watchmen, thief-takers, and Bow Street Runners.* The new officers were nicknamed *bobbies* in England and *peelers* in Ireland, where Peel had been secretary and had founded the Royal Irish Constabulary.

In the 1830s, when the uniformed bobbies hit the street, a new word appeared—*detective*. The English word *detect*, meaning to catch or discover someone in the act of committing a crime, dates from the first half of the fifteenth century in English, derived from the Latin *detectus*, the past participle of *detegere*, "to uncover." The new meaning described a new job. A centralized police force, charged with preventing and responding to crime, required a division assigned to solve crimes and hunt down their perpetrators—a detective bureau, including plainclothes detectives who could operate incognito. In 1842, after the public outcry over a scandalous case in London helped create a welcoming political atmosphere for it, Scotland Yard created the Criminal Investigation Department, comprising two inspectors and six sergeants.

---

*The Runners had been founded in 1749 by novelist Henry Fielding, author of *Tom Jones*. Fielding, who was also chief magistrate of London, directed the Runners out of his Bow Street office. Paid from allocated government funding, the Runners (only eight, originally) stood out from their predecessors and prepared the public for the idea of an organized metropolitan police.

The first officers to sign up for detective work included an enterprising young man named Charles Field, who soon rose to inspector. As you will discover herein, in my introduction to Charles Dickens's article "On Duty with Inspector Field," Dickens met and admired Field and soon wrote articles about him for his periodical *Household Words*, articles that helped promote in the public imagination the concept of vigilant police detectives. The word *detective* was still unfamiliar enough in 1850 for Dickens to wrap it in quotation marks in the title of the first article, but soon the term flourished in the thriving daily, weekly, and monthly periodicals. *The Dead Witness* includes other nonfictional glimpses of criminal investigation in the Victorian era. You will find one of the first newspaper accounts of, and a transcript from the coroner's inquest about, Jack the Ripper's first murder in 1888—before anyone had heard that chilling moniker, before anyone knew that this was only the first atrocity by a serial killer. The article and transcript reveal how familiar the Victorian public had become with real-life crime-solving. No wonder detective stories were becoming ever more sophisticated.

In another cross-pollination between fact and fiction, Inspector Field helped inspire the first important detective in a literary novel—Inspector Bucket, "a detective officer," in Dickens's 1852 novel *Bleak House*. Bucket materializes in a room without even a creak in the floorboards and seems to have an omniscient gaze: "he looks at Mr. Snagsby as if he were going to take his portrait." Some years later, Dickens's friend and colleague Wilkie Collins made a detective, Sergeant Cuff, one of the major characters in his popular 1868 novel *The Moonstone*. Following the style of the day, he indicated his detective's perception with a scientific gaze. His eyes, "of a steely light gray, had a very disconcerting trick, when they encountered your eyes, of looking as if they expected more from you than you were aware of yourself."

Collins was considered the king of the "sensation" writers. These authors included Mary Elizabeth Braddon, whose best-known book was the scandalous *Lady Audley's Secret*, and Ellen Wood (known then as Mrs. Henry Wood), the prolific author of *East Lynne* and the Johnny Ludlow stories. They were important contributors to the flourishing genre and helped establish themes that persist to this day, especially the mistakenly accused innocent and the labyrinths of family secrets. Such tales helped inspire what would come to be known in the early-twentieth century as the Had I But Known school of crime fiction—portentous retrospective tales by female narrators who had no interest in becoming detectives but were forced by circumstance to defend themselves. The narrator of Wilkie Collins's story "The Diary of Anne Rodway," which appears herein, is a pioneer example of this kind of story at its best.

Women were playing an important role beyond the sensation writers. The first significant female writer in the detective-story genre seems to have been a young Irishwoman named Mary Fortune. While living in Australia, in 1866, she published there her first story, "The Dead Witness; or, The Bush Waterhole." Narrated by a young policeman, it is a vivid and surprising adventure that reads like a hybrid between the Gothic dramas of the past and the rational detective stories that were soon to dominate the genre. Its pioneer position nominated it to play the title role in this anthology.

About the same time, an important innovator appeared across the Channel. Inspired by real-life policeman Vidocq, and by Balzac and Hugo, Frenchman Émile Gaboriau made his debut with *L'Affaire Lerouge,* usually referred to in English as *The Widow Lerouge* or *The Lerouge Case.* It introduced Monsieur Lecoq, who would appear in several subsequent novels. Lecoq was a detective who saw through crimes because, like his real-life inspiration, he had been a criminal himself. You will find Gaboriau represented in this anthology by a vivid, innovative story called "The Little Old Man of Batignolles," from his collection with the wonderful title *Other People's Money.* Another countryman influenced by Vidocq, Alexandre Dumas *père,* couldn't resist turning his famous musketeer d'Artagnan into a detective, in the last volume of his outings. This chapter is reproduced herein with a phrase from the text as title: "You Are Not Human, Monsieur d'Artagnan."

When a young American woman named Anna Katharine Green published her first novel in 1878, *The Leavenworth Case*, she deliberately violated expectations by making her detective, sardonic New York policeman Ebenezer Gryce, seem anything but energetic and observant. "Mr. Gryce, the detective, was not the thin, wiry individual with a shrewd eye that seems to plunge into the core of your being and pounce at once upon its hidden secret." His gaze never seems to rest on a person. "If it rested anywhere, it was always on some insignificant object in your vicinity, some vase, inkstand, book or button." Naturally, however, Gryce proves astute and indomitable.

Green was the first woman to write a full-fledged detective novel.★ *The Leavenworth Case* became a runaway bestseller in 1878 and was soon required reading at Yale's school of law because of its fascinating interpretation of circumstantial evidence. Green went on to write many more novels and dozens of stories. In 1897 she created her first female detective in the novel *That Affair Next Door*, introducing Amelia Butterworth, an upper-middle-class New Yorker who became the prototype of the aging spinster whose nosiness leads her to stumble across a crime. She was a direct influence on Agatha Christie and clearly the inspiration for Miss Marple, although Butterworth is a more convincing and nuanced creation. She appears in three novels that also feature Ebenezer Gryce. Green also created Violet Strange, a young New York socialite who secretly works as a detective; she can easily gain access to mansions and dinner parties to which no outsider could. Strange appears in the last story in this anthology, "An Intangible Clue."

★Some commentators credit an industrious hack named Seeley Regester, whose real name was Metta Victoria Fuller Victor, with the first detective novel by a woman, but Regester's 1867 novel *The Dead Letter* depends upon the psychic visions of the detective's young daughter—thus rejecting the underlying rational basis of detection—and is also poorly written in comparison with Green's work.

Amelia Butterworth and Violet Strange had many female colleagues in the business whose contribution to the genre has been forgotten or undervalued. These smart and courageous women include full-time professionals such as Loveday Brooke and Dorcas Dene, whom you will find herein. Unlike their male counterparts, many of the female detectives were provided with an excuse for their unladylike profession. Violet Strange is supporting a disinherited sister, and Dorcas Dene, a former actress, must work as a private detective because her artist husband has, in fine Victorian fashion, gone blind. Loveday Brooke, however, the unflappable protagonist that you will meet in C. L. Pirkis's 1897 story "The Murder at Troyte's Hill," is not presented as beautiful or supernaturally feminine, and she, unlike many of her colleagues, does not marry in the last installment. She remains a paid and respected private detective, the first female private investigator in fiction, and a character of Sherlockian insight and commitment to social justice.

When I get together with members of the Baker Street Irregulars or other fans of Victorian detective stories, many of us recall the pleasure we first experienced in the heroic teamwork of detectives such as Holmes and Watson or Dorcas Dene and Mr. Saxon. We talk about the narrative satisfactions in the genre, the opportunity to accompany characters who are intelligent and resourceful, even heroic. Conversation comes back to the triumph of rationality and virtue in a dark and violent world—the excitement and insight drawn from close observation, inferences from a cabman's boots and cigar ash, revelations from textures and artifacts and status symbols. In the pages ahead, Loveday Brooke infers her first glimmer of a theory from the arrangement of furniture in a room; November Joe reads stream currents and balsam boughs; blind Max Carrados listens and remembers. Dumas's swashbuckling D'Artagnan deciphers footprints and drops of blood, while Mark Twain's small-town lawyer Pudd'nhead Wilson becomes the first detective in literature to employ fingerprints to identify a villain.

We return to a favorite genre not only to revisit old friends but to renew a mood that we have found satisfying. Most genres are identified by the emotion they hope to evoke: mystery, love, horror, suspense. Detective stories, on the other hand, are about a certain kind of character. Paying such close attention to the physical world, the many detectives mentioned in this introduction remind us of cause and effect in this messy society, of the ripples that extend outward from our actions. I think that's why I sometimes find myself reading detective stories in the same mood in which I read natural history and science books. I know that if I climb the seventeen steps at 221B Baker Street on a cold night, I will find that Mrs. Hudson has built a roaring fire that glows like the light of reason to guard us from dangers that lurk in the fog. And nearby I will find Sherlock Holmes at his desk, peering with his scientist's eye into a magnifying glass as if it were a crystal ball—acting, as Thomas Huxley said, like a prophet looking not forward into the future but backward into the past.

The first essential value of the detective story lies in this, that it is the earliest and only form of popular literature in which is expressed some sense of the poetry of modern life. Men lived among mighty mountains and eternal forests for ages before they realized that they were poetical; it may reasonably be inferred that some of our descendants may see the chimney-pots as rich a purple as the mountain-peaks, and find the lamp-posts as old and natural as the trees. Of this realization of a great city itself as something wild and obvious the detective story is certainly the "Iliad."

—G. K. Chesterton,
"A Defence of Detective Stories," 1904

✴

William E. Burton

(1804–1860)

PRIOR TO ITS PUBLICATION in *The Dead Witness*, the following story has never been reprinted since its first appearance in 1837. "The Secret Cell" is wrapped in minor coincidences relevant to this anthology. It was published in the year that Victoria became queen; thus it perfectly opens a collection of Victorian detective stories. The narrator describes this case as having occurred eight years prior to publication of the story, which would have been 1829, the year that Sir Robert Peel established the metropolitan police in London. Its author, William E. Burton, was born in England but rose to fame in the newly minted United States, thus merging the two nations that would dominate the rise of the detective story as a nineteenth-century cultural phenomenon.

As discussed in the introduction, Edgar Allan Poe is almost universally acclaimed the inventor of the detective story, with the 1841 publication of his "Murders in the Rue Morgue." Although it is excellent, William Burton's story doesn't challenge Poe's preeminence. L——, the detective in "The Secret Cell," isn't the kind of eccentric genius, à la Dupin, that would ultimately capture the public imagination in the form of Sherlock Holmes. Realistic, flawed, hardworking but not brilliant, he is more of an ancestor to the "casebook" stories that would become popular three decades later—tales purporting to be based upon actual police cases. This story is clearly fiction, despite Burton's framing of it as reminiscence.

The son of an author and printer, William E. Burton was born in London in 1804. His father, author of books such as *Biblical Researches*, expected him to enter the ministry. The father died before the plan could be put into effect, however, leaving his eighteen-year-old son to make his way in the world on his own. Having worked as a printer and proofer in the family business, and as an editor after his father's death, Burton then tried his hand at acting. By the mid-1820s he was touring in the provinces and in 1831 first played London. "It may be said," noted an early biographer who had known Burton, "that his career was not free from the vicissitudes that frequently attend dramatic itinerancy." He was well known when he left England. In 1834 Burton arrived in Philadelphia and was soon starring in comedies at the Arch Street Theatre. He featured humorous ballads and performed in some of his own works. Burton went on to considerable acclaim as an actor, especially in comedies, and as a producer and theater manager, as well as attracting notice for his writings on Shakespeare and other topics.

In 1837 Burton founded his own periodical in Philadelphia, the *Gentleman's Magazine*. Two years later, he hired a brilliant but unstable thirty-year-old Baltimore writer named Edgar Allan Poe, who had already published "The Ms. Found in a Bottle" and "Ligeia" and other works. For not quite a year, Poe served as editor to Burton's publisher. His erratic behavior and growing unreliability locked horns with Burton's own volatile ways, and Burton fired him. (For more about Poe, see the next story, "The Murders in the Rue Morgue.") Shortly afterward, Burton sold his periodical to a young Philadelphia journalist and publisher named George Rex Graham, who merged it with another he had bought, *Atkinson's Casket*, and launched *Graham's Magazine*, which would publish Poe's "Murders in the Rue Morgue" in 1841. After Poe's death eight years later, Graham defended him against critics who denounced his literary preoccupations and real-life shortcomings.

In September 1837, just after Burton launched the *Gentleman's Magazine*, and only three months after eighteen-year-old Victoria acceded to the throne, the fourth issue included the first half of Burton's own story "The Secret Cell," which concluded the next month. The tale appeared as part of a series entitled "Leaves from a Life in London." It seems likely, considering the circumstances related above, that Poe read this tale before composing his own detective stories. It has many virtues: a lively and literate style, convincing dialogue, suspenseful legwork and fisticuffs, a detective who works in disguise and tails suspects. Probably Poe would have found it too realistic.

The epigraph is from George Crabbe's allegedly opium-induced poem "Sir Eustace Grey," set in part in a madhouse.

The Secret Cell

I'll know no more;—the heart is torn
By views of woe we cannot heal;
Long shall I see these things forlorn.
And oft again their griefs shall feel,
As each upon the mind shall steal;
That wan projector's mystic style,
That lumpish idiot leering by,
That peevish idler's ceaseless wile,
And that poor maiden's half-formed smile,
While struggling for the full-drawn sigh—

—Crabbe

ABOUT EIGHT YEARS AGO, I was the humble means of unravelling a curious piece of villainy that occurred in one of the suburbs of London; it is well worth recording in exemplification of
that portion of "Life" which is constantly passing in the holes and
corners of the Great Metropolis. My tale, although romantic
enough to be a fiction, is excessively common-place in some of the
details—it is a jumble of real life; a conspiracy, an abduction, a nun-
nery, and a lunatic asylum are mixed up with constables, hackney-
coaches, and an old washerwoman. I regret also that my heroine is

4

not only without a lover, but is absolutely free from the influence of the passion, and is not persecuted on account of her transcendent beauty.

Mrs. Lobenstein was the widow of a German coachman who had accompanied a noble family from the continent of Europe and, anticipating a lengthened stay, he had prevailed upon his wife to bring over their only child, a daughter, and settle down in the rooms apportioned to his use over the stable in one of the fashionable mews at the west end of London. But Mr. Lobenstein had scarcely embraced his family ere he was driven off, post-haste, to the other world, leaving his destitute relict, with a very young daughter, to buffet her way along the rugged path of life.

With a little assistance from the nobleman in whose employ her husband had for some time been settled, Mrs. Lobenstein was enabled to earn a respectable livelihood, and filled the honorable situation of laundress to many families of gentility, besides diverse stray bachelors, dandies, and men about town. The little girl grew to be an assistance, instead of a drag, to her mother, and the widow found that her path was not entirely desolate, nor "choked with the brambles of despair."

In the sixth year of her bereavement, Mrs. Lobenstein, who presided over the destinies of my linen, called at my rooms, in company with a lady of equal width, breadth, and depth. Mrs. L was of the genuine Hanseatic build—of the real Bremen beam; when in her presence, you felt the overwhelming nature of her pretensions to be considered a woman of some weight in the world and standing in society. On the occasion of the visit in question, her friend was equally adipose, and it would have puzzled a conjurer to have turned the party into a tallowy trio. Mrs. L begged leave to recommend her friend as her successor in the lavatorial line—for her own part, she was independent of work, thank heaven, and meant to retire from the worry of trade.

I congratulated her on the successful termination of her flourish with the wash tubs.

"Oh, I have not made the money, bless you! I might have scrubbed my fingers to the bones before I could have done more than earn my daily bread and get, maybe, a black silk gown or so for Sundays. No, no! My Mary has done more with her quiet, meeting-day face in one year than either the late Mr. Lobenstein or myself could compass in our lives."

Mary Lobenstein, an artless, merry, blue-eyed girl of seventeen had attracted the attention of a bed-ridden lady whose linen she was in the habit of carrying home; and in compliance with the importunities of the old lady, she agreed to reside in her house as the invalid's sole and especial attendant. The old lady, luckily, was almost friendless; an hypocritical hyena of a niece, who expected, and had been promised, the reversion of her fortune, would occasionally give an inquiry relative to the state of her aunt's health. But so miserably did she conceal her joy at the approach of the old lady's dissolution that the party in question perceived her selfish and mercenary nature and, disgusted at her evident security of purpose, called in an attorney and executed an entirely new will. There was no oilier relative to select—Mary Lobenstein had been kind and attentive and, more from revenge than good nature, the old lady bequeathed the whole of her property to the lucky little girl, excepting a trifling annuity to the old maid, her niece, who also held the chance of possession in case of Mary's death.

When this will was read by the man of law, who brought it forth in due season after the old lady's demise, Mary's wonder and delight almost equalled the rage and despair of the hyena of a niece, whom we shall beg leave to designate by the name of Elizabeth Bishop. She raved and swore the deadliest revenge against the innocent Mary, who one minute trembled at the denunciations of the thin and yellow spinster, and in the next chuckled and danced at the suddenness of her unexpected good fortune.

Mr. Wilson, the lawyer, desired the dis-inherited to leave the premises to the legal owner, and stayed by Miss Mary Lobenstein and her fat mama till they were in full and undisturbed possession.

The "good luck," as Mrs. L called it, had fallen so suddenly upon them that a very heavy wash was left unfinished to attend to the important business, and the complaints of the naked and destitute customers alone aroused the lucky laundress to a sense of her situation. The right and privilege of the routine of customers were sold to another fat lady, and Mrs. Lobenstein called upon me, among the rest of her friends, to solicit the continuance of my washing for her stout successor.

A year passed away. I was lying in bed one wintry morning and shivering with dread at the idea of poking my uncased legs into the cold air of the room when my landlady disturbed my cogitations by knocking loudly at the room door and requesting my instant appearance in the parlor, where "a fat lady in tears" wished my presence. The existence of the obese Mrs. Lobenstein had almost slipped my memory, and I was somewhat startled at seeing that lady, dressed in a gaudy-colored silk gown and velvet hat and feathers, in violent hysterics upon my crimson silk ottoman, that groaned beneath its burden. The attentions of my landlady and her domestic soon restored my ci-devant laundress to a state of comparative composure, when the distressed lady informed me that her daughter, her only child, had been missing for several days, and that, notwithstanding the utmost exertions of herself, her lawyer, and her friends, she had been unable to obtain the smallest intelligence respecting her beloved Mary. She had been to the police offices, had advertised in the newspapers, had personally inquired of all her friends or acquaintance, yet every exertion bad resulted in disappointment.

"Everybody pities me, but no one suggests a means of finding my darling, and I am almost distracted. She left me one evening—it was quite early—to carry a small present to the chandler's-shop woman, who was so kind to us when I was left a destitute widow. My dear girl had but three streets to go; and ran out without a cloak or shawl; she made her gift to the poor woman, and instantly set out to return home. She never reached home—and, woe is me,

I fear she never will. The magistrates at the police office said that she had eloped with some sweetheart; my Mary loved no one but her mother—and my heart tells me that my child could not willingly abandon her widowed parent for any new affection that might have entered her young breast. She had no followers—we were never for one hour apart, and I knew every thought of her innocent mind.

"One gentleman—he said he was a parson—called on me this morning to administer consolation; yet he hinted that my poor girl had probably committed self-destruction—that the light of grace had suddenly burst upon her soul, and the sudden knowledge of her sinful state had been too much for her to bear and, in desperation, she had hurried from the world. Alas, if my poor Mary is indeed no more, it was not by her own act that she appeared in haste before her Maker—God loved the little girl that He had made so good. The light of heavenly happiness glistened in her bright and pretty eyes; and she was too fond of this world's beauties, and the delights of life showered by the Almighty upon His children, to think of repaying Him by gloom and suicide! No, no! Upon her bended knees, morning and night, she prayed to her Father in Heaven that His will might be done; her religion, like her life, was simple, but pure. She was not of the creed professed by him who thought to cheer a parent's broken heart by speaking of a daughter's shameful death."

The plain but earnest eloquence of the poor lady excited my warmest sympathy. She had called on me for advice, but I resolved to give her my personal assistance and exert all my faculties in the clearance of this mystery. She denied the probability of anyone being concerned in kidnapping, or conveying away her daughter— for, as she simply expressed herself, "she was too insignificant to have created an enemy of such importance."

I had a friend in the police department—a man who suffered not his intimacy with the villainy of the world to dull the humanities of nature. At the period of my tale, he was but little known and the claims of a large family pressed hard upon him; yet his enemies have been unable to affix a stain upon his busy life. He has since attained a height of reputation that must ensure a sufficient income; he is established as the head of the private police of London—a body of men possessing rare and wonderful attainments. To this man I went and, in a few words, excited his sympathy for the heart-stricken mother and obtained a promise of his valuable assistance.

"The mother is rich," said I, "and if successful in your search, I can warrant you a larger reward than the sum total of your last year's earnings."

"A powerful inducement, I confess," replied L—, "but my professional pride is roused; it is a case deserving attention from its apparent inexplicability—to say nothing of the mother's misery, and that is something to a father and a son."

I mentioned every particular connected with the affair and, as he declined visiting Mrs. Lobenatein's house, invited her to a conference with the officer at my lodgings, where he was made acquainted with many a curious item that seemed to have no connection with the subject we were in consultation upon. But this minute curiosity pleased the mother, and she went on her way rejoicing, for she was satisfied in her own mind that the officer would discover the fate of her child. Strange to say, although L— declared that he possessed not the slightest clue, this feeling on the part of the mother daily became stronger; a presentiment of the officer's success became the leading feature of her life, and she waited for many days with a placid face and a contented mind. The prophetic fancies of her maternal heart were confirmed; and L— eventually restored the pretty Mary to her mother's arms.

About ten days after the consultation, he called on me and reported progress—requiring my presence at the police office for the purpose of making the affidavit necessary for the procuration of a search warrant.

"I have been hard at work," said he, and if I have not found out where the young lady is concealed, I have at least made a singular discovery. My own inquiries in the mother's neighborhood were not attended with any success. I therefore sent my wife, a shrewd woman, and well adapted for the business. She went without a shawl or bonnet, as if she had but stopped out from an adjacent house, into the baker's, the grocer's, the chandler's, and the beer shop, and while making her trifling purchases, she asked in a careless, gossiping way if any intelligence of Miss Lobenstein had been obtained? Everybody was willing to talk of such a remarkable circumstance, and my wife listened patiently to many different versions of the story, but without obtaining any useful intelligence. One day, the last attempt that I had determined she should make, she observed that a huckster woman who was standing in a baker's shop when the question was discussed betrayed a violence of speech against the bereaved parent, and seemed to rejoice in her misfortunes. The womanly feeling of the rest of the gossips put down her inhuman chucklings, but my wife, with considerable tact, I must say, joined the huckster in her vituperation, rightly judging that there must be some peculiar reason for disliking a lady who seems generally esteemed and who was then suffering under an affliction the most distressing to a female heart. The huckster invited my wife to walk down the street with her.

" 'I say—are you one of Joe's gang?' whispered the huckster.

" 'Yes,' said my wife.

" 'I thought so, when I seed you grinning at the fat old Dutchey's trouble. Did Joe come down with the rhino pretty well to you about this business?'

" 'Not to me,' said my wife, at a venture.

" 'Nor to me, neither, the shabby varmint. Where was your post?'

"This question rather bothered my wife, but she answered, 'I swore not to tell.'

" 'Oh, stuff! They've got the girl, and it's all over now, in course; though Sal Brown who giv'd Joe the information about the girl says that five pounds won't stop her mouth when there's a hundred offered for the information—so we thought of splitting upon Joe, and touching the rhino. If you knows any more nor we do, and can make your share of the work, you may join our party, and come in for your whacks.'

" 'Well, I know a good deal, if I liked to tell it—what do you know!'

" 'Why, I knows that four of us were employed to watch when Miss Lobenstein went out in the evening without her mother, and to let Joe know directly; and I know that we did watch for six months and more; and when Sal Brown did let him know, that the girl was missing that same night, and ha'n't been heard on since.'

" 'But do you know where she is?' said my wife in a whisper.

" 'Well, I can't say that I do. My stall is at the corner near the mother's house; and Sal Brown was walking past, up and down the street, a following her profession. She's of opinion that the girl has been sent over the herring pond to some place abroad; but my idea is that she ha'n't far off, fur Joe hasn't been away many hours together, I know.'

"My wife declared that she was acquainted with every particular and would join them in forcing Joe to be more liberal in his disbursements or give him up to justice and claim the reward. She regretted that she was compelled to go to Hornsey to her mother for the next few days, but agreed to call at the huckster's stall immediately on her return.

"There was one point more that my wife wished to obtain. 'I saw the girl alone one night when it was quite dark, but Joe was not to be found when I went after him. Where did Sal Brown meet with him when she told of the girl?'

" 'Why, at the Blue Lion beer-shop, to be sure,' said the other.

"I was waiting in the neighborhood, well-disguised. I received my wife's valuable information, and in a few minutes was sitting in the tap room of the Blue Lion, an humble public house of inferior pretension. I was dressed in a shooting jacket, breeches, and gaiters, with a shot belt and powder horn slung round me. A huge pair of red whiskers circled my face, and a dark red shock of hair peeped from the sides of my broad-rimmed hat. I waited in the dull room, stinking of beer and tobacco, till the house closed for the night, but heard nothing of my Joe, although I listened attentively to the conversation of the incomers, a strange, uncouth set, entirely composed of the lower order of laborers, and seemingly unacquainted with each other.

"The whole of the next day, I lounged about the sanded tap room and smoked my pipe and drank my beer in silent gloominess. The landlord asked me a few questions, but when his curiosity was satisfied he left me to myself. I pretended to be a runaway gamekeeper, hiding from my master's anger for selling his game without permission. The story satisfied the host, but I saw nothing of any stranger, nor did I hear any of the old faces called by the name I wished to hear. One of the visitors was an ill-looking thick-set fellow, and kept up a continual whispering with the landlord—I made sure that he was my man, when, to my great regret, I heard him hailed by the name of George.

"I was standing inside the bar, chattering with the landlord, and settling for my pipes and my beer, when a good-looking, fresh-colored, smiling-faced young fellow danced into the bar and was immediately saluted by the host, 'Hello, Joe, where have you been these two days?'

"'Heavy business on hand, my buck—occupies all my time, but pays well. So give up a mug of your best, and d—the expense.'

"I had no doubt but this was my man. I entered into conversation with him, in my assumed manner, and my knowledge of the Somersetshire dialect materially assisted my disguise. Joe was evidently a sharp-witted fellow who knew exactly what he was about. All my endeavors to draw him into talking of his own avocations completely failed; he would laugh, drink, and chatter, but not a word relative to the business that occupied his time could I induce him to utter.

"'Who's going to the hop in Saint John Street?' said the lively Joe.

'I mean to have eighteen-pennyworth of shake-a-leg there tonight, and have it directly too, for I must be back at my place at daybreak.'

"This was enough for me. I walked with Joe to the vicinity of the dancing-rooms when, pleading a prior engagement, I quitted him and returned home. My disguise was soon completely altered; my red wig and whiskers, drab hat, and shooting dress were exchanged for a suit of black, with a small French cloak of dark cloth, and plain black hat. Thus attired, I watched the entrance of the humble ball-room, fearing that my man might leave it at an early period, for I knew not how far he had to journey to his place in the country, where he was compelled to be by the break of day.

"I walked the pavement of Saint John Street for six long hours, and was obliged to make myself known to the watchman to prevent his interference, for he doubted the honesty of my intentions. Just before the dawn of day, my friend Joe, who seemed determined to have enough dancing for his money, appeared in the street with a lady on each arm. I had to keep him in sight till he had escorted the damsels to their domiciles; when, buttoning up his coat and pressing his hat down over his brows, he walked forward with a determined pace. I followed him at a convenient distance. I felt that he was in my power—that I was on the point of tracing the mystery of the girl's disappearance, and ascertaining the place of her detention.

"Joe walked rapidly towards Shoreditch Church. I was within a hundred feet of him when the early Cambridge coach dashed down the Kingsland Road. Joe seized the guard's hold at the side of the back boot, placed his feet upon the hind spring, and in one moment was on the top of the coach, and trundling away from me at the rate of twelve miles an hour.

"I was beaten. It was impossible for me to overtake the coach. I thought of hiring a hack, but the rapid progress of the stage defied all idea of overtaking it. I returned dispirited to my home.

"My courage rose with the conception of fresh schemes. In the course of the day, I called on a friend, a stage coachman, and telling him some of the particulars of my object, asked him to introduce me to the driver of the Cambridge coach. I met him on his return to town the next day and, by the help of my friend, overcame his repugnance to talk with strangers respecting the affairs of his passengers. I learnt, at last, that Joe never travelled more than half-a-dozen miles, but Elliott, the coachman, was unable to say who he was or where he went to. My plan was soon arranged, and Elliott was bribed to assist me.

"The next morning by daybreak, I was sitting on the top of the Cambridge coach, well wrapped-up in a large white top coat, with a shawl tied over my mouth. I got on the coach at the inn yard, and as we neared the church looked out anxiously for my friend Joe; but he was not to be seen, nor could I discern anything of him for six or seven miles along the road. The first stage was performed, and while the horses were being changed, Elliott, the coachman, pointed out a strange, ill-looking man in a close light waistcoat with white sleeves, white breeches, yarn stockings, and high-low shoes. That fellow,' said Elliott, 'is always in company with the man you have been inquiring about. I have seen them frequently together come from over that style; he is now waiting for Joe, I'll bet a pound.'

"I alighted and bargained with the landlord of the small roadside inn for the use of the front bedroom, upstairs. I took my post and, as the stage departed, began my watch. Joe did not appear till late in the afternoon—his friend eagerly seized him by the arm and began to relate something with great anxiety of look and energy of action. They moved off over the style. I glided out of the house and followed them. A footpath wound through an extensive meadow, and the men were rapidly nearing the farthest end. I hastened my pace and gained the centre of the field ere they were aware of my approach. I observed a telegraphic signal pass between them, and they instantly stopped their expedition and, turning back upon their path, sauntered slowly towards me. I kept on; we met—their eyes were searchingly bent upon me, but I maintained an easy gait and

undisturbed countenance and continued my walk for some minutes after they were past. As I climbed the farthest style, I observed
them watching me from the other end of the field. I saw no more of
Joe or his friend for the rest of that day and the whole of the next.

"I was much annoyed at my disappointment and resolved not to
be again out-witted. Every possible inquiry that could be made
without exciting the curiosity of the neighborhood was instituted,
but I was unable to obtain the smallest information, either of the
abducted lady or of Joe's individuality. His friend was known as a
vagabond of the first class—a discharged ostler, with a character
that marked him ready for the perpetration of every crime.

"I was hunting in the dark. I had nothing but surmises to go
upon, excepting the declaration of the huckster, that a man named
Joe was the means of Miss Lobenstein's absence, but I was not sure
that I was in pursuit of that identical Joe. The mystery attending
the object of my suspicion gave an appearance of probability to my
supposition, but it seemed as if I was not to proceed beyond the
limits of uncertainty. I resolved, after waiting till the evening of
the next day, to return to the tap room of the Blue Lion and the
impenetrability of my gamekeeper's disguise.

"Tying my rough coat up in my shawl, I clapped the bundle under
my arm and walked quietly along the road. As I passed through some
twists on the sidewalk, a post-chaise was coming through the adjoining toll-gate. A scuffle, accompanied with high oaths, in the interior of the chaise attracted my attention; a hand was dashed through
the carriage-window and cries for help were loudly vociferated. I ran
towards the chaise and ordered the postillion to stop; a coarse voice
desired him to drive on; the command was repeated with violent
imprecations and the horses, severely lashed, bounded rapidly
away. I was sufficiently near to catch hold of the back of the springs
as the vehicle moved; the motion was violent, but I kept my grasp.
The backboard of the chaise, where the footman should stand, had
been covered with a double row of iron spikes to prevent the intrusion of idle boys; but, determined not to lose sight of the ruffians

who were thus violating the peace of the realm, I pressed my bundle hard upon the spikes and, jumping nimbly up, found myself in a firm and pleasant seat.

"The carriage rolled speedily along. I determined, at the very first halting place, to summon assistance and desire an explanation of the outcries and demands for help. If, as there seemed but little doubt, some act of lawless violence was being perpetrated. I resolved to arrest the principals upon the spot. While cogitating on the probabilities of the result, I received a tremendous cut across the face from the thong of a heavy leather whip, jerked with considerable violence from the window of the post-chaise. A second well-directed blow drove me from my seat, and I fell into the road, severely lacerated and almost blind.

"I rolled upon the dusty ground and writhed in excessive agony. A thick wale crossed each cheek, and one of my eyes had been terrifically hit. It was yet early night, and the public nature of the road soon afforded me assistance. A young man passed me, driving a gig towards London; I hailed him and requested his services. A slight detail of the cause in which I had received my injuries induced him to turn round and receive me in the vacant seat. The promise of half-a-guinea tempted him to drive rapidly after the chaise, and in a few minutes we heard the sound of wheels. The young man cheered his horse to greater progress, but we were unable to pass the vehicle in advance, and it was not till we both drew up to the door of the roadside inn where I had previously stopped that we discovered that we had been in pursuit of a mail-coach instead of a post-chaise.

"The waiter declared that 'nothin'' of a four-veel natur, 'cept a vaggin and a nearse' had passed within the previous half-hour. Placing my gig friend over some brandy and water, I sought the recesses of the kitchen that I might procure some cooling liquid to bathe my face with. While busily employed at the yard pump, the sound of voices from an adjoining stable arrested my attention. The dim light of a lantern fell upon the figure of the ostler whom I had seen in company with mysterious Joe. I advanced lightly, in hopes of hearing the conversation. When I reached the door, I was startled by the sudden approach of someone from the other side of the yard, and compelled to hide behind the door. A stable helper popped his head into the building, and said, 'See here, Billet, vot I found sticking on the spikes of the chay you've left in the lane.'

"My luckless bundle was produced and speedily untied. Directly Billy, for so was the suspicious ostler named, saw my rough, white greatcoat, he exclaimed, with considerable energy, 'I'm blessed if ve haint been looked arter. I seed this ere toggery a valking arter Joe and me in the meadow yonder. Ve thought it suspectable, so ve mizzled back. And I'm jiggered if the owner vornt sitting behind our conweyance ven Joe hit him a vollop or two vith your vip to knock him off. Tommy, my tulip, I'll go back vi' you tonight, and vait a vhile till the vind changes.'

"It was evident then that Joe was connected with the abduction of the day—another convincing proof that he was the active agent in Miss Lobenstein's affair. With respect to my friend the ostler, I determined to try the effects of a little coercion, but concluded that it would be better to let him reach some distance from his usual jaunts to prevent alarming his co-mate Joe.

"In about an hour the post-chaise was driven to the door, and the ostler, much the worse for his potations, was placed within the body of the vehicle. I was soon after them, in company with the young man in the gig, and we kept the chaise in sight till it had entered the still and deserted streets of the city. It was nearly midnight; the drunken ostler desired the scarcely sober postillion to put him out at the door of a tavern. I walked up to the astonished couple and, arresting them on a charge of felony, slipped a pair of small but powerful spring handcuffs over the ostler's wrists.

"I conducted him, helpless and amazed, to an adjacent watch-house and, mentioning my name and office, desired his safe custody till I could demand his body. The postillion, who was guarded by my gig friend, became much alarmed and volunteered any information that I might desire. He confessed that he had been employed that afternoon by one Joseph Mills to carry a lunatic priest to the Franciscan Monastery at Enfield Chase, from whence it was asserted that he had made his escape. The existence of a religious establishment in that neighborhood was entirely unknown to me, and I questioned the postillion respecting the number of its inmates and the name of the superior, but he professed to know nothing beyond the locality of the building, and declared that he had never been inside the yard gate. He admitted that Joseph Mills had employed him several times upon the same business; and that, rather more than a fortnight ago, Billy, the ostler, had desired him to bring up a post-chaise from his master's yard at a minute's notice, and that a young lady was lifted, in a senseless state, into the chaise and driven down to the building at Enfield as rapidly as the horses could be made to go.

"I took down his directions respecting the house, and at daybreak this morning I reconnoitered the front and back of the building. If I am any judge, that house is not devoted to monastic purposes alone; but you will see it tomorrow, I trust, for I wish you to accompany me as early in the morning as we can start after procuring the warrants for a general search into the secrets of this most mysterious monastery."

It was nearly noon the next day before we were enabled to complete our necessary arrangements. L——, Mr. Wilson, the attorney, Mr. R——, a police magistrate of some distinction, and the reader's humble servant stepped into a private carriage, while a police officer, well-armed, sat with the driver. The magistrate had been interested in the details necessary for the procuration of the warrant and had invited himself to the development of the mystery. An hour's ride brought us to the entrance of a green lane that wound its mazy length between hedges of prickly holly and withered hawthorn trees. After traversing this lane for nearly two miles, we turned again to the left, by L——'s direction, and entered a narrow pass between a high brick wall and a huge bank, surmounted by a row of high and gloomy trees. The wall formed the boundary of the monastery grounds and, at a certain place, where an ascent in the narrow road favored the purpose, we were desired by L— to mount the roof of the coach and, by looking over the wall, to inspect the back front of the building. Massive bars of iron were fastened across every window of the house; in some places, the frames and glass were entirely removed, and the gratings were fixed in the naked brick-work; or the apertures were fitted with thick boarding, excepting a small place at the top for the admission of the smallest possible quantity of light and air. The windows of a range of outhouses, which extended down one side of the extensive yard, were also se-curely barred; and a small square stone building stood in the middle of the garden, which immediately adjoined the yard. Two sides of this singular construction were visible from our coach top, yet neither door nor window were to be discerned.

One of our party pointed out a pale and wild-looking face glar-ing at us from one of the grated windows of the house. "Let us away," said L—. "We are observed, and a further gratification of our curiosity may prevent a successful issue to my scheme."

"This looks more like a prison than a monastery or convent," said the magistrate.

"I fear that we shall find it worse than either," replied L—.

In a few minutes the carriage stopped at the gate of the building, the front of which exhibited but few points for the attachment of suspicion. The windows were shaded by blinds and curtains, but free from gratings or bars. The palings that enclosed a small fore court were of massive oak and, being mounted on a dwarf wall, effectually prevented the intrusion of un-invited guests. The gates were securely closed, but the handle of a small bell invited attention, and a lusty pull by the driver gave notice of our presence.

L—, who had quitted the vehicle by the off door, requested the magistrate to keep out of sight, and with his brother officer retired behind the coach. Our course of proceeding had been well-arranged; when the door of the house was opened, I put my head from the carriage window and requested to see the superior of the convent.

The attendant, a short, ill-looking follow in a fustian coat and gaiters, desired to know my business with him. "It is of great secrecy
and importance," I replied; "I cannot leave the carriage because I
have somebody here that requires my strictest attention. Give your
master this card, and he will know exactly who I am, and what I
require."

Our scheme succeeded. The fellow left his post and, unfasten-
ing the paling gate, advanced to the edge of the footpath, and put
his hand in at the window of the carriage for my card. L— and the
officer glided from their concealment and secured possession of the
outer gate and the door of the house before the fellow had time to
give the alarm. The driver, who had pretended to busy himself with
the horses, immediately opened the carriage door, and in a few
seconds the whole of our party were mustered in the entrance hall.
The man who had answered the bell, when he recovered his surprise,
rushed to the door, and attempted to force his way to the interior
of the house. The police officer stopped him, and an angry altercа-
tion ensued—he placed his finger in his mouth and gave a loud and
lengthy whistle. L—, who was busily engaged in searching for the
fastenings of an iron screen that crossed the width of the hall, observed the noise and turning round to his mate said quietly, "If he's
troublesome, Tommy, give him a pair of gloves." In two minutes,
the fellow was sitting helpless on the ground, securely handcuffed.

"Confound him," said L—, "he must have come out through
this grating; there is no other entrance to the hall, and yet I cannot
discover the door-way, and I am afraid that his signal has made it
worse, for I heard the click of spring work directly after he gave his
whistle."

"This grating is a common appendage to a convent or religious
house," said Mr. Wilson. "Perhaps we are giving ourselves unnecessary trouble—let us ring the bell again, and we may obtain admission
without the use of force."

The officer and the magistrate exchanged a smile. The latter went
to the man who had opened the door and said, in a low tone of

voice, "We must get into the house, my man; show us how we can pass this grating and I will give you five guineas. If you refuse, I shall commit you to jail, whether your connection with this establishment deserves it or no. I am a magistrate, and these, my officers, are acting under my direction."

The man spoke not; but, raising his manacled hands to his mouth, gave another whistle of peculiar shrillness and modulation.

The hall in which we were detained was of great height and extent. Beyond the iron screen, a heavy partition of woodwork cut off the lower end, and a door of heavy oak opened from the room thus formed into the body of the hall. An open, but grated, window was immediately above the door and extended almost from one end of the partition to the other. L——, observing this, climbed up the iron screen with the agility of the cat, and had scarcely attained the top ere we observed him level a pistol towards some object in the enclosure and exclaim, with a loud voice, "Move one step and I'll drive a couple of bullets through your skull."

"What do you require?" exclaimed a tremulous voice from within.

"Send your friend there, Joe Mills, to open the door of the grating. If you move hand or foot, I'll pull trigger, and your blood be upon your own head."

L—— afterwards informed me, that upon climbing the screen, he discerned a gentleman in black in close consultation with a group of men. They were standing at the farther end of the enclosure against a window, the light of which enabled him to pick out the superior, and to discern the physiognomy of his old acquaintance Joe.

"Come, come, Joe, make haste," said L——. "My fingers are cramped, and I may fire in mistake."

The threat was effectual in its operation. The man was afraid to move, and the door of the enclosure was opened by his direction. Joe walked trippingly across the hall and, touching a spring in one of the iron rails, removed the fastenings from a portion of the screen, and admitted our party.

"How do you do, Mr. Mills?" said L——. "How are our friends at

the Blue Lion! You must excuse me if I put you to a little inconvenience, but you are so volatile that we can't make sure of finding
you when we want you unless we take the requisite precaution.
Tommy, tackle him to his friend, and by way of greater security,
fasten them to the grating—but don't waste the gloves, for we have
several more to fit."

"Gentlemen," said the man in black, advancing to the door of
the enclosure, "what is the reason of this violence? Why is the
sanctity of this holy establishment thus defiled! Who are you, and
what seek you here?"

"I am a magistrate, sir, and these men are officers of justice armed
with proper authority to search this house for the person of Mary
Lobenstein, and we charge you with her unlawful detention. Give
her to our care, and you may save yourself much trouble."

"I know nothing of the person you mean, nor are we subject to
the supervision of your laws. This house is devoted to religious
purposes—it is the abode of penitents who have abjured the world
and all its vanities. We are under the protection of the Legate of
His Holiness, the Pope, and the laws of England do not forbid our
existence. Foreigners only dwell within these walls, and I cannot
allow the interference of any party un-authorised by the Head of
the Church."

"I shall not stop," said the magistrate, "to expose the errors of
your statement. I am furnished with sufficient power to demand a
right of search in any house in the Kingdom. Independent of ascertaining the safety of the individual with whose abduction you are
charged, it is my duty to inquire into the nature of an establishment
assuming the right to capture the subjects of the King of this realm
and detain them in a place having all the appointments of a common
prison, yet disowning the surveillance of the English laws. Mr. L—,
you will proceed in your search, and if any one attempts to oppose
you, he must take the consequences."

The countenance of the man in black betrayed the uneasiness he
felt; the attendants, six in number, who, with our friend Mills, had

formed the council whose deliberations were disturbed by the sight of L—'s pistol, were ranged beneath the window that looked into the yard, and waited the commands of the chief. This man, whose name we afterwards ascertained was Farrell, exchanged a look of cunning with his minions and, with apparent resignation, replied, "Well, sir, it is useless for me to contend with the authority you possess; Mr. Nares, throw open the yard door and, do you and your men attend the gentlemen round the circuit of the cells."

The person addressed unbolted the fastenings of a huge door that opened into the yard, and bowed to our party as if waiting their precedence. Mr. Wilson, being nearest the door, went first, and Nares, with a bend of his head, motioned two of his party to follow. As they passed him, he gave them a knowing wink and said, "Take the gentlemen to the stone house first." The magistrate was about to pass into the yard when L— seized him by the collar of his coat and violently pulling him back into the room, closed the door and jerked the principal bolt into its socket.

"Excuse my rudeness, sir, but you will soon perceive that it was necessary. Your plan, Mr. Nares, is a very good plan, but will scarcely answer your purpose. We do not intend placing ourselves at the mercy of your men in any of your stone houses, or cells with barred windows. You have the keys of the establishment at your girdle— go round with us yourself and let those five or six fellows remain here instead of dancing at our heels. Come, come, sir, we are not to be trifled with; no hesitation, or I shall possess myself of your keys and leave you securely affixed to your friend Mills."

Nares grinned defiance, but made no reply. Farrell, whose pale face exhibited his dismay, took courage from the dogged bearing of his official and stuttered out, "Mr. Nares, I desire that you will not give up your keys." The hint was sufficient. Nares and his fellows, who were all furnished with bludgeons, raised their weapons in an attitude of attack, and a general fight was inevitable. The closing of the yard door had cut off one of our friends, but it also excluded two of the enemy. Still the odds were fearfully against us, not only in point of numbers, which rated five to four, and our antagonists were all of them armed, while the magistrate and I were totally unprovided with the means of defense.

Hostilities commenced by one of the men striking me a violent blow upon the fleshy part of the left shoulder that sent me staggering to the other side of the room. Two of the ruffians simultaneously faced the police officer, as if to attack him; he received the blow of the nearest upon his mace or staff of office, and before the fellow had time to lift his guard, returned him a smashing rap upon the fingers of his right hand, compelling him to drop his cudgel and run howling into the corner of the room. The officer then turned his attention to the fellow who had assaulted me and who was flourishing his stick with the intent of repeating the blow—but receiving a severe crack across his shins from the officer's mace, he was unable to keep his legs and dropped upon the floor. I immediately wrested the bludgeon from his grasp, and left him *hors de combat*. The officer, while assisting me, received a knock-down blow from the fellow who had hesitated joining in the first attack, but, cat-like, had been watching his opportunity for a pounce. I gave him in return a violent thump upon his head, and drove his hat over his eyes—then, rushing in upon him. I pinioned his arms and held him till the officer rose and assisted me to secure him. While placing the handcuffs upon him, I was favored with a succession of kicks from the gentleman with the crippled hand.

L—, having drawn a pistol from his pocket, advanced to Nares and desired him to deliver up the keys; the ruffian answered him by striking a heavy blow on L—'s ear that immediately produced blood. The officer, exhibiting the utmost self-possession under these irritating circumstances, did not fire the pistol at his adversary, but dashed the weapon into his face and inflicted a painful wound. Nares was a man of bull-dog courage. He seized the pistol and struggled fearfully for its possession. His gigantic frame and strength over-powered his antagonist; the pistol was discharged in the scuffle, luckily without wounding anyone—and the ruffian, holding the conquered L— upon the ground, was twisting his cravat for the purpose of choking him when, having satisfactorily arranged our men, we arrived to the rescue and prevented the scoundrel from executing his villainous intention. But Nares, although defeated by numbers, evinced a determination to die game—it was with the utmost difficulty that we were enabled to secure his arms, and while slipping the handcuffs over his wrists, he continued to leave the marks of his teeth upon the fingers of the policeman.

While this furious melee was going on, the magistrate had been unceremoniously collared by the master of the house and thrust forth into that part of the hall which adjoined the iron screen. But his worship did not reverence this ungentlemanly proceeding, and turned valiantly upon his assailer. Both of them were un-provided with weapons, and a furious bout of fisticuffs ensued, wherein his worship was considerably worsted. Mills and the porter, who had been fastened by the policeman to the railing of the screen, encouraged Farrell by their cheers. The magistrate was severely punished and roared for help; Farrell, dreading collision with the conquerors of his party, left his man and started off through the open door of the grating; he ran down the lane with a speed that defied pursuit. The driver and the magistrate both endeavored to overtake him, but they soon lost sight of the nimble rogue, and returned discomforted to the house.

During the scuffle, the two men who, with Mr. Wilson, were shut out by the promptitude of L—, clamored loudly at the door for re-admission. The attorney, as he afterwards confessed, was much alarmed at the position in which he found himself—cut off from all communication with his friends and left at the mercy of two ill-looking scoundrels, in a strange place, and surrounded by a range of grated prisons, while a number of cadaverous, maniac looking faces glared at him from between the bars.

Upon mustering our party, we were all more or less wounded. The magistrate was outrageous in his denunciations of vengeance upon all the parties concerned; his discolored eye and torn apparel,

besides the bruises about his person, had inflamed his temper, and
he declared that it was his firm determination to offer a large reward for the apprehension of the chief ruffian, Farrell. L— was
much hurt, and for some time appeared unable to stand alone—his
ear bled profusely and relieved his head, which had been seriously
affected by Nares's attempt at strangulation. The other officer had
received a severe thumping, and his bitten hand gave him much pain.
My left arm was almost useless, and many bloody marks exhibited
the effects of the fellow's kicks upon my shins. Nevertheless, we had
fought a good fight, and had achieved a perilous victory.

The magistrate threw up the window sash and addressed the
men in the yard from between the iron gratings. "Harken, you sirs,
we have thrashed your fellows, and have them here in custody. If you
attempt resistance, we shall serve you exactly in the same manner.
But if either of you feel inclined to assist us in the discharge of our
duty, and will freely answer every question and render all the help
in his power, you shall not only be forgiven for any part you may
have taken in scenes of past violence, short of murder, but shall be
well rewarded into the bargain."

One of the men, and I must say that he was the most ill-looking
of the whole lot, immediately stepped forward, and offered to turn
"King's evidence" if the magistrate would swear to keep his promise.
The other fellow growled his contempt of the sneak "what would
snitch" and darted rapidly down the yard. As we never saw him
again, it is supposed that he got into the garden and found some
means of escaping over the walls.

The yard door was opened, and the lawyer and the informer
were admitted. The latter personage told us that his wife was the
matron of the establishment and, with her sister, would be found
upstairs. The keys were taken from Nares, and we began our search.
Mr. Wilson desired the man to conduct us to Mary Lobenstein's
room, but he positively denied the knowledge of any such person.
His wife, a coarse, pock-marked, snub-nosed woman with a loud,
masculine voice, also declared that no female answering to that

name had ever been within the house. L— remarked that no credit was to be attached to their assertions, and ordered them to lead the way to the search.

It would occupy too much space to describe minutely the nature of the persons and events that we encountered in our rounds. Suffice it to say, we soon discovered that the suspicions of the police officer and the magistrate barely reached the truth. Farrell's establishment had no connection with any religious house, nor could we discover either monk, friar, nun, or novice in any of the cells. But the name was a good cloak for the villainous usages practiced in the house, as it dis-armed suspicion and prevented the interference of the police. The house, in reality, was a private mad-house, but subject to the foulest abuses; wives who were tired of their husbands, and vice versa, reprobate sons wishing to dispose of fathers, or villains who wanted to remove their rivals, either in love or wealth, could secure safe lodgings for the obnoxious personages in Farrell's Farm, as it was termed by the knowing few. Farrell could always obtain a certificate of the lunacy of the person to be removed; Nares had been bred to the pestle and the mortar and, as the Act then stood, an apothecary's signature was sufficient authority for immuring a suspected person. Incurables of the worst description were received by Farrell and boarded at the lowest rate. He generally contracted for a sum down, guaranteeing that their friends should never again be troubled by them—and, as the informer said, "He gave them little enough to eat, and if they did not die, it wasn't his fault."

The house was also appropriated to other purposes of secrecy and crime. Ladies in a delicate situation were accommodated with private rooms for their accouchement, and the children effectually provided for. Fugitives from justice were sure of concealment if they could obtain admission to the Farm. In short, Farrell's doors, although closed to the world and the eye of the law, were open to all who could afford to pay, or be paid for—from the titled seducer and his victim, whose ruin was effected in the elegant suite of rooms fronting the lane, to the outcast bedlamite, the refuse of the poor-house and the asylum who was condemned to a slow but certain death in the secret cells of this horrible abode.

It would fill a volume to recount the history of the sufferers whom we released from their almost hopeless imprisonment—a volume of crime, of suffering, and of sorrow.

After a painful and fruitless search through all the various rooms, cells, and hiding places of that singular house, we were compelled to acknowledge that the assertions of the under-keeper and his wife were but too correct. Mary Lobenstein was not among the number of the detenues at the Farm, nor could we discover the slightest trace of her. Still L— clung to the hope that in the confusion necessarily attending our first search we had passed over some secret cell or dungeon in which the poor girl was immured. The square stone building in the centre of the garden afforded some ground for this surmise—we were unable to open the small iron-banded door that was fixed in the side of this apparently solid structure. The under-keeper declared that the key was always in the possession of Farrell, his principal; and that no one ever entered the place but Nares und his master. He was not aware that any person was ever confined in it, a spring of water bubbled up within the building, and he believed that Farrell used it as a wine cellar only. He had seen wine carried in and out of the place. Indeed, the whole appearance of the building corroborated the man's statement—there was no window, air hole, or aperture of any description, excepting the small door before mentioned; and the contracted size of the place itself prevented the possibility of its containing a hiding hole for a human being if a well or spring occupied the area, as the keeper affirmed.

Resigning this last hope of finding the poor girl, we gave our assistance to the magistrate in removing the prisoners and placing the unfortunates whom we had released in temporary but appropriate abodes. In this service, the under-keeper and his wife proved valuable auxiliaries in pointing out the incurable mad folks and those who, in his opinion, had been unjustly detained. The prisoners were placed in our carriage and conveyed to London, under the superintendence of L— himself, who promised to return during the evening with additional assistance. The policeman was dispatched to Enfield for several carriages and post-chaises. Some of the most desperate and confirmed maniacs were sent to the lunatic asylum, with the magistrate's order for their admittance, and two or three of the sick and sorrowing were removed to the Middlesex hospital.

I assisted the lawyer and the magistrate in taking the depositions of several of the sufferers who appeared sane enough to warrant the truth of their stories. As night approached, I prepared for a departure, and Mr. Wilson resolved to accompany me; we received the addresses of several persons from various inmates of the Farm, who requested us to let their families know of the place of their detention. As we drove down the lane, we met L— and a posse of police officers, who were to accompany the magistrate in his night sojourn at the house and assist him in the removal of the rest of the inmates in the morning.

During the evening I called, with a heavy heart, upon Mrs. Lobenstein and communicated the melancholy remit of our scheme. I related minutely the particulars of our transaction—she listened quietly to my story and occasionally interrupted me, when describing the zeal of the officer L—, by invoking the blessings of Heaven upon his head. When she learnt the unsuccessful issue of our search, she remained silent for a minute only—when, with a confident tone and a cheerful voice, she said, "My daughter Mary is in that stone house. The workings of the fingers of Providence are too evident in the wonderful train of circumstances that led to the discovery of Farrell and his infamous mansion. My child is there, but you have not been able to penetrate the secret of her cell. I will go with you in the morning, if you can spare another day to assist a bereaved mother."

I declared my readiness to accompany her, but endeavored to impress upon her mind the inutility of further search. She relied securely upon the faith of her divine impression, as she termed it, and declared that God would never suffer so good a man as L— to be disappointed in his wonderful exertions; the keenness of a mother's eye, the instinct of a mother's love would help him in the completion of his sacred trust. It was impossible to argue with her, and I agreed to be with her at an early hour.

I slept but little during the night, for my bruised shins and battered shoulder pained me considerably, and the strange excitement of the day's events materially assisted to heighten both my corporeal and mental fever. When I arose in the morning, I felt so badly that nothing but the earnest and confident tone of the poor childless widow induced me to undertake the annoyance of the trip—I could not bear to disappoint her. I found the carriage ready at the door—a couple of mechanics, with sledge hammers, crow bars, and huge bunches of skeleton keys occupied the front seat, and having placed myself beside Mrs. Lobenstein upon the other seat, the horses trotted briskly along the street.

During our ride she informed me that a lawyer had called upon her from Elizabeth Bishop, the disappointed spinster, who, it will be recollected, had lost her expected fortune by the intervention of the gentle Mary Lobenstein. The man stated that Miss Bishop had heard of the disappearance of the inheritor of her aunt's estate and had desired him to give notice that if proof was not forthcoming of Miss Lobenstein's existence, she should take possession of the property, agreeably to the provision existing in the will. "I am sure," said the mother, "that woman is at the bottom of this affair—she has concerted the abduction of my daughter to obtain possession of the estate—but I trust in God that she will be disappointed in her foul design. A fearful whisper comes across my heart that those who would rob a mother of a child for gold would not object to rob that child of her existence; but my trust is in the Most High, Who tempers the wind to the shorn lamb and will not consent to the spoliation of the widow and the fatherless."

The probability of the poor girl's murder had been suggested by L— at the termination of our unsuccessful search, and had occupied

a serious portion of my thoughts during the wakeful moments of
the past night. Expecting nothing from the mother's repetition of
the search, I determined to consult L— upon the feasibility of offering rewards to the villains Mills and Nares for a revelation of the
truth, and if we failed in eliciting any intelligence, to institute a
rigorous examination of the garden and the yard and discover, if
possible, the remains of the murdered girl.

The magistrate received Mrs. Lobenstein with tenderness and
respect, and sanctioned her desire to penetrate into the mystery of
the square stone house. L— had nothing new to disclose, excepting
that in one of the rooms several articles of female apparel had been
discovered, and he suggested that Mrs. L should inspect them as,
perhaps, something that belonged to her daughter might be among
them. The mother remarked that her daughter left home without a
bonnet or a shawl, and it was scarcely likely that her body-clothes
would be in the room. She, therefore, thought it useless to waste
time in going upstairs, but requested the locksmith to accompany
her to the stone house in the garden. It was impossible to help sym-
pathizing with Mrs. Lobenstein in her anxiety; the magistrate deferred his return to London, where his presence was absolutely
necessary to preside at the examination of Messrs. Nares, Mills,
and Co., and the warm-hearted L— wiped the moisture from his
eyes as he followed the mother across the yard and heard her
encourage the workmen to commence the necessary proceedings
for the release of her darling child. The lock of the stone house was
picked—the door was thrown wide open—and the maternal voice
was heard in loud citation, but the dull echo of the stone room was
the only reply—there was no living creature within the place.

We found the interior of the building to correspond with the
description given by the under-keeper. The walls were hollowed
into bins, which were filled with wine bottles packed in sawdust; a
circular well, bricked up a little above the level of the floor, filled
the centre of the room; the water rose to within a foot of the
ground—an old pulley and bucket, rotten from desuetude, clogged

up one side of the doorway, and two or three wine barrels filled up the remaining vacancy of space. It was impossible that a human being could be concealed in any part of the building.

Mrs. Lobenstein sighed, and her countenance told of her dismay; but the flame of hope had warmed her heart into a heat that was not to be immediately cooled. "Gentlemen," said she, "accompany me once more round the cells and secret places—let me be satisfied with my own eyes that a thorough search has been made, and it will remove my doubts that you have overlooked some obscure nook wherein the wretches have concealed my little girl."

The range of chambers was again traversed, but without success, and the widow was compelled to admit that every possible place had been looked into, and that a farther sojourn in the house was entirely useless. The old lady sat down upon the last stair of the second flight, and with a grievous expression of countenance looked into our several faces as we stood around her as if she was searching for that consolation it was not in our power to bestow. Tears rolled down her cheeks, and mighty sobs told of the anguish of her heart. I was endeavoring to rouse her to exertion as the only means of breaking the force of her grief, when my attention was drawn to the loud yelping of a dog, a small cocker spaniel, that had accompanied us in the carriage from Mrs. Lobenstein's house and in prowling round the building, had been accidentally shut up in one of the rooms.

"Poor Dash!" said the widow. "I must not lose you; my dear Mary was fond of you, and I ought to be careful of her favorite." I took the hint and walking down the gallery, opened the door of the room from whence the barking proceeded. It was the apartment that contained the articles of wearing apparel which Mrs. L had visited in her round without discovering any token of her daughter. But the animal's superior instinct enabled him to detect the presence of a pair of shoes that had graced the feet of the little Mary when she quitted her mother's house on the day of her abduction. Immediately the door was opened, the faithful creature gathered up the shoes in his mouth and ran to his mistress and dropped them at her feet, inviting her attention by a loud and sagacious bark. The old lady knew the shoes in a moment. "Yes, they are my girl's—I bought them myself for my darling. She has been here—has been murdered—and the body of my child is now moldering in the grave." A violent fit of hysterics ensued, and I consigned her to the care of the wife and sister of the under-keeper, who had not been allowed to leave the house.

I deemed the finding of the shoes to be of sufficient importance to recall the magistrate, who was in the carriage at the door and about to start for London. He immediately alighted and inquired into the particulars of the affair. Directly it was proved that Mary Lobenstein had been in the house, L— rushed up stairs and dragged the keeper into the presence of the magistrate, who sternly asked the man why he had deceived him in declaring that the girl had never been there. The fellow was evidently alarmed and protested vehemently that he knew no female of the name of Lobenstein—and the only clue he could give to the mystery of the shoes was that a young girl answering our description of Mary had been brought into the house at night time about a fortnight ago, but she was represented as an insane prostitute of the name of Hill who had been annoying some married gentlemen by riotous conduct at their houses—and it was said at first that she was to remain at the Farm for life—but that she had suddenly been removed by Nares, but where, he could not say.

L— shook his head ominously when he heard this statement, and it was evident to us all that the mother's suspicions were right, and that a deed of blood had been recently perpetrated. The best means of ascertaining the place of burial was consulted on, and we adjourned to the garden to search for any appearance of freshly disturbed ground, or other evidence that might lead to a discovery of her remains. When we had crossed the yard, and were about entering the garden gate, L— suggested the propriety of fetching the little dog, whose excellent nose had afforded the only clue we had been able to obtain. I went back for the animal, but he refused to leave his mistress, and it was not without some danger of a bite that I succeeded in catching him by the neck and carrying him out of the room. I put him on his feet when we were past the garden gate, and endeavored to excite him to sprightliness by running along the walk and whistling to him to follow, but he sneaked after me with a drooping tail and a bowed head, as if he felt his share of the general grief.

We walked round the garden without discovering any signs that warranted further search. We had traversed every path in the garden, excepting a narrow, transverse one that led from the gate to a range of green and hot houses that lined the farthest wall. We were on the point of leaving the place, satisfied that it was not in our power to remove the veil of mystery that shrouded the girl's disappearance, when the dog, who had strayed into the entrance of the narrow path, gave extraordinary signs of liveliness and emotion—his tail wagged furiously, his ears were thrown forward, and a short but earnest yaffle broke into a continuous bark as he turned rapidly from one tide of the path to another, and finally ran down toward the greenhouse with his nose bent to the ground. "He scents her," said L—. "There is still a chance."

Our party, consisting of the magistrate, L— and two other officers, the under-keeper, the locksmith, and myself, followed the dog down the narrow path into the center of a piece of ground containing three or four cucumber beds covered with sliding glass frames. The spaniel, after searching round the bed, jumped upon the center frame and howled piteously. It was evident that he had lost the scent. L— pointed out to our notice that the sliding lid was fastened to the frame by a large padlock—this extraordinary security increased our suspicions. He seized a crow-bar from one of the smiths, and the lock was soon removed. The top of the frame was pulled up and the dog jumped into the tank that filled the bed and commenced scratching with all his might.

L— thrust the bar into the yielding soil, and at the depth of a foot, the iron struck a solid substance. This intimation electrified us—we waited not for tools; our hands were dug into the bed and the tan and black mould were dragged from the frame with an eagerness that soon emptied it and exhibited the boarding of a large trap door, divided into two parts, but securely locked together. While the smiths essayed their skill upon the lock, the magistrate stood by with lifted hands and head uncovered—a tear was in the good man's eye, and he breathed short from the excess of his anxiety. Everyone was visibly excited, and the loud and cheerful bark of the dog was hailed as an omen of success. L—'s impatience could not brook delay. He seized the sledgehammer of the smiths and with a blow that might have knocked in the side of a house, demolished the lock and bolt, and the doors jumped apart in the recoil from the blow. They were raised—a black and yawning vault was below—and a small flight of wooden steps, green and moldy from the effects of the earth's dampness, led to the gloomy depths of the cavern.

The little dog dashed bravely down the stairway, and L—, requesting us to stand from between him and the light, picked his way down the narrow, slimy steps. One of the smiths followed, and the rest of us hung our heads anxiously over the edge of the vault's mouth, watching our friends as they receded in the distant gloom.

A pause ensued; the dog was heard barking, and an indistinct muttering between L— and the smith ascended to the surface of the earth. I shouted to them and was frightened at the reverberation of my voice. Our anxiety became painful in the extreme—the magistrate called to L—, but obtained no answer, and we were on the point of descending in a body when the officer appeared at the root of the stairs. "We have found her," said he—we gave a simultaneous shout. "But she is dead" was the appalling finish of his speech, as he emerged from the mouth of the vault.

The smith, with the lifeless body of Mary Lobenstein swung over his shoulder, was assisted up the stairs. The corpse of the little girl was placed on one of the garden settees and, with heavy hearts and gloomy faces, we carried the melancholy burden into the house. The mother had not recovered from the shock which the anticipation of her daughter's death had given to her feelings; she was lying senseless upon the bed where she had been placed by the keeper's wife. We laid the body of her daughter in an adjoining room and directed the woman to perform the last sad duties to the senseless clay while we awaited the parent's restoration. The magistrate returned to London; the smiths were packing up their tools preparatory to departure and I was musing in melancholy mood over the events of the day when the forbidding face of the keeper's wife peeped in at the half-opened door and we were beckoned from the room.

"Please your honor, I never seed a dead body look like that there corpse of the little girl upstair. I've seed a many corpses in my time, but there's something onnataral about that there one, not like a dead body ought to be."

"What do you mean?"

"Why, though her feet and hands are cold, her jaw ain't dropped, and her eyes ain't open—and there's a limberness in her limbs that I don't like. I really believe she's only swounded."

L— and I hurried up stairs, and the smiths, with their baskets of tools dangling at their backs, followed us into the room. I anxiously searched for any pulsation at the heart and the wrists of poor Mary, whose appearance certainly corroborated the woman's surmise, but the total absence of all visible signs of life denied us the encouragement of the flattering hope. One of the smiths took from his basket a tool of bright, fine-tempered steel; he held it for a few seconds against Mary's half-closed mouth, and upon withdrawing it, said, with a loud and energetic voice, "She is alive! Her breath has damped the surface of the steel!"

The man was right. Proper remedies were applied to the daughter and to her parent, and L— had the gratification of placing the lost Mary within her mother's arms.

Miss Lobenstein's explanation afforded but little additional information. When she was brought to the Farm by the villain Mills and his friend Billy the ostler, she was informed that it was to be the residence of her future life. She was subjected to the treatment of a maniac, her questions remained unanswered, and her supplications for permission to send to her mother were answered with a sneer. About three nights ago, she was ordered from her room, her shoes were taken off that she might noiselessly traverse the passages, and she was removed to the secret cell in the garden; some biscuits and a jug of water were placed beside her, and she had remained in undisturbed solitude till the instinct of her favorite dog led to her discovery shortly after she had fainted from exhaustion and terror.

There is little doubt but that the ruffians were alarmed at the watching and appearances of the indefatigable L——, and withdrew their victim to the securest hiding-place. I had the curiosity, in company with some of the officers, to descend into the secret cell; it had originally been dug out for the foundation of an intended house; the walls and partitions were solidly built, but the bankruptcy of the projector prevented any further progress. When Farrell and his gang took possession of the place, it was deemed easier to cover the rafters of the cellar with boards and earth than to fill it up—in time, the existence of the hole became forgotten, save by those most interested in its concealment. Farrell contrived the mode of entrance through the glass frame of the forcing bed, and when the adjacent greenhouses were constructed, an artificial flue or vent was introduced to the depths of the cell, and supplied it with a sufficiency of air.

Mrs. Lobenstein refused to prosecute the spinster Bishop, the malignancy of whose temper preyed upon her own heart, and speedily consigned her unlamented to the grave. The true particulars of this strange affair were never given to the public, although I believe that its occurrence mainly contributed to effect an alteration in the English laws respecting private mad houses and other receptacles for lunatics.

The magistracy of the county knew that they were to blame in permitting the existence of such a den as Farrell's Farm, and exerted themselves to quash proceedings against the fellows Mills and Nares, and their co-adjutors. A few months imprisonment was the only punishment awarded them, and that was in return for the assault upon the head of the police; but in Billy, the ostler, was recognized an old offender—various un-punished offences rose against him, and he was condemned to "seven pennorth" aboard the hulks at Chatham. The greatest rogue escaped the arm of justice for a time; but L— has since assured me he has every reason to believe that Farrell was, under a feigned name, executed in Somersetshire for horse stealing.

The Farm was converted into a Poor House for some of the adjacent parishes; L—received his reward, and when I left England, our heroine Mary was the blooming mother of a numerous family.

✲

Edgar Allan Poe

(1809–1849)

*Where is the ingenuity of unravelling a web which you yourself
have woven for the express purpose of unravelling? These tales of
ratiocination owe most of their popularity to being something in a
new key. I do not mean to say that they are not ingenious—but people
think they are more ingenious than they are—on account of the
method and air of method.*

—Poe

FEW WRITERS HAVE SO enriched the darker end of the literary
spectrum as Edgar Allan Poe. The images haunt our imaginations: a
premature burial, the gamble of mesmerism, a horrifying red plague,
a murderer haunted by the phantom heartbeat of his victim, William
Wilson's encounter with his doppelgänger, the code behind a search
for buried treasure, not to mention that annoying raven. Critics argue
over Poe's virtues and faults, but readers keep turning pages.

Born in Boston in 1809 to itinerant actors, both of whom died
while he was a toddler, Edgar Poe was then adopted by the Allan
family in Richmond, Virginia. He attended various schools in
England but was back in Virginia by the age of eleven. In 1826 he
enrolled in the University of Virginia and had by the next year
accumulated massive gambling debts that inspired him to leave

college, move to his family's roots in Baltimore, and join the army. The same year, 1827, he published his first book, *Tamerlane and Other Poems*, and he was off on a legendarily tempestuous career. At the age of twenty-seven, he married his thirteen-year-old cousin. He was reckless with love, money, alcohol, and other drugs, and by forty he was dead. Besides poetry and horror stories—including vampire tales at various levels of subtlety and quality—Poe wrote satire, literary criticism, and even science-minded essays. The latter include "Eureka: A Prose Poem," an insightful and lyrical analysis of a perennial bugbear for astronomers—the question of why the night sky is black if space holds an infinite number of stars.

Somehow Poe also found time to launch a genre. On April 1, 1841, the Philadelphia magazine *Graham's* published "The Murders in the Rue Morgue," which established the dominant characteristic of the detective-story field: a series of accounts featuring a recurring character and concentrating upon the investigative process. Poe's detective was an eccentric Frenchman named C. Auguste Dupin, a moody insomniac whose Romantic melancholy seems to have re-sulted in part from his family's pecuniary fall from grace. (For more background, see the introduction to "The Secret Cell.") Dupin is in some ways a typical Poe hero. Melancholy, literate, Dupin strolls like the embodiment of reason through all the bloody Gothic chaos of this story. Poe is almost universally credited with the invention of the detective story, and the pioneer virtues of "The Secret Cell" won't dethrone him.

Dupin's debut was followed by two more cases. "The Mystery of Marie Rogêt," which appeared in *Snowden's Ladies' Companion* in the winter of 1842–43, was inspired by the real-life murder of an American woman named Mary Cecilia Rogers. Poe moved the story to Dupin's Paris and gallicized the victim's name, but otherwise used many details from reality. While pretending to show how Dupin "unravelled the mystery of Marie's assassination," Poe later bragged, "I, in fact, enter into a very vigorous analysis of the real tragedy in New York." This "analysis" weakens the story; it doesn't begin to compare with "Rue Morgue" and the third Dupin outing, "The Purloined Letter." In December 1844, this final Dupin case appeared in a publication called *The Gift: A Christmas and New Year's Present for 1845*. In it Dupin famously outwits his adversary by daring to think the obvious.

With these three stories, Dupin stands as the first series detective, the first genius detective, and the star of the first locked-room mystery. Four and a half decades later, Arthur Conan Doyle shamelessly emulated Poe's approach, although he refined it and created a more versatile and appealing character than Dupin. But these stories weren't Poe's only contribution to crime fiction. In 1843 he won a prize from Philadelphia's *Dollar Newspaper* for his buried-treasure story "The Gold Bug," which featured the equally incisive William Legrand. Poe also wrote "The Man of the Crowd," in which the narrator shadows a suspect through the alleys of London, and "Thou Art the Man," in which a resurrection scene is staged to shock a confession from a murderer.

After the epigraph from Thomas Browne's seventeenth-century work *Urn Burial*, Poe prefaces the story with brief philosophical remarks, prior to the introduction of Dupin. He closes with a French quotation that, in context, becomes a sarcastic commentary upon the bureaucratic incompetence of the official police—a common theme in crime fiction ever since. The words *de nier ce qui est, et d'expliquer ce qui n'est pas* (to deny what is and to explain what is not) are from Jean-Jacques Rousseau's 1761 epistolary novel, *Julie, or the New Héloïse*, which was hugely popular despite, or perhaps because of, its strong philosophical themes about individual authenticity within an innately false society. It's the work credited with helping create the modern notion of authorial celebrity. Poe himself was one of the writers who helped launch the corollary idea of authors as disturbed geniuses, and even now our caped Vincent Price mental image of him towers over his ravens and plagues, his ghostly horses and brilliant amateur detectives.

The Murders in the Rue Morgue

What song the Syrens sang, or what name Achilles
assumed when he hid himself among women, although
puzzling Questions, are not beyond all conjecture.

—Sir Thomas Browne

THE MENTAL FEATURES DISCOURSED of as the analytical, are, in
themselves, but little susceptible of analysis. We appreciate them
only in their effects. We know of them, among other things, that
they are always to their possessor, when inordinately possessed, a
source of the liveliest enjoyment. As the strong man exults in his
physical ability, delighting in such exercises as call his muscles into
action, so glories the analyst in that moral activity which disen-
tangles. He derives pleasure from even the most trivial occupations
bringing his talent into play. He is fond of enigmas, of conun-
drums, hieroglyphics; exhibiting in his solutions of each a degree of
acumen which appears to the ordinary apprehension praeternatural.
His results, brought about by the very soul and essence of method,
have, in truth, the whole air of intuition.

The faculty of resolution is possibly much invigorated by mathematical study, and especially by that highest branch of it which,

unjustly, and merely on account of its retrograde operations, has been called, as if par excellence, analysis. Yet to calculate is not in itself to analyze. A chess-player, for example, does the one, without effort at the other. It follows that the game of chess, in its effects upon mental character, is greatly misunderstood. I am not now writing a treatise, but simply prefacing a somewhat peculiar narrative by observations very much at random; I will, therefore, take occasion to assert that the higher powers of the reflective intellect are more decidedly and more usefully tasked by the unostentatious game of draughts than by all the elaborate frivolity of chess. In this latter, where the pieces have different and bizarre motions, with various and variable values, what is only complex, is mistaken (a not unusual error) for what is profound. The attention is here called powerfully into play. If it flag for an instant, an oversight is committed, resulting in injury or defeat. The possible moves being not only manifold, but involute, the chances of such oversights are multiplied; and in nine cases out of ten, it is the more concentrative rather than the more acute player who conquers. In draughts, on the contrary, where the moves are unique and have but little variation, the probabilities of inadvertence are diminished, and the mere attention being left comparatively unemployed, what advantages are obtained by either party are obtained by superior acumen. To be less abstract, let us suppose a game of draughts where the pieces are reduced to four kings, and where, of course, no oversight is to be expected. It is obvious that here the victory can be decided (the players being at all equal) only by some recherché movement, the result of some strong exertion of the intellect. Deprived of ordinary resources, the analyst throws himself into the spirit of his opponent, identifies himself therewith, and not unfrequently sees thus, at a glance, the sole methods (sometimes indeed absurdly simple ones) by which he may seduce into error or hurry into miscalculation.

Whist has long been known for its influence upon what is termed the calculating power; and men of the highest order of intellect have been known to take an apparently unaccountable delight in it, while eschewing chess as frivolous. Beyond doubt there is nothing of a similar nature so greatly tasking the faculty of analysis. The best chess-player in Christendom may be little more than the best player of chess; but proficiency in whist implies a capacity for success in all these more important undertakings where mind struggles with mind. When I say proficiency, I mean that perfection in the game which includes a comprehension of all the sources whence legitimate advantage may be derived. These are not only manifold, but multiform, and lie frequently among recesses of thought altogether inaccessible to the ordinary understanding. To observe attentively is to remember distinctly; and, so far, the concentrative chess-player will do very well at whist; while the rules of Hoyle (themselves based upon the mere mechanism of the game) are sufficiently and generally comprehensible. Thus to have a retentive memory, and proceed by "the book" are points commonly regarded as the sum total of good playing. But it is in matters beyond the limits of mere rule that the skill of the analyst is evinced. He makes, in silence, a host of observations and inferences. So, perhaps, do his companions; and the difference in the extent of the information obtained, lies not so much in the validity of the inference as in the quality of the observation. The necessary knowledge is that of what to observe. Our player confines himself not at all; nor, because the game is the object, does he reject deductions from things external to the game. He examines the countenance of his partners, comparing it carefully with that of each of his opponents. He considers the mode of assorting the cards in each hand; often counting trump by trump, and honor by honor, through the glances bestowed by their holders upon each. He notes every variation of face as the play progresses, gathering a fund of thought from the differences in the expression of certainty, of surprise, of triumph, or chagrin. From the manner of gathering up a trick he judges whether the person taking it, can make another in the suit. He recognizes what is played through feint, by the manner with which it is thrown upon the table. A casual or inadvertent word; the accidental dropping or turning of a card, with the accompanying anxiety or carelessness in regard to its concealment; the counting of the tricks, with the order of their arrangement; embarrassment, hesitation, eagerness, or trepidation—all afford, to his apparently intuitive perception, indications of the true state of affairs. The first two or three rounds having been played, he is in full possession of the contents of each hand, and thenceforward puts down his cards with as absolute a precision of purpose as if the rest of the party had turned outward the faces of their own.

The analytical power should not be confounded with simple ingenuity; for while the analyst is necessarily ingenious, the ingenious man is often remarkably incapable of analysis. The constructive or combining power, by which ingenuity is usually manifested, and to which the phrenologists (I believe erroneously) have assigned a separate organ, supposing it a primitive faculty, has been so frequently seen in those whose intellect bordered otherwise upon idiocy, as to have attracted general observation among writers on morals. Between ingenuity and the analytic ability there exists a difference far greater, indeed, than that between the fancy and the imagination, but of a character very strictly analogous. It will be found, in fact, that the ingenious are always fanciful, and the truly imaginative never otherwise than analytic.

The narrative which follows will appear to the reader somewhat in the light of a commentary upon the propositions just advanced.

RESIDING IN PARIS DURING the spring and part of the summer of 18—, I there became acquainted with a Monsieur C. Auguste Dupin. This young gentleman was of an excellent, indeed of an illustrious family, but, by a variety of untoward events, had been reduced to such poverty that the energy of his character succumbed beneath it, and he ceased to bestir himself in this world, or to care for the retrieval of his fortunes. By courtesy of his creditors, there still remained in his possession a small remnant of his patrimony; and,

upon the income arising from this, he managed, by means of a rigorous economy, to procure the necessities of life, without troubling
himself about its superfluities. Books, indeed, were his sole luxuries, and in Paris these are easily obtained.

Our first meeting was at an obscure library in the Rue Mont-
martre, where the accident of our both being in search of the same
very rare and very remarkable volume, brought us into closer com-
munion. We saw each other again and again. I was deeply interested in the little family history which he detailed to me with all
that candor which a Frenchman indulges whenever mere self is the
theme. I was astonished, too, at the vast extent of his reading; and,
above all, I felt my soul enkindled within me by the wild fervor,
and the vivid freshness of his imagination. Seeking in Paris the
objects I then sought, I felt that the society of such a man would be
to me a treasure beyond price; and this feeling I frankly confided
to him. It was at length arranged that we should live together during
my stay in the city; and as my worldly circumstances were somewhat
less embarrassed than his own, I was permitted to be at the expense
of renting, and furnishing in a style which suited the rather fantastic gloom of our common temper, a time-eaten and grotesque mansion, long deserted through superstitions into which we did not
inquire, and tottering to its fall in a retired and desolate portion of
the Faubourg St. Germain.

Had the routine of our life at this place been known to the world,
we should have been regarded as madmen—although, perhaps, as
madmen of a harmless nature. Our seclusion was perfect. We admitted no visitors. Indeed the locality of our retirement had been
carefully kept a secret from my own former associates; and it had
been many years since Dupin had ceased to know or be known in
Paris. We existed within ourselves alone.

It was a freak of fancy in my friend (for what else shall I call it?)
to be enamored of the night for her own sake; and into this bi-
zarrerie, as into all his others, I quietly fell; giving myself up to his
wild whims with a perfect abandon. The sable divinity would not

herself dwell with us always; but we could counterfeit her presence. At the first dawn of the morning we closed all the massy shutters of our old building; lighted a couple of tapers which, strongly perfumed, threw out only the ghastliest and feeblest of rays. By the aid of these we then busied our souls in dreams—reading, writing, or conversing, until warned by the clock of the advent of the true Darkness. Then we sallied forth into the streets, arm in arm, continuing the topics of the day, or roaming far and wide until a late hour, seeking, amid the wild lights and shadows of the populous city, that infinity of mental excitement which quiet observation can afford.

At such times I could not help remarking and admiring (although from his rich ideality I had been prepared to expect it) a peculiar analytic ability in Dupin. He seemed, too, to take an eager delight in its exercise—if not exactly in its display—and did not hesitate to confess the pleasure thus derived. He boasted to me, with a low chuckling laugh, that most men, in respect to himself, wore windows in their bosoms, and was wont to follow up such assertions by direct and very startling proofs of his intimate knowledge of my own. His manner at these moments was frigid and abstract; his eyes were vacant in expression; while his voice, usually a rich tenor, rose into a treble which would have sounded petulant but for the deliberateness and entire distinctness of this enunciation. Observing him in these moods, I often dwelt meditatively upon the old philosophy of the Bi-Part Soul, and amused myself with the fancy of a double Dupin—the creative and the resolvent.

Let it not be supposed, from what I have just said, that I am detailing any mystery, or penning any romance. What I have described in the Frenchman was merely the result of an excited, or perhaps of a diseased, intelligence. But of the character of his remarks at the periods in question an example will best convey the idea.

We were strolling one night down a long dirty street, in the vicinity of the Palais Royal. Being both, apparently, occupied with thought, neither of us had spoken a syllable for fifteen minutes at least. All at once Dupin broke forth with these words:

"He is a very little fellow, that's true, and would do better for the Théâtre des Variétés."

"There can be no doubt of that," I replied, unwittingly, and not at first observing (so much had I been absorbed in reflection) the extraordinary manner in which the speaker had chimed in with my meditations. In an instant afterward I recollected myself, and my astonishment was profound.

"Dupin," said I, gravely, "this is beyond my comprehension. I do not hesitate to say that I am amazed, and can scarcely credit my senses. How was it possible you should know I was thinking of ————?" Here I paused, to ascertain beyond a doubt whether he really knew of whom I thought.

"———— of Chantilly," said he, "why do you pause? You were remarking to yourself that his diminutive figure unfitted him for tragedy."

This was precisely what had formed the subject of my reflections. Chantilly was a quondam cobbler of the Rue St. Denis, who, becoming stage-mad, had attempted the role of Xerxes, in Crébillon's tragedy so called, and been notoriously Pasquinaded for his pains.

"Tell me, for Heaven's sake," I exclaimed, "the method—if method there is—by which you have been enabled to fathom my soul in this matter." In fact, I was even more startled than I would have been willing to express.

"It was the fruiterer," replied my friend, "who brought you to the conclusion that the mender of soles was not of sufficient height for Xerxes *et id genus omne*."

"The fruiterer!—you astonish me—I know no fruiterer whomsoever."

"The man who ran up against you as we entered the street—it may have been fifteen minutes ago."

I now remember that, in fact, a fruiterer, carrying upon his head a large basket of apples, had nearly thrown me down, by accident, as we paused from the Rue C———— into the thoroughfare where we stood; but what this had to do with Chantilly I could not possibly understand.

There was not a particle of charlatanerie about Dupin. "I will explain," he said, "and that you may comprehend all clearly, we will first retrace the course of your meditations, from the moment in which I spoke to you until that of the rencontre with the fruiterer in question. The larger links of the chain run thus—Chantilly, Orion, Dr. Nichols, Epicurus, Stereotomy, the street stones, the fruiterer."

There are few persons who have not, at some period of their lives, amused themselves in retracing the steps by which particular conclusions of their own minds have been attained. The occupation is often full of interest; and he who attempts it for the first time is astonished by the apparently illimitable distance and incoherence between the starting-point and the goal. What, then, must have been my amazement, when I heard the Frenchman speak what he had just spoken, and when I could not help acknowledging that he spoke the truth. He continued:

"We had been talking of horses, if I remember aright, just before leaving the Rue C———. This was the last subject we discussed. As we crossed into this street, a fruiterer, with a large basket upon his head, brushing quickly past us, thrust you upon a pile of paving-stones collected at a spot where the causeway is undergoing repair. You stepped upon one of the loose fragments, slipped, slightly strained you ankle, appeared vexed or sulky, muttered a few words, turned to look at the pile, and then proceeded in silence. I was not particularly attentive to what you did; but observation has become with me, of late, a species of necessity.

"You kept your eyes upon the ground—glancing, with a petulant expression, at the holes and ruts in the pavement (so that I saw you were still thinking of the stones), until we reached the little alley called Lamartine, which has been paved, by way of experiment, with the overlapping and riveted blocks. Here your countenance brightened up, and, perceiving you lips move, I could not doubt that you murmured the word 'stereotomy,' a term very affectedly applied to this species of pavement. I knew that you could not say to yourself 'stereotomy' without being brought to think of atomies, and thus of the theories of Epicurus; and since, when we discussed this subject not very long ago, I mentioned to you how singularly, yet with how little notice, the vague guesses of that noble Greek had met with confirmation in the late nebular cosmogony, I felt that you could not avoid casting your eyes upward to the great nebula in Orion, and I certainly expected that you would do so. You did look up; and I was now assured that I correctly followed your steps. But in that bitter tirade upon Chantilly, which appeared in yesterday's 'Musée,' the satirist, making some disgraceful allusions to the cobbler's change of name upon assuming the buskin, quoted a Latin line about which we have often conversed. I mean the line *Perdidit antiquum litera prima sonum*. I had told you that this was in reference to Orion, formerly written Urion; and, from certain pungencies connected with this explanation, I was aware that you could not have forgotten it. It was clear, therefore, that you would not fail to combine the two ideas of Orion and Chantilly. That you did combine them I saw by the character of the smile which passed over your lips. You thought of the poor cobbler's immolation. So far, you had been stooping in your gait; but now I saw you draw yourself up to your full height. I was then sure that you reflected upon the diminutive figure of Chantilly. At this point I interrupted your meditations to remark that as, in fact, he was a very little fellow—that Chantilly—he would not do better at the Théâtre des Variétés."

Not long after this, we were looking over an evening edition of the *Gazette des Tribunaux*, when the following paragraphs arrested our attention.

"EXTRAORDINARY MURDERS.—This morning, about three o'clock, the inhabitants of the Quartier St. Roch were roused from sleep by a succession of terrific shrieks, issuing, apparently, from the fourth story of a house in the Rue Morgue, known to be in the sole occupancy of one Madame L'Espanaye, and her daughter, Mademoiselle Camille L'Espanaye. After some delay, occasioned by a fruitless attempt to procure admission in the usual manner, the gateway was broken in with a crowbar, and eight or ten of the neighbors entered, accompanied by two gendarmes. By this time the cries had ceased; but, as the party rushed up the first flight of stairs, two or more rough voices, in angry contention, were distinguished, and seemed to proceed from the upper part of the house. As the second landing was reached, these sounds, also, had ceased, and every thing remained perfectly quiet. The party spread themselves, and hurried from room to room. Upon arriving at a large back chamber in the fourth story (the door of which, being found locked, with the key inside, was forced open), a spectacle presented itself which struck every one present not less with horror than with astonishment.

"The apartment was in the wildest disorder—the furniture broken and thrown about in all directions. There was only one bedstead; and from this the bed had been removed, and thrown into the middle of the floor. On the chair lay a razor, besmeared with blood. On the hearth were two or three long and thick tresses of gray human hair, also dabbled with blood, and seeming to have been pulled out by the roots. Upon the floor were found four Napoleons, an ear-ring of topaz, three large silver spoons, three smaller of metal d'Alger, and two bags, containing nearly four thousand francs in gold. The drawers of a bureau, which stood in one corner, were open, and had been, apparently, rifled, although many articles still remained in them. A small iron safe was discovered under the bed (not under the bedstead). It was open, with the key still in the door. It had no contents beyond a few old letters, and other papers of little consequence.

"Of Madame L'Espanaye no traces were here seen; but an unusual quantity of soot being observed in the fire-place, a search was made in the chimney, and (horrible to relate!) the corpse of the daughter, head downward, was dragged therefrom; it having been thus forced up the narrow aperture for a considerable distance. The body was quite warm. Upon examining it, many excoriations were perceived, no doubt occasioned by the violence with which it had been thrust up and disengaged. Upon the face were many severe scratches, and, upon the throat, dark bruises, and deep indentations of finger nails, as if the deceased had been throttled to death.

"After a thorough investigation of every portion of the house without farther discovery, the party made its way into a small paved yard in the rear of the building, where lay the corpse of the old lady, with her throat so entirely cut that, upon an attempt to raise her, the head fell off. The body, as well as the head, was fearfully mutilated—the former so much so as scarcely to retain any semblance of humanity.

"To this horrible mystery there is not as yet, we believe, the slightest clew."

The next day's paper had these additional particulars:

"The Tragedy in the Rue Morgue.—Many individuals have been examined in relation to this most extraordinary and frightful affair," [the word 'affaire' has not yet, in France, that levity of import which it conveys with us] "but nothing whatever has transpired to throw light upon it. We give below all the material testimony elicited.

"Pauline Dubourg, laundress, deposes that she has known both the deceased for three years, having washed for them during that period. The old lady and her daughter seemed on good terms—very affectionate toward each other. They were excellent pay. Could not speak in regard to their mode or means of living. Believe that Madame L. told fortunes for a living. Was reputed to have money put by. Never met any person in the house when she called for the clothes or took them home. Was sure that they had no servant in employ. There appeared to be no furniture in any part of the building except in the fourth story.

"Pierre Moreau, tobacconist, deposes that he has been in the habit of selling small quantities of tobacco and snuff to Madame L'Espanaye for nearly four years. Was born in the neighborhood, and has always resided there. The deceased and her daughter had occupied the house in which the corpses were found, for more than six years. It was formerly occupied by a jeweller, who under-let the upper rooms to various persons. The house was the property of Madame L. She became dissatisfied with the abuse of the premises by her tenant, and moved into them herself, refusing to let any portion. The old lady was childish. Witness had seen the daughter some five or six times during the six years. The two lived an exceedingly retired life—were reputed to have money. Had heard it said among the neighbors that Madame L. told fortunes—did not believe it. Had never seen any person enter the door except the old lady and her daughter, a porter once or twice, and a physician some eight or ten times.

"Many other persons, neighbors, gave evidence to the same effect. No one was spoken of as frequenting the house. It was not known whether there were any living connections of Madame L. and her daughter. The shutters of the front windows were seldom opened. Those in the rear were always closed, with the exception of the large back room, fourth story. The house was a good house—not very old.

"Isidore Muset, gendarme, deposes that he was called to the house about three o'clock in the morning, and found some twenty or thirty persons at the gateway, endeavoring to gain admittance. Forced it open, at length, with a bayonet—not with a crowbar. Had but little difficulty in getting it open, on account of its being a double or folding gate, and bolted neither at bottom nor top. The shrieks were continued until the gate was forced—and then suddenly ceased. They seemed to be screams of some person (or persons) in great agony—were loud and drawn out, not short and quick. Witness led the way up stairs. Upon reaching the first landing, heard two voices in loud and angry contention—the one a gruff voice, the other much shriller—a very strange voice. Could distinguish some words of the former, which was that of a Frenchman. Was positive that it was not a woman's voice. Could distinguish the words 'sacré' and 'diable.' The shrill voice was that of a foreigner. Could not be sure whether it was the voice of a man or of a woman. Could not make out what was said but believed the language to be Spanish. The state of the room and of the bodies was described by this witness as we described them yesterday.

"Henri Duval, a neighbor, and by trade a silver-smith, deposes that he was one of the party who first entered the house. Corroborates the testimony of Muset in general. As soon as they forced an entrance, they reclosed the door, to keep out the crowd, which collected very fast, notwithstanding the lateness of the hour. The shrill voice, this witness thinks, was that of an Italian. Was certain it was not French. Could not be sure that it was a man's voice. It might have been a woman's. Was not acquainted with the Italian language. Could not distinguish the words, but was convinced by the intonation that the speaker was an Italian. Knew Madame L. and her daughter. Had conversed with both frequently. Was sure that the shrill voice was not that of either of the deceased.

"——— Odenheimer, restaurateur.—This witness volunteered his testimony. Not speaking French, was examined through an interpreter. Is a native of Amsterdam. Was passing the house at the time of the shrieks. They lasted for several minutes—probably ten. They were long and loud—very awful and distressing. Was one of those who entered the building. Corroborated the previous evidence in every respect but one. Was sure that the shrill voice was that of a man—of a Frenchman. Could not distinguish the words uttered. They were loud and quick—unequal—spoken apparently in fear as well as in anger. The voice was harsh—not so much shrill as harsh. Could not call it a shrill voice. The gruff voice said repeatedly, 'sacré,' 'diable,' and once 'mon Dieu.'

"Jules Mignaud, banker, of the firm of Mignaud et Fils, Rue Deloraine. Is the elder Mignaud. Madame L'Espanaye had some property. Had opened an account with his banking house in the spring of the year ——— (eight years previously). Made frequent deposits in small sums. Had checked for nothing until the third day before her death, when she took out in person the sum of 4,000 francs. This sum was paid in gold, and a clerk sent home with the money.

"Adolphe Le Bon, clerk to Mignaud et Fils, deposes that on the day in question, about noon, he accompanied Madame L'Espanaye to her residence with the 4,000 francs, put up in two bags. Upon the door being opened, Mademoiselle L. appeared and took from his hands one of the bags, while the old lady relieved him of the other. He then bowed and departed. Did not see any person in the street at the time. It is a by-street—very lonely.

"William Bird, tailor, deposes that he was one of the party who entered the house. Is an Englishman. Has lived in Paris two years. Was one of the first to ascend the stairs. Heard the voices in contention. The gruff voice was that of a Frenchman. Could make out several words, but cannot now remember all. Heard distinctly 'sacré' and 'mon Dieu.' There was a sound at the moment as if of several persons struggling—a scraping and scuffling sound. The shrill voice was very loud—louder than the gruff one. Is sure that it was not the voice of an Englishman. Appeared to be that of a German. Might have been a woman's voice. Does not understand German.

"Four of the above-named witnesses, being recalled, deposed that the door of the chamber in which was found the body of Mademoiselle L. was locked on the inside when the party reached it. Every thing was perfectly silent—no groans or noises of any kind. Upon forcing the door no person was seen. The windows, both of the back and front room, were down and firmly fastened from within. A door between the two rooms was closed but not locked. The door leading from the front room into the passage was locked, with the key on the inside. A small room in the front of the house, on the fourth story, at the head of the passage, was open, the door being ajar. This room was crowded with old beds, boxes, and so forth. These were carefully removed and searched. There was not an inch of any portion of the house which was not carefully searched.

Sweeps were sent up and down the chimneys. The house was a four-story one, with garrets (mansardes). A trap-door on the roof was nailed down very securely—did not appear to have been opened for years. The time elapsing between the hearing of the voices in contention and the breaking open of the room door was variously stated by the witnesses. Some made it as short as three minutes—some as long as five. The door was opened with difficulty.

"Alfonzo Garcio, undertaker, deposes that he resides in the Rue Morgue. Is a native of Spain. Was one of the party who entered the house. Did not proceed up stairs. Is nervous, and was apprehensive of the consequences of agitation. Heard the voices in contention. The gruff voice was that of a Frenchman. Could not distinguish what was said. The shrill voice was that of an Englishman—is sure of this. Does not understand the English language, but judges by the intonation.

"Alberto Montani, confectioner, deposes that he was among the first to ascend the stairs. Heard the voices in question. The gruff voice was that of a Frenchman. Distinguished several words. The speaker appeared to be expostulating. Could not make out the words of the shrill voice. Spoke quick and unevenly. Thinks it is the voice of a Russian. Corroborates the general testimony. Is an Italian. Never conversed with a native of Russia.

"Several witnesses, recalled, here testified that the chimneys of all the rooms of the fourth story were too narrow to admit the passage of a human being. By 'sweeps' were meant cylindrical sweeping-brushes, such as are employed by those who clean chimneys. These brushes were passed up and down every flue in the house. There is no back passage by which any one could have descended while the party proceeded upstairs. The body of Mademoiselle L'Espanaye was so firmly wedged in the chimney that it could not be got down until four or five of the party united their strength.

"Paul Dumas, physician, deposes that he was called to view the bodies about daybreak. They were both then lying on the sacking of the bedstead in the chamber where Mademoiselle L. was found.

The corpse of the young lady was much bruised and excoriated. The fact that it had been thrust up the chimney would sufficiently account for these appearances. The throat was greatly chafed. There were several deep scratches just below the chin, together with a series of livid spots which were evidently the impressions of fingers. The face was fearfully discolored, and the eyeballs protruded. The tongue had been partially bitten through. A large bruise was discovered upon the pit of the stomach, produced, apparently, by the pressure of a knee. In the opinion of M. Dumas, Mademoiselle L'Espanaye had been throttled to death by some person or persons unknown. The corpse of the mother was horribly mutilated. All the bones of the right leg and arm were more or less shattered. The left tibia much splintered, as well as all the ribs of the left side. Whole body dreadfully bruised and discolored. It was not possible to say how the injuries had been inflicted. A heavy club of wood, or a broad bar of iron—a chair—any large, heavy, and obtuse weapon would have produced such results, if wielded by the hands of a very powerful man. No woman could have inflicted the blows with any weapon. The head of the deceased, when seen by witness, was entirely separated from the body, and was also greatly shattered. The throat had evidently been cut with some very sharp instrument—probably with a razor.

"Alexandre Étienne, surgeon, was called with M. Dumas to view the bodies. Corroborated the testimony, and the opinions of M. Dumas.

"Nothing further of importance was elicited, although several other persons were examined. A murder so mysterious, and so perplexing in all its particulars, was never before committed in Paris—if indeed a murder had been committed at all. The police are entirely at fault—an unusual occurrence in affairs of this nature. There is not, however, the shadow of a clew apparent."

The evening edition of the paper stated that the greatest excitement still continued in the quartier St. Roch—that the premises in question had been carefully re-searched, and fresh examinations of witnesses instituted, but all to no purpose. A postscript, however, mentioned that Adolphe Le Bon had been arrested and imprisoned— although nothing appeared to criminate him beyond the facts already detailed.

Dupin seemed singularly interested in the progress of this affair— at least so I judged from his manner, for he made no comments. It was only after the announcement that Le Bon had been imprisoned, that he asked me my opinion respecting the murders.

I could merely agree with all Paris in considering them an insoluble mystery. I saw no means by which it would be possible to trace the murderer.

"We must not judge of the means," said Dupin, "by this shell of an examination. The Parisian police, so much extolled for acumen, are cunning, but no more. There is no method in their proceedings, beyond the method of the moment. They make a vast parade of measures; but, not infrequently, these are so ill-adapted to the objects proposed, as to put us in mind of Monsieur Jourdain's calling for his robe-de-chambre—*pour mieux entendre la musique.* The results attained by them are not unfrequently surprising, but for the most part, are brought about by simple diligence and activity. When these qualities are unavailing, their schemes fail. Vidocq, for example, was a good guesser, and the persevering man. But, without educated thought, he erred continually by the very intensity of his investigations. He impaired his vision by holding the object too close. He might see, perhaps, one or two points with unusual clearness, but in so doing he, necessarily, lost sight of the matter as a whole. Thus there is such a thing as being too profound. Truth is not always in a well. In fact, as regards the more important knowledge, I do believe that she is invariably superficial. The depth lies in the valleys where we seek her, and not upon the mountain-tops where she is found. The modes and sources of this kind of error are well typified in the contemplation of the heavenly bodies. To look at a star by glances— to view it in a side-long way, by turning toward it the exterior portions of the retina (more susceptible of feeble impressions of light than the interior), is to behold the star distinctly—is to have the best appreciation of its lustre—a lustre which grows dim just in proportion as we turn our vision fully upon it. A greater number of rays actually fall upon the eye in the latter case, but in the former, there is the more refined capacity for comprehension. By undue profundity we perplex and enfeeble thought; and it is possible to make even Venus herself vanish from the firmament by a scrutiny too sustained, too concentrated, or too direct.

"As for these murders, let us enter into some examinations for ourselves, before we make up an opinion respecting them. An inquiry will afford us amusement," [I thought this an odd term, so applied, but said nothing] "and besides, Le Bon once rendered me a service for which I am not ungrateful. We will go and see the premises with our own eyes. I know G———, the Prefect of Police, and shall have no difficulty in obtaining the necessary permission."

The permission was obtained, and we proceeded at once to the Rue Morgue. This is one of those miserable thoroughfares which intervene between the Rue Richelieu and the Rue St. Roch. It was late in the afternoon when we reached it, as this quarter is at a great distance from that in which we resided. The house was readily found; for there were still many persons gazing up at the closed shutters, with an objectless curiosity, from the opposite side of the way. It was an ordinary Parisian house, with a gateway, on one side of which was glazed watch-box, with a sliding panel in the window, indicating a loge de concierge. Before going in we walked up the street, turned down an alley, and then, again turning, passed in the rear of the building—Dupin, meanwhile, examining the whole neighborhood, as well as the house, with a minuteness of attention for which I could see no possible object.

Retracing our steps we came again to the front of the dwelling, rang, and, having shown our credentials, were admitted by the agents in charge. We went up stairs—into the chamber where the body of Mademoiselle L'Espanaye had been found, and where both the deceased still lay. The disorders of the room had, as usual, been suffered to exist. I saw nothing beyond what had been stated in the *Gazette des Tribunaux*. Dupin scrutinized every thing—not excepting the bodies of the victims. We then went into the other rooms, and into the yard; a gendarme accompanying us throughout. The examination occupied us until dark, when we took our departure. On our way home my companion stepped in for a moment at the office of one of the daily papers.

I have said that the whims of my friend were manifold, and that *Je les menagais:*—for this phrase there is no English equivalent. It was his humor, now, to decline all conversation on the subject of the murder, until about noon the next day. He then asked me, suddenly, if I had observed any thing peculiar at the scene of the atrocity.

There was something in his manner of emphasizing the word "peculiar," which caused me to shudder without knowing why.

"No, nothing peculiar," I said; "nothing more, at least, than we both saw stated in the paper."

"The *Gazette*," he replied, "has not entered, I fear, into the unusual horror of the thing. But dismiss the idle opinions of this print. It appears to me that this mystery is considered insoluble, for the very reason which should cause it to be regarded as easy of solution—I mean for the outré character of its features. The police are confounded by the seeming absence of motive—not for the murder itself—but for the atrocity of the murder. They are puzzled, too, by the seeming impossibility of reconciling the voices heard in contention, with the facts that no one was discovered upstairs but the assassinated Mademoiselle L'Espanaye, and that there were no means of egress without the notice of the party ascending. The wild disorder of the room; the corpse thrust, with the head downward, up the chimney; the frightful mutilation of the body of the old lady; these considerations, with those just mentioned, and others which I need not mention, have sufficed to paralyze the powers, by putting completely at fault the boasted acumen, of the government agents. They have fallen into the gross but common error of confounding the unusual with the abstruse. But it is by these deviations from the plane of the ordinary, that reason feels its way, if at all, in its search for the true. In investigations such as we are now pursuing, it should not be so much asked 'what has occurred,' as 'what has occurred that has never occurred before.' In fact, the facility with which I shall arrive, or have arrived, at the solution of this mystery, is in the direct ration of its apparent insolubility in the eyes of the police." I stared at the speaker in mute astonishment.

"I am now awaiting," continued he, looking toward the door of our apartment—"I am now awaiting a person who, although perhaps not the perpetrator of these butcheries, must have been in some measure implicated in their perpetration. Of the worst portion of the crimes committed, it is probable that he is innocent. I hope that I am right in this supposition; for upon it I build my expectation of reading the entire riddle. I look for the man here—in this room—every moment. It is true that he may not arrive; but the probability is that he will. Should he come, it will be necessary to detain him. Here are pistols; and we both know how to use them when occasion demands their use."

I took the pistols, scarcely knowing what I did, or believing what I heard, while Dupin went on, very much as if in a soliloquy. I have already spoken of his abstract manner at such times. His discourse was addressed to myself; but his voice, although by no means loud, had that intonation which is commonly employed in speaking to some one at a great distance. His eyes, vacant in expression, regarded only the wall.

"That the voices heard in contention," he said, "by the party upon the stairs, were not the voices of the women themselves, was fully proved by the evidence. This relieves us of all doubt upon the question whether the old lady could have first destroyed the daughter, and afterward have committed suicide. I speak of this point chiefly for the sake of method; for the strength of Madame L'Espanaye would have been utterly unequal to the task of thrusting her daughter's corpse up the chimney as it was found; and the nature of the wounds upon her own person entirely precludes the idea of self-destruction.

Murder, then, has been committed by some third party; and the voices of this third party were those heard in contention. Let me now advert—not to the whole testimony respecting these voices— but to what was peculiar in that testimony. Did you observe any thing peculiar about it?"

I remarked that, while all the witnesses agreed in supposing the gruff voice to be that of a Frenchman, there was much disagreement in regard to the shrill, or, as one individual termed it, the harsh voice.

"That was the evidence itself," said Dupin, "but it was not the peculiarity of the evidence. You have observed nothing distinctive. Yet there was something to be observed. The witnesses, as you remarked, agreed about the gruff voice; they were here unanimous. But in regard to the shrill voice, the peculiarity is—not that they disagreed—but that, while an Italian, an Englishman, a Spaniard, a Hollander, and a Frenchman attempted to describe it, each one spoke of it as that of a foreigner. Each is sure that it was not the voice of one of his own countrymen. Each likens it—not to the voice of an individual of any nation with whose language he is conversant— but the converse. The Frenchman supposes it is the voice of a Spaniard, and 'might have distinguished some words had he been acquainted with the Spanish.' The Dutchman maintains it to have been that of a Frenchman; but we find it stated that 'not under- standing French this witness was examined through an interpreter.' The Englishman thinks it the voice of a German, and 'does not understand German.' The Spaniard 'is sure' that it was that of an Englishman, but 'judges by the intonation' altogether, 'as he has no knowledge of the English.' The Italian believes it the voice of a Russian, but 'has never conversed with a native of Russia.' A second Frenchman differs, moreover, with the first, and is positive that the voice was that of an Italian; but, not being cognizant of that tongue, is, like the Spaniard, 'convinced by the intonation.' Now, how strangely unusual must that voice have really been, about which such testimony as this could have been elicited!—in whose tones, even, denizens of the five great divisions of Europe could recognize nothing familiar! You will say that it might have been the voice of an Asiatic—of an African. Neither Asiatics nor Africans abound in Paris; but, without denying the inference, I will now merely call your attention to three points. The voice is termed by one witness 'harsh rather than shrill.' It is represented by two others to have been 'quick and unequal.' No words—no sounds resembling words—were by any witness mentioned as distinguishable.

"I know not," continued Dupin, "what impression I may have made, so far, upon your own understanding; but I do not hesitate to say that legitimate deductions even from this portion of the testimony—the portion respecting the gruff and shrill voices—are in themselves sufficient to engender a suspicion which should give direction to all farther progress in the investigation of the mystery. I said 'legitimate deductions'; but my meaning is not thus fully expressed. I designed to imply that the deductions are the sole proper ones, and that the suspicion arises inevitably from them as the single result. What the suspicion is, however, I will not say just yet. I merely wish you to bear in mind that, with myself, it was sufficiently forcible to give a definite form—a certain tendency—to my inquiries in the chamber.

"Let us now transport ourselves, in fancy, to this chamber. What shall we first seek here? The means of egress employed by the murderers. It is not too much to say that neither of us believe in praeternatural events. Madame and Mademoiselle L'Espanaye were not destroyed by spirits. The doers of the deed were material and escaped materially. Then how? Fortunately there is but one mode of reasoning upon the point, and that mode must lead us to a definite decision. Let us examine, each by each, the possible means of egress. It is clear that the assassins were in the room where Mademoiselle L'Espanaye was found, or at least in the room adjoining, when the party ascended the stairs. It is, then, only from these two apartments that we have to seek issues. The police have laid bare the floors, the ceiling, and the masonry of the walls, in every direction. No secret issues could have escaped their vigilance. But, not trusting to their eyes, I examined with my own. There were, then, no secret issues. Both doors leading from the rooms into the passage were securely locked, with the keys inside. Let us turn to the chimneys. These, although of ordinary width for some eight or ten feet above the hearths, will not admit, throughout their extent, the body of a large cat. The impossibility of egress, by means already stated, being thus absolute, we are reduced to the windows. Through those of the front room no one could have escaped without notice from the crowd in the street. The murderers must have passed, then, through those of the back room. Now, brought to this conclusion in so unequivocal a manner as we are, it is not our part, as reasoners, to reject it on account of apparent impossibilities. It is only left for us to prove that these apparent 'impossibilities' are, in reality, not such.

"There are two windows in the chamber. One of them is unobstructed by furniture, and is wholly visible. The lower portion of the other is hidden from view by the head of the unwieldy bedstead which is thrust close up against it. The former was found securely fastened from within. It resisted the utmost force of those who endeavor to raise it. A large gimlet-hole had been pierced in its frame to the left, and a very stout nail was found fitted therein, nearly to the head. Upon examining the other window, a similar nail was seen similarly fitted in it; and a vigorous attempt to raise this sash failed also. The police were now entirely satisfied that egress had not been in these directions. And, therefore, it was thought a matter of supererogation to withdraw the nails and open the windows.

"My own examination was somewhat more particular, and was so for the reason I have just given—because here it was, I knew, that all apparent impossibilities must be proved to be not such in reality.

"I proceeded to think thus—a posteriori. The murderers did escape from one of these windows. This being so, they could not have re-fastened the sashes from the inside, as they were found fastened;—the consideration which put a stop, through its obviousness, to the scrutiny of the police in this quarter. Yet the sashes were fastened. They must, then, have the power of fastening themselves. There was no escape from this conclusion. I stepped to the unobstructed casement, withdrew the nail with some difficulty, and attempted to raise the sash. It resisted all my efforts, as I had anticipated. A concealed spring must, I now knew, exist; and this corroboration of my idea convinced me that my premises, at least, were correct, however mysterious still appeared the circumstances attending the nails. A careful search soon brought to light the hidden spring. I pressed it, and, satisfied with the discovery, forbore to upraise the sash.

"I now replaced the nail and regarded it attentively. A person passing out through this window might have reclosed it, and the spring would have caught—but the nail could not have been replaced. The conclusion was plain, and again narrowed in the field of my investigations. The assassins must have escaped through the other window. Supposing, then, the springs upon each sash to be the same, as was probable, there must be found a difference between the nails, or at least between the modes of their fixture. Getting upon the sacking of the bedstead, I looked over the head-board minutely at the second casement. Passing my hand down behind the board, I readily discovered and pressed the spring, which was, as I had supposed, identical in character with its neighbor. I now looked at the nail. It was as stout as the other, and apparently fitted in the same manner—driven in nearly up to the head.

"You will say that I was puzzled; but, if you think so, you must have misunderstood the nature of the inductions. To use a sporting phrase, I had not been once 'at fault.' The scent had never for an instant been lost. There was no flaw in any link in the chain. I had traced the secret to its ultimate result,—and that result was the nail. It had, I say, in every respect, the appearance of its fellow in the other window; but this fact was an absolute nullity (conclusive as it might seem to be) when compared with the consideration that here, at this point, terminated the clew. 'There must be something wrong,' I said, 'about the nail.' I touched it; and the head, with about a quarter of an inch of the shank, came off in my fingers. The rest of the shank was in the gimlet-hole, where it had been broken off. The fracture was an old one (for its edges were incrusted with rust), and had apparently been accomplished by the blow of a hammer, which had partially imbedded, in the top of the bottom sash, the head portion of the nail. I now carefully replaced this head portion in the indentation whence I had taken it, and the resemblance to a perfect nail was complete—the fissure was invisible. Pressing the spring, I gently raised the sash for a few inches; the head went up with it, remaining firm in its bed. I closed the window, and the semblance of the whole nail was again perfect.

"This riddle, so far, was now unriddled. The assassin had escaped through the window which looked upon the bed. Dropping of its own accord upon his exit (or perhaps purposely closed), it had become fastened by the spring; and it was the retention of this spring which had been mistaken by the police for that of the nail,—farther inquiry being thus considered unnecessary.

"The next question is that of the mode of descent. Upon this point I had been satisfied in my walk with you around the building. About five feet and a half from the casement in question there runs a lightning-rod. From this rod it would have been impossible for any one to reach to the window itself, to say nothing of entering it. I observed, however, that the shutters of the fourth story were of the peculiar kind called by Parisian carpenters ferrades—a kind rarely employed at the present day, but frequently seen upon very old mansions at Lyons and Bordeaux. They are in the form of an ordinary door (a single, not a folding door), except that the lower half is latticed or worked in open trellis—thus affording an excellent hold for the hands. In the present instance these shutters are fully three feet and a half broad. When we saw them from the rear of the house, they were both about half open—that is to say they stood off at right angles from the wall. It is probable that the police, as well as myself, examined the back of the tenement; but, if so, in looking at these ferrades in the line of their breadth (as they must have done), they did not perceive the great breadth itself, or, at all events, failed to take it into due consideration. In fact, having once satisfied themselves that no egress could have been made in this quarter, they would naturally bestow here a very cursory examination. It was clear to me, however, that the shutter belonging to the window at the head of the bed, would, if swung fully back to the wall, reach to within two feet of the lightning-rod. It was also evident that, by exertion of a very unusual degree of activity and courage, an entrance into the window, from the rod, might have been thus effected. By reaching to the distance of two feet and a half (we now suppose the shutter open to its whole extent) a robber might have taken a firm grasp upon the trellis-work. Letting go, then, his hold upon the rod, placing his feet securely against the wall, and springing boldly from it, he might have swung the shutter so as to close it, and, if we imagine the window open at the time, might even have swung himself into the room.

"I wish you to bear especially in mind that I have spoken of a very unusual degree of activity as requisite to success in so hazardous and so difficult a feat. It is my design to show you first, that the thing might possibly have been accomplished:—but, secondly and chiefly, I wish to impress upon your understanding the very extraordinary—the almost praeternatural character of that agility which could have accomplished it.

"You will say, no doubt, using the language of the law, that to make out my case, I should rather undervalue than insist upon a full estimation of the activity required in this matter. This may be the practice in the law, but it is not the usage of reason. My ultimate object is only the truth. My immediate purpose is to lead you to place in juxtaposition, that very unusual activity of which I have just spoken, with that very peculiar shrill (or harsh) and unequal voice, about whose nationality no two persons could be found to agree, and in whose utterance no syllabification could be detected."

At these words a vague and half-formed conception of the meaning of Dupin flitted over in my mind. I seemed to be upon the verge of comprehension, without power to comprehend—as men, at times, find themselves upon the brink of remembrance, without being able, in the end, to remember. My friend went on with his discourse.

"You will see," he said, "that I have shifted the question from the mode of egress to that of ingress. It was my design to convey the idea that both were effected in the same manner, at the same point. Let us now revert to the interior of the room. Let us survey the appearances here. The drawers of the bureau, it is said, had been rifled, although many articles of apparel still remained within them. The conclusion here is absurd. It is a mere guess—a very silly one—and no more. How are we to know that the articles found in the drawers were not all these drawers had originally contained? Madame L'Espanaye and her daughter lived an exceedingly retired life—saw no company—seldom went out—had little use for the numerous changes of habiliment. Those found were at least of as good quality as any likely to be possessed by these ladies. If a thief had taken any, why did he not take the best—why did he not take all? In a word, why did he abandon four thousand francs in gold to encumber himself with a bundle of linen? The gold was abandoned. Nearly the whole sum mentioned by Monsieur Mignaud, the banker, was discovered, in bags, upon the floor. I wish you therefore, to discard from your thoughts the blundering idea of motive, engendered in the brains of the police by that portion of the evidence which speaks of money delivered at the door of the house. Coincidences ten times as remarkable as this (the delivery of the money, and murder committed within these days upon the party receiving it), happen to all of us every hour of our lives, without attracting even momentary notice. Coincidences, in general, are great stumbling-blocks in the way of that class of thinkers who have been educated to know nothing of the theory of probabilities— that theory to which the most glorious objects of human research are indebted for the most glorious of illustration. In the present instance, had the gold been gone, the fact of its delivery three days before would have formed something more than a coincidence. It would have been corroborative of this idea of motive. But, under the real circumstances of the case, if we are to suppose gold the motive of this outrage, we must also imagine the perpetrator so vacillating an idiot as to have abandoned his gold and his motive altogether.

"Keeping now steadily in mind the points to which I have drawn your attention—that peculiar voice, that unusual agility, and that startling absence of motive in a murder so singularly atrocious as this—let us glance at the butchery itself. Here is a woman strangled to death by manual strength, and thrust up a chimney head downward. Ordinary assassins employ no such mode of murder as this. Least of all, do they thus dispose of the murdered. In this manner of thrusting the corpse up the chimney, you will admit that there was something excessively outré—something altogether irreconcilable with our common notions of human action, even when we suppose the actors the most depraved of men. Think, too, how great must have been that strength which could have thrust the body up such an aperture so forcibly that the united vigor of several persons was found barely sufficient to drag it down!

"Turn, now, to other indications of the employment of a vigor most marvellous. On the hearth were thick tresses—very thick tresses—of gray human hair. These had been torn out by the roots. You are aware of the great force necessary in tearing thus from the head even twenty or thirty hairs together. You saw the locks in question as well as myself. Their roots (a hideous sight!) were clotted with fragments of the flesh of the scalp—sure tokens of the prodigious power which had been exerted in uprooting perhaps half a million of hairs at a time. The throat of the old lady was not

merely cut, but the head absolutely severed from the body: the instrument was a mere razor. I wish you also to look at the brutal
ferocity of these deeds. Of the bruises upon the body of Madame
L'Espanaye I do not speak. Monsieur Dumas, and his worthy coadjutor Monsieur Étienne, have pronounced that they were inflicted
by some obtuse instrument; and so far these gentlemen are very
correct. The obtuse instrument was clearly the stone pavement in
the yard, upon which the victim had fallen from the window
which looked in upon the bed. This idea, however simple it may
now seem, escaped the police for the same reason that the breadth
of the shutters escaped them—because, by the affair of the nails,
their perceptions had been hermetically sealed against the possibility of the windows having ever been opened at all.

"If now, in addition to all these things, you have properly reflected upon the odd disorder of the chamber, we have gone so far
as to combine the ideas of an agility astounding, a strength superhuman, a ferocity brutal, a butchery without motive, a grotesque-
rie in horror absolutely alien from humanity, and a voice foreign in
tone to the ears of men of many nations, and devoid of all distinct
or intelligible syllabification. What result, then, has ensued? What
impression have I made upon your fancy?"

I felt a creeping of the flesh as Dupin asked me the question. "A
madman," I said, "has done this deed—some raving maniac, escaped from a neighboring Maison de Santé."

"In some respects," he replied, "your idea is not irrelevant. But
the voices of madmen, even in their wildest paroxysms, are never
found to tally with that peculiar voice heard upon the stairs. Madmen are of some nation, and their language, however incoherent in
its words, has always the coherence of syllabification. Besides, the
hair of a madman is not such as I now hold in my hand. I disen-
tangled this little tuft from the rigidly clutched fingers of Madame
L'Espanaye. Tell me what you can make of it."

"Dupin!" I said, completely unnerved; "this hair is most unusual—
this is no human hair."

"I have not asserted that it is," said he; "but, before we decide this point, I wish you to glance at the little sketch I have here traced upon this paper. It is a facsimile drawing of what has been described in one portion of the testimony as 'dark bruises and deep indentations of finger nails' upon the throat of Mademoiselle L'Espanaye, and in another (by Messrs. Dumas and Étienne) as a 'series of livid spots, evidently the impression of fingers.'

"You will perceive," continued my friend, spreading out the paper upon the table before us, "that this drawing gives the idea of a firm and fixed hold. There is no slipping apparent. Each finger has retained—possibly until the death of the victim—the fearful grasp by which it originally imbedded itself. Attempt, now, to place all your fingers, at the same time, in the respective impressions as you see them."

I made the attempt in vain.

"We are possibly not giving this matter a fair trial," he said. "The paper is spread out upon a plane surface; but the human throat is cylindrical. Here is a billet of wood, the circumference of which is about that of the throat. Wrap the drawing around it, and try the experiment again."

I did so; but the difficulty was even more obvious than before. "This," I said, "is the mark of no human hand."

"Read now," replied Dupin, "this passage from Cuvier."

It was a minute anatomical and generally descriptive account of the large fulvous Ourang-Outang of the East Indian Islands. The gigantic stature, the prodigious strength and activity, the wild ferocity, and the imitative propensities of these mammalia are sufficiently well known to all. I understood the full horrors of the murder at once.

"The description of the digits," said I, as I made an end of the reading, "is in exact accordance with this drawing. I see no animal but an Ourang-Outang, of the species here mentioned, could have impressed the indentations as you have traced them. This tuft of tawny hair, too, is identical in character with that of the beast of Cuvier.

But I cannot possibly comprehend the particulars of this frightful mystery. Besides, there were two voices heard in contention, and one of them was unquestionably the voice of a Frenchman."

"True; and you will remember an expression attributed almost unanimously, by the evidence, to this voice,—the expression, 'mon Dieu!' This, under the circumstances, has been justly characterized by one of the witnesses (Montani, the confectioner) as an expression of remonstrance or expostulation. Upon these two words, therefore, I have mainly built my hopes of a full solution of the riddle. A Frenchman was cognizant of the murder. It is possible—indeed it is far more than probable—that he was innocent of all participation in the bloody transactions which took place. The Ourang-Outang may have escaped from him. He may have traced it to the chamber; but, under the agitating circumstances which ensued, he could never have recaptured it. It is still at large. I will not pursue these guesses—for I have no right to call them more—since the shades of reflection upon which they are based are scarcely of sufficient depth to be appreciated by my own intellect, and since I could not pretend to make them intelligible to the understanding of another. We will call them guesses, then, and speak of them as such. If the Frenchman in question is indeed, as I suppose, innocent of this atrocity, this advertisement, which I left last night, upon our return home, at the office of *Le Monde* (a paper devoted to the shipping interest, and much sought by sailors), will bring him to our residence."

He handed me a paper, and I read thus:

"CAUGHT—In the Bois de Boulogne, early in the morning of the —— inst. (the morning of the murder), a very large, tawny Ourang-Outang of the Bornese species. The owner (who is ascertained to be a sailor, belonging to a Maltese vessel) may have the animal again, upon identifying it satisfactorily, and paying a few charges arising from its capture and keeping. Call at No. —— Rue ——, Faubourg St. Germain—au troisième."

"How was it possible," I asked, "that you should know the man to be a sailor, and belonging to a Maltese vessel?"

"I do not know it," said Dupin. "I am not sure of it. Here, however, is a small piece of ribbon, which from its form, and from its greasy appearance, has evidently been used in tying the hair in one of those long queues of which sailors are so fond. Moreover, this knot is one which few besides sailors can tie, and is peculiar to the Maltese. I picked the ribbon up at the foot of the lighting-rod. It could not have belonged to either of the deceased. Now if, after all, I am wrong in my induction from this ribbon, that the Frenchman was a sailor belonging to a Maltese vessel, still I can have done no harm in saying what I did in the advertisement. If I am in error, he will merely suppose that I had been misled by some circumstance into which he will not take the trouble to inquire. But if I am right, a great point is gained. Cognizant although innocent of the murder, the Frenchman will naturally hesitate about replying to the advertisement—about demanding the Ourang-Outang. He will reason thus:—'I am innocent; I am poor; my Ourang-Outang is of great value—to one in my circumstances a fortune of itself—why should I lose it through idle apprehensions of danger? Here it is, within my grasp. It was found in the Bois de Boulogne—at a vast distance from the scene of that butchery. How can it ever be suspected that a brute beast should have done the deed? The police are at fault—they have failed to procure the slightest clew. Should they even trace the animal, it would be impossible to prove me cognizant of the murder, or to implicate me in guilt on account of that cognizance. Above all, I am known. The advertiser designates me as the possessor of the beast. I am not sure to what limit his knowledge may extend. Should I avoid claiming a property of so great value, which is known that I possess, I will render the animal at least, liable to suspicion. It is not my policy to attract attention either to myself or to the beast. I will answer the advertisement, get the Ourang-Outang, and keep it close until this matter has blown over.'"

At this moment we heard a step upon the stairs.

"Be ready," said Dupin, "with your pistols, but neither use them nor show them until at a signal from myself."

The front door of the house had been left open, and the visitor had entered, without ringing, and advanced several steps upon the staircase. Now, however, he seemed to hesitate. Presently we heard him descending. Dupin was moving quickly to the door, when we again heard him coming up. He did not turn back a second time, but stepped up with decision, and rapped at the door of our chamber.

"Come in," said Dupin, in a cheerful and hearty tone.

A man entered. He was a sailor, evidently,—a tall, stout, and muscular-looking person, with a certain dare-devil expression of countenance, not altogether unprepossessing. His face, greatly sunburnt, was more than half hidden by whisker and mustachio. He had with him a huge oaken cudgel, but appeared to be otherwise unarmed. He bowed awkwardly, and bade us "good evening," in French accents, which, although somewhat Neufchâtelish, were still sufficiently indicative of a Parisian origin.

"Sit down, my friend," said Dupin. "I suppose you have called about the Ourang-Outang. Upon my word, I almost envy you the possession of him; a remarkably fine, and no doubt very valuable animal. How old do you suppose him to be?"

The sailor drew a long breath, with the air of a man relieved of some intolerable burden, and then replied in an assured tone:

"I have no way of telling—but he can't be more than four or five years old. Have you got him here?"

"Oh, no; we had no conveniences for keeping him here. He is at a livery stable in the Rue Dubourg, just by. You can get him in the morning. Of course you are prepared to identify the property?"

"To be sure I am, sir."

"I shall be sorry to part with him," said Dupin.

"I don't mean that you should be at all this trouble for nothing, sir," said the man. "Couldn't expect it. Am very willing to pay a reward for the finding of the animal—that is to say, any thing in reason."

"Well," replied my friend, "that is all very fair, to be sure. Let me think!—what should I have? Oh! I will tell you. My reward shall be this. You shall give me all the information in your power about these murders in the Rue Morgue."

Dupin said the last words in a very low tone, and very quietly. Just as quietly, too, he walked toward the door, locked it, and put the key in his pocket. He then drew a pistol from his bosom and placed it, without the least flurry, upon the table.

The sailor's face flushed up as if he were struggling with suffocation. He started to his feet and grasped his cudgel; but the next moment he fell back into his seat, trembling violently, and with the countenance of death itself. He spoke not a word. I pitied him from the bottom of my heart.

"My friend," said Dupin, in a kind tone, "you are alarming yourself unnecessarily—you are indeed. We mean you no harm whatever. I pledge you the honor of a gentleman, and of a Frenchman, that we intend you no injury. I perfectly well know that you are innocent of the atrocities in the Rue Morgue. It will not do, however, to deny that you are in some measure implicated in them. From what I have already said, you must know that I have had means of information about this matter—means of which you could never have dreamed. Now the thing stands thus. You have done nothing which you could have avoided—nothing, certainly, which renders you culpable. You were not even guilty of robbery, when you might have robbed with impunity. You have nothing to conceal. You have no reason for concealment. On the other hand, you are bound by every principle of honor to confess all you know. An innocent man is now imprisoned, charged with a crime of which you can point out the perpetrator."

The sailor had recovered his presence of mind, in a great measure, while Dupin uttered these words; but his original boldness of bearing was all gone.

"So help me God!" said he, after a brief pause, "I will tell you all I know about this affair;—but I do not expect you to believe one half I say—I would be a fool indeed if I did. Still, I am innocent, and I will make a clean breast if I die for it."

What he stated was, in substance, this. He had lately made a voyage to the Indian Archipelago. A party, of which he formed one, landed at Borneo, and passed into the interior on an excursion of pleasure. Himself and a companion had captured the Ourang-Outang. This companion dying, the animal fell into his own exclusive possession. After great trouble, occasioned by the intractable ferocity of his captive during the home voyage, he at length succeeded in lodging it safely at his own residence in Paris, where, not to attract toward himself the unpleasant curiosity of his neighbors, he kept it carefully secluded, until such time as it should recover from a wound in the foot, received from a splinter on board ship. His ultimate design was to sell it.

Returning home from some sailors' frolic on the night, or rather in the morning, of the murder, he found the beast occupying his own bedroom, into which it had broken from a closet adjoining, where it had been, as was thought, securely confined. Razor in hand, and fully lathered, it was sitting before a looking-glass, attempting the operation of shaving, in which it had no doubt previously watched its master through the keyhole of the closet. Terrified at the sight of so dangerous a weapon in the possession of an animal so ferocious, and so well able to use it, the man, for some moments, was at a loss what to do. He had been accustomed, however, to quiet the creature, even in its fiercest moods, by the use of a whip, and to this he now resorted. Upon sight of it, the Ourang-Outang sprang at once through the door of the chamber, down the stairs, and thence, through a window, unfortunately open, into the street.

The Frenchman followed in despair; the ape, razor still in hand, occasionally stopping to look back and gesticulate at his pursuer, until the latter had nearly come up with it. It then again made off. In this manner the chase continued for a long time. The streets were profoundly quiet, as it was nearly three o'clock in the morning. In passing down an alley in the rear of the Rue Morgue, the fugitive's attention was arrested by a light gleaming from the open window of Madame L'Espanaye's chamber, in the fourth story of her house.

Rushing to the building, it perceived the lightning-rod, clambered up with inconceivable agility, grasped the shutter, which was thrown fully back against the wall, and, by its means, swung itself directly upon the headboard of the bed. The whole feat did not occupy a minute. The shutter was kicked open again by the Ourang-Outang as it entered the room.

The sailor, in the meantime, was both rejoiced and perplexed. He had strong hopes of now recapturing the brute, as it could scarcely escape from the trap into which it had ventured, except by the rod, where it might be intercepted as it came down. On the other hand, there was much cause for anxiety as to what it might do in the house. This latter reflection urged the man still to follow the fugitive. A lightning-rod is ascended without difficulty, especially by a sailor; but when he had arrived as high as the window, which lay far to his left, his career was stopped; the most that he could accomplish was to reach over so as to obtain a glimpse of the interior of the room. At this glimpse he nearly fell from his hold through excess of horror. Now it was that those hideous shrieks arose upon the night, which had startled from slumber the inmates of the Rue Morgue. Madame L'Espanaye and her daughter, habited in their night clothes, had apparently been occupied in arranging some papers in the iron chest already mentioned, which had been wheeled into the middle of the room. It was open, and its contents lay beside it on the floor. The victims must have been sitting with their backs toward the window, and, from the time elapsing between the ingress of the beast and the screams, it seems probable that it was not immediately perceived. The flapping-to of the shutter would naturally have been attributed to the wind.

As the sailor looked in, the gigantic animal had seized Madame L'Espanaye by the hair (which was loose, as she had been combing it), and was flourishing the razor about her face, in imitation of the motions of a barber. The daughter lay prostrate and motionless; she had swooned. The screams and struggles of the old lady (during which the hair was torn from her head) had the effect of changing the probably pacific purposes of the Ourang-Outang into those of wrath. With one determined sweep of its muscular arm it nearly severed her head from her body. The sight of blood inflamed its anger into phrensy. Gnashing its teeth, and flashing fire from its eyes, it flew upon the body of the girl, and imbedded its fearful talons in her throat, retaining its grasp until she expired. Its wandering and wild glances fell at this moment upon the head of the bed, over which the face of its master, rigid with horror, was just discernible.

The fury of the beast, who no doubt bore still in mind the dreaded whip, was instantly converted into fear. Conscious of having deserved punishment, it seemed desirous of concealing its bloody deeds, and skipped about the chamber in an agony of nervous agitation; throwing down and breaking the furniture as it moved, and dragging the bed from the bedstead. In conclusion, it seized first the corpse of the daughter, and thrust it up the chimney, as it was found; then that of the old lady, which it immediately hurled through the window headlong.

As the ape approached the casement with its mutilated burden, the sailor shrank aghast to the rod, and, rather gliding than clambering down it, hurried at once home—dreading the consequences of the butchery, and gladly abandoning, in his terror, all solicitude about the fate of the Ourang-Outang. The words heard by the party upon the staircase were the Frenchman's exclamations of horror and affright, commingled with the fiendish jabberings of the brute.

I have scarcely any thing to add. The Ourang-Outang must have escaped from the chamber, by the rod, just before the breaking of the door. It must have closed the window as it passed through it. It was subsequently caught by the owner himself, who obtained for it a very large sum at the Jardin des Plantes. Le Bon was instantly released, upon our narration of the circumstances (with some comments from Dupin) at the bureau of the Prefect of Police. This functionary, however well disposed to my friend, could not altogether conceal his chagrin at the turn which affairs had taken, and was fain to indulge in a sarcasm or two about the propriety of every person minding his own business.

"Let him talk," said Dupin, who had not thought it necessary to reply. "Let him discourse; it will ease his conscience. I am satisfied with having defeated him in his own castle. Nevertheless, that he failed in the solution of this mystery, is by no means that matter for wonder which he supposes it; for, in truth, our friend the Prefect is somewhat too cunning to be profound. In his wisdom is no stamen. It is all head and no body, like the pictures of the Goddess Laverna—or, at best, all head and shoulders, like a codfish. But he is a good creature after all. I like him especially for one master stroke of cant, by which he has attained his reputation for ingenuity. I mean the way he has *'de nier ce qui est, et d'expliquer ce qui n'est pas.'*"

Charles Dickens

(1812–1870)

"ALTHOUGH I AM AN old man," says the narrator of *The Old Curiosity Shop*, "night is generally my time for walking." Night was Charles Dickens's favorite time for walking as well. In his letters and essays he often mentions nocturnal rambles across the countryside or down ill-lit London alleyways, for reasons ranging from his inability to sleep after hours of writing to cooling down from an argument with his wife. By 1851—fifteen years after attaining celebrity at the age of twenty-four, with *The Posthumous Papers of the Pickwick Club*—Dickens had long since achieved the status of household name. When he wanted to take a nighttime tour of London's most abject and frightening slums, he could depend upon a police escort. Dickens used this kind of anthropological safari in part to inform his role as adviser to philanthropist Angela Burdett-Coutts, with whom he had worked to rehabilitate prostitutes, create inexpensive housing, and launch other efforts at improving the lot of the poor. On the occasion described in this article, as on others, he was guided (and protected) by one Inspector Field.

Soon after Robert Peel formed the metropolitan police force in 1829, Charles Frederick Field was listed as a sergeant in the E Division, headquartered in Holborn in central London. Four years later he was promoted to inspector. When the Detective Department was created in 1842, he was one of the first to sign up, eventually rising to the rank of detective inspector. In the summer of 1850, Dickens wrote about his new acquaintance, barely disguised as Inspector Charley Wield, in two articles called "A Detective Police Party" and "Three 'Detective' Anecdotes." As noted in the introduction, the word *detective* began to be seen during the 1830s, but it was still unfamiliar enough in 1850 for Dickens to place quotation marks around it in his title. In the autumn of 1850, Field complained about the way Dickens quoted him in "Three 'Detective' Anecdotes," but Dickens insisted, as usual, that he was correct. Nonetheless, the next year, when fellow novelist Edward Bulwer-Lytton claimed that his ex-wife was threatening to disrupt a benefit performance of his play *Not So Bad as We Seem*, Dickens arranged for Field to provide security. "He is discretion itself," Dickens said, "and accustomed to the most delicate missions."

The always busy author would soon employ these nightmarish glimpses in *Bleak House*, especially as background for the slum called Tom-all-Alone's, where Jo the crossing sweeper makes his dreary way through the alley properties set adrift by the endless Chancery suit. Dickens used other experiences with Field in a different way: they helped inspire his most important detective character, Inspector Bucket, who is called in by Tulkinghorn to investigate Lady Dedlock. (See the introduction for more information about Bucket in the context of the genre.) Dickens called outings with the inspector "Field days," a term that next showed up as an inside joke in *Bleak House*, when the author repeatedly used "field-day" to describe Bucket's investigative expeditions. In 1852 Field retired from the police force and set up shop as a private inquiry agent. The same year, Dickens began publishing *Bleak House*.

Over the years you can see Dickens's determination to unify his narratives ever more, especially from the time of *Dombey and Son*, which began serial publication in 1846, and its immediate successors—*David Copperfield* and *Bleak House*. Gradually each book contains not only a tighter plot and more unified symbolism, but also less farce and more dark poetry. Plots become Byzantine and eventually, in the case of his penultimate novel, *Our Mutual Friend*, almost indecipherable—yet the lyricism and poignant imagery keep improving. Sadly for the genre, Dickens died halfway through the writing of what seems to have been planned as his first full-fledged detective novel, *The Mystery of Edwin Drood*.

Naturally detectives appealed to Dickens. Their authority came as much from street experience as official fiat; they understood the system well enough to work outside it when necessary; and their very identity was defined by savvy intelligence and attention to detail—all qualities that Dickens admired in himself. Before *Bleak House* he had brought a pair of blundering Bow Street Runners into *Oliver Twist* and a private investigator named Nadgett into *Martin Chuzzlewit*. Later an otherwise unnamed inspector investigates two deaths in *Our Mutual Friend* (although, in the postscript, Dickens explicitly denied constructing the book like a whodunit); and, although we will never know for certain, Dick Datchery in *Edwin Drood* may be a detective in disguise.

"On Duty with Inspector Field" appeared in the June 14, 1851, issue of Dickens's own weekly periodical, *Household Words*, filling both columns on the cover and continuing inside—followed, in the eclectic way that kept Dickens's journals lively and inviting, by a history of Madagascar. In lesser hands, this material would have been merely reportage or screed. With his usual playful imagination, however, Dickens brought it all to life. He even described scenes he didn't witness, as in what Field might have been doing at the British Museum before meeting him for their nighttime prowl: "Suspicious of the Elgin marbles, and not to be done by cat-faced Egyptian giants with their hands upon their knees, Inspector Field, sagacious, vigilant, lamp in hand, throwing monstrous shadows on the walls and ceilings, passes through the spacious rooms." Throughout, Dickens demonstrates his usual attentive curiosity, eye for vivid details, and compassion for the starving, abandoned poor who flocked in the alleys alongside rats and pigeons. Along the way, he quotes from *Macbeth*, demonstrates that he is so rich in analogies he can invest them in offhand remarks, and invents an entertaining way to represent profanity before it was legal to actually print it.

On Duty with Inspector Field

How goes the night? Saint Giles's clock is striking nine. The weather is dull and wet, and the long lines of street lamps are blurred, as if we saw them through tears. A damp wind blows and rakes the pieman's fire out, when he opens the door of his little furnace, carrying away an eddy of sparks.

Saint Giles's clock strikes nine. We are punctual. Where is Inspector Field? Assistant Commissioner of Police is already here, enwrapped in oil-skin cloak, and standing in the shadow of Saint Giles's steeple. Detective Sergeant, weary of speaking French all day to foreigners unpacking at the Great Exhibition, is already here. Where is Inspector Field?

Inspector Field is, to-night, the guardian genius of the British Museum. He is bringing his shrewd eye to bear on every corner of its solitary galleries, before he reports "all right." Suspicious of the Elgin marbles, and not to be done by cat-faced Egyptian giants with their hands upon their knees, Inspector Field, sagacious, vigilant, lamp in hand, throwing monstrous shadows on the walls and ceilings, passes through the spacious rooms. If a mummy trembled in an atom of its dusty covering, Inspector Field would say, "Come out of that, Tom Green. I know you!" If the smallest "Gonoph" about town were crouching at the bottom of a classic bath, Inspector Field would nose him with a finer scent than the ogre's, when adventurous Jack lay trembling in his kitchen copper. But all is quiet, and Inspector Field goes warily on, making little outward show of attending to anything in particular, just recognising the Ichthyosaurus as a familiar acquaintance, and wondering, perhaps, how the detectives did it in the days before the Flood.

Will Inspector Field be long about this work? He may be half-an-hour longer. He sends his compliments by Police Constable, and proposes that we meet at St. Giles's Station House, across the road. Good. It were as well to stand by the fire, there, as in the shadow of Saint Giles's steeple.

Anything doing here to-night? Not much. We are very quiet. A lost boy, extremely calm and small, sitting by the fire, whom we now confide to a constable to take home, for the child says that if you show him Newgate Street, he can show you where he lives—a raving drunken woman in the cells, who has screeched her voice away, and has hardly power enough left to declare, even with the passionate help of her feet and arms, that she is the daughter of a British officer, and, strike her blind and dead, but she'll write a letter to the Queen! but who is soothed with a drink of water—in another cell, a quiet woman with a child at her breast, for begging—in another, her husband in a smock-frock, with a basket of watercresses—in another, a pickpocket—in another, a meek tremulous old pauper man who has been out for a holiday "and has took but a little drop, but it has overcome him after so many months in the house"—and that's all as yet. Presently, a sensation at the Station House door. Mr. Field, gentlemen!

Inspector Field comes in, wiping his forehead, for he is of a burly figure, and has come fast from the ores and metals of the deep mines of the earth, and from the Parrot Gods of the South Sea Islands, and from the birds and beetles of the tropics, and from the Arts of Greece and Rome, and from the Sculptures of Nineveh, and from the traces of an elder world, when these were not. Is Rogers ready? Rogers is ready, strapped and great-coated, with a flaming eye in the middle of his waist, like a deformed Cyclops. Lead on, Rogers, to Rats' Castle!

How many people may there be in London, who, if we had brought them deviously and blindfold, to this street, fifty paces from the Station House, and within call of Saint Giles's church, would know it for a not remote part of the city in which their lives are passed? How many, who amidst this compound of sickening smells, these heaps of filth, these tumbling houses, with all their vile contents, animate, and inanimate, slimily overflowing into the black road, would believe that they breathe *this* air? How much Red Tape may there be, that could look round on the faces which now hem us in—for our appearance here has caused a rush from all points to a common centre—the lowering foreheads, the sallow cheeks, the brutal eyes, the matted hair, the infected, vermin-haunted heaps of rags—and say, "I have thought of this. I have not dismissed the thing. I have neither blustered it away, nor frozen it away, nor tied it up and put it away, nor smoothly said pooh, pooh! to it when it has been shown to me"?

This is not what Rogers wants to know, however. What Rogers wants to know, is, whether you *will* clear the way here, some of you, or whether you won't; because if you don't do it right on end, he'll lock you up! "What! *You* are there, are you, Bob Miles? You haven't had enough of it yet, haven't you? You want three months more, do you? Come away from that gentleman! What are you creeping round there for?"

"What am I a doing, thinn, Mr. Rogers?" says Bob Miles, appearing, villainous, at the end of a lane of light, made by the lantern.

"I'll let you know pretty quick, if you don't hook it. WILL you hook it?"

A sycophantic murmur rises from the crowd. "Hook it, Bob, when Mr. Rogers and Mr. Field tells you! Why don't you hook it, when you are told to?"

The most importunate of the voices strikes familiarly on Mr. Rogers's ear. He suddenly turns his lantern on the owner.

"What! *You* are there, are you, Mister Click? You hook it too—come!"

"What for?" says Mr. Click, discomfited.

"You hook it, will you!" says Mr. Rogers with stern emphasis.

Both Click and Miles *do* "hook it," without another word, or, in plainer English, sneak away.

"Close up there, my men!" says Inspector Field to two constables on duty who have followed.

"Keep together, gentlemen; we are going down here. Heads!"

Saint Giles's church strikes half-past ten. We stoop low, and creep down a precipitous flight of steps into a dark close cellar. There is a fire. There is a long deal table. There are benches. The cellar is full of company, chiefly very young men in various conditions of dirt and raggedness. Some are eating supper. There are no girls or women present. Welcome to Rats' Castle, gentlemen, and to this company of noted thieves!

"Well, my lads! How are you, my lads? What have you been doing to-day? Here's some company come to see you, my lads!—*There's* a plate of beefsteak, sir, for the supper of a fine young man! And there's a mouth for a steak, sir! Why, I should be too proud of such a mouth as that, if I had it myself! Stand up and show it, sir! Take off your cap. There's a fine young man for a nice little party, sir! An't he?"

Inspector Field is the bustling speaker. Inspector Field's eye is the roving eye that searches every corner of the cellar as he talks. Inspector Field's hand is the well-known hand that has collared half the people here, and motioned their brothers, sisters, fathers, mothers, male and female friends, inexorably to New South Wales. Yet Inspector Field stands in this den, the Sultan of the place. Every thief here cowers before him, like a schoolboy before his schoolmaster. All watch him, all answer when addressed, all laugh at his jokes, all seek to propitiate him. This cellar company alone—to say nothing of the crowd surrounding the entrance from the street above, and making the steps shine with eyes—is strong enough to murder us all, and willing enough to do it; but, let Inspector Field have a mind to pick out one thief here, and take him; let him produce that ghostly truncheon from his pocket, and say, with his business-air, "My lad, I want you!" and all Rats' Castle shall be stricken with paralysis, and not a finger move against him, as he fits the handcuffs on!

Where's the Earl of Warwick?—Here he is, Mr. Field! Here's the Earl of Warwick, Mr. Field!—O there you are, my Lord. Come for'ard. There's a chest, sir, not to have a clean shirt on. An't it? Take your hat off, my Lord. Why, I should be ashamed if I was you—and an Earl, too—to show myself to a gentleman with my hat on!—The Earl of Warwick laughs and uncovers. All the company laugh. One pickpocket, especially, laughs with great enthusiasm. O what a jolly game it is, when Mr. Field comes down—and don't want nobody!

So, *you* are here, too, are you, you tall, grey, soldierly-looking, grave man, standing by the fire?—Yes, sir. Good evening, Mr. Field!—Let us see. You lived servant to a nobleman once?—Yes, Mr. Field.—And what is it you do now; I forget?—Well, Mr. Field, I job about as well as I can. I left my employment on account of delicate health. The family is still kind to me. Mr. Wix of Piccadilly is also very kind to me when I am hard up. Likewise Mr. Nix of Oxford Street. I get a trifle from them occasionally, and rub on as well as I can, Mr. Field. Mr. Field's eye rolls enjoyingly, for this man is a notorious begging-letter writer.—Good night, my lads!—Good night, Mr. Field, and thank'ee, sir!

Clear the street here, half a thousand of you! Cut it, Mrs. Stalker—none of that—we don't want you! Rogers of the flaming eye, lead on to the tramps' lodging-house!

A dream of baleful faces attends to the door. Now, stand back all of you! In the rear Detective Sergeant plants himself, composedly whistling, with his strong right arm across the narrow passage. Mrs. Stalker, I am something'd that need not be written here, if you won't get yourself into trouble, in about half a minute, if I see that face of yours again!

Saint Giles's church clock, striking eleven, hums through our hand from the dilapidated door of a dark outhouse as we open it, and are stricken back by the pestilent breath that issues from within. Rogers to the front with the light, and let us look!

Ten, twenty, thirty—who can count them! Men, women, children, for the most part naked, heaped upon the floor like maggots in a cheese! Ho! In that dark corner yonder! Does anybody lie there? Me sir, Irish me, a widder, with six children. And yonder? Me sir, Irish me, with me wife and eight poor babes. And to the left there? Me sir, Irish me, along with two more Irish boys as is me friends. And to the right there? Me sir and the Murphy fam'ly, numbering five blessed souls. And what's this, coiling, now, about my foot? Another Irish me, pitifully in want of shaving, whom I have awakened from sleep—and across my other foot lies his wife—and by the shoes of Inspector Field lie their three eldest—and their three youngest are at present squeezed between the open door and the wall. And why is there no one on that little mat before the sullen fire? Because O'Donovan, with his wife and daughter, is not come in from selling Lucifers! Nor on the bit of sacking in the nearest corner? Bad luck! Because that Irish family is late to-night, a-cadging in the streets!

They are all awake now, the children excepted, and most of them sit up, to stare. Wheresoever Mr. Rogers turns the flaming eye, there is a spectral figure rising, unshrouded, from a grave of rags. Who is the landlord here?—I am, Mr. Field! says a bundle of ribs and parchment against the wall, scratching itself.—Will you spend this money fairly, in the morning, to buy coffee for 'em all?—Yes, sir, I will!—O he'll do it, sir, he'll do it fair. He's honest! cry the spectres. And with thanks and Good Night sink into their graves again.

Thus, we make our New Oxford Streets, and our other new streets, never heeding, never asking, where the wretches whom we clear out, crowd. With such scenes at our doors, with all the plagues of Egypt tied up with bits of cobweb in kennels so near our homes, we timorously make our Nuisance Bills and Boards of Health, nonentities, and think to keep away the Wolves of Crime and

Filth, by our electioneering ducking to little vestrymen and our gentlemanly handling of Red Tape!

Intelligence of the coffee-money has got abroad. The yard is full, and Rogers of the flaming eye is beleaguered with entreaties to show other Lodging Houses. Mine next! Mine! Mine! Rogers, military, obdurate, stiff-necked, immovable, replies not, but leads away; all falling back before him. Inspector Field follows. Detective Sergeant, with his barrier of arm across the little passage, deliberately waits to close the procession. He sees behind him, without any effort, and exceedingly disturbs one individual far in the rear by coolly calling out, "It won't do, Mr. Michael! Don't try it!"

After council holden in the street, we enter other lodging-houses, public-houses, many lairs and holes; all noisome and offensive; none so filthy and so crowded as where Irish are. In one, The Ethiopian party are expected home presently—were in Oxford Street when last heard of—shall be fetched, for our delight, within ten minutes. In another, one of the two or three Professors who drew Napoleon Buonaparte and a couple of mackerel, on the pavement and then let the work of art out to a speculator, is refreshing after his labours. In another, the vested interest of the profitable nuisance has been in one family for a hundred years, and the landlord drives in comfortably from the country to his snug little stew in town. In all, Inspector Field is received with warmth. Coiners and smashers droop before him; pickpockets defer to him; the gentle sex (not very gentle here) smile upon him. Half-drunken hags check themselves in the midst of pots of beer, or pints of gin, to drink to Mr. Field, and pressingly to ask the honour of his finishing the draught. One beldame in rusty black has such admiration for him, that she runs a whole street's length to shake him by the hand; tumbling into a heap of mud by the way, and still pressing her attentions when her very form has ceased to be distinguishable through it. Before the power of the law, the power of superior sense—for common thieves are fools beside these men—and the power of a perfect mastery of their character, the garrison of Rats'

Castle and the adjacent Fortresses make but a skulking show indeed when reviewed by Inspector Field.

Saint Giles's clock says it will be midnight in half-an-hour, and Inspector Field says we must hurry to the Old Mint in the Borough. The cab-driver is low-spirited, and has a solemn sense of his responsibility. Now, what's your fare, my lad?—O YOU know, Inspector Field, what's the good of asking ME!

Say, Parker, strapped and great-coated, and waiting in dim Borough doorway by appointment, to replace the trusty Rogers whom we left deep in Saint Giles's, are you ready? Ready, Inspector Field, and at a motion of my wrist behold my flaming eye.

This narrow street, sir, is the chief part of the Old Mint, full of low lodging-houses, as you see by the transparent canvas-lamps and blinds, announcing beds for travellers! But it is greatly changed, friend Field, from my former knowledge of it; it is infinitely quieter and more subdued than when I was here last, some seven years ago? O yes! Inspector Haynes, a first-rate man, is on this station now and plays the Devil with them!

Well, my lads! How are you to-night, my lads? Playing cards here, eh? Who wins?—Why, Mr. Field, I, the sulky gentleman with the damp flat side-curls, rubbing my bleared eye with the end of my neckerchief which is like a dirty eel-skin, am losing just at present, but I suppose I must take my pipe out of my mouth, and be submissive to YOU—I hope I see you well, Mr. Field?—Aye, all right, my lad. Deputy, who have you got up-stairs? Be pleased to show the rooms!

Why Deputy, Inspector Field can't say. He only knows that the man who takes care of the beds and lodgers is always called so. Steady, O Deputy, with the flaring candle in the blacking-bottle, for this is a slushy back-yard, and the wooden staircase outside the house creaks and has holes in it.

Again, in these confined intolerable rooms, burrowed out like the holes of rats or the nests of insect-vermin, but fuller of intolerable smells, are crowds of sleepers, each on his foul truckle-bed coiled up beneath a rug. Holloa here! Come! Let us see you! Show your face! Pilot Parker goes from bed to bed and turns their slumbering heads towards us, as a salesman might turn sheep. Some wake up with an execration and a threat.—What! who spoke? O! If it's the accursed glaring eye that fixes me, go where I will, I am helpless. Here! I sit up to be looked at. Is it me you want? Not you, lie down again! and I lie down, with a woful growl.

Whenever the turning lane of light becomes stationary for a moment, some sleeper appears at the end of it, submits himself to be scrutinised, and fades away into the darkness. There should be strange dreams here, Deputy. They sleep sound enough, says Deputy, taking the candle out of the blacking-bottle, snuffing it with his fingers, throwing the snuff into the bottle, and corking it up with the candle; that's all I know. What is the inscription, Deputy, on all the discoloured sheets? A precaution against loss of linen. Deputy turns down the rug of an unoccupied bed and discloses it. STOP THIEF!

To lie at night, wrapped in the legend of my slinking life; to take the cry that pursues me, waking, to my breast in sleep; to have it staring at me, and clamouring for me, as soon as consciousness returns; to have it for my first-foot on New-Year's day, my Valentine, my Birthday salute, my Christmas greeting, my parting with the old year. STOP THIEF!

And to know that I MUST be stopped, come what will. To know that I am no match for this individual energy and keenness, or this organised and steady system! Come across the street, here, and, entering by a little shop and yard, examine these intricate passages and doors, contrived for escape, flapping and counter-flapping, like the lids of the conjurer's boxes. But what avail they? Who gets in by a nod, and shows their secret working to us? Inspector Field.

Don't forget the old Farm House, Parker! Parker is not the man to forget it. We are going there, now. It is the old Manor-House of these parts, and stood in the country once. Then, perhaps, there was something, which was not the beastly street, to see from the shattered

low fronts of the overhanging wooden houses we are passing under—
shut up now, pasted over with bills about the literature and drama
of the Mint, and mouldering away. This long paved yard was a
paddock or a garden once, or a court in front of the Farm House.
Perchance, with a dovecot in the centre, and fowls peeking about—
with fair elm trees, then, where discoloured chimney-stacks and
gables are now—noisy, then, with rooks which have yielded to a
different sort of rookery. It's likelier than not, Inspector Field
thinks, as we turn into the common kitchen, which is in the yard,
and many paces from the house.

Well, my lads and lasses, how are you all? Where's Blackey, who
has stood near London Bridge these five-and-twenty years, with a
painted skin to represent disease?—Here he is, Mr. Field!—How
are you, Blackey?—Jolly, sa! Not playing the fiddle to-night,
Blackey?—Not a night, sa! A sharp, smiling youth, the wit of the
kitchen, interposes. He an't musical to-night, sir. I've been giving
him a moral lecture; I've been a talking to him about his latter end,
you see. A good many of these are my pupils, sir. This here young
man (smoothing down the hair of one near him, reading a Sunday
paper) is a pupil of mine. I'm a teaching of him to read, sir. He's a
promising cove, sir. He's a smith, he is, and gets his living by the
sweat of the brow, sir. So do I, myself, sir. This young woman is
my sister, Mr. Field. SHE's getting on very well too. I've a deal of
trouble with 'em, sir, but I'm richly rewarded, now I see 'em all a
doing so well, and growing up so creditable. That's a great comfort, that is, an't it, sir?—In the midst of the kitchen (the whole
kitchen is in ecstasies with this impromptu "chaff") sits a young,
modest, gentle-looking creature, with a beautiful child in her lap.
She seems to belong to the company, but is so strangely unlike it.
She has such a pretty, quiet face and voice, and is so proud to hear the
child admired—thinks you would hardly believe that he is only
nine months old! Is she as bad as the rest, I wonder? Inspectorial
experience does not engender a belief contrariwise, but prompts
the answer, Not a ha'porth of difference!

There is a piano going in the old Farm House as we approach. It stops. Landlady appears. Has no objections, Mr. Field, to gentlemen being brought, but wishes it were at earlier hours, the lodgers complaining of ill-conwenience. Inspector Field is polite and soothing—knows his woman and the sex. Deputy (a girl in this case) shows the way up a heavy, broad old staircase, kept very clean, into clean rooms where many sleepers are, and where painted panels of an older time look strangely on the truckle beds. The sight of whitewash and the smell of soap—two things we seem by this time to have parted from in infancy—make the old Farm House a phenomenon, and connect themselves with the so curiously misplaced picture of the pretty mother and child long after we have left it,— long after we have left, besides, the neighbouring nook with something of a rustic flavour in it yet, where once, beneath a low wooden colonnade still standing as of yore, the eminent Jack Sheppard condescended to regale himself, and where, now, two old bachelor brothers in broad hats (who are whispered in the Mint to have made a compact long ago that if either should ever marry, he must forfeit his share of the joint property) still keep a sequestered tavern, and sit o' nights smoking pipes in the bar, among ancient bottles and glasses, as our eyes behold them.

How goes the night now? Saint George of Southwark answers with twelve blows upon his bell. Parker, good night, for Williams is already waiting over in the region of Ratcliffe Highway, to show the houses where the sailors dance.

I should like to know where Inspector Field was born. In Ratcliffe Highway, I would have answered with confidence, but for his being equally at home wherever we go. HE does not trouble his head as I do, about the river at night. HE does not care for its creeping, black and silent, on our right there, rushing through sluice-gates, lapping at piles and posts and iron rings, hiding strange things in its mud, running away with suicides and accidentally drowned bodies faster than midnight funeral should, and acquiring such various experience between its cradle and its grave. It has no mystery for HIM. Is there not the Thames Police!

Accordingly, Williams leads the way. We are a little late, for some of the houses are already closing. No matter. You show us plenty. All the landlords know Inspector Field. All pass him, freely and good-humouredly, wheresoever he wants to go. So thoroughly are all these houses open to him and our local guide, that, granting that sailors must be entertained in their own way—as I suppose they must, and have a right to be—I hardly know how such places could be better regulated. Not that I call the company very select, or the dancing very graceful—even so graceful as that of the German Sugar Bakers, whose assembly, by the Minories, we stopped to visit—but there is watchful maintenance of order in every house, and swift expulsion where need is. Even in the midst of drunkenness, both of the lethargic kind and the lively, there is sharp landlord supervision, and pockets are in less peril than out of doors. These houses show, singularly, how much of the picturesque and romantic there truly is in the sailor, requiring to be especially addressed. All the songs (sung in a hailstorm of halfpence, which are pitched at the singer without the least tenderness for the time or tune—mostly from great rolls of copper carried for the purpose— and which he occasionally dodges like shot as they fly near his head) are of the sentimental sea sort. All the rooms are decorated with nautical subjects. Wrecks, engagements, ships on fire, ships passing lighthouses on iron-bound coasts, ships blowing up, ships going down, ships running ashore, men lying out upon the main-yard in a gale of wind, sailors and ships in every variety of peril, constitute the illustrations of fact. Nothing can be done in the fanciful way, without a thumping boy upon a scaly dolphin.

How goes the night now? Past one. Black and Green are waiting in Whitechapel to unveil the mysteries of Wentworth Street. Williams, the best of friends must part. Adieu!

Are not Black and Green ready at the appointed place? O yes!

They glide out of shadow as we stop. Imperturbable Black opens the cab-door; Imperturbable Green takes a mental note of the driver. Both Green and Black then open each his flaming eye, and marshal us the way that we are going.

The lodging-house we want is hidden in a maze of streets and courts. It is fast shut. We knock at the door, and stand hushed looking up for a light at one or other of the begrimed old lattice windows in its ugly front, when another constable comes up—supposes that we want "to see the school." Detective Sergeant meanwhile has got over a rail, opened a gate, dropped down an area, overcome some other little obstacles, and tapped at a window. Now returns. The landlord will send a deputy immediately.

Deputy is heard to stumble out of bed. Deputy lights a candle, draws back a bolt or two, and appears at the door. Deputy is a shivering shirt and trousers by no means clean, a yawning face, a shock head much confused externally and internally. We want to look for some one. You may go up with the light, and take 'em all, if you like, says Deputy, resigning it, and sitting down upon a bench in the kitchen with his ten fingers sleepily twisting in his hair.

Halloa here! Now then! Show yourselves. That'll do. It's not you. Don't disturb yourself any more! So on, through a labyrinth of airless rooms, each man responding, like a wild beast, to the keeper who has tamed him, and who goes into his cage. What, you haven't found him, then? says Deputy, when we came down. A woman mysteriously sitting up all night in the dark by the smouldering ashes of the kitchen fire, says it's only tramps and cadgers here; it's gonophs over the way. A man mysteriously walking about the kitchen all night in the dark, bids her hold her tongue. We come out. Deputy fastens the door and goes to bed again.

Black and Green, you know Bark, lodging-house keeper and receiver of stolen goods?—O yes, Inspector Field.—Go to Bark's next.

Bark sleeps in an inner wooden hutch, near his street door. As we parley on the step with Bark's Deputy, Bark growls in his bed. We enter, and Bark flies out of bed. Bark is a red villain and a wrathful, with a sanguine throat that looks very much as if it were expressly made for hanging, as he stretches it out, in pale defiance, over the half-door of his hutch. Bark's parts of speech are of an awful sort—principally adjectives. I won't, says Bark, have no adjective police and adjective strangers in my adjective premises! I won't, by adjective and substantive! Give me my trousers, and I'll send the whole adjective police to adjective and substantive! Give me, says Bark, my adjective trousers! I'll put an adjective knife in the whole bileing of 'em. I'll punch their adjective heads. I'll rip up their adjective substantives. Give me my adjective trousers! says Bark, and I'll spile the bileing of 'em!

Now, Bark, what's the use of this? Here's Black and Green, Detective Sergeant, and Inspector Field. You know we will come in.—I know you won't! says Bark. Somebody give me my adjective trousers! Bark's trousers seem difficult to find. He calls for them as Hercules might for his club. Give me my adjective trousers! says Bark, and I'll spile the bileing of 'em! Inspector Field holds that it's all one whether Bark likes the visit or don't like it. He, Inspector Field, is an Inspector of the Detective Police, Detective Sergeant IS Detective Sergeant, Black and Green are constables in uniform. Don't you be a fool, Bark, or you know it will be the worse for you.—I don't care, says Bark. Give me my adjective trousers!

At two o'clock in the morning, we descend into Bark's low kitchen, leaving Bark to foam at the mouth above, and Imperturbable Black and Green to look at him. Bark's kitchen is crammed full of thieves, holding a CONVERSAZIONE there by lamp-light. It is by far the most dangerous assembly we have seen yet. Stimulated by the ravings of Bark, above, their looks are sullen, but not a man speaks. We ascend again. Bark has got his trousers, and is in a state of madness in the passage with his back against a door that shuts off the upper staircase. We observe, in other respects, a ferocious individuality in Bark. Instead of "STOP THIEF!" on his linen, he prints "STOLEN FROM Bark's!"

Now, Bark, we are going up-stairs!—No, you ain't!—YOU refuse admission to the Police, do you, Bark?—Yes, I do! I refuse it to all the adjective police, and to all the adjective substantives. If the adjective coves in the kitchen was men, they'd come up now, and do for you! Shut me that there door! says Bark, and suddenly we are enclosed in the passage. They'd come up and do for you! cries Bark, and waits. Not a sound in the kitchen! They'd come up and do for you! cries Bark again, and waits. Not a sound in the kitchen! We are shut up, half-a-dozen of us, in Bark's house in the innermost recesses of the worst part of London, in the dead of the night—the house is crammed with notorious robbers and ruffians—and not a man stirs. No, Bark. They know the weight of the law, and they know Inspector Field and Co. too well.

We leave bully Bark to subside at leisure out of his passion and his trousers, and, I dare say, to be inconveniently reminded of this little brush before long. Black and Green do ordinary duty here, and look serious.

As to White, who waits on Holborn Hill to show the courts that are eaten out of Rotten Gray's Inn, Lane, where other lodging-houses are, and where (in one blind alley) the Thieves' Kitchen and Seminary for the teaching of the art to children is, the night has so worn away, being now

almost at odds with morning, which is which,

that they are quiet, and no light shines through the chinks in the shutters. As undistinctive Death will come here, one day, sleep comes now. The wicked cease from troubling sometimes, even in this life.

Wilkie Collins

(1824–1889)

"The Diary of Anne Rodway" is a transitional story in the genre. It captures the period in which detective stories were still emerging from earlier forms of fiction. Although it would be a few more years before the first *professional* female detective, Rodway unquestionably launches an investigation on her own in this often sad story. She does so, despite her fears and lack of experience, by drawing upon her considerable supply of what the Victorians called pluck. Rodway is an amateur who appears in no other story; and like a number of other nineteenth-century characters, she takes up detection to solve a mystery in which she herself is entangled. Although Collins wasn't yet writing a full-fledged detective story, he had already mastered the pacing and suspense that would make him famous.

The story came before Collins's acclaimed novels such as *The Woman in White* and *The Moonstone*. It was first published in 1856, under the title "Brother Owen's Story of Anne Rodway (Taken from Her Diary)," in the July 19 and 26 issues of *Household Words*, as part of an interconnected series. In the manner of *The Decameron* or its literary descendant *The Canterbury Tales*, characters in the series take turns recounting stories. From this cycle came such popular Collins tales as "The Biter Bit" and "Mad Monkton." In 1859 the series was reprinted in a three-volume edition of Collins's collection *The Queen of Hearts*, published by Hurst & Blackett.

Charles Dickens had launched the two-pence weekly *Household Words* six years earlier, with the official mission "to show to all, that in all familiar things, even in those which are repellant on the surface, there is Romance enough, if we will find it out." Its two-column format was unrelieved by illustrations. In his professional as well as his personal life, Dickens sought ever greater control, and when the magazine's publishers, Bradbury & Evans, disagreed with him about his proposed publication of an unfair public letter justifying his separation from his wife, Catherine, after many years of marriage, Dickens departed in a huff. In 1859 he shut down *Household Words* and incorporated it into his own new periodical, *All the Year Round*. Wilkie Collins's stories and serialized novels appeared in the pages of both. "Anne Rodway" was published the year he joined the staff of *Household Words*.

By the time of his death, William Wilkie Collins was considered the king of sensation novelists. He published thirty novels and sixty-plus stories and fourteen plays—and somehow squeezed in more than a hundred essays and articles. The son of William Collins, an acclaimed painter in the pastoral style of John Constable, he received the middle name Wilkie in honor of another artist, the Scottish history painter David Wilkie, his godfather. Naturally the young Wilkie Collins tried painting; he even exhibited at the Royal Academy in 1849. The first novel he wrote, *Iolani*, could not find a home and sat around unpublished for the next 150 years; his first published book was a biography of his father. Then he met Dickens in 1851—they were introduced by yet another painter, the memorably named Augustus Egg—and their lives became ever more entwined. He and Dickens were not only colleagues but close friends and occasional collaborators. Together they traveled Europe and, back home in England, performed in amateur theatricals, including a production of Collins's play *The Frozen Deep*, which had been inspired by an idea from Dickens. Collins's younger brother even married Dickens's daughter.

Anne Rodway's diary—a form of narration that would become

Wilkie Collins's trademark with the publication of *The Woman in White* in 1860 and *The Moonstone* in 1868—demonstrates the author's sympathy for female characters and also for the poor, even the drug-addicted poor. His account in *The Moonstone* of the delusory effects of opium grew out of his personal experience. He became addicted to laudanum to lessen the pain of his "rheumatic gout," a form of arthritis, and even wrote of his own paranoid hallucinations, including the existence of a "ghost Wilkie" who at times shadowed his every move. Collins's sympathy for the unconventional also emerged from his own bohemian life. He never married. Instead he lived for a decade with a widow, and when she married someone else, he began a romance with another woman, who bore his three children. When the widow returned to him, he didn't break off his new romance but instead continued both for almost two decades. Not a hypocrite, Collins was slow to judge others, in life and in fiction.

The Diary of Anne Rodway

... **MARCH 3d, 1840.** A long letter today from Robert, which surprised and vexed me so that I have been sadly behindhand with my work ever since. He writes in worse spirits than last time, and absolutely declares that he is poorer even than when he went to America, and that he has made up his mind to come home to London.

How happy I should be at this news, if he only returned to me a prosperous man! As it is, though I love him dearly, I cannot look forward to the meeting him again, disappointed and broken down, and poorer than ever, without a feeling almost of dread for both of us. I was twenty-six last birthday and he was thirty-three, and there seems less chance now than ever of our being married. It is all I can do to keep myself by my needle; and his prospects, since he failed in the small stationery business three years ago, are worse, if possible, than mine.

Not that I mind so much for myself; women, in all ways of life, and especially in my dressmaking way, learn, I think, to be more patient than men. What I dread is Robert's despondency, and the hard struggle he will have in this cruel city to get his bread, let alone making money enough to marry me. So little as poor people want to set up in housekeeping and be happy together, it seems hard that they can't get it when they are honest and hearty, and willing to work. The clergyman said in his sermon last Sunday evening that all things were ordered for the best, and we are all put into the stations in life that are properest for us. I suppose he was right, being a very clever gentleman who fills the church to crowding; but I think I should have understood him better if I had not been very hungry at the time, in consequence of my own station in life being nothing but plain needlewoman.

March 4th. Mary Mallinson came down to my room to take a cup of tea with me. I read her bits of Robert's letter, to show her that, if she has her troubles, I have mine too; but I could not succeed in cheering her. She says she is born to misfortune, and that, as long back as she can remember, she has never had the least morsel of luck to be thankful for. I told her to go and look in my glass, and to say if she had nothing to be thankful for then; for Mary is a very pretty girl, and would look still prettier if she could be more cheerful and dress neater. However, my compliment did no good. She rattled her spoon impatiently in her tea-cup, and said, "If I was only as good a hand at needle-work as you are, Anne, I would change faces with the ugliest girl in London." "Not you!" says I, laughing. She looked at me for a moment, and shook her head, and was out of the room before I could get up and stop her. She always runs off in that way when she is going to cry, having a kind of pride about letting other people see her in tears.

March 5th. A fright about Mary. I had not seen her all day, as she does not work at the same place where I do; and in the evening she never came down to have tea with me, or sent me word to go to her; so, just before I went to bed, I ran upstairs to say good-night.

She did not answer when I knocked; and when I stepped softly in the room I saw her in bed, asleep, with her work not half done, lying about the room in the untidiest way. There was nothing remarkable in that, and I was just going away on tiptoe, when a tiny bottle and wine-glass on the chair by her bedside caught my eye. I thought she was ill and had been taking physic, and looked at the bottle. It was marked in large letters, "Laudanum—Poison."

My heart gave a jump as if it was going to fly out of me. I laid hold of her with both hands, and shook her with all my might. She was sleeping heavily, and woke slowly, as it seemed to me—but still she did wake. I tried to pull her out of bed, having heard that people ought to be always walked up and down when they have taken laudanum but she resisted, and pushed me away violently.

"Anne!" says she, in a fright. "For gracious sake, what's come to you! Are you out of your senses?"

"Oh, Mary! Mary!" says I, holding up the bottle before her, "if I hadn't come in when I did—" And I laid hold of her to shake her again.

She looked puzzled at me for a moment—then smiled (the first time I had seen her do so for many a long day)—then put her arms round my neck.

"Don't be frightened about me, Anne," she says; "I am not worth it, and there is no need."

"No need!" says I, out of breath—"no need, when the bottle has got Poison marked on it!"

"Poison, dear, if you take it all," says Mary, looking at me very tenderly, "and a night's rest if you only take a little."

I watched her for a moment, doubtful whether I ought to believe what she said or to alarm the house. But there was no sleepiness now in her eyes, and nothing drowsy in her voice; and she sat up in bed quite easily, without anything to support her.

"You have given me a dreadful fright, Mary," says I, sitting down by her in the chair, and beginning by this time to feel rather faint after being startled so.

She jumped out of bed to get me a drop of water, and kissed me, and said how sorry she was, and how undeserving of so much interest being taken in her. At the same time, she tried to possess herself of the laudanum bottle which I still kept cuddled up tight in my own hands.

"No," says I. "You have got into a low-spirited, despairing way. I won't trust you with it."

"I am afraid I can't do without it," says Mary, in her usual quiet, hopeless voice. "What with work that I can't get through as I ought, and troubles that I can't help thinking of, sleep won't come to me unless I take a few drops out of that bottle. Don't keep it away from me, Anne; it's the only thing in the world that makes me forget myself."

"Forget yourself!" says I. "You have no right to talk in that way, at your age. There's something horrible in the notion of a girl of eighteen sleeping with a bottle of laudanum by her bedside every night. We all of us have our troubles. Haven't I got mine?"

"You can do twice the work I can, twice as well as me," says Mary. "You are never scolded and rated at for awkwardness with your needle, and I always am. You can pay for your room every week, and I am three weeks in debt for mine."

"A little more practice," says I, "and a little more courage, and you will soon do better. You have got all your life before you—"

"I wish I was at the end of it," says she, breaking in. "I am alone in the world, and my life's no good to me."

"You ought to be ashamed of yourself for saying so," says I. "Haven't you got me for a friend? Didn't I take a fancy to you when first you left your step-mother and came to lodge in this house? And haven't I been sisters with you ever since? Suppose you are alone in the world, am I much better off? I'm an orphan like you. I've almost as many things in pawn as you; and, if your pockets are empty, mine have only got ninepence in them, to last me for all the rest of the week."

"Your father and mother were honest people," says Mary, obstinately. "My mother ran away from home, and died in a hospital. My father was always drunk, and always beating me. My step-mother is as good as dead, for all she cares about me. My only brother is thousands of miles away in foreign parts, and never writes to me, and never helps me with a farthing. My sweetheart—"

She stopped, and the red flew into her face. I knew, if she went on that way, she would only get to the saddest part of her sad story, and give both herself and me unnecessary pain.

"*My* sweetheart is too poor to marry me, Mary," I said, "so I'm not so much to be envied even there. But let's give over disputing which is worst off. Lie down in bed, and let me tuck you up. I'll put a stitch or two into that work of yours while you go to sleep."

Instead of doing what I told her, she burst out crying (being very like a child in some of her ways), and hugged me so tight round the neck that she quite hurt me. I let her go on till she had worn herself out, and was obliged to lie down. Even then, her last few words before she dropped off to sleep were such as I was half sorry, half frightened to hear.

"I won't plague you long, Anne," she said. "I haven't courage to go out of the world as you seem to fear I shall; but I began my life wretchedly, and wretchedly I am sentenced to end it."

It was of no use lecturing her again, for she closed her eyes.

I tucked her up as neatly as I could, and put her petticoat over her, for the bedclothes were scanty, and her hands felt cold. She looked so pretty and delicate as she fell asleep that it quite made my heart ache to see her, after such talk as we had held together. I just waited long enough to be quite sure that she was in the land of dreams, then emptied the horrible laudanum bottle into the grate, took up her half-done work, and, going out softly, left her for that night.

March 6th. Sent off a long letter to Robert, begging and entreating him not to be so down-hearted, and not to leave America without making another effort. I told him I could bear any trial except the wretchedness of seeing him come back a helpless, broken-down man, trying uselessly to begin life again when too old for a change.

It was not till after I had posted my own letter, and read over part of Robert's again, that the suspicion suddenly floated across me, for the first time, that he might have sailed for England immediately after writing to me. There were expressions in the letter which seemed to indicate that he had some such headlong project in his mind. And yet, surely, if it were so, I ought to have noticed them at the first reading. I can only hope I am wrong in my present interpretation of much of what he has written to me—hope it earnestly for both our sakes.

This has been a doleful day for me. I have been uneasy about Robert and uneasy about Mary. My mind is haunted by those last words of hers: "I began my life wretchedly, and wretchedly I am sentenced to end it." Her usual melancholy way of talking never produced the same impression on me that I feel now. Perhaps the discovery of the laudanum-bottle is the cause of this. I would give many a hard day's work to know what to do for Mary's good. My heart warmed to her when we first met in the same lodging-house two years ago, and, although I am not one of the over-affectionate sort myself, I feel as if I could go to the world's end to serve that girl. Yet, strange to say, if I was asked why I was so fond of her, I don't think I should know how to answer the question.

March 7th. I am almost ashamed to write it down, even in this journal, which no eyes but mine ever look on; yet I must honestly confess to myself that here I am, at nearly one in the morning, sitting up in a state of serious uneasiness because Mary has not yet come home.

I walked with her this morning to the place where she works, and tried to lead her into talking of the relations she has got who are still alive. My motive in doing this was to see if she dropped anything in the course of conversation which might suggest a way of helping her interests with those who are bound to give her all reasonable assistance. But the little I could get her to say to me led to nothing. Instead of answering my questions about her stepmother and her brother, she persisted at first, in the strangest way, in talking of her father, who was dead and gone, and of one Noah Truscott, who had been the worst of all the bad friends he had, and had taught him to drink and game. When I did get her to speak of her brother, she only knew that he had gone out to a place called Assam, where they grew tea. How he was doing, or whether he was there still, she did not seem to know, never having heard a word from him for years and years past.

As for her step-mother, Mary not unnaturally flew into a passion the moment I spoke of her. She keeps an eating-house at Hammersmith, and could have given Mary good employment in it; but she seems always to have hated her, and to have made her life so wretched with abuse and ill usage that she had no refuge left but to go away from home, and do her best to make a living for herself. Her husband (Mary's father) appears to have behaved badly to her, and, after his death, she took the wicked course of revenging herself on her step-daughter. I felt, after this, that it was impossible Mary could go back, and that it was the hard necessity of her position, as it is of mine, that she should struggle on to make a decent livelihood without assistance from any of her relations. I confessed as much as this to her; but I added that I would try to get her employment with the persons for whom I work, who pay higher wages, and show a little more indulgence to those under them than the people to whom she is now obliged to look for support.

I spoke much more confidently than I felt about being able to do this, and left her, as I thought, in better spirits than usual. She promised to be back to-night to tea at nine o'clock, and now it is nearly one in the morning, and she is not home yet. If it was any other girl I should not feel uneasy, for I should make up my mind that there was extra work to be done in a hurry, and that they were keeping her late, and I should go to bed. But Mary is so unfortunate in everything that happens to her, and her own melancholy talk about herself keeps hanging on my mind so, that I have fears on her account which would not distress me about any one else. It seems inexcusably silly to think such a thing, much more to write it down; but I have a kind of nervous dread upon me that some accident—

What does that loud knocking at the street door mean? And those voices and heavy footsteps outside?

Some lodger who has lost his key, I suppose. And yet, my heart— What a coward I have become all of a sudden!

More knocking and louder voices. I must run to the door and

see what it is. Oh, Mary! Mary! I hope I am not going to have another fright about you, but I feel sadly like it.

March 8th.

March 9th.

March 10th.

March 11th. Oh me! all the troubles I have ever had in my life
are as nothing to the trouble I am in now. For three days I have not
been able to write a single line in this journal, which I have kept
so regularly ever since I was a girl. For three days I have not once
thought of Robert—I, who am always thinking of him at other
times.

My poor, dear, unhappy Mary! the worst I feared for you on that
night when I sat up alone was far below the dreadful calamity that
has really happened. How can I write about it, with my eyes full of
tears and my hand all of a tremble? I don't even know why I am
sitting down at my desk now, unless it is habit that keeps me to my
old every-day task, in spite of all the grief and fear which seem to
unfit me entirely for performing it.

The people of the house were asleep and lazy on that dreadful
night, and I was the first to open the door. Never, never could I
describe in writing, or even say in plain talk, though it is so much
easier, what I felt when I saw two policemen come in, carrying
between them what seemed to me to be a dead girl, and that girl
Mary! I caught hold of her, and gave a scream that must have
alarmed the whole house; for frightened people came crowding
downstairs in their night-dresses. There was a dreadful confusion
and noise of loud talking, but I heard nothing and saw nothing till
I had got her into my room and laid on my bed. I stooped down,
frantic-like, to kiss her, and saw an awful mark of a blow on the
left temple, and felt, at the same time, a feeble flutter of her breath
on my cheek. The discovery that she was not dead seemed to give
me back my senses again. I told one of the policemen where the
nearest doctor was to be found, and sat down by the bedside while
he was gone, and bathed her poor head with cold water. She never

opened her eyes, or moved, or spoke; but she breathed, and that was enough for me, because it was enough for life.

The policeman left in the room was a big, thick-voiced, pomp-ous man, with a horrible unfeeling pleasure in hearing himself talk before an assembly of frightened, silent people. He told us how he had found her, as if he had been telling a story in a tap-room, and began with saying: "I don't think the young woman was drunk."

Drunk! My Mary, who might have been a born lady for all the spirits she ever touched—drunk! I could have struck the man for uttering the word, with her lying—poor suffering angel—so white, and still, and helpless before him. As it was, I gave him a look, but he was too stupid to understand it, and went droning on, saying the same thing over and over again in the same words. And yet the story of how they found her was, like all the sad stories I have ever heard told in real life, so very, very short. They had just seen her lying along on the curbstone a few streets off, and had taken her to the station-house. There she had been searched, and one of my cards, that I gave to ladies who promise me employment, had been found in her pocket, and so they had brought her to our house. This was all the man really had to tell. There was nobody near her when she was found, and no evidence to show how the blow on her temple had been inflicted.

What a time it was before the doctor came, and how dreadful to hear him say, after he had looked at her, that he was afraid all the medical men in the world could be of no use here! He could not get her to swallow anything; and the more he tried to bring her back to her senses the less chance there seemed of his succeeding. He examined the blow on her temple, and said he thought she must have fallen down in a fit of some sort, and struck her head against the pavement, and so have given her brain what he was afraid was a fatal shake. I asked what was to be done if she showed any return to sense in the night. He said: "Send for me directly"; and stopped for a little while afterward stroking her head gently with his hand, and whispering to himself: "Poor girl, so young and so pretty!" I had felt, some minutes before, as if I could have struck the police-man, and I felt now as if I could have thrown my arms round the doctor's neck and kissed him. I did put out my hand when he took up his hat, and he shook it in the friendliest way. "Don't hope, my dear," he said, and went out.

The rest of the lodgers followed him, all silent and shocked, ex-cept the inhuman wretch who owns the house and lives in idleness on the high rents he wrings from poor people like us.

"She's three weeks in my debt," says he, with a frown and an oath. "Where the devil is my money to come from now?" Brute! brute!

I had a long cry alone with her that seemed to ease my heart a little. She was not the least changed for the better when I had wiped away the tears and could see her clearly again. I took up her right hand, which lay nearest to me. It was tight clinched. I tried to un-clasp the fingers, and succeeded after a little time. Something dark fell out of the palm of her hand as I straightened it.

I picked the thing up, and smoothed it out, and saw that it was an end of a man's cravat.

A very old, rotten, dingy strip of black silk, with thin lilac lines, all blurred and deadened with dirt, running across and across the stuff in a sort of trellis-work pattern. The small end of the cravat was hemmed in the usual way, but the other end was all jagged, as if the morsel then in my hands had been torn off violently from the rest of the stuff. A chill ran all over me as I looked at it; for that poor, stained, crumpled end of a cravat seemed to be saying to me, as though it had been in plain words: "If she dies, she has come to her death by foul means, and I am the witness of it."

I had been frightened enough before, lest she should die suddenly and quietly without my knowing it, while we were alone together; but I got into a perfect agony now, for fear this last worst affliction should take me by surprise. I don't suppose five minutes passed all that woful night through without my getting up and putting my cheek close to her mouth, to feel if the faint breaths still fluttered out of it. They came and went just the same as at first, though the fright I was in often made me fancy they were stilled forever.

Just as the church clocks were striking four I was startled by seeing the room door open. It was only Dusty Sal (as they call her in the house), the maid-of-all-work. She was wrapped up in the blanket off her bed; her hair was all tumbled over her face, and her eyes were heavy with sleep as she came up to the bedside where I was sitting.

"I've two hours good before I begin to work," says she, in her hoarse, drowsy voice, "and I've come to sit up and take my turn at watching her. You lay down and get some sleep on the rug. Here's my blanket for you. I don't mind the cold—it will keep me awake."

"You are very kind—very, very kind and thoughtful, Sally," says I, "but I am too wretched in my mind to want sleep, or rest, or to do anything but wait where I am, and try and hope for the best."

"Then I'll wait, too," says Sally. "I must do something; if there's nothing to do but waiting, I'll wait."

And she sat down opposite me at the foot of the bed, and drew the blanket close round her with a shiver.

"After working so hard as you do, I'm sure you must want all the little rest you can get," says I.

"Excepting only you," says Sally, putting her heavy arm very clumsily, but very gently at the same time, round Mary's feet, and looking hard at the pale, still face on the pillow. "Excepting you, she's the only soul in this house as never swore at me, or give me a hard word that I can remember. When you made puddings on Sundays, and give her half, she always give me a bit. The rest of 'em calls me Dusty Sal. Excepting only you, again, she always called me Sally, as if she knowed me in a friendly way. I ain't no good here, but I ain't no harm, neither; and I shall take my turn at the sitting up—that's what I shall do!"

She nestled her head down close at Mary's feet as she spoke those words, and said no more. I once or twice thought she had fallen asleep, but whenever I looked at her her heavy eyes were always wide open. She never changed her position an inch till the church clocks struck six; then she gave one little squeeze to Mary's feet with her arm, and shuffled out of the room without a word. A minute or two after, I heard her down below, lighting the kitchen fire just as usual.

A little later the doctor stepped over before his breakfast-time to see if there had been any change in the night. He only shook his head when he looked at her as if there was no hope. Having nobody else to consult that I could put trust in, I showed him the end of the cravat, and told him of the dreadful suspicion that had arisen in my mind when I found it in her hand.

"You must keep it carefully, and produce it at the inquest," he said. "I don't know, though, that it is likely to lead to anything. The bit of stuff may have been lying on the pavement near her, and her hand may have unconsciously clutched it when she fell. Was she subject to fainting-fits?"

"Not more so, sir, than other young girls who are hard-worked and anxious, and weakly from poor living," I answered.

"I can't say that she may not have got that blow from a fall," the doctor went on, looking at her temple again. "I can't say that it presents any positive appearance of having been inflicted by another person. It will be important, however, to ascertain what state of health she was in last night. Have you any idea where she was yesterday evening?"

I told him where she was employed at work, and said I imagined she must have been kept there later than usual.

"I shall pass the place this morning," said the doctor, "in going my rounds among my patients, and I'll just step in and make some inquiries."

I thanked him, and we parted. Just as he was closing the door he looked in again.

"Was she your sister?" he asked.

"No, sir, only my dear friend."

He said nothing more, but I heard him sigh as he shut the door softly. Perhaps he once had a sister of his own, and lost her? Perhaps she was like Mary in the face?

The doctor was hours gone away. I began to feel unspeakably forlorn and helpless, so much so as even to wish selfishly that Robert might really have sailed from America, and might get to London in time to assist and console me.

No living creature came into the room but Sally. The first time she brought me some tea; the second and third times she only looked in to see if there was any change, and glanced her eye toward the bed. I had never known her so silent before; it seemed almost as if this dreadful accident had struck her dumb. I ought to have spoken to her, perhaps, but there was something in her face that daunted me; and, besides, the fever of anxiety I was in began to dry up my lips, as if they would never be able to shape any words again. I was still tormented by that frightful apprehension of the past night, that she would die without my knowing it—die without saying one word to clear up the awful mystery of this blow, and set the suspicions at rest forever which I still felt whenever my eyes fell on the end of the old cravat.

At last the doctor came back.

"I think you may safely clear your mind of any doubts to which that bit of stuff may have given rise," he said. "She was, as you supposed, detained late by her employers, and she fainted in the workroom. They most unwisely and unkindly let her go home alone, without giving her any stimulant, as soon as she came to her senses again. Nothing is more probable, under these circumstances, than that she should faint a second time on her way here. A fall on the pavement, without any friendly arm to break it, might have produced even a worse injury than the injury we see. I believe that the only ill usage to which the poor girl was exposed was the neglect she met with in the work-room."

"You speak very reasonably, I own, sir," said I, not yet quite convinced. "Still, perhaps she may—"

"My poor girl, I told you not to hope," said the doctor, interrupting me. He went to Mary, and lifted up her eyelids, and looked at her eyes while he spoke; then added, "If you still doubt how she came by that blow, do not encourage the idea that any words of hers will ever enlighten you. She will never speak again."

"Not dead! Oh, sir, don't say she's dead!"

"She is dead to pain and sorrow—dead to speech and recognition. There is more animation in the life of the feeblest insect that flies than in the life that is left in her. When you look at her now, try to think that she is in heaven. That is the best comfort I can give you, after telling the hard truth."

I did not believe him. I could not believe him. So long as she breathed at all, so long I was resolved to hope. Soon after the doctor was gone, Sally came in again, and found me listening (if I may call it so) at Mary's lips. She went to where my little hand-glass hangs against the wall, took it down, and gave it to me.

"See if the breath marks it," she said.

Yes; her breath did mark it, but very faintly. Sally cleaned the glass with her apron, and gave it back to me. As she did so, she half stretched out her hand to Mary's face, but drew it in again suddenly, as if she was afraid of soiling Mary's delicate skin with her hard, horny fingers. Going out, she stopped at the foot of the bed, and scraped away a little patch of mud that was on one of Mary's shoes.

"I always used to clean 'em for her," said Sally, "to save her hands from getting blacked. May I take 'em off now, and clean 'em again?"

I nodded my head, for my heart was too heavy to speak. Sally took the shoes off with a slow, awkward tenderness, and went out.

An hour or more must have passed, when, putting the glass over her lips again, I saw no mark on it. I held it closer and closer. I dulled it accidentally with my own breath, and cleaned it. I held it over her again. Oh, Mary, Mary, the doctor was right! I ought to have only thought of you in heaven!

Dead, without a word, without a sign—without even a look to tell the true story of the blow that killed her! I could not call to anybody, I could not cry, I could not so much as put the glass down and give her a kiss for the last time. I don't know how long I had sat there with my eyes burning, and my hands deadly cold, when Sally came in with the shoes cleaned, and carried carefully in her apron for fear of a soil touching them. At the sight of that—

I can write no more. My tears drop so fast on the paper that I can see nothing.

March 12th. She died on the afternoon of the eighth. On the morning of the ninth, I wrote, as in duty bound, to her step-mother at Hammersmith. There was no answer. I wrote again; my letter was returned to me this morning unopened. For all that woman cares, Mary might be buried with a pauper's funeral; but this shall never be, if I pawn everything about me, down to the very gown that is on my back. The bare thought of Mary being buried by the workhouse gave me the spirit to dry my eyes, and go to the undertaker's, and tell him how I was placed. I said if he would get me an estimate of all that would have to be paid, from first to last, for the cheapest decent funeral that could be had, I would undertake to raise the money. He gave me the estimate, written in this way, like a common bill:

A Walking Funeral Complete	£1	13	8
Vestry	0	4	4
Rector	0	4	4
Clerk	0	1	0
Sexton	0	1	0
Beadle	0	1	0
Bell	0	1	0
Six Feet of Ground	0	2	0
Total	£2	8	4

If I had the heart to give any thought to it, I should be inclined to wish that the Church could afford to do without so many small charges for burying poor people, to whose friends even shillings are of consequence. But it is useless to complain; the money must be raised at once. The charitable doctor—a poor man himself, or he would not be living in our neighborhood—has subscribed ten shillings toward the expenses; and the coroner, when the inquest was over, added five more. Perhaps others may assist me. If not, I have fortunately clothes and furniture of my own to pawn. And I must set about parting with them without delay, for the funeral is to be to-morrow, the thirteenth.

The funeral—Mary's funeral! It is well that the straits and difficulties I am in keep my mind on the stretch. If I had leisure to grieve, where should I find the courage to face to-morrow?

Thank God they did not want me at the inquest. The verdict given, with the doctor, the policeman, and two persons from the place where she worked, for witnesses, was Accidental Death. The end of the cravat was produced, and the coroner said that it was certainly enough to suggest suspicion; but the jury, in the absence of any positive evidence, held to the doctor's notion that she had fainted and fallen down, and so got the blow on her temple. They reproved the people where Mary worked for letting her go home alone, without so much as a drop of brandy to support her, after she had fallen into a swoon from exhaustion before their eyes. The coroner added, on his own account, that he thought the reproof was thoroughly deserved. After that, the cravat-end was given back to me by my own desire, the police saying that they could make no investigations with such a slight clew to guide them. They may think so, and the coroner, and doctor, and jury may think so; but, in spite of all that has passed, I am now more firmly persuaded than ever that there is some dreadful mystery in connection with that blow on my poor lost Mary's temple which has yet to be revealed, and which may come to be discovered through this very fragment of a cravat that I found in her hand. I cannot give any good reason for why I think so, but I know that if I had been one of the jury at the inquest, nothing should have induced me to consent to such a verdict as Accidental Death.

After I had pawned my things, and had begged a small advance

of wages at the place where I work to make up what was still wanting to pay for Mary's funeral, I thought I might have had a little
quiet time to prepare myself as I best could for to-morrow. But this
was not to be. When I got home the landlord met me in the passage. He was in liquor, and more brutal and pitiless in his way of
looking and speaking than ever I saw him before.

"So you're going to be fool enough to pay for her funeral, are
you?" were his first words to me. I was too weary and heart-sick to
answer; I only tried to get by him to my own door.

"If you can pay for burying her," he went on, putting himself in
front of me, "you can pay her lawful debts. She owes me three weeks'
rent. Suppose you raise the money for that next, and hand it over to
me? I'm not joking, I can promise you. I mean to have my rent;
and, if somebody don't pay it, I'll have her body seized and sent to
the workhouse!"

Between terror and disgust, I thought I should have dropped to
the floor at his feet. But I determined not to let him see how he
had horrified me, if I could possibly control myself. So I mustered
resolution enough to answer that I did not believe the law gave
him any such wicked power over the dead.

"I'll teach you what the law is!" he broke in; "you'll raise money
to bury her like a born lady, when she's died in my debt, will you?
And you think I'll let my rights be trampled upon like that, do
you? See if I do! I'll give you till to-night to think about it. If I
don't have the three weeks she owes before to-morrow, dead or
alive, she shall go to the workhouse!"

This time I managed to push by him, and get to my own room,
and lock the door in his face. As soon as I was alone I fell into a
breathless, suffocating fit of crying that seemed to be shaking me
to pieces. But there was no good and no help in tears; I did my best
to calm myself after a little while, and tried to think who I should
run to for help and protection.

The doctor was the first friend I thought of; but I knew he was always out seeing his patients of an afternoon. The beadle was the next person who came into my head. He had the look of being a very dignified, unapproachable kind of man when he came about the inquest; but he talked to me a little then, and said I was a good girl, and seemed, I really thought, to pity me. So to him I determined to apply in my great danger and distress.

Most fortunately, I found him at home. When I told him of the landlord's infamous threats, and of the misery I was suffering in consequence of them, he rose up with a stamp of his foot, and sent for his gold-laced cocked hat that he wears on Sundays, and his long cane with the ivory top to it. "I'll give it to him," said the beadle. "Come along with me, my dear. I think I told you you were a good girl at the inquest—if I didn't, I tell you so now. I'll give it to him! Come along with me."

And he went out, striding on with his cocked hat and his great cane, and I followed him.

"Landlord!" he cries, the moment he gets into the passage, with a thump of his cane on the floor, "landlord!" with a look all round him as if he was King of England calling to a beast, "come out!"

The moment the landlord came out and saw who it was, his eye fixed on the cocked hat, and he turned as pale as ashes.

"How dare you frighten this poor girl?" says the beadle. "How dare you bully her at this sorrowful time with threatening to do what you know you can't do? How dare you be a cowardly, bullying, braggadocio of an unmanly landlord? Don't talk to me: I won't hear you. I'll pull you up, sir. If you say another word to the young woman, I'll pull you up before the authorities of this metropolitan parish. I've had my eye on you, and the authorities have had their eye on you, and the rector has had his eye on you. We don't like the look of your small shop round the corner; we don't like the look of some of the customers who deal at it; we don't like disorderly characters; and we don't by any manner of means like you. Go away. Leave the young woman alone. Hold your tongue, or I'll pull you up. If he says another word, or interferes with you again, my dear, come and tell me; and, as sure as he's a bullying, unmanly, bragga- docio of a landlord, I'll pull him up."

With those words the beadle gave a loud cough to clear his throat, and another thump of his cane on the floor, and so went striding out again before I could open my lips to thank him. The landlord slunk back into his room without a word. I was left alone and un- molested at last, to strengthen myself for the hard trial of my poor love's funeral to-morrow.

March 13th. It is all over. A week ago her head rested on my bosom. It is laid in the churchyard now; the fresh earth lies heavy over her grave. I and my dearest friend, the sister of my love, are parted in this world forever.

I followed her funeral alone through the cruel, hustling streets. Sally, I thought, might have offered to go with me, but she never so much as came into my room. I did not like to think badly of her for this, and I am glad I restrained myself; for, when we got into the churchyard, among the two or three people who were standing by the open grave I saw Sally, in her ragged gray shawl and her patched black bonnet. She did not seem to notice me till the last words of the service had been read and the clergyman had gone away; then she came up and spoke to me.

"I couldn't follow along with you," she said, looking at her ragged shawl, "for I haven't a decent suit of clothes to walk in. I wish I could get vent in crying for her like you, but I can't; all the crying's been drudged and starved out of me long ago. Don't you think about lighting your fire when you get home. I'll do that, and get you a drop of tea to comfort you."

She seemed on the point of saying a kind word or two more, when, seeing the beadle coming toward me, she drew back, as if she was afraid of him, and left the churchyard.

"Here's my subscription toward the funeral," said the beadle, giving me back his shilling fee. "Don't say anything about it, for it mightn't be approved of in a business point of view, if it came to some people's ears. Has the landlord said anything more to you? no, I thought not. He's too polite a man to give me the trouble of pulling him up. Don't stop crying here, my dear. Take the advice of a man familiar with funerals, and go home."

I tried to take his advice, but it seemed like deserting Mary to go away when all the rest forsook her.

I waited about till the earth was thrown in and the man had left the place, then I returned to the grave. Oh, how bare and cruel it was, without so much as a bit of green turf to soften it! Oh, how much harder it seemed to live than to die, when I stood alone looking at the heavy piled-up lumps of clay, and thinking of what was hidden beneath them!

I was driven home by my own despairing thoughts. The sight of Sally lighting the fire in my room eased my heart a little. When she was gone, I took up Robert's letter again to keep my mind employed on the only subject in the world that has any interest for it now.

This fresh reading increased the doubts I had already felt relative to his having remained in America after writing to me. My grief and forlornness have made a strange alteration in my former feelings about his coming back. I seem to have lost all my prudence and self-denial, and to care so little about his poverty, and so much about himself, that the prospect of his return is really the only comforting thought I have now to support me. I know this is weak in me, and that his coming back can lead to no good result for either of us; but he is the only living being left me to love; and—I can't explain it—but I want to put my arms round his neck and tell him about Mary.

March 14th. I locked up the end of the cravat in my writing-desk. No change in the dreadful suspicions that the bare sight of it rouses in me. I tremble if I so much as touch it.

March 15th, 16th, 17th. Work, work, work. If I don't knock up, I shall be able to pay back the advance in another week; and then, with a little more pinching in my daily expenses, I may succeed in saving a shilling or two to get some turf to put over Mary's grave, and perhaps even a few flowers besides to grow round it.

March 18th. Thinking of Robert all day long. Does this mean that he is really coming back? If it does, reckoning the distance he is at from New York, and the time ships take to get to England, I might see him by the end of April or the beginning of May.

March 19th. I don't remember my mind running once on the end of the cravat yesterday, and I am certain I never looked at it; yet I had the strangest dream concerning it at night. I thought it was lengthened into a long clew, like the silken thread that led to Rosamond's Bower. I thought I took hold of it, and followed it a little way, and then got frightened and tried to go back, but found that I was obliged, in spite of myself, to go on. It led me through a place like the Valley of the Shadow of Death, in an old print I remember in my mother's copy of the *Pilgrim's Progress*. I seemed to be months and months following it without any respite, till at last it brought me, on a sudden, face to face with an angel whose eyes were like Mary's. He said to me, "Go on, still; the truth is at the end, waiting for you to find it." I burst out crying, for the angel had Mary's voice as well as Mary's eyes, and woke with my heart throbbing and my cheeks all wet. What is the meaning of this? Is it always superstitious, I wonder, to believe that dreams may come true?

April 30th. I have found it! God knows to what results it may lead; but it is as certain as that I am sitting here before my journal that I have found the cravat from which the end in Mary's hand was torn. I discovered it last night; but the flutter I was in, and the nervousness and uncertainty I felt, prevented me from noting down this most extraordinary and unexpected event at the time when it happened. Let me try if I can preserve the memory of it in writing now.

I was going home rather late from where I work, when I suddenly remembered that I had forgotten to buy myself any candles the evening before, and that I should be left in the dark if I did not manage to rectify this mistake in some way. The shop close to me, at which I usually deal, would be shut up, I knew, before I could get to it; so I determined to go into the first place I passed where candles were sold. This turned out to be a small shop with two counters, which did business on one side in the general grocery way, and on the other in the rag and bottle and old iron line.

There were several customers on the grocery side when I went in, so I waited on the empty rag side till I could be served. Glancing about me here at the worthless-looking things by which I was surrounded, my eye was caught by a bundle of rags lying on the counter, as if they had just been brought in and left there. From mere idle curiosity, I looked close at the rags, and saw among them something like an old cravat. I took it up directly and held it under a gaslight. The pattern was blurred lilac lines running across and across the dingy black ground in a trellis-work form. I looked at the ends: one of them was torn off.

How I managed to hide the breathless surprise into which this discovery threw me I cannot say, but I certainly contrived to steady my voice somehow, and to ask for my candles calmly when the man and woman serving in the shop, having disposed of their other customers, inquired of me what I wanted.

As the man took down the candles, my brain was all in a whirl with trying to think how I could get possession of the old cravat without exciting any suspicion. Chance, and a little quickness on my part in taking advantage of it, put the object within my reach in a moment. The man, having counted out the candles, asked the woman for some paper to wrap them in. She produced a piece much too small and flimsy for the purpose, and declared, when he called for something better, that the day's supply of stout paper was all exhausted. He flew into a rage with her for managing so badly. Just as they were beginning to quarrel violently, I stepped back to the rag-counter, took the old cravat carelessly out of the bundle, and said, in as light a tone as I could possibly assume:

"Come, come, don't let my candles be the cause of hard words between you. Tie this ragged old thing round them with a bit of string, and I shall carry them home quite comfortably."

The man seemed disposed to insist on the stout paper being produced; but the woman, as if she was glad of an opportunity of spiting him, snatched the candles away, and tied them up in a moment in the torn old cravat. I was afraid he would have struck her before my face, he seemed in such a fury; but, fortunately, another customer came in, and obliged him to put his hands to peaceable and proper use.

"Quite a bundle of all-sorts on the opposite counter there," I said to the woman, as I paid her for the candles.

"Yes, and all hoarded up for sale by a poor creature with a lazy brute of a husband, who lets his wife do all the work while he spends all the money," answered the woman, with a malicious look at the man by her side.

"He can't surely have much money to spend, if his wife has no better work to do than picking up rags," said I.

"It isn't her fault if she hasn't got no better," says the woman, rather angrily. "She's ready to turn her hand to anything. Charing, washing, laying-out, keeping empty houses—nothing comes amiss to her. She's my half-sister, and I think I ought to know."

"Did you say she went out charing?" I asked, making believe as if I knew of somebody who might employ her.

"Yes, of course I did," answered the woman; "and if you can put a job into her hands, you'll be doing a good turn to a poor hard-working creature as wants it. She lives down the Mews here to the right—name of Horlick, and as honest a woman as ever stood in shoe-leather. Now, then, ma'am, what for you?"

Another customer came in just then, and occupied her attention. I left the shop, passed the turning that led down to the Mews, looked up at the name of the street, so as to know how to find it again, and then ran home as fast as I could. Perhaps it was the remembrance of my strange dream striking me on a sudden, or perhaps it was the shock of the discovery I had just made, but I began to feel frightened without knowing why, and anxious to be under shelter in my own room.

If Robert should come back! Oh, what a relief and help it would be now if Robert should come back!

May 1st. On getting indoors last night, the first thing I did, after striking a light, was to take the ragged cravat off the candles, and smooth it out on the table. I then took the end that had been in poor Mary's hand out of my writing-desk, and smoothed that out too. It matched the torn side of the cravat exactly. I put them together, and satisfied myself that there was not a doubt of it.

Not once did I close my eyes that night. A kind of fever got possession of me—a vehement yearning to go on from this first discovery and find out more, no matter what the risk might be. The cravat now really became, to my mind, the clew that I thought I saw in my dream—the clew that I was resolved to follow. I determined to go to Mrs. Horlick this evening on my return from work.

I found the Mews easily. A crook-backed dwarf of a man was lounging at the corner of it smoking his pipe. Not liking his looks, I did not inquire of him where Mrs. Horlick lived, but went down the Mews till I met with a woman, and asked her. She directed me to the right number. I knocked at the door, and Mrs. Horlick herself—a lean, ill-tempered, miserable-looking woman—answered it. I told her at once that I had come to ask what her terms were for charing. She stared at me for a moment, then answered my question civilly enough.

"You look surprised at a stranger like me finding you out," I said. "I first came to hear of you last night, from a relation of yours, in rather an odd way."

And I told her all that had happened in the chandler's shop, bringing in the bundle of rags, and the circumstance of my carrying home the candles in the old torn cravat, as often as possible.

"It's the first time I've heard of anything belonging to him turning out any use," said Mrs. Horlick, bitterly.

"What! the spoiled old neck-handkerchief belonged to your husband, did it?" said I, at a venture.

"Yes; I pitched his rotten rag of a neck-'andkercher into the bundle along with the rest, and I wish I could have pitched him in after it," said Mrs. Horlick. "I'd sell him cheap at any ragshop. There he stands, smoking his pipe at the end of the Mews, out of work for weeks past, the idlest humpbacked pig in all London!"

She pointed to the man whom I had passed on entering the Mews. My cheeks began to burn and my knees to tremble, for I knew that in tracing the cravat to its owner I was advancing a step toward a fresh discovery. I wished Mrs. Horlick good evening, and said I would write and mention the day on which I wanted her.

What I had just been told put a thought into my mind that I was afraid to follow out. I have heard people talk of being light-headed, and I felt as I have heard them say they felt when I retraced my steps up the Mews. My head got giddy, and my eyes seemed able to see nothing but the figure of the little crook-backed man, still smoking his pipe in his former place. I could see nothing but that; I could think of nothing but the mark of the blow on my poor lost Mary's temple. I know that I must have been light-headed, for as I came close to the crook-backed man I stopped without meaning it. The minute before, there had been no idea in me of speaking to him. I did not know how to speak, or in what way it would be safest to begin; and yet, the moment I came face to face with him, something out of myself seemed to stop me, and to make me speak without considering beforehand, without thinking of consequences, without knowing, I may almost say, what words I was uttering till the instant when they rose to my lips.

"When your old neck-tie was torn, did you know that one end of it went to the ragshop, and the other fell into my hands?"

I said these bold words to him suddenly, and, as it seemed, without my own will taking any part in them.

He started, stared, changed color. He was too much amazed by my sudden speaking to find an answer for me. When he did open his lips, it was to say rather to himself than me:

"You're not the girl."

"No," I said, with a strange choking at my heart, "I'm her friend."

By this time he had recovered his surprise, and he seemed to be aware that he had let out more than he ought.

"You may be anybody's friend you like," he said, brutally, "so long as you don't come jabbering nonsense here. I don't know you, and I don't understand your jokes."

He turned quickly away from me when he had said the last words. He had never once looked fairly at me since I first spoke to him.

Was it his hand that had struck the blow? I had only sixpence in my pocket, but I took it out and followed him. If it had been a five-pound note I should have done the same in the state I was in then.

"Would a pot of beer help you to understand me?" I said, and offered him the sixpence.

"A pot ain't no great things," he answered, taking the sixpence doubtfully.

"It may lead to something better," I said. His eyes began to twinkle, and he came close to me. Oh, how my legs trembled— how my head swam!

"This is all in a friendly way, is it?" he asked, in a whisper.

I nodded my head. At that moment I could not have spoken for worlds.

"Friendly, of course," he went on to himself, "or there would have been a policeman in it. She told you, I suppose, that I wasn't the man?"

I nodded my head again. It was all I could do to keep myself standing upright.

"I suppose it's a case of threatening to have him up, and make him settle it quietly for a pound or two? How much for me if you lay hold of him?"

"Half."

I began to be afraid that he would suspect something if I was still silent. The wretch's eyes twinkled again and he came yet closer.

"I drove him to the Red Lion, corner of Dodd Street and Rudgely Street. The house was shut up, but he was let in at the jug and bottle door, like a man who was known to the landlord. That's as much as I can tell you, and I'm certain I'm right. He was the last fare I took up at night. The next morning master gave me the sack—said I cribbed his corn and his fares. I wish I had."

I gathered from this that the crook-backed man had been a cab-driver.

"Why don't you speak?" he asked, suspiciously. "Has she been telling you a pack of lies about me? What did she say when she came home?"

"What ought she to have said?"

"She ought to have said my fare was drunk, and she came in the way as he was going to get into the cab. That's what she ought to have said to begin with."

"But after?"

"Well, after, my fare, by way of larking with her, puts out his leg for to trip her up, and she stumbles and catches at me for to save herself, and tears off one of the limp ends of my rotten old tie. 'What do you mean by that, you brute?' says she, turning round as soon as she was steady on her legs, to my fare. Says my fare to her: 'I means to teach you to keep a civil tongue in your head.' And he ups with his fist, and—what's come to you, now? What are you looking at me like that for? How do you think a man of my size was to take her part against a man big enough to have eaten me up? Look as much as you like, in my place you would have done what I done—drew off when he shook his fist at you, and swore he'd be the death of you if you didn't start your horse in no time."

I saw he was working himself up into a rage; but I could not, if my life had depended on it, have stood near him or looked at him any longer. I just managed to stammer out that I had been walking a long way, and that, not being used to much exercise, I felt faint and giddy with fatigue. He only changed from angry to sulky when I made that excuse. I got a little further away from him, and then added that if he would be at the Mews entrance the next evening I should have something more to say and something more to give him. He grumbled a few suspicious words in answer about doubting whether he should trust me to come back. Fortunately, at that moment, a policeman passed on the opposite side of the way. He slunk down the Mews immediately, and I was free to make my escape.

How I got home I can't say, except that I think I ran the greater part of the way. Sally opened the door, and asked if anything was the matter the moment she saw my face. I answered: "Nothing— nothing."

She stopped me as I was going into my room, and said:

"Smooth your hair a bit, and put your collar straight. There's a gentleman in there waiting for you."

My heart gave one great bound: I knew who it was in an instant, and rushed into the room like a mad woman.

"Oh, Robert, Robert!" All my heart went out to him in those two little words.

"Good God, Anne, has anything happened? Are you ill?"

"Mary! my poor, lost, murdered, dear, dear Mary!"

That was all I could say before I fell on his breast.

May 2d. Misfortunes and disappointments have saddened him a little, but toward me he is unaltered. He is as good, as kind, as gently and truly affectionate as ever. I believe no other man in the world could have listened to the story of Mary's death with such tenderness and pity as he. Instead of cutting me short anywhere, he drew me on to tell more than I had intended; and his first generous words when I had done were to assure me that he would see himself to the grass being laid and the flowers planted on Mary's grave. I could almost have gone on my knees and worshiped him when he made me that promise.

Surely this best, and kindest, and noblest of men cannot always be unfortunate! My cheeks burn when I think that he has come back with only a few pounds in his pocket, after all his hard and honest struggles to do well in America. They must be bad people there when such a man as Robert cannot get on among them. He now talks calmly and resignedly of trying for any one of the lowest employments by which a man can earn his bread honestly in this great city—he who knows French, who can write so beautifully! Oh, if the people who have places to give away only knew Robert as well as I do, what a salary he would have, what a post he would be chosen to occupy!

I am writing these lines alone while he has gone to the Mews to treat with the dastardly, heartless wretch with whom I spoke yesterday.

Robert says the creature—I won't call him a man—must be humored and kept deceived about poor Mary's end, in order that we may discover and bring to justice the monster whose drunken blow was the death of her. I shall know no ease of mind till her murderer is secured, and till I am certain that he will be made to suffer for his crimes. I wanted to go with Robert to the Mews, but he said it was best that he should carry out the rest of the investigation alone, for my strength and resolution had been too hardly taxed already. He said more words in praise of me for what I have been able to do up to this time, which I am almost ashamed to write down with my own pen. Besides, there is no need; praise from his lips is one of the things that I can trust my memory to preserve to the latest day of my life.

May 3d. Robert was very long last night before he came back to tell me what he had done. He easily recognized the hunchback at the corner of the Mews by my description of him; but he found it a hard matter, even with the help of money, to overcome the cowardly wretch's distrust of him as a stranger and a man. However, when this had been accomplished, the main difficulty was conquered.

The hunchback, excited by the promise of more money, went at once to the Red Lion to inquire about the person whom he had driven there in his cab. Robert followed him, and waited at the corner of the street. The tidings brought by the cabman were of the most unexpected kind. The murderer—I can write of him by no other name—had fallen ill on the very night when he was driven to the Red Lion, had taken to his bed there and then, and was still confined to it at that very moment. His disease was of a kind that is brought on by excessive drinking, and that affects the mind as well as the body. The people at the public house call it the Horrors.

Hearing these things, Robert determined to see if he could not find out something more for himself by going and inquiring at the public house, in the character of one of the friends of the sick man in bed upstairs. He made two important discoveries. First, he found out the name and address of the doctor in attendance. Secondly, he entrapped the barman into mentioning the murderous wretch by his name. This last discovery adds an unspeakably fearful interest to the dreadful misfortune of Mary's death. Noah Truscott, as she told me herself in the last conversation I ever had with her, was the name of the man whose drunken example ruined her father, and Noah Truscott is also the name of the man whose drunken fury killed her. There is something that makes one shudder, something supernatural in this awful fact. Robert agrees with me that the hand of Providence must have guided my steps to that shop from which all the discoveries since made took their rise. He says he believes we are the instruments of effecting a righteous retribution; and, if he spends his last farthing, he will have the investigation brought to its full end in a court of justice.

May 4th. Robert went to-day to consult a lawyer whom he knew in former times. The lawyer was much interested, though not so seriously impressed as he ought to have been by the story of Mary's death and of the events that have followed it. He gave Robert a confidential letter to take to the doctor in attendance on the double-dyed villain at the Red Lion. Robert left the letter, and called again and saw the doctor, who said his patient was getting better, and would most likely be up again in ten days or a fortnight. This statement Robert communicated to the lawyer, and the lawyer has undertaken to have the public house properly watched, and the hunchback (who is the most important witness) sharply looked after for the next fortnight, or longer if necessary. Here, then, the progress of this dreadful business stops for a while.

May 5th. Robert has got a little temporary employment in copying for his friend the lawyer. I am working harder than ever at my needle, to make up for the time that has been lost lately.

May 6th. To-day was Sunday, and Robert proposed that we should go and look at Mary's grave. He, who forgets nothing where a kindness is to be done, has found time to perform the promise he made to me on the night when we first met. The grave is already, by his orders, covered with turf, and planted round with shrubs. Some flowers, and a low headstone, are to be added, to make the place look worthier of my poor lost darling who is beneath it. Oh, I hope I shall live long after I am married to Robert! I want so much time to show him all my gratitude!

May 20th. A hard trial to my courage to-day. I have given evidence at the police-office, and have seen the monster who murdered her.

I could only look at him once. I could just see that he was a giant in size, and that he kept his dull, lowering, bestial face turned toward the witness-box, and his bloodshot, vacant eyes staring on me. For an instant I tried to confront that look; for an instant I kept my attention fixed on him—on his blotched face—on the short, grizzled hair above it—on his knotty, murderous right hand, hanging loose over the bar in front of him, like the paw of a wild beast over the edge of its den. Then the horror of him—the double horror of confronting him, in the first place, and afterward of seeing that he was an old man—overcame me, and I turned away, faint, sick, and shuddering. I never faced him again; and, at the end of my evidence, Robert considerately took me out.

When we met once more at the end of the examination, Robert told me that the prisoner never spoke and never changed his position. He was either fortified by the cruel composure of a savage, or his faculties had not yet thoroughly recovered from the disease that had so lately shaken them. The magistrate seemed to doubt if he was in his right mind; but the evidence of the medical man relieved this uncertainty, and the prisoner was committed for trial on a charge of manslaughter.

Why not on a charge of murder? Robert explained the law to me when I asked that question. I accepted the explanation, but it did not satisfy me. Mary Mallinson was killed by a blow from the hand of Noah Truscott. That is murder in the sight of God. Why not murder in the sight of the law also?

June 18th. To-morrow is the day appointed for the trial at the Old Bailey.

Before sunset this evening I went to look at Mary's grave. The turf has grown so green since I saw it last, and the flowers are springing up so prettily. A bird was perched dressing his feathers on the low white headstone that bears the inscription of her name and age. I did not go near enough to disturb the little creature. He looked innocent and pretty on the grave, as Mary herself was in her lifetime. When he flew away I went and sat for a little by the headstone, and read the mournful lines on it. Oh, my love! my love! what harm or wrong had you ever done in this world, that you should die at eighteen by a blow from a drunkard's hand?

June 19th. The trial. My experience of what happened at it is limited, like my experience of the examination at the police-office, to the time occupied in giving my own evidence. They made me say much more than I said before the magistrate. Between examination and cross-examination, I had to go into almost all the particulars about poor Mary and her funeral that I have written in this journal; the jury listening to every word I spoke with the most anxious attention. At the end, the judge said a few words to me approving of my conduct, and then there was a clapping of hands among the people in court. I was so agitated and excited that I trembled all over when they let me go out into the air again.

I looked at the prisoner both when I entered the witness-box and when I left it. The lowering brutality of his face was unchanged, but his faculties seemed to be more alive and observant than they were at the police-office. A frightful blue change passed over his face, and he drew his breath so heavily that the gasps were distinctly audible while I mentioned Mary by name and described the mark or the blow on her temple. When they asked me if I knew anything of the prisoner, and I answered that I only knew what Mary herself had told me about his having been her father's ruin, he gave a kind of groan, and struck both his hands heavily on the dock. And when I passed beneath him on my way out of court, he leaned over suddenly, whether to speak to me or to strike me I can't say, for he was immediately made to stand upright again by the turnkeys on either side of him. While the evidence proceeded (as Robert described it to me), the signs that he was suffering under superstitious terror became more and more apparent; until, at last, just as the lawyer appointed to defend him was rising to speak, he suddenly cried out, in a voice that startled every one, up to the very judge on the bench:

"Stop!"

There was a pause, and all eyes looked at him. The perspiration was pouring over his face like water, and he made strange, uncouth signs with his hands to the judge opposite. "Stop all this!" he cried again; "I've been the ruin of the father and the death of the child. Hang me before I do more harm! Hang me, for God's sake, out of the way!" As soon as the shock produced by this extraordinary interruption had subsided, he was removed, and there followed a long discussion about whether he was of sound mind or not. The matter was left to the jury to decide by their verdict. They found him guilty of the charge of manslaughter, without the excuse of insanity. He was brought up again, and condemned to transportation for life. All he did, on hearing the dreadful sentence, was to reiterate his desperate words: "Hang me before I do more harm! Hang me, for God's sake, out of the way!"

June 20th. I made yesterday's entry in sadness of heart, and I have not been better in my spirits to-day. It is something to have brought the murderer to the punishment that he deserves. But the knowledge that this most righteous act of retribution is accomplished brings no consolation with it. The law does indeed punish Noah Truscott for his crime, but can it raise up Mary Mallinson from her last resting-place in the churchyard?

While writing of the law, I ought to record that the heartless wretch who allowed Mary to be struck down in his presence without making an attempt to defend her is not likely to escape with perfect impunity. The policeman who looked after him to insure his attendance at the trial discovered that he had committed past offenses, for which the law can make him answer. A summons was executed upon him, and he was taken before the magistrate the moment he left the court after giving his evidence.

I had just written these few lines, and was closing my journal, when there came a knock at the door. I answered it, thinking that Robert had called on his way home to say good-night, and found myself face to face with a strange gentleman, who immediately asked for Anne Rodway. On hearing that I was the person inquired for, he requested five minutes' conversation with me. I showed him into the little empty room at the back of the house, and waited, rather surprised and fluttered, to hear what he had to say.

He was a dark man, with a serious manner, and a short, stern way of speaking. I was certain that he was a stranger, and yet there seemed something in his face not unfamiliar to me. He began by taking a newspaper from his pocket, and asking me if I was the person who had given evidence at the trial of Noah Truscott on a charge of manslaughter. I answered immediately that I was.

"I have been for nearly two years in London seeking Mary Mallinson, and always seeking her in vain," he said. "The first and only news I have had of her I found in the newspaper report of the trial yesterday."

He still spoke calmly, but there was something in the look of his eyes which showed me that he was suffering in spirit. A sudden nervousness overcame me, and I was obliged to sit down.

"You knew Mary Mallinson, sir?" I asked, as quietly as I could.

"I am her brother."

I clasped my hands and hid my face in despair. Oh, the bitterness of heart with which I heard him say those simple words!

"You were very kind to her," said the calm, tearless man. "In her name and for her sake, I thank you."

"Oh, sir," I said, "why did you never write to her when you were in foreign parts?"

"I wrote often," he answered; "but each of my letters contained a remittance of money. Did Mary tell you she had a step-mother? If she did, you may guess why none of my letters were allowed to reach her. I now know that this woman robbed my sister. Has she lied in telling me that she was never informed of Mary's place of abode?"

I remembered that Mary had never communicated with her step-mother after the separation, and could therefore assure him that the woman had spoken the truth.

He paused for a moment after that, and sighed. Then he took out a pocket-book, and said:

"I have already arranged for the payment of any legal expenses that may have been incurred by the trial, but I have still to reimburse you for the funeral charges which you so generously defrayed. Excuse my speaking bluntly on this subject; I am accustomed to look on all matters where money is concerned purely as matters of business."

I saw that he was taking several bank-notes out of the pocket-book, and stopped him.

"I will gratefully receive back the little money I actually paid, sir, because I am not well off, and it would be an ungracious act of pride in me to refuse it from you," I said; "but I see you handling bank-notes, any one of which is far beyond the amount you have to repay me. Pray put them back, sir. What I did for your poor lost sister I did from my love and fondness for her. You have thanked me for that, and your thanks are all I can receive."

He had hitherto concealed his feelings, but I saw them now begin to get the better of him. His eyes softened, and he took my hand and squeezed it hard.

"I beg your pardon," he said; "I beg your pardon, with all my heart."

There was silence between us, for I was crying, and I believe, at heart, he was crying too. At last he dropped my hand, and seemed to change back, by an effort, to his former calmness.

"Is there no one belonging to you to whom I can be of service?" he asked. "I see among the witnesses on the trial the name of a young man who appears to have assisted you in the inquiries which led to the prisoner's conviction. Is he a relation?"

"No, sir—at least, not now—but I hope—"

"What?"

"I hope that he may, one day, be the nearest and dearest relation to me that a woman can have." I said those words boldly, because I was afraid of his otherwise taking some wrong view of the connection between Robert and me

"One day?" he repeated. "One day may be a long time hence."

"We are neither of us well off, sir," I said. "One day means the day when we are a little richer than we are now."

"Is the young man educated? Can he produce testimonials to his character? Oblige me by writing his name and address down on the back of that card."

When I had obeyed, in a handwriting which I am afraid did me no credit, he took out another card and gave it to me.

"I shall leave England to-morrow," he said. "There is nothing now to keep me in my own country. If you are ever in any difficulty or distress (which I pray God you may never be), apply to my London agent, whose address you have there."

He stopped, and looked at me attentively, then took my hand again.

"Where is she buried?" he said, suddenly, in a quick whisper, turning his head away. I told him, and added that we had made the grave as beautiful as we could with grass and flowers. I saw his lips whiten and tremble.

"God bless and reward you!" he said, and drew me toward him

quickly and kissed my forehead. I was quite overcome, and sank down and hid my face on the table. When I looked up again he was gone.

June 25th, 1841. I write these lines on my wedding morning, when little more than a year has passed since Robert returned to England.

His salary was increased yesterday to one hundred and fifty pounds a year. If I only knew where Mr. Mallinson was, I would write and tell him of our present happiness. But for the situation which his kindness procured for Robert, we might still have been waiting vainly for the day that has now come.

I am to work at home for the future, and Sally is to help us in our new abode. If Mary could have lived to see this day! I am not ungrateful for my blessings; but oh, how I miss that sweet face on this morning of all others!

I got up to-day early enough to go alone to the grave, and to gather the nosegay that now lies before me from the flowers that grow round it. I shall put it in my bosom when Robert comes to fetch me to the church. Mary would have been my bridesmaid if she had lived; and I can't forget Mary, even on my wedding-day . . .

Alexandre Dumas, père

(1802–1870)

THE TITLES OF THE best-known historical adventure novels by Alexandre Dumas seem to be accompanied by an audible clash of swords—*The Count of Monte Cristo, The Three Musketeers, The Man in the Iron Mask.* The latter is actually only part of *The Vicomte de Bragelonne: Ten Years Later,* the huge, 268-chapter third volume in the d'Artagnan Romances, the wildly popular series begun with *Musketeers* in 1844 and continued the next year with *Twenty Years After.* The following selection comes from this final installment. Dumas was inspired by the adventures of the real-life Charles Ogier de Batz de Castelmore, the actual Comte d'Artagnan—or at least he was inspired by the already fictionalized version of d'Artagnan who had appeared in Gatien de Courtilz de Sandras's 1700 memoir-novel about him.

Dumas's son, laboring under the burden of parental fame, became a successful author in his own right, producing a couple of novels, including *The Lady of the Camellias,* and many plays, including a famous adaptation of the novel. Each writer was well enough known that they are remembered as Dumas *père* and *fils.* After beginning his career as a dramatist, Dumas *père* wrote, besides the d'Artagnan cycle, a series of novels about Marie Antoinette, many other novels, essays and articles on contemporary topics, and volumes recording his travels to Florence and Switzerland and elsewhere. One of his more surprising books is a monumental *Great Dictionary of Cuisine*, published in 1873, three years after his death. He intended the encyclopedic cookbook and compendium of cultural history "to be read by worldly people and to be used by professionals," and it is entertainingly browsable as well as packed with recipes that bring to life the cuisine and culture of a lost era.

The following selection, from *Louise de la Vallière*—the second part, named after the mistress of Louis XIV, of the huge novel *The Vicomte de Bragelonne*—comprises a bit more than a chapter from this last installment of the d'Artagnan series. The title comes from a phrase within the text. In these fast-moving scenes Dumas presents his favorite cocky, violent superhero swordsman as a brilliantly observant detective who reads footprints and matchsticks with Sherlockian aplomb at the command of the king. In the first brief scene, Saint-Aignan has served as a duplicitous messenger between the lovestruck king and his mistress, and he returns with bad news about a terrible hunting accident. Soon d'Artagnan investigates and learns the truth behind Saint-Aignan's account.

True, the action takes place in the third quarter of the seventeenth century, but the scene was written in the mid-nineteenth. While interested in the crime writing around him, Dumas was surely also paying tribute to his countryman Voltaire. Zadig's example hovers over d'Artagnan's every move.

You Are Not Human, Monsieur d'Artagnan

"THERE IS GREAT EXCITEMENT prevailing at Mademoiselle de la
Vallière's."

"What do you mean?"

"With her as with all the ladies of the court."

"Why?"

"On account of poor De Guiche's accident."

"Has anything serious happened to De Guiche, then?"

"Yes, sire, he has one hand nearly destroyed, a hole in his breast;
in fact, he is dying."

"Good heavens! who told you that?"

"Manicamp brought him back just now to the house of a doctor
here in Fontainebleau, and the rumor soon reached us all."

"Brought back! Poor De Guiche; and how did it happen?"

"Ah! that is the very question,—how did it happen?"

"You say that in a very singular manner, Saint-Aignan. Give me
the details. What does he say himself?"

"He says nothing, sire; but others do."

"What others?"

"Those who brought him back, sire."

"Who are they?"

"I do not know, sire; but M. de Manicamp knows. M. de Manicamp is one of his friends."

"As everybody is, indeed," said the king.

"Oh! no!" returned Saint-Aignan, "you are mistaken, sire; every one is not precisely a friend of M. de Guiche."

"How do you know that?"

"Does your majesty require me to explain myself?"

"Certainly I do."

"Well, sire, I believe I have heard something said about a quarrel between two gentlemen."

"When?"

"This very evening, before your majesty's supper was served."

"That can hardly be. I have issued such stringent and severe ordinances with respect to duelling, that no one, I presume, would dare to disobey them."

"In that case, Heaven preserve me from excusing any one!" exclaimed Saint-Aignan. "Your majesty commanded me to speak, and I spoke accordingly."

"Tell me, then, in what way the Comte de Guiche has been wounded?"

"Sire, it is said to have been at a boar-hunt."

"This evening?"

"Yes, sire."

"One of his hands shattered, and a hole in his breast. Who was at the hunt with M. de Guiche?"

"I do not know, sire; but M. de Manicamp knows, or ought to know."

"You are concealing something from me, Saint-Aignan."

"Nothing, sire, I assure you."

"Then, explain to me how the accident happened; was it a musket that burst?"

"Very likely, sire. But yet, on reflection, it could hardly have been that, for De Guiche's pistol was found close by him still loaded."

"His pistol? But a man does not go to a boar-hunt with a pistol, I should think."

"Sire, it is also said that De Guiche's horse was killed and that the horse is still to be found in the wide open glade in the forest."

"His horse?—Guiche go on horseback to a boar-hunt?—Saint-Aignan, I do not understand a syllable of what you have been telling me. Where did this affair happen?"

"At the Rond-point, in that part of the forest called the Bois-Rochin."

"That will do. Call M. d'Artagnan." Saint-Aignan obeyed, and the musketeer entered.

"Monsieur d'Artagnan," said the king, "you will leave this place by the little door of the private staircase."

"Yes, sire."

"You will mount your horse."

"Yes, sire."

"And you will proceed to the Rond-point du Bois-Rochin. Do you know the spot?"

"Yes, sire. I have fought there twice."

"What!" exclaimed the king, amazed at the reply.

"Under the edicts, sire, of Cardinal Richelieu," returned D'Artagnan, with his usual impassability.

"That is very different, monsieur. You will, therefore, go there, and will examine the locality very carefully. A man has been wounded there, and you will find a horse lying dead. You will tell me what your opinion is upon the whole affair."

"Very good, sire."

"As a matter of course, it is your own opinion I require, and not that of any one else."

"You shall have it in an hour's time, sire."

"I prohibit your speaking with any one, whoever it may be."

"Except with the person who must give me a lantern," said D'Artagnan.

"Oh! that is a matter of course," said the king, laughing at the liberty, which he tolerated in no one but his captain of the musketeers. D'Artagnan left by the little staircase.

"Now, let my physician be sent for," said Louis. Ten minutes afterwards the king's physician arrived, quite out of breath.

"You will go, monsieur," said the king to him, "and accompany M. de Saint-Aignan wherever he may take you; you will render me an account of the state of the person you may see in the house you will be taken to." The physician obeyed without a remark, as at that time people began to obey Louis XIV, and left the room preceding Saint-Aignan.

"Do you, Saint-Aignan, send Manicamp to me, before the physician can possibly have spoken to him." And Saint-Aignan left in his turn.

WHILE THE KING WAS engaged in making these last-mentioned arrangements in order to ascertain the truth, D'Artagnan, without losing a second, ran to the stable, took down the lantern, saddled his horse himself, and proceeded towards the place his majesty had indicated. According to the promise he had made, he had not accosted any one; and, as we have observed, he had carried his scruples so far as to do without the assistance of the stable-helpers altogether. D'Artagnan was one of those who in moments of difficulty pride themselves on increasing their own value. By dint of hard galloping, he in less than five minutes reached the wood, fastened his horse to the first tree he came to, and penetrated to the broad open space on foot. He then began to inspect most carefully, on foot and with his lantern in his hand, the whole surface of the Rond-point, went forward, turned back again, measured, examined, and after half an hour's minute inspection, he returned silently to where he had left his horse, and pursued his way in deep reflection and at a foot-pace to Fontainebleau. Louis was waiting in his cabinet; he was alone, and with a pencil was scribbling on paper certain lines which D'Artagnan at the first glance recognized as unequal and very much touched up. The conclusion he arrived at was, that they must be verses. The king raised his head and perceived D'Artagnan. "Well, monsieur," he said, "do you bring me any news?"

"Yes, sire."

"What have you seen?"

"As far as probability goes, sire—" D'Artagnan began to reply.

"It was certainty I requested of you."

"I will approach it as near as I possibly can. The weather was very well adapted for investigations of the character I have just made; it has been raining this evening, and the roads were wet and muddy—"

"Well, the result, M. d'Artagnan?"

"Sire, your majesty told me that there was a horse lying dead in the cross-road of the Bois-Rochin, and I began, therefore, by studying the roads. I say the roads, because the center of the cross-road is reached by four separate roads. The one that I myself took was the only one that presented any fresh traces. Two horses had followed it side by side; their eight feet were marked very distinctly in the clay. One of the riders was more impatient than the other, for the footprints of the one were invariably in advance of the other about half a horse's length."

"Are you quite sure they were traveling together?" said the king.

"Yes sire. The horses are two rather large animals of equal pace,— horses well used to maneuvers of all kinds, for they wheeled round the barrier of the Rond-point together."

"Well—and after?"

"The two cavaliers paused there for a minute, no doubt to arrange the conditions of the engagement; the horses grew restless and impatient. One of the riders spoke, while the other listened and seemed to have contented himself by simply answering. His horse pawed the ground, which proves that his attention was so taken up by listening that he let the bridle fall from his hand."

"A hostile meeting did take place then?"

"Undoubtedly."

"Continue; you are a very accurate observer."

"One of the two cavaliers remained where he was standing, the one, in fact, who had been listening; the other crossed the open

space, and at first placed himself directly opposite to his adversary.
The one who had remained stationary traversed the Rond-point at
a gallop, about two-thirds of its length, thinking that by this means
he would gain upon his opponent; but the latter had followed the
circumference of the wood."

"You are ignorant of their names, I suppose?"

"Completely so, sire. Only he who followed the circumference
of the wood was mounted on a black horse."

"How do you know that?"

"I found a few hairs of his tail among the brambles which bordered the sides of the ditch."

"Go on."

"As for the other horse, there can be no trouble in describing him,
since he was left dead on the field of battle."

"What was the cause of his death?"

"A ball which had passed through his brain."

"Was the ball that of a pistol or a gun?"

"It was a pistol-bullet, sire. Besides, the manner in which the
horse was wounded explained to me the tactics of the man who
had killed it. He had followed the circumference of the wood in
order to take his adversary in flank. Moreover, I followed his foot-
tracks on the grass."

"The tracks of the black horse, do you mean?"

"Yes, sire."

"Go on, Monsieur d'Artagnan."

"As your majesty now perceives the position of the two adver-
saries, I will, for a moment, leave the cavalier who had remained
stationary for the one who started off at a gallop."

"Do so."

"The horse of the cavalier who rode at full speed was killed on
the spot."

"How do you know that?"

"The cavalier had not time even to throw himself off his horse, and so fell with it. I observed the impression of his leg, which, with a great effort, he was enabled to extricate from under the horse. The spur, pressed down by the weight of the animal, had plowed up the ground."

"Very good; and what did he do as soon as he rose up again?"

"He walked straight up to his adversary."

"Who still remained upon the verge of the forest?"

"Yes, sire. Then, having reached a favorable distance, he stopped firmly, for the impression of both his heels are left in the ground quite close to each other, fired, and missed his adversary."

"How do you know he did not hit him?"

"I found a hat with a ball through it."

"Ah, a proof, then!" exclaimed the king.

"Insufficient, sire," replied D'Artagnan, coldly; "it is a hat without any letters indicating its ownership, without arms; a red feather, as all hats have; the lace, even, had nothing particular in it."

"Did the man with the hat through which the bullet had passed fire a second time?"

"Oh, sire, he had already fired twice."

"How did you ascertain that?"

"I found the waddings of the pistol."

"And what became of the bullet which did not kill the horse?"

"It cut in two the feather of the hat belonging to him against whom it was directed, and broke a small birch at the other end of the open glade."

"In that case, then, the man on the black horse was disarmed, whilst his adversary had still one more shot to fire?"

"Sire, while the dismounted rider was extricating himself from his horse, the other was reloading his pistol. Only, he was much agitated while he was loading it, and his hand trembled greatly."

"How do you know that?"

"Half the charge fell to the ground, and he threw the ramrod aside, not having time to replace it in the pistol."

"Monsieur d'Artagnan, this is marvellous you tell me."

"It is only close observation, sire, and the commonest highway-man could tell as much."

"The whole scene is before me from the manner in which you relate it."

"I have, in fact, reconstructed it in my own mind, with merely a few alterations."

"And now," said the king, "let us return to the dismounted cavalier. You were saying that he walked towards his adversary while the latter was loading his pistol."

"Yes; but at the very moment he himself was taking aim, the other fired."

"Oh!" said the king; "and the shot?"

"The shot told terribly, sire; the dismounted cavalier fell upon his face, after having staggered forward three or four paces."

"Where was he hit?"

"In two places; in the first place, in his right hand, and then, by the same bullet, in his chest."

"But how could you ascertain that?" inquired the king, full of admiration.

"By a very simple means; the butt end of the pistol was covered with blood, and the trace of the bullet could be observed, with frag-ments of a broken ring. The wounded man, in all probability, had the ring-finger and the little finger carried off."

"As far as the hand goes, I have nothing to say; but the chest?"

"Sire, there were two small pools of blood, at a distance of about two feet and a half from each other. At one of these pools of blood the grass was torn up by the clenched hand; at the other, the grass was simply pressed down by the weight of the body."

"Poor De Guiche!" exclaimed the king.

"Ah! it was M. de Guiche, then?" said the musketeer, quietly. "I suspected it, but did not venture to mention it to your majesty."

"And what made you suspect it?"

"I recognized the De Gramont arms upon the holsters of the dead horse."

"And you think he is seriously wounded?"

"Very seriously, since he fell immediately, and remained a long time in the same place; however, he was able to walk, as he left the spot, supported by two friends."

"You met him returning, then?"

"No; but I observed the footprints of three men; the one on the right and the one on the left walked freely and easily, but the one in the middle dragged his feet as he walked; besides, he left traces of blood at every step he took."

"Now, monsieur, since you saw the combat so distinctly that not a single detail seems to have escaped you, tell me something about De Guiche's adversary."

"Oh, sire, I do not know him."

"And yet you see everything very clearly."

"Yes, sire, I see everything; but I do not tell all I see; and, since the poor devil has escaped, your majesty will permit me to say that I do not intend to denounce him."

"And yet he is guilty, since he has fought a duel, monsieur."

"Not guilty in my eyes, sire," said D'Artagnan, coldly.

"Monsieur!" exclaimed the king, "are you aware of what you are saying?"

"Perfectly, sire; but, according to my notions, a man who fights a duel is a brave man; such, at least, is my own opinion; but your majesty may have another, it is but natural, for you are master here."

"Monsieur d'Artagnan, I ordered you, however—"

D'Artagnan interrupted the king by a respectful gesture. "You ordered me, sire, to gather what particulars I could, respecting a hostile meeting that had taken place; those particulars you have. If you order me to arrest M. de Guiche's adversary, I will do so; but do not order me to denounce him to you, for in that case I will not obey."

"Very well! Arrest him, then."

"Give me his name, sire."

The king stamped his foot angrily; but after a moment's reflection, he said, "You are right—ten times, twenty times, a hundred times right."

"That is my opinion, sire: I am happy that, this time, it accords with your majesty's."

"One word more. Who assisted Guiche?"

"I do not know, sire."

"But you speak of two men. There was a person present, then, as second."

"There was no second, sire. Nay, more than that, when M. de Guiche fell, his adversary fled without giving him any assistance."

"The miserable coward!" exclaimed the king.

"The consequence of your ordinances, sire. If a man has fought well, and fairly, and has already escaped one chance of death, he naturally wishes to escape a second. M. de Bouteville cannot be forgotten very easily."

"And so, men turn cowards."

"No, they become prudent."

"And he has fled, then, you say?"

"Yes; and as fast as his horse could possibly carry him."

"In what direction?"

"In the direction of the château."

"Well, and after that?"

"Afterwards, as I have had the honor of telling your majesty, two men on foot arrived, who carried M. de Guiche back with them."

"What proof have you that these men arrived after the combat?"

"A very evident proof, sire; at the moment the encounter took place, the rain had just ceased, the ground had not had time to imbibe the moisture, and was, consequently, soaked; the footsteps sank in the ground; but while M. de Guiche was lying there in a fainting condition, the ground became firm again, and the footsteps made a less sensible impression."

Louis clapped his hands together in sign of admiration. "Monsieur d'Artagnan," he said, "you are positively the cleverest man in my kingdom."

"The identical thing M. de Richelieu thought, and M. de Mazarin said, sire."

"And now, it remains for us to see if your sagacity is at fault."

"Oh! sire, a man may be mistaken; *humanum est errare*," said the musketeer, philosophically.

"In that case, you are not human, Monsieur d'Artagnan, for I believe you are never mistaken."

✤

Andrew Forrester Jr.

(dates unknown)

BETWEEN 1849 AND 1853, about the time that Dickens published "On Duty with Inspector Field," the British periodical *Chambers Magazine* launched a series of allegedly true criminal cases under the title "Recollections of a Police Officer." Attributed simply to Waters, the surname of the narrator, the "Recollections" were actually written by William Russell, a busy London journalist. A Waters collection appeared under the same title in 1856, a volume that crime fiction historian Howard Haycraft described as the first detective book to appear among the English "yellowbacks." These were cheap, magazine-like paperbacks, printed in eye-catching colors although not always yellow, targeted at rail travelers and the increasing numbers of literate, if not necessarily cultivated, masses. These were akin to the infamous penny dreadfuls, which were flashy, penny-apiece installments of serials, aimed primarily at working-class teenagers. London bookseller George Routledge launched his publishing empire with a "Railway Library" series of yellowbacks in 1849.

The contemporary attitude toward detectives was that they were troublemaking spies who invaded privacy and endangered liberty, so Russell made a point of demonstrating the civilized behavior of his detective. They still had little support behind them and tended to employ disguises and subterfuge in pursuit of evidence rather than interrogation and overt investigation. Waters is considered the founder of the "casebook" school of crime fiction— straightforward stories about police investigation of a crime, the ancestor of today's police procedurals. Not all of his descendants maintained the same level of realism. "Arrested on Suspicion," a suspenseful nonseries story about the narrator's fight to save his sister from being punished for a crime she didn't commit, concentrates upon the ratiocinative process in unraveling a crime and deciphering a code.

Andrew Forrester was a pseudonym employed by an important early writer whose real name is lost. In 1864, his story "The Unknown Weapon" introduced Mrs. G., narrator of a series of excellent stories in *The Female Detective*—one of the first female detectives in the genre, possibly the very first. "Arrested on Suspicion" appeared a year earlier, in Forrester's collection *The Revelations of a Private Detective*. The narrator explicitly cites his debt to Edgar Allan Poe in being able to solve the crime, and Forrester also cites him in "The Unknown Weapon." This sort of homage to predecessors remained common in nineteenth-century crime fiction, culminating perhaps in Sherlock Holmes's mocking dismissal of Auguste Dupin.

Arrested on Suspicion

I MAY AS WELL say, at once, that this statement never could have been made had I not been, as I remain, an admirer of Edgar Allan Poe; and if ever I have time, I hope to show that his acts were the result, not so much of a bad, as a diseased mind. For one thing, I believe his eyes were affected with an inequality of sight, which, in itself, was enough to overbalance a very exciteable brain.

But Poe has nothing to do with my statement, except as its prompter. My name is John Pendrath (Cornish man, as I dare say you see in a moment), my age is twenty-eight, and I live with my sister Annie. We are all that are left of our family, which you must see by the name was equally good and old. I need not say what I am; because, though I feel no shame for my work, I do not care about it, and hope, some day, when the Lord Chancellor wakes up, to be able to go back to Cornwall.

However, it seems I am writing about myself, and that is not my intention; which, indeed, is to show how much individual good such a writer as even the condemned Edgar Poe can do, and even on this side of the Atlantic.

As I and my sister cannot afford a house of our own, we live in apartments—two bedrooms and a sitting-room, generally second floor; Annie having the room behind our parlour, and I camping in a garret. I do not say we are very happy, because of our chancery affair; but we are generally cheerful—always so, except when we hear about costs, which is all we do hear of our famous suit.

When we had been in Aylesbury Terrace, Bayswater, about six weeks—on the second floor—I was coming home as usual, when, in the ordinary way, I found Annie at the usual meeting-place.

"Annie," said I, "what's the matter? Have you heard any good news?"

"No, Jack; but when I don't come to meet you, and I run down to open the door, you look twice before you give me my Cornwall kiss."

"Why, Annie," said I, "what do you mean?" for I hate a mystery without a statement. This arises, I suppose, through my liking for mathematics.

"Jack, dear," said she, "I have a double."

"No, Annie," I replied, "that can't be, or I shall go courting."

"Upon my word, Jack," said sister Annie, "I felt inclined to ask myself whether I had gone out and come home with a stout lady, aged forty, in black silk, when I saw them come to the door: and now I've left them behind, under our rooms, I ask myself—in fun, you know—whether I have come out to meet you."

Of course then, I understood. Annie had made a statement.

"Oh," said I, "a mother, with her daughter, apparently, has taken the first floor of No. 10, Aylesbury Terrace, and the supposed daughter is certainly something like you."

"That is the history itself, John," said sister Annie, "if you take out *apparently;* for I heard the younger call the elder, 'ma, dear'; and I am sure they have taken the first floor, because the door was open as I came down, and I could not help seeing that they were eating slices of bread and marmalade."

"Oh!" replied I; for I could say nothing else.

And when I saw the young person come up the house steps next morning (Sunday), it seemed to me that she resembled Annie in some degree; but my sister—like most women I think, had exaggerated the likeness. She would have passed for Annie with a stranger, but not with me.

Annie was also wrong in saying they had taken the first floor. The mother (apparent), alone lived in our house, and the daughter, said to be married, lived elsewhere.

Well, I hope my sister Annie has no more curiosity than most women; but, as I am away all day, and she is lonely, I can't blame her for looking out of the window, though I have, perhaps, sometimes told her it was a pity she could not find something better to do. So, she could not help noticing four daily facts:—

1. That the younger woman came every morning.

2. That the mother and daughter (apparent) went out together.

3. That they seldom left the house two days running in the same clothes, and frequently exchanged their cloaks and shawls on the same day.

4. That the occupant of the first floor always came home alone.

I put these premises before myself—though, perhaps, it would be, as a rule, below a man to interfere in such matters as these—and I came to this conclusion:—That the husband of the daughter had quarrelled with the mother; that, therefore, the mother and daughter went about together, while the husband was away at his business; and that they were rather vulgar, well-off women, who liked to go about and show their finery.

I had no need to tell Annie to avoid Mrs. Mountjoy and her daughter, Mrs. Lemmins. She felt neither was a companion for her. I mention this because Mrs. Mountjoy made advances to Annie, which, however, ended on her side; for in spite of the assurances of Mrs. Mountjoy's respectability by our landlady, Mrs. Blazhamey, Annie and I kept our own opinions.

I suppose Mrs. Mountjoy had been in the house about a month, when I noticed a little blue-stoned ring on Annie's left hand. Of course I said nothing about it, since she did not, though I saw it was new. I am not one of those men who pry into women's actions. You know we do not like them to pry into ours.

Well, the thunderclap came as suddenly as I am about stating its particulars to you. I was at work, when a cab drove up to the door, and out came Mrs. Blazhamey. I shoved her into the waiting-room for the public, and then listened for her to speak. The poor woman seemed quite overwhelmed for some moments, and though I did not move or utter a word, I dare say I was white enough.

"Oh, sir," at last, she said, "Miss Annie's took up for shopliftin'!"

If you ask me how I felt, I cannot tell you. But I am sure of this—that within ten seconds I was thinking wholly of my sister. I know Mrs. Blazhamey believes me to this day a brute; but I hope I am not cynical when I say, that most of the people who give way to a deal of emotion generally seem to have a quantity of big I's mixed up with their grief. I dare say, though, I am a cold sort of man.

What was to be done? See Annie, if possible. It was then ten minutes to four, the hour at which we closed. I obtained an easy permit to leave, and jumped into Mrs. Blazhamey's cab. I did not speak, after learning whither we had to go, till we met a hansom cab, into which I and the poor woman with me exchanged.

Of course, I am not going to give the particulars of the meeting. I have only to state facts, so I will only say that Annie, after a little while, was almost as cool as myself. She had been arrested at three, and now it was half-past four. That she would not be taken before the magistrate till half-past eleven the next morning was the first news I gained. Then I asked the inspector on duty, and the police-man who had brought Annie to that place, for the particulars of the case.

They were these: The prisoner, Annie—do not suppose I am going to conceal any fact, so I say prisoner—had been shoplifting the district for some time, in company with a companion about forty years of age. The prisoner had been identified by a jeweller who had been robbed; and one of the rings stolen from his shop was found on her left hand—it being sworn to by a private mark.

I may tell you that this statement was given to me with mock gravity by the inspector, on my calm representation that it was a case of mistaken identity. I need not add that I know my sister ran no chance of condemnation; but scandal has always got some weight, and therefore I had two ends to meet—her immediate liberation, and the arrest of the true depredators.

I need not state that both Annie and I saw how the ground lay—she had been arrested for Mrs. Lemmins (so called); and in a moment I comprehended the daily change of dress, and the return of the woman Mountjoy alone in order to avoid the greater chance of detection after a robbery by remaining with her companion.

Annie comprehended my warning glance as our eyes met, when the inspector, in the charging-office, stated the case; and I have no doubt he thought we knew the suspicion was strong. But I think I staggered him when I said—"Do thieves usually wear the jewellery they steal?"

"Good bye, Annie," I said; and I could not trust myself to kiss her—nor did she offer to touch my cheek.

Now, what was to be done? Here were the facts. Annie could not be released till the next day, and I had about eighteen hours in which to work for her, and procure the arrest of the women going by the names respectively of Mountjoy and Lemmins. Had they taken the alarm? If so, how long? If not, what extent of time would they require in which to learn how matters stood—when might they infer my sister and I would suspect them? So far, there had passed but two hours and a-half since the arrest. Had they heard of it in that time?

"Can I have a detective in my employ, if you please?" I said to the inspector.

"Two," the official said; who, in spite of the calmness of apparent fact against Annie Pendrath, was, I saw, interested by my action.

"One," I said; and a soft-looking, quiet, almost womanly man, with fair hair and weak, soft blue eyes, a man about thirty-five, was placed at my disposal.

We three—myself, the constable (named Birkley), and Mrs. Blazhamey—left that station in a cab called, and then I said—

"Mrs. Blazhamey, the real thieves are your precious drawing-room lodger and her friend."

"What, Mrs. Mountjoy!" screamed our landlady; "why, she's a lady."

"So she may be, but she's a thief."

"Then out o' my house she goes the moment I gets home."

Of course, this was just the kind of answer I expected. I had balanced it this way: if I do not tell Blazhamey, she will carry the whole history up to Mountjoy the moment we reach home; while if I inform her, she will put the woman on the alert.

"Mrs. Blazhamey," said I, "will you make five pounds? Yes, I see you will. Go to your daughter's at Kensington-park—don't come home till half-past ten, and I'll pay the note down to-morrow at twelve."

Of course, she made a thousand objections; but she was packed off, at last, in another cab, and I and the policeman drove to Aylesbury Terrace.

"Policeman," said I, "if this woman is still in the house, she must only leave it in your company. I'll take the responsibility of charging her; but I don't want you to take her (if she's there) till I give you the word. I want to catch her friend."

"Lor', sir! do yer think her frind'll turn up, and do yer think she's there? Lor' bless yer, sir! they takes an 'int in a hurry. They've hooked!"

"If she is still there," I said, "will you watch opposite till I've put a canary cage in the second-floor front right-hand window, looking *into*, and not from the street?"

The blue-eyed detective, the most innocent-looking man I ever saw, opened his azure eyes; and the end of it was, that he agreed to my proposal, which was but natural.

"It may be hours you'll have to wait," I said.

"Days," replied the man, with the best laconicism I ever witnessed.

We left the cab before reaching the house, and then separated to opposite sides of the street. It struck seven as I went up the garden path.

There she was, at the window, reading a yellow-covered book.

She could not have taken the alarm, I thought, or she would not be reading. I had up the servant directly. Did she know why her mistress had left the house in the afternoon?

"No," the girl replied. "She was very much flustered, and only said, 'It can't be—it can't be.'"

She (witness) did not know the beginning of the affair, because she had been out on an errand, and when she came back, missus had her every-day bonnet on. She went out with a policeman. I may here add, that Annie had sent the policeman to our lodgings to Mrs. Blazhamey; having forethought enough not to send to me at the establishment. I than asked the girl whether Mrs. Mountjoy was in at the time.

"No," the girl said; "she com'd in at five."

Had any letter arrived for her?

"No—not even a note, mister," the girl replied.

Now, I could have had Mountjoy arrested at once, but I had learnt that the criminal classes are, as a rule of business, very faithful to each other, and therefore I felt that the apprehension of Mountjoy might prevent that of Lemmins. If the latter heard of Annie's arrest first, I felt sure that Mountjoy would be in some way informed of the matter; while if our fellow-lodger was the first to acquire the knowledge, the accomplice would be in some way warned. The priority of information would chiefly depend upon this condition—to the residence of which woman was my sister nearest when she was arrested?

I went to the window, after dismissing the servant, and there was that blue-eyed man, who no one could take for a police-officer, eating nuts, and with a couple of newspapers under his right arm. I saw Mrs. Mountjoy was safe, but it was her accomplice I wanted to encompass.

Nothing occurred up to ten minutes to eight, except Mrs.

Mountjoy calling for some warm water; but at that time a woman limped up the garden, and carrying a basket of clothes, which, it seemed to me, was just home from the laundress. She did not come in, but she left the basket, and quietly went her way.

Almost immediately after she had closed the gate, the detective opened it, and before he reached the door I had my hand on the lock.

"Quick!" he said, pushing past me; "that's a 'complice—the letter's in the wash."

The girl was coming out of the drawing-room, having taken in the basket, as I ran down to the door; and as the policeman pushed past me and up the stairs without the waste of a moment, I am quite sure the basket had not been carried into the room more than a quarter of a minute, when the officer followed it.

Half a glance satisfied the man. The linen on the top of the basket had been roughly turned over. There was no letter in Mrs. Mountjoy's hand, but I saw it was trembling. She was seated in the chair near the window, exactly as I had seen her when I came home, but the book she had been reading was on the table.

The officer looked from me to the basket, flinging an expression into his blue eyes I never should have thought could characterize them; and then turning to the woman, he said—

"Come—the game's up."

"I don't understand you," said the woman.

"I does," added the officer; and continued to me—"will you go and fetch a cab, sir? I dare say the lady'ud rather not walk."

Upon the removal and charging of the woman I need not dilate, as those circumstances have nothing to do with my statement.

What I wanted was the letter, which I felt sure, without the help of the policeman, had been brought amongst the linen.

She had not had time to read it, and, therefore, it would not be destroyed, unless she had recognized the policeman's step at the bottom of the staircase, and had managed to annihilate it while he and I were ascending the staircase. The officer appeared to have been aware of the value of the letter equally with myself;

for when I returned to the house, he had manacled her hands, as he told me afterwards, to prevent her from touching the letter if she had it about her.

Under the policeman's directions, I kept my eyes on the ground from the drawing-room to the cab—(I seem to be writing the word "cab" very frequently; but the fact stands, that I was in one cab or another by far the better part of the score of hours between Annie's arrest and the end of my statement)—and I was quite sure the letter was not dropped during the passage. Again, when we reached the station-house, the vehicle was closely examined, and even the ground over which we passed to the charging-office.

Then the woman was closely searched. I was told that even her hair was examined minutely, and the basque of her stays taken out. But all to no purpose—the letter was not found. That some kind of communication had been made, or rather attempted, I was certain, for the policeman had recognized the apparent laundress as a hanger-on, and general thieves' go-between.

The conclusion both I and the officer came to before we left the station was, that the letter, or note, was in the drawing-room, and still in the basket.

It was clear she could not have found and read the warning, however short, in the few moments that elapsed while I ran down stairs and up again with the constable. It would take some seconds to reach the chair in which she was seated, and further time in which to hide the communication.

The constable said, "P'raps she swallered it," as a kind of preparation for the worst. But I was not inclined to accept this theory, notwithstanding he urged that it might have been a mere scrap of paper; because it seemed impossible that it could have been found, masticated, and swallowed in the time.

When the officer and I returned to the house, it wanted a quarter to nine. You see, time was progressing.

And now began the search for the letter. And here it was that I think my experience beat that of the police constable; for, after we had ransacked the basket, and were quite sure the letter was not within it, *he* began the ordinary routine search, while I sat down and began to *think*. The constable supposed I was broken down, and so he said—

"Chirrup, sir."

Whereupon I answered him—

"Go on, officer; I'm searching, too."

I suppose he was inclined to laugh, for he turned away to the stove. It was summer time (August), and so there was no fire in the grate. The officer, being at the stove, began examining it.

"Any ashes on the ground?" I asked.

"Why, you don't suppose she burnt it? It's hid," the man replied.

"Any soot on the hobs or hearth?"

"No," he replied.

"Then the top moveable flap of the stove has not been moved. Could a letter—take this card—be thrust between the damper and its frame?"

"No," said the man; "there's a hedge to it."

"Then, what are you staying about the stove for?" I asked.

The man turned, looked at me, his foolish-looking jaw dropped low, and then he said—

"You knows a thing or two, mister—you do."

Of course I do not wish to hide from the reader that I was trying to copy Edgar Poe's style of reasoning in this matter; for confessedly I am making this statement to show how a writer of fiction can aid the officers of the law.

"I shall do the regular round," said the officer, beginning to the right of the fire-place.

Now, as I sat, I was exerting all my reason to deduce the probabilities of the place of concealment from the facts known. I remembered that in the case of a search for a letter by the French police, recounted by Poe, that while the officers were hunting for the missive, even in the very legs and backs of the chairs, that it was stuck in a card rack, openly, with a dozen others; and though this knowledge was the basis upon which I built up my argument, yet, of itself, it was valueless, for I felt it would require a mind far beyond the common-place—a condition which did not distinguish Mountjoy—to imagine and rapidly complete a mode of concealment which should be successful by its very candour.

I felt that this woman had concealed the communication—if, indeed, it were not destroyed, a supposition I refused to entertain—in such a manner as a child would conceive, with the superaddition of some dexterity, the result of the shifting and elusive nature of her life.

I was still pondering, when the officer came to the bookcase, which was locked.

"Yere'll be a job, to hunt all through them books," said the blue-eyed, amiable officer, in a confidential tone.

Now, had the bookcase been opened? I got up, and looked at the projecting ledge of the escritoire portion, below the bookcase. The dust had been blowing that day, and the upper part of one of the windows was still open. A glance showed me the case had not been unclosed, for the particles of dust lay equally over the ledge; and I noticed that the opening, or key-door was furnished with an inner green silk curtain, which was shut in, and protruded below the bottom of the panel. Had it been opened, this curtain must have broken the regularity of the dust, which was *not* disturbed. So, again, the fine, white, pulverous particles lay on the upper part of the two knobs of the escritoire slide—a fact which proved to me that the escritoire had not been opened, as in that case both handles must have been touched.

My argument was so clear, that the officer did not even hesitate to admit I was right.

"And what about the cupboard under the askertor?" he asked.

"Search it," I said, "though I doubt if it's there. She was a stout woman, and would avoid stooping."

"Ha!" answered the officer approvingly; but he examined the cupboard, and found little else than china in it.

Still I sat, for I felt I could thus more easily concentrate my thoughts than by standing. And do not suppose that all this time I did not think of Annie. The fact is, I knew I could best serve her by acting exactly as though I was doing an ordinary duty, rather than one of love. Indeed, if people would but think of themselves a little less than they do, they would often-times get through more work than most men manage.

"Officer," I said, after a pause, in which he had looked over the chairs, under the table-cloth, and in all parts of the ebony inkstand—even fishing in the ink with a pen, and catching nothing worth the taking. "Officer, will you examine the joins of the wall-paper from the ground, to about six feet high?"

"Very well, mister; but will you help me move the heavy things?"

"Only note the joins you can see," I said, adding, with the first smile I had indulged in since the morning, "I don't think she had them out and back again in the time it took us to come upstairs—see if the joins fit and are flat."

This was a long piece of work for the officer, and dusk was coming on as he made half-way round the apartment.

"Look at the cracks in the mantelpiece, where the flat and the top of each pillar come together? Nothing! Well, and now the edge of the carpet all round the room, where the edge can easily be raised."

I dare say you will wonder that I did not help actively to search. I was hunting with my brains. Was it possible, I thought, that always anticipating a visit from the police, she had some easy place of concealment for pieces of jewellery and small articles of value, and into which she had conveyed the letter?—of the existence of which there could be no doubt, for we found that the tumbled linen belonged, some of it to children, and some of it to grown-up men, while a pair of stockings were unfolded, "and," said the constable, "somehow, a stockin' allers is the pest-bag among 'em."

Could such a place of immediate concealment be a slit in the carpet? This might be the case, and I suggested the idea to the officer.

"Then hadn't we better have the carpet up!" he asked.

"It will cause a great waste of time," answered I, "and we will not do so till we have done searching elsewhere."

But I found this idea so clung to my mind, that it impeded the progress of my thought. So, deciding that I must settle this point before I proceeded to another, I sat devising a means of ascertaining if there were a slit in the carpet without hauling it up. Soon I found one. If I took up one end of the carpet, and flapped the air under it, the dust you will always find under a lodging-house carpet would rise, and fly in a little cloud through any cutting.

The officer saw the force of this argument, and it was put into operation.

But nothing came of it; and I think it was at this point that my official friend began to break down, saying—

"Derpend upon it, she swallered it."

Then he began to hunt again—this time behind the pictures, but I soon called his attention from them by saying—

"The moderator-lamp."

"Ha! I didn't think o' the lamp," said the officer.

But we found nothing in the lamp beyond disappointment.

Time, however, had not been lost; for the field of observation was nearly gone over. The letter, or scrap of paper, was not below the wall-hangings, for not one of the seams was loose, or wet with paste or gum. It was not up the chimney, not even concealed in the paper ornament in the stove, nor about the bookcase, lamp, chairs, or table; nor, in all probability, was it under the carpet.

"The tea-caddy," I said, after a pause.

The caddy was easily opened, for Birkley had brought the woman's keys with him; but it was searched to no purpose. And when the night had well closed in, and Mrs. Blazhamey had come home (before her time, though), and hindered us, we were no nearer a satisfactory result than we had been at the commencement of the search. By this time, the carpet had been taken up, the pictures down and out of their frames, every loose book about nearly pulled to pieces with examination, and even the bell-pulls unripped. The sacking of the chairs, the bottom of the fender, the cornice of the bookcase—a hundred spots, nine-tenths of which must have been totally inaccessible to the woman in the time at her disposal, had been examined, and with equal want of success.

"Derpend upon it, sir, she swallered it," said the officer; and I think it was this persistency on his part which intensified my obstinacy in believing that the warning was in the room. I wanted to be by myself, to think without interruption, to follow the action of the woman; and with this end in view, I said to the officer—

"Go to the station, and see if they have heard anything."

"Holl right!" said he; "but, derpend upon it, she swallered of it *down.*"

The officer gone, and Mrs. Blazhamey almost forced out of the room, which by this time looked like a wreck, I sat down in the midst of the furniture, and asked what next was to be done. And then, with that repetitory process which, I am told, is common during intense thought, I began conceiving once more the idea of what the woman must have been about when she first supposed a police-officer in the house.

How many seconds had she been in doubt before the officer and I entered the room? I had accepted Birkley's theory that she had recognised the policeman's tramp when he was at the bottom of the stairs; but was I justified in accepting that theory? How if she had no suspicion till the door handle was turning? If such were the case, the scrap of paper would be within a foot of the right side of the chair in which we found her seated. You see, being left to myself, I was adding to the repetition of my thought.

Suppose I went through *her* actions from the opening of the linen basket to the entry of myself and the officer?

You may declare this action childish, but you are wrong.

I went to the basket, supposed that I opened a stocking, and then went to the chair, thinking to myself that she, a stout woman, and naturally agitated by the arrival of the warning, would take a seat; and what more natural, since she was going to read by the coming twilight, than to go to the window?

I took the chair, exactly as we had found her, my right side to the window, and then supposed myself startled by the opening of the door. This fright would be followed by the involuntary attempt to hide the letter *by the right hand.* I flung my hand behind me, and it lodged in the folds of the cord-knotted curtain.

The discovery was far easier than putting on a worn glove—which is sometimes a rather difficult operation. My fingers positively rested on the paper, a mere scrap, torn from a wide-margined newspaper, and which had been easily thrust into the folds where the damask was gathered.

We had been at fault by crediting the woman with too much cleverness. We had supposed that she had anticipated and prepared for our coming when we were at the bottom of the stairs; and acting upon that belief, we had been wandering all round the room when our investigation should have been confined to a square yard.

Nor was I blameless on another score. I had presupposed the woman to be not intellectual enough to avoid a distinct concealment; whereas, the rapidity of our coming had caused her to do by accident that which a clever and prepared criminal would do by premeditation—placing the letter where nobody would think it worth while to look, as being under one's very eyes.

Will you believe the statement that now I had found the scrap of paper I saw that it was *visible* as it lay in the folds of the curtain, which had positively been unhooked by the constable that he might examine the shutter-cases with facility?

But do not suppose my labours were over. Not that I refer to the perusal of the *cipher* as a labour; I defy an ignorant cipher to puzzle me. Exactly as you would never dream of looking for a hidden letter in a blotting-case, so a merely confused Roman-letter cipher (if the word in such an instance as this is applicable) is infinitely more difficult to analyse than a system of actual, arbitrary signs. I had always been able to read an arbitrary cipher after a study of twenty minutes. I was only twelve, when I found a little packet in my cousin's room containing a lock of hair and some words in arbitrary cipher, which I analysed in half a minute; for seeing two words flourished all about, I supposed they formed the lady's name, found that the fourth and sixth letters of the first, and the second and fifth of the second, were similar, so successfully guessed, in far less time than it takes to write about, that the MS. and lock referred to our neighbour Pheobe Reade.

Cunning, ignorant people, I am told, always use an arbitrary cipher, almost as easy to read as A B C. I may tell you that Mrs. Mountjoy's letter gave me little trouble. I found it at nearly a quarter-past nine, and at half-past it was written out for the benefit of the police. It was in a simple character.

And as I can have no secret in this matter, if you are willing to learn the process, which has few regular rules, here it is to study. You may acquire it in five minutes.

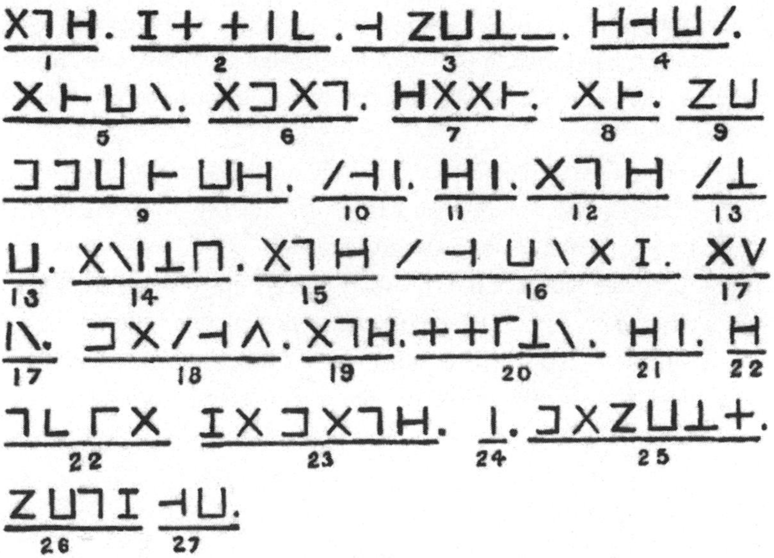

Now, I dare say all this appears very mysterious to the general reader. There never was a more candid arbitrary alphabet put together. In the first place, the straight-line character of the writing told me it was simple. Alphabets curve as they rise in the thought which they embody. It will be seen that here there is no curved line.

Now, when you are fairly sure you have a simple cipher, and written in the English language, you hold the key to it with this one piece of knowledge—that the most frequently used letter in our language is e. Very well, then, find that character which is most frequently repeated, and you may be pretty certain it is e. In this case, you will find the leading figure is X. It is repeated sixteen times.

Now, we have a more than merely supposed e. The next question is the frequency, if any, with which a series of characters is repeated. You will find that the first word marked by a stop is repeated four times in twenty-seven words, or better than one in seven. This, then, must be a common expression. Take the next newspaper, and you will find the word "the" the most frequently repeated. But here comes an important contradiction. The first word agreeing with "the" has certainly three letters, but then it begins, instead of ending, with X. Now, you will find that the character representing e begins many words in this sentence, and ends none; whereas, the rule in English is, that e rather ends than commences words.

Take this fact into connection with the known truth that the thieves talk "back," or reversed English, and the contradiction is cleared away—each word is begun to be written at the end. We have then three letters, t.h.e. Now, if you go on to the sixth word, you will find we have the characters representing t.h.e, and that they spell (in the right direction) he-e. Now, the only ordinary word with this combination is "here." Therefore, we have now four letters, t h e r. If we now hunt out a word in which all these characters occur, we shall find it at 23, which runs there-. The sixth character must be an s, because it's the only natural terminal to the word there's—short for "there is."

We have now five letters, t h e r s.

We will now take word 24, following "there's." It can't be I—
"There's I" is an impossible phrase. But there is only one other
ordinary English word of one letter besides "i"—it is "a." "There's a"
is a natural mode of expression. We have now six letters, t h e r s a.

Now, you must settle the short words before you can touch the
long. We have got "the" and "a," and the words in which t, h, and e
are commonly combined with one another. Let us now pass to other
short words. Take 21. One of the letters of this word we already
know to be "a"; what is the second? The two commonest words
with which a is combined, and at the same time not preceded by the
only letter word "i," thus as "I am," which is not the case here—are
"as," and "at." Now, this letter is already a direction, in the shape of
a warning. Every known circumstance in the case proves this, and
therefore the word "at" is more likely to be used than "as," which is
a word, when used grammatically, very seldom seen in common
letter-writing. We will suppose 21 to represent "at," and then we
shall find the same word at 11, which confirms the belief that these
characters represent "at." And this conclusion supports the supposition referring to the "s" and "t" character. To continue. The word
22, which follows 21, we now find to stand e--ht; and this partial
elucidation reciprocally acts with word 21, to form the likely phrase
in such a letter—"at eight."

Then we now have, as discovered letters—t h e r s a i g—eight
letters. There are now enough upon which to build up the first
skeleton of the revised letter, and thus it stands, the unknown letters being represented by small hyphens, and the words wholly
wanting by the figures with which they have been already allied:—

The ga - - s (3) - - -t - - -e here -eet -e   t - - - rr - -   a - -   at the (13)
  I   2   3   4   5   6   7   8   9   10   11 12 13
- - a - e   the se - - - - -   - a - e   - - -er the   - - i - -   at eight theres a   - - er
  14   15   16   17   18   19   20   21 22   23   24 25
sh - - (27).
  26   27

Now, 7 and 8 reciprocally suggest "meet me," and so we add "m"
to our list of letters—now nine; and the t - m - rr - - after "meet
me" confirms that reading, and which makes this word "to-morrow."
This gives the letters "o" and "w," making in all eleven letters. Taking 5, I find "o" and "m" are the second and third characters; therefore, I infer the first is "c." Now we have twelve letters. I also find
that the second letter of word 4 is "o," which gives "- o - t," which,
taken in connection with the letter being a warning, and the two following words, "come here," I take to be "don't." This rendering
yields me two more letters, "d" and "n," which make in all fourteen.

The elucidation now stands:—

The ga - - s - - own. Don't come here. Meet me to-morrow, and
   1   2   3   4   5   6   7   8   9   10
at the o - d - - ace, the second ca - e - nder the cl - - - at eight there's
11 12 13   14   15 16   17   18 19 20   21 22   23

a - - ower show on.
24   25   26   27

Now, putting aside the first sentence, the first words we have to
clear up are 13 and 14. Let us suppose it is "something place," and
we are right, for the "l" drops into the centre of word 13, and we
have "old place." This yields letter "p" and "l," and now we can
add a letter to word 3, which from "--own" becomes "-lown."

We now arrive at word 17, where there is one letter wanting,
and this we must for the present pass, and come to (18) - nder. This
must be "under," and so we add "u" to the list; but it is useless, for
it occurs only this once in the entire paragraph.

We now reach word 20, to which we can only add "l," which
makes it cli--. And it will be remarked that the two most important words in the letter are still defective. However, the word 20 is
soon elucidated, by going on to 25, to which we can now add the
letter "l"—thus we get - lower, which, taken with words 26 and
27, gives "flower show on." We therefore find that word 20 is
"cliff." The double "f" in word 2, makes it "gaff." We have now
only *two* characters to decipher; the composition standing thus:

"The gaffs -lown. Don't come here. Meet me tomorrow at the old place, the second ca-e under the cliff at eight. There's a flower show on."

Now it is clear the missing letters are two, neither of which is used more than once. Then we have only to find the missing letters, and see which will fit in, to solve the problem. These letters are b, j, k, v, x, y, z.

The only letter which will agree with -lown is b, by which we get the sentence "The gaffs blown"—pure thieves' English, perhaps even something like good Anglo-Saxon. It means, the meeting-place is discovered and overthrown. "Gaff" is doubtless the talking-place, from *gabian*, to talk; while, probably, the word "blown" is based upon the idea of giving a blow—to blow, when the past participle in Saxon English would be blown—"beaten down."

Coming to the word ca - e, we find that v only will fit, and so we get "the second cave under the cliff at eight to-morrow" as the gist of the missive slipped among the folds of the curtain.

One word before I proceed with my story. Give me little credit for reading that cipher. I did it in less than twenty minutes; though it strikes me I may as well give the alphabet of this cipher, and also the appearance of the missive when reduced to ordinary letters. Here, first, is the alphabet—very simple and elementary:

The back reading stood thus:—eht sffag nwolb tnod emoc ereh teem em worromot dna ta eht dlo ecalp eht dnoces evac rednu eht ffilc ta thgie sereht a rewolf wohs no.

You would hardly suppose this was merely reversed English—would you?

As I have said, the reading of the letter was nothing, but its application was another matter—another business to continue the thread of the clue in the nip of my mind till it was wound off the reel by the re-introduction, under the auspices of the police, of Mrs. Mountjoy to young Mrs. Lemmins.

What were the coming facts before me?

These—that Lemmins expected (since the go-between false laundress had got clear from the house)—Mountjoy to meet her at eight, in the second cave under the cliff, and that a flower show would take place.

Now, it was summer time, and, therefore, I might take the words "flower show" as literally meant; for, in connection with the correspondents, it meant theft at the *fête* in question. Now, where was this *fête* to be held? I was at a loss to tell whether it was next day or the following. If next day, the meeting for eight referred to the morning. If the following, it might mean eight in the evening.

But first for the spot. It must be populous, because the flower show was talked of in London, and because thieves thought it worth while to canvass the place. Secondly, it must be at the sea-side, because only at the sea or water-side is the cliff called by that name—at all events by Londoners.

Then I got at these suppositions, or rather facts. That a flower show was to take place either the next day or the following at a seaside place distinguished not only for cliffs, but with caverns, or caves, in them, and that Lemmins would be in the second either at eight in the morning of the following day, or at that hour in the evening.

Was the place far away? It seemed to me not, because the context of the letter so plainly inferred that the recipient could easily reach the spot, since the exact hour was named. Now, if I could only find out, by an advertisement, where a flower show was to take place within a couple of days, the locality being a cliffy, sea-side locality, in all probability full of visitors—for I had heard of thieves going to the sea-side with honest men—why, the chances were that I should trap the woman.

Where was the place, and how could I find it out?

It was clear it could not be on the *east coast*, because it is flat from the mouth of the river to Hull, or nearly so; neither, if very near home, could it be below Brighton, for thence the shore is level, or if not level, more or less unprovided with *cliffs* over a wide range of country.

Then the place in question, in all probability, stood either in Kent or Sussex. By this means I got my facts into a very narrow line, for I had but to examine the papers of both counties to ascertain whether or not a flower show was advertised. But here a new difficulty arose. It was now a quarter to ten, and all places of business, all reading-rooms were closed. Perhaps, however, the *fête* was advertised in the "Times," my second-day's copy of which was in our sitting-room. Ten minutes' search resulted in disappointment; but my eyes had caught an advertisement, all letters to be addressed to some initials, care of Messrs. Mitchell and Co., town and country newsagents, Red Lion Court, Fleet Street. The question I asked myself was, whether I should call at this office, in the faint chance of finding it still open, or go on at once to the London Bridge terminus, and take the night-mail to one of the several sea-side places, one of which I believed was the appointed place of meeting. My decision in favour of trying the office rested on the ground that, with a fast cab, to call on my road to the station, it would not delay me more than a quarter of an hour.

The cab (I find I must continually refer to cabs) took me into Fleet Street in considerably under the half-hour, and, to contract this portion of my narrative, for the simple reason that it is commonplace, I found a woman cleaning out the office. She was much flurried, and, I think, somewhat confused, in consequence of being so late at her work. With that extraordinary and simple belief of the very ignorant in the sacred nature of papers, she would not let me lay a finger upon one of the files of papers hung about the office; but with that other belief in the absolute power of money, I applied the great "progressive how much" argument with her, and which, supported by the assurance that print was not writing, led to my triumph upon another step of my journey; for at about the sixth hook I found a pile of (I think) *Kentish Observers*, or *Gazettes*, and soon I discovered (the information being in a prominent position) that a flower show was to be displayed on the very next day at the Tivoli Gardens, the context intimating that certain omnibuses would run at regular intervals from Ramsgate and Margate.

The inference stood that "the second cave under the cliff" was either at Ramsgate or Margate, and as I was driven on to the station, I turned over in my mind the various ways in which I could arrive at a just conclusion before I started, or while going down the line.

Absurd as was the question—"Are there any caves in the cliff at Ramsgate or at Margate?"—I put it to several railway porters; but they knew nothing about either place. And I have found generally that railway porters know nothing of their respective lines. In this strait, and after questioning the young woman in the refreshment department, and the policeman on duty, who, I think, felt somewhat inclined to arrest me on general grounds, I bethought me of buying a guide-book to the coast; but the railway book stall was blank with shutters, and the only acquisition I could make was the London and South Eastern Railway time-table; and this publication I was turning over, not so much disconsolately as with vexation, when an outline map fell open before me.

It was but natural that I should look at the relative positions of Ramsgate and Margate; and the investigation of the map formed another link in my chain of—may I say?—circumstantial evidence. The map showed me that the coast about Margate was more exposed to the action of the sea than the other marine town. Knowing that the indentation of the shore by sea water is, in a measure, effected by the formation of channels, or caves, the inference stood, that Margate was more likely to be the goal of my journey than the other town.

To Margate I went, making inquiries, however, when changing trains at Ramsgate, in order to ascertain if there were caves in the cliff of this latter place.

The reader who knows Margate is aware I was right.

But we did not catch our felon till ten a.m., for the tide was up, and the caves, which in the eyes of the children are such enormous caverns of darkness, were unapproachable. And, indeed, when the tide had receded sufficiently to allow of the approach of myself and the policeman I employed, I feared for my success, as I could discover no woman walking towards the "second cave," with her back towards me, and in whom I could trace a resemblance to the person called Lemmins. But the officer was right when he surmised that perhaps she had started from the "other end," referring to the break in the cliff at the point where the Preventive Service Station is built.

She was so surprised at the arrest, that she had not a word to say; for, as I implied from the copy of a telegraphic message we found on her, she had been informed that all was going well.

And as the magistrate of the district police court in which my sister had to appear was more than ordinarily late that morning, we reached the court before Annie was brought forward, and so when her eyes drifted round the court, they met mine. But we had already seen each other at the police cell door, and she knew that the actual thieves were in custody. Seen together, my sister and the younger prisoner were very distinguishable; but had the jeweller's man, upon oath, declared that Annie was Mrs. Mountjoy's companion, I do not think he should have been blamed.

I have now reached the end of my intended narrative. My purpose was to show that action in misfortune is better than grief. I have not referred to any pain, degradation, or consequence, which resulted either to my sister or myself, in consequence of her terrible arrest for shoplifting. I have merely stated, as logically as I could, a series of facts, inferences, and results, with the aim of pointing out that very frequently there is a deal of plain sailing where some people suppose no navigation can be effected.

W. W.
(Mary Fortune)

(c. 1833–c. 1910)

IN 1855 A YOUNG Irish-Canadian immigrant named Mary Fortune began publishing stories and poems in the goldfields newspapers of Australia. An editor at another of the fledgling newspapers
in the region, the *Mount Alexander Mail* in Victoria, admired her
writing and wrote to offer a position as sub-editor; but when she
revealed that he was addressing a woman, he canceled his offer. This
rejection seems to symbolize her career. Mary Fortune was successful and influential, but all of her work appeared under pseudonyms.

After missing out on the editor's position, Fortune continued to
write journalism and fiction, using various aliases. In late 1865 she
sent a story to a new Melbourne magazine called the *Australian
Journal*, the first periodical in the colonies to target the general
reader and the growing audience of female readers and teenagers.
It was modeled after successful British publications such as *Cassell's
Illustrated Family Paper* and *Family Herald*. Its founding editor, George
Arthur Walstab, was a former member of the Victoria Mounted
Police and a fan of crime stories; the *Journal* featured them from its
first issue.

In the January 20, 1866, issue there appeared a story entitled "The
Dead Witness; or, The Bush Waterhole"—the first known detective story written by a woman. The fifth entry in the series "Memoirs of an Australian Police Officer," it was the first written by

Fortune. The series, narrated by a young man named James Brooke, had been launched by James Skipp Borlase, a Cornish immigrant to Australia who is remembered now for stories such as "The Night Fossickers," set in the rough-and-tumble frontier of the goldfields. Borlase also wrote the penny dreadful *Ned Kelly, the Ironclad Australian Bushranger*, which the *Saturday Review* described in 1881 as "as disgraceful and disgusting a publication as has ever been printed." Borlase was a staff writer for the *Australian Journal*, but he was soon fired for plagiarism and the series discontinued. Later, when the stories were reprinted, he included Fortune's story without acknowledgment.

Under the poignant pseudonym Waif Wander, a nickname she had given herself, Fortune began to write regularly for the *Australian Journal*. In 1867 she launched a new series, "The Detective's Album," featuring a policeman named Mark Sinclair. For this series Walstab reduced Fortune's pen name to a genderless W. W. Not only bias against women kept her identity under wraps; the stories were narrated by a male detective and presented in a factual-sounding and realistic tone.

For the next four decades, Fortune wrote one story per month for this series, making her not only a pioneer in nineteenth-century crime fiction but one of its most prodigious contributors. The author's real identity was unknown to readers, however, until John Kinmont Moir, a Melbourne-based bibliophile and collector of Australian literature, unearthed it in the 1950s. Not until 1989 was an entire new volume devoted to her work—the collection *The Fortunes of Mary Fortune*, edited by Australian writer Lucy Sussex. It reveals the extent of Fortune's streetwise and literate talents, her skill at plotting and also at bringing characters to life.

Her style is literate and polished, with educated-looking flourishes including at least a nodding acquaintance with other languages, but it may have resulted from self-education, because there is no record of her attending college. The poignant tale of Mary Helena Wilson began in Belfast, but her family took her to Canada at an early age and she thought of it as home. The daughter of a Scottish engineer, she married in her late teens a man named Joseph Fortune. Four years later she followed her wandering father to Australia, where he had opened a store. When she gave birth to a second son, she listed Fortune as the father, but nothing indicates that he actually accompanied her to Australia, and he is known to have died in Canada. In 1858 she married a mounted policeman named Percy Rollo Brett, but this union, which may have taken place without a divorce from Fortune, also lasted only a short time. No glimpse of her personal life seems happy, and by the 1870s she was being jailed for vagrancy and alcoholism. Yet she continued writing, having launched her career in the genre with this dramatic milestone.

The Dead Witness;
or, The Bush Waterhole

I CAN SCARCELY FANCY anything more enjoyable to a mind at ease with itself than a spring ride through the Australian bush, if one is disposed to think he can do without any disturbing influence whatever from the outer world, for to a man accustomed to the sights and sounds of nature around him there is nothing distracting in the warble of the magpie or tinkle of the "bell bird." The little lizards that sit here and there upon logs and stumps, and look at the passerby with their heads on one side, and such a funny air of knowing stupidity in their small eyes, are such everyday affairs to an old colonist that they scarcely attract any notice from him, and even should a monstrous iguana dart across his path and trail his four feet length up a neighbouring tree, it is not a matter of much curiosity to him. A good horseman, with an easy going nag under him and plenty of time to journey at leisure through the park-like bush of Australia, has, to my notion, as good an opportunity of enjoying the Italians' *dolce far niente* as any fellow can have who does not regularly lie down to it.

Something like all this was coming home to me as I slowly rode through the forest of stringybark, box, peppermint, and other trees that creep close up to the bold ranges which divide as it were into two equal portions the district of Kooama. I had passed fifteen miles of bush and plain without seeing a face or a roof, and now, having but a mile or two before making the station to which I was bound, I loosened the reins and let my horse take his own time. While, however, I thoroughly enjoyed the calm tranquility of nature so unbroken around me, and felt the soothing influence more or less inseparable from such scenes, I cannot exactly say that my mind was enjoying the same "sweetness of doing nothing" as my body. My brain was busily at work, full of a professional case, on the investigation of which I was proceeding; still, thoughts of this kind cannot be said to trouble the mind, being as enjoyable to us, I dare say, as the pursuit of game to the hunter, or the search for gold to the miner.

The facts of the case were shortly these: a young photographic enthusiast, in search of colonial scenery upon which to employ his art, had taken a room in a public-house at the township of Kooama, in which he had arranged his photographic apparatus, and where he had perfected the views taken in trips to all the places within twenty or thirty miles that were likely to repay the trouble. The young fellow, who was a gentlemanly and exceedingly handsome youth of barely twenty years of age, became a general favourite at Kooama, his kindness to the children, especially in that out of the way township, endearing him to all the parents.

Well, one day this young artist, whose name was Edward Willis, left Kooama and returned no more. For a day or two the landlord of the house where he had put up thought but little of his absence, as he had upon more than one occasion before spent the night away on his excursions, but day after day passed, and they began to think it singular. He had himself expressed an intention of visiting some of the ranges to which I have alluded in search of some bolder "bits" of scenery than he had yet acquired, but otherwise they had not the slightest clue to guide them in any attempted search for the missing youth. His decision to leave Kooama, if he had made one, must have been sudden, as nothing was removed from his room. Camera, chemicals, plates, and all the paraphernalia of a photographer's handicraft, were still scattered about just as he had left them. A week passed away—a fortnight—consumed in guesses and wonders, and then came a letter from his mother in Adelaide to the landlord, inquiring the son's whereabouts, as they were getting uneasy at not hearing from so regular a correspondent. Then it was considered time to place the thing in the hands of the police, and I was sent for. As I was proceeding through the bush then, at the leisurely pace I have described, I heard the loud crack of a stock whip ring out like the sharp report of a rifle between me and the ranges to my left, and shortly after I heard the sound of rapidly advancing horse's hoof strokes, which was echoed and re-echoed from the rocks at either side of the horseman's route. The sound came nearer and nearer, and at last a young man, mounted on a half thoroughbred, and attired like a stock-driver or overseer on a station, galloped into the road which I was following a few yards behind me. Here he pulled up, and was soon by my side. The free-masonry of bush travellers in Australia would scarcely admit of one passing another without speaking, on a road where one might jour-ney for twenty miles without meeting a soul; so there was nothing singular in my addressing the newcomer with all the freedom of an old chum.

"Aren't you afraid of breaking your neck, mate," I inquired, "coming down those ranges at such a pace?"

"Not a bit of it," he replied "but at any rate I'm in a devil of a hurry, so had to risk it."

"Bound for Kooama, I suppose?"

"Yes, I'm for the police station, and if I don't look sharp, it'll be pitch dark before I get back, so I must go on, goodbye! I'll meet you again, I dare say."

"Stay!" I shouted, as the young fellow made a start, "I might save you a journey, as I'm a policeman myself, and am just on my way to Kooama. Is there anything wrong your way?"

The young horseman looked at me rather suspiciously, as, of course, I was in plain clothes. I dare say he did not half believe me.

"Well," he said, "it's nothing very particular, and if you *are* going to the police station, policeman or no policeman, you can tell all I have to say as well as I can, if you will be so kind, and I shall get home before sundown yet."

I assured him that I was really connected with the force, when he told me his errand to the camp.

"There's been the deuce of a talk at Kooama about a young picture-man who's been missing for a couple of weeks, and some think he's come to no good end. Now, I know myself that he has been on our station since he came to Kooama, for I saw him taking views over the range there, but I thought nothing of that, as it was when first he settled at Dycer's, and he has been photographing miles away since then. This afternoon, however, about ten miles from the home station, the cattle (we're mustering just now) kicked up such a devil of a row that I couldn't make it out until I concluded they had come across the scent of blood somehow. Sure enough when I came up to the mob they were bellowing and roaring like mad ones round a spot on the grass that must have been regularly soaked in blood, as it is as red and fresh looking as possible. What made it more suspicious to me was, that the place had been carefully covered up with branches, and no one would ever have noticed it, only the cattle had pawed and scraped the dead bushes quite off it. Heaven knows what might have caused it, or whether it was worth mentioning, but it's not far from where I saw the poor young chap. I thought I would run down to the camp and tell Cassel about it."

"Have you mentioned it to anyone else?" I inquired.

"No," he replied, "I haven't seen a soul since."

"Well, don't say a word, like a good fellow. It's very strange that I should have met you. I'm Brooke, the detective, and I'm on my way to Kooama about this very business. Will you meet me at sunrise tomorrow morning, and take me to the place?"

The young man readily promised, and I found that he was the son of a squatter whose station (called Minarra) was situated at the other side of the Rocky Ranges, to which I have so frequently alluded, and then we parted, and spurring my horse to a more rapid pace I soon reached the police camp, at Kooama, and got my horse

stalled and my supper, as well as all the information I could from
Constable Cassel before I turned in, which I did at an early hour.

There are a good many fellows—no matter in what anxiety of
mind they may be—who are able to forego it all when their usual
bedtime reminds them of sleep, and they seem to shake off their
troubles with their shoes, and draw up the blankets as an effectual
barrier between them and the world generally. It is not so with me,
I usually carry my perplexities to bed with me, and roll and tumble,
and tumble and roll, under their influence, unless some happy idea
of having hit the right nail on the head in my planning soothes me
into resignation to my fatigue. So it was on the night in question;
nevertheless, the sun was only beginning to shake himself out of the
horizon when I met the young squatter at the appointed place, and
together we proceeded to the indicated spot on Minarra station.

Over the range we went, and three or four miles through the
primeval forest beyond, and my companion, well acquainted with
the landmarks on his "run" stopped before what appeared to be a
few decaying branches fallen from a near gum tree. "This is it," he
said, dismounting and removing the dead boughs, "I covered it up
again yesterday."

Well, there was very little to see, a patch of blood-stained grass—
the colour was very evident still—and nothing more. I looked
round to see if perchance there was a view to make it worth an
artist's while to visit this spot, and soon perceived that from the
very place where we stood a photographer might catch a "bit" of
truly beautiful and entirely colonial scenery. At a distance of perhaps two miles the range over which we had come fell abruptly
down into the plain in a succession of sheer faces of rock, while at
the foot of what might be almost termed the precipice that termi-
nated the whole, a deep gorge or gully ran almost entirely at right
angles with it, up which the eye pierced through a vista of richly
foliaged and fantastically gnarled trees and huge boulders of grey
granite, altogether forming a scene that could scarcely fail to attract
the eye of an artist. The sun was up above the trees now, and,

closely scanning the ground at my feet, I perceived at a few yards distance a something that caught his brightness and reflected it, and stooping I picked it up; it was a small, a very small, piece of glass, and just such glass too, as might have been used in a camera. But near the piece of glass, which was not far from the blood spot on the grass, I found too, what I had been searching for, which was the triangular marks of the camera stand, which I thought it barely possible might be visible. The holes were indented deeper into the grass than the mere weight of the instrument would account for, especially two of them, the third was not so visible. We covered all up again as carefully yet as carelessly as possible, and after having again cautioned the young squatter to be silent, I parted with him for the present, and made the best of my way to Kooama.

An hour or so later, I was very busy in the deserted room of the young artist, of which I had taken possession, and into which to avoid disturbance I had locked myself. I was quite at home among the poor young fellow's chemicals, etc., as I happened to be a bit of an amateur photographer myself, and I have found my knowledge in that way of service to me on one or two occasions in connection with my professional duties already. The table and mantelpiece were littered with unfinished plates; they were leaning against the wall, and against every conceivable thing that would form a support for them. Naturally supposing that those last taken would be most *come-at-able*, I confined my search at first to the outside pictures, and before very long I fancied I was repaid for my trouble. My idea, it will readily be guessed, in searching the plates at all, was the one of finding a face or a view that might possibly be a clue in my hunt for the missing youth, or for the murderer, if murder had been done. Nothing would be more likely than that some chance encounter in his excursions might have resulted in a portrait, the original of which if discovered, might be able to give some useful information. Well, I found more than I hoped for. I lighted on a plate, only parts of which had "come out" under the after process, and which was rubbed in several places, and had evidently been thrown aside as worthless. There were two or three duplicate copies of the same view, and among the perfected and most clear pictures which the artist had laid away more carefully by themselves, was one apparently valued, as in case of danger of damage it was "cased" properly. It was a truly beautiful bit of entirely Australian bush scenery; a steep, rocky bank for a background; at its foot, a still, deep waterhole reflected every leaf of the twisted old white stemmed gum trees that hung over it and dipped their heavy branches in its dark waters, and to the left a reach of bush level, clustered with undergrowth on the slightly undulating ground, and shaded here and there with the tufty foliage of the stringybark. It was an excellent picture, every leaf had come out perfectly, and the shadows were as dark and cool as shadows could be, while the tone was all that could be wished; nevertheless on comparing this with the unfinished and imperfect one on which the artist's art had failed, my eye rested on a something in the latter which made it a hundred times more valuable to me.

In the shade of a heavy bush at the opposite side of this still, deep waterhole, there was the faint outline of a crouching human figure, an outline so faint and so shrouded in the obscurity of the faulty plate, that very likely no eye but that of a detective would have observed it, and it is more than probable that the poor lad whose art had fixed it in its place was quite unaware of its being there; but by the aid of a powerful microscope I made it out distinctly. We all know with what perfectness to every line of its object the camera fixes its light copies, even in the greatest failures as to perfect shading and tone, and there I had this crouching and malignant looking face peering from behind a shadowy bush, as recognisable as if he had been photographed in a Collins Street or George Street studio. Steadily I set to work reproducing this hiding figure, magnifying and photographing by aid of the good camera the young artist had left behind, and I succeeded at length in completing a likeness quite clear enough for my purpose; so after taking possession of the plate holding the view of the bush waterhole, I put it and my likeness into my pocket, and locking up the room, once more sought the camp.

The likeness of the missing youth himself was given to me by the landlady of the public-house; he had given it to her a few days before he took his last walk in search of subjects for his art. Poor fellow! he was very handsome and very youthful looking; a white, sickly, noble face, with large black eyes, and a profusion of curly black hair forming a frame to a high broad forehead. I felt sick at heart as I looked at it and thought of his empty home and the red pool of blood on Minarra station.

It was late in the day when I got thus far in my search, and I was rather glad that my young squatter acquaintance did not turn up at Kooama that evening, as he had intimated an intention of doing, for I was likely to require his assistance, and did not care to trust his young gossiping propensities with my secrets any longer than was absolutely necessary.

Early on the following morning, however, he rode up to the camp, and I so arranged that we should be left alone together. "I don't know your name, my young friend," I was commencing, when he interrupted me.

"My name is Derrick—Thomas Derrick."

"Well, Mr. Derrick, I am sure I need not tell you upon what a serious job I am engaged, nor that it is in your interest, as well as that of the public at large, that no crime should go unpunished, all this you know as well as I do, but what you do not know as well as I do, my dear fellow, is how very little will interfere with a search such as mine, and give a criminal a chance of escaping with impunity. All this I tell you because I am going to ask your assistance, and to beg that while you are affording it to me you will keep as secret as the grave anything that may pass between us until I accomplish my object, or fail in the endeavour to do so."

The young man promised faithful secrecy, and then I laid the picture of the bush waterhole before him.

"Is there any such place as that on your run?"

"To be sure there is; it's in Minarra Creek, about half a mile from where we found the flock."

"I thought it likely, and now I am almost sure you will be able to tell me who that is," and I handed him my copy of the hiding figure. He looked very much astonished, but replied immediately—

"It's Dick the Devil!"

"And who is Dick the Devil?"

"A crusty, cantankerous old wretch, one of our shepherds. Do you think *he's* in it!"

"Oh, of course, we are all abroad as to that yet. Where does this Dick live, and what does he do?"

"He minds a flock, and lives at an out-hut ten miles from the home station."

"Alone, or has he a hutkeeper?"

"Well, he's by himself this long time, he had two or three hutkeepers, but at last we were obliged to give it up—no one would live with him."

"Could you manage to get me in there as hutkeeper without exciting his suspicion."

"You! of course I could, he's always growling about not having one, but you could never stand it."

"No fear of me, it won't be for long at any rate."

Fancy me that same afternoon metamorphosed into a seedy, tired looking coon, accompanying the young squatter to Dick's hut, where he was going, or appeared to be obliged to go at any rate, with rations in a spring cart. Dick was within sight, letting his flock feed quietly foldwards, and his young employer led me to him.

"Now, you old growler, I hope you're satisfied! Here's a hutkeeper for you, and I hope you'll keep your ugly temper quiet for one week at any rate."

I should have recognised my man anywhere, sure enough; the villainous scowling face of the hider in the photograph was before me, and so determined a looking scoundrel I had not seen for a long time, familiar as I was with criminals. He was an elderly man—

about fifty perhaps—low sized, and strongly built; his years told on him in a slight stoop, and grizzled, coarse hair, that but added to his rascally appearance, and his character was but too plainly traced in his low, repulsive forehead, and heavy, dark beetling brows. I could have almost sworn he was an old hand the moment I set eyes on him.

"Thank ye for nothing, Tom," was his impudently given reply, "you didn't send to town for a hutkeeper for me, I'll swear."

"Well, you're about right. I met him as I was coming over with your rations, and as the poor fellow looked tired and hard up, I thought I'd give you another trial."

"You be d———d," was Dick the Devil's thanks, as the young fellow turned away with a "Well, so long, mate!" to me.

"Well," said my new mate, turning to me, "if you'll give me a hand to round up the flock, I'll get 'em all the sooner in, and then we can have a good yarn. I'm d———d if I'm not glad to see a fellow's face again, curse such a life as this, I say!"

"'Tis a slow one, I'm blessed if it ain't," I replied, doing as he wished; "have you no dog?"

"No, I haven't," he snapped out at me like a pistol shot, with such a look, half of terror and half of suspicion, that I was convinced about his dog there was something more to be learned.

After the billy was slung and the tea boiled, and the mutton and damper disposed of, Dick and I sat down in the still calm twilight outside the bush hut, and while puffing out volumes of tobacco smoke from dirty, black pipes managed to mutually interest ourselves, I dare say.

"Things are looking d——— bad in the country now, mate," rapped out Dick.

"You may say it," I replied, "I've tramped over many a hundred miles without the chance of a job."

"Where did you come from last?"

"Oh! I came from everywhere between this and Beechworth! I stopped at Kooama last night, there's a devil of a talk there about some murder."

"Murder!" said Dick, with a sort of gasp, and a short quick look at me, "what murder?"

"Some poor devil of a painter or picter-man, or something of that sort."

"Oh, d—— them ! they don't *know* he's murdered."

"I see you've heard about it then. Yes, I believe you're right. I think he's only missing, and they *guess* he's made away with."

"Let them guess and be d——d to them!" said the hardened wretch, and I thought fit to drop the subject.

"Oh, my lad!" thought I to myself, "if you only guessed who is sitting beside you, and what his object is here, wouldn't there be another pool of red blood under some tree in the Australian forest, eh?" And then I looked at my neighbour's muscular frame and determined criminal countenance, wondering in a battle for life and death between us should I be able to come off victor. Certainly, I could at any moment lay my hand upon my trusty revolver, and dexterity and self-possession might accomplish much with the hand-cuffs, but let a fellow be ever so little of a coward, he must feel a *little* at being so entirely isolated and so self-dependent as I was at this moment. Far out before us lay miles of almost level grass, dotted with tall-stemmed trees and patches of undergrowth. There wasn't a living soul within miles and not a sound save as night fell the scream of the distant curlew, that came, I guessed, from the vicinity of the black waterhole in the Minarra Creek, and I could not help picturing to myself the stillness of that night-gloomed water, its heavy, over-hanging foliage, and the white mangled face that *perhaps* lay below it. Altogether I was not sorry that Dick showed no disposition to prolong the conversation, but soon turned in, and I followed his example, not, however, without placing my revolver under my hand, and when I *did* sleep it was, as the saying is, with one eye open.

According to a concerted arrangement between me and my young assistant, the very earliest morning brought him to the hut at full gallop. His greeting to Dick was rather abrupt.

"What the devil's the reason you're running your flock up to the rock springs every day, Dick? Connel complains you don't leave him half enough for his sheep, and here's a waterhole close under your nose."

"Well, the cursed flock always head up that way, they're used to it, and it's d—— hard work to turn a thirsty mob when you've got no dog, in fact, it's onpossible."

"What the deuce have you *done* with your dog? You had a first rater."

"Done with him?" replied Dick, vindictively, "cut his throat! He was always giving me twice the work with his playin' up!"

"Well, you'll have to get another somewhere, at any rate take the flock to Minarra waterhole in future."

"I can't myself," was the response.

"Your mate will lend you a hand for a day or two, as the water is not far away, and the flock will soon get used to it."

I had been watching Dick as closely as I could, without being noticed by him, during this colloquy, and could easily see that he was much dissatisfied with this arrangement, but he could make no excuse, as the want of water was beginning to be complained of on all the surrounding runs, and so we headed the flock in the direction of Minarra waterhole. There was no opportunity for conversation on the way, as Dick and I were far apart, and the sheep were feeding quietly all the way; but when we neared the water, and the flock—which, by the way, showed no anxiety whatever to go in any other direction—had mob by mob satisfied their thirst, and were scattering out over the near pasture, I approached the waterhole, and, sitting down in almost the very spot where poor young Willis must have placed his camera to take the view I had in my pocket, I took out my pipe and commenced cutting tobacco for the purpose of filling it. All the time the sheep were drinking I could see that Dick was very uneasy. He kept away entirely, but when he saw me taking it so coolly he drew up slowly.

"D—— queer place to sit down, that," he said, "you'll be ate up with mosquitoes."

"No fear," I answered, "I'm thinking the mosquitoes have something more to their liking to eat down there."

"Down where?"

"Oh! about the water! What a devil of a lot of ugly things must be down at the bottom there, Dick! It's very deep."

I couldn't see the wretch, but I *fancied* his face was growing pale, and although I daren't look at him, neither durst I trust myself with my back to him, so, affecting an air of nonchalance I was far from feeling, I got up and faced him while I affected to be searching in my pocket for matches, my hand in reality clutching the revolver.

"I wonder if that picter-man ever *took* this place?" I added, "it would look first rate."

Dick's face flushed up with fury, he could stand the strain no longer.

"D—— the picter man!" he roared, "what the —— are you always talkin' about *him* for?"

I looked at him with affected surprise. "You get in a blessed pelter over it, mate! Anyone but me would be suspicious that you'd done it yourself!"

"And if I did —— to you?" he said, with a face fearful in its hardened ferocity. "And if I *did*, you couldn't prove it—you've no witnesses!"

While he was saying this, half a dozen bubbles rose to the surface of the water directly in front of us, followed by more and more, and I do not know to this day what unaccountable influence it was that as Dick ceased speaking urged me to seize him by the wrist, and while pointing to the bubbles before him with the other hand, to whisper in reply, "Haven't I?—Look!" For, of course, I had no more expectation of the awful scene that followed than has my reader at this moment.

A fearful, dripping *thing* rose to the surface—a white, ghastly face followed—and then, up—up—waist high out of the water, rose the corpse of the murdered artist!

It remained for a second or two standing, as it were, before us, with glaring, wide open eyeballs turned towards the bank on which we stood, and then, with a horrible *plump*, the body fell backward, the feet rose to the top, and there the terrible thing lay face upward— staring up, one might fancy, to the heavens, calling for justice on the murderer!

As I saw this awful sight, my grasp on Dick's wrist relaxed, although unconsciously I still pointed toward the white dripping terror; until it settled, as I have attempted to describe, and then Dick the Devil, with a wild cry that I shall never forget, threw both his hands up to his head and fell heavily to the ground.

To tell you how I felt in these few moments is impossible. I was horrorstruck. In all my experience of fearful and impressive sights, I never felt so completely stunned and awed. But it did not last long with me, for, of course, reason soon came to assure me that it required no supernatural agency to cause a corpse to rise from the bottom to the top of a waterhole, although the accounting for the way in which it had thus arisen would not be so simple.

With but a glance at the prostrate form of the insensible wretch beside me, I fired off one barrel of my revolver as a signal to young Derrick, who had promised to hang about, and I had soon the satisfaction of hearing in reply the echoed report of that young man's well given stock whip, and it was not long before he came galloping down to the side of the hole.

It may be supposed that this young fellow felt even more horrified than even I, more accustomed to deaths and murders, had done, and after I had shortly explained to him how matters stood, I do not think we had two opinions about the guilt of the still insensible old miserable. Be that as it may, I was heartless and unfeeling enough to handcuff him, even while he was unconscious, not choosing to risk an attempt at escape. And then we sprinkled water over him, and used all the means within our power for the purpose of restoring him. At length he sat up, but his first glance falling again on the floating corpse, he struggled to his feet, crying,

"Oh, my God! Take me out of this! Let me out of this!"

And, one on each side of him—he partly leading—we followed him three or four hundred yards, where, under the shade of a tree, he sat down weak as a child.

"I can't go any farther," he said. "You'll have to take me to the camp in a cart."

"Where's all your bounce now, mate?" I could not help inquiring, as I handed him a drop of grog out of a flask I carried.

He put it tremblingly to his lips and drained it, and then, with a heavily-drawn breath, replied, "It's in h—!"

This was awful, but he did not give us time to think for he immediately, and without any encouragement, added, "I'm goin' to tell you all about that lot while I'm able, for I feel all rotten like!"—and then he added again—"like *him*, down below."

We did not speak, either of us, and he went on—"One day, that chap came pictering up yonder, and my dog playin' up as usual, runnin' the sheep wrong, he got me in a pelter, and I outs with my knife and cut his b—— throat! The young picter chap sees me, and runs to try and save the dog; but he was too late, and he ups and told me I was a villain, and a cruel wretch, and all sorts, and I told him I'd cut his too if he gave me any more of his jaw, and when he went away I swore I'd be revenged on the cheeky pup. I watched him that day down at the Minarra waterhole, but couldn't get a good chance, and then he went home to Kooama. Well, about a week after, he was pictering down yonder."

Here he pointed in the direction of the blood marks, and I nodded, saying, "I know."

"You know!" he said, turning to me with something of his old ferocity, "how the —— do you know anything about it!"

"I know all about it," I said in reply, "I will finish your story for you and when I go wrong, you can set me right."

He looked at me stupidly—wonderingly. "Who are you?" he asked.

"I am Brooke, the detective."

"Oh!" Dick the Devil drew a hard breath.

"Well, he was taking views with his camera near that tree there, where you covered the blood up with the bushes—you know, and you stole behind him—"

"Yes," interrupted Dick, "when his head was under that black rag."

"And you struck him with something that stunned him."

"It was a waddy," said Dick.

"And the blow struck the camera also, capsized it, and broke it to shivers."

"Just so!" added the wretch, a hideous glee lighting up his ferocious countenance, "and then I took out my clasp knife and nagged his pipe, just as I did the dog's, and I asked him how he liked it, but he couldn't tell me!"

"Oh, you *awful* devil!" cried young Derrick, whose face I had remarked becoming paler and paler until I gave him a nobbler too, or I positively believe the poor fellow would have fainted.

"And then I carried him all the way to the hole on my back, and I got a rope and I rolled it round him in good knots, and then I tied the rope to a good sized boulder, and I rolled him and the boulder to the bottom together! But tell me now," he added, sinking his voice to a whisper, "how did he get up again? How *ever* did he get up again?"

Of course, this we can only surmise; the rope might have got damaged in the roll of rock and body down the bank, and remaining attached to the feet, had given below, and given until it allowed the unfastened part of the corpse to reach the surface, and then slackened more from the rock below until the feet also were able to find the surface. This is the most likely solution of the difficulty, for the rope, when the corpse was removed, was still found attached to both the body and the rock.

Dick the Devil was punished for his crime, but where and when, it is unnecessary for me to state.

�֎

James McGovan
(William Crawford Honeyman)

(1845–1919)

IN 1873 A SERIES of well-written articles began appearing in the *People's Journal* in Edinburgh. Narrated by local policeman James McGovan, they recounted the everyday working life of a metropolitan detective. "McGovan" was known to be an alias, to hide the identity of the insider who was providing these fascinating, realistic, and drily witty behind-the-scenes accounts. The series was compared to the autobiographical books by an earlier Edinburgh detective, James McLevy, which had begun appearing in 1849.

Five years after McGovan's series began, the first collection of cases appeared—*Brought to Bay; or, Experiences of a City Detective.* Other collections followed: *Hunted Down, Strange Clues, Traced and Tracked*, and a last one in 1888, *Solved Mysteries.* The next year the *Publishers' Circular* proclaimed McGovan's articles "the best detective stories (true stories, we esteem them) that we ever met with."

McGovan's realistic, straightforward approach—his lack of manufactured melodrama—can be seen even in his articles' titles: "A Servant's Heavy Trunk," "The Wrong Umbrella," "The Murdered Tailor's Watch." Many of his cases began with ordinary encounters on the Edinburgh streets. Readers glimpsed the detective's easy camaraderie with colleagues and even with the small-time crooks he arrested one day and sought information from the next. In one story, "The Romance of a Real Cremona," a grand ball provides enough confusing flurry to hide the theft of a musician's violin. Dragged reluctantly into this affair, McGovan makes little effort to conceal his impatience with fanatical musicians: "Mr. Turner had a craze for buying fiddles which he never did, and never could, play upon, and I mentally placed him in the same position as a bibliomaniac, who would sell his soul to get hold of some old musty volume not worth reading, simply because it happened to be the only copy in existence."

As he wrote this case, the author must have been smirking every time he dipped his quill into the ink, because he was actually a fanatical violinist himself. There was no James McGovan. The author behind the name did not work in a police department and never had. The stories were fiction. They were written by a violinist and orchestra leader at the Leith Theatre, who was also a writer and editor on the staff of the *People's Journal*—William Crawford Honeyman, described by a friend as a small, spade-bearded, bandy-legged man who was seldom seen without his violin case. Born in New Zealand, Honeyman had grown up in Edinburgh, where he performed often and served as judge of many traditional fiddle contests. The books under his own name don't sound likely to have generated the sort of income that the McGovan stories earned: *The Violin: How to Master It* and *Strathspey and Reel Tutor*, not to mention *Scottish Violin Makers Past and Present*. Fortunately for him and us, he was drawn to write fiction as well and bequeathed us stylish and amusing—and, in this case, somewhat horrific—entertainments.

The Mysterious Human Leg

THE LEG WAS FOUND by some boys in a backyard off the Grass-market, and as it was wrapped in a newspaper they thought it was a piece of beef, and each wanted it all to himself. The one who ran off with it, however, and got away from all the others by his superior swiftness, had no sooner examined his prize in a safe place than he felt weak about the legs, and set it down very hastily and tottered off to get a policeman. Then the place where it had been found had to be shown, and was easily identified by some blood stains; and the leg was brought to the Central, and the boy also, for examination. It was the left leg of a man neatly taken off at the knee joint with a bevelled slash off the flesh at each side for over-lapping purposes, which plainly pointed to the hand of a practised surgeon. The cause of the amputation was also plain, for the bone had been smashed and splintered beyond repair, as if by a bullet hitting it; but what was most puzzling was the presence of some dozens of common carpet tacks which had been propelled into the flesh and had remained there. The leg appeared to have been not many hours away from its original owner, so I naturally turned to the night policeman on the beat, whom I had to rouse out of bed for the purpose. I did not expect to get a clue of any kind, but I was surprised to get a very good one. The policeman had seen a man pass out of that close about three o'clock in the morning, and he had the idea that the man was a student who was sometimes sent to people who were too poor to pay a doctor. He did not know the student's name or his address, but he described him as red haired and having a slight limp, as if one leg were shorter than the other. He had spoken to the student in passing, but though he had gone into the close he had not thought of looking over a low wall into the yard where the leg was afterwards found. It seemed to me very unlikely that a student would throw away a good leg undissected, so I was doubtful of a connection, but I went out to the front of the College on chance and watched every student who entered. About one o'clock a troop of them came up from the Surgical Hospital in Infirmary Street, and I instantly spotted one who answered the description perfectly. He was a frank-faced, gentlemanly-looking fellow, and was laughing gaily with a companion when I accosted him, so I expected to have no difficulty whatever.

"You are a medical student I think, and attend cases of the poor?" I began as I drew him aside.

"Yes, sometimes," he said sobering down somewhat and summing me up on the spot as I could see.

"Were you at a case last night near the Grassmarket?" I continued.

"Are you a policeman in plain clothes?" he suddenly asked without replying to my question.

"Oh, well: something of that kind," I answered.

"Well," and he paused a little, and in the greatest good humour bestowed upon me a knowing wink, "I was not out last night at all."

I was staggered, and I must have looked the feeling for his grin became broader, and he was moving off when I suddenly held up a hand and said:—

"Are you sure?"

"Quite sure," he smilingly answered.

"And you know nothing about a lost human leg?" I continued.

"Nothing. What about it?" he answered with tantalising coolness and such widely opened eyes that I felt sure that he was laughing in his sleeve.

"Oh, nothing, except that I should like to get hold of the rest of the leg and the man at the end of it," I replied, feeling that he had the best of it. "He did not get a bullet through his bones for nothing, to say nothing of the carpet tacks. I suppose you cannot even explain the carpet tacks?"

"Quite out of my power, I assure you," he beamingly returned, "Might I ask your name?"

"M'Govan—James M'Govan," I responded, trying to look crusty, but not succeeding.

"Ah, I seem to have heard the name before—sort of detective or something, aren't you?" he airily continued. "Well, mine is Robert Manson, and I lodge in Lothian Street, No. 30. I'm rather pressed for time just now, so good-bye," and away he went quite undisturbed.

"The rascal knows all about it, but has made up his mind to keep the secret," was my thought as I watched him disappear. "However, no one has lodged a complaint as to a bullet smash or a lost leg, so things must develop a little before I can force his hand."

For some days after this failure I took to haunting the Grassmarket district after College hours in the hope of meeting Manson on a visit to the former owner of the leg, but fully a week elapsed before my wish was gratified, and then it was in a curious fashion. I was coming down the West Port at an easy pace when I heard the sound of two men in dispute near the foot of the Vennel, and I crossed the street into the shade to have a look at them, when I was surprised to find that one of them was Manson and the other a pickpocket named Pete Swift. The student was swearing at the other roundly, and telling him to be off, but a whisper from Swift seemed to pull him up, for he at length took some money from his pocket and gave it to the thief, and then moved off along the Grassmarket and vanished.

As soon as Manson was gone I crossed the street and intercepted Swift as he was moving away up the West Port.

"What have you been about now?" I sharply demanded.

"Nothing, s'elp me bob!" he protested, trying to edge past.

"You were begging—I saw you at it," I persisted.

"Begging? I never begged in my life!" he cried, looking as indignant as a clerk might look if accused of soiling his hands with manual labour. "Ye know that."

"I saw you get the money, so come along," I firmly answered, getting out the handcuffs, but he had a particular reason for disliking arrest just at that moment, and he made a bolt to get away, and, as I had to throw out the hand with the bracelets, he got an ugly bruise over the temple, which bled freely all the way to the Central, and caused him to lodge a complaint of having been treated with unnecessary violence. When he was searched, however, I began to have a dim idea of the nature of his crime, for in his breast pocket I found a letter addressed to a Mrs. Graham in Pitt Street, bearing an unobliterated stamp, and which was written in a strain not usually adopted when addressing a married woman. The letter began with "Dearest Nelly," and was signed "Your loving Bob," and was as like that of a lover addressing his sweetheart as any letter could be. The letter appeared to have been torn open with a rough hand, and was considerably soiled through being for some time in Pete's dirty pocket. When it was brought out Pete pulled on a stagey look of surprise to convey the idea that we had placed it there by some very clever conjuring.

"Where did you get this letter?" I said. "Is it your own?"

"Blest if I ever clapped eyes on it till this minute," he solemnly protested. "Must 'a' fallen into my pocket out o' some winder. Them things is al'ys flyin' about." And while we laughed consumedly Pete kept on a demure look of owl-like solemnity which would have done credit to a Judge at a murder trial.

"It doesn't belong to you then?" I continued.

"Certainly not," he said with a virtuous look. "I can't write."

"You can read," I sceptically remarked, "and I think I've seen you write your name. This letter seems to have been intended to be posted, but perhaps was intercepted. Letter-stealing is a very serious charge."

Pete winced at the hint, and coughed uneasily.

"Then I hopes you'll get the villin that put it into my pocket," he anxiously remarked.

"Maybe we've got him already," I cheerfully responded. "Any idea who wrote it?"

Pete had an appreciation of humour when the joke came from himself; he was as dull as ditch-water when it was levelled at him, so he assumed a stolid look and said:—

"Not the least."

"It might have been written by a student," I suggestively remarked.

Pete started painfully and eyed me with great concern. "Perhaps his name is Robert Manson," I continued. Pete's face grew sickly in hue, and he asked leave to sit down—he evidently wished, now that it was too late, that he had said nothing.

"But it will be easy to find that out by asking Manson himself," I calmly added, as Pete's silence grew painful. "Perhaps it has been a case of blackmailing."

Pete still had no reply to make, and so he was marched off to the cells till I could discover what he had been about. Students are noted for keeping late hours, so I had no scruples in making direct for Manson's lodgings in Lothian Street, in which I found him comfortably seated, smoking after his supper and studying a book at the same time. He seemed quite surprised on recognising me, but quickly recovered and offered me a chair.

"You did not tell me the strict truth the other day," I casually remarked as I took the seat. "I called here immediately after and learned that you had been called out the night before to an urgent case."

"Ah, indeed!" he said, affecting to make a powerful effort at recollecting his professional engagements. "Quite possible. I have so many calls of the kind. This is my last year at College."

"You took your amputating instruments with you," I pursued, "and also some chloroform—the landlady smelt it as you went out."

"Very likely," he musingly responded. "Have a cigar?" I took the cigar, and he hastened to help me to light it.

"I suppose you did nothing wrong, that you have any interest in concealing?" I said, at last.

"Oh dear, no—a doctor can't afford to do that," he firmly answered. "I never do anything wrong."

"Indeed, then you're an exception to most men," I laughingly observed. "Is it a professional secret?"

"Hem—well—yes, something of that kind," he cautiously answered, puffing hard at the cigar; "but, to tell you the truth, I wish now I had never gone out at all that night."

"You don't say so?" I exclaimed, trying to look astonished. "After complications?"

"Well, no, not in the case—that went all right," he gloomily answered; "but I lost some papers that night, or had them taken from me, of no use to any one but the owner, of course, but still such as I should rather have in my own possession."

"Some record of experiments, no doubt," I said, helpfully.

"Em—well, no," he answered, a little in doubt of me.

"Diploma maybe?" I continued.

"Oh, bless you, no—haven't taken that yet, but expect to at the end of the session," he hastily returned.

"Accounts, maybe—or letters?" I gently insinuated.

"Em—well, yes—something of that kind," he uneasily faltered.

"Nothing that I could get hold of for you, I suppose?" I suggested.

"I'm afraid not—it's too well guarded," he gloomily answered, "but I would do anything for you if you could get it. The fact is, Mr. M'Govan, it's a love letter, and one to be understood only by the lady to whom it was addressed."

"Most love letters are of that description," I sadly observed. "I used to write them once, so I know; to the callous outsider they are pure drivel."

I waited for him to say more, but he was fidgety and suspicious, and remained silent, so at last I said:—

"Are you afraid of a breach of promise case?"

"No; a breach of peace would be more likely," he grimly answered.

"Oh!—her father object?"

"No, no—she has no fathers—she's an old sweetheart, that's all."

I looked at him fixedly, and then said:—

"Do you mean that she is old, or that she was once your sweetheart?

"Once my sweetheart," he answered, flushing slightly.

"And now a widow, eh?"

"N—n—no—she's not a widow yet," he slowly admitted, and he signed drearily as if he wished she were.

I lay back and whistled aloud.

"Then you've been making love to another man's wife," I said at last.

"It would look like that to anyone who didn't under-stand," he hurriedly returned. "She and I know better."

"Imphm—they always say those things!" I dryly observed. "You seem to be in a tight place."

"Condemned tight!" he impressively rejoined, with a painfully troubled look. "If I once get out of this fix I'll never get into another."

"Well, I think I can help you out of the mess on two conditions," I quietly said at last, taking pity on him.

"Good!—I knew you were a good soul. I agree to them," he eagerly responded.

"The first is that you promise never to write to the same lady again, or to try to see her while she has a husband."

"Oh, I agree to that; it's really not safe, and scarcely right," he readily assented.

"And the second is that you tell me all about that amputation case. I have the leg, but want the other end of the man who owned it."

"And you'll get me the letter without the possibility of it reaching her husband?"

"I will."

"Then it's a bargain!" he said, in profoundest relief. "All I know about the business is that I was called up at one o'clock in the morning to see a man with a smashed leg. I was promised a sovereign to remain secret and the money was paid down before I started for the place. The man who came may have been a garroter or a house-breaker, for he had gallows bird written all over his face, and I took care to leave my watch and spare cash at home and to keep one of my amputating knives open and ready in my overcoat pocket. He said the leg might have to be cut off, so I took some chloroform with me. I have been sent to several cases among the poor down in the Grassmarket and the West Port, so I suppose they knew my address through that. Well, when we got to the Grassmarket my guide asked me to let myself be blindfolded, and I consented, and I was then led, so far as I could guess, to a house in the West Port, where I found my patient lying. He was a strong man, but he was weak enough with pain and loss of blood, and I saw in a minute that the leg had to go, and gave him the chloroform with the assistance of my guide, and soon had the leg off. I made a good job of it, considering that I worked almost alone and with a bad light, and then I asked for the leg as an extra perquisite, and took it away wrapped in a newspaper and hidden under my coat. I was again blindfolded and taken back to the Grassmarket, where my guide suddenly left me. When I snatched off the bandage I guessed the cause of his haste, for not far off was the night policeman, and I ducked into a close-mouth till he should pass; but in a little he came poking along shining his lamp in on me, and I got scared and threw the leg over a wall, and walked boldly out before him and got away home."

"But what about the carpet tacks?" I asked. "The leg was full of tacks."

"I know that, or rather my best amputating knife knows it, for some of them spoiled the edge of it," he said with energy; "but the people would not explain, so I know nothing of them. He had been shot by mistake, they said, and carried home by my guide—probably while breaking into some house."

"And how did you lose the letter?"

"I never knew—I had it in my overcoat pocket ready for post-ing, and I may have pulled it out when I took out my amputating knife—at any rate I was stopped on the street by the same villain who took me to the place, and he demanded money, saying he would give the letter to Mrs. Graham's husband if I refused, so I caved in and gave him half a sovereign. I appealed to his sense of gratitude for all I had done for them, but it was just a waste of breath."

"And have you never again seen your patient?"

"Oh, yes, once—I was taken to him in the same way, but by a different person, and he was progressing very well. I told him of the blackmailing, and he said he would have Pete's life for it; but that did not bring back the letter or my half-sovereign. He got an-other out of me to-night, and will be at me again before long."

"He won't, for he's in the lock-up now," I promptly answered, "and I have the letter safe."

"You have! Give me your hand! That takes a ton weight off my mind!" he joyously exclaimed. "You might hand it over and let me burn it."

"I cannot just now, but you will get it all right later on. Now you might get on your boots and try to take me as near to your patient's lodging as you can."

He started up and got on his things, and we went down to the Grassmarket together, where I blindfolded him, and he led me up the West Port for some distance, and then stopped near a street lamp.

"Is there a close-mouth near here?" he asked, and there was, so he led me into that, and some distance down he felt for a stair on the left hand.

"It was a place like this, but I'm not sure that we are in the right close," he said, but as I knew that on that stair was living a ticket-of-leave man named Ned Cooper, I decided to go up and give him a call. The keeper of the lodging declared that Cooper had not been there for weeks, but I soon proved that she was quite mistaken, for I found him—or at least a considerable part of him—in the inner room, with a basket over his left leg to keep the bedclothes off the tender stump. As the student did not appear with me, Ned rashly jumped to the conclusion that he had been betrayed by Pete Swift, and he straightway resolved to be even with the traitor.

"It's for that crib-cracking in Lauriston, I s'pose?" he inquiringly observed; "the one that Pete Swift planned and got me to help in?"

I nodded vaguely, and Ned clenched his fists, and swore at Pete till he was black in the face.

"It'll be seven years, I s'pose?" he gloomily added, "but seeing as I was drawed into it like a innercent lamb, and was shot by the man in the house and have lost a leg, I oughter get off easier nor Pete, eh?"

"Well, it seems fair that you should, and I daresay it may be managed," I said, and as my word was as good as a bond, Ned gave me the whole particulars of the housebreaking. They had thought the house empty; but it was not, for the owner was asleep in a back room, and had emptied a gun into Ned's leg before he even sighted him. There was no pursuit, and Ned was hauled out at the open window by Pete and borne off on his back. Ned knew nothing of the finding of his leg nor of the carpet tacks with which it had been filled; so I left him under guard, and next morning called at the house into which he had broken. The owner was at breakfast alone, and he started up in manifest alarm when he recognised my face.

"Is it about the man I shot?" he faintly asked, motioning me to a chair.

I nodded, and gravely said:—

"Why did you not report the matter to us?"

"Report it? I was nearly dead with remorse, and haven't had a solid night's rest ever since," he hurriedly answered. "Is he dead?"

"Oh, no; but how did it happen?"

"Well, I'm a light sleeper, and woke with the opening of the

front gate. Then I started up and listened, till I heard them trying
the front parlour window. There's been a lot of housebreaking about
here, so I had a gun ready loaded; but I'm no great shot, and as there
was only a bullet in it, I felt pretty sure I should miss the man. On
the mantlepiece, however, was a paper of tacks left by the uphol-
sterers a few weeks ago, and I groped for that in the dark, and
emptied them into the gun. I would have taken out the bullet, but
I had not time, for I heard the front window being shoved up. I
slipped along the lobby, and saw a man with one leg just inside the
window, and I let bang at that. I think the recoil knocked me over,
for when I came to again there was no sign of the man, and nothing but a great pool of blood to show what had happened. I think
there were two of them, but I only saw one inside."

I laughed at the poor soul's concern and terror, and hastened to
relieve his fears by stating the facts already set down. Ned Cooper
was removed as soon as possible, and was able to give such information against Pete that that worthy duly got off with the anticipated
seven years, while he himself got off with one. The case of the letter
and the blackmailing did not appear at the trial at all, and in due
time the letter was restored to Manson, who burned it before my
eyes, and declared that he would never again pen another of the
same kind.

✳

Émile Gaboriau

(1832–1873)

As mentioned in the introduction, Frenchman Émile Gaboriau was one of the many writers influenced by the "memoirs" of criminal-turned-policeman Eugène François Vidocq. Embellished or not, Vidocq's adventures left a considerable legacy. Gaboriau, however, was too good a writer to merely imitate either Vidocq or another of his idols, Poe's Dupin. His stylish and entertaining novels helped create the police procedural and influenced many later writers, from Anna Katharine Green to Arthur Conan Doyle. "Gaboriau had rather attracted me," Conan Doyle reminisced, "by the neat dovetailing of his plots."

Gaboriau was definitely good at plotting a mystery—he could plant clues and strew red herrings with the best of them—but he was just as interested in the investigative routine employed by his police detectives, the patient legwork and careful interrogation. He also spent more time than many of his colleagues in bringing characters to life, fleshing them out as individuals and conjuring the boulevards and countryside of France through which they make their cautious way. His dialogue is lively and his descriptions sparkle. In the story below, a snuffbox is "as large as that of a vaudeville capitalist." A candle at a crime scene "had burned down to the end, blackening the alabaster save-all in which it was placed." A prisoner in a cell "was ugly; smallpox had disfigured him, and his long straight nose and receding forehead gave him somewhat the stupid look of a sheep."

After years in the French cavalry, Gaboriau began the best possible training for a thriller writer. He served as secretary to the dramatist and novelist Paul Féval *père*, who wrote everything from swashbucklers to vampire stories. Gaboriau spent his time researching in police stations and morgues. A villain in one Féval novel was named Lecoq (the Rooster), and after he began writing on his own, Gaboriau resurrected the name for his protagonist. The French policeman called Monsieur Lecoq, whose surname would seem to also conjure the former head of the Sûreté (and whose given name is never revealed), appeared first as a relatively minor character in *L'Affaire Lerouge* (*The Widow Lerouge* or *The Lerouge Case*) and only rose to the marquee position in 1868 with a novel named after him and famously promoted all over Paris with mysterious posters bearing only the words *Monsieur Lecoq!* to build up advance interest.

Like many other writers at the time, Gaboriau tended to bifurcate his novels into detective story and Gothic family drama. In the first part a crime is discovered, an investigation carried out, and a culprit revealed; in the second part, he reveals the tangled history of mistakes and cruelties that led to the murder. They read like two related books joined together, not always the most compelling of structures. Anna Katharine Green, whose books clearly show Gaboriau's influence, sometimes used this approach. Three of Conan Doyle's four Sherlock Holmes novels are detective stories wrapping such flashback histories; only *The Hound of the Baskervilles* stays with Watson throughout, and even in it Holmes is offstage much of the time.

Gaboriau's most acclaimed shorter work, "The Little Old Man of Batignolles," which appears here in an anonymous nineteenth-century translation, was first published in 1868. It features not Lecoq but a tough and compassionate policeman named Mechinet.

The Little Old Man of Batignolles

I.

WHEN I HAD FINISHED my studies in order to become a health officer, a happy time it was, I was twenty-three years of age. I lived in the Rue Monsieur-le-Prince, almost at the corner of the Rue Racine.

There I had for thirty francs a month, service included, a furnished room, which to-day would certainly be worth a hundred francs; it was so spacious that I could easily put my arms in the sleeves of my overcoat without opening the window.

Since I left early in the morning to make the calls for my hospital, and since I returned very late, because the Café Leroy had irresistible attractions for me, I scarcely knew by sight the tenants in my house, peaceable people all; some living on their incomes, and some small merchants.

There was one, however, to whom, little by little, I became attached.

He was a man of average size, insignificant, always scrupulously shaved, who was pompously called "Monsieur Mechinet."

The doorkeeper treated him with a most particular regard, and never omitted quickly to lift his cap as he passed the lodge.

As M. Mechinet's apartment opened on my landing, directly

213

opposite the door of my room, we repeatedly met face to face. On such occasions we saluted one another.

One evening he came to ask me for some matches; another night I borrowed tobacco of him; one morning it happened that we both left at the same time, and walked side by side for a little stretch, talking.

Such were our first relations.

Without being curious or mistrusting—one is neither at the age I was then—we like to know what to think about people to whom we become attached.

Thus I naturally came to observe my neighbor's way of living, and became interested in his actions and gestures.

He was married. Madame Caroline Mechinet, blonde and fair, small, gay and plump, seemed to adore her husband.

But the husband's conduct was none too regular for that. Frequently he decamped before daylight, and often the sun had set before I heard him return to his domicile. At times he disappeared for whole weeks.

That the pretty little Madame Mechinet should tolerate this is what I could not understand.

Puzzled, I thought that our concierge, ordinarily as much a babbler as a magpie, would give me some explanation.

Not so! Hardly had I pronounced Mechinet's name than, without ceremony, he sent me about my business, telling me, as he rolled his eyes, that he was not in the habit of "spying" upon his tenants.

This reception doubled my curiosity to such an extent that, banishing all shame, I began to watch my neighbor.

I discovered things.

Once I saw him coming home dressed in the latest fashion, his buttonhole ornamented with five or six decorations; the next day I noticed him on the stairway dressed in a sordid blouse, on his head a cloth rag, which gave him a sinister air.

Nor was that all. One beautiful afternoon, as he was going out,

I saw his wife accompany him to the threshold of their apartment and there kiss him passionately, saying:

"I beg you, Mechinet, be prudent; think of your little wife."

Be prudent! Why? For what purpose? What did that mean? The wife must then be an accomplice.

It was not long before my astonishment was doubled.

One night, as I was sleeping soundly, some one knocked suddenly and rapidly at my door.

I arose and opened.

M. Mechinet entered, or rather rushed in, his clothing in disorder and torn, his necktie and the front of his shirt torn off, bareheaded, his face covered with blood.

"What has happened?" I exclaimed, frightened.

"Not so loud," said he; "you might be heard. Perhaps it is nothing, although I suffer devilishly. I said to myself that you, being a medical student would doubtless know how to help me."

Without saying a word, I made him sit down, and hastened to examine him and to do for him what was necessary.

Although he bled freely, the wound was a slight one—to tell the truth, it was only a superficial scratch, starting from the left ear and reaching to the corner of his mouth.

The dressing of the wound finished, "Well, here I am again healthy and safe for this time," M. Mechinet said to me. "Thousand thanks, dear Monsieur Godeuil. Above all, as a favor, do not speak to any one of this little accident, and—good night."

"Good night!" I had little thought of sleeping. When I remember all the absurd hypotheses and the romantic imaginations which passed through my brain, I can not help laughing.

In my mind, M. Mechinet took on fantastic proportions.

The next day he came to thank me again, and invited me to dinner.

That I was all eyes and ears when I entered my neighbor's home may be rightly guessed.

In vain did I concentrate my whole attention. I could not find out anything of a nature to dissipate the mystery which puzzled me so much.

However, from this dinner on, our relations became closer. M. Mechinet decidedly favored me with his friendship. Rarely a week passed without his taking me along, as he expressed it, to eat soup with him, and almost daily, at the time for absinthe, he came to meet me at the Café Leroy, where we played a game of dominoes.

Thus it was that on a certain evening in the month of July, on a Friday, at about five o'clock, when he was just about to beat me at "full double-six," an ugly-looking bully abruptly entered, and, approaching him, murmured in his ears some words I could not hear.

M. Mechinet rose suddenly, looking troubled.

"I am coming," said he; "run and say that I am coming."

The man ran off as fast as his legs could carry him, and then M. Mechinet offered me his hand.

"Excuse me," added my old neighbor, "duty before everything; we shall continue our game to-morrow."

Consumed with curiosity, I showed great vexation, saying that I regretted very much not accompanying him.

"Well," grumbled he, "why not? Do you want to come? Perhaps it will be interesting."

For all answer, I took my hat and we left.

II.

I WAS CERTAINLY FAR from thinking that I was then venturing on one of those apparently insignificant steps which, nevertheless, have a deciding influence on one's whole life.

For once, I thought to myself, I am holding the solution of the enigma!

And full of a silly and childish satisfaction, I trotted, like a lean cat, at the side of M. Mechinet.

I say "trotted," because I had all I could do not to be left behind.

He rushed along, down the Rue Racine, running against the passers-by, as if his fortune depended on his legs.

Luckily, on the Place de l'Odéon a cab came in our way.

M. Mechinet stopped it, and, opening the door, "Get in, Monsieur Godeuil," said he to me.

I obeyed, and he seated himself at my side, after having called to the coachman in a commanding voice: "39 Rue Lecluse, at Batignolles, and drive fast!"

The distance drew from the coachman a string of oaths. Nevertheless he whipped up his broken-down horses and the carriage rolled off.

"Oh! it is to Batignolles we are going?" I asked with a courtier's smile.

But M. Mechinet did not answer me; I even doubt that he heard me.

A complete change took place in him. He did not seem exactly agitated but his set lips and the contraction of his heavy, brushwood-like eyebrows betrayed a keen preoccupation. His look, lost in space, seemed to be studying there the meaning of some insolvable problem.

He had pulled out his snuff-box and continually took from it enormous pinches of snuff, which he kneaded between the index and thumb, rolled into a ball, and raised it to his nose; but he did not actually snuff.

It was a habit which I had observed, and it amused me very much.

This worthy man, who abhorred tobacco, always carried a snuff-box as large as that of a vaudeville capitalist.

If anything unforeseen happened to him, either agreeable or vexatious, in a trice he had it out, and seemed to snuff furiously.

Often the snuff-box was empty, but his gestures remained the same.

I learned later that this was a system with him for the purpose of concealing his impressions and of diverting the attention of his questioners.

In the mean time we rolled on. The cab easily passed up the Rue de Clichy; it crossed the exterior boulevard, entered the Rue de Lecluse, and soon stopped at some distance from the address given.

It was materially impossible to go farther, as the street was obstructed by a compact crowd.

In front of No. 39, two or three hundred persons were standing, their necks craned, eyes gleaming breathless with curiosity, and with difficulty kept in bounds by half a dozen *sergents de ville*, who were everywhere repeating in vain and in their roughest voices: "Move on, gentlemen, move on!"

After alighting from the carriage, we approached, making our way with difficulty through the crowd of idlers.

We already had our hands on the door of No. 39, when a police officer rudely pushed us back.

"Keep back! You can not pass!"

My companion eyed him from head to foot, and straightening himself up, said:

"Well, don't you know me? I am Mechinet, and this young man," pointing to me, "is with me."

"I beg your pardon! Excuse me!" stammered the officer, carrying his hand to his three-cocked hat. "I did not know; please enter."

We entered.

In the hall, a powerful woman, evidently the concierge, more red than a peony, was holding forth and gesticulating in the midst of a group of house tenants.

"Where is it?" demanded M. Mechinet gruffly.

"Third floor, monsieur," she replied; "third floor, door to the right. Oh! my God! What a misfortune. In a house like this. Such a good man."

I did not hear more. M. Mechinet was rushing up the stairs, and I followed him, four steps at a time, my heart thumping.

On the third floor the door to the right was open. We entered, went through an anteroom, a dining-room, a parlor, and finally reached a bedroom.

If I live a thousand years I shall not forget the scene which struck my eyes. Even at this moment as I am writing, after many years, I still see it down to the smallest details.

At the fireplace opposite the door two men were leaning on their elbows: a police commissary, wearing his scarf of office, and an examining magistrate.

At the right, seated at a table a young man, the judge's clerk, was writing.

In the centre of the room, on the floor, in a pool of coagulated and black blood, lay the body of an old man with white hair. He was lying on his back, his arms folded crosswise.

Terrified, I stopped as if nailed to the threshold, so nearly fainting that I was compelled to lean against the door-frame.

My profession had accustomed me to death; I had long ago overcome repugnance to the amphitheatre, but this was the first time that I found myself face to face with a crime.

For it was evident that an abominable crime had been committed.

Less sensitive than I, my neighbor entered with a firm step.

"Oh, it is you, Mechinet," said the police commissary; "I am very sorry to have troubled you."

"Why?"

"Because we shall not need your services. We know the guilty one; I have given orders; by this time he must have been arrested."

How strange!

From M. Mechinet's gesture one might have believed that this assurance vexed him. He pulled out his snuff-box, took two or three of his fantastic pinches, and said:

"Ah! the guilty one is known?"

It was the examining magistrate who answered:

"Yes, and known in a certain and positive manner; yes, M. Mechinet, the crime once committed, the assassin escaped, believing that his victim had ceased living. He was mistaken. Providence was watching; this unfortunate old man was still breathing. Gathering all his energy, he dipped one of his fingers in the blood which was flowing in streams from his wound, and there, on the floor, he wrote in his blood his murderer's name. Now look for yourself."

Then I perceived what at first I had not seen.

On the inlaid floor, in large, badly shaped, but legible letters, was written in blood: MONIS.

"Well?" asked M. Mechinet.

"That," answered the police commissary, "is the beginning of the name of a nephew of the poor man; of a nephew for whom he had an affection, and whose name is Monistrol."

"The devil!" exclaimed my neighbor.

"I can not suppose," continued the investigating magistrate, "that the wretch would attempt denying. The five letters are an overwhelming accusation. Moreover, who would profit by this cowardly crime? He alone, as sole heir of this old man, who, they say, leaves a large fortune. There is more. It was last evening that the murder was committed. Well, last evening none other but his nephew called on this poor old man. The concierge saw him enter the house at about nine o'cock and leave again a little before midnight."

"It is clear," said M. Mechinet approvingly; "it is very clear, this Monistrol is nothing but an idiot." And, shrugging his shoulders, asked:

"But did he steal anything, break some piece of furniture, anything to give us an idea as to the motive for the crime?"

"Up to now nothing seems to have been disturbed," answered the commissary. "As you said, the wretch is not clever; as soon as he finds himself discovered, he will confess."

Whereupon the police commissary and M. Mechinet withdrew to the window, conversing in low tones, while the judge gave some instructions to his clerk.

III.

I HAD WANTED TO know exactly what my enigmatic neighbor was doing. Now I knew it. Now everything was explained. The looseness of his life, his absences, his late homecomings, his sudden disappearances, his young wife's fears and complicity; the wound I had cured. But what did I care now about that discovery?

I examined with curiosity everything around me.

From where I was standing, leaning against the door-frame, my eye took in the entire apartment.

Nothing, absolutely nothing, evidenced a scene of murder. On the contrary, everything betokened comfort, and at the same time habits parsimonious and methodical.

Everything was in its place; there was not one wrong fold in the curtains; the wood of the furniture was brilliantly polished, show-ing daily care.

It seemed evident that the conjectures of the examining magis-trate and of the police commissary were correct, and that the poor old man had been murdered the evening before, when he was about to go to bed.

In fact, the bed was open, and on the blanket lay a shirt and a neckcloth.

On the table, at the head of the bed, I noticed a glass of sugared water, a box of safety matches, and an evening paper, the "Patrie."

On one corner of the mantelpiece a candlestick was shining brightly, a nice big, solid copper candlestick. But the candle which had illuminated the crime was burned out; the murderer had escaped without extinguishing it, and it had burned down to the end, black-ening the alabaster save-all in which it was placed.

I noticed all these details at a glance, without any effort, without my will having anything to do with it. My eye had become a photo-graphic objective; the stage of the murder had portrayed itself in my mind, as on a prepared plate, with such precision that no circum-stance was lacking, and with such depth that to-day, even, I can sketch the apartment of the "little old man of Batignolles" without omitting anything, not even a cork, partly covered with green wax, which lay on the floor under the chair of the judge's clerk.

It was an extraordinary faculty, which had been bestowed upon me—my chief faculty, which as yet I had not occasion to exercise and which all at once revealed itself to me.

I was then too agitated to analyze my impressions. I had but one obstinate, burning, irresistible desire: to get close to the body, which was lying two yards from me.

At first I struggled against the temptation. But fatality had something to do with it. I approached. Had my presence been remembered? I do not believe it.

At any rate, nobody paid any attention to me. M. Mechinet and the police commissary were still talking near the window; the clerk was reading his report in an undertone to the investigating magistrate.

Thus nothing prevented me from carrying out my intention. And, besides, I must confess I was possessed with some kind of a fever, which rendered me insensible to exterior circumstances and absolutely isolated me. So much so that I dared to kneel close to the body, in order to see better.

Far from expecting any one to call out: "What are you doing there?" I acted slowly and deliberately, like a man who, having received a mission, executes it.

The unfortunate old man seemed to me to have been between seventy and seventy-five years old. He was small and very thin, but solid and built to pass the hundred-year mark. He still had considerable hair, yellowish white and curly, on the nape of the neck. His gray beard, strong and thick, looked as if he had not been shaven for five or six days; it must have grown after his death. This circumstance did not surprise me, as I had often noticed it without subjects in the amphitheatres.

What did surprise me was the expression of the face. It was calm;

I should even say, smiling. His lips were parted, as for a friendly greeting. Death must have occurred then with terrible suddenness to preserve such a kindly expression! That was the first idea which came to my mind.

Yes, but how reconcile these two irreconcilable circumstances: a sudden death and those five letters—MONIS—which I saw in lines of blood on the floor? In order to write them, what effort must it have cost a dying man! Only the hope of revenge could have given him so much energy. And how great must his rage have been to feel himself expiring before being able to trace the entire name of his murderer! And yet the face of the dead seemed to smile at one.

The poor old man had been struck in the throat, and the weapon had gone right through the neck. The instrument must have been a dagger, or perhaps one of those terrible Catalan knives, as broad as the hand, which cut on both sides and are as pointed as a needle.

Never in my life before had I been agitated by such strange sensations. My temples throbbed with extraordinary violence, and my heart swelled as if it would break. What was I about to discover?

Driven by a mysterious and irresistible force, which annihilated my will-power, I took between my hands, for the purpose of examining them, the stiff and icy hands of the body.

The right hand was clean; it was one of the fingers of the left hand, the index, which was all blood-stained.

What! it was with the left hand that the old man had written? Impossible!

Seized with a kind of dizziness, with haggard eyes, my hair standing on end, paler than the dead lying at my feet, I rose with a terrible cry:

"Great God!"

At this cry all the others jumped up, surprised, frightened.

"What is it?" they asked me all together. "What has happened?"

I tried to answer, but the emotion was strangling me. All I could do was to show them the dead man's hands, stammering:

"There! There!"

Quick as lightning, M. Mechinet fell on his knees beside the body. What I had seen he saw, and my impression was also his, for, quickly rising, he said:

"It was not this poor old man who traced the letters there."

As the judge and the commissary looked at him with open mouths, he explained to them the circumstance of the left hand alone being blood-stained.

"And to think that I had not paid any attention to that," repeated the distressed commissary over and over again.

M. Mechinet was taking snuff furiously.

"So it is," he said, "the things that are not seen are those that are near enough to put the eyes out. But no matter. Now the situation is devilishly changed. Since it is not the old man himself who wrote, it must be the person who killed him."

"Evidently," approved the commissary.

"Now," continued my neighbor, "can any one imagine a murderer stupid enough to denounce himself by writing his own name beside the body of his victim? No; is it not so? Now, conclude—"

The judge had become anxious.

"It is clear," he said, "appearances have deceived us. Monistrol is not the guilty one. Who is it? It is your business, M. Mechinet, to discover him."

He stopped; a police officer had entered, and, addressing the commissary, said:

"Your orders have been carried out, sir. Monistrol has been arrested and locked up. He confessed everything."

IV.

IT IS IMPOSSIBLE TO describe our astonishment. What! While we were there, exerting ourselves to find proofs of Monistrol's innocence, he acknowledges himself guilty?

M. Mechinet was the first to recover.

Rapidly he raised his fingers from the snuff-box to his nose five or six times, and advancing toward the officer, said:

"Either you are mistaken, or you are deceiving us; one or the other."

"I'll take an oath, M. Mechinet."

"Hold your tongue. You either misunderstood what Monistrol said or got intoxicated by the hope of astonishing us with the announcement that the affair was settled."

The officer, up to then humble and respectful, now became refractory.

"Excuse me," he interrupted, "I am neither an idiot nor a liar, and I know what I am talking about."

The discussion came so near being a quarrel that the investigating judge thought best to interfere.

"Calm yourself, Monsieur Mechinet," he said, "and before expressing an opinion, wait to be informed."

Then turning toward the officer, he continued:

"And you, my friend, tell us what you know, and give us reasons for your assurance."

Thus sustained, the officer crushed M. Mechinet with an ironical glance, and with a very marked trace of conceit he began:

"Well, this is what happened: Monsieur the Judge and Monsieur the Commissary, both here present, instructed us—Inspector Goulard, my colleague Poltin, and myself—to arrest Monistrol, dealer in imitation jewelry, living at 75 Rue Vivienne, the said Monistrol being accused of the murder of his uncle."

"Exactly so," approved the commissary in a low voice.

"Thereupon," continued the officer, "we took a cab and had him drive us to the address given. We arrived and found M. Monistrol in the back of his shop, about to sit down to dinner with his wife, a woman of twenty-five or thirty years, and very beautiful.

"Seeing the three of us stand like a string of onions, our man got up. 'What do you want?' he asked us. Sergeant Goulard drew from his pocket the warrant and answered: 'In the name of the law, I arrest you!' "

Here M. Mechinet behaved as if he were on a gridiron.

"Could you not hurry up?" he said to the officer.

But the latter, as if he had not heard, continued in the same calm tone:

"I have arrested many people during my life. Well! I never saw any of them go to pieces like this one.

" 'You are joking,' he said to us, 'or you are making a mistake.'

" 'No, we are not mistaken!'

" 'But, after all, what do you arrest me for?'

"Goulard shrugged his shoulders.

" 'Don't act like a child,' he said, 'what about your uncle? The body has been found, and we have overwhelming proofs against you.'

"Oh! that rascal, what a disagreeable shock! He tottered and finally dropped on a chair, sobbing and stammering I can not tell what answer.

"Goulard, seeing him thus, shook him by the coat collar and said:

" 'Believe me, the shortest way is to confess everything.'

"The man looked at us stupidly and murmured:

" 'Well, yes, I confess everything.' "

"Well maneuvred, Goulard," said the commissary approvingly. The officer looked triumphant.

"It was now a matter of cutting short our stay in the shop," he continued. "We had been instructed to avoid all commotion, and some idlers were already crowding around. Goulard seized the prisoner by the arm, shouting to him: 'Come on, let us start; they are waiting for us at headquarters.' Monistrol managed to get on his shaking legs, and in the voice of a man taking his courage in both hands, said: 'Let us go.'

"We were thinking that the worst was over; we did not count on the wife.

"Up to that moment she had remained in an armchair, as in a faint, without breathing a word, without seeming even to understand what was going on.

"But when she saw that we were taking away her husband, she sprang up like a lioness, and throwing herself in front of the door, shouted: 'You shall not pass.'

"On my word of honor she was superb; but Goulard, who had seen others before, said to her: 'Come, come, little woman, don't let us get angry; your husband will be brought back.'

"However, far from giving way to us, she clung more firmly to the door-frame, swearing that her husband was innocent; declaring that if he was taken to prison she would follow him, at times threatening us and crushing us with invectives, and then again entreating in her sweetest voice.

"When she understood that nothing would prevent us from doing our duty, she let go the door, and, throwing herself on her husband's neck, groaned: 'Oh, dearest beloved, is it possible that you are accused of a crime? You—you! Please tell them, these men, that you are innocent.'

"In truth, we were all affected, except the man, who pushed his poor wife back so brutally that she fell in a heap in a corner of the back shop.

"Fortunately that was the end.

"The woman had fainted; we took advantage of it to stow the husband away in the cab that had brought us.

"To stow away is the right word, because he had become like an inanimate thing; he could no longer stand up; he had to be carried. To omit nothing, I should add that his dog, a kind of black cur, wanted actually to jump into the carriage with us, and that we had the greatest trouble to get rid of it.

"On the way, as by right, Goulard tried to entertain our prisoner and to make him blab. But it was impossible to draw one word from him. It was only when we arrived at police headquarters that he seemed to come to his senses. When he was duly installed in one of the 'close confinement' cells, he threw himself headlong on the bed, repeating: 'What have I done to you, my God! What have I done to you!'

"At this moment Goulard approached him, and for the second time asked: 'Well, do you confess your guilt?' Monistrol motioned with his head: 'Yes, yes.' Then in a hoarse voice said: 'I beg you, leave me alone.'

"That is what we did, taking care, however, to place a keeper on watch at the window of the cell, in case the fellow should attempt suicide.

"Goulard and Poltin remained down there, and I, here I am."

"That is precise," grumbled the commissary; "It could not be more precise."

That was also the judge's opinion, for he murmured:

"How can we, after all this, doubt Monistrol's guilt?"

As for me, though I was confounded, my convictions were still firm. I was just about to open my mouth to venture an objection, when M. Mechinet forestalled me.

"All that is well and good," exclaimed he. "Only if we admit that Monistrol is the murderer, we are forced also to admit that it was he who wrote his name there on the floor—and—well, that's a hard nut."

"Bosh!" interrupted the commissary, "since the accused confessed, what is the use of bothering about a circumstance which will be explained at the trial?"

But my neighbor's remark had again roused perplexities in the mind of the judge, and without committing himself, he said:

"I am going to the Prefecture. I want to examine Monistrol this very evening."

And after telling the commissary to be sure and fulfil all formalities and to await the arrival of the physicians called for the autopsy of the body, he left, followed by his clerk and by the officer who had come to inform us of the successful arrest.

"Provided these devils of doctors do not keep me waiting too long," growled the commissary, who was thinking of his dinner.

Neither M. Mechinet nor I answered him. We remained standing, facing one another, evidently beset by the same thought.

"After all," murmured my neighbor, "perhaps it was the old man who wrote——"—"With the left hand, then? Is that possible? Without considering that this poor fellow must have died instantly."—"Are you certain of it?"—"Judging by his wound I would take an oath on it. Besides, the physicians will come; they will tell you whether I am right or wrong."

With veritable frenzy M. Mechinet pretended to take snuff.

"Perhaps there is some mystery beneath this," said he; "that remains to be seen."

"It is an examination to be gone over again."—"Be it so, let us do it over; and to begin, let us examine the concierge."

Running to the staircase, M. Mechinet leaned over the balustrade, calling: "Concierge! Hey! Concierge! Come up, please."

V.

WHILE WAITING FOR THE concierge to come up, M. Mechinet proceeded with a rapid and able examination of the scene of the crime.

It was principally the lock of the main door to the apartment which attracted his attention; it was intact, and the key turned without difficulty. This circumstance absolutely discarded the thought that an evil-doer, a stranger, had entered during the night by means of false keys.

For my part, I had involuntarily, or rather inspired by the astonishing instinct which had revealed itself in me, picked up the cork, partly covered with green wax, which I had noticed on the floor.

It had been used, and on the side where the wax was showed traces of the corkscrew; but on the other end could be seen a kind of deepish notch, evidently produced by some sharp and pointed instrument.

Suspecting the importance of my discovery, I communicated it to M. Mechinet, and he could not avoid an exclamation of joy.

"At last," he exclaimed, "at last we have a clue! This cork, it's the murderer who dropped it here; he stuck in it the brittle point of the weapon he used. The conclusion is, that the instrument of the murder is a dagger with a fixed handle and not one of those knives which shut up. With this cork, I am certain to reach the guilty one, no matter who he is!"

The police commissary was just finishing his task in the room, M. Mechinet and I had remained in the parlor, when we were interrupted by the noise of heavy breathing.

Almost immediately appeared the powerful woman I had noticed holding forth in the hall in the midst of the tenants.

It was the concierge, if possible redder than at the time of our arrival.

"In what way can I serve you, monsieur?" she asked of M. Mechinet.

"Take a seat, madame," he answered.

"But, monsieur, I have people downstairs."

"They will wait for you. I tell you to sit down."

Nonplused by M. Mechinet's tone, she obeyed.

Then looking straight at her with his terrible, small, gray eyes, he began:

"I need certain information, and I'm going to question you. In your interest, I advise you to answer straightforwardly. Now, first of all, what is the name of this poor fellow who was murdered?"

"His name was Pigoreau, kind sir, but he was mostly known by the name of Antenor, which he had formerly taken as more suitable to his business."

"Did he live in this house a long time?"

"The last eight years."

"Where did he reside before?"

"Rue Richelieu, where he had his store; he had been a hair-dresser, and it was in that business that he made his money."

"He was then considered rich?"

"I heard him say to his niece that he would not let his throat be cut for a million."

As to this, it must have been known to the investigating magistrate, as the papers of the poor old man had been included in the inventory made.

"Now," M. Mechinet continued, "what kind of a man was this M. Pigoreau, called Antenor?"

"Oh! the cream of men, my dear, kind sir," answered the concierge. "It is true he was cantankerous, queer, as miserly as possible, but he was not proud. And so funny with all that. One could have spent whole nights listening to him, when he was in the right mood. And the number of stories he knew! Just think, a former hair-dresser, who, as he said, had dressed the hair of the most beautiful women in Paris!"

"How did he live?"

"As everybody else; as people do who have an income, you know, and who yet cling to their money."

"Can you give me some particulars?"

"Oh! As to that, I think so, since it was I who looked after his rooms, and that was no trouble at all for me, because he did almost everything himself—swept, dusted, and polished. Yes, it was his hobby. Well, every day at noon, I brought him up a cup of chocolate. He drank it; on top of that he took a large glass of water; that was his breakfast. Then he dressed and that took him until two o'clock, for he was a dandy, and careful of his person, more so than a newly married woman. As soon as he was dressed, he went out to take a walk through Paris. At six o'clock he went to dinner in a private boarding-house, the Mademoiselles Gomet, in the Rue de la Paix. After dinner he used to go to the Café Guerbois for his demitasse and to play his usual game, and at eleven he came home to go to bed. On the whole, the poor fellow had only one fault; he was fond of the other sex. I even told him often: 'At your age, are you not ashamed of yourself?' But no one is perfect, and after all it could be easily understood of a former perfumer, who in his life had had a great many good fortunes."

An obsequious smile strayed over the lips of the powerful concierge, but nothing could cheer up M. Mechinet.

"Did M. Pigoreau receive many calls?" he asked.

"Very few. I have hardly seen anybody call on him except his nephew, M. Monistrol, whom he invited every Sunday to dinner at Lathuile's."

"And how did they get along together, the uncle and the nephew?"

"Like two fingers of the same hand."

"Did they ever have any disputes?"

"Never, except that they were always wrangling about Madame Clara."

"Who is that Madame Clara?"

"Well, M. Monistrol's wife, a superb creature. The deceased, old Antenor, could not bear her. He said that his nephew loved that woman too much; that she was leading him by the end of his nose, and that she was fooling him in every way. He claimed that she did not love her husband; that she was too high and mighty for her position, and that finally she would do something foolish. Madame Clara and her uncle even had a falling out at the end of last year. She wanted the good fellow to lend a hundred thousand francs to M. Monistrol, to enable him to buy out a jeweler's stock at the Palais Royal. But he refused, saying that after his death they could do with his money whatever they wanted, but that until then, since he had earned it, he intended to keep and enjoy it."

I thought that M. Mechinet would dwell on this circumstance, which seemed to me very important. But no, in vain did I increase my signals; he continued:

"It remains now to be told by whom the crime was first discovered."

"By me, my kind monsieur, by me," moaned the concierge. "Oh! it is frightful! Just imagine, this morning, exactly at twelve, I brought up to old Antenor his chocolate, as usual. As I do the cleaning, I have a key to the apartment. I opened, I entered, and what did I see? Oh! my God!"

And she began to scream loudly.

"This grief proves that you have a good heart, madame," gravely said M. Mechinet. "Only, as I am in a great hurry, please try to overcome it. What did you think, seeing your tenant murdered?"

"I said to any one who wanted to hear: 'It is his nephew, the scoundrel, who has done it to inherit.'"

"What makes you so positive? Because after all to accuse a man of so great a crime, is to drive him to the scaffold."

"But, monsieur, who else would it be? M. Monistrol came to see his uncle last evening, and when he left it was nearly midnight. Besides, he nearly always speaks to me, but never said a word to me that night, neither when he came, nor when he left. And from that moment up to the time I discovered everything, I am sure nobody went up to M. Antenor's apartment."

I admit this evidence confused me. I would not have thought of continuing the examination. Fortunately, M. Mechinet's experience was great, and he was thoroughly master of the difficult art of drawing the whole truth from witnesses.

"Then, madame," he insisted, "you are certain that Monistrol came yesterday evening?"

"I am certain."

"Did you surely see him and recognize him?"

"Ah! wait. I did not look him in the face. He passed quickly, trying to hide himself, like the scoundrel he is, and the hallway is badly illuminated."

At this reply, of such incalculable importance, I jumped up and, approaching the concierge, exclaimed:

"If it is so, how dare you affirm that you recognized M. Mon-istrol?"

She looked me over from head to foot, and answered with an ironical smile:

"If I did not see the master's face, I did see the dog's nose. As I always pet him, he came into my lodge, and I was just going to give him a bone from a leg of mutton when his master whistled for him."

I looked at M. Mechinet, anxious to know what he thought of this, but his face faithfully kept the secret of his impressions.

He only added:

"Of what breed is M. Monistrol's dog?"

"It is a loulou, such as the drovers used formerly, all black, with a white spot over the ear; they call him 'Pluton.'"

M. Mechinet rose.

"You may retire," he said to the concierge; "I know all I want."

And when she had left, he remarked:

"It seems to me impossible that the nephew is not the guilty one."

During the time this long examination was taking place, the physicians had come. When they finished the autopsy they reached the following conclusion:

"M. Pigoreau's death had certainly been instantaneous." So it was not he who had lined out the five letters, MONIS, which we saw on the floor near the body.

So I was not mistaken.

"But if it was not he," exclaimed M. Mechinet, "who was it then? Monistrol—that is what nobody will ever succeed in putting into my brain."

And the commissary, happy at being free to go to dinner at last, made fun of M. Mechinet's perplexities—ridiculous perplexities, since Monistrol had confessed. But M. Mechinet said:

"Perhaps I am really nothing but an idiot; the future will tell. In the mean time, come, my dear Monsieur Godeuil, come with me to Police Headquarters."

VI.

IN LIKE MANNER, AS in going to Batignolles, we took a cab also to go to Police Headquarters.

M. Mechinet's preoccupation was great. His fingers continually traveled from the empty snuff-box to his nose, and I heard him grumbling between his teeth:

"I shall assure myself of the truth of this! I must find out the truth of this."

Then he took from his pocket the cork which I had given him, and turned it over and over like a monkey picking a nut, and murmured:

"This is evidence, however; there must be something gained by this green wax."

Buried in my corner, I did not breathe. My position was certainly one of the strangest, but I did not give it a thought. Whatever intelligence I had was absorbed in this affair; in my mind I went over its various and contradictory elements, and exhausted myself in trying to penetrate the secret of the tragedy, a secret of which I had a presentiment.

When our carriage stopped, it was night—dark.

The Quai des Orfèvres was deserted and quiet; not a sound, not a passer-by. The stores in the neighborhood, few and far between, were closed. All the life of the district had hidden itself in the little restaurant which almost forms the corner of the Rue de Jerusalem, behind the red curtains, on which were outlined the shadows of the patrons.

"Will they let you see the accused?" I asked M. Mechinet.

"Certainly," he answered. "Am I not charged with the following up of this affair? Is it not necessary, in view of unforeseen requirements at the inquest, that I be allowed to examine the prisoner at any hour of the day or night?"

And with a quick step he entered under the arch, saying to me:

"Come, come, we have no time to lose."

I did not require any encouragement from him. I followed, agitated by indescribable emotions and trembling with vague curiosity.

It was the first time I had ever crossed the threshold of the Police Headquarters, and God knows what my prejudices were then.

There, I said to myself, not without a certain terror, there is the secret of Paris!

I was so lost in thought, that, forgetting to look where I was going, I almost fell.

The shock brought me back to a sense of the situation.

We were going along an immense passageway, with damp walls and an uneven pavement. Soon my companion entered a small room where two men were playing cards, while three or four others, stretched on cots, were smoking pipes. M. Mechinet exchanged a few words with them—I could not hear, for I had remained outside. Then he came out again, and we continued our walk.

After crossing a court and entering another passageway, we soon came before an iron gate with heavy bolts and a formidable lock.

At a word from M. Mechinet, a watchman opened this gate for us; at the right we passed a spacious room, where it seemed to me I saw policemen and Paris guards; finally we climbed up a very steep stairway.

At the top of the stairs, at the entrance to a narrow passage with a number of small doors, was seated a stout man with a jovial face, that certainly had nothing of the classical jailer about it.

As soon as he noticed my companion, he exclaimed:

"Eh! it is M. Mechinet. Upon my word, I was expecting you. I bet you came for the murderer of the little old man of Batignolles."

"Precisely. Is there anything new?"

"No."

"But the investigating judge must have come."

"He has just gone."

"Well?"

"He did not stay more than three minutes with the accused, and when he left he seemed very much satisfied. At the bottom of the stairs he met the governor, and said to him: 'This is a settled case; the murderer has not even attempted to deny.'"

M. Mechinet jumped about three feet; but the jailer did not notice it, and continued:

"But then, that did not surprise me. At a mere glance at the individual as they brought him I said: 'Here is one who will not know how to hold out.'"

"And what is he doing now?"

"He moans. I have been instructed to watch him, for fear he should commit suicide, and as is my duty, I do watch him, but it is mere waste of time. He is another one of those fellows who care more for their own skin than for that of others."

"Let us go and see him," interrupted M. Mechinet; "and above all, no noise."

At once all three advanced on tiptoe till we reached a solid oak door, through which had been cut a little barred window about a man's height from the ground.

Through this little window could be seen everything that occurred in the cell, which was illuminated by a paltry gasburner.

The jailer glanced in first, M. Mechinet then looked, and at last my turn came.

On a narrow iron couch, covered with a gray woolen blanket with yellow stripes, I perceived a man lying flat, his head hidden between his partly folded arms.

He was crying; the smothered sound of his sobs reached me, and from time to time a convulsive trembling shook him from head to foot.

"Open now," ordered M. Mechinet of the watchman.

He obeyed, and we entered.

At the sound of the grating key, the prisoner had raised himself and, sitting on his pallet, his legs and arms hanging, his head inclined on his chest, he looked at us stupidly.

He was a man of thirty-five or thirty-eight years of age; his build a little above the average, but robust, with an apoplectic neck sunk between two broad shoulders. He was ugly; smallpox had disfigured him, and his long, straight nose and receding forehead gave him somewhat the stupid look of a sheep. However his blue eyes were very beautiful, and his teeth were of remarkable whiteness.

"Well! M. Monistrol," began M. Mechinet, "we are grieving, are we?"

As the unfortunate man did not answer, he continued:

"I admit that the situation is not enlivening. Nevertheless, if I were in your place, I would prove that I am a man. I would have common sense, and try to prove my innocence."

"I am not innocent."

This time there could not be any mistake, nor could the intelligence of the officer be doubted; it was from the very mouth of the accused that we gathered the terrible confession.

"What!" exclaimed M. Mechinet, "it was you who—"

The man stood up, staggering on his legs, his eyes bloodshot, his mouth foaming, prey to a veritable attack of rage.

"Yes, it was I," he interrupted; "I alone. How many times will I have to repeat it? Already, a while ago, a judge came; I confessed everything and signed my confession. What more do you ask? Go on, I know what awaits me, and I am not afraid. I killed, I must be killed! Well, cut my head off, the sooner the better."

Somewhat stunned at first, M. Mechinet soon recovered.

"One moment. You know," he said, "they do not cut people's heads off like that. First they must prove that they are guilty; after that the courts admit certain errors, certain fatalities, if you will, and it is for this very reason that they recognize 'extenuating circumstances.'"

An inarticulate moan was Monistrol's only answer. M. Mechinet continued:

"Did you have a terrible grudge against your uncle?"

"Oh, no."

THE LITTLE OLD MAN OF BATIGNOLLES 239

"Then why?"

"To inherit; my affairs were in bad shape—you may make inquiry. I needed money; my uncle, who was very rich, refused me some."

"I understand; you hoped to escape from justice?"

"I was hoping to."

Until then I had been surprised at the way M. Mechinet was conducting this rapid examination, but now it became clear to me. I guessed rightly what followed; I saw what trap he was laying for the accused.

"Another thing," he continued suddenly, "where did you buy the revolver you used in committing the murder?"

No surprise appeared on Monistrol's face.

"I had it in my possession for a long time," he answered.

"What did you do with it after the crime?"

"I threw it outside on the boulevard."

"All right," spoke M. Mechinet gravely, "we will make search and will surely find it."

After a moment of silence he added:

"What I can not explain to myself is, why is it that you had your dog follow you?"

"What! How! My dog?"

"Yes, Pluton. The concierge recognized him."

Monistrol's fists moved convulsively; he opened his mouth as if to answer, but a sudden idea crossing his mind, he threw himself back on his bed, and said in a tone of firm determination:

"You have tortured me enough; you shall not draw another word from me."

It was clear that to insist would be taking trouble for nothing.

We then withdrew.

Once outside on the quay, grasping M. Mechinet's arm, I said:

"You heard it, that unfortunate man does not even know how his uncle died. Is it possible to still doubt his innocence?"

But he was a terrible skeptic, that old detective.

"Who knows?" he answered. "I have seen some famous actors in my life. But we have had enough of it for to-day. This evening I will take you to eat soup with me. To-morrow it will be daylight, and we shall see."

VII.

IT WAS NOT FAR from ten o'clock when M. Mechinet, whom I was still accompanying, rang at the door of his apartment.

"I never carry any latch-key," he told me. "In our blessed business you can never know what may happen. There are many rascals who have a grudge against me, and even if I am not always careful for myself, I must be so for my wife."

My worthy neighbor's explanation was superfluous. I had understood. I even observed that he rang in a peculiar way, which must have been an agreed signal between his wife and himself.

It was the amiable Madame Mechinet who opened the door.

With a quick movement, as graceful as a kitten, she threw herself on her husband's neck, exclaiming:

"Here you are at last! I do not know why, but I was almost worried."

But she stopped suddenly; she had just noticed me. Her joyous expression darkened, and she drew back. Addressing both me and her husband:

"What!" she continued, "you come from the café at this hour? That is not common sense!"

M. Mechinet's lips wore the indulgent smile of the man who is sure of being loved, who knows how to appease by a word the quarrel picked with him.

"Do not scold us, Caroline," he answered; by this "us" associating me with his case. "We do not come from the café, and neither have we lost our time. They sent for me for an affair; for a murder committed at Batignolles."

With a suspicious look the young woman examined us—first her husband and then me; when she had persuaded herself that she was not being deceived, she said only:

"Ah!"

But it would take a whole page to give an inventory of all that was contained in that brief exclamation.

It was addressed to M. Mechinet, and clearly signified:

"What? you confided in this young man! You have revealed to him your position; you have initiated him into our secrets?"

Thus I interpreted that eloquent "Ah!" My worthy neighbor, too, must have interpreted it as I did, for he answered:

"Well, yes. Where is the wrong of it? I may have to dread the vengeance of wretches whom I give up to justice, but what have I to fear from honest people? Do you imagine perhaps that I hide myself; that I am ashamed of my trade?"

"You misunderstood me, my friend," objected the young woman.

M. Mechinet did not even hear her.

He had just mounted—I learned this detail later—on a favorite hobby that always carried the day.

"Upon my word," he continued, "you have some peculiar ideas, madame, my wife. What! I one of the sentinels of civilization! I, who assure society's safety at the price of my rest and at the risk of my life, and should I blush for it? That would be far too amusing. You will tell me that against us of the police there exist a number of absurd prejudices left behind by the past. What do I care? Yes, I know that there are some sensitive gentlemen who look down on us. But sacrebleu! How I should like to see their faces if tomorrow my colleagues and I should go on a strike, leaving the streets free to the army of rascals whom we hold in check."

Accustomed without doubt to explosions of this kind, Madame Mechinet did not say a word; she was right in doing so, for my good neighbor, meeting with no contradiction, calmed himself as if by magic.

"But enough of this," he said to his wife. "There is now a matter of far greater importance. We have not had any dinner yet; we are dying of hunger; have you anything to give us for supper?"

What happened that night must have happened too often for Madame Mechinet to be caught unprepared.

"In five minutes you gentlemen will be served," she answered with the most amiable smile.

In fact, a moment afterward we sat down at table before a fine cut of cold beef, served by Madame Mechinet, who did not stop filling our glasses with excellent Macon wine.

And while my worthy neighbor was conscientiously plying his fork I, looking at that peaceable home, which was his, that pretty, attentive little wife, which was his, kept asking myself whether I really saw before me one of those "savage" police agents who have been the heroes of so many absurd stories.

However, hunger soon satisfied, M. Mechinet started to tell his wife about our expedition. And he did not tell her about it lightly, but with the most minute details. She had taken a seat beside him, and by the way she listened and looked understandingly, asking for explanations when she had not well understood, one could recognize in her a plain "Egeria," accustomed to be consulted, and having a deliberative vote.

When M. Mechinet had finished, she said to him:

"You have made a great mistake, an irreparable mistake."

"Where?"

"It is not to Police Headquarters you should have gone, abandoning Batignolles."

"But Monistrol?"

"Yes, you wanted to examine him. What advantage did you get from that?"

"It was of use to me, my dear friend."

"For nothing. It was to the Rue Vivienne that you should have hurried, to the wife. You would have surprised her in a natural agitation caused by her husband's arrest, and if she is his accomplice, as we must suppose, with a little skill you would have made her confess."

At these words I jumped from my chair.

"What! madame," I exclaimed, "do you believe Monistrol guilty?"

After a moment's hesitation, she answered:

"Yes."

Then she added very vivaciously:

"But I am sure, do you hear, absolutely sure, that the murder was conceived by the woman. Of twenty crimes committed by men, fifteen have been conceived, planned and inspired by woman. Ask Mechinet. The concierge's deposition ought to have enlightened you. Who is that Madame Monistrol? They told you a remarkably beautiful person, coquettish, ambitious, affected with covetousness, and who was leading her husband by the end of his nose. Now what was her position? Wretched, tight, precarious. She suffered from it, and the proof of it is that she asked her uncle to loan her husband a hundred thousand francs. He refused them to her, thus shattering her hopes. Do you not think she had a deadly grudge against him? And when she kept seeing him in good health and sturdy as an oak, she must have said to herself fatally: 'He will live a hundred years; by the time he leaves us his inheritance we won't have any teeth left to munch it, and who knows even whether *he* will not bury *us!*' Is it so very far from this point to the conception of a crime? And the resolution once taken in her mind, she must have prepared her husband a long time before, she must have accustomed him to the thought of murder, she must have put, so to say, the knife in his hand. And he, one day, threatened with bankruptcy, crazed by his wife's lamentations, delivered the blow."

"All that is logical," approved M. Mechinet, "very logical, without a doubt, but what becomes of the circumstances brought to light by us?"

"Then, madame," I said, "you believe Monistrol stupid enough to denounce himself by writing down his name?"

She slightly shrugged her shoulders and answered:

"Is that stupidity? As for me, I maintain that it is not. Is not that point your strongest argument in favor of his innocence?"

This reasoning was so specious that for a moment I remained perplexed. Then recovering, I said, insisting:

"But he confesses his guilt, madame?"

"An excellent method of his for getting the authorities to prove him innocent."

"Oh!"

"You yourself are proof of its efficacy, dear M. Godeuil."

"Eh! madame, the unfortunate does not even know how his uncle was killed!"

"I beg your pardon; he *seemed* not to know it, which is not the same thing."

The discussion was becoming animated, and would have lasted much longer, had not M. Mechinet put an end to it.

"Come, come," he simply said to his wife, "you are too romantic this evening."

And addressing me, he continued:

"As for you, I shall come and get you to-morrow, and we shall go together to call on Madame Monistrol. And now, as I am dying for sleep, good night."

He may have slept. As for me, I could not close my eyes.

A secret voice within me seemed to say that Monistrol was innocent.

My imagination painted with painful liveliness the tortures of that unfortunate man, alone in his prison cell.

But why had he confessed?

VIII.

WHAT I THEN LACKED—I have had occasion to realize it hundreds of times since—was experience, business practise, and chiefly an exact knowledge of the means of action and of police investigation.

I felt vaguely that this particular investigation had been conducted wrongly, or rather superficially, but I would have been embarrassed to say why, and especially to say what should have been done.

None the less I was passionately interested in Monistrol.

It seemed to me that his cause was also mine, and it was only natural—my young vanity was at stake. Was it not one of my own remarks that had raised the first doubts as to the guilt of this unfortunate man?

I owed it to myself, I said, to prove his innocence.

Unfortunately the discussions of the evening troubled me to such an extent that I did not know precisely on which fact to build up my system.

And, as always happens when the mind is for too long a time applied to the solution of a problem, my thoughts became tangled, like a skein in the hands of a child; I could no longer see clearly; it was chaos.

Buried in my armchair, I was torturing my brain, when, at about nine o'clock in the morning, M. Mechinet, faithful to his promise of the evening before, came for me.

"Come, let us go," he said, shaking me suddenly, for I had not heard him enter. "Let us start!"

"I am with you," I said, getting up.

We descended hurriedly, and I noticed then that my worthy neighbor was more carefully dressed than usual.

He had succeeded in giving himself that easy and well-to-do appearance which more than anything else impresses the Parisian shopkeeper.

His cheerfulness was that of a man sure of himself, marching toward certain victory.

We were soon in the street, and while walking he asked me:

"Well, what do you think of my wife? I pass for a clever man at Police Headquarters, and yet I consult her—even Molière consulted his maid—and often I find it to my advantage. She has one weakness: for her, unreasonable crimes do not exist, and her imagination endows all scoundrels with diabolical plots. But as I have exactly the opposite fault, as I perhaps am a little too much matter-of-fact, it rarely happens that from our consultation the truth does not result somehow."

"What!" I exclaimed, "you think to have solved the mystery of the Monistrol case!"

He stopped short, drew out his snuff-box, inhaled three or four of his imaginary pinches, and in a tone of quiet vanity, answered:

"I have at least the means of solving it."

In the mean time we reached the upper end of the Rue Vivienne, not far from Monistrol's business place.

"Now look out," said M. Mechinet to me. "Follow me, and whatever happens do not be surprised."

He did well to warn me. Without the warning I would have been surprised at seeing him suddenly enter the store of an umbrella dealer.

Stiff and grave, like an Englishman, he made them show him everything there was in the shop, found nothing suitable, and finally inquired whether it was not possible for them to manufacture for him an umbrella according to a model which he would furnish.

They answered that it would be the easiest thing in the world, and he left, saying he would return the day following.

And most assuredly the half hour he spent in this store was not wasted.

While examining the objects submitted to him, he had artfully drawn from the dealers all they knew about the Monistrol couple.

Upon the whole, it was not a difficult task, as the affair of the "little old man of Batignolles" and the arrest of the imitation jeweler had deeply stirred the district and were the subject of all conversation.

"There, you see," he said to me, when we were outside, "how exact information is obtained. As soon as the people know with whom they are dealing, they pose, make long phrases, and then good-by to strict truth."

This comedy was repeated by Mr. Mechinet in seven or eight stores of the neighborhood.

In one of them, where the proprietors were disagreeable and not much inclined to talk, he even made a purchase amounting to twenty francs.

But after two hours of such practise, which amused me very much, we had gauged public opinion. We knew exactly what was thought of M. and Mme. Monistrol in the neighborhood, where they had lived since their marriage, that is, for the past four years.

As regards the husband, there was but one opinion—he was the most gentle and best of men, obliging, honest, intelligent, and hard-working. If he had not made a success in his business it was because luck does not always favor those who most deserve it. He did wrong in taking a shop doomed to bankruptcy, for, in the past fifteen years, four merchants had failed there.

Everybody knew and said that he adored his wife, but this great love had not exceeded the proper limits, and therefore no ridicule resulted for him.

Nobody could believe in his guilt.

His arrest, they said, must be a mistake made by the police.

As to Madame Monistrol, opinion was divided.

Some thought she was too stylish for her means; others claimed that a stylish dress was one of the requirements, one of the necessities, of a business dealing in luxuries.

In general, they were convinced that she loved her husband very much. For instance, they were unanimous in praising her modesty, the more meritorious, because she was remarkably beautiful, and because she was besieged by many admirers. But never had she given any occasion to be talked about, never had her immaculate reputation been glanced at by the lightest suspicion.

I noticed that this especially bewildered M. Mechinet.

"It is surprising," he said to me, "not one scandal, not one slander, not one calumny. Oh! this is not what Caroline thought. According to her, we were to find one of those lady shopkeepers, who occupy the principal place in the office, who display their beauty much more than their merchandise, and who banish to the back shop their husband—a blind idiot, or an indecent obliging scoundrel. But not at all."

I did not answer; I was not less disconcerted than my neighbor.

We were now far from the evidence the concierge of the Rue de Lecluse had given; so greatly varies the point of view according to the location. What at Batignolles is considered to be a blamable coquetry, is in the Rue Vivienne nothing more than an unreasonable requirement of position.

But we had already employed too much time for our investigations to stop and exchange impressions and to discuss our conjectures.

"Now," said M. Mechinet, "before entering the place, let us study its approaches."

And trained in carrying out discreet investigations in the midst of Paris bustle, he motioned to me to follow him under a carriage entrance, exactly opposite Monistrol's store.

It was a modest shop, almost poor, compared with those around it. The front needed badly a painter's brush. Above, in letters which were formerly gilt, now smoky and blackened, Monistrol's name was displayed. On the plate-glass windows could be read: "Gold and Imitation."

Alas! it was principally imitation that was glistening in the show window. On the rods were hanging many plated chains, sets of jet jewelry, diadems studded with rhinestones, then imitation coral necklaces and brooches and rings; and cuff buttons set with imitation stones in all colors.

All in all, a poor display, it could never tempt gimlet thieves.

"Let us enter," I said to M. Mechinet.

He was less impatient than I, or knew better how to keep back his impatience, for he stopped me by the arm, saying:

"One moment. I should like at least to catch a glimpse of Madame Monistrol."

In vain did we continue to stand for more than twenty minutes on our observation post; the shop remained empty, Madame Monistrol did not appear.

"Come, Monsieur Godeuil, let us venture," exclaimed my worthy neighbor at last, "we have been standing in one place long enough."

IX.

IN ORDER TO REACH Monistrol's store we had only to cross the street.

At the noise of the door opening, a little servant girl, from fifteen to sixteen years old, dirty and ill combed, came out of the back shop.

"What can I serve the gentlemen with?" she asked.

"Madame Monistrol?"

"She is there, gentlemen; I am going to notify her, because you see—"

M. Mechinet did not give her time to finish. With a movement, rather brutal, I must confess, he pushed her out of the way and entered the back shop saying:

"All right, since she is there, I am going to speak to her."

As for me, I walked on the heels of my worthy neighbor, convinced that we would not leave without knowing the solution of the riddle.

That back shop was a miserable room, serving at the same time as parlor, dining-room, and bedroom. Disorder reigned supreme; moreover there was that incoherence we notice in the house of the poor who endeavor to appear rich.

In the back there was a bed with blue damask curtains and with pillows adorned with lace; in front of the mantelpiece stood a table all covered with the remains of a more than modest breakfast.

In a large armchair was seated, or rather lying, a very blond young woman, who was holding in her hand a sheet of stamped paper.

It was Madame Monistrol.

Surely in telling us of her beauty, all the neighbors had come far below the reality. I was dazzled.

Only one circumstance displeased me. She was in full mourning, and wore a crape dress, slightly decolleté, which fitted her marvelously.

This showed too much presence of mind for so great a sorrow. Her attire seemed to me to be the contrivance of an actress dressing herself for the role she is to play.

As we entered, she stood up, like a frightened doe, and with a voice which seemed to be broken by tears, she asked:

"What do you want, gentlemen?"

M. Mechinet had also observed what I had noticed.

"Madame," he answered roughly, "I was sent by the Court; I am a police agent."

Hearing this, she fell back into her armchair with a moan that would have touched a tiger.

Then, all at once, seized by some kind of enthusiasm, with sparkling eyes and trembling lips, she exclaimed:

"So you have come to arrest me. God bless you. See! I am ready, take me. Thus I shall rejoin that honest man, arrested by you last evening. Whatever be his fate, I want to share it. He is as innocent as I am. No matter! If he is to be the victim of an error of human justice, it shall be for me a last joy to die with him."

She was interrupted by a low growl coming from one of the corners of the back shop.

I looked, and saw a black dog, with bristling hair and bloodshot eyes, showing his teeth, and ready to jump on us.

"Be quiet, Pluton!" called Madame Monistrol; "go and lie down; these gentlemen do not want to hurt me."

Slowly and without ceasing to glare at us furiously, the dog took refuge under the bed.

"You are right to say that we do not want to hurt you, madame," continued M. Mechinet, "we did not come to arrest you."

If she heard, she did not show it.

"This morning already," she said, "I received this paper here, commanding me to appear later in the day, at three o'clock, at the court-house, in the office of the investigating judge. What do they want of me? my God! What do they want of me?"

"To obtain explanations which will prove, I hope, your husband's innocence. So, madame, do not consider me an enemy. What I want is to get at the truth."

He produced his snuff-box, hastily poked his fingers therein, and in a solemn tone, which I did not recognize in him, he resumed:

"It is to tell you, madame, of what importance will be your answers to the questions which I shall have the honor of asking you. Will it be convenient for you to answer me frankly?"

For a long time she rested her large blue eyes, drowned in tears, on my worthy neighbor, and in a tone of painful resignation she said:

"Question me, monsieur."

For the third time I repeat it, I was absolutely without experience; I was troubled over the manner in which M. Mechinet had begun this examination.

It seemed to me that he betrayed his perplexity, and that, instead of pursuing an aim established in advance, he was delivering his blows at random.

Ah! if I were allowed to act! Ah! if I had dared.

He, impenetrable, had seated himself opposite Madame Monistrol.

"You must know, madame," he began, "that it was the night before last, at eleven o'clock, that M. Pigoreau, called Antenor, your husband's uncle, was murdered."

"Alas!"

"Where was M. Monistrol at that hour?"

"My God! that is fatality."

M. Mechinet did not wince.

"I am asking you, madame," he insisted, "where your husband spent the evening of the day before yesterday?"

The young woman needed time to answer, because she sobbed so that it seemed to choke her. Finally mastering herself, she moaned:

"The day before yesterday my husband spent the evening out of the house."

"Do you know where he was?"

"Oh! as to that, yes. One of our workmen, who lives in Montrouge, had to deliver for us a set of false pearls, and did not deliver it. We were taking the risk of being obliged to keep the order on our account, which would have been a disaster, as we are not rich. That is why, at dinner, my husband told me: 'I am going to see that fellow.' And, in fact, toward nine o'clock, he went out, and I even went with him as far as the omnibus, where he got in in my presence, Rue Richelieu."

I was breathing more easily. This, perhaps, was an alibi after all.

M. Mechinet had the same thought, and, more gently, he resumed:

"If it is so, your workman will be able to affirm that he saw M. Monistrol at his house at eleven o'clock."

"Alas! no."

"How? Why?"

"Because he had gone out. My husband did not see him."

"That is indeed fatal. But it may be that the concierge noticed M. Monistrol."

"Our workman lives in a house where there is no concierge."

That may have been the truth; it was certainly a terrible charge against the unfortunate prisoner.

"And at what time did your husband return?" continued M. Mechinet.

"A little after midnight."

"Did you not find that he was absent a very long time?"

"Oh! yes. And I even reproved him for it. He told me as an excuse that he had taken the longest way, that he had sauntered on the road, and that he had stopped in a café to drink a glass of beer."

"How did he look when he came home?"

"It seemed to me that he was vexed; but that was natural."

"What clothes did he wear?"

"The same he had on when he was arrested."

"You did not observe in him anything out of the ordinary?"

"Nothing."

Standing a little behind M. Mechinet, I could, at my leisure, observe Madame Monistrol's face and catch the most fleeting signs of her emotion.

She seemed overwhelmed by an immense grief, large tears rolled down her pale cheeks; nevertheless, it seemed to me at times that I could discover in the depth of her large blue eyes something like a flash of joy.

Is it possible that she is guilty? And as this thought, which had already come to me before, presented itself more obstinately, I quickly stepped forward, and in a rough tone asked her:

"But you, madame, where were you on that fatal evening at the time your husband went uselessly to Montrouge, to look for his workman?"

She cast on me a long look, full of stupor, and softly answered:

"I was here, monsieur; witnesses will confirm it to you."

"Witnesses!"

"Yes, monsieur. It was so hot that evening that I had a longing for ice-cream, but it vexed me to eat it alone. So I sent my maid to invite my neighbors, Madame Dorstrich, the bootmaker's wife, whose store is next to ours, and Madame Rivaille, the glove manufacturer, opposite us. These two ladies accepted my invitation and remained here until half-past eleven. Ask them, they will tell you. In the midst of such cruel trials that I am suffering, this accidental circumstance is a blessing from God."

Was it really an accidental circumstance?

That is what we were asking ourselves, M. Mechinet and I, with glances more rapid than a flash.

When chance is so intelligent as that, when it serves a cause so directly, it is very hard not to suspect that it had been somewhat prepared and led on.

But the moment was badly chosen for this discovery of our bottom thoughts.

"You have never been suspected, you, madame," imprudently stated M. Mechinet. "The worst that may be supposed is that your husband perhaps told you something of the crime before he committed it."

"Monsieur—if you knew us."

"Wait. Your business is not going very well, we were told; you were embarrassed."

"Momentarily, yes; in fact—"

"Your husband must have been unhappy and worried about this precarious condition. He must have suffered especially for you, whom he adores; for you who are so young and beautiful; for you, more than for himself, he must have ardently desired the enjoyments of luxury and the satisfactions of self-esteem, procured by wealth."

"Monsieur, I repeat it, my husband is innocent."

With an air of reflection, M. Mechinet seemed to fill his nose with tobacco; then all at once he said:

"Then, by thunder! how do you explain his confessions? An innocent man does not declare himself to be guilty at the mere mentioning of the crime of which he is suspected; that is rare, madame; that is prodigious!"

A fugitive blush appeared on the cheeks of the young woman. Up to then her look had been straight and clear; now for the first time it became troubled and unsteady.

"I suppose," she answered in an indistinct voice and with increased tears, "I believe that my husband, seized by fright and stupor at finding himself accused of so great a crime, lost his head."

M. Mechinet shook his head.

"If absolutely necessary," he said, "a passing delirium might be admitted; but this morning, after a whole long night of reflection, M. Monistrol persists in his first confessions."

Was this true? Was my worthy neighbor talking at random, or else had he before coming to get me been at the prison to get news?

However it was, the young woman seemed almost to faint; hiding her head between her hands, she murmured:

"Lord God! My poor husband has become insane."

Convinced now that I was assisting at a comedy, and that the great despair of this young woman was nothing but falsehood, I was asking myself whether for certain reasons which were escaping me she had not shaped the terrible determination taken by her husband; and whether, he being innocent, she did not know the real guilty one.

But M. Mechinet did not have the air of a man looking so far ahead.

After having given the young woman a few words of consolation too common to compromise him in any way, he gave her to understand that she would forestall many prejudices by allowing a minute and strict search through her domicile.

This opening she seized with an eagerness which was not feigned.

"Search, gentlemen!" she told us; "examine, search everywhere. It is a service which you will render me. And it will not take long. We have in our name nothing but the back shop where we are, our maid's room on the sixth floor, and a little cellar. Here are the keys for everything."

To my great surprise, M. Mechinet accepted; he seemed to be starting on one of the most exact and painstaking investigations.

What was his object? It was not possible that he did not have in view some secret aim, as his researches evidently had to end in nothing.

As soon as he had apparently finished he said:

"There remains the cellar to be explored."

"I am going to take you down, monsieur," said Madame Monistrol.

And immediately taking a burning candle, she made us cross a yard into which a door led from the back shop, and took us across a very slippery stairway to a door which she opened, saying:

"Here it is—enter, gentlemen."

I began to understand.

My worthy neighbor examined the cellar with a ready and trained look. It was miserably kept, and more miserably fitted out. In one corner was standing a small barrel of beer, and immediately opposite, fastened on blocks, was a barrel of wine, with a wooden tap to draw it. On the right side, on iron rods, were lined up about fifty filled bottles. These bottles M. Mechinet did not lose sight of, and found occasion to move them one by one.

And what I saw he noticed: not one of them was sealed with green wax.

Thus the cork picked up by me, and which served to protect the point of the murderer's weapon, did not come from the Monistrols' cellar.

"Decidedly," M. Mechinet said, affecting some disappointment, "I do not find anything; we can go up again."

We did so, but not in the same order in which we descended, for in returning I was the first.

Thus it was I who opened the door of the back shop. Immediately the dog of the Monistrol couple sprang at me, barking so furiously that I jumped back.

"The devil! Your dog is vicious," M. Mechinet said to the young woman.

She already called him off with a gesture of her hand.

"Certainly not, he is not vicious," she said, "but he is a good watchdog. We are jewelers, exposed more than others to thieves; we have trained him."

Involuntarily, as one always does after having been threatened by a dog, I called him by his name, which I knew:

"Pluton! Pluton!"

But instead of coming near me, he retreated growling, showing his sharp teeth.

"Oh, it is useless for you to call him," thoughtlessly said Madame Monistrol. "He will not obey you."

"Indeed! And why?"

"Ah! because he is faithful, as all of his breed; he knows only his master and me."

This sentence apparently did not mean anything. For me it was like a flash of light. And without reflecting I asked:

"Where then, madame, was that faithful dog the evening of the crime?"

The effect produced on her by this direct question was such that she almost dropped the candlestick she was still holding.

"I do not know," she stammered; "I do not remember."

"Perhaps he followed your husband."

"In fact, yes, it seems to me now I remember."

"He must then have been trained to follow carriages, since you told us that you went with your husband as far as the omnibus."

She remained silent, and I was going to continue when M. Mechinet interrupted me. Far from taking advantage of the young woman's troubled condition, he seemed to assume the task of reassuring her, and after having urged her to obey the summons of the investigating judge, he led me out.

Then when we were outside he said:

"Are you losing your head?"

The reproach hurt me.

"Is it losing one's head," I said, "to find the solution of the problem? Now I have it, that solution. Monistrol's dog shall guide us to the truth."

My hastiness made my worthy neighbor smile, and in a fatherly tone he said to me:

"You are right, and I have well understood you. Only if Madame Monistrol has penetrated into your suspicions, the dog before this evening will be dead or will have disappeared."

X.

I HAD COMMITTED AN enormous imprudence, it was true. Nevertheless, I had found the weak point; that point by which the most solid system of defense may be broken down.

I, voluntary recruit, had seen clearly where the old stager was losing himself, groping about. Any other would, perhaps, have been jealous and would have had a grudge against me. But not he.

He did not think of anything else but of profiting by my fortunate discovery; and, as he said, everything was easy enough now, since the investigation rested on a positive point of departure.

We entered a neighboring restaurant to deliberate while lunching.

The problem, which an hour before seemed unsolvable, now stood as follows:

It had been proved to us, as much as could be by evidence, that Monistrol was innocent. Why had he confessed to being guilty? We thought we could guess why, but that was not the question of the moment. We were equally certain that Madame Monistrol had not budged from her home the night of the murder. But everything tended to show that she was morally an accomplice to the crime; that she had known of it, even if she did not advise and prepare it, and that, on the other hand, she knew the murderer very well.

Who was he, that murderer?

A man whom Monistrol's dog obeyed as well as his master, since he had him follow him when he went to the Batignolles.

Therefore, it was an intimate friend of the Monistrol household. He must have hated the husband, however, since he had arranged everything with an infernal skill, so that the suspicion of the crime should fall on that unfortunate.

On the other hand, he must have been very dear to the woman, since, knowing him, she did not give him up, and without hesitation sacrificed to him her husband.

Well!

Oh! my God! The conclusion was all in a definite shape. The murderer could only be a miserable hypocrite, who had taken advantage of the husband's affection and confidence to take possession of the wife.

In short, Madame Monistrol, belieing her reputation, certainly had a lover, and that lover necessarily was the culprit.

All filled by this certitude, I was torturing my mind to think of some infallible stratagem which would lead us to this wretch.

"And this," I said to M. Mechinet, "is how I think we ought to operate. Madame Monistrol and the murderer must have agreed that after the crime they would not see each other for some time; this is the most elementary prudence. But you may believe that it will not be long before impatience will conquer the woman, and that she will want to see her accomplice. Now place near her an observer who will follow her everywhere, and before twice forty-eight hours have passed the affair will be settled."

Furiously fumbling after his empty snuff-box, M. Mechinet remained a moment without answering, mumbling between his teeth I know not what unintelligible words.

Then suddenly, leaning toward me, he said:

"That isn't it. You have the professional genius, that is certain, but it is practise that you lack. Fortunately, I am here. What! a phrase regarding the crime puts you on the trail, and you do not follow it."

"How is that?"

"That faithful dog must be made use of."

"I do not quite catch on."

"Then know how to wait. Madame Monistrol will go out at about two o'clock, in order to be at the court-house at three; the little maid will be alone in the shop. You will see. I only tell you that."

I insisted in vain; he did not want to say anything more, taking revenge for his defeat by this innocent spite. Willing or unwilling, I had to follow him to the nearest café, where he forced me to play dominoes.

Preoccupied as I was, I played badly, and he, without shame, was taking advantage of it to beat me, when the clock struck two.

"Up, men of the post," he said to me, letting go of his dice.

He paid, we went out, and a moment later we were again on duty under the carriage entrance from which we had before studied the front of the Monistrol store.

We had not been there ten minutes, when Madame Monistrol appeared in the door of her shop, dressed in black, with a long crape veil, like a widow.

"A pretty dress to go to an examination," mumbled M. Mechinet.

She gave a few instructions to her little maid, and soon left.

My companion patiently waited for five long minutes, and when he thought the young woman was already far away, he said to me:

"It is time."

And for the second time we entered the jewelry store.

The little maid was there alone, sitting in the office, for pastime nibbling some pieces of sugar stolen from her mistress.

As soon as we appeared she recognized us, and reddening and somewhat frightened, she stood up. But without giving her time to open her mouth, M. Mechinet asked:

"Where is Madame Monistrol?"

"Gone out, monsieur."

"You are deceiving me. She is there in the back shop."

"I swear to you, gentlemen, that she is not. Look in, please."

With the most disappointed looks, M. Mechinet was striking his forehead, repeating:

"How disagreeable. My God! how distressed that poor Madame Monistrol will be." And as the little maid was looking at him with her mouth wide open and with big, astonished eyes, he continued:

"But, in fact, you, my pretty girl, you can perhaps take the place of your mistress. I came back because I lost the address of the gentleman on whom she asked me to call."

"What gentleman?"

"You know. Monsieur—well, I have forgotten his name now. Monsieur—upon my word! you know, only him—that gentleman whom your devilish dog obeys so well."

"Oh! M. Victor?"

"That's just it. What is that gentleman doing?"

"He is a jeweler's workman; he is a great friend of monsieur; they were working together when monsieur was a jeweler's workman, before becoming proprietor, and that is why he can do anything he wants with Pluton."

"Then you can tell me where this M. Victor resides?"

"Certainly. He lives in the Rue du Roi-Doré, No. 23."

She seemed so happy, the poor girl, to be so well informed; but as for me, I suffered in hearing her so unwittingly denounce her mistress.

M. Mechinet, more hardened, did not have any such scruples. And even after we had obtained our information, he ended the scene with a sad joke.

As I opened the door for us to go out, he said to the young girl:

"Thanks to you. You have just rendered a great service to Madame Monistrol, and she will be very pleased."

XI.

As SOON AS I was on the sidewalk I had but one thought: and that was to shake out our legs and to run to the Rue du Roi-Doré and arrest this Victor, evidently the real culprit.

One word from M. Mechinet fell on my enthusiasm like a shower-bath.

"And the court," he said to me. "Without a warrant by the investigating judge I can not do anything. It is to the court-house that we must run."

"But we shall meet there Madame Monistrol, and if she sees us she will have her accomplice warned."

"Be it so," answered M. Mechinet, with a badly disguised bitterness. "Be it so, the culprit will escape and formality will have
been saved. However, I shall prevent that danger. Let us walk, let
us walk faster."

And, in fact, the hope of success gave him deer legs. Reaching
the court-house, he jumped, four steps at a time, up the steep stairway leading to the floor on which were the judges of investigation,
and, addressing the chief bailiff, he inquired whether the magistrate in charge of the case of the "little old man of Batignolles" was
in his room.

"He is there," answered the bailiff, "with a witness, a young lady
in black."

"It is she!" said my companion to me. Then to the bailiff: "You
know me," he continued. "Quick, give me something to write on,
a few words which you will take to the judge."

The bailiff went off with the note, dragging his boots along the
dusty floor, and was not long in returning with the announcement
that the judge was awaiting us in No. 9.

In order to see M. Mechinet, the magistrate had left Madame
Monistrol in his office, under his clerk's guard, and had borrowed
the room of one of his colleagues.

"What has happened?" he asked in a tone which enabled me to
measure the abyss separating a judge from a poor detective.

Briefly and clearly M. Mechinet described the steps taken by us,
their results and our hopes.

Must we say it? The magistrate did not at all seem to share our
convictions.

"But since Monistrol confesses," he repeated with an obstinacy
which was exasperating to me.

However, after many explanations, he said:

"At any rate, I am going to sign a warrant."

The valuable paper once in his possession, M. Mechinet escaped
so quickly that I nearly fell in precipitating myself after him down
the stairs. I do not know whether it took us a quarter of an hour to

reach the Rue du Roi-Doré. But once there: "Attention," said M. Mechinet to me.

And it was with the most composed air that he entered in the narrow passageway of the house bearing No. 23.

"M. Victor?" he asked of the concierge.

"On the fourth floor, the right-hand door in the hallway."

"Is he at home?"

"Yes."

M. Mechinet took a step toward the staircase, but seemed to change his mind, and said to the concierge:

"I must make a present of a good bottle of wine to that dear Victor. With which wine-merchant does he deal in this neighborhood?"

"With the one opposite."

We were there in a trice, and in the tone of a customer M. Mechinet ordered:

"One bottle, please, and of good wine—of that with the green seal."

Ah! upon my word! That thought would never have come to me at that time. And yet it was very simple.

When the bottle was brought, my companion exhibited the cork found at the home of M. Pigoreau, called Antenor, and we easily identified the wax.

To our moral certainty was now added a material certainty, and with a firm hand M. Mechinet knocked at Victor's door.

"Come in," cried a pleasant-sounding voice.

The key was in the door; we entered, and in a very neat room I perceived a man of about thirty, slender, pale, and blond, who was working in front of a bench.

Our presence did not seem to trouble him.

"What do you want?" he politely asked.

M. Mechinet advanced toward him, and, taking him by the arm, said:

"In the name of the law, I arrest you."

The man became livid, but did not lower his eyes.

"Are you making fun of me?" he said with an insolent air. "What have I done?"

M. Mechinet shrugged his shoulders.

"Do not act like a child," he answered; "your account is settled. You were seen coming out from old man Antenor's home, and in my pocket I have a cork which you made use of to prevent your dagger from losing its point."

It was like a blow of a fist in the neck of the wretch. Overwhelmed, he dropped on his chair, stammering:

"I am innocent."

"You will tell that to the judge," said M. Mechinet good-naturedly; "but I am afraid that he will not believe you. Your accomplice, the Monistrol woman, has confessed everything."

As if moved by a spring, Victor jumped up.

"That is impossible!" he exclaimed. "She did not know anything about it."

"Then you did the business all alone? Very well. There is at least that much confessed."

Then addressing me in a tone of a man knowing what he is talking about, M. Mechinet continued:

"Will you please look in the drawers, my dear Monsieur Godeuil; you will probably find there the dagger of this pretty fellow, and certainly also the love-letters and the picture of his sweetheart."

A flash of rage shone in the murderer's eyes, and he was gnashing his teeth, but M. Mechinet's broad shoulders and iron grip extinguished in him every desire for resistance.

I found in a drawer of the bureau all the articles my companion had mentioned. And twenty minutes later, Victor, "duly packed in," as the expression goes, in a cab, between M. Mechinet and myself, was driving toward Police Headquarters.

"What," I said to myself, astonished by the simplicity of the thing, "that is all there is to the arrest of a murderer; of a man destined for the scaffold!"

Later I had occasion to learn at my expense which of criminals is the most terrible.

This one, as soon as he found himself in the police cell, seeing that he was lost, gave up and told us all the details of his crime.

He knew for a long time, he said, the old man Pigoreau, and was known by him. His object in killing him was principally to cause the punishment of the crime to fall on Monistrol. That is why he dressed himself up like Monistrol and had Pluton follow him. The old man once murdered, he had had the terrible courage to dip in the blood a finger of the body, to trace these five letters, MONIS, which almost caused an innocent man to be lost.

"And that had been so nicely arranged," he said to us with cynic bragging. "If I had succeeded, I would have killed two birds with the same stone. I would have been rid of my friend Monistrol, whom I hate and of whom I am jealous, and I would have enriched the woman I love."

It was, in fact, simple and terrible.

"Unfortunately, my boy," M. Mechinet objected, "you lost your head at the last moment. Well, one is never perfect. It was the left hand of the body which you dipped in the blood."

With a jump, Victor stood up.

"What!" he exclaimed, "is that what betrayed me?"

"Exactly."

With a gesture of a misunderstood genius, the wretch raised his arm toward heaven.

"That is for being an artist," he exclaimed.

And looking us over with an air of pity, he added:

"Old man Pigoreau was left-handed!"

Thus it was due to a mistake made in the investigation that the culprit was discovered so promptly.

The day following Monistrol was released.

And when the investigating judge reproached him for his un-true confession, which had exposed the courts to a terrible error, he could not obtain any other answer than:

"I love my wife, and wanted to sacrifice myself for her. I thought she was guilty."

Was she guilty? I would have taken an oath on it. She was arrested, but was acquitted by the same judgment which sentenced Victor to forced labor for life.

M. and Mme. Monistrol to-day keep an ill-reputed wineshop on the Vincennes Road. Their uncle's inheritance has long ago disappeared; they live in terrible misery.

Arthur Conan Doyle

(1859–1930)

"It was very superficial, my dear Sacker, I assure you," said Sherrinford Holmes, as he and his companion, the physician and Sudan war veteran Ormond Sacker, sat before the cozy fire at 221B Upper Baker Street.

IT ALMOST TURNED OUT this way. Surviving pages from Arthur Conan Doyle's early notes for *A Study in Scarlet* indicate some of the names he considered for the characters. Eventually he not only changed Holmes's given name but altered even the country in which his assistant received a war wound and the street in which they lived together. With history's twenty-twenty hindsight, the memorable name *Sherlock* seems fated to be matched with *Holmes*. The sidekick, in contrast, needed a more mundane designation, to represent his role as admiring everyman. Therefore the novel included this title page note: "Being a reprint from the reminiscences of John H. Watson, M.D., late of the Army Medical Department."

In the same early notes, Conan Doyle was already thinking about Holmes's ancestors in the field. "Lecoq was a bungler," he scrawled in snippets of dialogue. "Dupin was better. Dupin was decidedly smart—his trick of following a train of thought was more sensational than clever but still he had superficial genius."

Eventually Holmes expresses these thoughts, in slightly different wording, to Watson, who dares to compare his new friend's feats of mental legerdemain to those of fictional forebears. In *The Dead Witness*, Holmes is represented by the opening chapters of the debut novel. One reason to reprint the early interactions between Holmes and Watson is to remind us how much Arthur Conan Doyle purloined, as he himself admitted, from Edgar Allan Poe. Compare Holmes with Dupin as he appears in "The Murders in the Rue Morgue" earlier in this volume.

Soon other authors were relating their protagonist to Holmes rather than Dupin. In 1894, immediately after Conan Doyle plunged Holmes and Moriarty over the Reichenbach Falls—because he was tired of detective stuff and wanted to move on to something that would make his name in literature—the *Strand* magazine launched a replacement. Arthur Morrison, author of *Tales of Mean Streets*, deliberately created the antithesis of Sherlock Holmes. Martin Hewitt is ordinary-looking, not hawk-nosed and eagle-eyed, and chubby, rather than whippet-skinny from Persian tobacco and cocaine. Some female detectives, such as Hugh Weir's Madelyn Mack, are presented as a kind of Holmes. Mack even consumes cola berries, her version of Holmes's 7 percent solution of cocaine, when the primary-colored excitement of crime-solving fades and she must face the pastel hues of everyday life.

Arthur Conan Doyle complained that his fictional detective's popularity kept the author from achieving better things. Whatever his other books' virtues, however, relatively few people today are reading *Micah Clarke* and *The White Company* instead of "The Adventure of the Speckled Band" and *The Hound of the Baskervilles*. Neither Conan Doyle's work as a missionary for spiritualism nor as a defender of the British Empire—not his work as physician, historical novelist, patriot, journalist, celebrity, or occasionally even sleuth asked to solve real-life crimes—can rival his creation of the immortal consulting detective invented during off hours waiting for patients to wander into his new medical office in Southsea, Portsmouth. He wrote the book in three weeks.

At first publishers did not applaud. "Verily," Conan Doyle sighed to his mother in 1885, "literature is a difficult oyster to open." A few months later he received one of the less promising publisher-to-author letters on record, from Ward, Lock & Co. in London: "We have read your story A Study in Scarlet, and are pleased with it. We could not publish this year, as the market is flooded at present with cheap fiction." They offered a flat £25 for full copyright if he was willing to wait until the following year. When he requested royalties, they turned him down. Poor and unknown, Conan Doyle nonetheless hesitated over this almost insulting offer. He worried more about the delay than anything else; he hoped this book might attract some attention. Finally he said yes. "I never at any time," he wrote in his autobiography, "received another penny for it."

The brief novel appeared in November 1887 as the cover story in a magazine called *Beeton's Christmas Annual.* (Today *Beeton's* is considered the most expensive magazine in collecting history. In 2007 one of the thirty-one known extant copies—few of which are in private hands—was auctioned at Sotheby's for $156,000.) In 1889, during a dinner at which Oscar Wilde was also a guest, Conan Doyle was commissioned to write a second Holmes novel, *The Sign of the Four.* In each, Holmes disappears during the middle half while a historical flashback unfolds. Although both books were popular, neither attracted as much attention as seemed to burst into flame when the first dozen stories began appearing monthly in *The Strand,* starting with "A Scandal in Bohemia" in 1891. Eventually there would be four novels and fifty-six stories.

Thanks in part to the TV series starring Jeremy Brett and the films starring Robert Downey Jr., there has been a resurgence of popular interest in the sage of Baker Street. But he has never faded in the crime fiction genre. During the second quarter of the twentieth century, Harold Ross, founder of *The New Yorker*, liked to instruct his writers to be specific in identifying allusions by reminding them that only two figures were known to everyone in Western culture at that time. One was real and the other fictional: Harry Houdini and Sherlock Holmes. Even Houdini has faded over time into a silent-movie montage, but Holmes remains as vivid as ever.

The Science of Deduction

Chapter 1

Mister Sherlock Holmes

IN THE YEAR 1878 I took my degree of Doctor of Medicine of the University of London, and proceeded to Netley to go through the course prescribed for surgeons in the army. Having completed my studies there, I was duly attached to the Fifth Northumberland Fusiliers as Assistant Surgeon. The regiment was stationed in India at the time, and before I could join it, the second Afghan war had broken out. On landing at Bombay, I learned that my corps had advanced through the passes, and was already deep in the enemy's country. I followed, however, with many other officers who were in the same situation as myself, and succeeded in reaching Candahar in safety, where I found my regiment, and at once entered upon my new duties.

The campaign brought honours and promotion to many, but for me it had nothing but misfortune and disaster. I was removed from my brigade and attached to the Berkshires, with whom I served at the fatal battle of Maiwand. There I was struck on the shoulder by a Jezail bullet, which shattered the bone and grazed the subclavian artery. I should have fallen into the hands of the murderous Ghazis had it not been for the devotion and courage shown by Murray, my orderly, who threw me across a pack-horse, and succeeded in bringing me safely to the British lines.

Worn with pain, and weak from the prolonged hardships which I had undergone, I was removed, with a great train of wounded sufferers, to the base hospital at Peshawar. Here I rallied, and had already improved so far as to be able to walk about the wards, and even to bask a little upon the verandah, when I was struck down by enteric fever, that curse of our Indian possessions. For months my life was despaired of, and when at last I came to myself and became convalescent, I was so weak and emaciated that a medical board determined that not a day should be lost in sending me back to England. I was dispatched, accordingly, in the troopship "Orontes," and landed a month later on Portsmouth jetty, with my health irretrievably ruined, but with permission from a paternal government to spend the next nine months in attempting to improve it.

I had neither kith nor kin in England, and was therefore as free as air—or as free as an income of eleven shillings and sixpence a day will permit a man to be. Under such circumstances, I naturally gravitated to London, that great cesspool into which all the loungers and idlers of the Empire are irresistibly drained. There I stayed for some time at a private hotel in the Strand, leading a comfortless, meaningless existence, and spending such money as I had, considerably more freely than I ought. So alarming did the state of my finances become, that I soon realized that I must either leave the metropolis and rusticate somewhere in the country, or that I must make a complete alteration in my style of living. Choosing the latter alternative, I began by making up my mind to leave the hotel, and to take up my quarters in some less pretentious and less expensive domicile.

On the very day that I had come to this conclusion, I was standing at the Criterion Bar, when some one tapped me on the shoulder, and turning round I recognized young Stamford, who had been a dresser under me at Barts. The sight of a friendly face in the great wilderness of London is a pleasant thing indeed to a lonely man. In old days Stamford had never been a particular crony of mine, but now I hailed him with enthusiasm, and he, in his turn, appeared to be delighted to see me. In the exuberance of my joy, I asked him to lunch with me at the Holborn, and we started off together in a hansom.

"Whatever have you been doing with yourself, Watson?" he asked in undisguised wonder, as we rattled through the crowded London streets. "You are as thin as a lath and as brown as a nut."

I gave him a short sketch of my adventures, and had hardly concluded it by the time that we reached our destination.

"Poor devil!" he said, commiseratingly, after he had listened to my misfortunes. "What are you up to now?"

"Looking for lodgings," I answered. "Trying to solve the problem as to whether it is possible to get comfortable rooms at a reasonable price."

"That's a strange thing," remarked my companion; "you are the second man to-day that has used that expression to me."

"And who was the first?" I asked.

"A fellow who is working at the chemical laboratory up at the hospital. He was bemoaning himself this morning because he could not get someone to go halves with him in some nice rooms which he had found, and which were too much for his purse."

"By Jove!" I cried, "if he really wants someone to share the rooms and the expense, I am the very man for him. I should prefer having a partner to being alone."

Young Stamford looked rather strangely at me over his wine-glass. "You don't know Sherlock Holmes yet," he said; "perhaps you would not care for him as a constant companion."

"Why, what is there against him?"

"Oh, I didn't say there was anything against him. He is a little queer in his ideas—an enthusiast in some branches of science. As far as I know he is a decent fellow enough."

"A medical student, I suppose?" said I.

"No—I have no idea what he intends to go in for. I believe he is well up in anatomy, and he is a first-class chemist; but, as far as I know, he has never taken out any systematic medical classes. His studies are very desultory and eccentric, but he has amassed a lot of out-of-the-way knowledge which would astonish his professors."

"Did you never ask him what he was going in for?" I asked.

"No; he is not a man that it is easy to draw out, though he can be communicative enough when the fancy seizes him."

"I should like to meet him," I said. "If I am to lodge with anyone, I should prefer a man of studious and quiet habits. I am not strong enough yet to stand much noise or excitement. I had enough of both in Afghanistan to last me for the remainder of my natural existence. How could I meet this friend of yours?"

"He is sure to be at the laboratory," returned my companion. "He either avoids the place for weeks, or else he works there from morning to night. If you like, we shall drive round together after luncheon."

"Certainly," I answered, and the conversation drifted away into other channels.

As we made our way to the hospital after leaving the Holborn, Stamford gave me a few more particulars about the gentleman whom I proposed to take as a fellow-lodger.

"You mustn't blame me if you don't get on with him," he said; "I know nothing more of him than I have learned from meeting him occasionally in the laboratory. You proposed this arrangement, so you must not hold me responsible."

"If we don't get on it will be easy to part company," I answered. "It seems to me, Stamford," I added, looking hard at my companion, "that you have some reason for washing your hands of the matter. Is this fellow's temper so formidable, or what is it? Don't be mealy-mouthed about it."

"It is not easy to express the inexpressible," he answered with a laugh. "Holmes is a little too scientific for my tastes—it approaches to cold-bloodedness. I could imagine his giving a friend a little pinch of the latest vegetable alkaloid, not out of malevolence, you understand, but simply out of a spirit of inquiry in order to have an accurate idea of the effects. To do him justice, I think that he would take it himself with the same readiness. He appears to have a passion for definite and exact knowledge."

"Very right too."

"Yes, but it may be pushed to excess. When it comes to beating the subjects in the dissecting-rooms with a stick, it is certainly taking rather a bizarre shape."

"Beating the subjects!"

"Yes, to verify how far bruises may be produced after death. I saw him at it with my own eyes."

"And yet you say he is not a medical student?"

"No. Heaven knows what the objects of his studies are. But here we are, and you must form your own impressions about him." As he spoke, we turned down a narrow lane and passed through a small side-door, which opened into a wing of the great hospital. It was familiar ground to me, and I needed no guiding as we ascended the bleak stone staircase and made our way down the long corridor with its vista of whitewashed wall and dun-coloured doors. Near the further end a low arched passage branched away from it and led to the chemical laboratory.

This was a lofty chamber, lined and littered with countless bottles. Broad, low tables were scattered about, which bristled with retorts, test-tubes, and little Bunsen lamps, with their blue flickering flames. There was only one student in the room, who was bending over a distant table absorbed in his work. At the sound of our steps he glanced round and sprang to his feet with a cry of pleasure. "I've found it! I've found it," he shouted to my companion, running towards us with a test-tube in his hand. "I have found a re-agent which is precipitated by hoemoglobin, and by nothing else." Had he discovered a gold mine, greater delight could not have shone upon his features.

"Dr. Watson, Mr. Sherlock Holmes," said Stamford, introducing us.

"How are you?" he said cordially, gripping my hand with a strength for which I should hardly have given him credit. "You have been in Afghanistan, I perceive."

"How on earth did you know that?" I asked in astonishment.

"Never mind," said he, chuckling to himself. "The question now is about hœmoglobin. No doubt you see the significance of this discovery of mine?"

"It is interesting, chemically, no doubt," I answered, "but practically—"

"Why, man, it is the most practical medico-legal discovery for years. Don't you see that it gives us an infallible test for blood stains. Come over here now!" He seized me by the coat-sleeve in his eagerness, and drew me over to the table at which he had been working. "Let us have some fresh blood," he said, digging a long bodkin into his finger, and drawing off the resulting drop of blood in a chemical pipette. "Now, I add this small quantity of blood to a litre of water. You perceive that the resulting mixture has the appearance of pure water. The proportion of blood cannot be more than one in a million. I have no doubt, however, that we shall be able to obtain the characteristic reaction." As he spoke, he threw into the vessel a few white crystals, and then added some drops of a transparent fluid. In an instant the contents assumed a dull mahogany colour, and a brownish dust was precipitated to the bottom of the glass jar.

"Ha! ha!" he cried, clapping his hands, and looking as delighted as a child with a new toy. "What do you think of that?"

"It seems to be a very delicate test," I remarked.

"Beautiful! beautiful! The old Guiacum test was very clumsy and uncertain. So is the microscopic examination for blood corpuscles. The latter is valueless if the stains are a few hours old. Now, this appears to act as well whether the blood is old or new.

Had this test been invented, there are hundreds of men now walking the earth who would long ago have paid the penalty of their crimes."

"Indeed!" I murmured.

"Criminal cases are continually hinging upon that one point. A man is suspected of a crime months perhaps after it has been committed. His linen or clothes are examined, and brownish stains discovered upon them. Are they blood stains, or mud stains, or rust stains, or fruit stains, or what are they? That is a question which has puzzled many an expert, and why? Because there was no reliable test. Now we have the Sherlock Holmes' test, and there will no longer be any difficulty."

His eyes fairly glittered as he spoke, and he put his hand over his heart and bowed as if to some applauding crowd conjured up by his imagination.

"You are to be congratulated," I remarked, considerably surprised at his enthusiasm.

"There was the case of Von Bischoff at Frankfort last year. He would certainly have been hung had this test been in existence. Then there was Mason of Bradford, and the notorious Muller, and Lefevre of Montpellier, and Samson of New Orleans. I could name a score of cases in which it would have been decisive."

"You seem to be a walking calendar of crime," said Stamford with a laugh. "You might start a paper on those lines. Call it the 'Police News of the Past.'"

"Very interesting reading it might be made, too," remarked Sherlock Holmes, sticking a small piece of plaster over the prick on his finger. "I have to be careful," he continued, turning to me with a smile, "for I dabble with poisons a good deal." He held out his hand as he spoke, and I noticed that it was all mottled over with similar pieces of plaster, and discoloured with strong acids.

"We came here on business," said Stamford, sitting down on a high three-legged stool, and pushing another one in my direction with his foot. "My friend here wants to take diggings, and as you were complaining that you could get no one to go halves with you, I thought that I had better bring you together."

Sherlock Holmes seemed delighted at the idea of sharing his rooms with me. "I have my eye on a suite in Baker Street," he said, "which would suit us down to the ground. You don't mind the smell of strong tobacco, I hope?"

"I always smoke 'ship's' myself," I answered.

"That's good enough. I generally have chemicals about, and occasionally do experiments. Would that annoy you?"

"By no means."

"Let me see—what are my other shortcomings. I get in the dumps at times, and don't open my mouth for days on end. You must not think I am sulky when I do that. Just let me alone, and I'll soon be right. What have you to confess now? It's just as well for two fellows to know the worst of one another before they begin to live together."

I laughed at this cross-examination. "I keep a bull pup," I said, "and I object to rows because my nerves are shaken, and I get up at all sorts of ungodly hours, and I am extremely lazy. I have another set of vices when I'm well, but those are the principal ones at present."

"Do you include violin-playing in your category of rows?" he asked, anxiously.

"It depends on the player," I answered. "A well-played violin is a treat for the gods—a badly-played one—"

"Oh, that's all right," he cried, with a merry laugh. "I think we may consider the thing as settled—that is, if the rooms are agreeable to you."

"When shall we see them?"

"Call for me here at noon to-morrow, and we'll go together and settle everything," he answered.

"All right—noon exactly," said I, shaking his hand.

We left him working among his chemicals, and we walked together towards my hotel.

"By the way," I asked suddenly, stopping and turning upon Stamford, "how the deuce did he know that I had come from Afghanistan?"

My companion smiled an enigmatical smile. "That's just his little peculiarity," he said. "A good many people have wanted to know how he finds things out."

"Oh! a mystery is it?" I cried, rubbing my hands. "This is very piquant. I am much obliged to you for bringing us together. 'The proper study of mankind is man,' you know."

"You must study him, then," Stamford said, as he bade me good-bye. "You'll find him a knotty problem, though. I'll wager he learns more about you than you about him. Good-bye."

"Good-bye," I answered, and strolled on to my hotel, considerably interested in my new acquaintance.

Chapter 2

The Science of Deduction

We met next day as he had arranged, and inspected the rooms at No. 221B, Baker Street, of which he had spoken at our meeting. They consisted of a couple of comfortable bed-rooms and a single large airy sitting-room, cheerfully furnished, and illuminated by two broad windows. So desirable in every way were the apartments, and so moderate did the terms seem when divided between us, that the bargain was concluded upon the spot, and we at once entered into possession. That very evening I moved my things round from the hotel, and on the following morning Sherlock Holmes followed me with several boxes and portmanteaus. For a day or two we were busily employed in unpacking and laying out our property to the best advantage. That done, we gradually began to settle down and to accommodate ourselves to our new surroundings.

Holmes was certainly not a difficult man to live with. He was quiet in his ways, and his habits were regular. It was rare for him to be up after ten at night, and he had invariably breakfasted and gone out before I rose in the morning. Sometimes he spent his day at the chemical laboratory, sometimes in the dissecting-rooms, and occasionally in long walks, which appeared to take him into the lowest portions of the City. Nothing could exceed his energy when the working fit was upon him; but now and again a reaction would seize him, and for days on end he would lie upon the sofa in the sitting-room, hardly uttering a word or moving a muscle from morning to night. On these occasions I have noticed such a dreamy, vacant expression in his eyes, that I might have suspected him of being addicted to the use of some narcotic, had not the temperance and cleanliness of his whole life forbidden such a notion.

As the weeks went by, my interest in him and my curiosity as to his aims in life, gradually deepened and increased. His very person and appearance were such as to strike the attention of the most casual observer. In height he was rather over six feet, and so excessively lean that he seemed to be considerably taller. His eyes were sharp and piercing, save during those intervals of torpor to which I have alluded; and his thin, hawk-like nose gave his whole expression an air of alertness and decision. His chin, too, had the prominence and squareness which mark the man of determination. His hands were invariably blotted with ink and stained with chemicals, yet he was possessed of extraordinary delicacy of touch, as I frequently had occasion to observe when I watched him manipulating his fragile philosophical instruments.

The reader may set me down as a hopeless busybody, when I confess how much this man stimulated my curiosity, and how often I endeavoured to break through the reticence which he showed on all that concerned himself. Before pronouncing judgment, however, be it remembered, how objectless was my life, and how little there was to engage my attention. My health forbade me from venturing out unless the weather was exceptionally genial, and I had no friends who would call upon me and break the monotony of my daily existence. Under these circumstances, I eagerly hailed the little mystery which hung around my companion, and spent much of my time in endeavouring to unravel it.

He was not studying medicine. He had himself, in reply to a question, confirmed Stamford's opinion upon that point. Neither did he appear to have pursued any course of reading which might fit him for a degree in science or any other recognized portal which would give him an entrance into the learned world. Yet his zeal for certain studies was remarkable, and within eccentric limits his knowledge was so extraordinarily ample and minute that his observations have fairly astounded me. Surely no man would work so hard or attain such precise information unless he had some definite end in view. Desultory readers are seldom remarkable for the exactness of their learning. No man burdens his mind with small matters unless he has some very good reason for doing so.

His ignorance was as remarkable as his knowledge. Of contemporary literature, philosophy and politics he appeared to know next to nothing. Upon my quoting Thomas Carlyle, he inquired in the naivest way who he might be and what he had done. My surprise reached a climax, however, when I found incidentally that he was ignorant of the Copernican Theory and of the composition of the Solar System. That any civilized human being in this nineteenth century should not be aware that the earth travelled round the sun appeared to be to me such an extraordinary fact that I could hardly realize it.

"You appear to be astonished," he said, smiling at my expression of surprise. "Now that I do know it I shall do my best to forget it."

"To forget it!"

"You see," he explained, "I consider that a man's brain originally is like a little empty attic, and you have to stock it with such furniture as you choose. A fool takes in all the lumber of every sort that he comes across, so that the knowledge which might be useful to him gets crowded out, or at best is jumbled up with a lot of other things so that he has a difficulty in laying his hands upon it.

Now the skilful workman is very careful indeed as to what he takes into his brain-attic. He will have nothing but the tools which may help him in doing his work, but of these he has a large assortment, and all in the most perfect order. It is a mistake to think that that little room has elastic walls and can distend to any extent. Depend upon it there comes a time when for every addition of knowledge you forget something that you knew before. It is of the highest importance, therefore, not to have useless facts elbowing out the useful ones."

"But the Solar System!" I protested.

"What the deuce is it to me?" he interrupted impatiently; "you say that we go round the sun. If we went round the moon it would not make a pennyworth of difference to me or to my work."

I was on the point of asking him what that work might be, but something in his manner showed me that the question would be an unwelcome one. I pondered over our short conversation, however, and endeavoured to draw my deductions from it. He said that he would acquire no knowledge which did not bear upon his object. Therefore all the knowledge which he possessed was such as would be useful to him. I enumerated in my own mind all the various points upon which he had shown me that he was exceptionally well-informed. I even took a pencil and jotted them down. I could not help smiling at the document when I had completed it. It ran in this way—

SHERLOCK HOLMES—his limits.

1. Knowledge of Literature.—Nil. 2. Philosophy.—Nil. 3. Astronomy.—Nil. 4. Politics.—Feeble. 5. Botany.—Variable. Well up in belladonna, opium, and poisons generally. Knows nothing of practical gardening. 6. Geology.—Practical, but limited. Tells at a glance different soils from each other. After walks has shown me splashes upon his trousers, and told me by their colour and consistence in what part of London he had received them. 7. Chemistry.—Profound.

8. Anatomy.—Accurate, but unsystematic. 9. Sensational Literature.—
Immense. He appears to know every detail of every horror perpetrated in the century. 10. Plays the violin well. 11. Is an expert
singlestick player, boxer, and swordsman. 12. Has a good practical
knowledge of British law.

WHEN I HAD GOT so far in my list I threw it into the fire in despair.
"If I can only find what the fellow is driving at by reconciling all
these accomplishments, and discovering a calling which needs them
all," I said to myself, "I may as well give up the attempt at once."

I see that I have alluded above to his powers upon the violin.
These were very remarkable, but as eccentric as all his other accomplishments. That he could play pieces, and difficult pieces, I
knew well, because at my request he has played me some of Men-
delssohn's Lieder, and other favourites. When left to himself, however, he would seldom produce any music or attempt any recognized
air. Leaning back in his arm-chair of an evening, he would close
his eyes and scrape carelessly at the fiddle which was thrown across
his knee. Sometimes the chords were sonorous and melancholy.
Occasionally they were fantastic and cheerful. Clearly they reflected the thoughts which possessed him, but whether the music
aided those thoughts, or whether the playing was simply the result
of a whim or fancy was more than I could determine. I might have
rebelled against these exasperating solos had it not been that
he usually terminated them by playing in quick succession a whole
series of my favourite airs as a slight compensation for the trial
upon my patience.

During the first week or so we had no callers, and I had begun
to think that my companion was as friendless a man as I was myself. Presently, however, I found that he had many acquaintances,
and those in the most different classes of society. There was one
little sallow rat-faced, dark-eyed fellow who was introduced to me
as Mr. Lestrade, and who came three or four times in a single
week. One morning a young girl called, fashionably dressed, and

stayed for half an hour or more. The same afternoon brought a grey-headed, seedy visitor, looking like a Jew pedlar, who appeared to me to be much excited, and who was closely followed by a slip-shod elderly woman. On another occasion an old white-haired gentleman had an interview with my companion; and on another a railway porter in his velveteen uniform. When any of these nondescript individuals put in an appearance, Sherlock Holmes used to beg for the use of the sitting-room, and I would retire to my bed-room. He always apologized to me for putting me to this inconvenience. "I have to use this room as a place of business," he said, "and these people are my clients." Again I had an opportunity of asking him a point blank question, and again my delicacy prevented me from forcing another man to confide in me. I imagined at the time that he had some strong reason for not alluding to it, but he soon dispelled the idea by coming round to the subject of his own accord.

It was upon the 4th of March, as I have good reason to remember, that I rose somewhat earlier than usual, and found that Sherlock Holmes had not yet finished his breakfast. The landlady had become so accustomed to my late habits that my place had not been laid nor my coffee prepared. With the unreasonable petulance of mankind I rang the bell and gave a curt intimation that I was ready. Then I picked up a magazine from the table and attempted to while away the time with it, while my companion munched silently at his toast. One of the articles had a pencil mark at the heading, and I naturally began to run my eye through it.

Its somewhat ambitious title was "The Book of Life," and it attempted to show how much an observant man might learn by an accurate and systematic examination of all that came in his way. It struck me as being a remarkable mixture of shrewdness and of absurdity. The reasoning was close and intense, but the deductions appeared to me to be far-fetched and exaggerated. The writer claimed by a momentary expression, a twitch of a muscle or a glance of an eye, to fathom a man's inmost thoughts. Deceit, according to him, was an impossibility in the case of one trained to observation and analysis. His conclusions were as infallible as so many propositions of Euclid. So startling would his results appear to the uninitiated that until they learned the processes by which he had arrived at them they might well consider him as a necromancer.

"From a drop of water," said the writer, "a logician could infer the possibility of an Atlantic or a Niagara without having seen or heard of one or the other. So all life is a great chain, the nature of which is known whenever we are shown a single link of it. Like all other arts, the Science of Deduction and Analysis is one which can only be acquired by long and patient study nor is life long enough to allow any mortal to attain the highest possible perfection in it. Before turning to those moral and mental aspects of the matter which present the greatest difficulties, let the enquirer begin by mastering more elementary problems. Let him, on meeting a fellow-mortal, learn at a glance to distinguish the history of the man, and the trade or profession to which he belongs. Puerile as such an exercise may seem, it sharpens the faculties of observation, and teaches one where to look and what to look for. By a man's finger-nails, by his coat-sleeve, by his boots, by his trouser-knees, by the callosities of his forefinger and thumb, by his expression, by his shirt-cuffs—by each of these things a man's calling is plainly revealed. That all united should fail to enlighten the competent enquirer in any case is almost inconceivable."

"What ineffable twaddle!" I cried, slapping the magazine down on the table, "I never read such rubbish in my life."

"What is it?" asked Sherlock Holmes.

"Why, this article," I said, pointing at it with my egg spoon as I sat down to my breakfast. "I see that you have read it since you have marked it. I don't deny that it is smartly written. It irritates me though. It is evidently the theory of some arm-chair lounger who evolves all these neat little paradoxes in the seclusion of his own study. It is not practical. I should like to see him clapped down in a third class carriage on the Underground, and asked to give the trades of all his fellow-travellers. I would lay a thousand to one against him."

"You would lose your money," Sherlock Holmes remarked calmly. "As for the article I wrote it myself."

"You!"

"Yes, I have a turn both for observation and for deduction. The theories which I have expressed there, and which appear to you to be so chimerical are really extremely practical—so practical that I depend upon them for my bread and cheese."

"And how?" I asked involuntarily.

"Well, I have a trade of my own. I suppose I am the only one in the world. I'm a consulting detective, if you can understand what that is. Here in London we have lots of Government detectives and lots of private ones. When these fellows are at fault they come to me, and I manage to put them on the right scent. They lay all the evidence before me, and I am generally able, by the help of my knowledge of the history of crime, to set them straight. There is a strong family resemblance about misdeeds, and if you have all the details of a thousand at your finger ends, it is odd if you can't unravel the thousand and first. Lestrade is a well-known detective. He got himself into a fog recently over a forgery case, and that was what brought him here."

"And these other people?"

"They are mostly sent on by private inquiry agencies. They are all people who are in trouble about something, and want a little enlightening. I listen to their story, they listen to my comments, and then I pocket my fee."

"But do you mean to say," I said, "that without leaving your room you can unravel some knot which other men can make nothing of, although they have seen every detail for themselves?"

"Quite so. I have a kind of intuition that way. Now and again a case turns up which is a little more complex. Then I have to bustle about and see things with my own eyes. You see I have a lot of special knowledge which I apply to the problem, and which facilitates matters wonderfully. Those rules of deduction laid down in that article which aroused your scorn, are invaluable to me in practical work. Observation with me is second nature. You appeared to be surprised when I told you, on our first meeting, that you had come from Afghanistan."

"You were told, no doubt."

"Nothing of the sort. I *knew* you came from Afghanistan. From long habit the train of thoughts ran so swiftly through my mind, that I arrived at the conclusion without being conscious of inter-mediate steps. There were such steps, however. The train of rea-soning ran, 'Here is a gentleman of a medical type, but with the air of a military man. Clearly an army doctor, then. He has just come from the tropics, for his face is dark, and that is not the natural tint of his skin, for his wrists are fair. He has undergone hardship and sickness, as his haggard face says clearly. His left arm has been in-jured. He holds it in a stiff and unnatural manner. Where in the tropics could an English army doctor have seen much hardship and got his arm wounded? Clearly in Afghanistan.' The whole train of thought did not occupy a second. I then remarked that you came from Afghanistan, and you were astonished."

"It is simple enough as you explain it," I said, smiling. "You remind me of Edgar Allan Poe's Dupin. I had no idea that such individuals did exist outside of stories."

Sherlock Holmes rose and lit his pipe. "No doubt you think that you are complimenting me in comparing me to Dupin," he observed. "Now, in my opinion, Dupin was a very inferior fellow. That trick of his of breaking in on his friends' thoughts with an apropos re-mark after a quarter of an hour's silence is really very showy and superficial. He had some analytical genius, no doubt; but he was by no means such a phenomenon as Poe appeared to imagine."

"Have you read Gaboriau's works?" I asked. "Does Lecoq come up to your idea of a detective?"

Sherlock Holmes sniffed sardonically. "Lecoq was a miserable bungler," he said, in an angry voice; "he had only one thing to recommend him, and that was his energy. That book made me positively ill. The question was how to identify an unknown prisoner. I could have done it in twenty-four hours. Lecoq took six months or so. It might be made a text-book for detectives to teach them what to avoid."

I felt rather indignant at having two characters whom I had admired treated in this cavalier style. I walked over to the window, and stood looking out into the busy street. "This fellow may be very clever," I said to myself, "but he is certainly very conceited."

"There are no crimes and no criminals in these days," he said, querulously. "What is the use of having brains in our profession. I know well that I have it in me to make my name famous. No man lives or has ever lived who has brought the same amount of study and of natural talent to the detection of crime which I have done. And what is the result? There is no crime to detect, or, at most, some bungling villainy with a motive so transparent that even a Scotland Yard official can see through it."

I was still annoyed at his bumptious style of conversation. I thought it best to change the topic.

"I wonder what that fellow is looking for?" I asked, pointing to a stalwart, plainly-dressed individual who was walking slowly down the other side of the street, looking anxiously at the numbers. He had a large blue envelope in his hand, and was evidently the bearer of a message.

"You mean the retired sergeant of Marines," said Sherlock Holmes.

"Brag and bounce!" thought I to myself. "He knows that I cannot verify his guess."

The thought had hardly passed through my mind when the man whom we were watching caught sight of the number on our door, and ran rapidly across the roadway. We heard a loud knock, a deep voice below, and heavy steps ascending the stair.

"For Mr. Sherlock Holmes," he said, stepping into the room and handing my friend the letter.

Here was an opportunity of taking the conceit out of him. He little thought of this when he made that random shot. "May I ask, my lad," I said, in the blandest voice, "what your trade may be?"

"Commissionaire, sir," he said, gruffly. "Uniform away for repairs."

"And you were?" I asked, with a slightly malicious glance at my companion.

"A sergeant, sir, Royal Marine Light Infantry, sir. No answer? Right, sir."

He clicked his heels together, raised his hand in a salute, and was gone.

※

Anonymous

IN THE DECADES FOLLOWING the 1851 appearance of Charles Dickens's article "On Duty with Inspector Field," both real and fictional police detectives became common. Detective fiction grew out of, responded to, and soon influenced the allegedly nonfictional accounts of crime in the popular press. Instructive examples of both news-media response to crime and official investigative techniques can be found in the following newspaper article and inquest transcript, both of which concern the most notorious criminal of the Victorian era—Jack the Ripper.

In the summer of 1888, London was agog over the recent dramatization of Robert Louis Stevenson's 1886 novella *Strange Case of Dr. Jekyll and Mr. Hyde.* As the following pages reveal, Stevenson's now iconic portrayal of a divided personality, a latent dark side of humanity, was cited by journalists as soon as the first murder occurred. Whitechapel was known for its high crime rate, but in the two years preceding the arrival of the Ripper, no homicides had been reported in the area. Thus the discovery of the viciously murdered and mutilated Mary Ann Nichols was all the more shocking. A crime of passion might have been understandable; premeditated slaughter was not. And gradually the killer's expertise with a knife led investigators to speculate that he was a medical professional, itself a kind of monstrous betrayal that made the crimes even more horrific.

The following article appeared in the London *Evening News* on September 1, 1888, the day after the first murder that is now considered among the five "canonical" Ripper murders—those, among eleven murders between 1888 and 1891, that seem most likely to have been perpetrated by the same villain. At the time, however, this murder was immediately linked to other recent crimes of a similar heinous nature. Frequent provocative subtitles were characteristic of sensational journalism at the time, the print equivalent of sound bites. Note that even in such an early account, journalists were turning to fiction and drama to help them explain the more horrific aspects of everyday life in the great unequal metropolis of London. By the end of this vivid and terrifying piece of daily Victorian journalism, the author is linking "homicidal mania" with the offhand cruelty of both monarchs and average citizens who walk among their fellow mortals without a flicker of compassion.

In the opening of this story there appears again, as it did in "On Duty with Inspector Field," the evocative image of a constable (in this case John Neil, officer 97J), alone in an ill-lit alley, shining the light of his bull's-eye lantern on a scene of poverty and crime. An oil lantern encased in a tin box, with on one side a bulging refractive lens that focused the light, the bull's-eye was held by a side handle like a large coffee mug. It performed the role of the later battery-powered torch or flashlight; the light from the burning wick was hidden until the bearer slid aside a metal panel.

Following the *Evening News* article is the *Daily Telegraph*'s transcript, from two days later, of the first day of inquest into the death of Mary Ann Nichols. It reminds us just how familiar, by this time, Victorians had become with the grisly details of criminal investigation, trial procedure, and forensic analysis, and also reveals how blatantly the investigation peered into the moral character of the victim. Real-life investigative technique, as opposed to the fanciful deductions of armchair sleuths, was messy and exhausting.

The Whitechapel Mystery

Fifth Edition.
The Whitechapel Mystery.
Horrible Murder in Buck's Row, Whitechapel.
Identification of the Body.
The Doctor's Statement.

THE LOCALITY OF WHITECHAPEL has long been associated with the committal of crimes of a brutal and at times almost incredible nature, in many of which women have been the victims. Some few months ago a woman was barbarously murdered near Whitechapel Church by being stabbed with a swordstick. On the night of last Bank Holiday a woman named Turner was found dead in George-yard, Whitechapel, with 30 stabs on her body. In both cases no clue to the perpetrators of the deed was discovered, and now even a more ghastly deed has come to light.

The Body Discovered.

AT A QUARTER TO four yesterday morning Police-constable Neil was on his beat in Buck's-row, Thomas-street, Whitechapel, when his attention was attracted to the body of a woman lying on the pavement close to the door of the stableyard in connection with Essex Wharf. Buck's-row, like many minor thoroughfares in this and similar neighbourhoods, is not overburdened with gas-lamps, and in the dim light the constable at first thought that the woman had fallen down in a drunken stupor, and was sleeping off the effects of a night's debauch. With the aid of the light from his bullseye lantern Neil at once perceived that the woman had been the victim of some horrible outrage. Her livid face was stained with blood, and her throat cut from ear to ear. The constable at once alarmed the people living in the house next to the stable-yard, occupied by a carter named Green and his family, and also knocked up Mr. Walter Perkins, the resident manager of the Essex Wharf, on the opposite side of the road, which is very narrow at this point.

No One Heard Anything.

NEITHER MR. PERKINS NOR any of the Green family, although the latter were sleeping within a few yards of where the body was discovered, had heard any sound of a struggle. Dr. Llewellyn, who lives only a short distance away in Whitechapel-road, was at once sent for and promptly arrived on the scene. He found the body lying on its back across the gateway, and the briefest possible examination was sufficient to prove that life was extinct. Death had not long ensued, because the extremities were still warm.

Most Brutal Murder.

WITH THE ASSISTANCE OF Police-sergeant Kirby and Police-constable Thane, the body was removed to the Whitechapel-road mortuary, and it was not until the unfortunate woman's clothes were removed that the horrible nature of the attack which had been made upon her transpired. It was then discovered that in addition to the gash in her throat, which had nearly severed the head from the body, the lower part of the abdomen had been ripped up, and the bowels were protruding. The abdominal wall, the whole length of the body, had been cut open, and on either side were two incised wounds, almost as severe as the centre one. This reached from the lower part of the abdomen to the breast bone. The instrument with which the wounds were inflicted must have been not only of the sharpness of a razor, but used with considerable ferocity.

Blood Stains on Both Sides of the Street.

A GENERAL OPINION IS now entertained that the spot where the body was found was not the scene of the murder. Buck's-row runs through from Thomas-street to Brady-street, and in the latter street what appeared to be blood stains were, early in the morning, found at irregular distances on the footpaths on either side of the street. Occasionally a larger splash was visible, and from the way in which the marks were scattered it seems as though the person carrying the mutilated body had hesitated where to deposit his ghastly burden, and gone from one side of the road to the other until the obscurity of Buck's-row afforded the shelter sought for. The street had been crossed twice within the space of about 120 yards. The point at which the stains were first visible is in front of the gateway to Honey's-mews, in Brady-street, about 150 yards from the point where Buck's-row commences. Several persons living in Brady-street state that early in the morning they heard screams, but this is a by no means uncommon incident in the neighbourhood, and, with one exception, nobody seems to have paid any particular attention to what was probably the death struggle of the unfortunate woman. The exception referred to was a Mrs. Colwell, who lives only a short distance from the foot of Buck's-row.

Awakened by the Children.

ACCORDING TO HER STATEMENT she was awakened early in the morning by her children, who said some one was trying to get into the house. She listened, and heard a woman screaming "Murder! Police!" five or six times. The voice faded away, as though the woman was going in the direction of Buck's-row, and all was quiet. She only heard the steps of one person. It is almost needless to point out that a person suffering from such injuries as the deceased had had inflicted upon her would be unable to traverse the distance from Honey's-mews to the gateway in Buck's-row, which is about 120 yards from Brady-street, making a total distance of at least 170 yards.

She Must Have Been Dragged.

THEREFORE THE WOMAN MUST have been carried or dragged there, and here the mystery becomes all the more involved. Even supposing that, with the severe abdominal wounds she had sufficient strength left to call out in the tones which Mrs. Colwell asserts she heard the deceased's throat could not have been cut at the spot where she was found lying dead, as that would have caused a considerably heavier flow of blood than was found there. As a matter of fact but a very small quantity of blood was to be seen at this spot, or found in Buck's-row at all, so the murderer could not have waited here to finish his ghastly task. If he had cut her throat on the onset the deceased could not have uttered a single cry afterwards. Mrs. Colwell's statement, looked at in the light of these circumstances, by no means totally clears up the mystery as to the exact locality which the murderer selected for the accomplishment of his foul deed.

An Unusually Quiet Night.

POLICE-CONSTABLE NEIL TRAVERSED BUCK'S-ROW about three-quarters of an hour before the body was discovered, so it must have been deposited there soon after he had patrolled that thoroughfare. Mrs. Green, Mr. and Mrs. Perkins, the watchman in Schneider's tar factory, and the watchman in a wool depot, which are both situated in Buck's-row, agree that the night was an unusually quiet one for the neighbourhood.

Two Spots of Blood.

SHORTLY AFTER MIDDAY SOME men who were searching the pavement in Buck's-row above the gateway found two spots of blood in the roadway. They were nine feet away from the gate, and they might have dropped from the hands or clothing of the murderer as he fled away. The stablery and the vicinity have been carefully searched in the hope of finding the weapon with which the crime was committed, but so far without success. A bridge over the Great Eastern Railway is close at hand, and the railway line was also fruitlessly searched for some distance.

The Doctor's Statement.

DR. LLEWELLYN MADE THE following statement yesterday: I was called to Buck's-row, about five minutes to four this morning by Police-constable Thane, who said a woman had been murdered. I went to the place at once, and found deceased lying on her back with her legs out straight as though she had been laid down. Police-constable Neil told me that the body had not been touched. The throat was cut from ear to ear, and the woman was quite dead.

On feeling the extremities of the body, I found that they were still warm, showing that death had not long ensued. A crowd was now gathering, and as it was undesirable to make a further examination in the street I ordered the removal of the body to the mortuary, telling the police to send for me again if anything of importance transpired.

The Murder Was Committed Elsewhere.

THERE WAS A VERY small pool of blood on the pathway, which had trickled from the wound in the throat, not more than would fill two wineglasses, or half a pint at the outside. This fact, and the way in which the deceased was lying, made me think at the time that it was at least probable that the murder was committed elsewhere, and the body conveyed to Buck's-row. There were no marks of blood on deceased's legs, and at the time I had no idea of the fearful abdominal wounds which had been inflicted upon the body. At half-past five I was summoned to the mortuary by the police, and was astonished at finding the other wounds.

A Brutal Affair.

I HAVE SEEN MANY horrible cases, but never such a brutal affair as this. From the nature of the cuts on the throat it is probable that they were inflicted with the left hand. There is a mark at the point of the jaw on the right side of deceased's face, as though made by a person's thumb, and a similar bruise on the left side as if the woman's head had been pushed back and her throat then cut. There is a gash under the left ear reaching nearly to the centre of the throat, and another cut apparently starting from the right ear. The neck is severed back to the vertebra, which is also slightly injured. The abdominal wounds are extraordinary for their length and the severity with which they have been inflicted. One cut extends from the base of the abdomen to the breastbone. Deceased's clothes were loose, and the wounds could have been inflicted while she was dressed.

The Theory of the Murder.

INSPECTOR HELSON, WHO HAS charge of the case, is making every effort to trace the murderer, but there is so little to guide the police that at present there does not seem much likelihood of success. The theory that the murder is the work of a lunatic, who is also the perpetrator of the other two murders of women which have occurred in Whitechapel during the last six months, meets with very general acceptance amongst the inhabitants of the district, the female portion of which is greatly alarmed. The more probable theory is that the murder has been committed by one or more of a gang of men, who are in the habit of frequenting the streets at late hours of the night and levying blackmail on women. No money was found upon deceased, and all she had in the pocket of her dress was a handkerchief, a small comb, and a piece of looking-glass.

Identification of the Woman.

THE CENTRAL NEWS SAYS: It was not until late in the evening that the first real clue towards the solution of the mystery was found—namely, the identification of the deceased. During the day some half-dozen women who thought that they knew deceased visited the mortuary and viewed the body, but without being able to recognise it. The energetic efforts of Inspector Helson and Detective-sergeants Enright and Godley were eventually successful in clearing up this point. It transpires that deceased is a married woman, named Mary Ann Nichols, who has been living apart from her husband for some years. Her real age is 36 years, and she had been an inmate of Lambeth Workhouse, off and on, for the past seven years. She was first admitted to the workhouse seven years ago as a patient into the lying-in ward, and from this point seems to have entered upon a downward career. Some few months ago she left the workhouse, after having temporarily sojourned there, to go into domestic service at Rose-hill-road, Wandsworth. She left suddenly, under suspicious circumstances, and for the last seven weeks or so seems to have been frequenting the neighbourhood of Whitechapel. She was last seen in the Whitechapel-road at half-past two yesterday morning, and was then under the influence of drink. The inquest will be held by Mr. Wynne E. Baxter, the coroner for the district, at the Working Lads' Institute, Whitechapel-road, this afternoon.

THE EXCHANGE TELEGRAPH COMPANY, on inquiry this morning at Scotland Yard, were informed that no arrests had been made in connection with the brutal murder at Whitechapel up to eleven o'clock to-day.

Homicidal Maniacs.

THE POLICE, IT APPEARS, have already abandoned their theory that the latest, as well as the previous, murder in Whitechapel is the deed of a homicidal maniac. The theories of the police about most things connected with the detection of crime are not deserving of much attention at any time, not even on the principle laid down by "Novalis" (Baron von Hardenberg): "It is certain my belief gains infinitely the moment I can convince another mind thereof." They, therefore, showed much cuteness in not insisting too long upon the possible fact of there being a fiend in human shape, such as Mr. Stevenson describes, roaming about the metropolis. The fierce light supposed to beat upon a throne would have been a farthing rushlight compared to the glare of public curiosity that would have

been turned on Scotland Yard had the assumption been maintained. This glare would not only have proceeded from a laudable
and natural desire to see the author of such dastardly and foul
crimes securely under lock and key, and thus rendered powerless to
pursue his monstrous career. The glare would have owed much of
its blinding effulgence to the expectation of seeing in the flesh so
terrible a scourge of humanity. It boots not to inquire whether the
police would have been capable of gratifying this curiosity. In fact,
it boots little to inquire at this hour of what the London detective
force are capable, except the almost miraculous execution of Dickens's precept, "How not to do it." Certain is it that beings, out-
wardly human, one such as was suggested to the police by either
the performance or perusal of "Dr. Jekyll and Mr. Hyde," do exist;
nay more, that Mr. Louis Stevenson himself did not altogether
evolve his hero from his own inner consciousness. The late Dr.
Strauss, better known to the majority of readers of periodicals, as
"The Old Bohemian," who died a year or two ago, published, a
decade since, a story in *Tinsley's Magazine*, dealing with the murders committed by such an irresponsible homicide. It was a startling tale, almost too ghastly to be believed. Dr. Strauss was a
friend of the writer of these lines and was assured that the narrative
was founded upon fact. The thing happened at one of the German
Universities, and the murderer was a professor there. He made
about half-a-dozen victims before he was discovered. Unlike Mr.
Hyde, he attacked the unwary passer-by with a small hammer.
Woodman and Tidy and Taylor in their "Medical Jurisprudence"
record more than one instance of special and general homicidal
mania. By special is meant the impulse towards a particular victim;
by general the equally irresistible but more extended desire to kill,
no matter whom. It must not be supposed, though, that fiendish
cruelty is always the impelling factor to the deed; on the contrary.
Esquirol, Pinel, and several other French savants have given it as
their firm conviction that the mania for destroying whether human life or inorganic things may have its cause in what—for want

of a better term—one might call hyper-philanthropy. One will demolish the walls of a room because to him they appear to totter on their bases, and in their fall bury so many of his cherished fellow-creatures beneath them; another will hack to pieces a bedstead because the fragments thereof are of inestimable value as charms against an otherwise incurable malady; a third will inflict the most revolting mutilations in the furtherance of morality; a fourth will slay outright because he fancies himself possessed of the gifts to immediately resuscitate his victim, and procure for him the ineffable joys and gratifications of everlasting life. To this latter category of homicides appears to have belonged the Hungarian noble who in the course of a few years murdered several young girls ranging from six to fourteen. Immediately the deed was done and the contemplated resuscitation failed, he used to writhe in the agony of most poignant remorse on the floor.

Others kill for killing sake. They have not the least resentment against their victim, nor are they moved by any feeling of benevolence. The "Chourineur" in Eugène Sue's "Mysteries of Paris" belongs to this class, and, it may be interesting to the reader to know that the "Chourineur" was not a creation of Sue's brain any more than "Prince Rodolphe." The latter character suggested to the novelist by an adventure of Louis Napoleon long before he was President of the Second Republic. The first chapter of "The Mysteries of Paris" is an absolute fact. The future Emperor of France found himself in the crime-laden atmosphere of the old [cité] because one of his boon companions, who, at his advent to power, became a high functionary, was a Don Juan, who sought his conquests indiscriminately, either in the gutter or in the drawing-room. The "Chourineur," it may be remembered, killed because a mist of blood not only perverted his physical but also his moral vision. His protector diverted his mania to the killing of animals, and started him in business as a butcher, in which station of life he prospered. In a trial for murder that took place years ago in Paris it was proved that one of the accomplices—a well-to-do tradesman—had merely lent the miscreants a hand "for the fun of the thing," as he expressed it himself. He had not benefited by the spoliation of the victim; until the moment of the crime he had never set eyes upon either the murdered man or his assassins. As a matter of course the experts had no difficulty in establishing his irresponsibility. He was suffering from a sudden and acute access of homicidal mania. The disease, it would further appear, does not always translate itself into deeds of sudden violence. If my memory does not play me false, the lady who purchased chocolate creams in West-street, Brighton, stuffed them with poison, and afterwards distributed them to any and every one, turned out to be an irresponsible homicidal maniac. Under such conditions the alienation is described as chronic and continued—albeit that there are periods of suspension and returns to perfect sanity of mind.

There remains homicidal mania whose cause is downright cruelty—cruelty that remained unchecked probably in its first manifestations owing to the social position of the offender, as in the case of Louis XI., who, when a child, amused himself by gouging out the eyes of birds with a red hot needle. Half of the pious monarch's victims, when he had grown to a man's estate, were victims of his cruelty that had developed into a mania to kill, though vicariously, for their removal from this earth was neither dictated by political nor private vengeance. Historians, and even savants have endeavoured to whitewash Robespierre, Carnier of Natès, and several other actors in the Reign of Terror, by putting forth this plea. In how far this plea is to be admitted is a problem with which only the most competent psychologists can deal. In his "Voyage to the Sources of the Nile" Captain Speke recorded the following incident: Having made a present of a breech-loader to Mtesa, King of Uganda, the latter handed the weapon to an officer, telling him to try its effect on one or more of those who were assembled in the courtyard. The order was strictly executed without exciting the disgust of any of the king's courtiers. They were not more squeamish than the courtiers of Cambyses, than Prexaspes himself, the latter of whom not only stood tamely by when his son was killed à la William Tell by the Persian monarch "just to show his steadiness of hand" even when drunk, but who paid his master a compliment on his skill; they were less squeamish than the Regent of France. The latter's son, who became the grandfather of Louis-Philippe, one day, out of mere passion, or perhaps to test the accuracy of his gun, shot a shopkeeper standing at his own door. Philippe d'Orleans pretended to forgive him. "A sudden access of homicidal mania, I suppose. You are irresponsible, but I shall apply the same tenet to the one who happens to kill you."

In fact, it becomes difficult in dealing with tyrants and irresponsible monarchs of times gone by to distinguish excessive cruelty, utter indifference to the sacredness of human life, from homicidal mania. The "high rippers" which flourished not so very long ago in Liverpool were perhaps a gang of homicidal maniacs though it would be difficult to imagine Nature to have brought together such an association, all the members of which were moved by the same invincible impulse. The revelations in connection with the late Marylebone murder have, however, given the police a plausible pretext for the theory they contemplated starting. It is difficult to believe in our days that human beings not utterly callous to all feelings would deliberately slay their fellow men without the incentive of gain, without the at least comprehensible pretext of enmity. The police on the spur of the moment nursed the idea of increasing our astonishment. Second thoughts showed them that even homicidal maniacs must be caught, and that the public look to them for the capture. So the theory was dropped. Our astonishment has vanished, may be at the same time, and will only be revived when they effect the capture of the miscreants, whether they be homicidal maniacs, or simply malefactors who levied blackmail [at] the most degraded class of unfortunates.

THE FOLLOWING INQUEST TRANSCRIPT *is from the* Daily Telegraph *of Monday, September 3, 1888.*

Inquest: Mary Ann "Polly" Nichols

Day 1, Saturday, September 1, 1888

On Saturday Mr. Wynne E. Baxter, the coroner for South-East Middlesex, opened an inquiry at the Working Lads' Institute, Whitechapel-road, into the circumstances attending the death of a woman supposed to be Mary Ann Nichols, who was discovered lying dead on the pavement in Buck's-row, Baker's-row, White-chapel, early on Friday morning. Her throat was cut, and she had other terrible injuries.

INSPECTOR HELSTON, WHO HAS the case in hand, attended, with other officers, on behalf of the Criminal Investigation Department.

> EDWARD WALKER deposed: I live at 15, Maidwell-street, Albany-road, Camberwell, and have no occupation. I was a smith when I was at work, but I am not now. I have seen the body in the mortuary, and to the best of my belief it is my daughter; but I have not seen her for three years. I recognise her by her general appearance and by a little mark she has had on her forehead since she was a child. She also had either one or two teeth out, the same as the woman I have just seen. My daughter's name was Mary Ann Nichols, and she had been married twenty-two years. Her husband's name is William Nichols, and he is alive. He is a machinist. They have been living apart about seven or eight years. I last heard of her before Easter. She was forty-two years of age.
>
> THE CORONER: How did you see her?
>
> WITNESS: She wrote to me.
>
> THE CORONER: Is this letter in her handwriting?
>
> WITNESS: Yes, that is her writing.
>
> The letter, which was dated April 17, 1888, was read by the

Coroner, and referred to a place which the deceased had gone to at Wandsworth.

THE CORONER: When did you last see her alive?

WITNESS: Two years ago last June.

THE CORONER: Was she then in a good situation?

WITNESS: I don't know. I was not on speaking terms with her. She had been living with me three or four years previously, but thought she could better herself, so I let her go.

THE CORONER: What did she do after she left you?

WITNESS: I don't know.

THE CORONER: This letter seems to suggest that she was in a decent situation.

WITNESS: She had only just gone there.

THE CORONER: Was she a sober woman?

WITNESS: Well, at times she drank, and that was why we did not agree.

THE CORONER: Was she fast?

WITNESS: No; I never heard of anything of that sort. She used to go with some young women and men that she knew, but I never heard of anything improper.

THE CORONER: Have you any idea what she has been doing lately?

WITNESS: I have not the slightest idea.

THE CORONER: She must have drunk heavily for you to turn her out of doors?

WITNESS: I never turned her out. She had no need to be like this while I had a home for her.

THE CORONER: How is it that she and her husband were not living together?

WITNESS: When she was confined her husband took on with the young woman who came to nurse her, and they parted, he living with the nurse, by whom he has another family.

THE CORONER: Have you any reasonable doubt that this is your daughter?

WITNESS: No, I have not. I know nothing about her acquaintances, or what she had been doing for a living. I had no idea she was over here in this part of the town. She has had five children, the eldest being twenty-one years old and the youngest eight or nine years. One of them lives with me, and the other four are with their father.

THE CORONER: Has she ever lived with anybody since she left her husband?

WITNESS: I believe she was once stopping with a man in York-street, Walworth. His name was Drew, and he was a smith by trade. He is living there now, I believe. The parish of Lambeth summoned her husband for the keep of the children, but the summons was dismissed, as it was proved that she was then living with another man. I don't know who that man was.

THE CORONER: Was she ever in the workhouse?

WITNESS: Yes, sir; Lambeth Workhouse, in April last, and went from there to a situation at Wandsworth.

BY THE JURY: The husband resides at Coburg-road, Old Kent-road. I don't know if he knows of her death.

CORONER: Is there anything you know of likely to throw any light upon this affair?

WITNESS: No; I don't think she had any enemies, she was too good for that.

JOHN NEIL, police-constable, 97J, said: Yesterday morning I was proceeding down Buck's-row, Whitechapel, going towards Brady-street. There was not a soul about. I had been round there half an hour previously, and I saw no one then. I was on the right-hand side of the street, when I noticed a figure lying in the street. It was dark at the time, though there was a street lamp shining at the end of the row. I went across and found deceased lying outside a gateway, her head towards the east. The gateway was closed. It was about nine or ten feet high, and led to some stables. There were houses from the gateway eastward, and the School Board school occupies the westward. On the opposite side of the road is Essex Wharf. Deceased was lying lengthways along the street, her left hand touching the gate. I examined the body by the aid of my lamp, and noticed blood oozing from a wound in the throat. She was lying on her back, with her clothes disarranged. I felt her arm, which was quite warm from the joints upwards. Her eyes were wide open. Her bonnet was off and lying at her side, close to the left hand. I heard a constable passing Brady-street, so I called him. I did not whistle. I said to him, "Run at once for Dr. Llewellyn," and, seeing another constable in Baker's-row, I sent him for the ambulance. The doctor arrived in a very short time. I had, in the meantime, rung the bell at Essex Wharf, and asked if any disturbance had been heard. The reply was "No." Sergeant Kirby came after, and he knocked. The doctor looked at the woman and then said, "Move her to the mortuary. She is dead, and I will make a further examination of her." We placed her on the ambulance, and moved her there. Inspector Spratley came to the mortuary, and while taking a description of the deceased turned up her clothes, and found that she was disembowelled. This had not been noticed by any of them before. On the body was found a piece of comb and a bit of looking-glass. No money was found, but an unmarked white handkerchief was found in her pocket.

THE CORONER: Did you notice any blood where she was found?

WITNESS: There was a pool of blood just where her neck was lying. It was running from the wound in her neck.

THE CORONER: Did you hear any noise that night?

WITNESS: No; I heard nothing. The farthest I had been that night was just through the Whitechapel-road and up Baker's-row. I was never far away from the spot.

THE CORONER: Whitechapel-road is busy in the early morning, I believe. Could anybody have escaped that way?

WITNESS: Oh yes, sir. I saw a number of women in the main road going home. At that time any one could have got away.

THE CORONER: Some one searched the ground, I believe?

WITNESS: Yes; I examined it while the doctor was being sent for.

INSPECTOR SPRATLEY: I examined the road, sir, in daylight.

A JURYMAN (to witness): Did you see a trap in the road at all?

WITNESS: No.

A JURYMAN: Knowing that the body was warm, did it not strike you that it might just have been laid there, and that the woman was killed elsewhere?

WITNESS: I examined the road, but did not see the mark of wheels. The first to arrive on the scene after I had discovered the body were two men who work at a slaughterhouse opposite. They said they knew nothing of the affair, and that they had not heard any screams. I had previously seen the men at work. That would be about a quarter-past three, or half an hour before I found the body.

HENRY LLEWELLYN, surgeon, said: On Friday morning I was called to Buck's-row about four o'clock. The constable told me what I was wanted for. On reaching Buck's-row I found the deceased woman lying flat on her back in the pathway, her legs extended. I found she was dead, and that she had severe injuries to her throat. Her hands and wrists were cold, but the body and lower extremities were warm. I examined her chest and felt the heart. It was dark at the time. I believe she had not been dead more than half-an-hour. I am quite certain that the injuries to her neck were not self-inflicted. There was very little blood round the neck. There were no marks of any struggle or of blood, as if the body had been dragged. I told the police to take her to the mortuary, and I would make another examination. About an hour later I was sent for by the Inspector to see the injuries he had discovered on the body. I went, and saw that the abdomen was cut very

extensively. I have this morning made a post-mortem examination of the body. I found it to be that of a female about
forty or forty-five years. Five of the teeth are missing, and
there is a slight laceration of the tongue. On the right side of
the face there is a bruise running along the lower part of the
jaw. It might have been caused by a blow with the fist or
pressure by the thumb. On the left side of the face there was
a circular bruise, which also might have been done by the
pressure of the fingers. On the left side of the neck, about an
inch below the jaw, there was an incision about four inches
long and running from a point immediately below the ear.
An inch below on the same side, and commencing about an
inch in front of it, was a circular incision terminating at a
point about three inches below the right jaw. This incision
completely severs all the tissues down to the vertebrae. The
large vessels of the neck on both sides were severed. The
incision is about eight inches long. These cuts must have
been caused with a long-bladed knife, moderately sharp, and
used with great violence. No blood at all was found on the
breast either of the body or clothes. There were no injuries
about the body till just about the lower part of the abdomen.
Two or three inches from the left side was a wound running
in a jagged manner. It was a very deep wound, and the tissues were cut through. There were several incisions running
across the abdomen. On the right side there were also three
or four similar cuts running downwards. All these had been
caused by a knife, which had been used violently and been
used downwards. The wounds were from left to right, and
might have been done by a left-handed person. All the injuries had been done by the same instrument.

The inquiry was adjourned till to-morrow.

Mark Twain

(1835–1910)

HUMORIST, JOURNALIST, NOVELIST, TRAVEL writer, public figure, lecturer, suffragist, abolitionist, quotable curmudgeon—and, in his white-suited old age, playmate of the rich and famous—Mark Twain grew during his lifetime into one of the most recognizable figures of American literature. His star hasn't faded since. Thanks to such publicity boons as actor Hal Holbrook's long-running one-man show about Twain, the recent publication of Twain's unfinished autobiography, and a new edition of *Huckleberry Finn* that controversially tones down the author's language, his position in the public imagination seems unlikely to fade soon. Twain has his shortcomings; he admitted, for example, that he couldn't really satirize and tended to attack instead. At his best, however, he was not only amusing and intelligent but a superb stylist, demonstrating constantly his dictum that "the difference between the almost right word and the right word is really a large matter—'tis the difference between the lightning-bug and the lightning."

Born in the tiny village of Florida, Missouri, in 1835, a few months after his family moved there from a farm in Jamestown, Tennessee, Samuel Clemens was raised in nearby Hannibal. He immortalized the town as St. Petersburg in both *Tom Sawyer* and *Huckleberry Finn*, and a version of it reappeared in different form in *Pudd'nhead Wilson*. Over the years Twain rejected most of the small-town

Southern ideas of his upbringing. Most notably, in *Huckleberry Finn* and elsewhere he promoted greater equality between whites and blacks. He became a staunch abolitionist and also a supporter of women's voting rights and of suffrage in general. "I would like to see that whiplash, the ballot," he declared in 1901, "in the hands of women."

Twain was interested in detective stories but couldn't resist lampooning their stylized, formulaic ways. Twenty years after their first outing, he brought back Tom and Huck in *Tom Sawyer Abroad* and *Tom Sawyer, Detective*, both narrated by Huck. Neither rises to the level of the original novel, but the latter has some amusing mockery of detective fiction. Twain reserved most of his interest in detectives for his novel *Pudd'nhead Wilson*. After serialization in *Century Magazine*, beginning in 1893 and concluding the next year, the book appeared in November 1894. The following is an excerpt from the last chapter, "Doom."

Twain created several memorable characters quite unlike Huck and Tom. Hank Morgan, the titular Connecticut Yankee, gets hit with a crowbar during a fight and wakes up in King Arthur's court— starring in a time-travel novel six years ahead of H. G. Wells's protagonist in *The Time Machine*. Twain's last novel, and his own favorite, was a humorless take on Joan of Arc. In *Pudd'nhead Wilson* he returned to the theme of identical twins that he had used in *The Prince and the Pauper* to satirize social strata and notions of fated birth; this time he used the provocative image of identical human beings switched at birth to skewer the assumptions behind racism.

Twain was preoccupied with twins and other symbols of the divided self; he even wrote a story about Chang and Eng, the original "Siamese" twins (who were actually of Chinese ancestry). He first conceived the story "Those Extraordinary Twins," featuring Angelo and Luigi Capello, based upon the so-called Italian Twins, Giovanni Batista and Giacomo Tocci, who were conjoined, with two heads on a single body. Only later did these two characters become smaller players in *Pudd'nhead Wilson*, which is about the racist delusions and self-justifications that helped maintain slavery and a general inequality among races. The novel opens as lawyer David Wilson moves to the Mississippi River hamlet of Dawson's Landing, Missouri, in 1830. He is soon nicknamed Pudd'nhead by townspeople who mistake his sense of humor for stupidity. From childhood Wilson has been fascinated by what we would now call fingerprints—and in a dramatic courtroom scene worthy of Perry Mason, Wilson uses his old hobby to unmask the villain. Twain was ahead of his time again. The first legal conviction based upon fingerprint evidence didn't occur in the real world until 1902.

The Assassin's Natal Autograph

I HAVE NOW DONE with my theory, and will proceed to the evidences by which I propose to try to prove its soundness." Wilson took up several of his strips of glass. When the audience recognized these familiar mementos of Pudd'nhead's old time childish "puttering" and folly, the tense and funereal interest vanished out of their faces, and the house burst into volleys of relieving and refreshing laughter, and Tom chirked up and joined in the fun himself; but Wilson was apparently not disturbed. He arranged his records on the table before him, and said:

"I beg the indulgence of the court while I make a few remarks in explanation of some evidence which I am about to introduce, and which I shall presently ask to be allowed to verify under oath on the witness stand. Every human being carries with him from his cradle to his grave certain physical marks which do not change their character, and by which he can always be identified—and that without shade of doubt or question. These marks are his signature, his physiological autograph, so to speak, and this autograph can not be counterfeited, nor can he disguise it or hide it away, nor can it become illegible by the wear and mutations of time. This signature is not his face—age can change that beyond recognition; it is not his hair, for that can fall out; it is not his height, for duplicates of that exist; it is not his form, for duplicates of that exist also,

313

whereas this signature is each man's very own—there is no duplicate of it among the swarming populations of the globe! [The audience were interested once more.]

"This autograph consists of the delicate lines or corrugations
with which Nature marks the insides of the hands and the soles of
the feet. If you will look at the balls of your fingers—you that have
very sharp eyesight—you will observe that these dainty curving
lines lie close together, like those that indicate the borders of oceans
in maps, and that they form various clearly defined patterns, such as
arches, circles, long curves, whorls, etc., and that these patters differ
on the different fingers. [Every man in the room had his hand up to
the light now, and his head canted to one side, and was minutely
scrutinizing the balls of his fingers; there were whispered ejaculations of "Why, it's so—I never noticed that before!"] The patterns
on the right hand are not the same as those on the left. [Ejacula-
tions of "Why, that's so, too!"] Taken finger for finger, your patterns differ from your neighbor's. [Comparisons were made all
over the house—even the judge and jury were absorbed in this
curious work.] The patterns of a twin's right hand are not the same
as those on his left. One twin's patterns are never the same as his
fellow twin's patterns—the jury will find that the patterns upon
the finger balls of the twins' hands follow this rule. [An examination of the twins' hands was begun at once.] You have often heard
of twins who were so exactly alike that when dressed alike their
own parents could not tell them apart. Yet there was never a twin
born in to this world that did not carry from birth to death a sure
identifier in this mysterious and marvelous natal autograph. That
once known to you, his fellow twin could never personate him and
deceive you."

Wilson stopped and stood silent. Inattention dies a quick and
sure death when a speaker does that. The stillness gives warning
that something is coming. All palms and finger balls went down
now, all slouching forms straightened, all heads came up, all eyes
were fastened upon Wilson's face. He waited yet one, two, three

moments, to let his pause complete and perfect its spell upon the house; then, when through the profound hush he could hear the ticking of the clock on the wall, he put out his hand and took the Indian knife by the blade and held it aloft where all could see the sinister spots upon its ivory handle; then he said, in a level and passionless voice:

"Upon this haft stands the assassin's natal autograph, written in the blood of that helpless and unoffending old man who loved you and whom you all loved. There is but one man in the whole earth whose hand can duplicate that crimson sign"—he paused and raised his eyes to the pendulum swinging back and forth—"and please God we will produce that man in this room before the clock strikes noon!"

Stunned, distraught, unconscious of its own movement, the house half rose, as if expecting to see the murderer appear at the door, and a breeze of muttered ejaculations swept the place. "Order in the court!—sit down!" This from the sheriff. He was obeyed, and quiet reigned again. Wilson stole a glance at Tom, and said to himself, "He is flying signals of distress now; even people who despise him are pitying him; they think this is a hard ordeal for a young fellow who has lost his benefactor by so cruel a stroke—and they are right." He resumed his speech:

"For more than twenty years I have amused my compulsory leisure with collecting these curious physical signatures in this town. At my house I have hundreds upon hundreds of them. Each and every one is labeled with name and date; not labeled the next day or even the next hour, but in the very minute that the impression was taken. When I go upon the witness stand I will repeat under oath the things which I am now saying. I have the fingerprints of the court, the sheriff, and every member of the jury. There is hardly a person in this room, white or black, whose natal signature I cannot produce, and not one of them can so disguise himself that I cannot pick him out from a multitude of his fellow creatures and unerringly identify him by his hands. And if he and

I should live to be a hundred I could still do it. [The interest of the audience was steadily deepening now.]

"I have studied some of these signatures so much that I know them as well as the bank cashier knows the autograph of his oldest customer. While I turn my back now, I beg that several persons will be so good as to pass their fingers through their hair, and then press them upon one of the panes of the window near the jury, and that among them the accused may set THEIR finger marks. Also, I beg that these experimenters, or others, will set their fingers upon another pane, and add again the marks of the accused, but not placing them in the same order or relation to the other signatures as before—for, by one chance in a million, a person might happen upon the right marks by pure guesswork, ONCE, therefore I wish to be tested twice."

He turned his back, and the two panes were quickly covered with delicately lined oval spots, but visible only to such persons as could get a dark background for them—the foliage of a tree, outside, for instance. Then upon call, Wilson went to the window, made his examination, and said:

"This is Count Luigi's right hand; this one, three signatures below, is his left. Here is Count Angelo's right; down here is his left. How for the other pane: here and here are Count Luigi's, here and here are his brother's." He faced about. "Am I right?"

A deafening explosion of applause was the answer. The bench said:

"This certainly approaches the miraculous!"

Wilson turned to the window again and remarked, pointing with his finger:

"This is the signature of Mr. Justice Robinson. [Applause.] This, of Constable Blake. [Applause.] This of John Mason, juryman. [Applause.] This, of the sheriff. [Applause.] I cannot name the others, but I have them all at home, named and dated, and could identify them all by my fingerprint records."

He moved to his place through a storm of applause—which the

sheriff stopped, and also made the people sit down, for they were all standing and struggling to see, of course. Court, jury, sheriff, and everybody had been too absorbed in observing Wilson's performance to attend to the audience earlier.

"Now then," said Wilson, "I have here the natal autographs of the two children—thrown up to ten times the natural size by the pantograph, so that anyone who can see at all can tell the markings apart at a glance. We will call the children A and B. Here are A's finger marks, taken at the age of five months. Here they are again taken at seven months. [Tom started.] They are alike, you see. Here are B's at five months, and also at seven months. They, too, exactly copy each other, but the patterns are quite different from A's, you observe. I shall refer to these again presently, but we will turn them face down now.

"Here, thrown up ten sizes, are the natal autographs of the two persons who are here before you accused of murdering Judge Driscoll. I made these pantograph copies last night, and will so swear when I go upon the witness stand. I ask the jury to compare them with the finger marks of the accused upon the windowpanes, and tell the court if they are the same."

He passed a powerful magnifying glass to the foreman.

One juryman after another took the cardboard and the glass and made the comparison. Then the foreman said to the judge:

"Your honor, we are all agreed that they are identical."

Wilson said to the foreman:

"Please turn that cardboard face down, and take this one, and compare it searchingly, by the magnifier, with the fatal signature upon the knife handle, and report your finding to the court."

Again the jury made minute examinations, and again reported:

"We find them to be exactly identical, your honor."

Wilson turned toward the counsel for the prosecution, and there was a clearly recognizable note of warning in his voice when he said:

"May it please the court, the state has claimed, strenuously and persistently, that the bloodstained fingerprints upon that knife handle were left there by the assassin of Judge Driscoll. You have heard us grant that claim, and welcome it." He turned to the jury: "Compare the fingerprints of the accused with the fingerprints left by the assassin—and report."

The comparison began. As it proceeded, all movement and all sound ceased, and the deep silence of an absorbed and waiting suspense settled upon the house; and when at last the words came, "THEY DO NOT EVEN RESEMBLE," a thundercrash of applause followed and the house sprang to its feet, but was quickly repressed by official force and brought to order again. Tom was altering his position every few minutes now, but none of his changes brought repose nor any small trifle of comfort. When the house's attention was become fixed once more, Wilson said gravely, indicating the twins with a gesture:

"These men are innocent—I have no further concern with them. [Another outbreak of applause began, but was promptly checked.] We will now proceed to find the guilty. [Tom's eyes were starting from their sockets—yes, it was a cruel day for the bereaved youth, everybody thought.] We will return to the infant autographs of A and B. I will ask the jury to take these large pantograph facsimilies of A's marked five months and seven months. Do they tally?"

The foreman responded: "Perfectly."

"Now examine this pantograph, taken at eight months, and also marked A. Does it tally with the other two?"

The surprised response was:

"NO—THEY DIFFER WIDELY!"

"You are quite right. Now take these two pantographs of B's autograph, marked five months and seven months. Do they tally with each other?"

"Yes—perfectly."

"Take this third pantograph marked B, eight months. Does it tally with B's other two?"

"BY NO MEANS!"

"Do you know how to account for those strange discrepancies? I will tell you. For a purpose unknown to us, but probably a selfish one, somebody changed those children in the cradle."

This produced a vast sensation, naturally; Roxana was astonished at this admirable guess, but not disturbed by it. To guess the exchange was one thing, to guess who did it quite another. Pudd'nhead Wilson could do wonderful things, no doubt, but he couldn't do impossible ones. Safe? She was perfectly safe. She smiled privately.

"Between the ages of seven months and eight months those children were changed in the cradle"—he made one of his effect-collecting pauses, and added—"and the person who did it is in this house!"

Roxy's pulses stood still! The house was thrilled as with an electric shock, and the people half rose as if to seek a glimpse of the person who had made that exchange. Tom was growing limp; the life seemed oozing out of him. Wilson resumed:

"A was put into B's cradle in the nursery; B was transferred to the kitchen and became a Negro and a slave [Sensation—confusion of angry ejaculations]—but within a quarter of an hour he will stand before you white and free! [Burst of applause, checked by the officers.] From seven months onward until now, A has still been a usurper, and in my finger record he bears B's name. Here is his pantograph at the age of twelve. Compare it with the assassin's signature upon the knife handle. Do they tally?"

The foreman answered:

"TO THE MINUTEST DETAIL!"

Wilson said, solemnly:

"The murderer of your friend and mine—York Driscoll of the generous hand and the kindly spirit—sits in among you. Valet de Chambre, Negro and slave—falsely called Thomas a Becket Driscoll—make upon the window the fingerprints that will hang you!"

Tom turned his ashen face imploring toward the speaker, made some impotent movements with his white lips, then slid limp and lifeless to the floor.

Wilson broke the awed silence with the words:

"There is no need. He has confessed."

C. L. Pirkis

(1841–1910)

CATHERINE LOUISA PIRKIS OCCUPIES a unique position in crime fiction. She was the first known female writer to create a female detective: an intelligent and resourceful young woman with the curious name of Loveday Brooke. And Brooke has the distinction of being not only a salaried professional private investigator but one who isn't presented as hyperfeminine to balance out her allegedly unfeminine career—unlike characters such as Madelyn Mack, created by Hugh Weir, or Dora Myrl, created by M. McDonnell Bodkin. Nor is Brooke working to support a disowned sister, like Violet Strange, or because her husband went blind, like Dorcas Dene, both of whom appear in this anthology. Brooke is simply a professional. Pirkis describes her as "neither handsome nor ugly," and in fact "nondescript," which seems a virtue for a real-life detective but a shocking anomaly for a fictional woman in the field. Brooke's adventures also stand alone rather than forming a story cycle, a popular unifying gimmick at the time.

Brooke is also unusual in her social mobility. Her work requires that she make her way through Victorian society, from parlor to alley, unaccompanied by a man. Brooke's adroit navigation of various levels of society, thanks to a talent for disguise and mimicry, gives Pirkis an opportunity to quietly critique the social conventions of her time. Throughout the series, Pirkis views the world around her—the backroom labor of forgotten poor women, the casual dehumanization of immigrants, the poverty in the streets—with a clearheaded gaze unusual among the mostly escapist crime writers of her era. Brooke and her boss, Ebenezer Dyer, "chief of the well-known detective agency in Lynch Court, Fleet Street," often argue, but he respects her talents and hard work. Although in one story Brooke gets rescued at the last minute by men, it was she who went in after the villain and arranged for the men's arrival.

Pirkis's first of fourteen volumes of fiction was published in 1877 and her last, a collection of stories about Brooke, in 1894. In 1891 she and her husband, a retired naval officer, founded the National Canine Defence League. After Loveday Brooke, Pirkis devoted the remaining sixteen years of her life to campaigning for the better welfare of the nation's countless dogs. The organization became the major educational and lobbying force against everything from casual abuse and neglect to science-minded exploitation such as vivisection and, eventually, the use of dogs in early space exploration. In 2003, more than a century after Pirkis founded it, the National Canine Defence League became the Dogs Trust.

A series of six Loveday Brooke stories appeared between February and July of 1893 in the newly founded *Ludgate Monthly*, which identified itself as a "family magazine," part of the targeted marketing aimed at new female readers. "The Murder at Troyte's Hill," the second installment, was published in the March issue. Pirkis added a seventh story that appeared in March 1894, after the periodical had changed its name to reflect the times and become *The Ludgate Illustrated Magazine*. The same year, Hutchinson & Company published the seven stories in *The Experiences of Loveday Brooke, Lady Detective*. Like the debut story, "The Black Bag Left on a Door-Step," this one takes off in the first sentence, in a lively dialogue between Brooke and her boss, Ebenezer Dyer. The opening description of Brooke that begins this selection comes from the debut story. "The Murder at Troyte's Hill" actually begins after the row of asterisks.

The Murder at Troyte's Hill

LOVEDAY BROOKE, AT THIS period of her career, was a little over thirty years of age, and could be best described in a series of negations.

She was not tall, she was not short; she was not dark, she was not fair; she was neither handsome nor ugly. Her features were altogether nondescript; her one noticeable trait was a habit she had, when absorbed in thought, of dropping her eyelids over her eyes till only a line of eyeball showed, and she appeared to be looking out at the world through a slit, instead of through a window.

Her dress was invariably black, and was almost Quaker-like in its neat primness. Some five or six years previously, by a jerk of Fortune's wheel, Loveday had been thrown upon the world penniless and all but friendless. Marketable accomplishments she had found she had none, so she had forthwith defied convention, and had chosen for herself a career that had cut her off sharply from her former associates and her position in society. For five or six years she drudged away patiently in the lower walks of her profession; then chance, or, to speak more precisely, an intricate criminal case, threw her in the way of the experienced head of the flourishing detective agency in Lynch Court. He quickly enough found out the stuff she was made of, and threw her in the way of better-class work—work, indeed, that brought increase of pay and of reputation alike to him and to Loveday.

Ebenezer Dyer was not, as a rule, given to enthusiasm; but he would at times wax eloquent over Miss Brooke's qualifications for the profession she had chosen.

"Too much of a lady, do you say?" he would say to anyone who chanced to call in question those qualifications. "I don't care twopence-halfpenny whether she is or is not a lady. I only know she is the most sensible and practical woman I ever met. In the first place, she has the faculty—so rare among women—of carrying out orders to the very letter; in the second place, she has a clear, shrewd brain, unhampered by any hard-and-fast theories; thirdly, and most important item of all, she has so much common sense that it amounts to genius—positively to genius, sir."

★　★　★　★　★

"Griffiths, of the Newcastle Constabulary, has the case in hand," said Mr. Dyer; "those Newcastle men are keen-witted, shrewd fellows, and very jealous of outside interference. They only sent to me under protest, as it were, because they wanted your sharp wits at work inside the house."

"I suppose throughout I am to work with Griffiths, not with you?" said Miss Brooke.

"Yes; when I have given you in outline the facts of the case, I simply have nothing more to do with it, and you must depend on Griffiths for any assistance of any sort that you may require."

Here, with a swing, Mr. Dyer opened his big ledger and turned rapidly over its leaves till he came to the heading "Troyte's Hill" and the date "September 6th."

"I'm all attention," said Loveday, leaning back in her chair in the attitude of a listener.

"The murdered man," resumed Mr. Dyer, "is a certain Alexander Henderson—usually known as old Sandy—lodge-keeper to

Mr. Craven, of Troyte's Hill, Cumberland. The lodge consists merely of two rooms on the ground floor, a bedroom and a sitting-room; these Sandy occupied alone, having neither kith nor kin of any degree. On the morning of September 6th, some children going up to the house with milk from the farm, noticed that Sandy's bed-room window stood wide open. Curiosity prompted them to peep in; and then, to their horror, they saw old Sandy, in his night-shirt, lying dead on the floor, as if he had fallen backwards from the window. They raised an alarm; and on examination, it was found that death had ensued from a heavy blow on the temple, given either by a strong fist or some blunt instrument. The room, on being entered, presented a curious appearance. It was as if a herd of monkeys had been turned into it and allowed to work their impish will. Not an article of furniture remained in its place: the bed-clothes had been rolled into a bundle and stuffed into the chimney; the bedstead—a small iron one—lay on its side; the one chair in the room stood on the top of the table; fender and fire-irons lay across the washstand, whose basin was to be found in a farther corner, holding bolster and pillow. The clock stood on its head in the middle of the mantelpiece; and the small vases and ornaments, which flanked it on either side, were walking, as it were, in a straight line towards the door. The old man's clothes had been rolled into a ball and thrown on the top of a high cupboard in which he kept his savings and whatever valuables he had. This cupboard, however, had not been meddled with, and its contents remained intact, so it was evident that robbery was not the motive for the crime. At the inquest, subsequently held, a verdict of 'willful murder' against some person or persons unknown was returned. The local police are diligently investigating the affair, but, as yet, no arrests have been made. The opinion that at present prevails in the neighbourhood is that the crime has been perpetrated by some lunatic, escaped or otherwise, and enquiries are being made at the local asylums as to missing or lately released inmates. Griffiths, however, tells me that his suspicions set in another direction."

"Did anything of importance transpire at the inquest?"

"Nothing specially important. Mr. Craven broke down in giving his evidence when he alluded to the confidential relations that had always subsisted between Sandy and himself, and spoke of the last time that he had seen him alive. The evidence of the butler, and one or two of the female servants, seems clear enough, and they let fall something of a hint that Sandy was not altogether a favourite among them, on account of the overbearing manner in which he used his influence with his master. Young Mr. Craven, a youth of about nineteen, home from Oxford for the long vacation, was not present at the inquest; a doctor's certificate was put in stating that he was suffering from typhoid fever, and could not leave his bed without risk to his life. Now this young man is a thoroughly bad sort, and as much a gentleman-blackleg as it is possible for such a young fellow to be. It seems to Griffiths that there is something suspicious about this illness of his. He came back from Oxford on the verge of delirium tremens, pulled round from that, and then suddenly, on the day after the murder, Mrs. Craven rings the bell, announces that he has developed typhoid fever and orders a doctor to be sent for."

"What sort of man is Mr. Craven senior?"

"He seems to be a quiet old fellow, a scholar and learned philologist. Neither his neighbours nor his family see much of him; he almost lives in his study, writing a treatise, in seven or eight volumes, on comparative philology. He is not a rich man. Troyte's Hill, though it carries position in the county, is not a paying property, and Mr. Craven is unable to keep it up properly. I am told he has had to cut down expenses in all directions in order to send his son to college, and his daughter from first to last has been entirely educated by her mother. Mr. Craven was originally intended for the church, but for some reason or other, when his college career came to an end, he did not present himself for ordination—went out to Natal instead, where he obtained some civil appointment and where he remained for about fifteen years. Henderson was his servant during the latter portion of his Oxford career, and must have been greatly respected by him, for although the remuneration derived from his appointment at Natal was small, he paid Sandy a regular yearly allowance out of it. When, about ten years ago, he succeeded to Troyte's Hill, on the death of his elder brother, and returned home with his family, Sandy was immediately installed as lodge-keeper, and at so high a rate of pay that the butler's wages were cut down to meet it."

"Ah, that wouldn't improve the butler's feelings towards him," ejaculated Loveday.

Mr. Dyer went on: "But, in spite of his high wages, he doesn't appear to have troubled much about his duties as lodge-keeper, for they were performed, as a rule, by the gardener's boy, while he took his meals and passed his time at the house, and, speaking generally, put his finger into every pie. You know the old adage respecting the servant of twenty-one years' standing: 'Seven years my servant, seven years my equal, seven years my master.' Well, it appears to have held good in the case of Mr. Craven and Sandy. The old gentleman, absorbed in his philological studies, evidently let the reins slip through his fingers, and Sandy seems to have taken easy possession of them. The servants frequently had to go to him for orders, and he carried things, as a rule, with a high hand."

"Did Mrs. Craven never have a word to say on the matter?"

"I've not heard much about her. She seems to be a quiet sort of person. She is a Scotch missionary's daughter; perhaps she spends her time working for the Cape mission and that sort of thing."

"And young Mr. Craven: did he knock under to Sandy's rule?"

"Ah, now you're hitting the bull's eye and we come to Griffiths' theory. The young man and Sandy appear to have been at logger-heads ever since the Cravens took possession of Troyte's Hill. As a schoolboy Master Harry defied Sandy and threatened him with his hunting-crop; and subsequently, as a young man, has used strenu-ous endeavours to put the old servant in his place. On the day before the murder, Griffiths says, there was a terrible scene between the

two, in which the young gentleman, in the presence of several witnesses, made use of strong language and threatened the old man's
life. Now, Miss Brooke, I have told you all the circumstances of the
case so far as I know them. For fuller particulars I must refer you to
Griffiths. He, no doubt, will meet you at Grenfell—the nearest station to Troyte's Hill, and tell you in what capacity he has procured
for you an entrance into the house. By-the-way, he has wired to me
this morning that he hopes you will be able to save the Scotch express to-night."

Loveday expressed her readiness to comply with Mr. Griffiths'
wishes.

"I shall be glad," said Mr. Dyer, as he shook hands with her at the
office door, "to see you immediately on your return—that, however, I suppose, will not be yet awhile. This promises, I fancy, to be
a longish affair?" This was said interrogatively.

"I haven't the least idea on the matter," answered Loveday. "I start
on my work without theory of any sort—in fact, I may say, with
my mind a perfect blank."

And anyone who had caught a glimpse of her blank, expression-
less features, as she said this, would have taken her at her word.

Grenfell, the nearest post-town to Troyte's Hill, is a fairly busy,
populous little town—looking south towards the black country,
and northwards to low, barren hills. Pre-eminent among these
stands Troyte's Hill, famed in the old days as a border keep, and
possibly at a still earlier date as a Druid stronghold.

At a small inn at Grenfell, dignified by the title of "The Station
Hotel," Mr. Griffiths, of the Newcastle Constabulary, met Loveday
and still further initiated her into the mysteries of the Troyte's Hill
murder.

"A little of the first excitement has subsided," he said, after pre-
liminary greetings had been exchanged; "but still the wildest ru-
mours are flying about and repeated as solemnly as if they were
Gospel truths. My chief here and my colleagues generally adhere
to their first conviction, that the criminal is some suddenly crazed

tramp or else an escaped lunatic, and they are confident that sooner or later we shall come upon his traces. Their theory is that Sandy, hearing some strange noise at the park gates, put his head out of the window to ascertain the cause and immediately had his death blow dealt him; then they suppose that the lunatic scrambled into the room through the window and exhausted his frenzy by turning things generally upside down. They refuse altogether to share my suspicions respecting young Mr. Craven."

Mr. Griffiths was a tall, thin-featured man, with iron-grey hair, but so close to his head that it refused to do anything but stand on end. This gave a somewhat comic expression to the upper portion of his face and clashed oddly with the melancholy look that his mouth habitually wore.

"I have made all smooth for you at Troyte's Hill," he presently went on. "Mr. Craven is not wealthy enough to allow himself the luxury of a family lawyer, so he occasionally employs the services of Messrs. Wells and Sugden, lawyers in this place, and who, as it happens, have, off and on, done a good deal of business for me. It was through them I heard that Mr. Craven was anxious to secure the assistance of an amanuensis. I immediately offered your services, stating that you were a friend of mine, a lady of impoverished means, who would gladly undertake the duties for the munificent sum of a guinea a month, with board and lodging. The old gentleman at once jumped at the offer, and is anxious for you to be at Troyte's Hill at once."

Loveday expressed her satisfaction with the programme that Mr. Griffiths had sketched for her, then she had a few questions to ask.

"Tell me," she said, "what led you, in the first instance, to suspect young Mr. Craven of the crime?"

"The footing on which he and Sandy stood towards each other, and the terrible scene that occurred between them only the day before the murder," answered Griffiths, promptly. "Nothing of this, however, was elicited at the inquest, where a very fair face was put on Sandy's relations with the whole of the Craven family. I have subsequently unearthed a good deal respecting the private life of Mr. Harry Craven, and, among other things, I have found out that on the night of the murder he left the house shortly after ten o'clock, and no one, so far as I have been able to ascertain, knows at what hour he returned. Now I must draw your attention, Miss Brooke, to the fact that at the inquest the medical evidence went to prove that the murder had been committed between ten and eleven at night."

"Do you surmise, then, that the murder was a planned thing on the part of this young man?"

"I do. I believe that he wandered about the grounds until Sandy shut himself in for the night, then aroused him by some outside noise, and, when the old man looked out to ascertain the cause, dealt him a blow with a bludgeon or loaded stick, that caused his death."

"A cold-blooded crime that, for a boy of nineteen?"

"Yes. He's a good-looking, gentlemanly youngster, too, with manners as mild as milk, but from all accounts is as full of wickedness as an egg is full of meat. Now, to come to another point—if, in connection with these ugly facts, you take into consideration the suddenness of his illness, I think you'll admit that it bears a suspicious appearance and might reasonably give rise to the surmise that it was a plant on his part, in order to get out of the inquest."

"Who is the doctor attending him?"

"A man called Waters; not much of a practitioner, from all accounts, and no doubt he feels himself highly honoured in being summoned to Troyte's Hill. The Cravens, it seems, have no family doctor. Mrs. Craven, with her missionary experience, is half a doctor herself, and never calls in one except in a serious emergency."

"The certificate was in order, I suppose?"

"Undoubtedly. And, as if to give colour to the gravity of the case, Mrs. Craven sent a message down to the servants, that if any of them were afraid of the infection they could at once go to their homes. Several of the maids, I believe, took advantage of her permission, and packed their boxes. Miss Craven, who is a delicate girl, was sent away with her maid to stay with friends at Newcastle, and Mrs. Craven isolated herself with her patient in one of the disused wings of the house."

"Has anyone ascertained whether Miss Craven arrived at her destination at Newcastle?"

Griffiths drew his brows together in thought.

"I did not see any necessity for such a thing," he answered. "I don't quite follow you. What do you mean to imply?"

"Oh, nothing. I don't suppose it matters much: it might have been interesting as a side-issue." She broke off for a moment, then added:

"Now tell me a little about the butler, the man whose wages were cut down to increase Sandy's pay."

"Old John Hales? He's a thoroughly worthy, respectable man; he was butler for five or six years to Mr. Craven's brother, when he was master of Troyte's Hill, and then took duty under this Mr. Craven. There's no ground for suspicion in that quarter. Hales's exclamation when he heard of the murder is quite enough to stamp him as an innocent man: 'Serve the old idiot right,' he cried: 'I couldn't pump up a tear for him if I tried for a month of Sundays!' Now I take it, Miss Brooke, a guilty man wouldn't dare make such a speech as that!"

"You think not?"

Griffiths stared at her. "I'm a little disappointed in her," he thought. "I'm afraid her powers have been slightly exaggerated if she can't see such a straight-forward thing as that."

Aloud he said, a little sharply, "Well, I don't stand alone in my thinking. No one yet has breathed a word against Hales, and if they did, I've no doubt he could prove an *alibi* without any trouble, for he lives in the house, and everyone has a good word for him."

"I suppose Sandy's lodge has been put into order by this time?"

"Yes; after the inquest, and when all possible evidence had been taken, everything was put straight."

"At the inquest it was stated that no marks of footsteps could be traced in any direction?"

"The long drought we've had would render such a thing impossible, let alone the fact that Sandy's lodge stands right on the graveled drive, without flower-beds or grass borders of any sort around it. But look here, Miss Brooke, don't you be wasting your time over the lodge and its surroundings. Every iota of fact on that matter has been gone through over and over again by me and my chief. What we want you to do is to go straight into the house and concentrate attention on Master Harry's sick-room, and find out what's going on there. What he did outside the house on the night of the 6th, I've no doubt I shall be able to find out for myself. Now, Miss Brooke, you've asked me no end of questions, to which I have replied as fully as it was in my power to do; will you be good enough to answer one question that I wish to put, as straightforwardly as I have answered yours? You have had fullest particulars given you of the condition of Sandy's room when the police entered it on the morning after the murder. No doubt, at the present moment, you can see it all in your mind's eye—the bedstead on its side, the clock on its head, the bed-clothes half-way up the chimney, the little vases and ornaments walking in a straight line towards the door?"

Loveday bowed her head.

"Very well. Now will you be good enough to tell me what this scene of confusion recalls to your mind before anything else?"

"The room of an unpopular Oxford freshman after a raid upon it by undergrads," answered Loveday promptly.

Mr. Griffiths rubbed his hands.

"Quite so!" he ejaculated. "I see, after all, we are one at heart in this matter, in spite of a little surface disagreement of ideas. Depend upon it, by-and-bye, like the engineers tunneling from different quarters under the Alps, we shall meet at the same point and shake hands. By-the-way, I have arranged for daily communication between us through the postboy who takes the letters to Troyte's Hill.

He is trustworthy, and any letter you give him for me will find its way into my hands within the hour."

It was about three o'clock in the afternoon when Loveday drove in through the park gates of Troyte's Hill, past the lodge where old Sandy had met with his death. It was a pretty little cottage, covered with Virginia creeper and wild honeysuckle, and showing no outward sign of the tragedy that had been enacted within.

The park and pleasure-grounds of Troyte's Hill were extensive, and the house itself was a somewhat imposing red-brick structure, built, possibly, at the time when Dutch William's taste had grown popular in the country. Its frontage presented a somewhat forlorn appearance, its centre windows—a square of eight—alone seeming to show signs of occupation. With the exception of two windows at the extreme end of the bedroom floor of the north wing, where, possibly, the invalid and his mother were located, and two windows at the extreme end of the ground floor of the south wing, which Loveday ascertained subsequently were those of Mr. Craven's study, not a single window in either wing owned blind or curtain. The wings were extensive, and it was easy to understand that at the extreme end of the one the fever patient would be isolated from the rest of the household, and that at the extreme end of the other Mr. Craven could secure the quiet and freedom from interruption which, no doubt, were essential to the due prosecution of his philological studies.

Alike on the house and ill-kept grounds were present the stamp of the smallness of the income of the master and owner of the place. The terrace, which ran the length of the house in front, and on to which every window on the ground floor opened, was miserably out of repair: not a lintel or door-post, window-ledge or balcony but what seemed to cry aloud for the touch of the painter. "Pity me! I have seen better days," Loveday could fancy written as a legend across the red-brick porch that gave entrance to the old house.

The butler, John Hales, admitted Loveday, shouldered her port-manteau and told her he would show her to her room. He was a tall, powerfully-built man, with a ruddy face and dogged expression of countenance. It was easy to understand that, off and on, there must have been many a sharp encounter between him and old Sandy. He treated Loveday in an easy, familiar fashion, evidently considering that an amanuensis took much the same rank as a nursery governess—that is to say, a little below a lady's maid and a little above a house-maid.

"We're short of hands, just now," he said, in broad Cumberland dialect, as he led the way up the wide stair case. "Some of the lasses downstairs took fright at the fever and went home. Cook and I are single-handed, for Moggie, the only maid left, has been told off to wait on Madam and Master Harry. I hope you're not afeared of fever?"

Loveday explained that she was not, and asked if the room at the extreme end of the north wing was the one assigned to "Madam and Master Harry."

"Yes," said the man; "it's convenient for sick nursing; there's a flight of stairs runs straight down from it to the kitchen quarters. We put all Madam wants at the foot of those stairs and Moggie herself never enters the sick-room. I take it you'll not be seeing Madam for many a day, yet awhile."

"When shall I see Mr. Craven? At dinner to-night?"

"That's what naebody could say," answered Hales. "He may not come out of his study till past midnight; sometimes he sits there till two or three in the morning. Shouldn't advise you to wait till he wants his dinner—better have a cup of tea and a chop sent up to you. Madam never waits for him at any meal."

As he finished speaking he deposited the portmanteau outside one of the many doors opening into the gallery.

"This is Miss Craven's room," he went on; "cook and me thought you'd better have it, as it would want less getting ready than the other rooms, and work is work when there are so few hands to do it. Oh, my stars! I do declare there is cook putting it straight for you now." The last sentence was added as the opened door laid bare to view, the cook, with a duster in her hand, polishing a mirror; the bed had been made, it is true, but otherwise the room must have been much as Miss Craven left it, after a hurried packing up.

To the surprise of the two servants Loveday took the matter very lightly.

"I have a special talent for arranging rooms and would prefer getting this one straight for myself," she said. "Now, if you will go and get ready that chop and cup of tea we were talking about just now, I shall think it much kinder than if you stayed here doing what I can so easily do for myself."

When, however, the cook and butler had departed in company, Loveday showed no disposition to exercise the "special talent" of which she had boasted.

She first carefully turned the key in the lock and then proceeded to make a thorough and minute investigation of every corner of the room. Not an article of furniture, not an ornament or toilet accessory, but what was lifted from its place and carefully scrutinized. Even the ashes in the grate, the debris of the last fire made there, were raked over and well looked through.

This careful investigation of Miss Craven's late surroundings occupied in all about three quarters of an hour, and Loveday, with her hat in her hand, descended the stairs to see Hales crossing the hall to the dining-room with the promised cup of tea and chop.

In silence and solitude she partook of the simple repast in a dining-hall that could with ease have banqueted a hundred and fifty guests.

"Now for the grounds before it gets dark," she said to herself, as she noted that already the outside shadows were beginning to slant.

The dining-hall was at the back of the house; and here, as in the front, the windows, reaching to the ground, presented easy means of egress. The flower-garden was on this side of the house and sloped downhill to a pretty stretch of well-wooded country.

Loveday did not linger here even to admire, but passed at once round the south corner of the house to the windows which she had ascertained, by a careless question to the butler, were those of Mr. Craven's study.

Very cautiously she drew near them, for the blinds were up, the curtains drawn back. A side glance, however, relieved her apprehensions, for it showed her the occupant of the room, seated in an easy-chair, with his back to the windows. From the length of his outstretched limbs he was evidently a tall man. His hair was silvery and curly, the lower part of his face was hidden from her view by the chair, but she could see one hand was pressed tightly across his eyes and brows. The whole attitude was that of a man absorbed in deep thought. The room was comfortably furnished, but presented an appearance of disorder from the books and manuscripts scattered in all directions. A whole pile of torn fragments of foolscap sheets, overflowing from a waste-paper basket beside the writing-table, seemed to proclaim the fact that the scholar had of late grown weary of, or else dissatisfied with his work, and had condemned it freely.

Although Loveday stood looking in at this window for over five minutes, not the faintest sign of life did that tall, reclining figure give, and it would have been as easy to believe him locked in sleep as in thought.

From here she turned her steps in the direction of Sandy's lodge. As Griffiths had said, it was graveled up to its doorstep. The blinds were closely drawn, and it presented the ordinary appearance of a disused cottage.

A narrow path beneath over-arching boughs of cherry-laurel and arbutus, immediately facing the lodge, caught her eye, and down this she at once turned her footsteps.

This path led, with many a wind and turn, through a belt of shrubbery that skirted the frontage of Mr. Craven's grounds, and eventually, after much zig-zagging, ended in close proximity to the stables. As Loveday entered it, she seemed literally to leave daylight behind her.

"I feel as if I were following the course of a circuitous mind," she said to herself as the shadows closed around her. "I could not fancy Sir Isaac Newton or Bacon planning or delighting in such a wind-about-alley as this!"

The path showed greyly in front of her out of the dimness. On and on she followed it; here and there the roots of the old laurels, struggling out of the ground, threatened to trip her up. Her eyes, however, had now grown accustomed to the half-gloom, and not a detail of her surroundings escaped her as she went along.

A bird flew from out the thicket on her right hand with a startled cry. A dainty little frog leaped out of her way into the shriveled leaves lying below the laurels. Following the movements of this frog, her eye was caught by something black and solid among those leaves. What was it? A bundle—a shiny black coat? Loveday knelt down, and using her hands to assist her eyes, found that they came into contact with the dead, stiffened body of a beautiful black retriever. She parted, as well as she was able, the lower boughs of the evergreens, and minutely examined the poor animal. Its eyes were still open, though glazed and bleared, and its death had, undoubtedly, been caused by the blow of some blunt, heavy instrument, for on one side its skull was almost battered in.

"Exactly the death that was dealt to Sandy," she thought, as she groped hither and thither beneath the trees in hopes of lighting upon the weapon of destruction.

She searched until increasing darkness warned her that search was useless. Then, still following the zig-zagging path, she made her way out by the stables and thence back to the house.

She went to bed that night without having spoken to a soul beyond the cook and butler. The next morning, however, Mr. Craven introduced himself to her across the breakfast-table. He was a man of really handsome personal appearance, with a fine carriage of the head and shoulders, and eyes that had a forlorn, appealing look in them. He entered the room with an air of great energy, apologized to Loveday for the absence of his wife, and for his own remissness in not being in the way to receive her on the previous day. Then he bade her make herself at home at the breakfast-table, and expressed his delight in having found a coadjutor in his work.

"I hope you understand what a great—a stupendous work it is?" he added, as he sank into a chair. "It is a work that will leave its impress upon thought in all the ages to come. Only a man who has studied comparative philology as I have for the past thirty years, could gauge the magnitude of the task I have set myself."

With the last remark, his energy seemed spent, and he sank back in his chair, covering his eyes with his hand in precisely the same attitude as that in which Loveday had seen him over-night, and utterly oblivious of the fact that breakfast was before him and a stranger-guest seated at table. The butler entered with another dish. "Better go on with your breakfast," he whispered to Loveday, "he may sit like that for another hour."

He placed his dish in front of his master.

"Captain hasn't come back yet, sir," he said, making an effort to arouse him from his reverie.

"Eh, what?" said Mr. Craven, for a moment lifting his hand from his eyes.

"Captain, sir—the black retriever," repeated the man.

The pathetic look in Mr. Craven's eyes deepened.

"Ah, poor Captain!" he murmured; "the best dog I ever had."

Then he again sank back in his chair, putting his hand to his forehead.

The butler made one more effort to arouse him.

"Madam sent you down a newspaper, sir, that she thought you would like to see," he shouted almost into his master's ear, and at the same time laid the morning's paper on the table beside his plate.

"Confound you! leave it there," said Mr. Craven irritably. "Fools! dolts that you all are! With your trivialities and interruptions you are sending me out of the world with my work undone!"

And again he sank back in his chair, closed his eyes and became lost to his surroundings.

Loveday went on with her breakfast. She changed her place at table to one on Mr. Craven's right hand, so that the newspaper sent down for his perusal lay between his plate and hers. It was folded into an oblong shape, as if it were wished to direct attention to a certain portion of a certain column.

A clock in a corner of the room struck the hour with a loud, resonant stroke. Mr. Craven gave a start and rubbed his eyes.

"Eh, what's this?" he said. "What meal are we at?" He looked around with a bewildered air. "Eh!—who are you?" he went on, staring hard at Loveday. "What are you doing here? Where's Nina?— Where's Harry?"

Loveday began to explain, and gradually recollection seemed to come back to him.

"Ah, yes, yes," he said. "I remember; you've come to assist me with my great work. You promised, you know, to help me out of the hole I've got into. Very enthusiastic, I remember they said you were, on certain abstruse points in comparative philology. Now, Miss—Miss—I've forgotten your name—tell me a little of what you know about the elemental sounds of speech that are common to all languages. Now, to how many would you reduce those elemental sounds—to six, eight, nine? No, we won't discuss the matter here, the cups and saucers distract me. Come into my den at the other end of the house; we'll have perfect quiet there."

And utterly ignoring the fact that he had not as yet broken his fast, he rose from the table, seized Loveday by the wrist, and led her out of the room and down the long corridor that led through the south wing to his study.

But seated in that study his energy once more speedily exhausted itself.

He placed Loveday in a comfortable chair at his writing-table, consulted her taste as to pens, and spread a sheet of foolscap before her. Then he settled himself in his easy-chair, with his back to the light, as if he were about to dictate folios to her.

In a loud, distinct voice he repeated the title of his learned work, then its sub-division, then the number and heading of the chapter that was at present engaging his attention. Then he put his hand to his head. "It's the elemental sounds that are my stumbling-block," he said. "Now, how on earth is it possible to get a notion of a sound of agony that is not in part a sound of terror? or a sound of surprise that is not in part a sound of either joy or sorrow?"

With this his energies were spent, and although Loveday remained seated in that study from early morning till daylight began to fade, she had not ten sentences to show for her day's work as amanuensis.

Loveday in all spent only two clear days at Troyte's Hill.

On the evening of the first of those days Detective Griffiths received, through the trustworthy postboy, the following brief note from her:

"I have found out that Hales owed Sandy close upon a hundred pounds, which he had borrowed at various times. I don't know whether you will think this fact of any importance.—L. B."

Mr. Griffiths repeated the last sentence blankly. "If Harry Craven were put upon his defence, his counsel, I take it, would consider the fact of first importance," he muttered. And for the remainder of that day Mr. Griffiths went about his work in a perturbed state of mind, doubtful whether to hold or to let go his theory concerning Harry Craven's guilt.

The next morning there came another brief note from Loveday which ran thus:

"As a matter of collateral interest, find out if a person, calling himself Harold Cousins, sailed two days ago from London Docks for Natal in the *Bonnie Dundee*?"

To this missive Loveday received, in reply, the following somewhat lengthy dispatch:

"I do not quite see the drift of your last note, but have wired to our agents in London to carry out its suggestion. On my part, I have important news to communicate. I have found out what Harry Craven's business out of doors was on the night of the murder, and at my instance a warrant has been issued for his arrest. This warrant it will be my duty to serve on him in the course of to-day. Things are beginning to look very black against him, and I am convinced his illness is all a sham. I have seen Waters, the man who is supposed to be attending him, and have driven him into a corner and made him admit that he has only seen young Craven once—on the first day of his illness—and that he gave his certificate entirely on the strength of what Mrs. Craven told him of her son's condition. On the occasion of this, his first and only visit, the lady, it seems, also told him that it would not be necessary for him to continue his attendance, as she quite felt herself competent to treat the case, having had so much experience in fever cases among the blacks at Natal.

"As I left Waters's house, after eliciting this important information, I was accosted by a man who keeps a low-class inn in the place, McQueen by name. He said that he wished to speak to me on a matter of importance. To make a long story short, this McQueen stated that on the night of the sixth, shortly after eleven o'clock, Harry Craven came to his house, bringing with him a valuable piece of plate—a handsome epergne—and requested him to lend him a hundred pounds on it, as he hadn't a penny in his pocket. McQueen complied with his request to the extent of ten sovereigns, and now, in a fit of nervous terror, comes to me to confess himself a receiver of stolen goods and play the honest man! He says he noticed that the young gentleman was very much agitated as he made the request, and he also begged him to mention his visit to no one. Now, I am curious to learn how Master Harry will get over the fact that he passed the lodge at the hour at which the murder was most probably committed; or how he will get out of the dilemma of having repassed the lodge on his way back to the house, and not noticed the wide-open window with the full moon shining down on it?

"Another word! Keep out of the way when I arrive at the house, somewhere between two and three in the afternoon, to serve the warrant. I do not wish your professional capacity to get wind, for you will most likely yet be of some use to us in the house."

Loveday read this note, seated at Mr. Craven's writing-table, with the old gentleman himself reclining motionless beside her in his easy-chair. A little smile played about the corners of her mouth as she read over again the words—"for you will most likely yet be of some use to us in the house."

Loveday's second day in Mr. Craven's study promised to be as unfruitful as the first. For fully an hour after she had received Griffiths' note, she sat at the writing-table with her pen in her hand, ready to transcribe Mr. Craven's inspirations. Beyond, however, the phrase, muttered with closed eyes—"It's all here, in my brain, but I can't put it into words"—not a half-syllable escaped his lips.

At the end of that hour the sound of footsteps on the outside gravel made her turn her head towards the window. It was Griffiths approaching with two constables. She heard the hall door opened to admit them, but, beyond that, not a sound reached her ear, and she realized how fully she was cut off from communication with the rest of the household at the farther end of this unoccupied wing.

Mr. Craven, still reclining in his semi-trance, evidently had not the faintest suspicion that so important an event as the arrest of his only son on a charge of murder was about to be enacted in the house.

Meantime, Griffiths and his constables had mounted the stairs leading to the north wing, and were being guided through the corridors to the sick-room by the flying figure of Moggie, the maid.

"Hoot, mistress!" cried the girl, "here are three men coming up the stairs—policemen, every one of them—will ye come and ask them what they be wanting?"

Outside the door of the sick-room stood Mrs. Craven—a tall, sharp-featured woman with sandy hair going rapidly grey.

"What is the meaning of this? What is your business here?" she said haughtily, addressing Griffiths, who headed the party.

Griffiths respectfully explained what his business was, and requested her to stand on one side that he might enter her son's room.

"This is my daughter's room; satisfy yourself of the fact," said the lady, throwing back the door as she spoke.

And Griffiths and his confrères entered, to find pretty Miss Craven, looking very white and scared, seated beside a fire in a long flowing robe de chambre.

Griffiths departed in haste and confusion, without the chance of a professional talk with Loveday. That afternoon saw him telegraphing wildly in all directions, and dispatching messengers in all quarters. Finally he spent over an hour drawing up an elaborate report to his chief at Newcastle, assuring him of the identity of one Harold Cousins, who had sailed in the *Bonnie Dundee* for Natal, with Harry Craven, of Troyte's Hill, and advising that the police authorities in that far-away district should be immediately communicated with.

The ink had not dried on the pen with which this report was written before a note, in Loveday's writing, was put into his hand.

Loveday evidently had had some difficulty in finding a messenger for this note, for it was brought by a gardener's boy, who informed Griffiths that the lady had said he would receive a gold sovereign if he delivered the letter all right.

Griffiths paid the boy and dismissed him, and then proceeded to read Loveday's communication.

It was written hurriedly in pencil, and ran as follows:

"Things are getting critical here. Directly you receive this, come up to the house with two of your men, and post yourselves anywhere in the grounds where you can see and not be seen. There will be no difficulty in this, for it will be dark by the time you are able to get there. I am not sure whether I shall want your aid to-night, but you had better keep in the grounds until morning, in case of need; and above all, never once lose sight of the study windows." (This was underscored.) "If I put a lamp with a green shade in one of those windows, do not lose a moment in entering by that window, which I will contrive to keep unlocked."

Detective Griffiths rubbed his forehead—rubbed his eyes, as he finished reading this.

"Well, I daresay it's all right," he said, "but I'm bothered, that's all, and for the life of me I can't see one step of the way she is going."

He looked at his watch: the hands pointed to a quarter past six. The short September day was drawing rapidly to a close. A good five miles lay between him and Troyte's Hill—there was evidently not a moment to lose.

At the very moment that Griffiths, with his two constables, were once more starting along the Grenfell High Road behind the best horse they could procure, Mr. Craven was rousing himself from his long slumber, and beginning to look around him. That slumber, however, though long, had not been a peaceful one, and it was sundry of the old gentleman's muttered exclamations, as he had started uneasily in his sleep, that had caused Loveday to open, and then to creep out of the room to dispatch, her hurried note.

What effect the occurrence of the morning had had upon the household generally, Loveday, in her isolated corner of the house, had no means of ascertaining. She only noted that when Hales brought in her tea, as he did precisely at five o'clock, he wore a particularly ill-tempered expression of countenance, and she heard him mutter, as he set down the tea-tray with a clatter, something about being a respectable man, and not used to such "goings on."

It was not until nearly an hour and a half after this that Mr. Craven had awakened with a sudden start, and, looking wildly around him, had questioned Loveday, who had entered the room.

Loveday explained that the butler had brought in lunch at one, and tea at five, but that since then no one had come in.

"Now that's false," said Mr. Craven, in a sharp, unnatural sort of voice; "I saw him sneaking round the room, the whining, canting hypocrite, and you must have seen him, too! Didn't you hear him say, in his squeaky old voice: 'Master, I knows your secret—'" He broke off abruptly, looking wildly round. "Eh, what's this?" he cried. "No, no, I'm all wrong—Sandy is dead and buried—they held an inquest on him, and we all praised him up as if he were a saint."

"He must have been a bad man, that old Sandy," said Loveday sympathetically.

"You're right! you're right!" cried Mr. Craven, springing up excitedly from his chair and seizing her by the hand. "If ever a man deserved his death, he did. For thirty years he held that rod over my head, and then—ah where was I?"

He put his hand to his head and again sank, as if exhausted, into his chair.

"I suppose it was some early indiscretion of yours at college that he knew of?" said Loveday, eager to get at as much of the truth as possible while the mood for confidence held sway in the feeble brain.

"That was it! I was fool enough to marry a disreputable girl—a barmaid in the town—and Sandy was present at the wedding, and then—" Here his eyes closed again and his mutterings became incoherent.

For ten minutes he lay back in his chair, muttering thus; "A yelp—a groan," were the only words Loveday could distinguish among those mutterings, then suddenly, slowly and distinctly, he said, as if answering some plainly-put question: "A good blow with the hammer and the thing was done."

"I should like amazingly to see that hammer," said Loveday; "do you keep it anywhere at hand?"

His eyes opened with a wild, cunning look in them.

"Who's talking about a hammer? I did not say I had one. If any-one says I did it with a hammer, they're telling a lie."

"Oh, you've spoken to me about the hammer two or three times," said Loveday calmly; "the one that killed your dog, Captain, and I should like to see it, that's all."

The look of cunning died out of the old man's eye—"Ah, poor Captain! splendid dog that! Well, now, where were we? Where did we leave off? Ah, I remember, it was the elemental sounds of speech that bothered me so that night. Were you here then? Ah, no! I remember. I had been trying all day to assimilate a dog's yelp of pain to a human groan, and I couldn't do it. The idea haunted me—followed me about wherever I went. If they were both elemental sounds, they must have something in common, but the link between them I could not find; then it occurred to me, would a well-bred, well-trained dog like my Captain in the stables, there, at the moment of death give an unmitigated currish yelp; would there not be something of a human note in his death-cry? The thing was worth putting to the test. If I could hand down in my treatise a fragment of fact on the matter, it would be worth a dozen dogs' lives. So I went out into the moonlight—ah, but you know all about it—now, don't you?"

"Yes. Poor Captain! did he yelp or groan?"

"Why, he gave one loud, long, hideous yelp, just as if he had been a common cur. I might just as well have let him alone; it only set that other brute opening his window and spying out on me, and saying in his cracked old voice: 'Master, what are you doing out here at this time of night?'"

Again he sank back in his chair, muttering incoherently with half-closed eyes.

Loveday let him alone for a minute or so; then she had another question to ask.

"And that other brute—did he yelp or groan when you dealt him his blow?"

"What, old Sandy—the brute? he fell back—Ah, I remember, you said you would like to see the hammer that stopped his babbling old tongue—now didn't you?"

He rose a little unsteadily from his chair, and seemed to drag his long limbs with an effort across the room to a cabinet at the farther end. Opening a drawer in this cabinet, he produced, from amidst some specimens of strata and fossils, a large-sized geological hammer.

He brandished it for a moment over his head, then paused with his finger on his lip.

"Hush!" he said, "we shall have the fools creeping in to peep at us if we don't take care."

And to Loveday's horror he suddenly made for the door, turned the key in the lock, withdrew it and put it into his pocket.

She looked at the clock; the hands pointed to half-past seven. Had Griffiths received her note at the proper time, and were the men now in the grounds? She could only pray that they were.

"The light is too strong for my eyes," she said, and rising from her chair, she lifted the green-shaded lamp and placed it on a table that stood at the window.

"No, no, that won't do," said Mr. Craven; "that would show everyone outside what we're doing in here." He crossed to the window as he spoke and removed the lamp thence to the mantelpiece.

Loveday could only hope that in the few seconds it had remained in the window it had caught the eye of the outside watchers.

The old man beckoned to Loveday to come near and examine his deadly weapon. "Give it a good swing round," he said, suiting the action to the word, "and down it comes with a splendid crash." He brought the hammer round within an inch of Loveday's forehead.

She started back.

"Ha, ha," he laughed harshly and unnaturally, with the light of madness dancing in his eyes now; "did I frighten you? I wonder what sort of sound you would make if I were to give you a little tap just there." Here he lightly touched her forehead with the hammer. "Elemental, of course, it would be, and—"

Loveday steadied her nerves with difficulty. Locked in with this lunatic, her only chance lay in gaining time for the detectives to reach the house and enter through the window.

"Wait a minute," she said, striving to divert his attention; "you have not yet told me what sort of an elemental sound old Sandy made when he fell. If you'll give me pen and ink, I'll write down a full account of it all, and you can incorporate it afterwards in your treatise."

For a moment a look of real pleasure flitted across the old man's face, then it faded. "The brute fell back dead without a sound," he answered; "it was all for nothing, that night's work; yet not altogether for nothing. No, I don't mind owning I would do it all over again to get the wild thrill of joy at my heart that I had when I looked down into that old man's dead face and felt myself free at last! Free at last!" his voice rang out excitedly—once more he brought his hammer round with an ugly swing.

"For a moment I was a young man again; I leaped into his room—the moon was shining full in through the window—I thought of my old college days, and the fun we used to have at Pembroke—topsy turvey I turned everything—" He broke off abruptly, and drew a step nearer to Loveday. "The pity of it all was," he said, suddenly dropping from his high, excited tone to a low, pathetic one, "that he fell without a sound of any sort." Here he drew another step nearer. "I wonder—" he said, then broke off again, and came close to Loveday's side. "It has only this moment occurred to me," he said, now with his lips close to Loveday's ear, "that a woman, in her death agony, would be much more likely to give utterance to an elemental sound than a man."

He raised his hammer, and Loveday fled to the window, and was lifted from the outside by three pairs of strong arms.

"I thought I was conducting my very last case—I never had such a narrow escape before!" said Loveday, as she stood talking with Mr. Griffiths on the Grenfell platform, awaiting the train to carry her back to London. "It seems strange that no one before suspected the old gentleman's sanity—I suppose, however, people were so used to his eccentricities that they did not notice how they had deepened into positive lunacy. His cunning evidently stood him in good stead at the inquest."

"It is possible," said Griffiths thoughtfully, "that he did not absolutely cross the very slender line that divided eccentricity from madness until after the murder. The excitement consequent upon the discovery of the crime may just have pushed him over the border. Now, Miss Brooke, we have exactly ten minutes before your train comes in. I should feel greatly obliged to you if you would explain one or two things that have a professional interest for me."

"With pleasure," said Loveday. "Put your questions in categorical order and I will answer them."

"Well, then, in the first place, what suggested to your mind the old man's guilt?"

"The relations that subsisted between him and Sandy seemed to me to savour too much of fear on the one side and power on the other. Also the income paid to Sandy during Mr. Craven's absence in Natal bore, to my mind, an unpleasant resemblance to hush-money."

"Poor wretched being! And I hear that, after all, the woman he married in his wild young days died soon afterwards of drink. I have no doubt, however, that Sandy sedulously kept up the fiction of her existence, even after his master's second marriage. Now for another question: how was it you knew that Miss Craven had taken her brother's place in the sick-room?"

"On the evening of my arrival I discovered a rather long lock of fair hair in the unswept fireplace of my room, which, as it happened, was usually occupied by Miss Craven. It at once occurred to me that the young lady had been cutting off her hair and that there must be some powerful motive to induce such a sacrifice. The suspicious circumstances attending her brother's illness soon supplied me with such a motive."

"Ah! that typhoid fever business was very cleverly done. Not a servant in the house, I verily believe, but who thought Master Harry was upstairs, ill in bed, and Miss Craven away at her friends' in Newcastle. The young fellow must have got a clear start off within an hour of the murder. His sister, sent away the next day to

Newcastle, dismissed her maid there, I hear, on the plea of no ac-
commodation at her friends' house—sent the girl to her own home
for a holiday and herself returned to Troyte's Hill in the middle of
the night, having walked the five miles from Grenfell. No doubt
her mother admitted her through one of those easily-opened front
windows, cut her hair and put her to bed to personate her brother
without delay. With Miss Craven's strong likeness to Master Harry,
and in a darkened room, it is easy to understand that the eyes of a
doctor, personally unacquainted with the family, might easily be
deceived. Now, Miss Brooke, you must admit that with all this
elaborate chicanery and double dealing going on, it was only natural that my suspicions should set in strongly in that quarter."

"I read it all in another light, you see," said Loveday. "It seemed
to me that the mother, knowing her son's evil proclivities, believed
in his guilt, in spite, possibly, of his assertions of innocence. The
son, most likely, on his way back to the house after pledging the
family plate, had met old Mr. Craven with the hammer in his hand.
Seeing, no doubt, how impossible it would be for him to clear
himself without incriminating his father, he preferred flight to Natal
to giving evidence at the inquest."

"Now about his alias?" said Mr. Griffiths briskly, for the train
was at that moment steaming into the station. "How did you know
that Harold Cousins was identical with Harry Craven, and had
sailed in the *Bonnie Dundee*?"

"Oh, that was easy enough," said Loveday, as she stepped into
the train; "a newspaper sent down to Mr. Craven by his wife, was
folded so as to direct his attention to the shipping list. In it I saw
that the *Bonnie Dundee* had sailed two days previously for Natal.
Now it was only natural to connect Natal with Mrs. Craven, who
had passed the greater part of her life there; and it was easy to understand her wish to get her scapegrace son among her early friends.
The alias under which he sailed came readily enough to light. I
found it scribbled all over one of Mr. Craven's writing pads in his
study; evidently it had been drummed into his ears by his wife as

his son's alias, and the old gentleman had taken this method of fixing it in his memory. We'll hope that the young fellow, under his new name, will make a new reputation for himself—at any rate, he'll have a better chance of doing so with the ocean between him and his evil companions. Now it's good-bye, I think."

"No," said Mr. Griffiths; "it's au revoir, for you'll have to come back again for the assizes, and give the evidence that will shut old Mr. Craven in an asylum for the rest of his life."

George R. Sims

(1847–1922)

In the mid-1870s, George Sims began his writing career with brief contributions to the comic weekly *Fun*, a rival to *Punch*, along with William S. Gilbert and Ambrose Bierce and others who later gained fame. He seems to have never stopped writing for the next half century. Sims was best known in his own time as the author of many successful plays, from farce to melodrama to musical burlesques such as *Faust up to Date* and *Carmen up to Data*, performed at the West End's famous Gaiety Theatre, the influential home of English musical comedy until World War I. A number of these plays Sims co-wrote with collaborators, and some were adapted from French farces and other sources. He was also a popular reform-minded journalist in the Dickens tradition, writing about child abuse and the troubles of the urban poor and contributing a vast three-volume survey of London that is still considered a valuable historical text.

Sims liked variety. He wrote poetry, or at least verse, including the collection *The Dagonet Ballads*, which ranges from lighthearted ballads in dialect to shamelessly saturated pathos. Dagonet was his pseudonym for a column, "Mustard and Cress," in the sports paper *The Referee*. One poem, for example, entitled "Fellow Feeling," features a man explaining to his only remaining son why they must not drown a litter of puppies. Even in his verse Sims was a born reformer. In 1879 he wrote a Dickensian plea on behalf of the poor, the famous poem that opens with the line "It was Christmas Day in the workhouse . . ."

He also translated Balzac, barely evaded a libel suit after he satirized the popular actor Henry Irving, founded charities, raised bulldogs, marketed a hair-growing tonic, and quickly spent just about every shilling he earned. A friend of Arthur Conan Doyle's, Sims was also interested in criminology and crime fiction. He wrote a magazine series about Scotland Yard detectives, as well as a couple of detective novels, *The Case of George Candlemas* and *The Death Gamble*. In 1897 Sims launched a series of stories about a female detective named Dorcas Dene. Formerly the actress Dorcas Lester, she married artist Paul Dene, but when he went blind, she needed work. A friend, a retired police superintendent, invites her to help him. "You want me to be a lady detective?" she gasps in fine Victorian fashion. He explains that he wants her to help him solve a problem that is tearing apart a family and adds, "That is surely a business transaction in which an angel could engage without soiling its wings."

She accepts and becomes quite good at her job, eventually evolving into, as she describes herself, "a professional lady detective." One of the skills that Sherlock Holmes often emphasizes is the importance in a detective of employing disguises. George Sims took this idea to its logical extreme by making Dorcas Dene start out as an actress, so that disguise comes naturally to her. He brought to his Dene stories, with their abused wives and lost children, the same concern for the disadvantaged that marks his journalism and his nonfiction books. Sims had a light touch, but these stories were not lighthearted.

The Haverstock Hill Murder

THE BLINDS HAD BEEN down at the house in Elm Tree Road and the house shut for nearly six weeks. I had received a note from Dorcas saying that she was engaged on a case which would take her away for some little time, and that as Paul had not been very well lately she had arranged that he and her mother should accompany her. She would advise me as soon as they returned. I called once at Elm Tree Road and found it was in charge of the two servants and Toddlekins, the bulldog. The housemaid informed me that Mrs. Dene had not written, so that she did not know where she was or when she would be back, but that letters which arrived for her were forwarded by her instructions to Mr. Jackson of Penton Street, King's Cross.

Mr. Jackson, I remembered, was the ex-police-sergeant who was generally employed by Dorcas when she wanted a house watched or certain inquiries made among tradespeople. I felt that it would be unfair to go to Jackson. Had Dorcas wanted me to know where she was she would have told me in her letter.

The departure had been a hurried one. I had gone to the North in connection with a business matter of my own on a Thursday evening, leaving Dorcas at Elm Tree Road, and when I returned on Monday afternoon I found Dorcas's letter at my chambers. It was written on the Saturday, and evidently on the eve of departure.

But something that Dorcas did not tell me I learned quite accidentally from my old friend Inspector Swanage, of Scotland Yard, whom met one cold February afternoon at Kempton Park Steeplechases.

Inspector Swanage has a much greater acquaintance with the fraternity known as "the boys" than any other officer. He has attended race meetings for years, and the "boys" always greet him respectfully, though they wish him further. Many a prettily-planned coup of theirs has he nipped in the bud, and many an unsuspecting greenhorn has he saved from pillage by a timely whisper that the well-dressed young gentlemen who are putting their fivers on so merrily and coming out of the enclosure with their pockets stuffed full of bank-notes are men who get their living by clever swindling, and are far more dangerous than the ordinary vulgar pick-pocket.

On one occasion not many years ago I found a well-known publisher at a race meeting in earnest conversation with a beautifully-dressed, grey-haired sportsman. The publisher informed me that his new acquaintance was the owner of a horse which was certain to win the next race, and that it would start at ten to one. Only in order not to shorten the price nobody was to know the name of the horse, as the stable had three in the race. He had obligingly taken a fiver off the publisher to put on with his own money.

I told the publisher that he was the victim of a "tale-pitcher," and that he would never see his fiver again. At that moment Inspector Swanage came on the scene, and the owner of racehorses disappeared as if by magic. Swanage recognized the man instantly, and having heard my publisher's story said, "If I have the man taken will you prosecute?" The publisher shook his head. He didn't want to send his authors mad with delight at the idea that somebody had eventually succeeded in getting a fiver the best of him. So Inspector Swanage strolled away. Half an hour later he came to us in the enclosure and said, "Your friend's horse doesn't run, so he's given me that fiver back again for you." And with a broad grin he handed my friend a bank-note.

It was Inspector Swanage's skill and kindness on this occasion that made me always eager to have a chat with him when I saw him at a race meeting, for his conversation was always interesting.

The February afternoon had been a cold one, and soon after the commencement of racing there were signs of fog. Now a foggy afternoon is dear to the hearts of the "boys." It conceals their operations, and helps to cover their retreat. As the fog came up the Inspector began to look anxious, and I went up to him.

"You don't like the look of things?" I said.

"No, if this gets worse the band will begin to play—there are some very warm members of it here this afternoon. It was a day just like this last year that they held up a bookmaker going to the station, and eased him of over £500. Hullo?"

As he uttered the exclamation the Inspector pulled out his race card and seemed to be anxiously studying it.

But under his voice he said to me, "Do you see that tall man in a fur coat talking to a bookmaker? See, he's just handed him a bank-note?"

"Where?—I don't see him."

"Yonder. Do you see that old gipsy-looking woman with race cards? She has just thrust her hand through the railings and offered one to the man."

"Yes, yes—I see him now."

"That's Flash George. I've missed him lately, and I heard he was broke, but he's in funds again evidently by his get-up."

"One of the boys?"

"Has been—but he's been on another lay lately. He was mixed up in that big jewel case—£10,000 worth of diamonds stolen from a demimondaine. He got rid of some of the jewels for the thieves, but we could never bring it home to him. But he was watched for a long time afterwards and his game was stopped. The last we heard of him he was hard up and borrowing from some of his pals. He's gone now. I'll just go and ask the bookie what he's betting to."

The Inspector stepped across to the bookmaker and presently returned.

"He *is* in luck again," he said. "He's put a hundred ready on the favourite for this race. By the bye, how's your friend Mrs. Dene getting on with her case?"

I confessed my ignorance as to what Dorcas was doing at the present moment—all I knew was that she was away.

"Oh, I thought you'd have known all about it," said the Inspector. "She's on the Hannaford case."

"What, the murder?"

"Yes."

"But surely that was settled by the police? The husband was arrested immediately after the inquest."

"Yes, and the case against him was very strong, but we know that Dorcas Dene has been engaged by Mr. Hannaford's family, who have made up their minds that the police, firmly believing him guilty, won't look anywhere else for the murderer—of course they are convinced of his innocence. But you must excuse me— the fog looks like thickening, and may stop racing—I must go and put my men to work."

"One moment before you go—why did you suddenly ask me how Mrs. Dene was getting on? Was it anything to do with Flash George that put it in your head?"

The Inspector looked at me curiously.

"Yes," he said, "though I didn't expect you'd see the connection. It was a mere coincidence. On the night that Mrs. Hannaford was murdered, Flash George, who had been lost sight of for some time by our people, was reported to have been seen by the Inspector who was going his rounds in the neighbourhood. He was seen about half-past two o'clock in the morning looking rather dilapidated and seedy. When the report of the murder came in, the Inspector at once remembered that he had seen Flash George in Haverstock Hill. But there was nothing in it—as the house hadn't been broken into and there was nothing stolen. You understand now why seeing Flash George carried my train of thought on to the Hannaford murder and Dorcas Dene. Good-bye."

The Inspector hurried away and a few minutes afterwards the favourite came in alone for the second race on the card. The stewards immediately afterwards announced that racing would be abandoned on account of the fog increasing, and I made my way to the railway station and went home by the members' train.

Directly I reached home I turned eagerly to my newspaper file and read up the Hannaford murder. I knew the leading features, but every detail of it had now a special interest to me, seeing that Dorcas Dene had taken the case up.

These were the facts as reported in the Press:

Early in the morning of January 5 a maid-servant rushed out of the house, standing in its own grounds on Haverstock Hill, calling "Murder!" Several people who were passing instantly came to her and inquired what was the matter, but all she could gasp was, "Fetch a policeman." When the policeman arrived he followed the terrified girl into the house and was conducted to the drawing-room, where he found a lady lying in her nightdress in the centre of the room covered with blood, but still alive. He sent one of the servants for a doctor, and another to the police-station to inform the superintendent. The doctor came immediately and declared that the woman was dying. He did everything that could be done for her, and presently she partially regained consciousness. The superintendent had by this time arrived, and in the presence of the doctor asked her who had injured her.

She seemed anxious to say something, but the effort was too much for her, and presently she relapsed into unconsciousness. She died two hours later, without speaking.

The woman's injuries had been inflicted with some heavy instrument. On making a search of the room the poker was found lying between the fireplace and the body. The poker was found to have blood upon it, and some hair from the unfortunate lady's head.

The servants stated that their master and mistress, Mr. and Mrs. Hannaford, had retired to rest at their usual time, shortly before midnight. The housemaid had seen them go up together. She had been working at a dress which she wanted for next Sunday, and sat up late, using her sewing-machine in the kitchen. It was one o'clock in the morning when she passed her master and mistress's door, and she judged by what she heard that they were quarrelling. Mr. Hannaford was not in the house when the murder was discovered. The house was searched thoroughly in every direction, the first idea of the police being that he had committed suicide. The telegraph was then set to work, and at ten o'clock a man answering Mr. Hannaford's description was arrested at Paddington Station, where he was taking a ticket for Uxbridge.

Taken to the police-station and informed that he would be charged with murdering his wife, he appeared to be horrified, and for some time was a prey to the most violent emotion. When he had recovered himself and was made aware of the serious position in which he stood, he volunteered a statement. He was warned, but he insisted on making it. He declared that he and his wife had quarrelled violently after they had retired to rest. Their quarrel was about a purely domestic matter, but he was in an irritable, nervous condition, owing to his health, and at last he had worked himself up into such a state, that he had risen, dressed himself, and gone out into the street. That would be about two in the morning. He had wandered about in a state of nervous excitement until daybreak. At seven he had gone into a coffee-house and had breakfast, and had then gone into the park and sat on a seat and fallen asleep. When he woke up it was nine o'clock. He had taken a cab to Paddington, and had intended to go to Uxbridge to see his mother, who resided there. Quarrels between himself and his wife had been frequent of late, and he was ill and wanted to get away, and he thought perhaps if he went to his mother for a day or two he might get calmer and feel better. He had been very much worried lately over business matters. He was a stock-jobber, and the market in the securities in which he had been speculating was against him.

At the conclusion of the statement, which was made in a nervous, excited manner, he broke down so completely that it was deemed desirable to send for the doctor and keep him under close observation.

Police investigations of the premises failed to find any further clue. Everything pointed to the supposition that the result of the quarrel had been an attack by the husband—possibly in a sudden fit of homicidal mania—on the unfortunate woman. The police suggestion was that the lady, terrified by her husband's behaviour, had risen in the night and run down the stairs to the drawing-room, and that he had followed her there, picked up the poker, and furiously attacked her. When she fell, apparently lifeless, he had run back to his bedroom, dressed himself, and made his escape quietly from the house. There was nothing missing so far as could be ascertained—nothing to suggest in any way that any third party, a burglar from outside or some person inside, had had anything to do with the matter.

The coroner's jury brought in a verdict of wilful murder, and the husband was charged before a magistrate and committed for trial. But in the interval his reason gave way, and, the doctors certifying that he was undoubtedly insane, he was sent to Broadmoor.

Nobody had the slightest doubt of his guilt, and it was his mother who, broken-hearted, and absolutely refusing to believe in her son's guilt, had come to Dorcas Dene and requested her to take up the case privately and investigate it. The poor old lady declared that she was perfectly certain that her son could not have been guilty of such a deed, but the police were satisfied, and would make no further investigation.

This I learnt afterwards when I went to see Inspector Swanage. All I knew when I had finished reading up the case in the newspapers was that the husband of Mrs. Hannaford was in Broadmoor, practically condemned for the murder of his wife, and that Dorcas Dene had left home to try and prove his innocence.

The history of the Hannafords as given in the public Press was as follows: Mrs. Hannaford was a widow when Mr. Hannaford, a man of six-and-thirty, married her. Her first husband was a Mr. Charles Drayson, a financier, who had been among the victims of the disastrous fire in Paris. His wife was with him in the rue Jean Goujon that fatal night. When the fire broke out they both tried to escape together. They became separated in the crush. She was only slightly injured, and succeeded in getting out; he was less fortunate. His gold watch, a presentation one, with an inscription, was found among a mass of charred unrecognizable remains when the ruins were searched.

Three years after this tragedy the widow married Mr. Hannaford. The death of her first husband did not leave her well off. It was found that he was heavily in debt, and had he lived a serious charge of fraud would undoubtedly have been preferred against him. As it was, his partner, a Mr. Thomas Holmes, was arrested and sentenced to five years penal servitude in connection with a joint fraudulent transaction.

The estate of Mr. Drayson went to satisfy the creditors, but Mrs. Drayson, the widow, retained the house at Haverstock Hill, which he had purchased and settled on her, with all the furniture and contents, some years previously. She wished to continue living in the house when she married again, and Mr. Hannaford consented, and they made it their home. Hannaford himself, though not a wealthy man, was a fairly successful stock-jobber, and until the crisis, which had brought on great anxiety and helped to break down his health, had had no financial worries. But the marriage, so it was alleged, had not been a very happy one and quarrels had been frequent. Old Mrs. Hannaford was against it from the first, and to her her son always turned in his later matrimonial troubles. Now that his life had probably been spared by this mental breakdown, and he had been sent to Broadmoor, she had but one object in life—to set her son free, some day restored to reason, and with his innocence proved to the world.

IT WAS ABOUT A fortnight after my interview with Inspector Swanage, and my study of the details of the Haverstock Hill murder, that one morning I opened a telegram and to my intense delight

found that it was from Dorcas Dene. It was from London, and informed me that in the evening they would be very pleased to see
me at Elm Tree Road.

In the evening I presented myself about eight o'clock. Paul was
alone in the drawing-room when I entered, and his face and his
voice when he greeted me showed me plainly that he had benefited
greatly by the change.

"Where have you been, to look so well?" I asked. "The South of
Europe, I suppose—Nice or Monte Carlo?"

"No," said Paul smiling, "we haven't been nearly so far as that.
But I mustn't tell tales out of school. You must ask Dorcas."

At that moment Dorcas came in and gave me a cordial greeting.

"Well," I said, after the first conversational preliminaries, "who
committed the Haverstock Hill murder?"

"Oh, so you know that I have taken that up, do you? I imagined
it would get about through the Yard people. You see, Paul dear,
how wise I was to give out that I had gone away."

"Give out!" I exclaimed. "*Haven't* you been away then?"

"No, Paul and mother have been staying at Hastings, and I have
been down whenever I have been able to spare a day, but as a matter of fact I have been in London the greater part of the time."

"But I don't see the use of your pretending you were going away."

"I did it on purpose. I knew the fact that old Mrs. Hannaford had
engaged me would get about in certain circles, and I wanted certain
people to think that I had gone away to investigate some clue which
I thought I had discovered. In order to baulk all possible inquirers I
didn't even let the servants forward my letters. They went to Jackson, who sent them on to me."

"Then you were really investigating in London?"

"Now shall I tell you where you heard that I was on this case?"

"Yes."

"You heard it at Kempton Park Steeplechases, and your infor-
mant was Inspector Swanage."

"You have seen him and he has told you."

"No; I saw you there talking to him."

"*You* saw me? You were at Kempton Park? I never saw you."

"Yes, you did, for I caught you looking full at me. I was trying to sell some race cards just before the second race, and was holding them between the railings of the enclosure."

"What! You were that old gipsy woman? I'm certain Swanage didn't know you."

"I didn't want him to, or anybody else."

"It was an astonishing disguise. But come, aren't you going to tell me anything about the Hannaford case? I've been reading it up, but I fail entirely to see the slightest suspicion against any one but the husband. Everything points to his having committed the crime in a moment of madness. The fact that he has since gone completely out of his mind seems to me to show that conclusively."

"It is a good job he did go out of his mind—but for that I am afraid he would have suffered for the crime, and the poor broken-hearted old mother for whom I am working would soon have followed him to the grave."

"Then you don't share the general belief in his guilt?"

"I did at first, but I don't now."

"You have discovered the guilty party?"

"No—not yet—but I hope to."

"Tell me exactly all that has happened—there may still be a chance for your 'assistant.' "

"Yes, it is quite possible that now I may be able to avail myself of your services. You say you have studied the details of this case—let us just run through them together, and see what you think of my plan of campaign so far as it has gone. When old Mrs. Hannaford came to me, her son had already been declared insane and unable to plead, and had gone to Broadmoor. That was nearly a month after the commission of the crime, so that much valuable time had been lost. At first I declined to take the matter up—the police had so thoroughly investigated the affair. The case seemed so absolutely conclusive that I told her that it would be useless for her to incur the heavy expense of a private investigation. But she pleaded so earnestly—her faith in her son was so great—and she seemed such a sweet, dear old lady, that at last she conquered my scruples, and I consented to study the case, and see if there was the slightest alternative theory to go on. I had almost abandoned hope, for there was nothing in the published reports to encourage it, when I determined to go to the fountain-head, and see the Superintendent who had had the case in hand.

"He received me courteously, and told me everything. He was certain that the husband committed the murder. There was an entire absence of motive for any one else in the house to have done it, and the husband's flight from the house in the middle of the night was absolutely damning. I inquired if they had found any one who had seen the husband in the street—any one who could fix the time at which he had left the house. He replied that no such witness had been found. Then I asked if the policeman on duty that night had made any report of any suspicious characters being seen about. He said that the only person he had noticed at all was a man well known to the police—a man named Flash George. I asked what time Flash George had been seen and whereabouts, and I ascertained that it was at half-past two in the morning, and about a hundred yards below the scene of the crime, that when the policeman spoke to him he said he was coming from Hampstead, and was going to Covent Garden Market. He walked away in the direction of the Chalk Farm Road. I inquired what Flash George's record was, and ascertained that he was the associate of thieves and swindlers, and he was suspected of having disposed of some jewels, the proceeds of a robbery which had made a nine days' sensation. But the police had failed to bring the charge home to him, and the jewels had never been traced. He was also a gambler, a frequenter of racecourses and certain night-clubs of evil repute, and had not been seen about for some time previous to that evening."

"And didn't the police make any further investigations in that direction?"

"No. Why should they? There was nothing missing from the house—not the slightest sign of an attempted burglary. All their efforts were directed to proving the guilt of the unfortunate woman's husband."

"And you?"

"I had a different task—mine was to prove the husband's innocence. I determined to find out something more of Flash George. I shut the house up, gave out that I had gone away, and took, amongst other things, to selling cards and pencils on racecourses. The day that Flash George made his reappearance on the turf after a long absence was the day that he backed the winner of the second race at Kempton Park for a hundred pounds."

"But surely that proves that if he had been connected with any crime it must have been one in which money was obtained. No one has attempted to associate the murder of Mrs. Hannaford with robbery."

"No. But one thing is certain—that on the night of the crime Flash George was in the neighbourhood. Two days previously he had borrowed a few pounds of a pal because he was 'stony broke.' When he reappears as a racing man he has on a fur coat, is evidently in first-class circumstances, and he bets in hundred-pound notes. He is a considerably richer man after the murder of Mrs. Hannaford than he was before, and he was seen within a hundred yards of the house at half-past two o'clock on the night that the crime was committed."

"That might have been a mere accident. His sudden wealth may be the result of a lucky gamble, or a swindle of which you know nothing. I can't see that it can possibly have any bearing on the Hannaford crime, because nothing was taken from the house."

"Quite true. But here is a remarkable fact. When he went up to the betting man he went to one who was betting close to the rails. When he pulled out that hundred-pound note I was at the rails, and I pushed my cards in between and asked him to buy one. Flash George is a 'suspected character,' and quite capable on a foggy day of trying to swindle a bookmaker. The bookmaker took the precaution to open that note, it being for a hundred pounds, and examined it carefully. That enabled me to see the number. I had sharpened pencils to sell, and with one of them I hastily took down the number of that note—35421."

"That was clever. And you have traced it?"

"Yes."

"And has that furnished you with any clue?"

"It has placed me in possession of a most remarkable fact The hundred-pound note which was in Flash George's possession on Kempton Park racecourse was one of a number which were paid over the counter of the Union Bank of London for a five-thousand-pound cheque over ten years ago. And that cheque was drawn by the murdered woman's husband."

"Mr. Hannaford!"

"No; her first husband—Mr. Charles Drayson."

When Dorcas Dene told me that the £100 note Flash George had handed to the bookmaker at Kempton Park was one which had some years previously been paid to Mr. Charles Drayson, the first husband of the murdered woman, Mrs. Hannaford, I had to sit still and think for a moment.

It was curious certainly, but after all much more remarkable coincidences than that occur daily. I could not see what practical value there was in Dorcas's extraordinary discovery, because Mr. Charles Drayson was dead, and it was hardly likely that his wife would have kept a £100 note of his for several years. And if she had, she had not been murdered for that, because there were no signs of the house having been broken into. The more I thought the business over the more confused I became in my attempt to establish a clue from it, and so after a minute's silence I frankly confessed to Dorcas that I didn't see where her discovery led to.

"I don't say that it leads very far by itself," said Dorcas. "But you must look at *all* the circumstances. During the night of January 5 a lady is murdered in her own drawing-room. Round about the time that the attack is supposed to have been made upon her a well-known bad character is seen close to the house. That person, who just previously has been ascertained to have been so hard up that he had been borrowing of his associates, reappears on the turf a few weeks later expensively dressed and in possession of money. He bets with a £100 note, and that £100 note I have traced to the previous possession of the murdered woman's first husband, who lost his life in the disastrous fire in Paris, while oh a short visit to that capital."

"Yes, it certainly is curious, but—"

"Wait a minute—I haven't finished yet. Of the bank-notes—several of them for £100—which were paid some years ago to Mr. Charles Drayson, not one had come back to the bank *before* the murder."

"Indeed!"

"Since the murder *several* of them have come in. Now, is it not a remarkable circumstance that during all those years £5,000 worth of bank-notes should have remained out!"

"It is remarkable, but after all bank-notes circulate—they may pass through hundreds of hands before returning to the bank."

"Some may, undoubtedly, but it is highly improbable that *all* would under ordinary circumstances—especially notes for £100. These are sums which are not passed from pocket to pocket. As a rule they go to the bank of one of the early receivers of them, and from that bank into the Bank of England."

"You mean that it is an extraordinary fact that for many years not one of the notes paid to Mr. Charles Drayson by the Union Bank came back to the Bank of England."

"Yes, that *is* an extraordinary fact, but there is a fact which is more extraordinary still, and that is that soon after the murder of Mrs. Hannaford that state of things alters. It looks as though the murderer had placed the notes in circulation again."

"It does, certainly. Have you traced back any of the other notes that have come in?"

"Yes; but they have been cleverly worked. They have nearly all been circulated in the betting ring; those that have not have come in from money-changers in Paris and Rotterdam. My own belief is that before long the whole of those notes will come back to the bank."

"Then, my dear Dorcas, it seems to me that your course is plain, and you ought to go to the police and ask them to get the bank to circulate a list of the notes."

Dorcas shook her head. "No, thank you," she said. "I'm going to carry this case through on my own account. The police are convinced that the murderer is Mr. Hannaford, who is at present in Broadmoor, and the bank has absolutely no reason to interfere. No question has been raised of the notes having been stolen. They were paid to the man who died over ten years ago, not to the woman who was murdered last January."

"But you have traced one note to Flash George, who is a bad lot, and he was near the house on the night of the tragedy. You suspect Flash George and—"

"I do not suspect Flash George of the actual murder," she said, "and I don't see how he is to be arrested for being in possession of a bank-note which forms no part of the police case, and which he might easily say he had received in the betting ring."

"Then what *are* you going to do?"

"Follow up the clue I have. I have been shadowing Flash George all the time I have been away. I know where he lives—I know who are his companions."

"And do you think the murderer is among them?"

"No. They are all a little astonished at his sudden good fortune. I have heard them 'chip' him, as they call it, on the subject. I have carried my investigations up to a certain point and there they stop short. I am going a step further to-morrow evening, and it is in that step that I want assistance."

"And you have come to me?" I said eagerly.

"Yes."

"What do you want me to do?"

"To-morrow morning I am going to make a thorough examination of the room in which the murder was committed. To-morrow evening I have to meet a gentleman of whom I know nothing but his career and his name. I want you to accompany me."

"Certainly; but if I am your assistant in the evening I shall expect to be your assistant in the morning—I should very much like to see the scene of the crime."

"I have no objection. The house on Haverstock Hill is at present shut up and in charge of a caretaker, but the solicitors who are managing the late Mrs. Hannaford's estate have given me permission to go over it and examine it."

The next day at eleven o'clock I met Dorcas outside Mrs. Hannaford's house, and the caretaker, who had received his instructions, admitted us. He was the gardener, and an old servant, and had been present during the police investigation.

The bedroom in which Mr. Hannaford and his wife slept on the fatal night was on the floor above. Dorcas told me to go upstairs, shut the door, lie down on the bed, and listen. Directly a noise in the room below attracted my attention, I was to jump up, open the door and call out.

I obeyed her instructions and listened intently, but lying on the bed I heard nothing for a long time. It must have been quite a quarter of an hour when suddenly I heard a sound as of a door opening with a cracking sound. I leapt up, ran to the balusters, and called over, "I heard that!"

"All right, then, come down," said Dorcas, who was standing in the hall with the caretaker.

She explained to me that she had been moving about the drawing-room with the man, and they had both made as much noise with their feet as they could. They had even opened and shut the drawing-room door, but nothing had attracted my attention. Then Dorcas had sent the man to open the front door. It had opened with the cracking sound that I had heard.

"Now," said Dorcas to the caretaker, "you were here when the police were coming and going—did the front door always make a sound like that?"

"Yes, madam. The door had swollen or warped, or something, and it was always difficult to open. Mrs. Hannaford spoke about it once and was going to have it eased."

"That's it, then," said Dorcas to me. "The probability is that it was the noise made by the opening of that front door which first attracted the attention of the murdered woman."

"That was Hannaford going out—if his story is correct."

"No; Hannaford went out in a rage. He would pull the door open violently, and probably bang it to. That she would understand. It was when the door *opened again* with a sharp crack that she listened, thinking it was her husband come back."

"But she was murdered in the drawing-room!"

"Yes. My theory, therefore, is that after the opening of the front door she expected her husband to come upstairs. He didn't do so, and she concluded that he had gone into one of the rooms downstairs to spend the night, and she got up and came down to find him and ask him to get over his temper and come back to bed. She went into the drawing-room to see if he was there, and was struck down from behind before she had time to utter a cry. The servants heard nothing, remember."

"They said so at the inquest—yes."

"Now come into the drawing-room. This is where the caretaker tells me the body was found—here in the centre of the room—the poker with which the fatal blow had been struck was lying between the body and the fireplace. The absence of a cry and the position of the body show that when Mrs. Hannaford opened the door she *saw no one* (I am of course presuming that the murderer was *not* her husband) and she came in further. But there must have been some one in the room or she couldn't have been murdered in it."

"That is indisputable; but he might not have been in the room at the time—the person might have been hiding in the hall and followed her in."

"To suppose that we must presume that the murderer came into the room, took the poker from the fireplace, and went out again in order to come in again. That poker was secured, I am convinced, when the intruder heard footsteps coming down the stair. He picked up the poker and then concealed himself *here*."

"Then why, my dear Dorcas, shouldn't he have remained concealed until Mrs. Hannaford had gone out of the room again?"

"I think she was turning to go when he rushed out and struck her down. He probably thought that she had heard the noise of the door, and might go and alarm the servants."

"But just now you said she came in believing that her husband had returned and was in one of the rooms."

"The intruder could hardly be in possession of *her thoughts*."

"In the meantime he could have got out at the front door."

'Yes; but if his object was robbery he would have to go without the plunder. He struck the woman down in order to have time to get what he wanted."

"Then you think he left her here senseless while he searched the house?"

"Nobody got anything by searching the house, ma'am," broke in the caretaker. "The police satisfied themselves that nothing had been disturbed. Every door was locked, the plate was all complete, not a bit of jewellery or anything was missing. The servants were all examined about that, and the detectives went over every room and every cupboard to prove it wasn't no burglar broke in or anything of that sort. Besides, the windows were all fastened."

"What he says is quite true," said Dorcas to me, "but something alarmed Mrs. Hannaford in the night and brought her to the drawing-room in her nightdress. If it was, as I suspect, the opening of the front door, that is how the guilty person got in."

"The caretaker shook his head. "It was the poor master as did it, ma'am, right enough. He was out of his mind."

Dorcas shrugged her shoulders. "If he had done it, it would have been a furious attack, there would have been oaths and cries, and the poor lady would have received a rain of blows. The medical evidence shows that death resulted from *one* heavy blow on the *back* of the skull. But let us see where the murderer could have concealed himself ready armed with the poker here in the drawing-room."

In front of the drawing-room window were heavy curtains, and I at once suggested that curtains were the usual place of concealment on the stage and might be in real life.

As soon as I had asked the question Dorcas turned to the caretaker. "You are certain that every article of furniture is in its place exactly as it was that night?"

"Yes; the police prepared a plan of the room for the trial, and since then by the solicitors' orders we have not touched a thing."

"That settles the curtains then," continued Dorcas. "Look at the windows for yourself. In front of one, close by the curtains, is an ornamental table covered with china and glass and bric-à-brac; and in front of the other a large settee. No man could have come from behind those curtains without shifting that furniture out of his way. That would have immediately attracted Mrs. Hannaford's attention and given her time to scream and rush out of the room. No, we must find some other place for the assassin. Ah—I wonder if—"

Dorcas's eyes were fixed on a large brown bear which stood nearly against the wall by the fireplace. The bear, a very fine, big specimen, was supported in its upright position by an ornamental iron pole, at the top of which was fixed an oil lamp covered with a yellow silk shade.

"That's a fine bear lamp," exclaimed Dorcas.

"Yes," said the caretaker, "it's been here ever since I've been in the family's service. It was bought by the poor mistress's first husband, Mr. Drayson, and he thought a lot of it. But," he added, looking at it curiously, "I always thought it stood closer to the wall than that. It used to—right against it."

"Ah," exclaimed Dorcas, "that's interesting. Pull the curtains right back and give me all the light you can."

As the man obeyed her directions she went down on her hands and knees and examined the carpet carefully.

"You are right," she said. "This has been moved a little forward, and not so very long ago—the carpet for a square of some inches is a different colour to the rest. The brown bear stands on a square mahogany stand, and the exact square now shows in the colour of the carpet that has been hidden by it. Only here is a discoloured portion and the bear does not now stand on it."

The evidence of the bear having been moved forward from a position it had long occupied was indisputable. Dorcas got up and went to the door of the drawing-room.

"Go and stand behind that bear," she said. "Stand as compact as you can, as though you were endeavouring to conceal yourself."

I obeyed, and Dorcas, standing in the drawing-room doorway, declared that I was completely hidden.

"Now," she said, coming to the centre of the room and turning her back to me, "reach down from where you are and see if you can pick up the shovel from the fire-place without making a noise."

I reached out carefully and had the shovel in my hand without making a sound.

"I have it," I said.

"That's right. The poker would have been on the same side as the shovel, and much easier to pick up quietly. Now, while my back is turned, grasp the shovel by the handle, leap out at me, and raise the shovel as if to hit me—but don't get excited and do it, because I don't want to realize the scene *too* completely."

I obeyed. My footsteps were scarcely heard on the heavy-pile drawing-room carpet. When Dorcas turned round the shovel was above her head ready to strike.

"Thank you for letting me off," she said, with a smile. Then her face becoming serious again, she exclaimed: "The murderer of Mrs. Hannaford concealed himself behind that brown bear lamp, and attacked her in exactly the way I have indicated. But why had he moved the bear two or three inches forward?"

"To conceal himself behind it."

"Nonsense! His concealment was a sudden act That bear is heavy—the glass chimney of the lamp would have rattled if it had been done violently and hurriedly while Mrs. Hannaford was coming downstairs—that would have attracted her attention and she would have called out, 'Who's there?' at the doorway, and not have come in looking about for her husband."

Dorcas looked the animal over carefully, prodded it with her fingers, and then went behind it.

After a minute or two's close examination, she uttered a little cry and called me to her side.

She had found in the back of the bear a small straight slit. This was quite invisible. She had only discovered it by an accidentally violent thrust of her fingers into the animal's fur. Into this slit she thrust her hand, and the aperture yielded sufficiently for her to thrust her arm in. The interior of the bear was hollow, but Dorcas's hand as it went down struck against a wooden bottom. Then she withdrew her arm and the aperture closed up. It had evidently been specially prepared as a place of concealment, and only the most careful examination would have revealed it.

"Now," exclaimed Dorcas, triumphantly, "I think we are on a straight road! This, I believe, is where those missing bank-notes lay concealed for years. They were probably placed there by Mr. Drayson with the idea that some day his frauds might be discovered or he might be made a bankrupt. This was his little nest-egg, and his death in Paris before his fraud was discovered prevented him making use of them. Mrs. Hannaford evidently knew nothing of the hidden treasure, or she would speedily have removed it. But *some one* knew, and that some one put his knowledge to practical use the night that Mrs. Hannaford was murdered. The man who got in at the front door that night, got in to relieve the bear of its valuable stuffing; he moved the bear to get at the aperture, and was behind it when Mrs. Hannaford came in. The rest is easy to understand."

"But how did he get in at the front door?"

"That's what I have to find out. I am sure now that Flash George was in it. He was seen outside, and some of the notes that were concealed in the brown bear lamp have been traced to him. Who was Flash George's accomplice we may discover to-night. I think I have an idea, and if that is correct we shall have the solution of the whole mystery before dawn to-morrow morning."

"Why do you think you will learn so much to-night?"

"Because Flash George met a man two nights ago outside the Criterion. I was selling wax matches, and followed them up, pestering them. I heard George say to his companion, whom I had never seen with him before, 'Tell him Hungerford Bridge, midnight, Wednesday. Tell him to bring the lot and I'll cash up for them!'"

"And you think the 'him'—?"

"Is the man who rifled the brown bear and killed Mrs. Hannaford."

AT ELEVEN O'CLOCK THAT evening I met Dorcas Dene in Villiers Street. I knew what she would be like, otherwise her disguise would have completely baffled me. She was dressed as an Italian street musician, and was with a man who looked like an Italian organ-grinder.

Dorcas took my breath away by her first words.

"Allow me to introduce you," she said, "to Mr. Thomas Holmes. This is the gentleman who was Charles Drayson's partner, and was sentenced to five years' penal servitude over the partnership frauds."

"Yes," replied the organ-grinder in excellent English. "I suppose I deserved it for being a fool, but the villain was Drayson—he had all my money, and involved me in a fraud at the finish."

"I have told Mr. Holmes the story of our discovery," said Dorcas. "I have been in communication with him ever since I discovered the notes were in circulation. He knew Drayson's affairs, and he has given me some valuable information. He is with us to-night because he knew Mr. Drayson's former associates, and he may be able to identify the man who knew the secret of the house at Haverstock Hill."

"You think that is the man Flash George is to meet?"

"I do. What else can 'Tell him to bring the lot and I'll cash up' mean but the rest of the bank-notes?"

Shortly before twelve we got on to Hungerford Bridge—the narrow footway that runs across the Thames by the side of the railway.

I was to walk ahead and keep clear of the Italians until I heard a signal.

We crossed the bridge after that once or twice, I coming from one end and the Italians from the other, and passing each other about the centre.

At five minutes to midnight I saw Flash George come slowly along from the Middlesex, side. The Italians were not far behind. A minute later an old man with a grey beard, and wearing an old Inverness cape, passed me, coming from the Surrey side. When he met Flash George the two stopped and leant over the parapet, apparently interested in the river. Suddenly I heard Dorcas's signal. She began to sing the Italian song, "Santa Lucia."

I had my instructions. I jostled up against the two men and begged their pardon.

Flash George turned fiercely round. At the same moment I seized the old man and shouted for help. The Italians came hastily up. Several foot passengers rushed to the scene and inquired what was the matter.

"He was going to commit suicide," I cried. "He was just going to jump into the water."

The old man was struggling in my grasp. The crowd were keeping back Flash George. They believed the old man was struggling to get free to throw himself into the water.

The Italian rushed up to me.

"Ah, poor old man!" he said. "Don't let him get away!"

He gave a violent tug to the grey beard. It came off in his hands.

Then with an oath he seized the supposed would-be suicide by the throat.

"You infernal villain!" he said.

"Who is he?" asked Dorcas.

"Who is he!" exclaimed Thomas Holmes, "why, the villain who brought me to ruin—*my precious partner—Charles Drayson!*"

As the words escaped from the supposed Italian's lips, Charles Drayson gave a cry of terror, and leaping on to the parapet, plunged into the river.

Flash George turned to run, but was stopped by a policeman who had just come up.

Dorcas whispered something in the man's ear, and the officer, thrusting his hand in the rascal's pocket, drew out a bundle of banknotes.

A few minutes later the would-be suicide was brought ashore. He was still alive, but had injured himself terribly in his fall, and was taken to the hospital.

Before he died he was induced to confess that he had taken advantage of the Paris fire to disappear. He had flung his watch down in order that it might be found as evidence of his death. He had, previously to visiting the rue Jean Goujon, received a letter at his hotel which told him pretty plainly the game was up, and he knew that at any moment a warrant might be issued against him. After reading his name amongst the victims, he lived as best he could abroad, but after some years, being in desperate straits, he determined to do a bold thing, return to London and endeavour to get into his house and obtain possession of the money which was lying unsuspected in the interior of the brown bear lamp. He had concealed it, well knowing that at any time the crash might come, and everything belonging to him be seized. The hiding-place he had selected was one which neither his creditors nor his relatives would suspect.

On the night he entered the house, Flash George, whose acquaintance he had made in London, kept watch for him *while he let himself in with his latch-key*, which he had carefully preserved. Mr. Hannaford's leaving the house was one of those pieces of good fortune which occasionally favour the wicked.

With his dying breath Charles Drayson declared that he had no intention of killing his wife. He feared that, having heard a noise, she had come to see what it was, and might alarm the house in her terror, and as she turned to go out of the drawing-room he struck her, intending only to render her senseless until he had secured the booty.

MR. HANNAFORD, COMPLETELY RECOVERED and in his right mind, was in due time released from Broadmoor. The letter from his mother to Dorcas Dene, thanking her for clearing her son's character and proving his innocence of the terrible crime for which he had been practically condemned, brought tears to my eyes as Dorcas read it aloud to Paul and myself. It was touching and beautiful to a degree.

As she folded it up and put it away, I saw that Dorcas herself was deeply moved.

"These are the *rewards* of my profession," she said. "They compensate for everything."

Bret Harte

(1836–1902)

"THERE ARE PROBABLY MORE imitations of Sherlock Holmes,"
wrote Paul D. Herbert, "than of any other character from literature."
Aside from the admiring pastiches that seek—with wildly varying
results—to honor the style and atmosphere of the original Conan
Doyle stories, there have been uncountable numbers of parodies.
Only four months after Arthur Conan Doyle launched the series of
Holmes stories in 1891 in the *Strand,* with "A Scandal in Bohemia,"
the first parody appeared. O. Henry took a shot at the sage of Baker
Street and so did Mark Twain. The best, however, was "The Stolen
Cigar-Case," written by Twain's contemporary and occasional rival,
Bret Harte.

Harte led a colorful life. As a journalist on the *Northern Califor-
nian* he publicly damned the infamous 1860 massacre of the Wiyot,
a Native American tribe centered around Humboldt Bay and among
the last natives to face the violent onslaught of white invaders—
and he had to flee death threats. He was quick to condemn racism.
He wrote his poem "Plain Language from Truthful James," later
reprinted as "The Heathen Chinee," which he modeled upon a
Swinburne poem, as a parody of Irish immigrants' bias against
Chinese immigrants who had suddenly become their competitors
for jobs, but it was quickly adopted by the racists themselves as an
anthem. Harte's life was a roller coaster of good and bad fortune.

At one point he was one of the highest-paid authors in America, on salary for the *Atlantic Monthly,* but a few years later he was reduced to writing marketing jingles. Beginning in the late 1870s, he was appointed as a consul to Germany and later to Scotland and wound up settling in England. He is remembered now mostly for stories such as "The Luck of Roaring Camp" and "The Outcasts of Poker Flat." The following story appeared as part of his series of parodies, *Later Condensed Novels.* In the original publication, under "The Stolen Cigar-Case" appeared the words "by A. C---n D--le."

The Stolen Cigar-Case

I FOUND HEMLOCK JONES in the old Brook Street lodgings, musing before the fire. With the freedom of an old friend I at once threw myself in my old familiar attitude at his feet, and gently caressed his boot. I was induced to do this for two reasons; one that it enabled me to get a good look at his bent, concentrated face, and the other that it seemed to indicate my reverence for his superhuman insight. So absorbed was he, even then, in tracking some mysterious clue, that he did not seem to notice me. But therein I was wrong—as I always was in my attempt to understand that powerful intellect.

"It is raining," he said, without lifting his head.

"You have been out then?" I said quickly.

"No. But I see that your umbrella is wet, and that your overcoat, which you threw off on entering, has drops of water on it."

I sat aghast at his penetration. After a pause he said carelessly, as if dismissing the subject: "Besides, I hear the rain on the window. Listen."

I listened. I could scarcely credit my ears, but there was the soft pattering of drops on the pane. It was evident, there was no deceiving this man!

"Have you been busy lately?" I asked, changing the subject. "What new problem—given up by Scotland Yard as inscrutable—has occupied that gigantic intellect?"

He drew back his foot slightly, and seemed to hesitate ere he returned it to its original position. Then he answered wearily: "Mere trifles—nothing to speak of. The Prince Kapoli has been here to get my advice regarding the disappearance of certain rubies from the Kremlin; the Rajah of Pootibad, after vainly beheading his entire bodyguard, has been obliged to seek my assistance to recover a jewelled sword. The Grand Duchess of Pretzel-Brauntswig is desirous of discovering where her husband was on the night of the 14th of February, and last night"—he lowered his voice slightly—"a lodger in this very house, meeting me on the stairs, wanted to know 'Why they don't answer his bell.'"

I could not help smiling—until I saw a frown gathering on his inscrutable forehead.

"Pray to remember," he said coldly, "that it was through such an apparently trivial question that I found out, 'Why Paul Ferroll killed his Wife,' and 'What happened to Jones!'"

I became dumb at once. He paused for a moment, and then suddenly changing back to his usual pitiless, analytical style, he said: "When I say these are trifles—they are so in comparison to an affair that is now before me. A crime has been committed, and, singularly enough, against myself. You start," he said; "you wonder who would have dared attempt it! So did I; nevertheless, it has been done. I have been robbed!"

"You robbed—you, Hemlock Jones, the Terror of Peculators!" I gasped in amazement, rising and gripping the table as I faced him.

"Yes; listen. I would confess it to no other. But you who have followed my career, who know my methods; yea, for whom I have partly lifted the veil that conceals my plans from ordinary humanity; you, who have for years rapturously accepted my confidences, passionately admired my inductions and inferences, placed yourself at my beck and call, become my slave, grovelled at my feet, given up your practice except those few unremunerative and rapidly-decreasing patients to whom, in moments of abstraction over my problems, you have administered strychnine for quinine and arsenic for Epsom salts; you, who have sacrificed everything and every-body to me—*you* I make my confidant!"

I rose and embraced him warmly, yet he was already so engrossed in thought that at the same moment he mechanically placed his hand upon his watch chain as if to consult the time. "Sit down," he said; "have a cigar?"

"I have given up cigar smoking," I said.

"Why?" he asked.

I hesitated, and perhaps coloured. I had really given it up be-cause, with my diminished practice, it was too expensive. I could only afford a pipe. "I prefer a pipe," I said laughingly. "But tell me of this robbery. What have you lost?"

He rose, and planting himself before the fire with his hands un-der his coat tails, looked down upon me reflectively for a moment. "Do you remember the cigar-case presented to me by the Turkish Ambassador for discovering the missing favourite of the Grand Vizier in the fifth chorus girl at the Hilarity Theatre? It was that one. It was incrusted with diamonds. I mean the cigar-case."

"And the largest one had been supplanted by paste," I said.

"Ah," he said with a reflective smile, "you know that?"

"You told me yourself. I remember considering it a proof of your extraordinary perception. But, by Jove, you don't mean to say you have lost it?"

He was silent for a moment. "No; it has been stolen, it is true, but I shall still find it. And by myself alone! In your profession, my dear fellow, when a member is severely ill he does not prescribe for himself, but calls in a brother doctor. Therein we differ. I shall take this matter in my own hands."

"And where could you find better?" I said enthusiastically. "I should say the cigar-case is as good as recovered already."

"I shall remind you of that again," he said lightly. "And now, to show you my confidence in your judgment, in spite of my deter-mination to pursue this alone, I am willing to listen to any sugges-tions from you."

He drew a memorandum book from his pocket, and, with a grave smile, took up his pencil.

I could scarcely believe my reason. He, the great Hemlock Jones! accepting suggestions from a humble individual like myself! I kissed his hand reverently, and began in a joyous tone:

"First I should advertise, offering a reward. I should give the same information in handbills, distributed at the 'pubs' and the pastry-cooks. I should next visit the different pawnbrokers; I should give notice at the police station. I should examine the servants. I should thoroughly search the house and my own pockets. I speak relatively," I added with a laugh, "of course I mean *your* own."

He gravely made an entry of these details.

"Perhaps," I added, "you have already done this?"

"Perhaps," he returned enigmatically. "Now, my dear friend," he continued, putting the notebook in his pocket, and rising—"would you excuse me for a few moments? Make yourself perfectly at home until I return; there may be some things," he added with a sweep of his hand towards his heterogeneously filled shelves, "that may interest you, and while away the time. There are pipes and tobacco in that corner and whiskey on the table." And nodding to me with the same inscrutable face, he left the room. I was too well accustomed to his methods to think much of his unceremonious withdrawal, and made no doubt he was off to investigate some clue which had suddenly occurred to his active intelligence.

Left to myself, I cast a cursory glance over his shelves. There were a number of small glass jars, containing earthy substances labeled "Pavement and road sweepings," from the principal thoroughfares and suburbs of London, with the sub-directions "For identifying foot tracks." There were several other jars labeled "Fluff from omnibus and road-car seats," "Cocoanut fibre and rope strands from mattings in public places," "Cigarette stumps and match ends from floor of Palace Theatre, Row A, 1 to 50." Everywhere were evidences of this wonderful man's system and perspicacity.

I was thus engaged when I heard the slight creaking of a door, and I looked up as a stranger entered. He was a rough-looking man, with a shabby overcoat, a still more disreputable muffler round his throat, and a cap on his head. Considerably annoyed at his intrusion I turned upon him rather sharply, when, with a mumbled, growling apology for mistaking the room, he shuffled out again and closed the door. I followed him quickly to the landing and saw that he disappeared down the stairs.

With my mind full of the robbery, the incident made a singular impression on me. I knew my friend's habits of hasty absences from his room in his moments of deep inspiration; it was only too probable that with his powerful intellect and magnificent perceptive genius concentrated on one subject, he should be careless of his own belongings, and, no doubt, even forget to take the ordinary precaution of locking up his drawers. I tried one or two and found I was right—although for some reason I was unable to open one to its fullest extent. The handles were sticky, as if someone had opened them with dirty fingers. Knowing Hemlock's fastidious cleanliness, I resolved to inform him of this circumstance, but I forgot it, alas! until—but I am anticipating my story.

His absence was strangely prolonged. I at last seated myself by the fire, and lulled by warmth and the patter of the rain on the window, I fell asleep. I may have dreamt, for during my sleep I had a vague semi-consciousness as of hands being softly pressed on my pockets—no doubt induced by the story of the robbery. When I came fully to my senses, I found Hemlock Jones sitting on the other side of the hearth, his deeply concentrated gaze fixed on the fire.

"I found you so comfortably asleep that I could not bear to waken you," he said with a smile.

I rubbed my eyes. "And what news?" I asked. "How have you succeeded?"

"Better than I expected," he said, "and I think," he added, tapping his note-book—"I owe much to *you*."

Deeply gratified, I awaited more. But in vain. I ought to have remembered that in his moods Hemlock Jones was reticence itself. I told him simply of the strange intrusion, but he only laughed.

Later, when I rose to go, he looked at me playfully. "If you were a married man," he said, "I would advise you not to go home until you had brushed your sleeve. There are a few short, brown seal-skin hairs on the inner side of the fore-arm—just where they would have adhered if your arm had encircled a seal-skin sacque with some pressure!"

"For once you are at fault," I said triumphantly, "the hair is my own as you will perceive; I had just had it cut at the hair-dressers, and no doubt this arm projected beyond the apron."

He frowned slightly, yet nevertheless, on my turning to go he embraced me warmly—a rare exhibition in that man of ice. He even helped me on with my overcoat and pulled out and smoothed down the flaps of my pockets. He was particular, too, in fitting my arm in my overcoat sleeve, shaking the sleeve down from the arm-hole to the cuff with his deft fingers. "Come again soon!" he said, clapping me on the back.

"At any and all times," I said enthusiastically. "I only ask ten minutes twice a day to eat a crust at my office and four hours sleep at night, and the rest of my time is devoted to you always—as you know."

"It is, indeed," he said, with his impenetrable smile.

Nevertheless I did not find him at home when I next called. One afternoon, when nearing my own home I met him in one of his favourite disguises—a long, blue, swallow-tailed coat, striped cotton trousers, large turn-over collar, blacked face, and white hat, carrying a tambourine. Of course to others the disguise was perfect, although it was known to myself, and I passed him—according to an old understanding between us—without the slightest recognition, trusting to a later explanation. At another time, as I was making a professional visit to the wife of a publican at the East

End, I saw him in the disguise of a broken down artisan looking into the window of an adjacent pawnshop. I was delighted to see that he was evidently following my suggestions, and in my joy I ventured to tip him a wink; it was abstractedly returned.

Two days later I received a note appointing a meeting at his lodgings that night. That meeting, alas! was the one memorable occurrence of my life, and the last meeting I ever had with Hemlock Jones! I will try to set it down calmly, though my pulses still throb with the recollection of it.

I found him standing before the fire with that look upon his face which I had seen only once or twice in our acquaintance—a look which I may call an absolute concatenation of inductive and deductive ratiocination—from which all that was human, tender, or sympathetic, was absolutely discharged. He was simply an icy algebraic symbol! Indeed his whole being was concentrated to that extent that his clothes fitted loosely, and his head was absolutely so much reduced in size by his mental compression that his hat tipped back from his forehead and literally hung on his massive ears.

After I had entered, he locked the doors, fastened the windows, and even placed a chair before the chimney. As I watched those significant precautions with absorbing interest, he suddenly drew a revolver and presenting it to my temple, said in low, icy tones:

"Hand over that cigar-case!"

Even in my bewilderment, my reply was truthful, spontaneous, and involuntary. "I haven't got it," I said.

He smiled bitterly, and threw down his revolver. "I expected that reply! Then let me now confront you with something more awful, more deadly, more relentless and convincing than that mere lethal weapon—the damning inductive and deductive proofs of your guilt!" He drew from his pocket a roll of paper and a notebook.

"But surely," I gasped, "you are joking! You could not for a moment believe—"

"Silence!" he roared. "Sit down!"

I obeyed.

"You have condemned yourself," he went on pitilessly. "Condemned yourself on my processes—processes familiar to you, applauded by you, accepted by you for years! We will go back to the time when you first saw the cigar-case. Your expressions," he said in cold, deliberate tones, consulting his paper, "were: 'How beautiful! I wish it were mine.' This was your first step in crime—and my first indication. From 'I *wish* it were mine' to 'I *will* have it mine,' and the mere detail, 'How *can* I make it mine,' the advance was obvious. Silence! But as in my methods, it was necessary that there should be an overwhelming inducement to the crime, that unholy admiration of yours for the mere trinket itself was not enough. You are a smoker of cigars."

"But," I burst out passionately, "I told you I had given up smoking cigars."

"Fool!" he said coldly, "that is the *second* time you have committed yourself. Of course, you *told* me! what more natural than for you to blazon forth that prepared and unsolicited statement to *prevent* accusation. Yet, as I said before, even that wretched attempt to cover up your tracks was not enough. I still had to find that overwhelming, impelling motive necessary to affect a man like you. That motive I found in *passion*, the strongest of all impulses—love, I suppose you would call it," he added bitterly; "that night you called! You had brought the damning proofs of it in your sleeves."

"But," I almost screamed.

"Silence," he thundered, "I know what you would say. You would say that even if you had embraced some young person in a sealskin sacque what had that to do with the robbery. Let me tell you then, that that sealskin sacque represented the quality and character of your fatal entanglement! If you are at all conversant with light sporting literature you would know that a sealskin sacque indicates a love induced by sordid mercenary interests. You bartered your honour for it—that stolen cigar-case was the purchaser of the sealskin sacque! Without money, with a decreasing practice, it was the only way you could insure your passion being returned by that young person, whom, for your sake, I have not even pursued. Silence! Having thoroughly established your motive, I now proceed to the commission of the crime itself. Ordinary people would have begun with that—with an attempt to discover the whereabouts of the missing object. These are not my methods."

So overpowering was his penetration, that although I knew myself innocent, I licked my lips with avidity to hear the further details of this lucid exposition of my crime.

"You committed that theft the night I showed you the cigar-case and after I had carelessly thrown it in that drawer. You were sitting in that chair, and I had risen to take something from that shelf. In that instant you secured your booty without rising. Silence! Do you remember when I helped you on with your overcoat the other night? I was particular about fitting your arm in. While doing so I measured your arm with a spring tape measure from the shoulder to the cuff. A later visit to your tailor confirmed that measurement. It proved to be *the exact distance between your chair and that drawer!*"

I sat stunned.

"The rest are mere corroborative details! You were again tampering with the drawer when I discovered you doing so. Do not start! The stranger that blundered into the room with the muffler on—was myself. More, I had placed a little soap on the drawer handles when I purposely left you alone. The soap was on your hand when I shook it at parting. I softly felt your pockets when you were asleep for further developments. I embraced you when you left—that I might feel if you had the cigar-case, or any other articles, hidden on your body. This confirmed me in the belief that you had already disposed of it in the manner and for the purpose I have shown you. As I still believed you capable of remorse and confession, I allowed you to see I was on your track twice, once in the garb of an itinerant negro minstrel, and the second time as a workman looking in the window of the pawnshop where you pledged your booty."

"But," I burst out, "if you had asked the pawnbroker you would have seen how unjust—"

"Fool!" he hissed; "that was one of *your* suggestions to search the pawnshops. Do you suppose I followed any of your suggestions—the suggestions of the thief? On the contrary, they told me what to avoid."

"And I suppose," I said bitterly, "you have not even searched your drawer."

"No," he said calmly.

I was for the first time really vexed. I went to the nearest drawer and pulled it out sharply. It stuck as it had before, leaving a part of the drawer unopened. By working it, however, I discovered that it was impeded by some obstacle that had slipped to the upper part of the drawer, and held it firmly fast. Inserting my hand, I pulled out the impeding object. It was the missing cigar-case. I turned to him with a cry of joy.

But I was appalled at his expression. A look of contempt was now added to his acute, penetrating gaze. "I have been mistaken," he said slowly. "I had not allowed for your weakness and coward-ice. I thought too highly of you even in your guilt; but I see now why you tampered with that drawer the other night. By some in-credible means—possibly another theft—you took the cigar-case out of pawn, and like a whipped hound restored it to me in this feeble, clumsy fashion. You thought to deceive me, Hemlock Jones: more, you thought to destroy my infallibility. Go! I give you your liberty. I shall not summon the three policemen who wait in the adjoining room—but out of my sight for ever."

As I stood once more dazed and petrified, he took me firmly by the ear and led me into the hall, closing the door behind him. This re-opened presently wide enough to permit him to thrust out my hat, overcoat, umbrella and overshoes, and then closed against me for ever!

I never saw him again. I am bound to say, however, that thereafter my business increased—I recovered much of my old practice—and a few of my patients recovered also. I became rich. I had a brougham and a house in the West End. But I often wondered, pondering on that wonderful man's penetration and insight, if, in some lapse of consciousness, I had not really stolen his cigar-case!

✣

Robert Barr

(1849–1912)

SOMETIMES A PERFECTLY GOOD character gets demoted to mere
ancestor when a descendant comes along who is more colorful and
more successful. Such has been the case with Robert Barr's amusing,
vainglorious detective Eugène Valmont, who seems likely to have
inspired Agatha Christie's Hercule Poirot. In the entertaining series
of stories about him, Valmont is a smart and energetic detective
whose vanity sometimes gets in his way. The Frenchman's outsider
take on English life afforded Barr an opportunity for gentle satire.

About a year after the publication of the first Valmont story,
"The Mystery of the Five Hundred Diamonds," the *Saturday Evening Post* published "The Absent-Minded Coterie" in its May 13,
1905, issue. The story then appeared in England in the May 1906
issue of the *Windsor Magazine*. Barr wrote only eight Valmont stories, which in 1906 he gathered into an ironically titled collection,
The Triumphs of Eugène Valmont. The series opens with Valmont in
Paris, ultimately losing his high position in the French police because of what can only be described as flamboyant incompetence.
He retires to London and launches a second career as a private investigator. Christie's Poirot is Belgian, not French, and he winds
up in England as a World War I refugee, but he too metamorphoses from continental policeman to English private detective.

Barr was born in Glasgow but his family moved to Ontario

when he was five. He began his writing career by contributing to *Grip*, a satirical weekly magazine published in Toronto by pioneer Canadian cartoonist John Wilson Bengough. (Bengough named the periodical after the talking raven in Charles Dickens's novel *Barnaby Rudge*—who was in turn named after Dickens's own pet raven.) Barr studied teaching in Toronto and by 1874 was principal of Windsor's Central School. Two years later he went to work for the *Detroit Free Press* as a reporter and columnist. His nomadic life took him to England in the early 1880s, and in 1892 he founded an illustrated glossy monthly, *The Idler*, specifically aimed at "gentlemen," who by definition had plenty of idle time on their hands. Barr hired humorist Jerome K. Jerome, famous for the farcical novel *Three Men in a Boat*, as editor. During its almost twenty-year run of lightweight entertainment, *The Idler* published contributions by renowned writers such as Barr's friends Rudyard Kipling and Arthur Conan Doyle, along with many stories by Barr and Jerome themselves. Barr knew everyone from Joseph Conrad to Mark Twain.

Barr was a prolific writer and his stories show up in the contents pages of many Victorian and Edwardian magazines in the U.K. and the United States—*McClure's*, *The Strand*, *Everybody's*, *Argosy*. Valmont is not Barr's only contribution to detective stories. He also wrote collections such as *Revenge!* and *The Face and the Mask*. His many novels include *A Woman Intervenes* and *The Speculations of John Steele*. Today most of his work is completely forgotten, except among crime-fiction fans who are determined to keep alive the memory of Eugène Valmont, as in this surprising outing about a clever con artist.

The Absent-Minded Coterie

SOME YEARS AGO I enjoyed the unique experience of pursuing a man for one crime, and getting evidence against him of another. He was innocent of the misdemeanor, the proof of which I sought, but was guilty of another most serious offense, yet he and his confederates escaped scot-free in circumstances which I now purpose to relate.

You may remember that in Rudyard Kipling's story, "Bedalia Herodsfoot," the unfortunate woman's husband ran the risk of being arrested as a simple drunkard, at a moment when the blood of murder was upon his boots. The case of Ralph Summertrees was rather the reverse of this. The English authorities were trying to fasten upon him a crime almost as important as murder, while I was collecting evidence which proved him guilty of an action much more momentous than that of drunkenness.

The English authorities have always been good enough, when they recognize my existence at all, to look down upon me with amused condescension. If to-day you ask Spenser Hale, of Scotland Yard, what he thinks of Eugène Valmont, that complacent man will put on the superior smile which so well becomes him, and if you are a very intimate friend of his, he may draw down the lid of his right eye as he replies: "Oh, yes; a very decent fellow, Valmont, but he's a Frenchman!" as if, that said, there was no need of further inquiry.

Myself, I like the English detective very much, and if I were to be in a melee to-morrow, there is no man I would rather find beside me than Spenser Hale. In any situation where a fist that can fell an ox is desirable, my friend Hale is a useful companion, but for intellectuality, mental acumen, finesse—ah, well! I am the most modest of men, and will say nothing.

It would amuse you to see this giant come into my room during an evening, on the bluff pretense that he wishes to smoke a pipe with me. There is the same difference between this good-natured giant and myself as exists between that strong black pipe of his and my delicate cigarette, which I smoke feverishly, when he is present, to protect myself from the fumes of his terrible tobacco. I look with delight upon the huge man, who, with an air of the utmost good humor, and a twinkle in his eye as he thinks he is twisting me about his finger, vainly endeavors to obtain a hint regarding whatever case is perplexing him at that moment. I baffle him with the ease that an active greyhound eludes the pursuit of a heavy mastiff, then at last I say to him, with a laugh: "Come, mon ami Hale, tell me all about it, and I will help you if I can."

Once or twice at the beginning he shook his massive head, and replied the secret was not his. The last time he did this I assured him that what he said was quite correct, and then I related full particulars of the situation in which he found himself, excepting the names, for these he had not mentioned. I had pieced together his perplexity from scraps of conversation in his half-hour's fishing for my advice, which, of course, he could have had for the plain asking. Since that time he has not come to me except with cases he feels at liberty to reveal, and one or two complications I have happily been enabled to unravel for him.

But, stanch as Spenser Hale holds the belief that no detective service on earth can excel that centering in Scotland Yard, there is one department of activity in which even he confesses that Frenchmen are his masters, although he somewhat grudgingly qualifies his admission, by adding that we in France are constantly allowed to do what is prohibited in England. I refer to the minute search of a house during the owner's absence. If you read that excellent story entitled "The Purloined Letter," by Edgar Allan Poe, you will find a record of the kind of thing I mean, which is better than any description I, who have so often taken part in such a search, can set down.

Now, these people among whom I live are proud of their phrase, "The Englishman's house is his castle," and into that castle even a policeman cannot penetrate without a legal warrant. This may be all very well in theory, but if you are compelled to march up to a man's house, blowing a trumpet and rattling a snare drum, you need not be disappointed if you fail to find what you are in search of when all the legal restrictions are complied with. Of course, the English are a very excellent people, a fact to which I am always proud to bear testimony, but it must be admitted that for cold common sense the French are very much their superiors. In Paris, if I wish to obtain an incriminating document, I do not send the possessor a carte postale to inform him of my desire, and in this procedure the French people sanely acquiesce. I have known men who, when they go out to spend an evening on the boulevards, toss their bunch of keys to the concierge, saying: "If you hear the police rummaging about while I'm away, pray assist them, with an expression of my distinguished consideration."

I remember, while I was chief detective in the service of the French Government, being requested to call at a certain hour at the private hotel of the Minister for Foreign Affairs. It was during the time that Bismarck meditated a second attack upon my country, and I am happy to say that I was instrumental in supplying the Secret Bureau with documents which mollified that iron man's purpose, a fact which I think entitled me to my country's gratitude, not that I ever even hinted such a claim when a succeeding ministry forgot my services. The memory of a republic, as has been said by a greater man than I, is short. However, all that has nothing to do with the incident I am about to relate. I merely mention the crisis to excuse a momentary forgetfulness on my part which in any country might have been followed by serious results to myself. But in France—ah, we understand those things, and nothing happened.

I am the last person in the world to give myself away, as they say in the great West. I am usually the calm, collected Eugène Valmont whom nothing can perturb, but this was a time of great tension, and I had become absorbed. I was alone with the minister in his private house, and one of the papers he wished was in his bureau at the Ministry for Foreign Affairs; at least, he thought so, and said: "Ah! it is in my desk at the bureau. How annoying! I must send for it!"

"No, Excellency," I cried, springing up in a self-oblivion the most complete; "it is here."

Touching the spring of a secret drawer, I opened it, and taking out the document he wished, handed it to him.

It was not until I met his searching look, and saw the faint smile on his lips, that I realized what I had done.

"Valmont," he said quietly, "on whose behalf did you search my house?"

"Excellency," I replied in tones no less agreeable than his own, "to-night at your orders I pay a domiciliary visit to the mansion of Baron Dumoulaine, who stands high in the estimation of the President of the French Republic. If either of those distinguished gentlemen should learn of my informal call, and should ask me in whose interests I made the domiciliary visit, what is it you wish that I should reply?"

"You should reply, Valmont, that you did it in the interests of the Secret Service."

"I shall not fail to do so, Excellency, and in answer to your question just now, I had the honor of searching this mansion in the interests of the Secret Service of France."

The Minister for Foreign Affairs laughed; a hearty laugh that expressed no resentment.

"I merely wished to compliment you, Valmont, on the efficiency of your search and the excellence of your memory. This is indeed the document which I thought was left in my office."

I wonder what Lord Lansdowne would say if Spenser Hale showed an equal familiarity with his private papers! But now that we have returned to our good friend Hale, we must not keep him waiting any longer.

Mr. Spenser Hale of Scotland Yard

I WELL REMEMBER THE November day when I first heard of the Summertrees case, because there hung over London a fog so thick that two or three times I lost my way, and no cab was to be had at any price. The few cabmen then in the streets were leading their animals slowly along, making for their stables. It was one of those depressing London days which filled me with ennui and a yearning for my own clear city of Paris, where, if we are ever visited by a slight mist, it is at least clean, white vapor, and not this horrible London mixture saturated with suffocating carbon.

The fog was too thick for any passer to read the contents bills of the newspapers plastered on the pavement, and as there were probably no races that day the newsboys were shouting what they considered the next most important event—the election of an American President. I bought a paper and thrust it into my pocket. It was late when I reached my flat, and, after dining there, which was an unusual thing for me to do, I put on my slippers, took an easy-chair before the fire, and began to read my evening journal. I was distressed to learn that the eloquent Mr. Bryan had been defeated. I knew little about the silver question, but the man's oratorical powers had appealed to me, and my sympathy was aroused because he owned many silver mines, and yet the price of the metal was so low that apparently he could not make a living through the operation

of them. But, of course, the cry that he was a plutocrat, and a reputed millionaire over and over again, was bound to defeat him in
a democracy where the average voter is exceedingly poor and not
comfortably well-to-do, as is the case with our peasants in France.
I always took great interest in the affairs of the huge republic to the
west, having been at some pains to inform myself accurately regarding its politics; and although, as my readers know, I seldom
quote anything complimentary that is said of me, nevertheless, an
American client of mine once admitted that he never knew the true
inwardness—I think that was the phrase he used—of American
politics until he heard me discourse upon them. But then, he added,
he had been a very busy man all his life.

I had allowed my paper to slip to the floor, for in very truth the
fog was penetrating even into my flat, and it was becoming difficult to read, notwithstanding the electric light. My man came in,
and announced that Mr. Spenser Hale wished to see me, and, indeed, any night, but especially when there is rain or fog outside, I
am more pleased to talk with a friend than to read a newspaper.

"Mon Dieu, my dear Monsieur Hale, it is a brave man you are
to venture out in such a fog as is abroad to-night."

"Ah, Monsieur Valmont," said Hale with pride, "you cannot raise
a fog like this in Paris!"

"No. There you are supreme," I admitted, rising and saluting my
visitor, then offering him a chair.

"I see you are reading the latest news," he said, indicating my
newspaper. "I am very glad that man Bryan is defeated. Now we
shall have better times."

I waved my hand as I took my chair again. I will discuss many
things with Spenser Hale, but not American politics; he does not
understand them. It is a common defect of the English to suffer complete ignorance regarding the internal affairs of other countries.

"It is surely an important thing that brought you out on such a
night as this. The fog must be very thick in Scotland Yard."

This delicate shaft of fancy completely missed him, and he answered stolidly: "It's thick all over London, and, indeed, throughout most of England."

"Yes, it is," I agreed, but he did not see that either.

Still, a moment later, he made a remark which, if it had come from some people I know, might have indicated a glimmer of comprehension.

"You are a very, very clever man, Monsieur Valmont, so all I need say is that the question which brought me here is the same as that on which the American election was fought. Now, to a countryman, I should be compelled to give further explanation, but to you, monsieur, that will not be necessary."

There are times when I dislike the crafty smile and partial closing of the eyes which always distinguishes Spenser Hale when he places on the table a problem which he expects will baffle me. If I said he never did baffle me, I would be wrong, of course, for sometimes the utter simplicity of the puzzles which trouble him leads me into an intricate involution entirely unnecessary in the circumstances.

I pressed my finger tips together, and gazed for a few moments at the ceiling. Hale had lit his black pipe, and my silent servant placed at his elbow the whisky and soda, then tiptoed out of the room. As the door closed my eyes came from the ceiling to the level of Hale's expansive countenance.

"Have they eluded you?" I asked quietly.

"Who?"

"The coiners."

Hale's pipe dropped from his jaw, but he managed to catch it before it reached the floor. Then he took a gulp from the tumbler.

"That was just a lucky shot," he said.

"Parfaitement," I replied carelessly.

"Now, own up, Valmont, wasn't it?"

I shrugged my shoulders. A man cannot contradict a guest in his own house.

"Oh, stow that!" cried Hale impolitely. He is a trifle prone to strong and even slangy expressions when puzzled. "Tell me how you guessed it."

"It is very simple, mon ami. The question on which the American election was fought is the price of silver, which is so low that it has ruined Mr. Bryan, and threatens to ruin all the farmers of the West who possess silver mines on their farms. Silver troubled America, ergo silver troubles Scotland Yard.

"Very well; the natural inference is that some one has stolen bars of silver. But such a theft happened three months ago, when the metal was being unloaded from a German steamer at Southampton, and my dear friend Spenser Hale ran down the thieves very cleverly as they were trying to dissolve the marks off the bars with acid. Now crimes do not run in series, like the numbers in roulette at Monte Carlo. The thieves are men of brains. They say to themselves, 'What chance is there successfully to steal bars of silver while Mr. Hale is at Scotland Yard?' Eh, my good friend?"

"Really, Valmont," said Hale, taking another sip, "sometimes you almost persuade me that you have reasoning powers."

"Thanks, comrade. Then it is not a theft of silver we have now to deal with. But the American election was fought on the price of silver. If silver had been high in cost, there would have been no silver question. So the crime that is bothering you arises through the low price of silver, and this suggests that it must be a case of illicit coinage, for there the low price of the metal comes in. You have, perhaps, found a more subtle illegitimate act going forward than heretofore. Some one is making your shillings and your half crowns from real silver, instead of from baser metal, and yet there is a large profit which has not hitherto been possible through the high price of silver. With the old conditions you were familiar, but this new element sets at naught all your previous formulas. That is how I reasoned the matter out."

"Well, Valmont, you have hit it, I'll say that for you; you have hit it. There is a gang of expert coiners who are putting out real silver money, and making a clear shilling on the half crown. We can find no trace of the coiners, but we know the man who is shoving the stuff."

"That ought to be sufficient," I suggested.

"Yes, it should, but it hasn't proved so up to date. Now I came to-night to see if you would do one of your French tricks for us, right on the quiet."

"What French trick, Monsieur Spenser Hale?" I inquired with some asperity, forgetting for the moment that the man invariably became impolite when he grew excited.

"No offense intended," said this blundering officer, who really is a good-natured fellow, but always puts his foot in it, and then apologizes. "I want some one to go through a man's house without a search warrant, spot the evidence, let me know, and then we'll rush the place before he has time to hide his tracks."

"Who is this man, and where does he live?"

"His name is Ralph Summertrees, and he lives in a very natty little bijou residence, as the advertisements call it, situated in no less a fashionable street than Park Lane."

"I see. What has aroused your suspicions against him?"

"Well, you know, that's an expensive district to live in; it takes a bit of money to do the trick. This Summertrees has no ostensible business, yet every Friday he goes to the United Capital Bank in Piccadilly, and deposits a bag of swag, usually all silver coin."

"Yes; and this money?"

"This money, so far as we can learn, contains a good many of these new pieces which never saw the British Mint."

"It's not all the new coinage, then?"

"Oh, no, he's a bit too artful for that! You see, a man can go round London, his pockets filled with new-coined five-shilling pieces, buy this, that, and the other, and come home with his change in legitimate coins of the realm—half crowns, florins, shillings, six-pences, and all that."

"I see. Then why don't you nab him one day when his pockets are stuffed with illegitimate five-shilling pieces?"

"That could be done, of course, and I've thought of it, but, you see, we want to land the whole gang. Once we arrested him without knowing where the money came from, the real coiners would take flight."

"How do you know he is not the real coiner himself?"

Now poor Hale is as easy to read as a book. He hesitated before answering this question, and looked confused as a culprit caught in some dishonest act.

"You need not be afraid to tell me," I said soothingly, after a pause. "You have had one of your men in Mr. Summertrees's house, and so learned that he is not the coiner. But your man has not succeeded in getting you evidence to incriminate other people."

"You've about hit it again, Monsieur Valmont. One of my men has been Summertrees's butler for two weeks, but, as you say, he has found no evidence."

"Is he still butler?"

"Yes."

"Now tell me how far you have got. You know that Summertrees deposits a bag of coin every Friday in the Piccadilly Bank, and I suppose the bank has allowed you to examine one or two of the bags."

"Yes, sir, they have, but, you see, banks are very difficult to treat with. They don't like detectives bothering round, and while they do not stand out against the law, still they never answer any more questions than they're asked, and Mr. Summertrees has been a good customer at the United Capital for many years."

"Haven't you found out where the money comes from?"

"Yes, we have; it is brought there night after night by a man who looks like a respectable city clerk, and he puts it into a large safe, of which he holds the key, this safe being on the ground floor, in the dining room."

"Haven't you followed the clerk?"

"Yes. He sleeps in the Park Lane house every night and goes up in the morning to an old curiosity shop in Tottenham Court

Road, where he stays all day, returning with his bag of money in the evening."

"Why don't you arrest and question him?"

"Well, Monsieur Valmont, there is just the same objection to his arrest as to that of Summertrees himself. We could easily arrest both, but we have not the slightest evidence against either of them, and then, although we put the go-betweens in clink, the worst criminals of the lot would escape."

"Nothing suspicious about the old curiosity shop?"

"No. It appears to be perfectly regular."

"This game has been going on under your noses for how long?"

"For about six weeks."

"Is Summertrees a married man?"

"No."

"Are there any women servants in the house?"

"No, except that three charwomen come in every morning to do up the rooms."

"Of what is his household comprised?"

"There is the butler, then the valet, and last the French cook."

"Ah," cried I, "the French cook! This case interests me. So Summertrees has succeeded in completely disconcerting your man? Has he prevented him going from top to bottom of the house?"

"Oh, no! He has rather assisted him than otherwise. On one occasion he went to the safe, took out the money, had Podgers—that's my chap's name—help him to count it, and then actually sent Podgers to the bank with the bag of coin."

"And Podgers has been all over the place?"

"Yes."

"Saw no signs of a coining establishment?"

"No. It is absolutely impossible that any coining can be done there. Besides, as I tell you, that respectable clerk brings him the money."

"I suppose you want me to take Podgers's position?"

"Well, Monsieur Valmont, to tell you the truth, I would rather you didn't. Podgers has done everything a man can do, but I thought if you got into the house, Podgers assisting, you might go through it night after night at your leisure."

"I see. That's just a little dangerous in England. I think I should prefer to assure myself the legitimate standing of being amiable Podgers's successor. You say that Summertrees has no business?"

"Well, sir, not what you might call a business. He is by way of being an author, but I don't count that any business."

"Oh, an author, is he? When does he do his writing?"

"He locks himself up most of the day in his study."

"Does he come out for lunch?"

"No; he lights a little spirit lamp inside, Podgers tells me, and makes himself a cup of coffee, which he takes with a sandwich or two."

"That's rather frugal fare for Park Lane."

"Yes, Monsieur Valmont, it is, but he makes it up in the evening, when he has a long dinner, with all them foreign kickshaws you people like, done by his French cook."

"Sensible man! Well, Hale, I see I shall look forward with pleasure to making the acquaintance of Mr. Summertrees. Is there any restriction on the going and coming of your man Podgers?"

"None in the least. He can get away either night or day."

"Very good, friend Hale; bring him here to-morrow, as soon as our author locks himself up in his study, or rather, I should say, as soon as the respectable clerk leaves for Tottenham Court Road, which I should guess, as you put it, is about half an hour after his master turns the key of the room in which he writes."

"You are quite right in that guess, Valmont. How did you hit it?"

"Merely a surmise, Hale. There is a good deal of oddity about that Park Lane house, so it doesn't surprise me in the least that the master gets to work earlier in the morning than the man. I have also a suspicion that Ralph Summertrees knows perfectly well what the estimable Podgers is there for."

"What makes you think that?"

"I can give no reason except that my opinion of the acuteness of Summertrees has been gradually rising all the while you were speaking, and at the same time my estimate of Podgers's craft has been as steadily declining. However, bring the man here to-morrow, that I may ask him a few questions."

The Strange House in Park Lane

NEXT DAY, ABOUT ELEVEN o'clock, the ponderous Podgers, hat in hand, followed his chief into my room. His broad, impassive, immobile, smooth face gave him rather more the air of a genuine butler than I had expected, and this appearance, of course, was enhanced by his livery. His replies to my questions were those of a well-trained servant who will not say too much unless it is made worth his while. All in all, Podgers exceeded my expectations, and really my friend Hale had some justification for regarding him, as he evidently did, a triumph in his line.

"Sit down, Mr. Hale, and you, Podgers."

The man disregarded my invitation, standing like a statue until his chief made a motion; then he dropped into a chair. The English are great on discipline.

"Now, Mr. Hale, I must first congratulate you on the make-up of Podgers. It is excellent. You depend less on artificial assistance than we do in France, and in that I think you are right."

"Oh, we know a bit over here, Monsieur Valmont!" said Hale, with pardonable pride.

"Now then, Podgers, I want to ask you about this clerk. What time does he arrive in the evening?"

"At prompt six, sir."

"Does he ring, or let himself in with a latchkey?"

"With a latchkey, sir."

"How does he carry the money?"

"In a little locked leather satchel, sir, flung over his shoulder."

"Does he go direct to the dining room?"

"Yes, sir."

"Have you seen him unlock the safe, and put in the money?"

"Yes, sir."

"Does the safe unlock with a word or a key?"

"With a key, sir. It's one of the old-fashioned kind."

"Then the clerk unlocks his leather money bag?"

"Yes, sir."

"That's three keys used within as many minutes. Are they separate or in a bunch?"

"In a bunch, sir."

"Did you ever see your master with this bunch of keys?"

"No, sir."

"You saw him open the safe once, I am told?"

"Yes, sir."

"Did he use a separate key, or one of a bunch?"

Podgers slowly scratched his head, then said: "I don't just remember, sir."

"Ah, Podgers, you are neglecting the big things in that house! Sure you can't remember?"

"No, sir."

"Once the money is in and the safe locked up, what does the clerk do?"

"Goes to his room, sir."

"Where is this room?"

"On the third floor, sir."

"Where do you sleep?"

"On the fourth floor with the rest of the servants, sir."

"Where does the master sleep?"

"On the second floor, adjoining his study."

"The house consists of four stories and a basement, does it?"

"Yes, sir."

"I have somehow arrived at the suspicion that it is a very narrow house. Is that true?"

"Yes, sir."

"Does the clerk ever dine with your master?"

"No, sir. The clerk don't eat in the house at all, sir."

"Does he go away before breakfast?"

"No, sir."

"No one takes breakfast to his room?"

"No, sir."

"What time does he leave the house?"

"At ten o'clock, sir."

"When is breakfast served?"

"At nine o'clock, sir."

"At what hour does your master retire to his study?"

"At half past nine, sir."

"Locks the door on the inside?"

"Yes, sir."

"Never rings for anything during the day?"

"Not that I know of, sir."

"What sort of a man is he?"

Here Podgers was on familiar ground, and he rattled off a description minute in every particular.

"What I meant was, Podgers, is he silent, or talkative, or does he get angry? Does he seem furtive, suspicious, anxious, terrorized, calm, excitable, or what?"

"Well, sir, he is by way of being very quiet, never has much to say for hisself; never saw him angry or excited."

"Now, Podgers, you've been at Park Lane for a fortnight or more. You are a sharp, alert, observant man. What happens there that strikes you as unusual?"

"Well, I can't exactly say, sir," replied Podgers, looking rather helplessly from his chief to myself, and back again.

"Your professional duties have often compelled you to enact the part of butler before, otherwise you wouldn't do it so well. Isn't that the case?"

Podgers did not reply, but glanced at his chief. This was evidently a question pertaining to the service, which a subordinate was not allowed to answer. However, Hale said at once:

"Certainly. Podgers has been in dozens of places."

"Well, Podgers, just call to mind some of the other households where you have been employed, and tell me any particulars in which Mr. Summertrees's establishment differs from them."

Podgers pondered a long time.

"Well, sir, he do stick to writing pretty close."

"Ah, that's his profession, you see, Podgers. Hard at it from half past nine till toward seven, I imagine?"

"Yes, sir."

"Anything else, Podgers? No matter how trivial."

"Well, sir, he's fond of reading, too; leastways, he's fond of newspapers."

"When does he read?"

"I never seen him read 'em, sir; indeed, so far as I can tell, I never knew the papers to be opened, but he takes them all in, sir."

"What, all the morning papers?"

"Yes, sir, and all the evening papers, too."

"Where are the morning papers placed?"

"On the table in his study, sir."

"And the evening papers?"

"Well, sir, when the evening papers come, the study is locked. They are put on a side table in the dining room, and he takes them upstairs with him to his study."

"This has happened every day since you've been there?"

"Yes, sir."

"You reported that very striking fact to your chief, of course?"

"No, sir, I don't think I did," said Podgers confused.

"You should have done so. Mr. Hale would have known how to make the most of a point so vital."

"Oh, come now, Valmont," interrupted Hale, "you're chaffing us! Plenty of people take in all the papers!"

"I think not. Even clubs and hotels subscribe to the leading journals only. You said all, I think, Podgers?"

"Well, nearly all, sir."

"But which is it? There's a vast difference."

"He takes a good many, sir."

"How many?"

"I don't just know, sir."

"That's easily found out, Valmont," cried Hale, with some impatience, "if you think it really important."

"I think it so important that I'm going back with Podgers myself. You can take me into the house, I suppose, when you return?"

"Oh, yes, sir!"

"Coming back to these newspapers for a moment, Podgers. What is done with them?"

"They are sold to the ragman, sir, once a week."

"Who takes them from the study?"

"I do, sir."

"Do they appear to have been read very carefully?"

"Well, no, sir; leastways, some of them seem never to have been opened, or else folded up very carefully again."

"Did you notice that extracts have been clipped from any of them?"

"No, sir."

"Does Mr. Summertrees keep a scrapbook?"

"Not that I know of, sir."

"Oh, the case is perfectly plain!" said I, leaning back in my chair, and regarding the puzzled Hale with that cherubic expression of self-satisfaction which I know is so annoying to him.

"What's perfectly plain?" he demanded, more gruffly perhaps than etiquette would have sanctioned.

"Summertrees is no coiner, nor is he linked with any band of coiners."

"What is he, then?"

"Ah, that opens another avenue of inquiry! For all I know to the contrary, he may be the most honest of men. On the surface it would appear that he is a reasonably industrious tradesman in Tottenham Court Road, who is anxious that there should be no visible connection between a plebeian employment and so aristocratic a residence as that in Park Lane."

At this point Spenser Hale gave expression to one of those rare flashes of reason which are always an astonishment to his friends.

"That is nonsense, Monsieur Valmont," he said; "the man who is ashamed of the connection between his business and his house is one who is trying to get into society, or else the women of his family are trying it, as is usually the case. Now Summertrees has no family. He himself goes nowhere, gives no entertainments, and accepts no invitations. He belongs to no club; therefore, to say that he is ashamed of his connection with the Tottenham Court Road shop is absurd. He is concealing the connection for some other reason that will bear looking into."

"My dear Hale, the Goddess of Wisdom herself could not have made a more sensible series of remarks. Now, mon ami, do you want my assistance, or have you enough to go on with?"

"Enough to go on with? We have nothing more than we had when I called on you last night."

"Last night, my dear Hale, you supposed this man was in league with coiners. To-day you know he is not."

"I know you say he is not."

I shrugged my shoulders, and raised my eyebrows, smiling at him.

"It is the same thing, Monsieur Hale."

"Well, of all the conceited—" and the good Hale could get no farther.

"If you wish my assistance, it is yours."

"Very good. Not to put too fine a point upon it, I do."

"In that case, my dear Podgers, you will return to the residence of our friend Summertrees, and get together for me in a bundle all of yesterday's morning and evening papers that were delivered to the house. Can you do that, or are they mixed up in a heap in the coal cellar?"

"I can do it, sir. I have instructions to place each day's papers in a pile by itself in case they should be wanted again. There is always one week's supply in the cellar, and we sell the papers of the week before to the ragman."

"Excellent. Well, take the risk of abstracting one day's journals, and have them ready for me. I will call upon you at half past three o'clock exactly, and then I want you to take me upstairs to the clerk's bedroom in the third story, which I suppose is not locked during the daytime?"

"No, sir, it is not."

With this the patient Podgers took his departure. Spenser Hale rose when his assistant left.

"Anything further I can do?" he asked.

"Yes; give me the address of the shop in Tottenham Court Road. Do you happen to have about you one of those new five-shilling pieces which you believe to be illegally coined?"

He opened his pocketbook, took out the bit of white metal, and handed it to me.

"I'm going to pass this off before evening," I said, putting it in my pocket, "and I hope none of your men will arrest me."

"That's all right," laughed Hale as he took his leave.

At half past three Podgers was waiting for me, and opened the front door as I came up the steps, thus saving me the necessity of ringing. The house seemed strangely quiet. The French cook was evidently down in the basement, and we had probably all the upper part to ourselves, unless Summertrees was in his study, which I doubted. Podgers led me directly upstairs to the clerk's room on the third floor, walking on tiptoe, with an elephantine air of silence and secrecy combined, which struck me as unnecessary.

"I will make an examination of this room," I said. "Kindly wait for me down by the door of the study."

The bedroom proved to be of respectable size when one considers the smallness of the house. The bed was all nicely made up, and there were two chairs in the room, but the usual washstand and swing mirror were not visible. However, seeing a curtain at the farther end of the room, I drew it aside, and found, as I expected, a fixed lavatory in an alcove of perhaps four feet deep by five in width. As the room was about fifteen feet wide, this left two-thirds of the space unaccounted for. A moment later I opened a door which exhibited a closet filled with clothes hanging on hooks. This left a space of five feet between the clothes closet and the lavatory. I thought at first that the entrance to the secret stairway must have issued from the lavatory, but examining the boards closely, although they sounded hollow to the knuckles, they were quite evidently plain match boarding, and not a concealed door. The entrance to the stairway, therefore, must issue from the clothes closet. The right-hand wall proved similar to the match boarding of the lavatory, so far as the casual eye or touch was concerned, but I saw at once it was a door. The latch turned out to be somewhat ingeniously operated by one of the hooks which held a pair of old trousers. I found that the hook, if pressed upward, allowed the door to swing outward, over the stairhead. Descending to the second floor, a similar latch let me into a similar clothes closet in the room beneath. The two rooms were identical in size, one directly above the other, the only difference being that the lower-room door gave into the study, instead of into the hall, as was the case with the upper chamber.

The study was extremely neat, either not much used, or the abode of a very methodical man. There was nothing on the table except a pile of that morning's papers. I walked to the farther end, turned the key in the lock, and came out upon the astonished Podgers.

"Well, I'm blowed!" exclaimed he.

"Quite so," I rejoined; "you've been tiptoeing past an empty room for the last two weeks. Now, if you'll come with me, Podgers, I'll show you how the trick is done."

When he entered the study I locked the door once more, and led the assumed butler, still tiptoeing through force of habit, up the stair into the top bedroom, and so out again, leaving everything exactly as we found it. We went down the main stair to the front hall, and there Podgers had my parcel of papers all neatly wrapped up. This bundle I carried to my flat, gave one of my assistants some instructions, and left him at work on the papers.

The Queer Shop in Tottenham Court Road

I TOOK A CAB to the foot of Tottenham Court Road, and walked up that street till I came to J. Simpson's old curiosity shop. After gazing at the well-filled windows for some time, I stepped inside, having selected a little iron crucifix displayed behind the pane; the work of some ancient craftsman.

I knew at once from Podgers's description that I was waited upon by the veritable respectable clerk who brought the bag of money each night to Park Lane, and who, I was certain, was no other than Ralph Summertrees himself.

There was nothing in his manner differing from that of any other quiet salesman. The price of the crucifix proved to be seven-and-six, and I threw down a sovereign to pay for it.

"Do you mind the change all in silver, sir?" he asked, and I answered without any eagerness, although the question aroused a suspicion that had begun to be allayed: "Not in the least."

He gave me half a crown, three two-shilling pieces, and four separate shillings, all coins being well-worn silver of the realm, the undoubted inartistic product of the reputable British Mint. This seemed to dispose of the theory that he was palming off illegitimate money. He asked me if I were interested in any particular branch of antiquity, and I replied that my curiosity was merely general, and exceedingly amateurish, whereupon he invited me to look around. This I proceeded to do, while he resumed the addressing and stamping of some wrapped-up pamphlets which I surmised to be copies of his catalogue.

He made no attempt either to watch me or to press his wares upon me. I selected at random a little inkstand, and asked its price. It was two shillings, he said, whereupon I produced my fraudulent five-shilling piece. He took it, gave me the change without comment, and the last doubt about his connection with coiners flickered from my mind.

At this moment a young man came in who, I saw at once, was not a customer. He walked briskly to the farther end of the shop, and disappeared behind a partition which had one pane of glass in it that gave an outlook toward the front door.

"Excuse me a moment," said the shopkeeper, and he followed the young man into the private office.

As I examined the curious heterogeneous collection of things for sale, I heard the clink of coins being poured out on the lid of a desk or an uncovered table and the murmur of voices floated out to me. I was now near the entrance of the shop, and by a sleight-of-hand trick, keeping the corner of my eye on the glass pane of the private office, I removed the key of the front door without a sound, and took an impression of it in wax, returning the key to its place unobserved. At this moment another young man came in, and walked straight past me into the private office. I heard him say: "Oh, I beg pardon, Mr. Simpson! How are you, Rogers?"

"Hello, Macpherson," saluted Rogers, who then came out, bidding good night to Mr. Simpson, and departed, whistling, down the street, but not before he had repeated his phrase to another young man entering, to whom he gave the name of Tyrrel.

I noted these three names in my mind. Two others came in together, but I was compelled to content myself with memorizing their features, for I did not learn their names. These men were evidently collectors, for I heard the rattle of money in every case; yet here was a small shop, doing apparently very little business, for I had been within it for more than half an hour, and yet remained the only customer. If credit were given, one collector would certainly have been sufficient, yet five had come in, and had poured their contributions into the pile Summertrees was to take home with him that night.

I determined to secure one of the pamphlets which the man had been addressing. They were piled on a shelf behind the counter, but I had no difficulty in reaching across and taking the one on top, which I slipped into my pocket. When the fifth young man went down the street Summertrees himself emerged, and this time he carried in his hand the well-filled locked leather satchel, with the straps dangling. It was now approaching half past five, and I saw he was eager to close up and get away.

"Anything else you fancy, sir?" he asked me.

"No, or, rather, yes and no. You have a very interesting collection here, but it's getting so dark I can hardly see."

"I close at half past five, sir."

"Ah! in that case," I said, consulting my watch, "I shall be pleased to call some other time."

"Thank you, sir," replied Summertrees quietly, and with that I took my leave.

From the corner of an alley on the other side of the street I saw him put up the shutters with his own hands, then he emerged with overcoat on, and the money satchel slung across his shoulder. He locked the door, tested it with his knuckles, and walked down the street, carrying under one arm the pamphlets he had been addressing. I followed him at some distance, saw him drop the pamphlets into the box at the first post office he passed, and walk rapidly toward his house in Park Lane.

When I returned to my flat and called in my assistant, he said: "After putting to one side the regular advertisements of pills, soap, and what not, here is the only one common to all the newspapers, morning and evening alike. The advertisements are not identical, sir, but they have two points of similarity, or perhaps I should say three. They all profess to furnish a cure for absent-mindedness;

they all ask that the applicant's chief hobby shall be stated, and they all bear the same address: Dr. Willoughby, in Tottenham Court Road."

"Thank you," said I, as he placed the scissored advertisements before me.

I read several of the announcements. They were all small, and perhaps that is why I had never noticed one of them in the newspapers, for certainly they were odd enough. Some asked for lists of absent-minded men, with the hobbies of each, and for these lists, prizes of from one shilling to six were offered. In other clippings Dr. Willoughby professed to be able to cure absent-mindedness. There were no fees and no treatment, but a pamphlet would be sent, which, if it did not benefit the receiver, could do no harm. The doctor was unable to meet patients personally, nor could he enter into correspondence with them. The address was the same as that of the old curiosity shop in Tottenham Court Road. At this juncture I pulled the pamphlet from my pocket, and saw it was entitled, "Christian Science and Absent-Mindedness," by Dr. Stamford Willoughby, and at the end of the article was the statement contained in the advertisements, that Dr. Willoughby would neither see patients nor hold any correspondence with them.

I drew a sheet of paper toward me, wrote to Dr. Willoughby, alleging that I was a very absent-minded man, and would be glad of his pamphlet, adding that my special hobby was the collecting of first editions. I then signed myself, "Alport Webster, Imperial Flats, London, W." I may here explain that it is often necessary for me to see people under some other name than the well-known appellation of Eugène Valmont. There are two doors to my flat, and on one of these is painted, "Eugène Valmont"; on the other there is a receptacle, into which can be slipped a sliding panel bearing any nom de guerre I choose. The same device is arranged on the ground floor, where the names of all the occupants of the building appear on the right-hand wall. I sealed, addressed, and stamped my letter, then told my man to put out the name of Alport Webster, and if I did not happen to be in when anyone called upon that mythical person, he was to make an appointment for me.

It was nearly six o'clock next afternoon when the card of Angus Macpherson was brought in to Mr. Alport Webster. I recognized the young man at once as the second who had entered the little shop, carrying his tribute to Mr. Simpson the day before. He held three volumes under his arm, and spoke in such a pleasant, insinuating sort of way, that I knew at once he was an adept in his profession of canvasser.

"Will you be seated, Mr. Macpherson? In what can I serve you?"

He placed the three volumes, backs upward, on my table.

"Are you interested at all in first editions, Mr. Webster?"

"It is the one thing I am interested in," I replied; "but unfortunately they often run into a lot of money."

"That is true," said Macpherson sympathetically, "and I have here three books, one of which is an exemplification of what you say. This one costs a hundred pounds. The last copy that was sold by auction in London brought a hundred and twenty-three pounds. This next one is forty pounds, and the third ten pounds. At these prices I am certain you could not duplicate three such treasures in any bookshop in Britain."

I examined them critically, and saw at once that what he said was true. He was still standing on the opposite side of the table.

"Please take a chair, Mr. Macpherson. Do you mean to say you go round London with a hundred and fifty pounds' worth of goods under your arm in this careless way?"

The young man laughed.

"I run very little risk, Mr. Webster. I don't suppose anyone I meet imagines for a moment there is more under my arm than perhaps a trio of volumes I have picked up in the fourpenny box to take home with me."

I lingered over the volume for which he asked a hundred pounds, then said, looking across at him: "How came you to be possessed of this book, for instance?"

He turned upon me a fine, open countenance, and answered without hesitation in the frankest possible manner: "I am not in actual possession of it, Mr. Webster. I am by way of being a connoisseur in rare and valuable books myself, although, of course, I have little money with which to indulge in the collection of them. I am acquainted, however, with the lovers of desirable books in different quarters of London. These three volumes, for instance, are from the library of a private gentleman in the West End. I have sold many books to him, and he knows I am trustworthy. He wishes to dispose of them at something under their real value, and has kindly allowed me to conduct the negotiations. I make it my business to find out those who are interested in rare books, and by such trading I add considerably to my income."

"How, for instance, did you learn that I was a bibliophile?"

Mr. Macpherson laughed genially.

"Well, Mr. Webster, I must confess that I chanced it. I do that very often. I take a flat like this, and send in my card to the name on the door. If I am invited in, I ask the occupant the question I asked you just now: 'Are you interested in rare editions?' If he says no, I simply beg pardon and retire. If he says yes, then I show my wares."

"I see," said I, nodding. What a glib young liar he was, with that innocent face of his, and yet my next question brought forth the truth.

"As this is the first time you have called upon me, Mr. Macpherson, you have no objection to my making some further inquiry, I suppose. Would you mind telling me the name of the owner of these books in the West End?"

"His name is Mr. Ralph Summertrees, of Park Lane."

"Of Park Lane? Ah, indeed!"

"I shall be glad to leave the books with you, Mr. Webster, and if you care to make an appointment with Mr. Summertrees, I am sure he will not object to say a word in my favor."

"Oh, I do not in the least doubt it, and should not think of troubling the gentleman."

"I was going to tell you," went on the young man, "that I have a friend, a capitalist, who, in a way, is my supporter; for, as I said, I have little money of my own. I find it is often inconvenient for people to pay down any considerable sum. When, however, I strike a bargain, my capitalist buys the books, and I make an arrangement with my customer to pay a certain amount each week, and so even a large purchase is not felt, as I make the installments small enough to suit my client."

"You are employed during the day, I take it?"

"Yes, I am a clerk in the City."

Again we were in the blissful realms of fiction!

"Suppose I take this book at ten pounds, what installments should I have to pay each week?"

"Oh, what you like, sir. Would five shillings be too much?"

"I think not."

"Very well, sir; if you pay me five shillings now, I will leave the book with you, and shall have pleasure in calling this day week for the next installment."

I put my hand into my pocket, and drew out two half crowns, which I passed over to him.

"Do I need to sign any form or undertaking to pay the rest?"

The young man laughed cordially.

"Oh, no, sir, there is no formality necessary. You see, sir, this is largely a labor of love with me, although I don't deny I have my eye on the future. I am getting together what I hope will be a very valuable connection with gentlemen like yourself who are fond of books, and I trust some day that I may be able to resign my place with the insurance company and set up a choice little business of my own, where my knowledge of values in literature will prove useful."

And then, after making a note in a little book he took from his pocket, he bade me a most graceful good-by and departed, leaving me cogitating over what it all meant.

Next morning two articles were handed to me. The first came

by post and was a pamphlet on "Christian Science and Absent-Mindedness," exactly similar to the one I had taken away from the old curiosity shop; the second was a small key made from my wax impression that would fit the front door of the same shop—a key fashioned by an excellent anarchist friend of mine in an obscure street near Holborn.

That night at ten o'clock I was inside the old curiosity shop, with a small storage battery in my pocket, and a little electric glowlamp at my buttonhole, a most useful instrument for either burglar or detective.

I had expected to find the books of the establishment in a safe, which, if it was similar to the one in Park Lane, I was prepared to open with the false keys in my possession, or to take an impression of the keyhole and trust to my anarchist friend for the rest. But to my amazement I discovered all the papers pertaining to the concern in a desk which was not even locked. The books, three in number, were the ordinary daybook, journal, and ledger referring to the shop; bookkeeping of the older fashion; but in a portfolio lay half a dozen foolscap sheets, headed, "Mr. Rogers's List," "Mr. Macpherson's," "Mr. Tyrrel's," the names I had already learned, and three others. These lists contained in the first column, names; in the second column, addresses; in the third, sums of money; and then in the small, square places following were amounts ranging from two-and-sixpence to a pound. At the bottom of Mr. Macpherson's list was the name Alport Webster, Imperial Flats, 10 pounds; then in the small, square place, five shillings. These six sheets each headed by a canvasser's name, were evidently the record of current collections, and the innocence of the whole thing was so apparent that, if it were not for my fixed rule never to believe that I am at the bottom of any case until I have come on something suspicious, I would have gone out empty-handed as I came in.

The six sheets were loose in a thin portfolio, but standing on a shelf above the desk were a number of fat volumes, one of which I took down, and saw that it contained similar lists running back several years. I noticed on Mr. Macpherson's current list the name of Lord Semptam, an eccentric old nobleman whom I knew slightly. Then turning to the list immediately before the current one the name was still there; I traced it back through list after list until I found the first entry, which was no less than three years previous, and there Lord Semptam was down for a piece of furniture costing fifty pounds, and on that account he had paid a pound a week for more than three years, totaling a hundred and seventy pounds at the least, and instantly the glorious simplicity of the scheme dawned upon me, and I became so interested in the swindle that I lit the gas, fearing my little lamp would be exhausted before my investigation ended, for it promised to be a long one.

In several instances the intended victim proved shrewder than old Simpson had counted upon, and the word "Settled" had been written on the line carrying the name when the exact number of installments was paid. But as these shrewd persons dropped out, others took their places, and Simpson's dependence on their absent-mindedness seemed to be justified in nine cases out of ten. His collectors were collecting long after the debt had been paid. In Lord Semptam's case, the payment had evidently become chronic, and the old man was giving away his pound a week to the suave Macpherson two years after his debt had been liquidated. From the big volume I detached the loose leaf, dated 1893, which recorded Lord Semptam's purchase of a carved table for fifty pounds, and on which he had been paying a pound a week from that time to the date of which I am writing, which was November, 1896. This single document, taken from the file of three years previous, was not likely to be missed, as would have been the case if I had selected a current sheet. I nevertheless made a copy of the names and addresses of Macpherson's present clients; then, carefully placing everything exactly as I had found it, I extinguished the gas, and went out of the shop, locking the door behind me. With the 1893 sheet in my pocket I resolved to prepare a pleasant little surprise for

my suave friend Macpherson when he called to get his next installment of five shillings.

Late as was the hour when I reached Trafalgar Square, I could
not deprive myself of the felicity of calling on Mr. Spenser Hale,
who I knew was then on duty. He never appeared at his best during
office hours, because officialism stiffened his stalwart frame. Mentally he was impressed with the importance of his position, and
added to this he was not then allowed to smoke his big black pipe
and terrible tobacco. He received me with the curtness I had been
taught to expect when I inflicted myself upon him at his office. He
greeted me abruptly with: "I say, Valmont, how long do you expect
to be on this job?"

"What job?" I asked mildly.

"Oh, you know what I mean: the Summertrees affair?"

"Oh, that!" I exclaimed, with surprise. "The Summertrees case
is already completed, of course. If I had known you were in a hurry,
I should have finished up everything yesterday, but as you and
Podgers, and I don't know how many more, have been at it sixteen
or seventeen days, if not longer, I thought I might venture to take as
many hours, as I am working entirely alone. You said nothing about
haste, you know."

"Oh, come now, Valmont, that's a bit thick. Do you mean to say
you have already got evidence against the man?"

"Evidence absolute and complete."

"Then who are the coiners?"

"My most estimable friend, how often have I told you not to
jump at conclusions? I informed you when you first spoke to me
about the matter that Summertrees was neither a coiner nor a confederate of coiners. I secured evidence sufficient to convict him of
quite another offense, which is probably unique in the annals of
crime. I have penetrated the mystery of the shop, and discovered
the reason for all those suspicious actions which quite properly set
you on his trail. Now I wish you to come to my flat next Wednesday night at a quarter to six, prepared to make an arrest."

"I must know whom I am to arrest and on what counts."

"Quite so, mon ami Hale; I did not say you were to make an arrest, but merely warned you to be prepared. If you have time now to listen to the disclosures, I am quite at your service. I promise you there are some original features in the case. If, however, the present moment is inopportune, drop in on me at your convenience, previously telephoning so that you may know whether I am there or not, and thus your valuable time will not be expended purposelessly." With this I presented to him my most courteous bow, and although his mystified expression hinted a suspicion that he thought I was chaffing him, as he would call it, official dignity dissolved somewhat, and he intimated his desire to hear all about it then and there. I had succeeded in arousing my friend Hale's curiosity. He listened to the evidence with perplexed brow, and at last ejaculated he would be blessed.

"This young man," I said, in conclusion, "will call upon me at six on Wednesday afternoon, to receive his second five shillings. I propose that you, in your uniform, shall be seated there with me to receive him, and I am anxious to study Mr. Macpherson's countenance when he realizes he has walked in to confront a policeman. If you will then allow me to cross-examine him for a few moments, not after the manner of Scotland Yard, with a warning lest he incriminate himself, but in the free and easy fashion we adopt in Paris, I shall afterwards turn the case over to you to be dealt with at your discretion."

"You have a wonderful flow of language, Monsieur Valmont," was the officer's tribute to me. "I shall be on hand at a quarter to six on Wednesday."

"Meanwhile," said I, "kindly say nothing of this to anyone. We must arrange a complete surprise for Macpherson. That is essential. Please make no move in the matter at all until Wednesday night."

Spenser Hale, much impressed, nodded acquiescence, and I took a polite leave of him.

The Absent-Minded Coterie

THE QUESTION OF LIGHTING is an important one in a room such as mine, and electricity offers a good deal of scope to the ingenious. Of this fact I have taken full advantage. I can manipulate the lighting of my room so that any particular spot is bathed in brilliancy, while the rest of the space remains in comparative gloom, and I arranged the lamps so that the full force of their rays impinged against the door that Wednesday evening, while I sat on one side of the table in semidarkness and Hale sat on the other, with a light beating down on him from above which gave him the odd, sculptured look of a living statue of Justice, stern and triumphant. Anyone entering the room would first be dazzled by the light, and next would see the gigantic form of Hale in the full uniform of his order.

When Angus Macpherson was shown into this room, he was quite visibly taken aback, and paused abruptly on the threshold, his gaze riveted on the huge policeman. I think his first purpose was to turn and run, but the door closed behind him, and he doubtless heard, as we all did, the sound of the bolt being thrust in its place, thus locking him in.

"I—I beg your pardon," he stammered, "I expected to meet Mr. Webster."

As he said this, I pressed the button under my table, and was instantly enshrouded with light. A sickly smile overspread the countenance of Macpherson as he caught sight of me, and he made a very creditable attempt to carry off the situation with nonchalance.

"Oh, there you are, Mr. Webster; I did not notice you at first."

It was a tense moment. I spoke slowly and, impressively.

"Sir, perhaps you are not unacquainted with the name of Eugène Valmont."

He replied brazenly: "I am sorry to say, sir, I never heard of the gentleman before."

At this came a most inopportune "Haw-haw" from that blockhead Spenser Hale, completely spoiling the dramatic situation I had elaborated with such thought and care. It is little wonder the English possess no drama, for they show scant appreciation of the sensational moments in life; they are not quickly alive to the lights and shadows of events.

"Haw-haw," brayed Spenser Hale, and at once reduced the emotional atmosphere to a fog of commonplace. However, what is a man to do? He must handle the tools with which it pleases Providence to provide him. I ignored Hale's untimely laughter.

"Sit down, sir," I said to Macpherson, and he obeyed.

"You have called on Lord Semptam this week," I continued sternly.

"Yes, sir."

"And collected a pound from him?"

"Yes, sir."

"In October, 1893, you sold Lord Semptam a carved antique table for fifty pounds?"

"Quite right, sir."

"When you were here last week you gave me Ralph Summertrees as the name of a gentleman living in Park Lane. You knew at the time that this man was your employer?" Macpherson was now looking fixedly at me, and on this occasion made no reply. I went on calmly: "You also knew that Summertrees, of Park Lane, was identical with Simpson, of Tottenham Court Road?"

"Well, sir," said Macpherson, "I don't exactly see what you're driving at, but it's quite usual for a man to carry on a business under an assumed name. There is nothing illegal about that."

"We will come to the illegality in a moment, Mr. Macpherson. You and Rogers and Tyrrel and three others are confederates of this man Simpson."

"We are in his employ; yes, sir, but no more confederates than clerks usually are."

"I think, Mr. Macpherson, I have said enough to show you that the game is what you call up. You are now in the presence of Mr.

Spenser Hale, from Scotland Yard, who is waiting to hear your confession." Here the stupid Hale broke in with his: "And remember, sir, that anything you be—"

"Excuse me, Mr. Hale," I interrupted hastily, "I shall turn over the case to you in a very few moments, but I ask you to remember our compact, and to leave it for the present entirely in my hands. Now, Mr. Macpherson, I want your confession, and I want it at once."

"Confession? Confederates?" protested Macpherson, with admirably simulated surprise. "I must say you use extraordinary terms, Mr.—Mr.— What did you say the name was?"

"Haw-haw," roared Hale. "His name is Monsieur Valmont."

"I implore you, Mr. Hale, to leave this man to me for a very few moments. Now, Macpherson, what have you to say in your defense?"

"There nothing criminal has been alleged, Monsieur Valmont, I see no necessity for defense. If you wish me to admit that somehow you have acquired a number of details regarding our business, I am perfectly willing to do so, and to subscribe to their accuracy. If you will be good enough to let me know of what you complain, I shall endeavor to make the point clear to you, if I can. There has evidently been some misapprehension, but for the life of me, without further explanation, I am as much in a fog as I was on my way coming here, for it is getting a little thick outside."

Macpherson certainly was conducting himself with great discretion, and presented, quite unconsciously, a much more diplomatic figure than my friend Spenser Hale, sitting stiffly opposite me. His tone was one of mild expostulation, mitigated by the intimation that misunderstanding speedily would be cleared away. To outward view he offered a perfect picture of innocence neither protesting too much nor too little. I had, however, another surprise in store for him, a trump card, as it were, and I played it down on the table.

"There!" I cried with vim, "have you ever seen that sheet before?"

He glanced at it without offering to take it in his hand.

"Oh, yes," he said, "that has been abstracted from our file. It is what I call my visiting list."

"Come, come, sir," I cried sternly, "you refuse to confess, but I warn you we know all about it. You never heard of Dr. Willoughby, I suppose?"

"Yes, he is the author of the silly pamphlet on Christian Science."

"You are in the right, Mr. Macpherson; on Christian Science and Absent-Mindedness."

"Possibly. I haven't read it for a long while."

"Have you ever met this learned doctor, Mr. Macpherson?"

"Oh, yes. Dr. Willoughby is the pen name of Mr. Summertrees. He believes in Christian Science and that sort of thing, and writes about it."

"Ah, really. We are getting your confession bit by bit, Mr. Macpherson. I think it would be better to be quite frank with us."

"I was just going to make the same suggestion to you, Monsieur Valmont. If you will tell me in a few words exactly what is your charge against either Mr. Summertrees or myself, I will know then what to say."

"We charge you, sir, with obtaining money under false pretenses, which is a crime that has landed more than one distinguished financier in prison."

Spenser Hale shook his fat forefinger at me, and said: "Tut, tut, Valmont; we mustn't threaten, we mustn't threaten, you know"; but I went on without heeding him.

"Take, for instance, Lord Semptam. You sold a table for fifty pounds, on the installment plan. He was to pay a pound a week, and in less than a year the debt was liquidated. But he is an absent-minded man, as all your clients are. That is why you came to me. I had answered the bogus Willoughby's advertisement. And so you kept on collecting and collecting for something more than three years. Now do you understand the charge?"

Mr. Macpherson's head, during this accusation, was held slightly inclined to one side. At first his face was clouded by the most clever imitation of anxious concentration of mind I had ever seen, and this was gradually cleared away by the dawn of awakening perception. When I had finished, an ingratiating smile hovered about his lips.

"Really, you know," he said, "that is rather a capital scheme. The absent-minded league, as one might call them. Most ingenious. Summertrees, if he had any sense of humor, which he hasn't, would be rather taken by the idea that his innocent fad for Christian Science had led him to be suspected of obtaining money under false pretenses. But, really, there are no pretensions about the matter at all. As I understand it, I simply call and receive the money through the forgetfulness of the persons on my list, but where I think you would have both Summertrees and myself, if there was anything in your audacious theory, would be an indictment for conspiracy. Still, I quite see how the mistake arises. You have jumped to the conclusion that we sold nothing to Lord Semptam except that carved table three years ago. I have pleasure in pointing out to you that his lordship is a frequent customer of ours, and has had many things from us at one time or another. Sometimes he is in our debt; sometimes we are in his. We keep a sort of running contract with him by which he pays us a pound a week. He and several other customers deal on the same plan, and in return, for an income that we can count upon, they get the first offer of anything in which they are supposed to be interested. As I have told you, we call these sheets in the office our visiting lists, but to make the visiting lists complete you need what we term our encyclopedia. We call it that because it is in so many volumes; a volume for each year, running back I don't know how long. You will notice little figures here from time to time above the amount stated on this visiting list. These figures refer to the page of the encyclopedia for the current year, and on that page is noted the next sale and the amount as it might be set down, say, in a ledger."

"That is a very entertaining explanation, Mr. Macpherson. I suppose this encyclopedia, as you call it, is in the shop at Tottenham Court Road?"

"Oh, no, sir. Each volume of the encyclopedia is self-locking. These books contain the real secret of our business, and they are kept in the safe at Mr. Summertrees's house in Park Lane. Take Lord Semptam's account, for instance. You will find in faint figures under a certain date, 102. If you turn to page 102 of the encyclopedia for that year, you will then see a list of what Lord Semptam has bought, and the prices he was charged for them. It is really a very simple matter. If you will allow me to use your telephone for a moment I will ask Mr. Summertrees, who has not yet begun dinner, to bring with him here the volume for 1893, and within a quarter of an hour you will he perfectly satisfied that everything is quite legitimate." I confess that the young man's naturalness and confidence staggered me, the more so as I saw by the sarcastic smile on Hale's lips that he did not believe a single word spoken. A portable telephone stood on the table, and as Macpherson finished his explanation, he reached over and drew it toward him. Then Spenser Hale interfered.

"Excuse me," he said, "I'll do the telephoning. What is the call number of Mr. Summertrees?"

"One forty Hyde Park."

Hale at once called up Central, and presently was answered from Park Lane. We heard him say: "Is this the residence of Mr. Summertrees? Oh, is that you, Podgers? Is Mr. Summertrees in? Very well. This is Hale. I am in Valmont's flat—Imperial Flats—you know. Yes, where you went with me the other day. Very well, go to Mr. Summertrees, and say to him that Mr. Macpherson wants the encyclopedia for 1893. Do you get that? Yes, encyclopedia. Oh, don't understand what it is. Mr. Macpherson. No, don't mention my name at all. Just say Mr. Macpherson wants the encyclopedia for the year 1893, and that you are to bring it. Yes, you may tell him that Mr. Macpherson is at Imperial Flats, but don't mention my name at all. Exactly. As soon as he gives you the book, get into a cab, and come here as quickly as possible with it. If Summertrees doesn't want to let the book go, then tell him to come with you. If he won't do that, place him under arrest, and bring both him and the book here. All right. Be as quick as you can; we're waiting."

Macpherson made no protest against Hale's use of the telephone; he merely sat back in his chair with a resigned expression on his face which, if painted on canvas, might have been entitled, "The Falsely Accused." When Hale rang off, Macpherson said: "Of course you know your own business best, but if your man arrests Summertrees, he will make you the laughingstock of London. There is such a thing as unjustifiable arrest, as well as getting money under false pretenses, and Mr. Summertrees is not the man to forgive an insult. And then, if you will allow me to say so, the more I think over your absent-minded theory, the more absolutely grotesque it seems, and, if the case ever gets into the newspapers, I am sure, Mr. Hale, you'll experience an uncomfortable half hour with your chiefs at Scotland Yard."

"I'll take the risk of that, thank you," said Hale stubbornly.

"Am I to consider myself under arrest?" inquired the young man.

"No, sir."

"Then, if you will pardon me, I shall withdraw. Mr. Summertrees will show you everything you wish to see in his books, and can explain his business more capably than I, because he knows more about it; therefore, gentlemen, I bid you good night."

"No you don't. Not just yet awhile," exclaimed Hale, rising to his feet simultaneously with the young man.

"Then I am under arrest," protested Macpherson.

"You're not going to leave this room until Podgers brings that book."

"Oh, very well," and he sat down again.

And now, as talking is dry work, I set out something to drink, a box of cigars, and a box of cigarettes. Hale mixed his favorite brew, but Macpherson, shunning the wine of his country, contented himself with a glass of plain mineral water, and lit a cigarette. Then he awoke my high regard by saying pleasantly, as if nothing had happened: "While we are waiting, Monsieur Valmont, may I remind you that you owe me five shillings?"

I laughed, took the coin from my pocket, and paid him, whereupon he thanked me.

"Are you connected with Scotland Yard, Monsieur Valmont?" asked Macpherson, with the air of a man trying to make conversation to bridge over a tedious interval; but before I could reply Hale blurted out: "Not likely!"

"You have no official standing as a detective, then, Monsieur Valmont?"

"None whatever," I replied quickly, thus getting in my oar ahead of Hale.

"That is a loss to our country," pursued this admirable young man, with evident sincerity.

I began to see I could make a good deal of so clever a fellow if he came under my tuition.

"The blunders of our police," he went on, "are something deplorable. If they would but take lessons in strategy, say, from France, their unpleasant duties would be so much more acceptably performed, with much less discomfort to their victims."

"France," snorted Hale in derision, "why, they call a man guilty there until he's proven innocent."

"Yes, Mr. Hale, and the same seems to be the case in Imperial Flats. You have quite made up your mind that Mr. Summertrees is guilty, and will not be content until he proves his innocence. I venture to predict that, you will hear from him before long in a manner that may astonish you."

Hale grunted and looked at his watch. The time passed very slowly as we sat there smoking and at last even I began to get uneasy. Macpherson, seeing our anxiety, said that when he came in the fog was almost as thick as it had been the week before, and that there might be some difficulty in getting a cab. Just as he was speaking the door was unlocked from the outside, and Podgers entered, bearing a thick volume in his hand. This he gave to his superior, who turned over its pages in amazement, and then looked at the back, crying:

"*Encyclopedia of Sport, 1893!* What sort of a joke is this, Mr. Macpherson?"

There was a pained look on Mr. Macpherson's face as he reached forward and took the book. He said with a sigh: "If you had allowed me to telephone, Mr. Hale, I should have made it perfectly plain to Summertrees what was wanted. I might have known this mistake was liable to occur. There is an increasing demand for out-of-date books of sport, and no doubt Mr. Summertrees thought this was what I meant. There is nothing for it but to send your man back to Park Lane and tell Mr. Summertrees that what we want is the locked volume of accounts for 1893, which we call the encyclopedia. Allow me to write an order that will bring it. Oh, I'll show you what I have written before your man takes it," he said, as Hale stood ready to look over his shoulder.

On my note paper he dashed off a request such as he had outlined; and handed it to Hale, who read it and gave it to Podgers.

"Take that to Summertrees, and get back as quickly as possible. Have you a cab at the door?"

"Yes, sir."

"Is it foggy outside?"

"Not so much, sir, as it was an hour ago. No difficulty about the traffic now, sir."

"Very well, get back as soon as you can."

Podgers saluted, and left with the book under his arm. Again the door was locked, and again we sat smoking in silence until the stillness was broken by the tinkle of the telephone. Hale put the receiver to his ear.

"Yes, this is the Imperial Flats. Yes. Valmont. Oh, yes; Macpherson is here. What? Out of what? Can't hear you. Out of print. What, the encyclopedia's out of print? Who is that speaking? Dr. Willoughby; thanks."

Macpherson rose as if he would go to the telephone, but instead (and he acted so quietly that I did not notice what he was doing until the thing was done) he picked up the sheet which he called his visiting list, and walking quite without haste, held it in the glowing coals of the fireplace until it disappeared in a flash of flame up the chimney. I sprang to my feet indignant, but too late to make even a motion toward saving the sheet. Macpherson regarded us both with that self-depreciatory smile which had several times lighted up his face.

"How dared you burn that sheet?" I demanded.

"Because, Monsieur Valmont, it did not belong to you; because you do not belong to Scotland Yard; because you stole it; because you had no right to it; and because you have no official standing in this country. If it had been in Mr. Hale's possession I should not have dared, as you put it, to destroy the sheet, but as this sheet was abstracted from my master's premises by you, an entirely un-authorized person, whom he would have been justified in shooting dead if he had found you housebreaking; and you had resisted him on his discovery, I took the liberty of destroying the document. I have always held that these sheets should not have been kept, for, as has been the case, if they fell under the scrutiny of so intelligent a person as Eugène Valmont, improper inferences might have been drawn. Mr. Summertrees, however, persisted in keeping them, but made this concession, that if I ever telegraphed him or telephoned him the word 'Encyclopedia,' he would at once burn these records, and he, on his part, was to telegraph or telephone to me 'The en-cyclopedia is out of print,' whereupon I would know that he had succeeded.

"Now, gentlemen, open this door, which will save me the trouble of forcing it. Either put me formally under arrest, or cease to restrict my liberty. I am very much obliged to Mr. Hale for telephoning, and I have made no protest to so gallant a host as Monsieur Valmont is, because of the locked door. However, the farce is now termi-nated. The proceedings I have sat through were entirely illegal, and if you will pardon me, Mr. Hale, they have been a little too French to go down here in old England, or to make a report in the newspapers that would be quite satisfactory to your chiefs. I demand either my formal arrest or the unlocking of that door."

In silence I pressed a button, and my man threw open the door. Macpherson walked to the threshold, paused, and looked back at Spenser Hale, who sat there silent as a sphinx.

"Good evening, Mr. Hale."

There being no reply, he turned to me with the same ingratiating smile:

"Good evening, Monsieur Eugène Valmont," he said. "I shall give myself the pleasure of calling next Wednesday at six for my five shillings."

G. K. Chesterton

(1874–1936)

IN MARCH OF 1904, when he was a few months shy of thirty years old, G. K. Chesterton visited the village of Keighley, at the confluence of the Worth and Aire Rivers in West Yorkshire—Brontë country, a bleakly romantic land of gritstone tors and remote villages. He was there to speak about literature. Although he had not yet grown the rotund silhouette that later inspired P. G. Wodehouse to describe a loud crash as sounding "like Chesterton falling onto a sheet of tin"—he was six feet four inches tall and eventually weighed close to three hundred pounds—with his anarchic hair and pince-nez on a cord he already looked every inch the absent-minded intellectual.

After Chesterton's lecture he met and immediately became friends with a man only a few years older than himself, John O'Connor, the Catholic priest of St. Cuthbert's in nearby Bradford. The next morning they hiked together across the windy moor to Ilkley. Along the way they discussed penny dreadfuls, modern notions of society, the psychology of the rich, mathematics versus literature in education, and the priest's horrific recitations of the depravity he encountered in his work. They found the air exhilarating and even tone-deaf Chesterton burst into song. Soon they were continuing their lively conversation over shepherd's pie in Ilkley. O'Connor later recalled that Chesterton expressed "an ambition to increase and improve the breed of detective stories."

O'Connor had a huge influence on the life and work of Chesterton and they remained friends until the author's death. It was he who guided Chesterton's conversion to Catholicism in 1922. Much earlier, however, the priest inspired the sole Chestertonian character that most of us are familiar with nowadays—Father Brown. From his insight into character and his sympathy for wrongdoers to his flat-brimmed hat, decrepit umbrella, and penchant for carrying brown paper parcels, the fictional priest owes many of his attributes to this real-life inspiration. Once when O'Connor arrived at the Chesterton household for lunch, he gradually realized that a young woman present, Maria Zimmern, was unobtrusively sketching him for what turned out to be a portrait of the crime-attracting curate that wound up adorning *The Innocence of Father Brown*, the first collection, which was published in 1911. O'Connor was proud of both his friendship with Chesterton and his unwitting influence on detective stories. In 1937, the year after Chesterton died, O'Connor recounted their friendship in a little book entitled *Father Brown on Chesterton*.

Chesterton became a well-known public intellectual, writing eighty books, some of them composed of his columns and occasional writings for newspapers such as the *Illustrated London News* and the *Daily News*. He served as editor of the *New Witness* and in 1925 launched his own paper, *G. K.'s Weekly*, which ran until his death. Novelist, poet, and essayist, he also wrote insightful critical prefaces to each of Dickens's novels, as well as full-length studies of Dickens and other authors. By 1911, when he launched the Father Brown series—which eventually ran to fifty-two stories—he was already well known as the author of, among other books, the philosophical and satirical thriller *The Man Who Was Thursday*.

"At a time when the crime story might have drifted into romantic theatricalism and pseudo-science," wrote R. T. Bond in his 1935

introduction to *The Father Brown Omnibus*, "Chesterton gave it se-
riousness and validity . . . Thus to Poe, Dickens, Collins and Doyle
as proponents of the detective story was added the name of Chesterton, and it took on thereby an added consequence and literary
stature." Chesterton is remembered in crime fiction not only for
his creation of Father Brown but also for his idiosyncratic élan. His
style is precisely phrased, rich in paradox, and concerned with
more than whodunit.

The Hammer of God

THE LITTLE VILLAGE OF Bohun Beacon was perched on a hill so steep that the tall spire of its church seemed only like the peak of a small mountain. At the foot of the church stood a smithy, generally red with fires and always littered with hammers and scraps of iron; opposite to this, over a rude cross of cobbled paths, was "The Blue Boar," the only inn of the place. It was upon this crossway, in the lifting of a leaden and silver daybreak, that two brothers met in the street and spoke; though one was beginning the day and the other finishing it. The Rev. and Hon. Wilfred Bohun was very devout, and was making his way to some austere exercises of prayer or contemplation at dawn. Colonel the Hon. Norman Bohun, his elder brother, was by no means devout, and was sitting in evening dress on the bench outside "The Blue Boar," drinking what the philosophic observer was free to regard either as his last glass on Tuesday or his first on Wednesday. The colonel was not particular.

The Bohuns were one of the very few aristocratic families really dating from the Middle Ages, and their pennon had actually seen Palestine. But it is a great mistake to suppose that such houses stand high in chivalric tradition. Few except the poor preserve traditions. Aristocrats live not in traditions but in fashions. The Bohuns had been Mohocks under Queen Anne and Mashers under Queen Victoria. But like more than one of the really ancient houses, they had rotted in the last two centuries into mere drunkards and dandy degenerates, till there had even come a whisper of insanity. Certainly there was something hardly human about the colonel's wolfish pursuit of pleasure, and his chronic resolution not to go home till morning had a touch of the hideous clarity of insomnia. He was a tall, fine animal, elderly, but with hair still startlingly yellow. He would have looked merely blonde and leonine, but his blue eyes were sunk so deep in his face that they looked black. They were a little too close together. He had very long yellow moustaches; on each side of them a fold or furrow from nostril to jaw, so that a sneer seemed cut into his face. Over his evening clothes he wore a curious pale yellow coat that looked more like a very light dressing gown than an overcoat, and on the back of his head was stuck an extraordinary broad-brimmed hat of a bright green colour, evidently some oriental curiosity caught up at random. He was proud of appearing in such incongruous attires—proud of the fact that he always made them look congruous.

His brother the curate had also the yellow hair and the elegance, but he was buttoned up to the chin in black, and his face was clean-shaven, cultivated, and a little nervous. He seemed to live for nothing but his religion; but there were some who said (notably the blacksmith, who was a Presbyterian) that it was a love of Gothic architecture rather than of God, and that his haunting of the church like a ghost was only another and purer turn of the almost morbid thirst for beauty which sent his brother raging after women and wine. This charge was doubtful, while the man's practical piety was indubitable. Indeed, the charge was mostly an ignorant misunderstanding of the love of solitude and secret prayer, and was founded on his being often found kneeling, not before the altar, but in peculiar places, in the crypts or gallery, or even in the belfry. He was at the moment about to enter the church through the yard of the smithy, but stopped and frowned a little as he saw his brother's cavernous eyes staring in the same direction. On the hypothesis that the colonel was interested in the church he did not waste any speculations. There only remained the blacksmith's shop, and though the blacksmith was a Puritan and none of his people, Wilfred Bohun had heard some scandals about a beautiful and rather celebrated wife. He flung a suspicious look across the shed, and the colonel stood up laughing to speak to him.

"Good morning, Wilfred," he said. "Like a good landlord I am watching sleeplessly over my people. I am going to call on the blacksmith."

Wilfred looked at the ground, and said: "The blacksmith is out. He is over at Greenford."

"I know," answered the other with silent laughter; "that is why I am calling on him."

"Norman," said the cleric, with his eye on a pebble in the road, "are you ever afraid of thunderbolts?"

"What do you mean?" asked the colonel. "Is your hobby meteorology?"

"I mean," said Wilfred, without looking up, "do you ever think that God might strike you in the street?"

"I beg your pardon," said the colonel; "I see your hobby is folklore."

"I know your hobby is blasphemy," retorted the religious man, stung in the one live place of his nature. "But if you do not fear God, you have good reason to fear man."

The elder raised his eyebrows politely. "Fear man?" he said.

"Barnes the blacksmith is the biggest and strongest man for forty miles round," said the clergyman sternly. "I know you are no coward or weakling, but he could throw you over the wall."

This struck home, being true, and the lowering line by mouth and nostril darkened and deepened. For a moment he stood with the heavy sneer on his face. But in an instant Colonel Bohun had recovered his own cruel good humour and laughed, showing two dog-like front teeth under his yellow moustache. "In that case, my dear Wilfred," he said quite carelessly, "it was wise for the last of the Bohuns to come out partially in armour."

And he took off the queer round hat covered with green, showing that it was lined within with steel. Wilfred recognised it indeed
as a light Japanese or Chinese helmet torn down from a trophy that
hung in the old family hall.

"It was the first hat to hand," explained his brother airily; "always the nearest hat—and the nearest woman."

"The blacksmith is away at Greenford," said Wilfred quietly;
"the time of his return is unsettled."

And with that he turned and went into the church with bowed
head, crossing himself like one who wishes to be quit of an unclean
spirit. He was anxious to forget such grossness in the cool twilight
of his tall Gothic cloisters; but on that morning it was fated that his
still round of religious exercises should be everywhere arrested by
small shocks. As he entered the church, hitherto always empty at
that hour, a kneeling figure rose hastily to its feet and came towards
the full daylight of the doorway. When the curate saw it he stood
still with surprise. For the early worshipper was none other than the
village idiot, a nephew of the blacksmith, one who neither would
nor could care for the church or for anything else. He was always
called "Mad Joe," and seemed to have no other name; he was a
dark, strong, slouching lad, with a heavy white face, dark straight
hair, and a mouth always open. As he passed the priest, his moon-
calf countenance gave no hint of what he had been doing or thinking of. He had never been known to pray before.

What sort of prayers was he saying now? Extraordinary prayers
surely.

Wilfred Bohun stood rooted to the spot long enough to see the
idiot go out into the sunshine, and even to see his dissolute brother
hail him with a sort of avuncular jocularity. The last thing he saw
was the colonel throwing pennies at the open mouth of Joe, with
the serious appearance of trying to hit it.

This ugly sunlit picture of the stupidity and cruelty of the earth
sent the ascetic finally to his prayers for purification and new
thoughts. He went up to a pew in the gallery, which brought him

under a coloured window which he loved and always quieted his spirit; a blue window with an angel carrying lilies. There he began to think less about the half-wit, with his livid face and mouth like a fish. He began to think less of his evil brother, pacing like a lean lion in his horrible hunger. He sank deeper and deeper into those cold and sweet colours of silver blossoms and sapphire sky.

In this place half an hour afterwards he was found by Gibbs, the village cobbler, who had been sent for him in some haste. He got to his feet with promptitude, for he knew that no small matter would have brought Gibbs into such a place at all. The cobbler was, as in many villages, an atheist, and his appearance in church was a shade more extraordinary than Mad Joe's. It was a morning of theological enigmas.

"What is it?" asked Wilfred Bohun rather stiffly, but putting out a trembling hand for his hat.

The atheist spoke in a tone that, coming from him, was quite startlingly respectful, and even, as it were, huskily sympathetic.

"You must excuse me, sir," he said in a hoarse whisper, "but we didn't think it right not to let you know at once. I'm afraid a rather dreadful thing has happened, sir. I'm afraid your brother—"

Wilfred clenched his frail hands. "What devilry has he done now?" he cried in voluntary passion.

"Why, sir," said the cobbler, coughing, "I'm afraid he's done nothing, and won't do anything. I'm afraid he's done for. You had really better come down, sir."

The curate followed the cobbler down a short winding stair which brought them out at an entrance rather higher than the street. Bohun saw the tragedy in one glance, flat underneath him like a plan. In the yard of the smithy were standing five or six men mostly in black, one in an inspector's uniform. They included the doctor, the Presbyterian minister, and the priest from the Roman Catholic chapel, to which the blacksmith's wife belonged. The latter was speaking to her, indeed, very rapidly, in an undertone, as she, a magnificent woman with red-gold hair, was sobbing blindly on a bench. Between these two groups, and just clear of the main heap of hammers, lay a man in evening dress, spread-eagled and flat on his face. From the height above Wilfred could have sworn to every item of his costume and appearance, down to the Bohun rings upon his fingers; but the skull was only a hideous splash, like a star of blackness and blood. Wilfred Bohun gave but one glance, and ran down the steps into the yard. The doctor, who was the family physician, saluted him, but he scarcely took any notice. He could only stammer out:

"My brother is dead. What does it mean? What is this horrible mystery?" There was an unhappy silence; and then the cobbler, the most outspoken man present, answered: "Plenty of horror, sir," he said; "but not much mystery."

"What do you mean?" asked Wilfred, with a white face.

"It's plain enough," answered Gibbs. "There is only one man for forty miles round that could have struck such a blow as that, and he's the man that had most reason to."

"We must not prejudge anything," put in the doctor, a tall, black-bearded man, rather nervously; "but it is competent for me to corroborate what Mr. Gibbs says about the nature of the blow, sir; it is an incredible blow. Mr. Gibbs says that only one man in this district could have done it. I should have said myself that nobody could have done it."

A shudder of superstition went through the slight figure of the curate. "I can hardly understand," he said.

"Mr. Bohun," said the doctor in a low voice, "metaphors literally fail me. It is inadequate to say that the skull was smashed to bits like an eggshell. Fragments of bone were driven into the body and the ground like bullets into a mud wall. It was the hand of a giant."

He was silent a moment, looking grimly through his glasses; then he added: "The thing has one advantage—that it clears most people of suspicion at one stroke. If you or I or any normally made man in the country were accused of this crime, we should be acquitted as an infant would be acquitted of stealing the Nelson column."

"That's what I say," repeated the cobbler obstinately; "there's only one man that could have done it, and he's the man that would have done it. Where's Simeon Barnes, the blacksmith?"

"He's over at Greenford," faltered the curate.

"More likely over in France," muttered the cobbler.

"No; he is in neither of those places," said a small and colourless voice, which came from the little Roman priest who had joined the group. "As a matter of fact, he is coming up the road at this moment."

The little priest was not an interesting man to look at, having stubbly brown hair and a round and stolid face. But if he had been as splendid as Apollo no one would have looked at him at that moment. Everyone turned round and peered at the pathway which wound across the plain below, along which was indeed walking, at his own huge stride and with a hammer on his shoulder, Simeon the smith. He was a bony and gigantic man, with deep, dark, sinister eyes and a dark chin beard. He was walking and talking quietly with two other men; and though he was never specially cheerful, he seemed quite at his ease.

"My God!" cried the atheistic cobbler, "and there's the hammer he did it with."

"No," said the inspector, a sensible-looking man with a sandy moustache, speaking for the first time. "There's the hammer he did it with over there by the church wall. We have left it and the body exactly as they are."

All glanced round and the short priest went across and looked down in silence at the tool where it lay. It was one of the smallest and the lightest of the hammers, and would not have caught the eye among the rest; but on the iron edge of it were blood and yellow hair.

After a silence the short priest spoke without looking up, and there was a new note in his dull voice. "Mr. Gibbs was hardly right," he said, "in saying that there is no mystery. There is at least the mystery of why so big a man should attempt so big a blow with so little a hammer."

"Oh, never mind that," cried Gibbs, in a fever. "What are we to do with Simeon Barnes?"

"Leave him alone," said the priest quietly. "He is coming here of himself. I know those two men with him. They are very good fellows from Greenford, and they have come over about the Presbyterian chapel."

Even as he spoke the tall smith swung round the corner of the church, and strode into his own yard. Then he stood there quite still, and the hammer fell from his hand. The inspector, who had preserved impenetrable propriety, immediately went up to him.

"I won't ask you, Mr. Barnes," he said, "whether you know anything about what has happened here. You are not bound to say. I hope you don't know, and that you will be able to prove it. But I must go through the form of arresting you in the King's name for the murder of Colonel Norman Bohun."

"You are not bound to say anything," said the cobbler in officious excitement. "They've got to prove everything. They haven't proved yet that it is Colonel Bohun, with the head all smashed up like that."

"That won't wash," said the doctor aside to the priest. "That's out of the detective stories. I was the colonel's medical man, and I knew his body better than he did. He had very fine hands, but quite peculiar ones. The second and third fingers were the same length. Oh, that's the colonel right enough."

As he glanced at the brained corpse upon the ground the iron eyes of the motionless blacksmith followed them and rested there also.

"Is Colonel Bohun dead?" said the smith quite calmly. "Then he's damned."

"Don't say anything! Oh, don't say anything," cried the atheist cobbler, dancing about in an ecstasy of admiration of the English legal system. For no man is such a legalist as the good Secularist.

The blacksmith turned on him over his shoulder the august face of a fanatic.

"It's well for you infidels to dodge like foxes because the world's law favours you," he said; "but God guards His own in His pocket, as you shall see this day."

Then he pointed to the colonel and said: "When did this dog die in his sins?"

"Moderate your language," said the doctor.

"Moderate the Bible's language, and I'll moderate mine. When did he die?"

"I saw him alive at six o'clock this morning," stammered Wilfred Bohun.

"God is good," said the smith. "Mr. Inspector, I have not the slightest objection to being arrested. It is you who may object to arresting me. I don't mind leaving the court without a stain on my character. You do mind perhaps leaving the court with a bad setback in your career."

The solid inspector for the first time looked at the blacksmith with a lively eye; as did everybody else, except the short, strange priest, who was still looking down at the little hammer that dealt the dreadful blow.

"There are two men standing outside this shop," went on the blacksmith with ponderous lucidity, "good tradesmen in Greenford whom you all know, who will swear that they saw me from before midnight till daybreak and long after in the committee room of our Revival Mission, which sits all night, we save souls so fast. In Greenford itself twenty people could swear to me for all that time. If I were a heathen, Mr. Inspector, I would let you walk on to your downfall. But as a Christian man I feel bound to give you your chance, and ask you whether you will hear my alibi now or in court."

The inspector seemed for the first time disturbed, and said, "Of course I should be glad to clear you altogether now."

The smith walked out of his yard with the same long and easy stride, and returned to his two friends from Greenford, who were indeed friends of nearly everyone present. Each of them said a few words which no one ever thought of disbelieving. When they had spoken, the innocence of Simeon stood up as solid as the great church above them.

One of those silences struck the group which are more strange and insufferable than any speech. Madly, in order to make conversation, the curate said to the Catholic priest:

"You seem very much interested in that hammer, Father Brown."

"Yes, I am," said Father Brown; "why is it such a small hammer?"

The doctor swung round on him.

"By George, that's true," he cried; "who would use a little hammer with ten larger hammers lying about?"

Then he lowered his voice in the curate's ear and said: "Only the kind of person that can't lift a large hammer. It is not a question of force or courage between the sexes. It's a question of lifting power in the shoulders. A bold woman could commit ten murders with a light hammer and never turn a hair. She could not kill a beetle with a heavy one."

Wilfred Bohun was staring at him with a sort of hypnotised horror, while Father Brown listened with his head a little on one side, really interested and attentive. The doctor went on with more hissing emphasis:

"Why do these idiots always assume that the only person who hates the wife's lover is the wife's husband? Nine times out of ten the person who most hates the wife's lover is the wife. Who knows what insolence or treachery he had shown her—look there!"

He made a momentary gesture towards the red-haired woman on the bench. She had lifted her head at last and the tears were drying on her splendid face. But the eyes were fixed on the corpse with an electric glare that had in it something of idiocy.

The Rev. Wilfred Bohun made a limp gesture as if waving away all desire to know; but Father Brown, dusting off his sleeve some ashes blown from the furnace, spoke in his indifferent way.

"You are like so many doctors," he said; "your mental science is really suggestive. It is your physical science that is utterly impossible. I agree that the woman wants to kill the co-respondent much more than the petitioner does. And I agree that a woman will always pick up a small hammer instead of a big one. But the difficulty is one of physical impossibility. No woman ever born could have smashed a man's skull out flat like that." Then he added reflectively, after a pause: "These people haven't grasped the whole of it. The man was actually wearing an iron helmet, and the blow scattered it like broken glass. Look at that woman. Look at her arms."

Silence held them all up again, and then the doctor said rather sulkily: "Well, I may be wrong; there are objections to everything. But I stick to the main point. No man but an idiot would pick up that little hammer if he could use a big hammer."

With that the lean and quivering hands of Wilfred Bohun went up to his head and seemed to clutch his scanty yellow hair. After an instant they dropped, and he cried: "That was the word I wanted; you have said the word."

Then he continued, mastering his discomposure: "The words you said were, 'No man but an idiot would pick up the small hammer.'"

"Yes," said the doctor. "Well?"

"Well," said the curate, "no man but an idiot did." The rest stared at him with eyes arrested and riveted, and he went on in a febrile and feminine agitation.

"I am a priest," he cried unsteadily, "and a priest should be no shedder of blood. I—I mean that he should bring no one to the gallows. And I thank God that I see the criminal clearly now— because he is a criminal who cannot be brought to the gallows."

"You will not denounce him?" inquired the doctor.

"He would not be hanged if I did denounce him," answered Wilfred with a wild but curiously happy smile. "When I went into the church this morning I found a madman praying there—that poor Joe, who has been wrong all his life. God knows what he prayed; but with such strange folk it is not incredible to suppose that their prayers are all upside down. Very likely a lunatic would pray before killing a man. When I last saw poor Joe he was with my brother. My brother was mocking him."

"By Jove!" cried the doctor, "this is talking at last. But how do you explain—"

The Rev. Wilfred was almost trembling with the excitement of his own glimpse of the truth. "Don't you see; don't you see," he cried feverishly; "that is the only theory that covers both the queer things, that answers both the riddles. The two riddles are the little hammer and the big blow. The smith might have struck the big blow, but would not have chosen the little hammer. His wife would have chosen the little hammer, but she could not have struck the big blow. But the madman might have done both. As for the little hammer— why, he was mad and might have picked up anything. And for the big blow, have you never heard, doctor, that a maniac in his paroxysm may have the strength of ten men?"

The doctor drew a deep breath and then said, "By golly, I believe you've got it."

Father Brown had fixed his eyes on the speaker so long and steadily as to prove that his large grey, ox-like eyes were not quite so insignificant as the rest of his face. When silence had fallen he said with marked respect: "Mr. Bohun, yours is the only theory yet propounded which holds water every way and is essentially unassailable. I think, therefore, that you deserve to be told, on my positive knowledge, that it is not the true one." And with that the old little man walked away and stared again at the hammer.

"That fellow seems to know more than he ought to," whispered the doctor peevishly to Wilfred. "Those popish priests are deucedly sly."

"No, no," said Bohun, with a sort of wild fatigue. "It was the lunatic. It was the lunatic."

The group of the two clerics and the doctor had fallen away from the more official group containing the inspector and the man he had arrested. Now, however, that their own party had broken up, they heard voices from the others. The priest looked up quietly and then looked down again as he heard the blacksmith say in a loud voice:

"I hope I've convinced you, Mr. Inspector. I'm a strong man, as you say, but I couldn't have flung my hammer bang here from Greenford. My hammer hasn't got wings that it should come flying half a mile over hedges and fields."

The inspector laughed amicably and said: "No, I think you can be considered out of it, though it's one of the rummiest coincidences I ever saw. I can only ask you to give us all the assistance you can in finding a man as big and strong as yourself. By George! you might be useful, if only to hold him! I suppose you yourself have no guess at the man?"

"I may have a guess," said the pale smith, "but it is not at a man." Then, seeing the scared eyes turn towards his wife on the bench, he put his huge hand on her shoulder and said: "Nor a woman either."

"What do you mean?" asked the inspector jocularly. "You don't think cows use hammers, do you?"

"I think no thing of flesh held that hammer," said the blacksmith in a stifled voice; "mortally speaking, I think the man died alone."

Wilfred made a sudden forward movement and peered at him with burning eyes.

"Do you mean to say, Barnes," came the sharp voice of the cobbler, "that the hammer jumped up of itself and knocked the man down?"

"Oh, you gentlemen may stare and snigger," cried Simeon; "you clergymen who tell us on Sunday in what a stillness the Lord smote Sennacherib. I believe that One who walks invisible in every house defended the honour of mine, and laid the defiler dead before the door of it. I believe the force in that blow was just the force there is in earthquakes, and no force less."

Wilfred said, with a voice utterly undescribable: "I told Norman myself to beware of the thunderbolt."

"That agent is outside my jurisdiction," said the inspector with a slight smile.

"You are not outside His," answered the smith; "see you to it," and, turning his broad back, he went into the house.

The shaken Wilfred was led away by Father Brown, who had an

easy and friendly way with him. "Let us get out of this horrid place, Mr. Bohun," he said. "May I look inside your church? I hear it's one of the oldest in England. We take some interest, you know," he added with a comical grimace, "in old English churches."

Wilfred Bohun did not smile, for humour was never his strong point. But he nodded rather eagerly, being only too ready to explain the Gothic splendours to someone more likely to be sympathetic than the Presbyterian blacksmith or the atheist cobbler.

"By all means," he said; "let us go in at this side." And he led the way into the high side entrance at the top of the flight of steps. Father Brown was mounting the first step to follow him when he felt a hand on his shoulder, and turned to behold the dark, thin figure of the doctor, his face darker yet with suspicion.

"Sir," said the physician harshly, "you appear to know some secrets in this black business. May I ask if you are going to keep them to yourself?"

"Why, doctor," answered the priest, smiling quite pleasantly, "there is one very good reason why a man of my trade should keep things to himself when he is not sure of them, and that is that it is so constantly his duty to keep them to himself when he is sure of them. But if you think I have been discourteously reticent with you or anyone, I will go to the extreme limit of my custom. I will give you two very large hints."

"Well, sir?" said the doctor gloomily.

"First," said Father Brown quietly, "the thing is quite in your own province. It is a matter of physical science. The blacksmith is mistaken, not perhaps in saying that the blow was divine, but certainly in saying that it came by a miracle. It was no miracle, doctor, except in so far as man is himself a miracle, with his strange and wicked and yet half-heroic heart. The force that smashed that skull was a force well known to scientists—one of the most frequently debated of the laws of nature."

The doctor, who was looking at him with frowning intentness, only said: "And the other hint?"

"The other hint is this," said the priest. "Do you remember the blacksmith, though he believes in miracles, talking scornfully of the impossible fairy tale that his hammer had wings and flew half a mile across country?"

"Yes," said the doctor, "I remember that."

"Well," added Father Brown, with a broad smile, "that fairy tale was the nearest thing to the real truth that has been said today." And with that he turned his back and stumped up the steps after the curate.

The Reverend Wilfred, who had been waiting for him, pale and impatient, as if this little delay were the last straw for his nerves, led him immediately to his favourite corner of the church, that part of the gallery closest to the carved roof and lit by the wonderful window with the angel. The little Latin priest explored and admired everything exhaustively, talking cheerfully but in a low voice all the time. When in the course of his investigation he found the side exit and the winding stair down which Wilfred had rushed to find his brother dead, Father Brown ran not down but up, with the agility of a monkey, and his clear voice came from an outer platform above.

"Come up here, Mr. Bohun," he called. "The air will do you good."

Bohun followed him, and came out on a kind of stone gallery or balcony outside the building, from which one could see the illimitable plain in which their small hill stood, wooded away to the purple horizon and dotted with villages and farms. Clear and square, but quite small beneath them, was the blacksmith's yard, where the inspector still stood taking notes and the corpse still lay like a smashed fly.

"Might be the map of the world, mightn't it?" said Father Brown.

"Yes," said Bohun very gravely, and nodded his head.

Immediately beneath and about them the lines of the Gothic building plunged outwards into the void with a sickening swiftness akin to suicide. There is that element of Titan energy in the architecture of the Middle Ages that, from whatever aspect it be seen, it always seems to be rushing away, like the strong back of some maddened horse. This church was hewn out of ancient and silent stone, bearded with old fungoids and stained with the nests of birds. And yet, when they saw it from below, it sprang like a fountain at the stars; and when they saw it, as now, from above, it poured like a cataract into a voiceless pit. For these two men on the tower were left alone with the most terrible aspect of Gothic; the monstrous foreshortening and disproportion, the dizzy perspectives, the glimpses of great things small and small things great; a topsy-turvydom of stone in the mid-air. Details of stone, enormous by their proximity, were relieved against a pattern of fields and farms, pygmy in their distance. A carved bird or beast at a corner seemed like some vast walking or flying dragon wasting the pastures and villages below. The whole atmosphere was dizzy and dangerous, as if men were upheld in air amid the gyrating wings of colossal genii; and the whole of that old church, as tall and rich as a cathedral, seemed to sit upon the sunlit country like a cloudburst.

"I think there is something rather dangerous about standing on these high places even to pray," said Father Brown. "Heights were made to be looked at, not to be looked from."

"Do you mean that one may fall over?" asked Wilfred.

"I mean that one's soul may fall if one's body doesn't," said the other priest.

"I scarcely understand you," remarked Bohun indistinctly.

"Look at that blacksmith, for instance," went on Father Brown calmly; "a good man, but not a Christian—hard, imperious, unforgiving. Well, his Scotch religion was made up by men who prayed on hills and high crags, and learnt to look down on the world more than to look up at heaven. Humility is the mother of giants. One sees great things from the valley; only small things from the peak."

"But he—he didn't do it," said Bohun tremulously.

"No," said the other in an odd voice; "we know he didn't do it."

After a moment he resumed, looking tranquilly out over the

plain with his pale grey eyes. "I knew a man," he said, "who began by worshipping with others before the altar, but who grew fond of high and lonely places to pray from, corners or niches in the belfry or the spire. And once in one of those dizzy places, where the whole world seemed to turn under him like a wheel, his brain turned also, and he fancied he was God. So that, though he was a good man, he committed a great crime."

Wilfred's face was turned away, but his bony hands turned blue and white as they tightened on the parapet of stone.

"He thought it was given to him to judge the world and strike down the sinner. He would never have had such a thought if he had been kneeling with other men upon a floor. But he saw all men walking about like insects. He saw one especially strutting just below him, insolent and evident by a bright green hat—a poisonous insect."

Rooks cawed round the corners of the belfry; but there was no other sound till Father Brown went on.

"This also tempted him, that he had in his hand one of the most awful engines of nature; I mean gravitation, that mad and quickening rush by which all earth's creatures fly back to her heart when released. See, the inspector is strutting just below us in the smithy. If I were to toss a pebble over this parapet it would be something like a bullet by the time it struck him. If I were to drop a hammer— even a small hammer—"

Wilfred Bohun threw one leg over the parapet, and Father Brown had him in a minute by the collar.

"Not by that door," he said quite gently; "that door leads to hell."

Bohun staggered back against the wall, and stared at him with frightful eyes.

"How do you know all this?" he cried. "Are you a devil?"

"I am a man," answered Father Brown gravely; "and therefore have all devils in my heart. Listen to me," he said after a short pause. "I know what you did—at least, I can guess the great part of it. When you left your brother you were racked with no unrighteous rage, to the extent even that you snatched up a small hammer, half inclined to kill him with his foulness on his mouth. Recoiling, you thrust it under your buttoned coat instead, and rushed into the church. You pray wildly in many places, under the angel window, upon the platform above, and a higher platform still, from which you could see the colonel's Eastern hat like the back of a green beetle crawling about. Then something snapped in your soul, and you let God's thunderbolt fall."

Wilfred put a weak hand to his head, and asked in a low voice: "How did you know that his hat looked like a green beetle?"

"Oh, that," said the other with the shadow of a smile, "that was common sense. But hear me further. I say I know all this; but no one else shall know it. The next step is for you; I shall take no more steps; I will seal this with the seal of confession. If you ask me why, there are many reasons, and only one that concerns you. I leave things to you because you have not yet gone very far wrong, as assassins go. You did not help to fix the crime on the smith when it was easy; or on his wife, when that was easy. You tried to fix it on the imbecile because you knew that he could not suffer. That was one of the gleams that it is my business to find in assassins. And now come down into the village, and go your own way as free as the wind; for I have said my last word."

They went down the winding stairs in utter silence, and came out into the sunlight by the smithy. Wilfred Bohun carefully un-latched the wooden gate of the yard, and going up to the inspector, said: "I wish to give myself up; I have killed my brother."

※

Melville Davisson Post

(1869–1930)

In 1911, the same year that G. K. Chesterton introduced Father Brown, Melville Davisson Post published his first story about a Bible-toting Virginia mountain man called Uncle Abner. Although not a clergyman, Abner was no less preoccupied with sin and retribution than Chesterton's priest. In most ways, however, these two amateur crime fighters could not be more different. Father Brown is short and modest and serene, Uncle Abner a giant who walks through the world with the courage of an Old Testament prophet. What they have in common is that the creator of each possessed a vivid, straightforward literary style and larger moral preoccupations than many crime writers.

Most fans of the genre are familiar with Father Brown, but Uncle Abner has acquired an antique patina he does not deserve. In the late twentieth century, John F. Suter resurrected Abner for a series of pastiches, as Barry Perowne did with Raffles and Robert Goldsborough with Nero Wolfe, which may help renew attention to the original tales. Post invents clever clues—in one story, for example, Abner notices that a note allegedly written by a deaf man contains a phonetic misspelling—yet these adventures are notable mostly for their style and atmosphere. There are flashes of dark humor, but mostly Post writes with a primary-colored voice equal to the thundering pronouncements and apocalyptic vision of Abner.

This antebellum vigilante can be a troublemaker. The narrator, Abner's nephew, mentions that once his uncle beat up a group of men who mocked his fireside Bible reading in a tavern. (When detective-story fan William Faulkner created his recurring character Gavin Stevens, his own small-town Southern detective and the hero of the series of stories in *Knight's Gambit*, he often used Stevens's nephew as narrator.)

Post's turn toward religious themes seems to have followed the death of his son in 1906 and to have intensified after the death of his wife in 1919. In earlier stories Post was certainly no moral crusader. He began his crime-fiction career in 1896, with *The Strange Schemes of Randolph Mason*. In an original twist, Mason is an unscrupulous attorney who works within legal loopholes to help criminals evade justice. "Crime is a technical word," Mason explains. "It is the law's term for certain acts which it is pleased to define and punish with a penalty. What the law permits is right, else it would prohibit it." Uncle Abner would have railed at such sophistry. A year later, jurist Oliver Wendell Holmes distinguished law from morality: "If you want to know the law and nothing else, you must look at it as a bad man, who cares only for the material consequences which such knowledge will enable him to predict, not as a good one, who finds his reasons for conduct, whether inside the law or outside of it, in the vaguer sanctions of conscience." Crime fiction scholar Francis M. Nevins has linked such attitudes to prevailing notions of social Darwinism at the time.

Post also created Sir Henry Marquis, the head of Scotland Yard's Criminal Investigation Department; no deskbound administrator, he travels around the world solving crimes. But Post is remembered mostly for Uncle Abner. The *Saturday Evening Post* published the following story, the memorable debut of Abner, in its June 3, 1911, issue, as "The Broken Stirrup-Leather." Seventeen other Abner stories appeared before, in 1918, they were gathered in the collection *Uncle Abner, Mastery of Mysteries*—"second only to Poe's tales," wrote Ellery Queen, "among all the books of detective short stories written by American authors." In this powerful collection, the story appeared as the third adventure in the book, under the title "The Angel of the Lord." (A decade later, Post wrote four more stories about Abner.) Post sets an old-fashioned religious tone before the book opens. "To my father," reads the book's dedication page, "whose unfailing faith in an ultimate justice behind the moving of events has been to the writer a wonder and an inspiration." Yet the stories aren't didactic or pious, but lively, adventurous, suspenseful, and filled with thoughtful investigation.

Although Post was considered a master of the detective-story formula, his stories weren't predictable. In this one, we have only one suspect—in fact, only one other character besides Abner and the narrator—so Abner reveals his earlier detective work only after he confronts the villain. In this story as in others, Abner doesn't hestitate to serve as judge and jury. Part of the suspense in this story derives from Abner's confrontation with the villain. His calm way of speaking to murderers is one of his many unnerving traits.

The Angel of the Lord

IALWAYS THOUGHT MY father took a long chance, but somebody had to take it and certainly I was the one least likely to be suspected. It was a wild country. There were no banks. We had to pay for the cattle, and somebody had to carry the money. My father and my uncle were always being watched. My father was right, I think.

"Abner," he said, "I'm going to send Martin. No one will ever suppose that we would trust this money to a child."

My uncle drummed on the table and rapped his heels on the floor. He was a bachelor, stern and silent. But he could talk . . . and when he did, he began at the beginning and you heard him through; and what he said—well, he stood behind it.

"To stop Martin," my father went on, "would be only to lose the money; but to stop you would be to get somebody killed."

I knew what my father meant. He meant that no one would undertake to rob Abner until after he had shot him to death.

I ought to say a word about my Uncle Abner. He was one of those austere, deeply religious men who were the product of the Reformation. He always carried a Bible in his pocket and he read it where he pleased. Once the crowd at Roy's Tavern tried to make sport of him when he got his book out by the fire; but they never tried it again. When the fight was over Abner paid Roy eighteen silver dollars for the broken chairs and the table—and he was the

only man in the tavern who could ride a horse. Abner belonged to
the church militant and his God was a war lord.

So that is how they came to send me. The money was in green-
backs in packages. They wrapped it up in newspaper and put it into
a pair of saddle-bags, and I set out. I was about nine years old. No,
it was not as bad as you think. I could ride a horse all day when I
was nine years old—most any kind of a horse. I was tough as whit'-
leather, and I knew the country I was going into. You must not
picture a little boy rolling a hoop in the park.

It was an afternoon in early autumn. The clay roads froze in the
night; they thawed out in the day and they were a bit sticky. I was
to stop at Roy's Tavern, south of the river, and go on in the morning. Now and then I passed some cattle driver, but no one overtook me on the road until almost sundown; then I heard a horse
behind me and a man came up. I knew him. He was a cattleman
named Dix. He had once been a shipper, but he had come in for a
good deal of bad luck. His partner, Alkire, had absconded with a
big sum of money due the grazers. This had ruined Dix; he had
given up his land, which wasn't very much, to the grazers. After
that he had gone over the mountain to his people, got together a
pretty big sum of money and bought a large tract of grazing land.
Foreign claimants had sued him in the courts on some old title and
he had lost the whole tract and the money that he had paid for it. He
had married a remote cousin of ours and he had always lived on her
lands, adjoining those of my Uncle Abner.

Dix seemed surprised to see me on the road.

"So it's you, Martin," he said; "I thought Abner would be going
into the upcountry."

One gets to be a pretty cunning youngster, even at this age, and
I told no one what I was about.

"Father wants the cattle over the river to run a month," I returned
easily, "and I'm going up there to give his orders to the grazers."

He looked me over, then he rapped the saddlebags with his knuckles. "You carry a good deal of baggage, my lad."

I laughed. "Horse feed," I said. "You know my father! A horse must be fed at dinner time, but a man can go till he gets it."

One was always glad of any company on the road, and we fell into an idle talk. Dix said he was going out into the Ten Mile country; and I have always thought that was, in fact, his intention. The road turned south about a mile our side of the tavern. I never liked Dix; he was of an apologetic manner, with a cunning, irresolute face.

A little later a man passed us at a gallop. He was a drover named Marks, who lived beyond my Uncle Abner, and he was riding hard to get in before night. He hailed us, but he did not stop; we got a shower of mud and Dix cursed him. I have never seen a more evil face. I suppose it was because Dix usually had a grin about his mouth, and when that sort of face gets twisted there's nothing like it.

After that he was silent. He rode with his head down and his fingers plucking at his jaw, like a man in some perplexity. At the crossroads he stopped and sat for some time in the saddle, looking before him. I left him there, but at the bridge he overtook me. He said he had concluded to get some supper and go on after that.

Roy's Tavern consisted of a single big room, with a loft above it for sleeping quarters. A narrow covered way connected this room with the house in which Roy and his family lived. We used to hang our saddles on wooden pegs in this covered way. I have seen that wall so hung with saddles that you could not find a place for another stirrup. But tonight Dix and I were alone in the tavern. He looked cunningly at me when I took the saddle-bags with me into the big room and when I went with them up the ladder into the loft. But he said nothing—in fact, he had scarcely spoken. It was cold; the road had begun to freeze when we got in. Roy had lighted a big fire. I left Dix before it. I did not take off my clothes, because Roy's beds were mattresses of wheat straw covered with heifer skins—good enough for summer but pretty cold on such a night, even with the heavy, hand-woven coverlet in big white and black checks.

I put the saddle-bags under my head and lay down. I went at

once to sleep, but I suddenly awaked. I thought there was a candle in the loft, but it was a gleam of light from the fire below, shining through a crack in the floor. I lay and watched it, the coverlet pulled up to my chin. Then I began to wonder why the fire burned so brightly. Dix ought to be on his way some time and it was a custom for the last man to rake out the fire. There was not a sound. The light streamed steadily through the crack.

Presently it occurred to me that Dix had forgotten the fire and that I ought to go down and rake it out. Roy always warned us about the fire when he went to bed. I got up, wrapped the great coverlet around me, went over to the gleam of light and looked down through the crack in the floor. I had to lie out at full length to get my eye against the board. The hickory logs had turned to great embers and glowed like a furnace of red coals.

Before this fire stood Dix. He was holding out his hands and turning himself about as though he were cold to the marrow; but with all that chill upon him, when the man's face came into the light I saw it covered with a sprinkling of sweat.

I shall carry the memory of that face. The grin was there at the mouth, but it was pulled about; the eyelids were drawn in; the teeth were clamped together. I have seen a dog poisoned with strychnine look like that.

I lay there and watched the thing. It was as though something potent and evil dwelling within the man were in travail to re-form his face upon its image. You cannot realize how that devilish labor held me—the face worked as though it were some plastic stuff, and the sweat oozed through. And all the time the man was cold; and he was crowding into the fire and turning himself about and putting out his hands. And it was as though the heat would no more enter in and warm him than it will enter in and warm the ice.

It seemed to scorch him and leave him cold—and he was fearfully and desperately cold! I could smell the singe of the fire on him, but it had no power against this diabolic chill. I began myself to shiver, although I had the heavy coverlet wrapped around me.

The thing was a fascinating horror; I seemed to be looking down into the chamber of some abominable maternity. The room was filled with the steady red light of the fire. Not a shadow moved in it. And there was silence. The man had taken off his boots and he twisted before the fire without a sound. It was like the shuddering tales of possession or transformation by a drug. I thought the man would burn himself to death. His clothes smoked. How could he be so cold?

Then, finally, the thing was over! I did not see it for his face was in the fire. But suddenly he grew composed and stepped back into the room. I tell you I was afraid to look! I do not know what thing I expected to see there, but I did not think it would be Dix.

Well, it was Dix; but not the Dix that any of us knew. There was a certain apology, a certain indecision, a certain servility in that other Dix, and these things showed about his face. But there was none of these weaknesses in this man.

His face had been pulled into planes of firmness and decision; the slack in his features had been taken up; the furtive moving of the eye was gone. He stood now squarely on his feet and he was full of courage. But I was afraid of him as I have never been afraid of any human creature in this world! Something that had been servile in him, that had skulked behind disguises, that had worn the habiliments of subterfuge, had now come forth; and it had molded the features of the man to its abominable courage.

Presently he began to move swiftly about the room. He looked out at the window and he listened at the door; then he went softly into the covered way. I thought he was going on his journey; but then he could not be going with his boots there beside the fire. In a moment he returned with a saddle blanket in his hand and came softly across the room to the ladder.

Then I understood the thing that he intended, and I was motionless with fear. I tried to get up, but I could not. I could only lie there with my eye strained to the crack in the floor. His foot was on the ladder, and I could already feel his hand on my throat and that blanket on my face, and the suffocation of death in me, when far away on the hard road I heard a horse!

He heard it, too, for he stopped on the ladder and turned his evil face about toward the door. The horse was on the long hill beyond the bridge, and he was coming as though the devil rode in his saddle. It was a hard, dark night. The frozen road was like flint; I could hear the iron of the shoes ring. Whoever rode that horse rode for his life or for something more than his life, or he was mad. I heard the horse strike the bridge and thunder across it. And all the while Dix hung there on the ladder by his hands and listened. Now he sprang softly down, pulled on his boots and stood up before the fire, his face—this new face—gleaming with its evil courage. The next moment the horse stopped.

I could hear him plunge under the bit, his iron shoes ripping the frozen road; then the door leaped back and my Uncle Abner was in the room. I was so glad that my heart almost choked me and for a moment I could hardly see—everything was in a sort of mist.

Abner swept the room in a glance, then he stopped. "Thank God!" he said; "I'm in time." And he drew his hand down over his face with the fingers hard and close as though he pulled something away.

"In time for what?" said Dix.

Abner looked him over. And I could see the muscles of his big shoulders stiffen as he looked. And again he looked him over. Then he spoke and his voice was strange. "Dix," he said, "is it you?"

"Who would it be but me?" said Dix.

"It might be the devil," said Abner. "Do you know what your face looks like?"

"No matter what it looks like!" said Dix.

"And so," said Abner, "we have got courage with this new face."

Dix threw up his head.

"Now, look here, Abner," he said, "I've had about enough of your big manner. You ride a horse to death and you come plunging in here; what the devil's wrong with you?"

"There's nothing wrong with me," replied Abner, and his voice was low. "But there's something damnably wrong with you, Dix."

"The devil take you," said Dix, and I saw him measure Abner with his eye. It was not fear that held him back; fear was gone out of the creature; I think it was a kind of prudence.

Abner's eyes kindled, but his voice remained low and steady.

"Those are big words," he said.

"Well," cried Dix, "get out of the door then and let me pass!"

"Not just yet," said Abner; "I have something to say to you."

"Say it then," cried Dix, "and get out of the door."

"Why hurry?" said Abner. "It's a long time until daylight, and I have a good deal to say."

"You'll not say it to me," said Dix. "I've got a trip to make to-night; get out of the door."

Abner did not move. "You've got a longer trip to make tonight than you think, Dix," he said; "but you're going to hear what I have to say before you set out on it."

I saw Dix rise on his toes and I knew what he wished for. He wished for a weapon; and he wished for the bulk of bone and muscle that would have a chance against Abner. But he had neither the one nor the other. And he stood there on his toes and began to curse—low, vicious, withering oaths, that were like the swish of a knife.

Abner was looking at the man with a curious interest.

"It is strange," he said, as though speaking to himself, "but it explains the thing. While one is the servant of neither, one has the courage of neither; but when he finally makes his choice he gets what his master has to give him."

Then he spoke to Dix.

"Sit down!" he said; and it was in that deep, level voice that Abner used when he was standing close behind his words. Every man in the hills knew that voice; one had only a moment to decide after he heard it. Dix knew that, and yet for one instant he hung there on his toes, his eyes shimmering like a weasel's, his mouth twisting. He was not afraid! If he had had the ghost of a chance against Abner he would have taken it. But he knew he had not, and with an oath he threw the saddle blanket into a corner and sat down by the fire.

Abner came away from the door then. He took off his great coat. He put a log on the fire and he sat down across the hearth from Dix. The new hickory sprang crackling into flames. For a good while there was silence; the two men sat at either end of the hearth without a word. Abner seemed to have fallen into a study of the man before him. Finally he spoke:

"Dix," he said, "do you believe in the providence of God?"

Dix flung up his head.

"Abner," he cried, "if you are going to talk nonsense I promise you upon my oath that I will not stay to listen."

Abner did not at once reply. He seemed to begin now at another point.

"Dix," he said, "you've had a good deal of bad luck . . . Perhaps you wish it put that way."

"Now, Abner," he cried, "you speak the truth; I have had hell's luck."

"Hell's luck you have had," replied Abner. "It is a good word. I accept it. Your partner disappeared with all the money of the grazers on the other side of the river; you lost the land in your lawsuit; and you are tonight without a dollar. That was a big tract of land to lose. Where did you get so great a sum of money?"

"I have told you a hundred times," replied Dix. "I got it from my people over the mountains. You know where I got it."

"Yes," said Abner. "I know where you got it, Dix. And I know another thing. But first I want to show you this," and he took a little penknife out of his pocket. "And I want to tell you that I believe in the providence of God, Dix."

"I don't care a fiddler's damn what you believe in," said Dix.

"But you do care what I know," replied Abner.

"What do you know?" said Dix.

"I know where your partner is," replied Abner.

I was uncertain about what Dix was going to do, but finally he answered with a sneer.

"Then you know something that nobody else knows."

"Yes," replied Abner, "there is another man who knows."

"Who?" said Dix.

"You," said Abner.

Dix leaned over in his chair and looked at Abner closely.

"Abner," he cried, "you are talking nonsense. Nobody knows where Alkire is. If I knew I'd go after him."

"Dix," Abner answered, and it was again in that deep, level voice, "if I had got here five minutes later you would have gone after him. I can promise you that, Dix.

"Now, listen! I was in the upcountry when I got your word about the partnership; and I was on my way back when at Big Run I broke a stirrup-leather. I had no knife and I went into the store and bought this one; then the storekeeper told me that Alkire had gone to see you. I didn't want to interfere with him and I turned back . . . So I did not become your partner. And so I did not disappear . . . What was it that prevented? The broken stirrup-leather? The knife? In old times, Dix, men were so blind that God had to open their eyes before they could see His angel in the way before them . . . They are still blind, but they ought not to be that blind . . . Well, on the night that Alkire disappeared I met him on his way to your house. It was out there at the bridge. He had broken a stirrup-leather and he was trying to fasten it with a nail. He asked me if I had a knife, and I gave him this one. It was beginning to rain and I went on, leaving him there in the road with the knife in his hand."

Abner paused; the muscles of his great iron jaw contracted.

"God forgive me," he said; "it was His angel again! I never saw Alkire after that."

"Nobody ever saw him after that," said Dix. "He got out of the hills that night."

"No," replied Abner; "it was not in the night when Alkire started on his journey; it was in the day."

"Abner," said Dix, "you talk like a fool. If Alkire had traveled the road in the day somebody would have seen him."

"Nobody could see him on the road he traveled," replied Abner.

"What road?" said Dix.

"Dix," replied Abner, "you will learn that soon enough."

Abner looked hard at the man.

"You saw Alkire when he started on his journey," he continued; "but did you see who it was that went with him?"

"Nobody went with him," replied Dix; "Alkire rode alone."

"Not alone," said Abner; "there was another."

"I didn't see him," said Dix.

"And yet," continued Abner, "you made Alkire go with him."

I saw cunning enter Dix's face. He was puzzled, but he thought Abner off the scent.

"And I made Alkire go with somebody, did I? Well, who was it? Did you see him?"

"Nobody ever saw him."

"He must be a stranger."

"No," replied Abner, "he rode the hills before we came into them."

"Indeed!" said Dix. "And what kind of a horse did he ride?"

"White!" said Abner.

Dix got some inkling of what Abner meant now, and his face grew livid.

"What are you driving at?" he cried. "You sit here beating around the bush. If you know anything, say it out; let's hear it. What is it?"

Abner put out his big sinewy hand as though to thrust Dix back into his chair. "Listen!" he said. "Two days after that I wanted to get out into the Ten Mile country and I went through your lands; I rode a path through the narrow valley west of your house. At a point on the path where there is an apple tree something caught my eye and I stopped. Five minutes later I knew exactly what had happened under that apple tree . . . Someone had ridden there; he had stopped under that tree; then something happened and the horse had run away—I knew that by the tracks of a horse on this path. I knew that the horse had a rider and that it had stopped under this tree, because there was a limb cut from the tree at a certain height. I knew the horse had remained there, because the small twigs of the apple limb had been pared off, and they lay in a heap on the path. I knew that something had frightened the horse and that it had run away, because the sod was torn up where it had jumped . . . Ten minutes later I knew that the rider had not been in the saddle when the horse jumped; I knew what it was that had frightened the horse; and I knew that the thing had occurred the day before. Now, how did I know that?

"Listen! I put my horse into the tracks of that other horse under the tree and studied the ground. Immediately I saw where the weeds beside the path had been crushed, as though some animal had been lying down there, and in the very center of that bed I saw a little heap of fresh earth. That was strange, Dix, that fresh earth where the animal had been lying down! It had come there after the animal had got up, or else it would have been pressed flat. But where had it come from?

"I got off and walked around the apple tree, moving out from it in an ever-widening circle. Finally I found an ant heap, the top of which had been scraped away as though one had taken up the loose earth in his hands. Then I went back and plucked up some of the earth. The under clods of it were colored as with red paint . . . No, it wasn't paint.

"There was a brush fence some fifty yards away. I went over to it and followed it down.

"Opposite the apple tree the weeds were again crushed as though some animal had lain there. I sat down in that place and drew a line with my eye across a log of the fence to a limb of the apple tree. Then I got on my horse and again put him in the tracks of that other horse under the tree; the imaginary line passed through the pit of my stomach! . . . I am four inches taller than Alkire."

It was then that Dix began to curse. I had seen his face work

while Abner was speaking and that spray of sweat had reappeared.
But he kept the courage he had got.

"Lord Almighty, man!" he cried. "How prettily you sum it up!
We shall presently have Lawyer Abner with his brief. Because my
renters have killed a calf; because one of their horses frightened at
the blood has bolted, and because they cover the blood with earth
so the other horses traveling the path may not do the like; straightway I have shot Alkire out of his saddle . . . Man! What a mare's
nest! And now, Lawyer Abner, with your neat little conclusions,
what did I do with Alkire after I had killed him? Did I cause him
to vanish into the air with a smell of sulphur or did I cause the
earth to yawn and Alkire to descend into its bowels?"

"Dix," replied Abner, "your words move somewhat near the
truth."

"Upon my soul," cried Dix, "you compliment me. If I had that
trick of magic, believe me, you would be already some distance
down."

Abner remained a moment silent.

"Dix," he said, "what does it mean when one finds a plot of earth
resodded?"

"Is that a riddle?" cried Dix. "Well, confound me, if I don't answer it! You charge me with murder and then you fling in this neat
conundrum. Now, what could be the answer to that riddle, Abner?
If one had done a murder this sod would overlie a grave and Alkire
would be in it in his bloody shirt. Do I give the answer?"

"You do not," replied Abner.

"No!" cried Dix. "Your sodded plot no grave, and Alkire not
within it waiting for the trump of Gabriel! Why, man, where are
your little damned conclusions?"

"Dix," said Abner, "you do not deceive me in the least; Alkire is
not sleeping in a grave."

"Then in the air," sneered Dix, "with the smell of sulphur?"

"Nor in the air," said Abner.

"Then consumed with fire, like the priests of Baal?"

"Nor with fire," said Abner.

Dix had got back the quiet of his face; this banter had put him where he was when Abner entered. "This is all fools' talk," he said; "if I had killed Alkire, what could I have done with the body? And the horse! What could I have done with the horse? Remember, no man has ever seen Alkire's horse any more than he has seen Alkire—and for the reason that Alkire rode him out of the hills that night. Now, look here, Abner, you have asked me a good many questions. I will ask you one. Among your little conclusions do you find that I did this thing alone or with the aid of others?"

"Dix," replied Abner, "I will answer that upon my own belief you had no accomplice."

"Then," said Dix, "how could I have carried off the horse? Alkire I might carry; but his horse weighed thirteen hundred pounds!"

"Dix," said Abner, "no man helped you do this thing; but there were men who helped you to conceal it."

"And now," cried Dix, "the man is going mad! Who could I trust with such work, I ask you? Have I a renter that would not tell it when he moved on to another's land, or when he got a quart of cider in him? Where are the men who helped me?"

"Dix," said Abner, "they have been dead these fifty years." I heard Dix laugh then, and his evil face lighted as though a candle were behind it. And, in truth, I thought he had got Abner silenced.

"In the name of Heaven!" he cried. "With such proofs it is a wonder that you did not have me hanged."

"And hanged you should have been," said Abner.

"Well," cried Dix, "go and tell the sheriff, and mind you lay before him those little, neat conclusions: How from a horse track and the place where a calf was butchered you have reasoned on Alkire's murder, and to conceal the body and the horse you have reasoned on the aid of men who were rotting in their graves when I was born; and see how he will receive you!"

Abner gave no attention to the man's flippant speech. He got his

great silver watch out of his pocket, pressed the stem and looked.
Then he spoke in his deep, even voice.

"Dix," he said, "it is nearly midnight; in an hour you must be
on your journey, and I have something more to say. Listen! I knew
this thing had been done the previous day because it had rained on
the night that I met Alkire, and the earth of this ant heap had been
disturbed after that. Moreover, this earth had been frozen, and that
showed a night had passed since it had been placed there. And I
knew the rider of that horse was Alkire because, beside the path
near the severed twigs lay my knife, where it had fallen from his
hand. This much I learned in some fifteen minutes; the rest took
somewhat longer.

"I followed the track of the horse until it stopped in the little
valley below. It was easy to follow while the horse ran, because the
sod was torn; but when it ceased to run there was no track that I
could follow. There was a little stream threading the valley, and I
began at the wood and came slowly up to see if I could find where
the horse had crossed. Finally I found a horse track and there was
also a man's track, which meant that you had caught the horse and
were leading it away. But where?

"On the rising ground above there was an old orchard where
there had once been a house. The work about that house had been
done a hundred years. It was rotted down now. You had opened
this orchard into the pasture. I rode all over the face of this hill
and finally I entered this orchard. There was a great, flat, moss-
covered stone lying a few steps from where the house had stood. As
I looked I noticed that the moss growing from it into the earth had
been broken along the edges of the stone, and then I noticed that
for a few feet about the stone the ground had been resodded. I got
down and lifted up some of this new sod. Under it the earth had
been soaked with that . . . red paint.

"It was clever of you, Dix, to resod the ground; that took only a
little time and it effectually concealed the place where you had

killed the horse; but it was foolish of you to forget that the broken moss around the edges of the great flat stone could not be mended."

"Abner!" cried Dix. "Stop!" And I saw that spray of sweat, and his face working like kneaded bread, and the shiver of that abominable chill on him.

Abner was silent for a moment and then he went on, but from another quarter.

"Twice," said Abner, "the Angel of the Lord stood before me and I did not know it; but the third time I knew it. It is not in the cry of the wind, nor in the voice of many waters that His presence is made known to us. That man in Israel had only the sign that the beast under him would not go on. Twice I had as good a sign, and tonight, when Marks broke a stirrup-leather before my house and called me to the door and asked me for a knife to mend it, I saw and I came!"

The log that Abner had thrown on was burned down, and the fire was again a mass of embers; the room was filled with that dull red light. Dix had got on to his feet, and he stood now twisting before the fire, his hands reaching out to it, and that cold creeping in his bones, and the smell of the fire on him.

Abner rose. And when he spoke his voice was like a thing that has dimensions and weight.

"Dix," he said, "you robbed the grazers; you shot Alkire out of his saddle; and a child you would have murdered!"

And I saw the sleeve of Abner's coat begin to move, then it stopped. He stood staring at something against the wall. I looked to see what the thing was, but I did not see it. Abner was looking beyond the wall, as though it had been moved away.

And all the time Dix had been shaking with that hellish cold, and twisting on the hearth and crowding into the fire. Then he fell back, and he was the Dix I knew—his face was slack; his eye was furtive; and he was full of terror.

It was his weak whine that awakened Abner. He put up his hand and brought the fingers hard down over his face, and then he looked at this new creature, cringing and beset with fears.

"Dix," he said, "Alkire was a just man; he sleeps as peacefully in that abandoned well under his horse as he would sleep in the churchyard. My hand has been held back; you may go. Vengeance is mine, I will repay, saith the Lord."

"But where shall I go, Abner?" the creature wailed; "I have no money and I am cold."

Abner took out his leather wallet and flung it toward the door.

"There is money," he said—"a hundred dollars—and there is my coat. Go! But if I find you in the hills tomorrow, or if I ever find you, I warn you in the name of the living God that I will stamp you out of life!"

I saw the loathsome thing writhe into Abner's coat and seize the wallet and slip out through the door; and a moment later I heard a horse. And I crept back on to Roy's heifer skin.

When I came down at daylight my Uncle Abner was reading by the fire.

Hesketh Prichard

(1876–1922)

SEVERAL OF MYSTERY FICTION'S distinguished writers hailed from Canada while setting most of their fiction elsewhere. This group includes, for example, Ross Macdonald, the creator of twentieth-century detective Lew Archer, and the great Victorian crime writer Grant Allen, creator of master con artist Colonel Clay. A different genus comprises writers from elsewhere who set some of their fiction in Canada. In this group we find Hesketh Prichard, an outsider who placed in the wilds of the north an original and intriguing variation on the Sherlock Holmes type of detective—November Joe.

Like Natty Bumppo, the hero of James Fenimore Cooper's Leatherstocking Tales, November Joe notices seemingly irrelevant minutiae in the woods. Like Sherlock Holmes, he turns coy about the clues' importance until he's ready to talk—and, when he solves a case, doesn't hesitate to serve as a vigilante judge and jury. Although Hesketh Prichard doesn't specify to which native people Joe belongs, and the text is even vague about whether his ancestry is only half-native, mostly he portrays Joe without the usual Anglo-Saxon condescension of the era. Our narrator's primary response to Joe, in time-honored Watson fashion, is dazzled admiration.

Joe's interpretations of the clues seem reasonable in part because Hesketh Prichard understood outdoor life. He was also the author of *Through Trackless Labrador* and *Hunting-Camps in Wood and Wilderness.*

Born in India to a Scottish officer in the British military, he grew up to become an acclaimed cricket bowler and then a big-game hunter, restless explorer, and travel writer. He contracted malaria in the Caribbean, named a Patagonian river in honor of his mother, and discovered a South American species of grass that soon bore the species name *prichardii*. He is even credited with improving marksmanship and sniper training in the British army during World War I. He may refer to a moose's "horns" when he means "antlers," but he knows which part of a canoe's hull is called the stem, that balsam boughs make soft bedding, and that in this region of North America ruffed grouse are known as hardwood partridges. Prichard also wrote under a pseudonym, H. Heron, collaborating with his mother, who wrote as E. Heron. Together they created the pioneer psychic detective Flaxman Low, and also Don Q, a figure similar to Robin Hood who later appeared in Hollywood films as *Don Q, Son of Zorro*, starring swashbuckling Douglas Fairbanks.

"The Crime at Big Tree Portage" originally appeared as the third chapter of *November Joe: Detective of the Woods*, which Houghton Mifflin published in Boston in 1913. Like so many detective series of the time, it progresses from chapter to chapter although, after the first two set the scene, each chapter is a self-contained case. This first recorded adventure is set in the early autumn of 1908. The narrator, a harried Quebec businessman named James Quaritch, has been prescribed a three-month hunting trip in the wilderness to calm his money-stressed nerves. On earlier expeditions he met a smart teenage assistant guide named November Joe. When Quaritch's doctor recommends a hunting trip, he explains that Joe is now a man of twenty-four who is not only a respected guide but has become something of a legend as a hawkeyed woodlands detective. Later a friend of Joe's reveals that the tracker was offered a thousand dollars a month to move to New York City and become a detective—but he turned the offer down, declaring that "he would rather be tied to a tree in the woods for the rest of his life than live on Fifth Avenue." Joe lives twenty-seven miles from the nearest telegraph office, so Quaritch heads off to meet him at his camp, only to be asked to deliver to Joe the message that a man named Henry Lyon has been found murdered in his woodland camp and that tracking down the culprit will result in a fifty-dollar reward for November Joe. Quaritch talks Joe into letting him tag along and thus becomes the first backwoods Watson, in a vivid and suspenseful series that has been unfairly forgotten in the decades since its debut.

The Crime at Big Tree Portage

I HAVE SOMETIMES WONDERED whether he was not irked at the prospect of my proffered companionship, and whether he did not at first intend to shake me off by obvious and primitive methods.

He has in later days assured me that neither of my suppositions was correct, but there has been a far-off look in his eyes while he denied them, which leaves me still half-doubtful.

However these things may be, it is certain that I had my work, and more than my work, cut out for me in keeping up with November who, although he was carrying a pack while I was unloaded, travelled through the woods at an astonishing pace.

He moved from the thighs, bending a little forward. However thick the underbrush and the trees, he never once halted or even wavered, but passed onward with neither check nor pause. Meanwhile, I blundered in his tracks until at last, when we came out on the bank of a strong and swiftly flowing river, I was fairly done, and felt that, had the journey continued much longer, I must have been forced to give in.

November threw down his pack and signed to me to remain beside it, while he walked off downstream, only to reappear with a canoe.

We were soon aboard her. Of the remainder of our journey I am sorry to say I can recall very little. The rustle of the water as it hissed against our stem, and the wind in the birches and junipers on the banks, soon lulled me. I was only awakened by the canoe touching the bank at Big Tree.

Big Tree Portage is a recognized camping place, situated between the great main lumber-camp of Briston and Harpur and the settlement of St. Amiel, and it lies about equidistant from both. Old fire-scars in the clearing showed black not more than thirty yards from the water. From the canoe we were in full sight of the scene of the tragedy.

A small shelter of boughs stood beneath the spreading branches of a large fir; the ground all about was strewn with tins and debris. On a bare space in front of the shelter, beside the charred logs of a camp-fire, a patch of blue caught my eye. This, as my sight grew accustomed to the light, resolved itself into the shape of a huge man. He lay upon his face, and the wind fluttered the blue blouse which he was wearing. It came upon me with a shock that I was looking at the body of Henry Lyon, the murdered man.

November, standing up in the canoe, a wood picture in his buckskin shirt and jeans, surveyed the scene in silence, then pushed off again and paddled up and down, staring at the bank. After a bit he put in and waded ashore.

In obedience to a sign I stayed in the canoe, from which I watched the movements of my companion. First, he went to the body and examined it with minute care; next, he disappeared within the shelter, came out, and stood for a minute staring towards the river; finally, he called to me to come ashore.

I had seen November turn the body over, and as I came up I was aware of a great ginger-bearded face, horribly pale, confronting the sky. It was easy to see how the man had died, for the bullet had torn a hole at the base of the neck. The ground beside him was torn up as if by some small sharp instruments.

The idea occurred to me that I would try my hand at detection. I went into the shelter. There I found a blanket, two freshly flayed bearskins, and a pack, which lay open. I came out again and carefully examined the ground in all directions. Suddenly looking up,

I saw November Joe watching me with a kind of grim and covert amusement.

"What are you looking for?" said he.

"The tracks of the murderer."

"You won't find them."

"Why?"

"He didn't make none."

I pointed out the spot where the ground was torn.

"The lumberman that found him—spiked boots," said November.

"How do you know he was not the murderer?"

"He didn't get here till Lyon had been dead for hours. Compare his tracks with Lyon's . . . much fresher. No, Mr. Sport, that cock won't fight."

"Then, as you seem to know so much, tell me what you do know."

"I know that Lyon reached here in the afternoon of the day before yesterday. He'd been visiting his traps upstream. He hadn't been here more'n a few minutes, and was lighting his pipe in the shelter there, when he hears a voice hail him. He comes out and sees a man in a canoe shoved into the bank. That man shot him dead and cleared off—without leaving a trace."

"How can you be sure of all this?" I asked, for not one of these things had occurred to my mind.

"Because I found a pipe of tobacco not rightly lit, but just charred on top, beside Lyon's body, and a newly used match in this shack. The man that killed him come downstream and surprised him."

"How can you tell he came downstream?"

"Because, if he'd come upstream Lyon would 'a' seen him from the shack," said November with admirable patience.

"You say the shot was fired from a canoe?"

"The river's too wide to shoot across; and, anyway, there's the mark of where the canoe rested agin the bank. No, this is the work of a right smart woodsman, and he's not left me one clue as to who he is. But I'm not through with him, mister. Such men as he needs catching . . . Let's boil the kettle."

We laid the dead man inside the shack, and then, coming out once more into the sunlight, sat down beside a fire which we built among the stones on the bank of the river. Here November made tea in true woods fashion, drawing all the strength and bitterness from the leaves by boiling them. I was wondering what he would do next, for it appeared that our chance of catching the murderer was infinitesimal, since he had left no clue save the mark on the bank where his canoe had rested among the reeds while he fired his deadly bullet. I put my thoughts into words.

"You're right," said November. "When a chap who's used to the woods life takes to crime, he's harder to lay hands on than a lynx in a alder patch."

"There is one thing which I don't understand," said I. "Why did not the murderer sink Lyon's body in the water? It would have been well hidden there."

The young woodsman pointed to the river, which foamed in low rapids about dark heads of rock.

"He couldn't trust her; the current's sharp, and would put the dead man ashore as like as not," he replied. "And if he'd landed to carry it down to his canoe, he'd have left tracks. No, he's done his work to rights from his point of view."

I saw the force of the argument, and nodded.

"And more'n that, there's few people," he went on, "travel up and down this river. Lyon might 'a' laid in that clearing till he was a skeleton, but for the chance of that lumber-jack happening along."

"Then which way do you think the murderer has fled?"

"Can't say," said he, "and, anyhow, he's maybe eighty miles away by this time."

"Will you try and follow him?"

"No, not yet. I must find out something about him first. But, look here, mister, there's one fact you haven't given much weight to. This shooting was pre-meditated. The murderer knew that Lyon would camp here. The chances are a hundred to one against their having met by accident. The chap that killed him followed him downstream. Now, suppose I can find Lyon's last camp, I may learn something more. It can't be very far off, for he had a tidy-sized pack to carry, besides those green skins, which loaded him a bit . . . And, anyway, it's my only chance."

So we set out upon our walk. November soon picked up Lyon's trail, leading from Big Tree Portage to a disused tote-road, which again led us due west between the aisles of the forest. From midday on through the whole of the afternoon we travelled. Squirrels chattered and hissed at us from the spruces, hardwood partridges drummed in the clearings, and once a red-deer buck bounded across our path with its white flag waving and dipping as it was swallowed up in the sun-speckled orange and red of the woods.

Lyon's trail was, fortunately, easy to follow, and it was only where, at long intervals, paths from the north or south broke into the main logging-road that November had reason to pause. But one by one we passed these by, until at last the tracks we were following shot away among the trees, and after a mile of deadfalls and moss de-bouched into a little clearing beside a backwater grown round with high yellow grass, and covered over the larger part of its surface with lily-pads.

The trail, after leading along the margin of this water, struck back to a higher reach of the same river that ran by Big Tree Portage, and then we were at once on the site of the deserted camp.

The very first thing my eye lit upon caused me to cry out in excitement, for side by side were two beds of balsam branches, that had evidently been placed under the shelter of the same tent cover. November, then, was right; Lyon had camped with someone on the night before he died.

I called out to him. His quiet patience and an attitude as if rather detached from events fell away from him like a cloak, and with al-most uncanny swiftness he was making his examination of the camp.

I entirely believe that he was unconscious of my presence, so concentrated was he on his work as I followed him from spot to spot with an interest and excitement that no form of big-game shooting has ever given me. Now, man was the quarry, and, as it seemed, a man more dangerous than any beast. But I was destined to disappointment, for, as far as I could see, Joe discovered neither clue nor anything unusual.

To begin with, he took up and sifted through the layers of balsam boughs which had composed the beds, but apparently made no find. From them he turned quickly to kneel down by the ashy remains of the fire, and to examine the charred logs one by one. After that he followed a well-marked trail that led away from the lake to a small marsh in the farther part of which masts of dead timber were standing in great profusion. Nearer at hand a number of stumps showed where the campers had chopped the wood for their fire.

After looking closely at these stumps, November went swiftly back to the camp and spent the next ten minutes in following the tracks which led in all directions. Then once more he came back to the fire and methodically lifted off one charred stick after another. At the time I could not imagine why he did this, but, when I understood it, the reason was as simple and obvious as was that of his every action when once it was explained.

Before men leave a camp they seem instinctively to throw such trifles as they do not require or wish to carry on with them in the fire, which is generally expiring, for a first axiom of the true camper in the woods is never to leave his fire alight behind him, in case of a chance ember starting a forest conflagration.

In this case November had taken off nearly every bit of wood before I heard him utter a smothered exclamation as he held up a piece of stick.

I took it into my own hands and looked it over. It was charred, but I saw that one end had been split and the other end sharpened.

"What in the world is it?" I asked, puzzled.

November smiled. "Just evidence," he answered.

I was glad he had at last found something to go upon, for, so far, the camp had appeared to produce parsimoniously little that was suggestive. Nevertheless, I did not see how this little bit of spruce, crudely fashioned and split as it was, would lead us very far.

November spent another few minutes in looking everything over a second time, then he took up his axe and split a couple of logs and lit the fire. Over it he hung his inevitable kettle and boiled up the leaves of our morning brew with a liberal handful freshly added.

"Well," I said, as he touched the end of a burning ember to his pipe, "has this camp helped you?"

"Some," said November. "And you?"

He put the question quite seriously, though I suspect not without some inward irony.

"I can see that two men slept under one tent cover, that they cut the wood for their fire in that marsh we visited, and that they were here for a day, perhaps two."

"One was here for three days, the other one night," corrected November.

"How can you tell that?"

November pointed to the ground at the far side of the fire.

"To begin with, number 1 had his camp pitched over there," said he; then, seeing my look of perplexity, he added pityingly: "We've a westerly wind these last two days, but before that the wind was east, and he camped the first night with his back to it. And in the new camp one bed o' boughs is fresher than the other."

The thing seemed so absurdly obvious that I was nettled.

"I suppose there are other indications I haven't noticed," I said.

"There might be some you haven't mentioned," he answered warily.

"What are they?"

"That the man who killed Lyon is thick-set and very strong; that he has been a good while in the woods without having gone to a settlement; that he owns a blunt hatchet such as we woods chaps call 'tomahawk, number 3'; that he killed a moose last week; that he can read; that he spent the night before the murder in great trouble of mind, and that likely he was a religious kind o' chap."

As November reeled off these details in his quiet, low-keyed voice, I stared at him in amazement.

"But how can you have found out all that?" I said at last. "If it's correct, it's wonderful!"

"I'll tell you, if you still want to hear, when I've got my man—if ever I do get him. One thing more is sure, he is a chap who knew Lyon well. The rest of the job lies in the settlement of St. Amiel, where Lyon lived."

We walked back to Big Tree Portage, and from there ran down in the canoe to St. Amiel, arriving the following evening. About half a mile short of the settlement, November landed and set up our camp. After-wards we went on. I had never before visited the place, and I found it to be a little colony of scattered houses, straggling beside the river. It possessed two stores and one of the smallest churches I have ever seen.

"You can help me here if you will," said November as we paused before the larger of the stores.

"Of course I will. How?"

"By letting 'em think you've engaged me as your guide and we've come in to St. Amiel to buy some grub and gear we've run short of."

"All right." And with this arrangement we entered the store.

I will not make any attempt to describe by what roundabout courses of talk November learned all the news of desolate little St. Amiel and of the surrounding countryside. Had I not known exactly what he wanted, I should never have dreamed that he was seeking information. He played the desultory uninterested listener to perfection. The Provincial Police had evidently found means to close the mouth of the lumber-jack for the time, at least, as no hint of Lyon's death had yet drifted back to his native place.

Little by little it came out that only five men were absent from the settlement. Two of these, Fitz and Baxter Gurd, were brothers who had gone on an extended trapping expedition. The other absentees were Highamson, Lyon's father-in-law; Thomas Miller, a professional guide and hunter; and, lastly, Henry Lyon himself, who had gone up-river to visit his traps, starting on the previous Friday. The other men had all been away three weeks or more, and all had started in canoes, except Lyon, who, having sold his, went on foot.

Next, by imperceptible degrees, the talk slid round to the subject of Lyon's wife. They had been married four years and had no child. She had been the belle of St. Amiel, and there had been no small competition for her hand. Of the absent men, both Miller and Fitz Gurd had been her suitors, and the former and Lyon had never been on good terms since the marriage. The younger Gurd was a wild fellow, and only his brother's influence kept him straight.

So much we heard before November wrapped up our purchases and we took our leave.

No sooner were we away than I put my eager question: "What do you think of it?"

Joe shrugged his shoulders.

"Do you know any of these men?"

"All of them."

"How about the fellow who is on bad terms with—"

November seized my arm. A man was approaching through the dusk. As he passed, my companion hailed him.

"Hullo, Baxter! Didn't know you'd come back. Where you been?"

"Right up on the headwaters."

"Fitz come down with you?"

"No; stayed on the line of traps. Did you want him, November?"

"Yes, but it can wait. See any moose?"

"Nary one—nothing but red deer."

"Good-night."

"So long."

"That settles it," said November. "If he speaks the truth, as I believe he does, it wasn't either of the Gurds shot Lyon."

"Why not?"

"Didn't you hear him say they hadn't seen any moose? And I

told you that the man that shot Lyon had killed a moose quite recent. That leaves just Miller and Highamson and it weren't Miller."

"You're sure of that?"

"Stark certain. One reason is that Miller's above six foot, and the man as camped with Lyon wasn't as tall by six inches. Another reason. You heard the storekeeper say how Miller and Lyon wasn't on speaking terms; yet the man who shot Lyon camped with him— slep' beside him—must 'a' talked to him. That weren't Miller."

His clear reasoning rang true.

"Highamson lives alone away up above Lyon's," continued November; "he'll make back home soon."

"Unless he's guilty and has fled the country," I suggested.

"He won't 'a' done that. It'ud be as good as a confession. No, he thinks he's done his work to rights and has nothing to fear. Like as not he's back home now. There's not much coming and going between these up-river places and St. Amiel, and he might easy be there and no one know it yet down to the settlement. We'll go up to-night and make sure. But first we'll get back to camp and take a cup o' tea."

The night had become both wild and blustering before we set out for Highamson's hut, and all along the forest paths which led to it the sleet and snow of what November called "a real mean night" beat in our faces.

As we travelled on in silence, my mind kept going over and over the events of the last two days. I had already seen enough to assure me that my companion was a very skilful detective, but the most ingenious part of his work, namely, the deductions by which he had pretended to reconstruct the personality of the criminal, had yet to be put to the test.

It was black dark, or nearly so, when at last a building loomed up in front of us, a faint light showing under the door.

"You there, Highamson?" called out November.

As there was no answer, my companion pushed it open and we entered the small wooden room, where, on a single table, a lamp

burned dimly. He turned it up and looked around. A pack lay on
the floor unopened, and a gun leant up in a corner.

"Just got in," commented November. "Hasn't loosed up his pack
yet."

He turned it over. A hatchet was thrust through the wide thongs
which bound it. November drew it out.

"Put your thumb along that edge," he said. "Blunt? Yes? Yet he
drove that old hatchet as deep in the wood as Lyon drove his sharp
one: he's a strong man."

As he spoke he was busying himself with the pack, examining its
contents with deft fingers. It held little save a few clothes, a little tea
and salt, and other fragments of provisions, and a Bible. The finding
of the last was, I could see, no surprise to November, though the
reason why he should have suspected its presence remained hidden
from me. But I had begun to realize that much was plain to him
which to the ordinary man was invisible.

Having satisfied himself as to every article in the pack, he rapidly replaced them, and tied it up as he had found it, when I, glancing out of the small window, saw a light moving low among the
trees, to which I called November Joe's attention.

"It's likely Highamson," he said, "coming home with a lantern.
Get you into that dark corner."

I did so, while November stood in the shadow at the back of the
closed door. From my position I could see the lantern slowly approaching until it flung a gleam of light through the window into
the hut. The next moment the door was thrust open, and the
heavy breathing of a man became audible.

It happened that at first Highamson saw neither of us, so that the
first intimation that he had of our presence was November's "Hello!"

Down crashed the lantern, and its bearer started back with a
quick hoarse gasp.

"Who's there?" he cried, "who—"

"Them as is sent by Hal Lyon."

Never have I seen words produce so tremendous an effect.

Highamson gave a bellow of fury, and the next instant he and
November were struggling together.

I sprang to my companion's aid, and even then it was no easy
task for the two of us to master the powerful old man. As we held
him down I caught my first sight of his ash-grey face. His mouth
grinned open, and there was a terrible intention in his staring eyes.
But all changed as he recognized his visitor.

"November! November Joe!" cried he.

"Get up!" And as Highamson rose to his feet, "Whatever for did
you do it?" asked November in his quiet voice. But now its quiet-
ness carried a menace.

"Do what? I didn't—I—" Highamson paused, and there was
something unquestionably fine about the old man as he added:
"No, I won't lie. It's true I shot Hal Lyon. And, what's more, if it
was to do again, I'd do it again! It's the best deed I ever done; yes,
I say that, though I know it's written in the book: 'Whoso shed-
deth man's blood, by man shall his blood be shed.'"

"Why did you do it?" repeated November.

Highamson gave him a look.

"I'll tell you. I did it for my little Janey's sake. He was her husband. See here! I'll tell you why I shot Hal Lyon. Along of the first
week of last month I went away back into the woods trapping
musk-rats. I was gone more 'n the month, and the day I come back
I did as I did to-night, as I always do first thing when I gets in—I
went over to see Janey. Hal Lyon weren't there; if he had been, I
shouldn't never 'a' needed to travel so far to get even with him. But
that's neither here nor there. He'd gone to his bear traps above Big
Tree; but the night before he left he'd got in one of his quarrels
with my Janey. Hit her—he did—there was one tooth gone where
his—fist fell."

Never have I seen such fury as burned in the old man's eyes as
he groaned out the last words.

"Janey, that had the prettiest face for fifty miles around. She
tried to hide it from me, didn't want me to know, but there was

poor face all swole, and black and blue, and the gap among her white teeth. Bit by bit it all came out. It weren't the first time Lyon'd took his hands to her, no, nor the third, nor the fourth. There on the spot, as I looked at her, I made up my mind I'd go after him, and I'd make him promise me, aye, swear to me, on the Holy Book, never to lay hand on her again. If he wouldn't swear I'd put him where his hands couldn't reach her. I found him camped away up alongside a backwater near his traps, and I told him I'd seen Janey and that he must swear . . . He wouldn't! He said he'd learn her to tell on him, he'd smash her in the mouth again. Then he lay down and slep'. I wonder now he weren't afraid of me, but I suppose that was along of me being a quiet, God-fearing chap.

"Hour by hour I lay awake, and then I couldn't stand it no more, and I got up and pulled a bit of candle I had from my pack, fixed up a candlestick, and looked in my Bible for guidance. And the words I lit on were: 'Thou shalt break them with a rod of iron.' That was the gun clear enough . . . Then I blew out the light, and I think I slep', for I dreamed.

"Next morning Lyon was up early. He had two or three green skins that he'd took off the day before, and he said he was going straight home to smash Janey. I lay there and I said nothing, black nor white. His judgment was set. I knew he couldn't make all the distance in one day, and I was pretty sure he'd camp at Big Tree. I arrived there just after him, as I could travel faster by canoe than him walking, and so kep' near him all day. It was nigh sunset, and I bent down under the bank so he couldn't see me. He went into the old shack. I called out his name. I heard him cursing at my voice, and when he showed his face I shot him dead. I never landed, I never left no tracks, I thought I was safe, sure. You've took me; yet only for Janey's sake I wouldn't care. I did right, but she won't like them to say her father's a murderer . . . That's all."

November sat on the edge of the table. His handsome face was grave. Nothing more was said for a good while. Then Highamson stood up.

"I'm ready, November, but you'll let me see Janey again before you give me over to the police."

November looked him in the eyes. "Expect you'll see a good deal of Janey yet. She'll be lonesome over there now that her brute husband's gone. She'll want you to live with her," he said.

"D'ye mean . . ."

November nodded. "If the police can catch you for themselves, let 'em. And you'd lessen the chance of that wonderful deal if you was to burn them moose-shank moccasins you're wearing. When did you kill your moose?"

"Tuesday's a week. And my moccasins was wore out, so I fixed 'em up woods fashion."

"I know. The hair on 'em is slipping. I found some of it in your tracks in the camp, away above Big Tree. That's how I knew you'd killed a moose. I found your candlestick too. Here it is." He took from his pocket the little piece of spruce stick, which had puzzled me so much, and turned towards me.

"This end's sharp to stick into the earth, that end's slit and you fix the candle in with a bit o' birch bark. Now it can go into the stove along o' the moccasins." He opened the stove door and thrust in the articles.

"Only three know your secret, Highamson, and if I was you I wouldn't make it four, not even by adding a woman to it."

Highamson held out his hand.

"You always was a white man, Nov," said he.

Hours later, as we sat drinking a final cup of tea at the campfire, I said:—

"After you examined Lyon's upper camp, you told me seven things about the murderer. You've explained how you knew them, all but three."

"What are the three?"

"First, how did you know that Highamson had been a long time in the woods without visiting a settlement?"

"His moccasins was wore out and patched with raw moose-hide. The tracks of them was plain," replied November.

I nodded. "And how could you tell that he was religious and spent the night in great trouble of mind?"

November paused in filling his pipe. "He couldn't sleep," said he, "and so he got up and cut that candlestick. What'd he want to light a candle for but to read by? And why should he want to read in the middle of the night if he was not in trouble? And if he was in trouble, what book would he want to read? Besides, not one trapper in a hundred carries any book but the Bible."

"I see. But how did you know it was in the middle of the night?"

"Did you notice where he cut his candlestick?"

"No," said I.

"I did, and he made two false cuts where his knife slipped in the dark. You're wonderful at questions."

"And you at answers."

November stirred the embers under the kettle, and the firelight lit up his fine face as he turned with a yawn.

"My!" said he, "but I'm glad Highamson had his reasons. I'd 'a' hated to think of that old man shut in where he couldn't see the sun rise. Wouldn't you?"

※

Ernest Bramah

(1868–1942)

ERNEST BRAMAH IS REMEMBERED nowadays for two characters he created. The first appeared in his 1900 book *The Wallet of Kai Lung.* Kai Lung is an itinerant Chinese storyteller whose flowery, elegant style represents not exactly a Western parody but at least a Western stylization of formal Chinese mannerisms when speaking English. Bramah had never been to China and the stories are fanciful fables, featuring many colorful characters such as gentlemanly highwaymen, as well as occasional appearances by dragons or ghosts. Certainly the stories can be criticized as imperial British condescension, but Bramah played the language for laughs, not mockery. "It has been said," Kai Lung remarks, "there are few situations in life that cannot be honourably settled, and without loss of time, either by suicide, a bag of gold or by thrusting a despised antagonist over the edge of a precipice on a dark night." The stories are sprinkled with epigrams that are about as authentic as the Polish proverbs on the old detective TV series *Banacek*, but then realism was never Bramah's goal.

Bramah's second memorable character was Max Carrados, the protagonist of the following story. Carrados is in the fortunate position of having inherited great wealth from an American relative, so he is free to amuse himself as he wishes. He is a renowned numismatist, and his first case, "The Coin of Dionysus," revolves around this field. Blinded in a horseback-riding incident twelve years before the series begins, Carrados has developed the kind of hyperacute senses that would later be further exaggerated in the blind superhero Daredevil. Nor did Bramah keep other elements of the Carrados stories confined to realism. "The Tragedy at Brookbend Cottage" involves an elaborate murder plot worthy of a James Bond movie in its reckless disregard for plausibility, despite the tragic tone. The Carrados stories were gathered into the collection *Max Carrados*, published by Methuen & Company in 1914; "The Tragedy at Brookbend Cottage" appears late in the book. A second collection, *The Eyes of Max Carrados*, appeared nine years later.

Bramah was acclaimed for the level of his work in many categories. His 1907 dystopian science fiction novel, *What Might Have Been* (also published as *The Secret of the League*), helped prepare the way for *1984*, as George Orwell himself pointed out. In creating Max Carrados, Bramah was merely exaggerating the kind of almost superhuman skills attributed to historical and contemporary figures whom he admired. One of the most renowned blind people in English history was John Fielding, brother of novelist Henry Fielding. Henry, as noted in the introduction, was also a magistrate and founder of the Bow Street Runners. John Fielding famously could identify many people (including, it was said, hundreds of criminals) by their voice alone, after only one meeting. He helped found the idea of a criminal records department in police offices by printing a police gazette featuring descriptions of known criminals. Fielding was a worthy example for Bramah to follow.

The Tragedy at Brookbend Cottage

M AX," SAID MR. CARLYLE, when Parkinson had closed the door behind him, "this is Lieutenant Hollyer, whom you consented to see."

"To hear," corrected Carrados, smiling straight into the healthy and rather embarrassed face of the stranger before him. "Mr. Hollyer knows of my disability?"

"Mr. Carlyle told me," said the young man, "but, as a matter of fact, I had heard of you before, Mr. Carrados, from one of our men. It was in connection with the foundering of the *Ivan Saratov*."

Carrados wagged his head in good-humoured resignation.

"And the owners were sworn to inviolable secrecy!" he exclaimed. "Well, it is inevitable, I suppose. Not another scuttling case, Mr. Hollyer?"

"No, mine is quite a private matter," replied the lieutenant. "My sister, Mrs. Creake—but Mr. Carlyle would tell you better than I can. He knows all about it."

"No, no; Carlyle is a professional. Let me have it in the rough, Mr. Hollyer. My ears are my eyes, you know."

"Very well, sir. I can tell you what there is to tell, right enough, but I feel that when all's said and done it must sound very little to another, although it seems important to me."

"We have occasionally found trifles of significance ourselves," said Carrados encouragingly. "Don't let that deter you."

This was the essence of Lieutenant Hollyer's narrative:

"I have a sister, Millicent, who is married to a man called Creake. She is about twenty-eight now and he is at least fifteen years older. Neither my mother (who has since died) nor I cared very much about Creake. We had nothing particular against him, except, perhaps, the moderate disparity of age, but none of us appeared to have anything in common. He was a dark, taciturn man, and his moody silence froze up conversation. As a result, of course, we didn't see much of each other."

"This, you must understand, was four or five years ago, Max," interposed Mr. Carlyle officiously.

Carrados maintained an uncompromising silence. Mr. Carlyle blew his nose and contrived to impart a hurt significance into the operation. Then Lieutenant Hollyer continued:

"Millicent married Creake after a very short engagement. It was a frightfully subdued wedding—more like a funeral to me. The man professed to have no relations and apparently he had scarcely any friends or business acquaintances. He was an agent for something or other and had an office off Holborn. I suppose he made a living out of it then, although we knew practically nothing of his private affairs, but I gather that it has been going down since, and I suspect that for the past few years they have been getting along almost entirely on Millicent's little income. You would like the particulars of that?"

"Please," assented Carrados.

"When our father died about seven years ago, he left three thousand pounds. It was invested in Canadian stock and brought in a little over a hundred a year. By his will my mother was to have the income of that for life and on her death it was to pass to Millicent, subject to the payment of a lump sum of five hundred pounds to me. But my father privately suggested to me that if I should have no particular use for the money at the time, he would propose my letting Millicent have the income of it until I did want it, as she would not be particularly well off. You see, Mr. Carrados, a great deal more had been spent on my education and advancement than on her; I had my pay, and, of course, I could look out for myself better than a girl could."

"Quite so," agreed Carrados.

"Therefore I did nothing about that," continued the lieutenant. "Three years ago I was over again but I did not see much of them. They were living in lodgings. That was the only time since the marriage that I have seen them until last week. In the meanwhile our mother had died and Millicent had been receiving her income. She wrote me several letters at the time. Otherwise we did not correspond much, but about a year ago she sent me their new address—Brookbend Cottage, Mulling Common—a house that they had taken. When I got two months' leave I invited myself there as a matter of course, fully expecting to stay most of my time with them, but I made an excuse to get away after a week. The place was dismal and unendurable, the whole life and atmosphere indescribably depressing." He looked round with an instinct of caution, leaned forward earnestly, and dropped his voice. "Mr. Carrados, it is my absolute conviction that Creake is only waiting for a favourable opportunity to murder Millicent."

"Go on," said Carrados quietly. "A week of the depressing surroundings of Brookbend Cottage would not alone convince you of that, Mr. Hollyer."

"I am not so sure," declared Hollyer doubtfully. "There was a feeling of suspicion and—before me—polite hatred that would have gone a good way towards it. All the same there *was* something more definite. Millicent told me this the day after I went there. There is no doubt that a few months ago Creake deliberately planned to poison her with some weed-killer. She told me the circumstances in a rather distressed moment, but afterwards she refused to speak of it again—even weakly denied it—and, as a matter of fact, it was with the greatest of difficulty that I could get her at any time to talk about her husband or his affairs. The gist of it was that she had the strongest suspicion that Creake doctored a bottle of stout which he expected she would drink for her supper when she was alone. The weed-killer, properly labelled, but also in a beer bottle, was kept with other miscellaneous liquids in the same cupboard as the beer but on a high shelf. When he found that it had miscarried he poured away the mixture, washed out the bottle and put in the dregs from another. There is no doubt in my mind that if he had come back and found Millicent dead or dying he would have contrived it to appear that she had made a mistake in the dark and drunk some of the poison before she found out."

"Yes," assented Carrados. "The open way; the safe way."

"You must understand that they live in a very small style, Mr. Carrados, and Millicent is almost entirely in the man's power. The only servant they have is a woman who comes in for a few hours every day. The house is lonely and secluded. Creake is sometimes away for days and nights at a time, and Millicent, either through pride or indifference, seems to have dropped off all her old friends and to have made no others. He might poison her, bury the body in the garden, and be a thousand miles away before anyone began even to inquire about her. What am I to do, Mr. Carrados?"

"He is less likely to try poison than some other means now," pondered Carrados. "That having failed, his wife will always be on her guard. He may know, or at least suspect, that others know. No . . . The common-sense precaution would be for your sister to leave the man, Mr. Hollyer. She will not?"

"No," admitted Hollyer, "she will not. I at once urged that." The young man struggled with some hesitation for a moment and then blurted out: "The fact is, Mr. Carrados, I don't understand Millicent. She is not the girl she was. She hates Creake and treats him with a silent contempt that eats into their lives like acid, and yet she is so jealous of him that she will let nothing short of death part them. It is a horrible life they lead. I stood it for a week and

I must say, much as I dislike my brother-in-law, that he has something to put up with. If only he got into a passion like a man and killed her it wouldn't be altogether incomprehensible."

"That does not concern us," said Carrados. "In a game of this kind one has to take sides and we have taken ours. It remains for us to see that our side wins. You mentioned jealousy, Mr. Hollyer. Have you any idea whether Mrs. Creake has real ground for it?"

"I should have told you that," replied Lieutenant Hollyer. "I happened to strike up with a newspaper man whose office is in the same block as Creake's. When I mentioned the name he grinned. 'Creake,' he said, 'oh, he's the man with the romantic typist, isn't he?' 'Well, he's my brother-in-law,' I replied. 'What about the typist?' Then the chap shut up like a knife. 'No, no,' he said, 'I didn't know he was married. I don't want to get mixed up in anything of that sort. I only said that he had a typist. Well, what of that? So have we; so has everyone.' There was nothing more to be got out of him, but the remark and the grin meant—well, about as usual, Mr. Carrados."

Carrados turned to his friend. "I suppose you know all about the typist by now, Louis?"

"We have had her under efficient observation, Max," replied Mr. Carlyle with severe dignity.

"Is she unmarried?"

"Yes; so far as ordinary repute goes, she is."

"That is all that is essential for the moment. Mr. Hollyer opens up three excellent reasons why this man might wish to dispose of his wife. If we accept the suggestion of poisoning—though we have only a jealous woman's suspicion for it—we add to the wish the determination. Well, we will go forward on that. Have you got a photograph of Mr. Creake?"

The lieutenant took out his pocket-book. "Mr. Carlyle asked me for one. Here is the best I could get."

Carrados rang the bell. "This, Parkinson," he said, when the man appeared, "is a photograph of a Mr. —— What first name, by the way?"

"Austin," put in Hollyer, who was following everything with a boyish mixture of excitement and subdued importance.

"—of a Mr. Austin Creake. I may require you to recognize him." Parkinson glanced at the print and returned it to his master's hand. "May I inquire if it is a recent photograph of the gentleman, sir?" he asked.

"About six years ago," said the lieutenant, taking in this new actor in the drama with frank curiosity. "But he is very little changed."

"Thank you, sir. I will endeavour to remember Mr. Creake, sir."

Lieutenant Hollyer stood up as Parkinson left the room. The interview seemed to be at an end. "Oh, there's one other matter," he remarked. "I am afraid that I did rather an unfortunate thing while I was at Brookbend. It seemed to me that as all Millicent's money would probably pass into Creake's hands sooner or later I might as well have my five hundred pounds, if only to help her with afterwards. So I broached the subject and said that I should like to have it now as I had an opportunity for investing."

"And you think?"

"It may possibly influence Creake to act sooner than he otherwise might have done. He may have got possession of the principal even and find it very awkward to replace it."

"So much the better. If your sister is going to be murdered it may as well be done next week as next year so far as I am concerned. Excuse my brutality, Mr. Hollyer, but this is simply a case to me and I regard it strategically. Now Mr. Carlyle's organization can look after Mrs. Creake for a few weeks, but it cannot look after her for ever. By increasing the immediate risk we diminish the permanent risk."

"I see," agreed Hollyer. "I'm awfully uneasy but I'm entirely in your hands."

"Then we will give Mr. Creake every inducement and every opportunity to get to work. Where are you staying now?"

"Just now with some friends at St. Albans."

"That is too far." The inscrutable eyes retained their tranquil depth but a new quality of quickening interest in the voice made Mr. Carlyle forget the weight and burden of his ruffled dignity. "Give me a few minutes, please. The cigarettes are behind you, Mr. Hollyer." The blind man walked to the window and seemed to look out over the cypress-shaded lawn. The lieutenant lit a cigarette and Mr. Carlyle picked up *Punch*. Then Carrados turned round again.

"You are prepared to put your own arrangements aside?" he demanded of his visitor.

"Certainly."

"Very well. I want you to go down now—straight from here—to Brookbend Cottage. Tell your sister that your leave is unexpectedly cut short and that you sail to-morrow."

"The *Martian*?"

"No, no; the *Martian* doesn't sail. Look up the movements on your way there and pick out a boat that does. Say you are transferred. Add that you expect to be away only two or three months and that you really want the five hundred pounds by the time of your return. Don't stay in the house long, please."

"I understand, sir."

"St. Albans is too far. Make your excuse and get away from there to-day. Put up somewhere in town, where you will be in reach of the telephone. Let Mr. Carlyle and myself know where you are. Keep out of Creake's way. I don't want actually to tie you down to the house, but we may require your services. We will let you know at the first sign of anything doing and if there is nothing to be done we must release you."

"I don't mind that. Is there nothing more that I can do now?"

"Nothing. In going to Mr. Carlyle you have done the best thing possible; you have put your sister into the care of the shrewdest man in London." Whereat the object of this quite unexpected eulogy found himself becoming covered with modest confusion.

"Well, Max?" remarked Mr. Carlyle tentatively when they were alone.

"Well, Louis?"

"Of course it wasn't worth while rubbing it in before young Hollyer, but, as a matter of fact, every single man carries the life of any other man—only one, mind you—in his hands, do what you will."

"Provided he doesn't bungle," acquiesced Carrados.

"Quite so."

"And also that he is absolutely reckless of the consequences."

"Of course."

"Two rather large provisos. Creake is obviously susceptible to both. Have you seen him?"

"No. As I told you, I put a man on to report his habits in town. Then, two days ago, as the case seemed to promise some interest—for he certainly is deeply involved with the typist, Max, and the thing might take a sensational turn at any time—I went down to Mulling Common myself. Although the house is lonely it is on the electric tram route. You know the sort of market garden rurality that about a dozen miles out of London offers—alternate bricks and cabbages. It was easy enough to get to know about Creake locally. He mixes with no one there, goes into town at irregular times but generally every day, and is reputed to be devilish hard to get money out of. Finally I made the acquaintance of an old fellow who used to do a day's gardening at Brookbend occasionally. He has a cottage and a garden of his own with a greenhouse, and the business cost me the price of a pound of tomatoes."

"Was it—a profitable investment?"

"As tomatoes, yes; as information, no. The old fellow had the fatal disadvantage from our point of view of labouring under a grievance. A few weeks ago Creake told him that he would not require him again as he was going to do his own gardening in future."

"That is something, Louis."

"If only Creake was going to poison his wife with hyoscyamine and bury her, instead of blowing her up with a dynamite cartridge and claiming that it came in among the coal."

"True, true. Still—"

"However, the chatty old soul had a simple explanation for everything that Creake did. Creake was mad. He had even seen him flying a kite in his garden where it was found to get wrecked among the trees. A lad of ten would have known better, he declared. And certainly the kite did get wrecked, for I saw it hanging over the road myself. But that a sane man should spend his time 'playing with a toy' was beyond him."

"A good many men have been flying kites of various kinds lately," said Carrados. "Is he interested in aviation?"

"I dare say. He appears to have some knowledge of scientific subjects. Now what do you want me to do, Max?"

"Will you do it?"

"Implicitly—subject to the usual reservations."

"Keep your man on Creake in town and let me have his reports after you have seen them. Lunch with me here now. Phone up to your office that you are detained on unpleasant business and then give the deserving Parkinson an afternoon off by looking after me while we take a motor run round Mulling Common. If we have time we might go on to Brighton, feed at the 'Ship,' and come back in the cool."

"Amiable and thrice lucky mortal," sighed Mr. Carlyle, his glance wandering round the room.

But, as it happened, Brighton did not figure in that day's itinerary. It had been Carrados's intention merely to pass Brookbend Cottage on this occasion, relying on his highly developed faculties, aided by Mr. Carlyle's description, to inform him of the surroundings. A hundred yards before they reached the house he had given an order to his chauffeur to drop into the lowest speed and they were leisurely drawing past when a discovery by Mr. Carlyle modified their plans.

"By Jupiter!" that gentleman suddenly exclaimed, "there's a board up, Max. The place is to be let."

Carrados picked up the tube again. A couple of sentences passed and the car stopped by the roadside, a score of paces past the limit of the garden. Mr. Carlyle took out his notebook and wrote down the address of a firm of house agents.

"You might raise the bonnet and have a look at the engines, Harris," said Carrados. "We want to be occupied here for a few minutes."

"This is sudden; Hollyer knew nothing of their leaving," remarked Mr. Carlyle.

"Probably not for three months yet. All the same, Louis, we will go on to the agents and get a card to view whether we use it to-day or not." A thick hedge, in its summer dress effectively screening the house beyond from public view, lay between the garden and the road. Above the hedge showed an occasional shrub; at the corner nearest to the car a chestnut flourished. The wooden gate, once white, which they had passed, was grimed and rickety. The road itself was still the unpretentious country lane that the advent of the electric car had found it.

When Carrados had taken in these details there seemed little else to notice. He was on the point of giving Harris the order to go on when his ear caught a trivial sound. "Someone is coming out of the house, Louis," he warned his friend.

"It may be Hollyer, but he ought to have gone by this time."

"I don't hear anyone," replied the other, but as he spoke a door banged noisily and Mr. Carlyle slipped into another seat and ensconced himself behind a copy of *The Globe*. "Creake himself," he whispered across the car, as a man appeared at the gate. "Hollyer was right; he is hardly changed. Waiting for a car, I suppose."

But a car very soon swung past them from the direction in which Mr. Creake was looking and it did not interest him. For a minute or two longer he continued to look expectantly along the road. Then he walked slowly up the drive back to the house.

"We will give him five or ten minutes," decided Carrados. "Harris is behaving very naturally."

Before even the shorter period had run out they were repaid. A telegraph-boy cycled leisurely along the road, and, leaving his machine at the gate, went up to the cottage. Evidently there was no reply, for in less than a minute he was trundling past them back again. Round the bend an approaching tram clanged its bell noisily, and, quickened by the warning sound, Mr. Creake again appeared, this time with a small portmanteau in his hand. With a backward glance he hurried on towards the next stopping-place, and, boarding the car as it slackened down, he was carried out of their knowledge.

"Very convenient of Mr. Creake," remarked Carrados, with quiet satisfaction. "We will now get the order and go over the house in his absence. It might be useful to have a look at the wire as well."

"It might, Max," acquiesced Mr. Carlyle a little dryly. "But if it is, as it probably is in Creake's pocket, how do you propose to get it?"

"By going to the post office, Louis."

"Quite so. Have you ever tried to see a copy of a telegram addressed to someone else?"

"I don't think I have ever had occasion yet," admitted Carrados. "Have you?"

"In one or two cases I have perhaps been an accessory to the act. It is generally a matter either of extreme delicacy or considerable expenditure."

"Then for Hollyer's sake we will hope for the former here." And Mr. Carlyle smiled darkly and hinted that he was content to wait for a friendly revenge.

A little later, having left the car at the beginning of the straggling High Street, the two men called at the village post office. They had already visited the house agent and obtained an order to view Brookbend Cottage, declining with some difficulty the clerk's persistent offer to accompany them. The reason was soon forthcoming. "As a matter of fact," explained the young man, "the present tenant is under *our* notice to leave."

"Unsatisfactory, eh?" said Carrados encouragingly.

"He's a corker," admitted the clerk, responding to the friendly tone. "Fifteen months and not a doit of rent have we had. That's why I should have liked—"

"We will make every allowance," replied Carrados.

The post office occupied one side of a stationer's shop. It was not without some inward trepidation that Mr. Carlyle found himself committed to the adventure. Carrados, on the other hand, was the personification of bland unconcern.

"You have just sent a telegram to Brookbend Cottage," he said to the young lady behind the brasswork lattice. "We think it may have come inaccurately and should like a repeat." He took out his purse. "What is the fee?"

The request was evidently not a common one. "Oh," said the girl uncertainly, "wait a minute, please." She turned to a pile of telegram duplicates behind the desk and ran a doubtful finger along the upper sheets. "I think this is all right. You want it repeated?"

"Please." Just a tinge of questioning surprise gave point to the courteous tone.

"It will be fourpence. If there is an error the amount will be refunded."

Carrados put down his coin and received his change. "Will it take long?" he inquired carelessly, as he pulled on his glove.

"You will most likely get it within a quarter of an hour," she replied.

"Now you've done it," commented Mr. Carlyle as they walked back to their car. "How do you propose to get that telegram, Max?"

"Ask for it," was the laconic explanation. And, stripping the artifice of any elaboration, he simply asked for it and got it. The car, posted at a convenient bend in the road, gave him a warning note as the telegraph-boy approached. Then Carrados took up a convincing attitude with his hand on the gate while Mr. Carlyle lent himself to the semblance of a departing friend. That was the inevitable impression when the boy rode up.

"Creake, Brookbend Cottage?" inquired Carrados, holding out his hand, and without a second thought the boy gave him the envelope and rode away on the assurance that there would be no reply.

"Some day, my friend," remarked Mr. Carlyle, looking nervously toward the unseen house, "your ingenuity will get you into a tight corner."

"Then my ingenuity must get me out again," was the retort. "Let us have our 'view' now. The telegram can wait."

An untidy workwoman took their order and left them standing at the door. Presently a lady whom they both knew to be Mrs. Creake appeared.

"You wish to see over the house?" she said, in a voice that was utterly devoid of any interest. Then, without waiting for a reply, she turned to the nearest door and threw it open.

"This is the drawing-room," she said, standing aside.

They walked into a sparsely furnished, damp-smelling room and made a pretence of looking round, while Mrs. Creake remained silent and aloof.

"The dining-room," she continued, crossing the narrow hall and opening another door. Mr. Carlyle ventured a genial commonplace in the hope of inducing conversation. The result was not encouraging. Doubtless they would have gone through the house under the same frigid guidance had not Carrados been at fault in a way that Mr. Carlyle had never known him fail before. In crossing the hall he stumbled over a mat and almost fell.

"Pardon my clumsiness," he said to the lady. "I am, unfortunately, quite blind. But," he added, with a smile, to turn off the mishap, "even a blind man must have a house."

The man who had eyes was surprised to see a flood of colour rush into Mrs. Creake's face. "Blind!" she exclaimed, "oh, I beg your pardon. Why did you not tell me? You might have fallen."

"I generally manage fairly well," he replied. "But, of course, in a strange house—"

She put her hand on his arm very lightly. "You must let me

guide you, just a little," she said. The house, without being large, was full of passages and inconvenient turnings. Carrados asked an occasional question and found Mrs. Creake quite amiable without effusion. Mr. Carlyle followed them from room to room in the hope, though scarcely the expectation, of learning something that might be useful.

"This is the last one. It is the largest bedroom," said their guide. Only two of the upper rooms were fully furnished and Mr. Carlyle at once saw, as Carrados knew without seeing, that this was the one which the Creakes occupied.

"A very pleasant outlook," declared Mr. Carlyle.

"Oh, I suppose so," admitted the lady vaguely. The room, in fact, looked over the leafy garden and the road beyond. It had a French window opening on to a small balcony, and to this, under the strange influence that always attracted him to light, Carrados walked.

"I expect that there is a certain amount of repair needed?" he said, after standing there a moment.

"I am afraid there would be," she confessed.

"I ask because there is a sheet of metal on the floor here," he continued. "Now that, in an old house, spells dry rot to the wary observer."

"My husband said that the rain, which comes in a little under the window, was rotting the boards there," she replied. "He put that down recently. I had not noticed anything myself."

It was the first time she had mentioned her husband; Mr. Carlyle pricked up his ears.

"Ah, that is a less serious matter," said Carrados. "May I step out on to the balcony?"

"Oh yes, if you like to." Then, as he appeared to be fumbling at the catch, "Let me open it for you."

But the window was already open, and Carrados, facing the various points of the compass, took in the bearings.

"A sunny, sheltered corner," he remarked. "An ideal spot for a deck-chair and a book."

She shrugged her shoulders half contemptuously. "I dare say," she replied, "but I never use it."

"Sometimes, surely," he persisted mildly. "It would be my favourite retreat. But then—"

"I was going to say that I had never even been out on it, but that would not be quite true. It has two uses for me, both equally romantic; I occasionally shake a duster from it, and when my husband returns late without his latchkey he wakes me up and I come out here and drop him mine."

Further revelation of Mr. Creake's nocturnal habits was cut off, greatly to Mr. Carlyle's annoyance, by a cough of unmistakable significance from the foot of the stairs. They had heard a trade cart drive up to the gate, a knock at the door, and the heavy-footed woman tramp along the hall.

"Excuse me a minute, please," said Mrs. Creake.

"Louis," said Carrados, in a sharp whisper, the moment they were alone, "stand against the door."

With extreme plausibility Mr. Carlyle began to admire a picture so situated that while he was there it was impossible to open the door more than a few inches. From that position he observed his confederate go through the curious procedure of kneeling down on the bedroom floor and for a full minute pressing his ear to the sheet of metal that had already engaged his attention. Then he rose to his feet, nodded, dusted his trousers, and Mr. Carlyle moved to a less equivocal position.

"What a beautiful rose-tree grows up your balcony," remarked Carrados, stepping into the room as Mrs. Creake returned. "I suppose you are very fond of gardening?"

"I detest it," she replied.

"But this *Gloire*, so carefully trained—?"

"Is it?" she replied. "I think my husband was nailing it up recently."

By some strange fatality Carrados's most aimless remarks seemed to involve the absent Mr. Creake. "Do you care to see the garden?"

The garden proved to be extensive and neglected. Behind the house was chiefly orchard. In front, some semblance of order had been kept up; here it was lawn and shrubbery, and the drive they had walked along. Two things interested Carrados: the soil at the foot of the balcony, which he declared on examination to be particularly suitable for roses, and the fine chestnut-tree in the corner by the road.

As they walked back to the car Mr. Carlyle lamented that they had learned so little of Creake's movements.

"Perhaps the telegram will tell us something," suggested Carrados. "Read it, Louis."

Mr. Carlyle cut open the envelope, glanced at the enclosure, and in spite of his disappointment could not restrain a chuckle.

"My poor Max," he explained, "you have put yourself to an amount of ingenious trouble for nothing. Creake is evidently taking a few days' holiday and prudently availed himself of the Meteorological Office forecast before going. Listen: '*Immediate prospect for London warm and settled. Further outlook cooler but fine.*' Well, well; I did get a pound of tomatoes for *my* fourpence."

"You certainly scored there, Louis," admitted Carrados, with humorous appreciation. "I wonder," he added speculatively, "whether it is Creake's peculiar taste usually to spend his weekend holiday in London."

"Eh?" exclaimed Mr. Carlyle, looking at the words again, "by gad, that's rum, Max. They go to Weston-super-Mare. Why on earth should he want to know about London?"

"I can make a guess, but before we are satisfied I must come here again. Take another look at that kite, Louis. Are there a few yards of string hanging loose from it?"

"Yes, there are."

"Rather thick string—unusually thick for the purpose?"

"Yes, but how do you know?"

As they drove home again Carrados explained, and Mr. Carlyle sat aghast, saying incredulously: "Good God, Max, is it possible?"

An hour later he was satisfied that it was possible. In reply to his inquiry someone in his office telephoned him the information that "they" had left Paddington by the four-thirty for Weston.

It was more than a week after his introduction to Carrados that Lieutenant Hollyer had a summons to present himself at The Turrets again. He found Mr. Carlyle already there and the two friends were awaiting his arrival.

"I stayed in all day after hearing from you this morning, Mr. Carrados," he said, shaking hands. "When I got your second message I was all ready to walk straight out of the house. That's how I did it in the time. I hope everything is all right?"

"Excellent," replied Carrados. "You'd better have something before we start. We probably have a long and perhaps an exciting night before us."

"And certainly a wet one," assented the lieutenant. "It was thundering over Mulling way as I came along."

"That is why you are here," said his host. "We are waiting for a certain message before we start, and in the meantime you may as well understand what we expect to happen. As you saw, there is a thunderstorm coming on. The Meteorological Office morning forecast predicted it for the whole of London if the conditions remained. That is why I kept you in readiness. Within an hour it is now inevitable that we shall experience a deluge. Here and there damage will be done to trees and buildings; here and there a person will probably be struck and killed."

"Yes."

"It is Mr. Creake's intention that his wife should be among the victims."

"I don't exactly follow," said Hollyer, looking from one man to the other. "I quite admit that Creake would be immensely relieved if such a thing did happen, but the chance is surely an absurdly remote one."

"Yet unless we intervene it is precisely what a coroner's jury will decide has happened. Do you know whether your brother-in-law has any practical knowledge of electricity, Mr. Hollyer?"

"I cannot say. He was so reserved, and we really knew so little of him—"

"Yet in 1896 an Austin Creake contributed an article on 'Alternating Currents' to the American *Scientific World*. That would argue a fairly intimate acquaintanceship."

"But do you mean that he is going to direct a flash of lightning?"

"Only into the minds of the doctor who conducts the post-mortem, and the coroner. This storm, the opportunity for which he has been waiting for weeks, is merely the cloak to his act. The weapon which he has planned to use—scarcely less powerful than lightning but much more tractable—is the high voltage current of electricity that flows along the tram wire at his gate."

"Oh!" exclaimed Lieutenant Hollyer, as the sudden revelation struck him.

"Some time between eleven o'clock to-night—about the hour when your sister goes to bed—and one thirty in the morning—the time up to which he can rely on the current—Creake will throw a stone up at the balcony window. Most of his preparation has long been made; it only remains for him to connect up a short length to the window handle and a longer one at the other end to tap the live wire. That done, he will wake his wife in the way I have said. The moment she moves the catch of the window—and he has carefully filed its parts to ensure perfect contact—she will be electrocuted as effectually as if she sat in the executioner's chair in Sing Sing prison."

"But what are we doing here!" exclaimed Hollyer, starting to his feet, pale and horrified.

"It is past ten now and anything may happen."

"Quite natural, Mr. Hollyer," said Carrados reassuringly, "but you need have no anxiety. Creake is being watched, the house is being watched, and your sister is as safe as if she slept to-night in Windsor Castle. Be assured that whatever happens he will not be

allowed to complete his scheme; but it is desirable to let him implicate himself to the fullest limit. Your brother-in-law, Mr. Hollyer,
is a man with a peculiar capacity for taking pains."

"He is a damned cold-blooded scoundrel!" exclaimed the young
officer fiercely. "When I think of Millicent five years ago—"

"Well, for that matter, an enlightened nation has decided that
electrocution is the most humane way of removing its superfluous
citizens," suggested Carrados mildly. "He is certainly an ingenious-
minded gentleman. It is his misfortune that in Mr. Carlyle he was
fated to be opposed by an even subtler brain—"

"No, no! Really, Max!" protested the embarrassed gentleman.

"Mr. Hollyer will be able to judge for himself when I tell him
that it was Mr. Carlyle who first drew attention to the significance
of the abandoned kite," insisted Carrados firmly. "Then, of course,
its object became plain to me—as indeed to anyone. For ten minutes, perhaps, a wire must be carried from the overhead line to the
chestnut-tree. Creake has everything in his favour, but it is just
within possibility that the driver of an inopportune train might
notice the appendage. What of that? Why, for more than a week he
has seen a derelict kite with its yards of trailing string hanging in
the tree. A very calculating mind, Mr. Hollyer. It would be interesting to know what line of action Mr. Creake has mapped out
for himself afterwards. I expect he has half-a-dozen artistic little
touches up his sleeve. Possibly he would merely singe his wife's hair,
burn her feet with a red-hot poker, shiver the glass of the French
window, and be content with that to let well alone. You see, lightning is so varied in its effects that whatever he did or did not do
would be right. He is in the impregnable position of the body
showing all the symptoms of death by lightning shock and nothing
else but lightning to account for it—a dilated eye, heart contracted
in systole, bloodless lungs shrunk to a third the normal weight, and
all the rest of it. When he has removed a few outward traces of his
work Creake might quite safely 'discover' his dead wife and rush
off for the nearest doctor. Or he may have decided to arrange a

convincing alibi, and creep away, leaving the discovery to another. We shall never know; he will make no confession."

"I wish it was well over," admitted Hollyer, "I'm not particularly jumpy, but this gives me a touch of the creeps."

"Three more hours at the worst, lieutenant," said Carrados cheerfully. "Ah-ha, something is coming through now."

He went to the telephone and received a message from one quarter; then made another connection and talked for a few minutes with someone else.

"Everything working smoothly," he remarked between times over his shoulder. "Your sister has gone to bed, Mr. Hollyer."

Then he turned to the house telephone and distributed his orders. "So we," he concluded, "must get up." By the time they were ready a large closed motor car was waiting.

The lieutenant thought he recognised Parkinson in the well-swathed form beside the driver, but there was no temptation to linger for a second on the steps. Already the stinging rain had lashed the drive into the semblance of a frothy estuary; all round the lightning jagged its course through the incessant tremulous glow of more distant lightning, while the thunder only ceased its muttering to turn at close quarters and crackle viciously.

"One of the few things I regret missing," remarked Carrados tranquilly; "but I hear a good deal of colour in it."

The car slushed its way down to the gate, lurched a little heavily across the dip into the road, and, steadying as it came upon the straight, began to hum contentedly along the deserted highway.

"We are not going direct?" suddenly inquired Hollyer, after they had travelled perhaps half-a-dozen miles. The night was bewildering enough but he had the sailor's gift for location.

"No; through Hunscott Green and then by a field-path to the orchard at the back," replied Carrados. "Keep a sharp look out for the man with the lantern about here, Harris," he called through the tube.

"Something flashing just ahead, sir," came the reply, and the car slowed down and stopped. Carrados dropped the near window as a man in glistening waterproof stepped from the shelter of a lich-gate and approached.

"Inspector Beedel, sir," said the stranger, looking into the car. "Quite right, Inspector," said Carrados. "Get in."

"I have a man with me, sir."

"We can find room for him as well."

"We are very wet."

"So shall we all be soon."

The lieutenant changed his seat and the two burly forms took places side by side. In less than five minutes the car stopped again, this time in a grassy country lane.

"Now we have to face it," announced Carrados. "The inspector will show us the way."

The car slid round and disappeared into the night, while Beedel led the party to a stile in the hedge. A couple of fields brought them to the Brookbend boundary. There a figure stood out of the black foliage, exchanged a few words with their guide and piloted them along the shadows of the orchard to the back door of the house.

"You will find a broken pane near the catch of the scullery window," said the blind man.

"Right, sir," replied the inspector. "I have it. Now who goes through?"

"Mr. Hollyer will open the door for us. I'm afraid you must take off your boots and all wet things, Lieutenant. We cannot risk a single spot inside."

They waited until the back door opened, then each one divested himself in a similar manner and passed into the kitchen, where the remains of a fire still burned. The man from the orchard gathered together the discarded garments and disappeared again.

Carrados turned to the lieutenant.

"A rather delicate job for you now, Mr. Hollyer. I want you to go up to your sister, wake her, and get her into another room with as little fuss as possible. Tell her as much as you think fit and let her understand that her very life depends on absolute stillness when she is alone. Don't be unduly hurried, but not a glimmer of a light, please."

Ten minutes passed by the measure of the battered old alarum on the dresser shelf before the young man returned.

"I've had rather a time of it," he reported, with a nervous laugh, "but I think it will be all right now. She is in the spare room."

"Then we will take our places. You and Parkinson come with me to the bedroom. Inspector, you have your own arrangements. Mr. Carlyle will be with you."

They dispersed silently about the house. Hollyer glanced apprehensively at the door of the spare room as they passed it, but within was as quiet as the grave. Their room lay at the other end of the passage.

"You may as well take your place in the bed now, Hollyer," directed Carrados when they were inside and the door closed. "Keep well down among the clothes. Creake has to get up on the balcony, you know, and he will probably peep through the window, but he dare come no farther. Then when he begins to throw up stones slip on this dressing-gown of your sister's. I'll tell you what to do after."

The next sixty minutes drew out into the longest hour that the lieutenant had ever known. Occasionally he heard a whisper pass between the two men who stood behind the window curtains, but he could see nothing. Then Carrados threw a guarded remark in his direction.

"He is in the garden now."

Something scraped slightly against the outer wall. But the night was full of wilder sounds, and in the house the furniture and the boards creaked and sprung between the yawling of the wind among the chimneys, the rattle of the thunder and the pelting of the rain. It was a time to quicken the steadiest pulse, and when the crucial moment came, when a pebble suddenly rang against the pane with a sound that the tense waiting magnified into a shivering crash, Hollyer leapt from the bed on the instant.

"Easy, easy," warned Carrados feelingly. "We will wait for another knock." He passed something across. "Here is a rubber glove. I have cut the wire but you had better put it on. Stand just for a moment at the window, move the catch so that it can blow open a little, and drop immediately. Now."

Another stone had rattled against the glass. For Hollyer to go through his part was the work merely of seconds, and with a few touches Carrados spread the dressing-gown to more effective disguise about the extended form. But an unforeseen and in the circumstances rather horrible interval followed, for Creake, in accordance with some detail of his never-revealed plan, continued to shower missile after missile against the panes until even the unimpressionable Parkinson shivered.

"The last act," whispered Carrados, a moment after the throwing had ceased. "He has gone round to the back. Keep as you are. We take cover now." He pressed behind the arras of an extemporized wardrobe, and the spirit of emptiness and desolation seemed once more to reign over the lonely house.

From half-a-dozen places of concealment ears were straining to catch the first guiding sound. He moved very stealthily, burdened, perhaps, by some strange scruple in the presence of the tragedy that he had not feared to contrive, paused for a moment at the bedroom door, then opened it very quietly, and in the fickle light read the consummation of his hopes.

"At last!" they heard the sharp whisper drawn from his relief. "At last!"

He took another step and two shadows seemed to fall upon him from behind, one on either side. With primitive instinct a cry of terror and surprise escaped him as he made a desperate movement to wrench himself free, and for a short second he almost succeeded in dragging one hand into a pocket. Then his wrists slowly came together and the handcuffs closed.

"I am Inspector Beedel," said the man on his right side. "You are charged with the attempted murder of your wife, Millicent Creake."

"You are mad," retorted the miserable creature, falling into a desperate calmness. "She has been struck by lightning."

"No, you blackguard, she hasn't," wrathfully exclaimed his brother-in-law, jumping up. "Would you like to see her?"

"I also have to warn you," continued the inspector impassively, "that anything you say may be used as evidence against you."

A startled cry from the farther end of the passage arrested their attention.

"Mr. Carrados," called Hollyer, "oh, come at once."

At the open door of the other bedroom stood the lieutenant, his eyes still turned towards something in the room beyond, a little empty bottle in his hand.

"Dead!" he exclaimed tragically, with a sob, "with this beside her. Dead just when she would have been free of the brute."

The blind man passed into the room, sniffed the air, and laid a gentle hand on the pulseless heart.

"Yes," he replied. "That, Hollyer, does not always appeal to the woman, strange to say."

Harvey O'Higgins

(1876–1929)

ONE OF THE MORE realistic detectives in this anthology is also one of the youngest.

Journalist Harvey O'Higgins, who was also a playwright and fiction writer, worked hard and didn't like to waste material. Born in London, Ontario, he began his career writing for newspapers such as the *Toronto Star* and the *New York Globe*. In the early years of the twentieth century he wrote a series of articles about a real-life investigator, William J. Burns, nicknamed "America's Sherlock Holmes." Burns was head of the Burns Detective Agency in New York. Later he would become director of the Bureau of Investigation, the predecessor of the FBI, until J. Edgar Hoover took over in 1924—after Burns was ousted for assigning BOI agents to various illegal tasks, including the intimidation of critical journalists. After his articles, O'Higgins recycled some of his factual material on the Burns agency as background for a series in *Collier's* about a sixteen-year-old boy named Barney Cook, who, in the first story, gets a job working for a famous New York detective, Walter Babbing.

Eight years ago Barney's father, patrolman Robert Cook, was killed. Barney lives now with his mother and sister, on Hudson Street in Greenwich Village, and delivers telegrams and does other small jobs until he is hired as an assistant detective. Streetwise but youthfully reckless, alternately cocky and timid, Barney is a more

convincing character than most of his descendants, including the
Hardy Boys or, later, the boys of the Three Investigators. Barney's
mental image of detectives was formed, naturally, by the fictional
adventures of characters such as Nick Carter—which mind-
destroying trash his new employer warns him against, while also
forbidding cigarettes. The series is also realistic in that Barney isn't
usually involved in murder cases. In the following story he helps
find a wily con man—and cons him in turn. A less happy touch of
realism is the casual use of an offensive racist term.

With Harriet Ford, O'Higgins co-wrote several plays, including
a popular four-act comedy, *The Dummy*, which featured Barney
Cook but wasn't based upon the stories. The play was soon adapted
as a silent film and then as an early talkie. O'Higgins liked variety.
His collection *The Smoke-Eaters* is about New York City's firefight-
ers; his critical analysis of how urban children are socialized was
entitled *The Beast*. During World War I he became associate chair-
man of the Committee on Public Information. For a few months in
1918 he wrote "The Daily German Lie," which provided a forum
for U.S. government officials to refute anti-American propaganda
and promote the United States' own propaganda machine. In 1914,
the same year that he launched the Barney Cook stories, O'Higgins's
play about Mormon marriage, *Polygamy*, was first staged; earlier he
had written an undercover exposé of the Mormon church. In re-
viewing one of his more serious plays, the *New York Times* called
O'Higgins "a reporter, an investigator, a social diagnostician."

Somehow he also managed to write another volume of crime
stories, *Detective Duff Unravels It*, but he is remembered now for the
Barney Cook series. The opening pages below, about how Barney
discovered the job opening and sought the position, are from the
first story, "The Blackmailers"; "The Case of Padages Palmer" actually begins after the row of asterisks.

The Case of Padages Palmer

THE WANT AD—AFTER THE manner of want ads—had read simply: "Boy, over 14, intelligent, trustworthy, for confidential office work, references. Address B-67 *Evening Express*."

Several scores of boys, who were neither very intelligent nor peculiarly trustworthy, exposed their disqualifications—after the manner of boys—in the written applications that they made. Of these scores, a dozen boys received typewritten requests to call next morning at room 1056, in the Cranmer Building, on Broadway, for a personal interview with "H. M. Archibald." But of the dozen, only one knew what sort of confidential office work might be waiting for him in room 1056.

He was little Barney Cook. And he kept his information to himself.

The directory, on the wall of the building's entrance, did not assign 1056 to any of the names on its list. The elevator boys did not know who occupied 1056. The door of 1056 had nothing on its glass panel but the painted number; and the neighboring doors were equally discreet. The "Babbing Bureau" was the nearest name in the corridor, but its doors were marked "Private. Entrance at 1070."

Nor was there anything in the interior aspect of 1056 to enlighten any of Barney Cook's competitors when they came there to be interviewed. It was an ordinary outer office of the golden-oak variety, with a railing of spindles separating a telephone switchboard and two typewriter desks from two public settles and a brass cuspidor. There were girls at the desks and the switchboard. The boys were on the settles or at the railing. The girls were busy, indifferent, chatty (among themselves) and very much at home. The boys, of course, were quite otherwise. They might have been suspected of having assumed a common expression of inert and anxious stupidity in order that each might conceal from all the others the required intelligence with which he hoped to win the "job."

Barney Cook alone betrayed the workings of mind. He sat erect—stretching his neck—at the end of a settle nearest the gate of the railing, watching the door of an inner room and scrutinizing every one who came out of it. He paid no heed to the girls; he knew that they were merely clerks. But when he saw a rough-looking man appear, with a red handkerchief around his neck, he stared excitedly. Surely the bandana was a disguise! Perhaps the black mustache was false!

Forty-eight hours earlier, in the uniform of a telegraph boy, Barney had been in the public office of the Babbing Detective Bureau, and he had been asked to deliver an envelope to the advertising department of the *Evening Express* as he went back. The envelope was not sealed. It did stick slightly in places—but it was not sealed. And it contained the want ad. "Confidential office work"! For the famous Walter Babbing!

Young Barney had been delivering telegrams to the Babbing Bureau for months, without ever getting past the outer office at 1070, and without so much as suspecting the existence of these operatives' rooms and inner chambers down the hall. He had seen Babbing only once; "the great detective" came out with one of his men while Barney was getting his book signed. Babbing stood in the doorway long enough to say: "I'll meet you at the station. Get the tickets. I'll send Jim down with my suit-case." The operative replied: "All right, Chief." And Barney knew that this was Walter Babbing.

He was a brisk-looking, clean-shaven, little fat man—rather "a dude" to Barney—with a mild expression and vague eyes.

Barney knew nothing of the scientific theory of "protective coloring" in detectives; he did not know that the most successful among them naturally look least like anything that might be expected of their kind. He went out with his book open in his hand, absorbed in study of the picture of Babbing that had been photographed on his instantaneous young mind.

Subsequently, he decided that he had seen Babbing without any make-up, in the private appearance that he reserved for office use among his men. And he was assisted to this conclusion by his knowledge of the adventures of Nick Carter which he read on the street cars, in the subways, on the benches in the waiting room of the telegraph office, or wherever else he had leisure. And it was the influence of these Nick Carter stories that had brought him now to 1056 in his Sunday best, with his hair brushed and his shoes polished, as guiltily excited as a truant, having lied to his mother and absented himself from his work in the wild hope of getting employment—confidential and mysterious employment—in the office of the great Babbing.

He was a rather plump and sturdy youth of sixteen with an innocent brightness of face, brown-eyed, black-haired, not easily abashed and always ready with a smile. It was a dimpled smile, too; and he understood its value. In spite of his boyish ignorance of many things of immediate experience—such as famous detectives, for example—he knew his world and his way about in it; he met the events of his day with a practical understanding; and when he did not understand them he disarmed them with a grin. He was confident that he could get this job in the Babbing Bureau, in competition with any of the "boobs" who were waiting to dispute it with him, unless some one among them had a "pull." Being an experienced New Yorker, it was the fear of the pull that worried him.

★　★　★　★　★

I

BARNEY, AS A TELEGRAPH boy, had once been summoned to a dressing room in Daly's Theatre, by an indignant star who had refused to entrust his message to any but official hands. And he had once been called to a grated office in the Tombs to take a telegram from a prosperous-looking elderly gentleman in handcuffs. It was chiefly from the memories of these two experiences that Barney constructed his expectation of what he was to find when he should enter the private offices and operatives' rooms of the Babbing Detective Bureau, to report for duty.

As, for example:— Babbing, in his sanctum, at a make-up table, gumming a false mustache to his lip; his dresser waiting to hand him a wig and a revolver; the room picturesquely hung with costumes and disguises, handcuffs and leg-irons, dodgers that offered rewards for desperate captures ("dead or alive") and sets of burglar's tools and the weapons of outlawry—the latter arranged decoratively on the walls after the manner of a collection of trophies.

And Barney's better judgment accepted that picture from his inebriated young imagination without really knowing that he had accepted it—until he was called from the outer public office of the bureau into Babbing's private room, and found the famous detective sitting at a table-desk, in a swivel chair, reading his morning mail like the manager of any successful business at work in the office of any successful business manager. "Sit down," Babbing said, without looking at him.

Barney sat down, against the wall. He was conscious of the stimulating disappointment—the interested surprise in disillusion—that reality gives to the alert romantic mind. So to speak.

The office was as commonplace and average as Babbing's conventional business clothes. There was nothing on the walls but some framed photographs of office groups. There was no furniture but the desk and the chairs. There was nothing on the desk but telephone instruments, pens and ink, paper-weights, and some shallow

wire baskets that were filled with letters, telegrams and typewritten reports. There was, in fact, nothing interesting in the room but
Babbing; and Babbing looked as uninteresting and ordinary as the
room.

His letters had been opened for him, the pages flattened out,
and the envelopes attached to them with paper-clips. His right
hand reached a sheet from a wire basket at one side of the desk, and
put it on the blotter before him; his left hand held it a moment for
his eyes to read it, and then carried it to one of the baskets on the
other side of the desk and dropped it automatically in its proper
place; his right hand, meanwhile, had produced the next letter. His
eyes moved only from sheet to sheet. "Did you tell your mother
about the case you were on yesterday?"

"No, sir."

The left hand passed a letter back to the right. The right hand
dropped it in the waste basket. "What did you tell her?"

"I tol' her I had a new job."

"As a detective?"

"I was scared to tell her that. She 'd 'a' thought it was the same
as a policeman."

"Well?" The left hand pressed a call button. "Suppose she did?"

"She 'd 'a' thought I was goin' to get killed."

Babbing turned his head to look over his glasses at the boy.
"Like your father?"

Barney smiled an apology for the absurdity of mothers. "Yes, sir."

A clerk opened the door. Babbing tossed a letter across the table
to him. "Find out who that fellow is. Right away."

The clerk reported: "Mr. Snider has just come in." Babbing
continued with his reading. The clerk went out, ignored even by
Barney—as the commander's civilian secretary would be ignored
by a young uniform.

"So you told her what?"

"I tol' her I was waitin' in an office with a telegram yeste'day, 'n'—They wanted an office boy, 'n'—They offered me twelve a week. An' I took it."

Babbing apparently forgot him in the perusal of a two-page letter closely typed. His eyes parted with it reluctantly. "Did you tell any one else?"

"No, sir."

"I see," Babbing said. And Barney was not aware that he had stood a test of character and passed an examination in discretion. He had no suspicion that Babbing's absent-minded manner was almost as much a disguise as if it had been put on with spirit-gum. He was waiting for Babbing to finish with the letters and direct him to his work.

"Don't use the public office, hereafter," Babbing said. "Come in at 1056." He turned to a 'phone. "Tell Snider I'll see him." He pressed a call button. "You'll have to start by learning to speak the English language," he admonished Barney. "We haven't cases enough on the Bowery to keep you working where people say 'I toler I was waiten' when they mean 'I told her I was waiting.'" He changed the switches on an office 'phone. "Bring me my schedule." He said to Barney: "Stay where you are. I'll have something for you in a moment."

Doors began to open, unexpectedly, on all sides. A stenographer appeared, with a note book, sat down to face Babbing across the desk, and prepared himself and his fountain pen to take dictation. Archibald, the office manager—a grizzled old man, with the lean mouth of a prelate—brought a list of Babbing's appointments for the day and discussed them with him, deferentially. An operative, who proved to be "Chal" Snider from Chicago, drifted in as if he were casually interested, and shook hands with "The Chief," and drew a chair up at one side of the desk, and made himself at home, with his ankle on his knee and his hat on his ankle. The day's work had begun.

To Barney, watching, it became as bewildering as the smoothly intricate activity of a complicated machine. Babbing dictated letters in a leisurely undertone that was continually intermitted for

telephone calls, the arrival of opened telegrams, corroboratory
references to filed records, consultations with Archibald, directions
to operatives, and above and around and under it all an interested
reciprocation of talk with Snider. "Hello? Yes. Where are you?
Have you got the goods on him? I see. Who's with you? Can you
get in to see me? I 'll relieve you with Corcoran. Three-thirty this
afternoon." . . . "Take this. William P. Sarrow, and so forth. Dear
Sir. Yours of the fifteenth. Regret that I'm unable to meet you and
so forth. Previous engagements in Chicago on that date. Suggest
the twenty-seventh." . . . "Wire that fellow to stop sending me telegrams or he'll queer the whole plant. Sign it Adam Hansen." . . .
"Yes, Chal? Did he bite?"

And because Snider was telling a connected story—a patiently
connected story in spite of all distractions—Barney's confused attention slowly concentrated on *him*.

Snider was becoming bald; his hair was parted down the middle
with mathematical precision, as perfectly aligned as the ribs and
backbone of a kippered herring. He spoke rather mincingly, smiling,
but never moving his hands. He had an air of pudgy inertia—an
inoffensive sedentary air, good-natured—and a look of credulity.
He made a specialty of confidence men. He was telling about one
who had been operating in Chicago under the name of Charles Q.
Palmer.

Palmer had advertised, in the want columns, that he wished to
buy a hotel property in Chicago, and the owner of the old Stilton
House had answered the ad. Palmer was living in splendor at the La
Salle; the owner of the Stilton lunched with him there, talked
terms, and convinced himself that Palmer had money and knew
something about the hotel business. They inspected the moribund
Stilton House together. Palmer saw possibilities in it. He paid $200
for a two weeks' option on the property and took the only good
room in the house, in order to audit the books at his leisure and consider a plan of business rehabilitation. The proprietor assisted him,

deferred to him, flattered him, and secretly chuckled over him. A price of $50,000 was agreed upon. Palmer affected a brand of expensive Havana cigars, called Padages Palmas; and the proprietor added a box of them to his show-case stock for Palmer's use. They became as intimately friendly as it is possible to become in a business deal where the seller has to maintain a consistent indifference because he is getting too much for his goods.

"The thing that sticks in *his* crop," Snider said, "is those millionaire cigars. Palmer smoked two boxes of them. The old mail squeals about it worse than anything."

"What are they? A perfecto?" Babbing asked, with the air of a teetotaler showing curiosity about wines.

"No," Snider explained, "they're like a panatela, only longer. They're a little longer than a lead pencil and about as thick. They're some smoke."

Babbing gave Archibald a telegram that he had been reading. "Wire them I can't take it up personally, but if they'll turn it over to our branch office there, I'll be on later, to direct the investigation . . . What was it, Chal? The same old game?"

"Sure." Snider smiled. "At noon on the fifteenth, the day the option expired, he bought the hotel with a New York draft for fifty-five thousand, and opened an account at the old man's bank with a check for the extra five thousand which the old man wrote. He was carrying a little black handbag full of furniture catalogues and decorator's estimates and plans he had drawn for remodeling the ground floor of the Stilton. He got five hundred under the old man's nose, put it in the bag, and went off to make a deposit with the contractor who was to do the remodeling. One of the boys from the hotel happened to be at the Central depot about three o'clock and he thought he saw Palmer going through the gates; but he didn't speak of it until the old man began to worry because Palmer hadn't turned up for dinner. He was afraid Palmer had been black-jacked!

"Next morning, he found out, at the bank, that Palmer had

drawn all but fifty dollars of his five thousand. And the New York draft turned out to be phoney.

"They brought the case to us, but Palmer had made a clean get-away. There was nothing in his trunk but some hotel sheets and bundles of old newspapers to give it weight. Our boys are at work on it."

Babbing had finished his correspondence. He began to walk up and down the room in an idle interval. "He's probably in town here, now."

"What makes you think so, Chief?"

"Why didn't you wire us? That three o'clock train is one of the slowest on the line. It doesn't get here till eight-thirty next night."

"We didn't have the case till late yesterday morning. And there was nothing to show he came this way."

"He'd arrive last night. Did you get a good description of him?"

"Yes, but he was wearing a beard and mustache."

"How old?"

"They say about thirty-five, and heavy—a hundred and seventy or may be more. Five foot eight or nine. Dressed to look like a prosperous hotel man. Light eyes, bluish gray. Nothing peculiar about him."

Babbing was standing at the window looking out over the lower roofs of wholesale houses to the ferries of the North River and the docks and chimneys of the Jersey shore. It was an invitingly clean and bright Spring day. "I'd like to try a long shot at that fellow," he said. And little Barney's heart leaped with the blind instinct of a setter pup who sees preparations for the hunt.

Snider took his hat from his ankle and his ankle from his knee. "At Palmer?"

Babbing drifted back to his desk and sat down.

"Got a hunch, Chief?"

Snider asked it in the wistful manner of envy interrogating the inscrutable. Babbing stared at him, thoughtfully. Snider blinked and waited. Babbing said, at last: "It was raining hard last night at eight-thirty . . . He wouldn't shave on the train."

Snider put his hat on the floor and leaned forward intently. "We couldn't run out all the barber shops in town, could we?"

"He'd go to a hotel, and get it off in his room."

Snider's expression indicated that there were almost as many hotels as barber shops.

Babbing glanced at his watch. "I can locate him in an hour if I can locate him at all." He rose briskly. "Explain to Archibald. I'll 'phone to tell you where I am, as soon as I get in touch with anything. Where's my bag? Dump those reports into it." He opened the door of a clothes closet in a corner by the window and took out a soft black felt, a black raincoat, and an umbrella. He put on the coat, and it looked as provincial as a linen duster. He shook out the rolled umbrella, untidily. "Come on, boy," he said to Barney. "Carry that bag." Barney grabbed it eagerly. "This is no day to be in school, is it?" Babbing said to him at the door. And Barney's throat was so choked with excitement that he could only gulp and grin.

Snider, seeing them go, had the puzzled eyebrows and the doubtful smile of the man who does not believe that you can do it but would like to know how you propose to begin. To find, in the city of New York, a swindler whom you have never seen, of whom you have no accurate description, who may not have come to New York at all, and who will be carefully concealing himself if he *has* come!

II

NO SUCH DOUBTS AS Snider's occupied Barney's mind, of course. He had other things to think of. He had his first ride up Broadway in a taxi-cab, for instance—whirring along in a bouncing rush of luxury whose incredible cost grew on the taximeter so fast that it took his breath away like a Coney Island chute, and he held back against the cushions, with his eyes on the dial, delightfully appalled. And he had the confused emotions of being outfitted in a round felt hat, such as college boys are supposed to favor, and a pair of enameled-leather shoes, which Babbing bought for him in a Broadway shop while the cab waited at the door. Two dollars for the hat and five dollars for the shoes! Gee! And then the meter began again—measuring Fifth Avenue in dimes.

He had been aware in the shop that Babbing was posing as his father and enjoying the part; and he had had an awful moment of fear that there might be holes in his stockings when the clerk unlaced his shoes. There were none. A woman, whom he vaguely recalled as his mother, had darned those stockings for him in a Cinderella world that had since been lost in the whirr of a fairy godfather's golden chariot. He caught Babbing smiling at him in the chariot; and he snickered excitedly.

When the cab stopped, Babbing reached for the handle of the door and said, "Keep right up with me, now, but don't open your mouth"; and Barney stepped out of the cab as if it had been an aeroplane, and found himself on the earth again, in front of the Hotel Haarlem on 42nd Street near the Grand Central station. He defended Babbing's satchel from the doorman while Babbing ransomed himself from the taximeter.

The detective, in his raincoat, with his umbrella, wandered into the gilded lobby of the Haarlem, looking about him simply. He found the cigar stand, and approached it, with Barney, as if it were a booth at a county fair. The clerk saw them coming. It showed in his face.

Babbing said: "Padages Palmas."

The clerk did not move. He was New York accosted by the provinces. "What did you say?"

Babbing regarded him a moment, mildly thoughtful. He cleared his throat. "Young man," he said, "I want a seegar called the Padages Palmas. It's a fairly well-known Havana, but the easiest way for you to tell it, when you see it, is to read the name on the band around the middle."

The clerk had turned his back to get a box from the shelves behind him. His ears were red.

"Yes," Babbing said, "that's the one. Are these fresh?"

"I opened it myself yesterday." The box was still full.

"I don't much like them fresh."

The clerk tried to look his indifference. "We don't keep—"

"You can keep four of those," Babbing cut in cheerfully and passed on. Barney followed him. And Barney could feel the clerk's eyes witheringly on his back.

This was good fun, but Barney did not see the drift of it. When they issued on 42nd Street again and started to cross towards the Beaumont, he began to understand.

They mounted the Beaumont's marble steps together and approached the cigar counter. The clerk, here, was an older man who was perhaps accustomed to serving millionaires in shabbiness. Babbing found the box in the showcase and pointed to it. The clerk whisked it out deftly. Babbing took two. "Do you sell many of these?"

"Yes, sir," he said. "Quite a number."

"How many?"

"Well, I couldn't say, exactly. I've sold six this morning."

Babbing was slow about getting the cigars into his waistcoat pocket; and he was slow about getting his money out. "Six, eh? Counting mine?"

"Yes. Another gentleman took four."

"I'll bet that was Charlie," Babbing commented to Barney. "Clean-shaven man with blue eyes?" he asked the clerk. "Heavy set?"

"I think you're right," the clerk replied, busying himself with his cash register. "I didn't notice his eyes, but I think you're right . . . Thank you. Nice day?"

Babbing grunted, non-committally, and went to the desk. He gave Barney his umbrella to hold, while he put on his glasses to consult the register. He turned to the arrivals of the previous night. Among the names of visitors from Buffalo and Albany, there was the florid signature of a Spenserian caligraphist who had arrived singularly from Washington, D.C. He was "Thos. Sullivan."

Babbing put up his glasses, resumed his umbrella and led the way to a leather sofa. "I think our man is here," he said to Barney, "under the name of Thomas Sullivan. He writes like a forger, anyway. We've got to pick him up and feel him out. I'm going outside to telephone to him. If he's in his room, I'll give him a stall. If he isn't, I'll have him paged. Thomas Sullivan. You follow the boy around. Nobody'll notice you. They'll think you're looking for some one. Spot Sullivan if the boy finds him, and show him to me when I come back. Then we'll get together and rope him."

"Yes, sir," Barney said.

"The telephone booths are down that hall at the left of the desk. There's a parcel rack there, and you'd better check this bag till we know what we're going to do. The dining-room's at the end of the hall. Sullivan may be at breakfast. If any one asks you any questions, you're looking for your uncle. I'm your uncle. Sit here for two minutes. Then get over by the call desk."

"Yes, sir," Barney said.

Babbing pursued his placid way to the door, and Barney sat back in the sofa. He had no doubt that Sullivan was the swindler Palmer, but he could not guess how Babbing had come almost directly to the Beaumont to locate him. He puzzled over it, happily. In the background of his thoughts, he was saying to himself: "Gee, this job's *great!*"

When his two minutes had measured themselves on the clock, he went to check his bag. He located the telephone booths. He made sure that the dining-room had not been shifted. As he returned to the lobby, a call boy, circulating among the easy chairs and smoking tables in front of the news stand, suddenly began to crow "Mr. Sullah-*van!* Mr. Sullah-*van!*" A cold tingle of excitement ran down Barney's spine and struck forward into his solar plexus. His vital organs sank inside him, rallied, and rose exultingly.

"Mr. Sullah-*van!* Mr. Sullah-*van!*"

Mr. Sullivan did not reply. The boy turned down the hall to the dining-room, and Barney sauntered after him. "Mr. Sullah-*van!*"

The head waiter at the door bent indulgently to ask Barney: "One?" Barney mumbled that he was looking for his uncle. Standing in the doorway, he searched the tables anxiously. "Mr. Sullah-*van!*" A man sitting alone at a far window, signaled to the bell boy. They conferred together. The man shook his head. The boy went on. "Mr. Sullah-*van!*"

Barney had seen his float bob to a nibble.

The boy passed him on his way out, and Barney followed. But there were no more nibbles—neither in the bar, the café, the grill, the barber shop, the wash-room, nor anywhere else. The boy went back to the desk. Barney returned to the telephones and stood looking regretfully down the hall at the door of the dining-room where he had seen his hope. If it had only been Palmer! If they had only landed that bite!

Babbing joined him there. "He didn't get him," Barney reported. Babbing nodded. They went to their seats on the sofa. "He'll be back," Babbing said. "He hasn't given up his room."

Barney sighed. "I thought we had him."

"How so?"

"A man in the dinin' room stopped that bell-hop an' then turned him down."

Babbing rose at once. "That's our man."

"But he turned him down."

"Come on. Show me where he is. You're asleep." They were crossing the lobby, and Babbing was talking in a low, indifferent, chatty tone. "His name isn't Sullivan. As soon as he learned that the boy had a telephone call, he knew it couldn't be for him. None of his friends in town would call for him by that name. Is there an empty table near him?"

"I—I don't know."

Babbing slowed his pace. "My name's Thomas Oliphant," he said. "We'll get a table near him. Then you go to the telephone and call up the office—one-seven-three-one Desbrosses—and get Chal Snider. Tell him I'm in the dining-room here, and I want to be paged as Thomas Sullivan. Make him insist on the 'Thomas.' Don't forget that. Tell him they've paged me as Sullivan and I don't answer. Then join me at the table. Sullivan'll stop the boy again. I'll break in on him. I'm expecting a call. There's probably a mistake in the name. Thomas Sullivan for Thomas Oliphant. Do you understand? That'll give us an introduction to him. Where is he? Don't point."

They were at the dining-room door. "There he is. Over at that last window."

"I see. I'm your rich uncle from Kansas City. You're Barney Cook, my New York nephew. Go ahead and telephone. Get me a *Tribune*." And Babbing, refusing the offices of the girl at the coat rack, went to meet the head-waiter with all his encumbrances of hat, rain-coat and umbrella. He had evidently a somewhat countrified reluctance to trust his things out of his sight.

The multiplicity of instructions which Barney had to remember weighed him down to deliberate and cautious movement. He went slowly to the telephone; it took him some time to get the Babbing Bureau; he gave his message to Snider hesitatingly, cautiously, in veiled terms, for fear some one might overhear him; and he was almost back to the dining-room before he recollected that he was to get a *Tribune*. Consequently, Babbing, in his spectacles, seated at a side-table, back to back with the suspected Sullivan, was concluding his order to the waiter when Barney joined them; and it was evident that there had been some difficulty over the menu. "Now, oatmeal porridge; mind that!" Babbing said. "Real oatmeal. No cattle mashes or health mashes for me. Sit here, boy." He put Barney at right angles to him. "And cream. Plenty of it. I don't care what it costs. And here. Wait a minute. I don't want my bacon fried to a cinder, either."

He was talking in an insistent, querulous grumble. The waiter kept saying "No, sir. Yes, sir," with a sort of cool servility that was professional to the point of contempt. Barney glanced at Mr. Sullivan. He was sipping his coffee, with his head turned slightly. Barney could see that he was "getting an ear full." The waiter departed.

"Well," Babbing asked, "did you get them?"

"Yes, sir."

"What did they say?"

"They said they'd call you up."

"Well, they'd better hurry," he blustered. "If they don't want my money, I can find lots of people in this town that do. Did they say they had those Bonanza shares for me?"

"They didn't say."

"Huh! Give me that *Tribune*." He spread the pages impatiently. "I don't see why these New York papers don't have some Western news in them." And Sullivan, turning, took an appraising look at him over the shoulder.

"There isn't a line here from Kansas City," Babbing complained. "A New York newspaper's the most provincial sheet in the universe, bar none!"

"Aw, gee, Uncle," Barney laughed. "Quit knockin' little ol' New York."

"Boy!" Babbing said sternly, "you talk as if your maw had raised you on the Bowery. Where did you ever learn to speak like that? If that's the sort of grammar you get in your New York public schools, y' ought to be ashamed of them."

Barney had no reply to make, and his uncle's eye forbade him to make any. He had "caught on to" the game that Babbing was playing, and he was enjoying it precociously; but Babbing was evidently not willing to have him join in it. They waited, in silence, for the call boy.

And when the call boy came, crying "Mr. *Thomas* Sullivan" the game developed with the most prosperous rapidity. Babbing interrupted the colloquy between the uneasy Sullivan and the boy, and claimed the call. "My name's Oliphant. I've been waiting here all morning for a telephone message, and these idiots go around bawling 'Sullivan! Sullivan' when I bet they want Oliphant. If you've no objection, I'll take this call Mr. Sullivan—"

"None whatever," Sullivan said affably. "I'm sure it's not for me."

"Come on, boy. Show me the 'phone."

As he passed, he laid his hand on Barney's shoulder, and gave him a warning squeeze. It was needed, for as soon as he was out of hearing, Sullivan turned to Barney with a plump, suave smile. "Isn't that Thomas Oliphant of Kansas City?"

Barney nodded cheerfully.

"I *thought* so. I've heard of him. Well, well! So that's Thomas Oliphant."

Barney grinned. "I guess everybody out there knows Uncle Tom."

"Did I understand that he's buying mining stock."

"Yep. I guess so. He's got money to burn."

"*You're* not from Kansas City?"

Barney shook his head scornfully.

"I wonder if he knows my brother-in-law, Billy Smith."

"I dunno. You better ask him."

"What does he do?"

"What does *who* do?"

"Your uncle."

"What does he *do!*"

"Yes. What business is he in?"

"Say!" Barney answered. "What are you tryin' to do to me? You know what he does as well as I do."

Sullivan said hastily: "Well, I thought he might have retired, and— Well, well! I must speak to him when he comes back. Tom Oliphant, eh? It 's a small world. Well, well!" And Barney saw their fish on the hook.

The fish proceeded to climb up the line and fight his way into the creel as soon as Babbing returned; and Babbing at first held him off, suspiciously. Yes, he was Thomas Oliphant of Kansas City. No, not cattle. Leather, sir; leather. William Smith? No, he didn't know William Smith. He thought he had heard of William Smith, but couldn't place him. His brother-in-law? A pleasure. A pleasure. Much obliged to Mr. Sullivan for letting him take that telephone call. It was pressing business. They had been trying all morning to get him on the 'phone.

In ten minutes the engaging Sullivan had moved to the vacant chair opposite Barney, had lighted one of his Padages Palmas rather gaudily, and was listening to Babbing with a flattering admiration showing in his bluish-gray eyes. It developed that Sullivan was interested in Cobalt mines, heavily interested; in fact, he owned one in partnership with some New York mining experts. Being questioned by Babbing upon the rating of the Bonanza mine in the Beaver district, he remarked that it was a hole in the ground, hopeless as an investment. It was not a mine at all but merely a trap for suckers. Babbing was much taken aback. He drank in Sullivan's knowledge and advice greedily—with occasional hasty gulps of oatmeal porridge and noisy draughts of hot coffee; and Barney's innocent hunger and absorbed attention were not more childish and convincing than his uncle's.

Sullivan blossomed and expanded in that atmosphere of trust. He and his partners were building a hotel for the tourist trade near their mine. He had been working on the plans for the building. They had discovered one of the finest, if not *the* finest spring of mineral water on the continent. And so forth.

He leaned back in his chair, making large gestures with his cigar and smiling a broad indulgent smile. He flattered Barney. "A mighty bright boy, your nephew. A mighty bright boy. I'd like to have a boy like that in my business."

"Not much!" Barney said pertly. "I'm goin' in with uncle."

Some of Babbing's coffee got in his windpipe at that moment, and he coughed himself red in the face. Barney kept a straight mouth.

"I don't know that you'll ever be as successful as your uncle," Sullivan said. "But you'll succeed. You've got it in you! I can see that."

He exacted a promise from Babbing that he should go no further in the matter of the Bonanza mine until he had come to the office of Sullivan's friends, with Sullivan, to look into the "proposition" there. "Excuse me a moment," he said, when Babbing had paid the waiter. "I'll just run upstairs and get the plans of our hotel. I want to take them with me. I'll meet you at the desk."

He strutted off importantly. Babbing sat a moment. "If he brings down his satchel with those plans in it," he said, "you'll get it to carry. And, at the first opportunity, you'll cut away with it. Understand? Take it to the office. They'll have keys to open it there. I'll get in touch with Chal as soon as I can, by 'phone. If he's still carrying his Chicago outfit in that bag, we've got our case complete. Now, don't get cheeky. If you're not careful, you'll stub your toe!"

III

A HALF HOUR LATER, a round-faced and sturdy youth of sixteen, breathing hard because he had been running, sat in a downtown express on the Subway, holding a small black handbag on his knees. He was struggling with a dimpled smile that continually escaped control and exploded in a snort. The other passengers smiled at him, amusedly. He retreated to the back platform, giggling, and grinned at his ease out the door.

He was still grinning and still breathing hard when he entered the Babbing Bureau at room 1056, and hurried into Babbing's private office to find Chal Snider reading a morning paper at Babbing's desk. "Here's his bag!"

Snider looked over the top of his newspaper.

"Whose bag?"

"Palmer's."

"What!" The cry was not wholly incredulous; it had the quality, too, of envious amazement.

"Sure! Hurry up an' see what's in it. The Chief wants to know. Hurry up. He's got him."

Snider dropped his paper and grabbed the 'phone. "Hello? Hello! Bring me in a bunch of skeletons for a small satchel. Quick."

He caught the bag from Barney. "Well, I'll be switched. How the hell?"

Barney wiped the perspiration of haste from his forehead with his coat cuff. "We roped him at the Beaumont. He'd been buyin' them long cigars."

"Well, the old devil!" He sat with the satchel on his lap, expressing a profane admiration to it in a sort of dumbfounded undertone. "The damn old fox! How did he think of *that!*"

"Search *me!*" Barney grinned.

A clerk came in with the keys. Snider had the bag opened in a jiffy. He dumped its contents on the desk—blue-prints, catalogues, a scratch block, loose sheets of memoranda, an assortment of blank checks, and a roll of money in a rubber band. "The old man's wad!" Snider exulted. "By G— he's got the swag back too! Where is he?"

"He's off with Palmer. He's goin' to 'phone you. He tol' me to grab the bag an' beat it. That boob was tryin' to sell him stock in some fake hotel he's buildin' some'rs, when *I* dropped off."

Snider went through the swindler's papers with appropriate remarks, and then began thoughtfully to pack them back in the bag. "Where did you go from here?"

Barney told the story in an excited incoherency. Snider nodded and nodded. "He's slick!" he commented primly, again and again. "He's pretty damn slick!"

"Well, how did he know the guy was at the Beaumont?" Barney asked.

"He didn't know. He took a chance. He figured that Palmer wouldn't go far from the depot in the rain. Didn't you hear him say it was raining hard last night at eight-thirty? He just played a hunch and got away with it."

"What's he goin' to do next?" Barney demanded in the delighted impatience of youth to know the end of the story.

The ringing of the telephone bell interrupted them with what proved to be the answer. "Hello?" Snider said. "Yes, Chief. Yes. His whole outfit's in it. And four thousand of the old man's money.

Yes. Yes." He tittered. He shook over the 'phone silently. "Ye-e-s.
I'll ha-ave them." And he dropped the receiver into its hook and
lay back in his chair in a grimacing sputter of fat laughter. "He's
bringing him hee-here. He 's pretending he thinks you—you've
been ki-ki-kidnapped. Hee-hee-hee!" He wiped his wet eyes helplessly. "Palmer won't let him go to the police station. They're co-
coming here to get us out to find you." He jumped up, suddenly, and
slapped himself on top of the head with a comical gesture. "I've got
to get papers for him. Put Archibald wise to what's coming." He
darted out the door with unexpected agility, and Barney hastened to
find Archibald.

Either Archibald had no sense of humor or it was inhibited by a
stronger sense of dignity. Barney's story provoked no smile from him.
"Wait in the operatives' room," he said drily. "If we need you,
we'll call you. Leave the bag here."

The operatives' room was a large inner office fitted up with desks
that showed inky evidences of long use, typewriters that rattled
loosely, and battered filing cabinets. Two men were getting out
reports on their typewriters; a third was searching the pages of a
telephone directory, page after page, slowly, as if he had been at it
for hours and expected to continue it for hours. Barney sat down in
a corner and waited. No call came for him. He imagined the scene
between Archibald, Babbing, and Mr. Thomas Sullivan, when they
should put the swindled swindler under arrest; but he had to take it
out in imagining. The operatives came and went as busily as reporters turning in their copy, but no one spoke to him.

And Barney became vaguely aware of one fact about the life of
detectives for which fiction had not prepared him. Like the private
soldier in a campaign, the operative of a detective bureau obeys
orders without knowing the reason for them and executes commands without seeing their results. He participates in events of which
he does not always understand the beginning and sometimes never
learns the end. He comes in for a single scene in one drama, and
leaves it to play an equally brief part in another. Barney was no

longer needed in the affair of Charles Q. Palmer, and he was not invited to watch the swindler's astonishment when his bag was produced as evidence against him and the police arrived with the warrant for his arrest.

It was nearly midday when Babbing appeared, and Barney stood up smiling to greet him.

"Go home and tell your mother what you're doing," Babbing said. "And tell her to keep it to herself. I want you to come to Philadelphia with me to-night. Get yourself a suit-case. And bring a suit of old clothes—the shabbiest you've got . . . Here, Clark!" he called. "Show this boy how to make out a requisition for expense money. He'll need twenty-five or thirty dollars. Be back here at four o'clock."

"Yes, sir." Barney hesitated. "Did you get him?"

"Who? Palmer? Oh, yes. Yes. He's held for return to Chicago. Run along now. Be here sharp at four, with your bag packed. And tell your mother not to mark your linen—except with your initials. Understand?"

"Yes, sir."

Babbing regarded him whimsically. "How do you like being a detective?"

"Oh, gee!" Barney grinned. "It's great, Chief."

Babbing gave him a parting pat on the shoulder. "All right, boy," he said. "I'm glad you like it." And Barney did not understand why his tone of voice was depreciative!

❈

Anna Katharine Green

(1846–1935)

AFTER MARY FORTUNE'S 1866 milestone—the first full-fledged detective story by a woman—Anna Katharine Green stands as the next important female writer in the genre. She was the author of the first known detective novel by a woman, *The Leavenworth Case*, published in 1878. This charming and fast-paced adventure introduced Ebenezer Gryce, a sardonic New York City policeman who would reappear in several novels, and launched one of the most successful careers in nineteenth-century crime writing. As noted in the introduction, the book became a bestseller and was soon required reading at Yale's school of law, in part because of Green's adroit handling of circumstantial evidence. Not bad for a book she had begun just after college and written on the sly in varicolored notebooks, until she was two-thirds finished, before showing it to her lawyer father, whose professional life had helped inspire it.

Some critics nominate an 1866 novel as the first book-length detective story by a woman: *The Dead Letter*, by Seeley Regester, the pen name of Metta Victoria Fuller Victor. But Regester's detective, Mr. Burton, relies upon the psychic visions of his daughter (which he demands of her despite their toll on her health and psyche). Supernatural or psychic detection has a long history, but it is a category of its own; the intrusion of such irrational plot elements disqualifies *The Dead Letter* from consideration as a true detective story. Regester was also an inferior writer who depended upon coincidence, exhibited little wit, and had a poor sense of pacing.

In 1897, in the clever and amusing novel *That Affair Next Door*, Green created her first female detective, Amelia Butterworth, who starred in two sequels. She didn't create her third detective until 1915, when G. P. Putnam's Sons published *The Golden Slipper and Other Problems for Violet Strange*. Although appearing in the generation following the Victorian era, this beautiful young New York socialite recalled the Victorian habit of supplying lady detectives with excuses for their unladylike prying and snooping. Through a cycle of ten stories, Green gradually revealed that Strange performs her secretive detective work to support a disinherited sister, a laughably noble motive worthy of her ancestors in the field. Strange must keep her investigations secret or risk losing the very attribute that makes them possible—her position in upper-crust Gotham society.

In the first story, "The Golden Slipper," Strange's boss, Mr. Driscoll, explains to a man who needs a discreet private detective within his own household that Violet Strange is the person for the job. The two men are at the opera and Driscoll indicates a box across the way. The potential client peers through his opera glasses.

"She? Why those are the Misses Pratt and—"

"Miss Violet Strange; no other."

"And do you mean to say—"

"I do—"

"That yon silly little chit, whose father I know, whose fortune I know, who is seen everywhere, and who is called one of the season's belles is an agent of yours; a—a—"

"No names here, please. You want a mystery solved. It is not a matter for the police—that is, as yet,—and so you come to me, and when I ask for the facts, I find that women and only women are involved, and that these women are not only young but one and all of the highest society. Is it a man's work to go to the bottom of a combination like this? No. Sex against sex, and, if possible, youth against youth. Happily, I know such a person—a girl of gifts and extraordinarily well placed for the purpose. Why she uses her talents in this direction—why, with means enough to play the part natural to her as a successful debutante, she consents to occupy herself with social and other mysteries, you must ask her, not me. Enough that I promise you her aid if you want it. That is, if you can interest her. She will not work otherwise."

An Intangible Clue

"HAVE YOU STUDIED THE CASE?"

"Not I."

"Not studied the case which for the last few days has provided the papers with such conspicuous headlines?"

"I do not read the papers. I have not looked at one in a whole week."

"Miss Strange, your social engagements must be of a very pressing nature just now?"

"They are."

"And your business sense in abeyance?"

"How so?"

"You would not ask if you had read the papers."

To this she made no reply save by a slight toss of her pretty head. If her employer felt nettled by this show of indifference, he did not betray it save by the rapidity of his tones as, without further preamble and possibly without real excuse, he proceeded to lay before her the case in question. "Last Tuesday night a woman was murdered in this city; an old woman, in a lonely house where she has lived for years. Perhaps you remember this house? It occupies a not inconspicuous site in Seventeenth Street—a house of the olden time?"

"No, I do not remember."

The extreme carelessness of Miss Strange's tone would have

been fatal to her socially; but then, she would never have used it socially. This they both knew, yet he smiled with his customary indulgence.

"Then I will describe it."

She looked around for a chair and sank into it. He did the same.

"It has a fanlight over the front door."

She remained impassive.

"And two old-fashioned strips of parti-coloured glass on either side."

"And a knocker between its panels which may bring money some day."

"Oh, you do remember! I thought you would, Miss Strange."

"Yes. Fanlights over doors are becoming very rare in New York."

"Very well, then. That house was the scene of Tuesday's tragedy. The woman who has lived there in solitude for years was foully murdered. I have since heard that the people who knew her best have always anticipated some such violent end for her. She never allowed maid or friend to remain with her after five in the afternoon; yet she had money—some think a great deal—always in the house."

"I am interested in the house, not in her."

"Yet, she was a character—as full of whims and crotchets as a nut is of meat. Her death was horrible. She fought—her dress was torn from her body in rags. This happened, you see, before her hour for retiring; some think as early as six in the afternoon. And"—here he made a rapid gesture to catch Violet's wandering attention—"in spite of this struggle; in spite of the fact that she was dragged from room to room—that her person was searched—and everything in the house searched—that drawers were pulled out of bureaus— doors wrenched off of cupboards—china smashed upon the floor— whole shelves denuded and not a spot from cellar to garret left unransacked, no direct clue to the perpetrator has been found— nothing that gives any idea of his personality save his display of strength and great cupidity. The police have even deigned to consult me,—an unusual procedure—but I could find nothing, either. Evidences of fiendish purpose abound—of relentless search—but no clue to the man himself. It's uncommon, isn't it, not to have any clue?"

"I suppose so." Miss Strange hated murders and it was with difficulty she could be brought to discuss them. But she was not going to be let off; not this time.

"You see," he proceeded insistently, "it's not only mortifying to the police but disappointing to the press, especially as few reporters believe in the No-thoroughfare business. They say, and we cannot but agree with them, that no such struggle could take place and no such repeated goings to and fro through the house without some vestige being left by which to connect this crime with its daring perpetrator."

Still she stared down at her hands—those little hands so white and fluttering, so seemingly helpless under the weight of their many rings, and yet so slyly capable.

"She must have queer neighbours," came at last, from Miss Strange's reluctant lips. "Didn't they hear or see anything of all this?"

"She has no neighbours—that is, after half-past five o'clock. There's a printing establishment on one side of her, a deserted mansion on the other side, and nothing but warehouses back and front. There was no one to notice what took place in her small dwelling after the printing house was closed. She was the most courageous or the most foolish of women to remain there as she did. But nothing except death could budge her. She was born in the room where she died; was married in the one where she worked; saw husband, father, mother, and five sisters carried out in turn to their graves through the door with the fanlight over the top—and these memories held her."

"You are trying to interest me in the woman. Don't."

"No, I'm not trying to interest you in her, only trying to explain her. There was another reason for her remaining where she did so long after all residents had left the block. She had a business."

"Oh!"

"She embroidered monograms for fine ladies."

"She did? But you needn't look at me like that. She never embroidered any for me."

"No? She did first-class work. I saw some of it. Miss Strange, if I could get you into that house for ten minutes—not to see her but to pick up the loose intangible thread which I am sure is floating around in it somewhere—wouldn't you go?"

Violet slowly rose—a movement which he followed to the letter.

"Must I express in words the limit I have set for myself in our affair?" she asked. "When, for reasons I have never thought myself called upon to explain, I consented to help you a little now and then with some matter where a woman's tact and knowledge of the social world might tell without offence to herself or others, I never thought it would be necessary for me to state that temptation must stop with such cases, or that I should not be asked to touch the sordid or the bloody. But it seems I was mistaken, and that I must stoop to be explicit. The woman who was killed on Tuesday might have interested me greatly as an embroiderer, but as a victim, not at all. What do you see in me, or miss in me, that you should drag me into an atmosphere of low-down crime?"

"Nothing, Miss Strange. You are by nature, as well as by breeding, very far removed from everything of the kind. But you will allow me to suggest that no crime is low-down which makes imperative demand upon the intellect and intuitive sense of its investigator. Only the most delicate touch can feel and hold the thread I've just spoken of, and you have the most delicate touch I know."

"Do not attempt to flatter me. I have no fancy for handling befouled spider webs. Besides, if I had—if such elusive filaments fascinated me—how could I, well-known in person and name, enter upon such a scene without prejudice to our mutual compact?"

"Miss Strange"—she had reseated herself, but so far he had failed to follow her example (an ignoring of the subtle hint that her interest might yet be caught, which seemed to annoy her a trifle),

"I should not even have suggested such a possibility had I not seen a way of introducing you there without risk to your position or mine. Among the boxes piled upon Mrs. Doolittle's table—boxes of finished work, most of them addressed and ready for delivery— was one on which could be seen the name of—shall I mention it?"

"Not mine? You don't mean mine? That would be too odd— too ridiculously odd. I should not understand a coincidence of that kind; no, I should not, notwithstanding the fact that I have lately sent out such work to be done."

"Yet it was your name, very clearly and precisely written—your whole name, Miss Strange. I saw and read it myself."

"But I gave the order to Madame Pirot on Fifth Avenue. How came my things to be found in the house of this woman of whose horrible death we have been talking?"

"Did you suppose that Madame Pirot did such work with her own hands?—or even had it done in her own establishment? Mrs. Doolittle was universally employed. She worked for a dozen firms. You will find the biggest names on most of her packages. But on this one—I allude to the one addressed to you—there was more to be seen than the name. These words were written on it in another hand. Send without opening. This struck the police as suspicious; sufficiently so, at least, for them to desire your presence at the house as soon as you can make it convenient."

"To open the box?"

"Exactly."

The curl of Miss Strange's disdainful lip was a sight to see.

"You wrote those words yourself," she coolly observed. "While someone's back was turned, you whipped out your pencil and—"

"Resorted to a very pardonable subterfuge highly conducive to the public's good. But never mind that. Will you go?"

Miss Strange became suddenly demure.

"I suppose I must," she grudgingly conceded. "However obtained, a summons from the police cannot be ignored even by Peter Strange's daughter."

Another man might have displayed his triumph by smile or gesture; but this one had learned his role too well. He simply said:

"Very good. Shall it be at once? I have a taxi at the door."

But she failed to see the necessity of any such hurry. With sudden dignity she replied:

"That won't do. If I go to this house it must be under suitable conditions. I shall have to ask my brother to accompany me."

"Your brother!"

"Oh, he's safe. He—he knows."

"Your brother knows?" Her visitor, with less control than usual, betrayed very openly his uneasiness.

"He does and—approves. But that's not what interests us now, only so far as it makes it possible for me to go with propriety to that dreadful house."

A formal bow from the other and the words:

"They may expect you, then. Can you say when?"

"Within the next hour. But it will be a useless concession on my part," she pettishly complained. "A place that has been gone over by a dozen detectives is apt to be brushed clean of its cobwebs, even if such ever existed."

"That's the difficulty," he acknowledged; and did not dare to add another word; she was at that particular moment so very much the great lady, and so little his confidential agent. He might have been less impressed, however, by this sudden assumption of manner, had he been so fortunate as to have seen how she employed the three quarters of an hour's delay for which she had asked.

She read those neglected newspapers, especially the one containing the following highly coloured narration of this ghastly crime:

"A door ajar—an empty hall—a line of sinister looking blotches marking a guilty step diagonally across the flagging—silence—and an unmistakable odour repugnant to all humanity,—such were the indications which met the eyes of Officer O'Leary on his first round last night, and led to the discovery of a murder which will long thrill the city by its mystery and horror.

"Both the house and the victim are well known." Here followed a description of the same and of Mrs. Doolittle's manner of life in her ancient home, which Violet hurriedly passed over to come to the following:

"As far as one can judge from appearances, the crime happened in this wise: Mrs. Doolittle had been in her kitchen, as the tea-kettle found singing on the stove goes to prove, and was coming back through her bedroom, when the wretch, who had stolen in by the front door which, to save steps, she was unfortunately in the habit of leaving on the latch till all possibility of customers for the day was over, sprang upon her from behind and dealt her a swinging blow with the poker he had caught up from the hearthstone.

"Whether the struggle which ensued followed immediately upon this first attack or came later, it will take medical experts to determine. But, whenever it did occur, the fierceness of its character is shown by the grip taken upon her throat and the traces of blood which are to be seen all over the house. If the wretch had lugged her into her workroom and thence to the kitchen, and thence back to the spot of first assault, the evidences could not have been more ghastly. Bits of her clothing torn off by a ruthless hand, lay scattered over all these floors. In her bedroom, where she finally breathed her last, there could be seen mingled with these a number of large but worthless glass beads; and close against one of the base-boards, the string which had held them, as shown by the few remaining beads still clinging to it. If in pulling the string from her neck he had hoped to light upon some valuable booty, his fury at his disappointment is evident. You can almost see the frenzy with which he flung the would-be necklace at the wall, and kicked about and stamped upon its rapidly rolling beads.

"Booty! That was what he was after; to find and carry away the poor needlewoman's supposed hoardings. If the scene baffles description—if, as some believe, he dragged her yet living from spot to spot, demanding information as to her places of concealment under threat of repeated blows, and, finally baffled, dealt the finishing stroke and proceeded on the search alone, no greater devastation could have taken place in this poor woman's house or effects. Yet such was his precaution and care for himself that he left no finger-print behind him nor any other token which could lead to personal identification. Even though his footsteps could be traced in much the order I have mentioned, they were of so indeterminate and shapeless a character as to convey little to the intelligence of the investigator.

"That these smears (they could not be called footprints) not only crossed the hall but appeared in more than one place on the stair-case proves that he did not confine his search to the lower storey; and perhaps one of the most interesting features of the case lies in the indications given by these marks of the raging course he took through these upper rooms. As the accompanying diagram will show he went first into the large front chamber, thence to the rear where we find two rooms, one unfinished and filled with accumu-lated stuff most of which he left lying loose upon the floor, and the other plastered, and containing a window opening upon an alley-way at the side, but empty of all furniture and without even a car-pet on the bare boards.

"Why he should have entered the latter place, and why, having entered he should have crossed to the window, will be plain to those who have studied the conditions. The front chamber win-dows were tightly shuttered, the attic ones cumbered with boxes and shielded from approach by old bureaus and discarded chairs. This one only was free and, although darkened by the proximity of the house neighbouring it across the alley, was the only spot on the storey where sufficient light could be had at this late hour for the examination of any object of whose value he was doubtful. That he had come across such an object and had brought it to this win-dow for some such purpose is very satisfactorily demonstrated by the discovery of a worn out wallet of ancient make lying on the floor directly in front of this window—a proof of his cupidity but also proof of his ill-luck. For this wallet, when lifted and opened, was found to contain two hundred or more dollars in old bills, which, if not the full hoard of their industrious owner, was certainly worth the taking by one who had risked his neck for the sole purpose of theft.

"This wallet, and the flight of the murderer without it, give to this affair, otherwise simply brutal, a dramatic interest which will be appreciated not only by the very able detectives already hot upon the chase, but by all other inquiring minds anxious to solve a mystery of which so estimable a woman has been the unfortunate victim. A problem is presented to the police—"

There Violet stopped.

When, not long after, the superb limousine of Peter Strange stopped before the little house in Seventeenth Street, it caused a veritable sensation, not only in the curiosity-mongers lingering on the sidewalk, but to the two persons within—the officer on guard and a belated reporter.

Though dressed in her plainest suit, Violet Strange looked much too fashionable and far too young and thoughtless to be observed, without emotion, entering a scene of hideous and brutal crime. Even the young man who accompanied her promised to bring a most incongruous element into this atmosphere of guilt and horror, and, as the detective on guard whispered to the man beside him, might much better have been left behind in the car.

But Violet was great for the proprieties and young Arthur followed her in.

Her entrance was a coup du theatre. She had lifted her veil in crossing the sidewalk and her interesting features and general air of timidity were very fetching. As the man holding open the door noted the impression made upon his companion, he muttered with sly facetiousness:

"You think you'll show her nothing; but I'm ready to bet a fiver that she'll want to see it all and that you'll show it to her."

The detective's grin was expressive, notwithstanding the shrug with which he tried to carry it off.

And Violet? The hall into which she now stepped from the most vivid sunlight had never been considered even in its palmiest days as possessing cheer even of the stately kind. The ghastly green light infused through it by the coloured glass on either side of the doorway seemed to promise yet more dismal things beyond.

"Must I go in there?" she asked, pointing, with an admirable simulation of nervous excitement, to a half-shut door at her left. "Is there where it happened? Arthur, do you suppose that there is where it happened?"

"No, no, Miss," the officer made haste to assure her. "If you are Miss Strange" (Violet bowed), "I need hardly say that the woman was struck in her bedroom. The door beside you leads into the parlour, or as she would have called it, her work-room. You needn't be afraid of going in there. You will see nothing but the disorder of her boxes. They were pretty well pulled about. Not all of them though," he added, watching her as closely as the dim light permitted.

"There is one which gives no sign of having been tampered with. It was done up in wrapping paper and is addressed to you, which in itself would not have seemed worthy of our attention had not these lines been scribbled on it in a man's handwriting: 'Send without opening.'"

"How odd!" exclaimed the little minx with widely opened eyes and an air of guileless innocence. "Whatever can it mean? Nothing serious I am sure, for the woman did not even know me. She was employed to do this work by Madame Pirot."

"Didn't you know that it was to be done here?"

"No. I thought Madame Pirot's own girls did her embroidery for her."

"So that you were surprised—"

"Wasn't I!"

"To get our message."

"I didn't know what to make of it."

The earnest, half-injured look with which she uttered this disclaimer, did its appointed work. The detective accepted her for what she seemed and, oblivious to the reporter's satirical gesture, crossed to the work-room door, which he threw wide open with the remark:

"I should be glad to have you open that box in our presence. It is undoubtedly all right, but we wish to be sure. You know what the box should contain?"

"Oh, yes, indeed; pillow-cases and sheets, with a big S embroidered on them."

"Very well. Shall I undo the string for you?"

"I shall be much obliged," said she, her eye flashing quickly about the room before settling down upon the knot he was deftly loosening.

Her brother, gazing indifferently in from the doorway, hardly noticed this look; but the reporter at his back did, though he failed to detect its penetrating quality.

"Your name is on the other side," observed the detective as he drew away the string and turned the package over.

The smile which just lifted the corner of her lips was not in answer to this remark, but to her recognition of her employer's handwriting in the words under her name: Send without opening. She had not misjudged him.

"The cover you may like to take off yourself," suggested the officer, as he lifted the box out of its wrapper.

"Oh, I don't mind. There's nothing to be ashamed of in embroidered linen. Or perhaps that is not what you are looking for?"

No one answered. All were busy watching her whip off the lid and lift out the pile of sheets and pillow-cases with which the box was closely packed.

"Shall I unfold them?" she asked.

The detective nodded.

Taking out the topmost sheet, she shook it open. Then the next and the next till she reached the bottom of the box. Nothing of a criminating nature came to light. The box as well as its contents was without mystery of any kind. This was not an unexpected result of

course, but the smile with which she began to refold the pieces
and throw them back into the box, revealed one of her dimples
which was almost as dangerous to the casual observer as when it
revealed both.

"There," she exclaimed, "you see! Household linen exactly as I
said. Now may I go home?"

"Certainly, Miss Strange."

The detective stole a sly glance at the reporter. She was not going in for the horrors then after all.

But the reporter abated nothing of his knowing air, for while
she spoke of going, she made no move towards doing so, but continued to look about the room till her glances finally settled on a
long dark curtain shutting off an adjoining room.

"There's where she lies, I suppose," she feelingly exclaimed. "And
not one of you knows who killed her. Somehow, I cannot understand that. Why don't you know when that's what you're hired
for?" The innocence with which she uttered this was astonishing.
The detective began to look sheepish and the reporter turned aside
to hide his smile. Whether in another moment either would have
spoken no one can say, for, with a mock consciousness of having
said something foolish, she caught up her parasol from the table and
made a start for the door.

But of course she looked back.

"I was wondering," she recommenced, with a half wistful, half
speculative air, "whether I should ask to have a peep at the place
where it all happened."

The reporter chuckled behind the pencil-end he was chewing, but
the officer maintained his solemn air, for which act of self-restraint
he was undoubtedly grateful when in another minute she gave a
quick impulsive shudder not altogether assumed, and vehemently
added: "But I couldn't stand the sight; no, I couldn't! I'm an awful
coward when it comes to things like that. Nothing in all the world
would induce me to look at the woman or her room. But I should
like"—here both her dimples came into play though she could not

be said exactly to smile—"just one little look upstairs, where he went poking about so long without any fear it seems of being interrupted. Ever since I've read about it I have seen, in my mind, a picture of his wicked figure sneaking from room to room, tearing open drawers and flinging out the contents of closets just to find a little money—a little, little money! I shall not sleep to-night just for wondering how those high up attic rooms really look."

Who could dream that back of this display of mingled childishness and audacity there lay hidden purpose, intellect, and a keen knowledge of human nature. Not the two men who listened to this seemingly irresponsible chatter. To them she was a child to be humoured and humour her they did. The dainty feet which had already found their way to that gloomy staircase were allowed to ascend, followed it is true by those of the officer who did not dare to smile back at the reporter because of the brother's watchful and none too conciliatory eye.

At the stair head she paused to look back.

"I don't see those horrible marks which the papers describe as running all along the lower hall and up these stairs."

"No, Miss Strange; they have gradually been rubbed out, but you will find some still showing on these upper floors."

"Oh! oh! where? You frighten me—frighten me horribly! But—but—if you don't mind, I should like to see."

Why should not a man on a tedious job amuse himself? Piloting her over to the small room in the rear, he pointed down at the boards. She gave one look and then stepped gingerly in.

"Just look!" she cried; "a whole string of marks going straight from door to window. They have no shape, have they,—just blotches? I wonder why one of them is so much larger than the rest?"

This was no new question. It was one which everybody who went into the room was sure to ask, there was such a difference in the size and appearance of the mark nearest the window. The reason—well, minds were divided about that, and no one had a satisfactory theory. The detective therefore kept discreetly silent.

This did not seem to offend Miss Strange. On the contrary it gave her an opportunity to babble away to her heart's content.

"One, two, three, four, five, six," she counted, with a shudder at every count. "And one of them bigger than the others." She might have added, "It is the trail of one foot, and strangely, intermingled at that," but she did not, though we may be quite sure that she noted the fact. "And where, just where did the old wallet fall? Here? or here?"

She had moved as she spoke, so that in uttering the last "here," she stood directly before the window. The surprise she received there nearly made her forget the part she was playing. From the character of the light in the room, she had expected, on looking out, to confront a near-by wall, but not a window in that wall. Yet that was what she saw directly facing her from across the old-fashioned alley separating this house from its neighbour; twelve unshuttered and uncurtained panes through which she caught a darkened view of a room almost as forlorn and devoid of furniture as the one in which she then stood.

When quite sure of herself, she let a certain portion of her surprise appear.

"Why, look!" she cried, "if you can't see right in next door! What a lonesome-looking place! From its desolate appearance I should think the house quite empty."

"And it is. That's the old Shaffer homestead. It's been empty for a year."

"Oh, empty!" And she turned away, with the most inconsequent air in the world, crying out as her name rang up the stair, "There's Arthur calling. I suppose he thinks I've been here long enough. I'm sure I'm very much obliged to you, officer. I really shouldn't have slept a wink to-night, if I hadn't been given a peep at these rooms, which I had imagined so different." And with one additional glance over her shoulder, that seemed to penetrate both windows and the desolate space beyond, she ran quickly out and down in response to her brother's reiterated call.

"Drive quickly!—as quickly as the law allows, to Hiram Brown's office in Duane Street."

Arrived at the address named, she went in alone to see Mr. Brown. He was her father's lawyer and a family friend.

Hardly waiting for his affectionate greeting, she cried out quickly. "Tell me how I can learn anything about the old Shaffer house in Seventeenth Street. Now, don't look so surprised. I have very good reasons for my request and—and—I'm in an awful hurry."

"But—"

"I know, I know; there's been a dreadful tragedy next door to it; but it's about the Shaffer house itself I want some information. Has it an agent, a—"

"Of course it has an agent, and here is his name."

Mr. Brown presented her with a card on which he had hastily written both name and address.

She thanked him, dropped him a mocking curtsey full of charm, whispered "Don't tell father," and was gone.

Her manner to the man she next interviewed was very different. As soon as she saw him she subsided into her usual society manner. With just a touch of the conceit of the successful debutante, she announced herself as Miss Strange of Seventy-second Street. Her business with him was in regard to the possible renting of the Shaffer house. She had an old lady friend who was desirous of living downtown.

In passing through Seventeenth Street, she had noticed that the old Shaffer house was standing empty and had been immediately struck with the advantages it possessed for her elderly friend's occupancy. Could it be that the house was for rent? There was no sign on it to that effect, but—etc.

His answer left her nothing to hope for.

"It is going to be torn down," he said.

"Oh, what a pity!" she exclaimed. "Real colonial, isn't it! I wish I could see the rooms inside before it is disturbed. Such doors and such dear old-fashioned mantelpieces as it must have! I just dote on the colonial. It brings up such pictures of the old days; weddings, you know, and parties;—all so different from ours and so much more interesting."

Is it the chance shot that tells? Sometimes. Violet had no especial intention in what she said save as a prelude to a pending request, but nothing could have served her purpose better than that one word, wedding. The agent laughed and giving her his first indulgent look, remarked genially:

"Romance is not confined to those ancient times. If you were to enter that house to-day you would come across evidences of a wedding as romantic as any which ever took place in all the seventy odd years of its existence. A man and a woman were married there day before yesterday who did their first courting under its roof forty years ago. He has been married twice and she once in the interval; but the old love held firm and now at the age of sixty and over they have come together to finish their days in peace and happiness. Or so we will hope."

"Married! married in that house and on the day that—"

She caught herself up in time. He did not notice the break.

"Yes, in memory of those old days of courtship, I suppose. They came here about five, got the keys, drove off, went through the ceremony in that empty house, returned the keys to me in my own apartment, took the steamer for Naples, and were on the sea before midnight. Do you not call that quick work as well as highly romantic?"

"Very." Miss Strange's cheek had paled. It was apt to when she was greatly excited. "But I don't understand," she added, the moment after. "How could they do this and nobody know about it? I should have thought it would have got into the papers."

"They are quiet people. I don't think they told their best friends. A simple announcement in the next day's journals testified to the fact of their marriage, but that was all. I would not have felt at liberty to mention the circumstances myself, if the parties were not well on their way to Europe."

"Oh, how glad I am that you did tell me! Such a story of constancy and the hold which old associations have upon sensitive minds! But—"

"Why, Miss? What's the matter? You look very much disturbed."

"Don't you remember? Haven't you thought? Something else happened that very day and almost at the same time on that block. Something very dreadful—"

"Mrs. Doolittle's murder?"

"Yes. It was as near as next door, wasn't it? Oh, if this happy couple had known—"

"But fortunately they didn't. Nor are they likely to, till they reach the other side. You needn't fear that their honeymoon will be spoiled that way."

"But they may have heard something or seen something before leaving the street. Did you notice how the gentleman looked when he returned you the keys?"

"I did, and there was no cloud on his satisfaction."

"Oh, how you relieve me!" One—two dimples made their appearance in Miss Strange's fresh, young cheeks. "Well! I wish them joy. Do you mind telling me their names? I cannot think of them as actual persons without knowing their names."

"The gentleman was Constantin Amidon; the lady, Marian Shaffer. You will have to think of them now as Mr. and Mrs. Amidon."

"And I will. Thank you, Mr. Hutton, thank you very much. Next to the pleasure of getting the house for my friend, is that of hearing this charming bit of news its connection."

She held out her hand and, as he took it, remarked:

"They must have had a clergyman and witnesses."

"Undoubtedly."

"I wish I had been one of the witnesses," she sighed sentimentally.

"They were two old men."

"Oh, no! Don't tell me that."

"Fogies; nothing less."

"But the clergyman? He must have been young. Surely there was some one there capable of appreciating the situation?"

"I can't say about that; I did not see the clergyman."

"Oh, well! it doesn't matter." Miss Strange's manner was as non-chalant as it was charming. "We will think of him as being very young."

And with a merry toss of her head she flitted away.

But she sobered very rapidly upon entering her limousine.

"Hello!"

"Ah, is that you?"

"Yes, I want a Marconi sent."

"A Marconi?"

"Yes, to the *Cretic*, which left dock the very night in which we are so deeply interested."

"Good. Whom to? The Captain?"

"No, to a Mrs. Constantin Amidon. But first be sure there is such a passenger."

"Mrs.! What idea have you there?"

"Excuse my not stating over the telephone. The message is to be to this effect. Did she at any time immediately before or after her marriage to Mr. Amidon get a glimpse of any one in the adjoining house? No remarks, please. I use the telephone because I am not ready to explain myself. If she did, let her send a written description to you of that person as soon as she reaches the Azores."

"You surprise me. May I not call or hope for a line from you early to-morrow?"

"I shall be busy till you get your answer."

He hung up the receiver. He recognized the resolute tone.

But the time came when the pending explanation was fully given to him. An answer had been returned from the steamer, favourable to Violet's hopes. Mrs. Amidon had seen such a person and would send a full description of the same at the first opportunity. It was news to fill Violet's heart with pride; the filament of a clue which had led to this great result had been so nearly invisible and had felt so like nothing in her grasp.

To her employer she described it as follows:

"When I hear or read of a case which contains any baffling features, I am apt to feel some hidden chord in my nature thrill to one fact in it and not to any of the others. In this case the single fact which appealed to my imagination was the dropping of the stolen wallet in that upstairs room. Why did the guilty man drop it? and why, having dropped it, did he not pick it up again? but one answer seemed possible. He had heard or seen something at the spot where it fell which not only alarmed him but sent him in flight from the house."

"Very good; and did you settle to your own mind the nature of that sound or that sight?"

"I did." Her manner was strangely businesslike. No show of dimples now. "Satisfied that if any possibility remained of my ever doing this, it would have to be on the exact place of this occurrence or not at all, I embraced your suggestion and visited the house."

"And that room no doubt."

"And that room. Women, somehow, seem to manage such things."

"So I've noticed, Miss Strange. And what was the result of your visit? What did you discover there?"

"This: that one of the blood spots marking the criminal's steps through the room was decidedly more pronounced than the rest; and, what was even more important, that the window out of which I was looking had its counterpart in the house on the opposite side of the alley. In gazing through the one I was gazing through the other; and not only that, but into the darkened area of the room beyond. Instantly I saw how the latter fact might be made to explain the former one. But before I say how, let me ask if it is quite settled among you that the smears on the floor and stairs mark the passage of the criminal's footsteps!"

"Certainly; and very bloody feet they must have been too. His shoes—or rather his one shoe—for the proof is plain that only the right one left its mark—must have become thoroughly saturated to carry its traces so far."

"Do you think that any amount of saturation would have done this? Or, if you are not ready to agree to that, that a shoe so covered with blood could have failed to leave behind it some hint of its shape, some imprint, however faint, of heel or toe? But nowhere did it do this. We see a smear—and that is all."

"You are right, Miss Strange; you are always right. And what do you gather from this?" She looked to see how much he expected from her, and, meeting an eye not quite as free from ironic suggestion as his words had led her to expect, faltered a little as she proceeded to say:

"My opinion is a girl's opinion, but such as it is you have the right to have it. From the indications mentioned I could draw but this conclusion: that the blood which accompanied the criminal's footsteps was not carried through the house by his shoes;—he wore no shoes; he did not even wear stockings; probably he had none. For reasons which appealed to his judgment, he went about his wicked work barefoot; and it was the blood from his own veins and not from those of his victim which made the trail we have followed with so much interest. Do you forget those broken beads;—how he kicked them about and stamped upon them in his fury? One of them pierced the ball of his foot, and that so sharply that it not only spurted blood but kept on bleeding with every step he took. Otherwise, the trail would have been lost after his passage up the stairs."

"Fine!" There was no irony in the bureau-chief's eye now. "You are progressing, Miss Strange. Allow me, I pray, to kiss your hand. It is a liberty I have never taken, but one which would greatly relieve my present stress of feeling."

She lifted her hand toward him, but it was in gesture, not in recognition of his homage.

"Thank you," said she, "but I claim no monopoly on deductions so simple as these. I have not the least doubt that not only yourself but every member of the force has made the same. But there is a little matter which may have escaped the police, may even have escaped you. To that I would now call your attention since through it I have been enabled, after a little necessary groping, to reach the open. You remember the one large blotch on the upper floor where the man dropped the wallet? That blotch, more or less commingled with a fainter one, possessed great significance for me from the first moment I saw it. How came his foot to bleed so much more profusely at that one spot than at any other? There could be but one answer: because here a surprise met him—a surprise so startling to him in his present state of mind, that he gave a quick spring backward, with the result that his wounded foot came down suddenly and forcibly instead of easily as in his previous wary tread. And what was the surprise? I made it my business to find out, and now I can tell you that it was the sight of a woman's face staring upon him from the neighbouring house which he had probably been told was empty. The shock disturbed his judgment. He saw his crime discovered—his guilty secret read, and fled in unreasoning panic. He might better have held on to his wits. It was this display of fear which led me to search after its cause, and consequently to discover that at this especial hour more than one person had been in the Shaffer house; that, in fact, a marriage had been celebrated there under circumstances as romantic as any we read of in books, and that this marriage, privately carried out, had been followed by an immediate voyage of the happy couple on one of the White Star steamers. With the rest you are conversant. I do not need to say anything about what has followed the sending of that Marconi."

"But I am going to say something about your work in this matter, Miss Strange. The big detectives about here will have to look sharp if—"

"Don't, please! Not yet." A smile softened the asperity of this interruption. "The man has yet to be caught and identified. Till that is done I cannot enjoy any one's congratulations. And you will see that all this may not be so easy. If no one happened to meet the desperate wretch before he had an opportunity to retie his shoe-laces, there will be little for you or even for the police to go upon but his wounded foot, his undoubtedly carefully prepared alibi, and later, a woman's confused description of a face seen but for a moment only and that under a personal excitement precluding minute attention. I should not be surprised if the whole thing came to nothing."

But it did not. As soon as the description was received from Mrs. Amidon (a description, by the way, which was unusually clear and precise, owing to the peculiar and contradictory features of the man), the police were able to recognize him among the many suspects always under their eye. Arrested, he pleaded, just as Miss Strange had foretold, an alibi of a seemingly unimpeachable character; but neither it, nor the plausible explanation with which he endeavoured to account for a freshly healed scar amid the callouses of his right foot, could stand before Mrs. Amidon's unequivocal testimony that he was the same man she had seen in Mrs. Doolittle's upper room on the afternoon of her own happiness and of that poor woman's murder. The moment when, at his trial, the two faces again confronted each other across a space no wider than that which had separated them on the dread occasion in Seventeenth Street, is said to have been one of the most dramatic in the annals of that ancient court room.

✳

Acknowledgments

FIRST, MY THANKS TO George Gibson, my extraordinary editor and publisher at Walker & Company; his assistants, Margaret Maloney and Lea Beresford; and the great team at Walker: production editor Nate Knaebel, copy editor Steve Boldt, jacket designer Mark Melnick, and publicist Jonathan Kroberger.

My thanks to various scholars who contributed ideas for *The Dead Witness* or critiqued parts of my earlier anthologies in ways that later helped with this book: Gwen Enstam at the Association for Scottish Literary Studies in Edinburgh, Elizabeth Carolyn Miller at the University of California, Davis, Caroline Elizabeth McCracken-Flesher at the University of Wyoming, and Donna Heddle at Orkney College in Scotland.

My thanks to Olivia Wierum, who helped me proof, and to fellow writer Isa Wierum. Several other people generously provided sources, suggested authors, discussed the issues, or otherwise assisted: Laura Carpenter, Michael Dirda, Dennis Drabelle, Jon Erickson, Jerry Felton, Michele Flynn, Collier Goodlett, Leslie S. Klinger, Robert Majcher, Greg Nemec, Otto Penzler, Michele B. Slung, John Spurlock, Art Taylor, Mark Wait, Carey Wallace, Alana White, Robin and Craig Wierum, and Nancy Wolff. Once again Karissa Kilgore proved invaluable. Perpetual gratitude to the staff of the Greensburg Hempfield Area Library, especially interlibrary loan book detective Linda Matey, library director Cesare Muccari, and Diana Ciabattoni.

First and last, in this book and many others, I thank the amazing Laura Sloan Patterson—scholar, wit, pal, and wife.

Bibliography and Suggested Further Reading

THIS BIBLIOGRAPHY INCLUDES ALL sources cited in, or useful in the writing of, this book's introductory essay or its individual story introductions. It also includes selected biographies, general introductions to the topics of detective fiction or specialized categories such as female detectives, a handful of recommended original volumes of stories featuring detectives reluctantly omitted from *The Dead Witness*, and other commentaries on particular authors and themes. It excludes works by those authors whose stories or excerpts appear in this anthology and thus receive attention in the biographical note that introduces their contribution. Web sites appear separately at the end.

Ackroyd, Peter. *Dickens*. New York: HarperCollins, 1990.

Allen, Grant. *Miss Cayley's Adventures*. London: Putnam's Sons, 1899.

Auden, W. H. "The Guilty Vicarage: Notes on the Detective Story, by an Addict." *Harper's*, May 1948.

Bargainnier, Earl F., ed. *10 Women of Mystery*. Bowling Green, OH: Bowling Green State University Popular Press, 1981.

Beckson, Karl. *London in the 1890s: A Cultural History*. New York: W. W. Norton, 1992.

Bentley, Nicolas. *The Victorian Scene: 1837–1901*. London: Weidenfeld and Nicolson, 1968.

Bodkin, M. McDonnell. *Dora Myrl, the Lady Detective.* London: Chatto & Windus, 1900.

Chesterton, G. K. *A Century of Detective Stories.* London: Hutchinson, 1935.

Clodd, Edward. *Grant Allen: A Memoir.* London: Grant Richards, 1900.

Corey, Melinda, and George Ochoa. *The Encyclopedia of the Victorian World.* New York: Henry Holt, 1996.

Cornillon, John. "A Case for Violet Strange." In *Images of Women in Fiction: Feminist Perspectives.* Bowling Green, OH: Bowling Green University Popular Press, 1972. A brief survey of Anna Katharine Green's socialite detective Violet Strange.

Cunningham, Gail. *The New Woman and the Victorian Novel.* New York: Barnes & Noble, 1979.

Dictionary of Literary Biography. Various volumes, and the numerous sources listed therein. Consult under each author's name.

Ensor, Sir Robert. *England 1870–1914.* London: Oxford University Press, 1936.

Flanders, Judith. *The Victorian House: Domestic Life from Childbirth to Deathbed.* London: HarperCollins, 2003.

Forrester, Andrew, Jr. *The Female Detective.* London: Ward & Lock, 1864. Featuring detective Mrs. Paschal, by the pseudonymous author of "Arrested on Suspicion."

Fortune, Mary. *The Detectives' Album.* Edited by Lucy Sussex. Sauk City, WI: Broken Silicon Dispatch Box, 2003. Stories by the author of "The Dead Witness."

Frank, Lawrence. "'The Murders in the Rue Morgue': Edgar Allan Poe's Evolutionary Reverie." *Nineteenth-Century Literature* 50, no. 2 (September 1995).

Garforth, John. *A Day in the Life of a Victorian Policeman.* London: Allen Unwin, 1974.

Ginzburg, Carlo. "Morelli, Freud, and Sherlock Holmes: Clues and Scientific Method." *History Workshop Journal* 9, no. 1 (1980).

Hadfield, John. *Victorian Delights.* London: Herbert Press, 1987.

Haining, Peter, ed. *Hunted Down: The Detective Stories of Charles Dickens*. London: Peter Owen, 1996.

Haycraft, Howard. *Murder for Pleasure: The Life and Times of the Detective Story*. 1941, revised 1951. Reprint, New York: Carroll & Graf, 1984.

Hayward, W. S. *Revelations of a Lady Detective*. London: George Vickers, 1864.

Heron-Maxwell, Beatrice. *The Adventures of a Lady Pearl-Broker*. London: Century Press, 1899.

Hume, Fergus. *Hagar of the Pawn-shop*. London: Skeffington, 1899.

———. *The Mystery of a Hansom Cab*. Melbourne: Fergus Hume, 1866.

Kaplan, Fred. *Dickens: A Biography*. New York: William Morrow, 1988.

Keese, William L. *William E. Burton: Actor, Author, and Manager, with Recollections of His Performances*. New York: G. P. Putnam's Sons/The Knickerbocker Press, 1885. About the author of "The Secret Cell."

Keppel, Robert D. "The Jack the Ripper Murders: A *Modus Operandi* and Signature Analysis of the 1888–1891 Whitechapel Murders." *Journal of Investigative Psychology and Offender Profiling* 2 (2005).

Kestner, Joseph A. *The Edwardian Detective, 1901–1915*. Aldershot: Ashgate, 2000.

———. *Sherlock's Sisters: The British Female Detective, 1864–1913*. Aldershot: Ashgate, 2003. More survey than analysis, this comprehensive volume tours female investigators, professional and unofficial, throughout this decisive period.

Klein, Kathleen Gregory. *The Woman Detective: Gender and Genre*. 2nd ed. Urbana and Chicago: University of Illinois Press, 1995. See especially chapter 3, "Britain's Turn-of-the-Century 'Lady Detective': 1891–1910," and chapter 4, "The Lady Detective's Yankee Cousin: 1906–15."

Knight, Stephen. *Crime Fiction, 1800–2000*. London: Palgrave Macmillan, 2003.

————, ed. *Dead Witness: Best Australian Mystery Stories.* Victoria: Penguin Australia, 1989. See especially the first story, "Dead Witness," by W. W. (Mary Fortune).

La Cour, Tage, and Harald Mogensen. *The Murder Book: An Illustrated History of the Detective Story.* New York: Herder & Herder, 1971.

Lock, Joan. *The British Policewoman: Her Story.* London: Robert Hale, 1979.

Maida, Patricia D. *Mother of Detective Fiction: The Life and Works of Anna Katharine Green.* Bowling Green, OH: Bowling Green State University Popular Press, 1989. About the creator of Violet Strange, Ebenezer Gryce, and Amelia Butterfield.

Marcus, Laura, with Chris Willis. *12 Women Detective Stories.* Oxford: Oxford University Press, 1997. See Marcus's introduction.

Matz, B. W. "Through Whitechapel with Dickens." *The Dickensian* 1, no. 9 (September 1905).

Meade, L. T., and Robert Eustace. *The Detections of Miss Florence Cusack.* Edited by Jack Adrian. 1899–1900. Reprint, Shelburne, ON: Battered Silicon Dispatch Box, 1998.

Miller, Elizabeth Carolyn. *Framed: The New Woman Criminal in British Culture at the Fin de Siècle.* Ann Arbor: University of Michigan Press, 2008.

————. "Trouble with She-Dicks: Private Eyes and Public Women in *The Adventures of Loveday Brooke, Lady Detective.*" *Victorian Literature and Culture* 33 (2005): 47–65.

Murch, Alma E. *The Development of the Detective Novel.* Westport, CT: Greenwood, 1981.

Nevins, Francis M. "From Darwinian to Biblical Lawyering: The Stories of Melville Davisson Post." *Legal Studies Forum* 18, no. 2 (1994). About the creator of Uncle Abner.

Nickerson, Catherine Ross. *The Web of Iniquity: Early Detective Fiction by American Women.* Chapel Hill, NC: Duke University Press, 1998.

Norton, Charles A. *Melville Davisson Post: Man of Many Mysteries.* Bowling Green, OH: Bowling Green University Popular Press, 1974. A biography of the creator of Uncle Abner.

Panek, LeRoy Lad. *The Origins of the American Detective Story*. Jefferson, NC: McFarland, 2006.

Queen, Ellery. *101 Years Entertainment: The Great Detective Stories, 1841–1941*. New York: Modern Library, 1941.

Sayers, Dorothy L. *Introduction to Omnibus of Crime*. New York: Payson & Clarke, 1929.

Sims, Michael, ed. *Arsène Lupin, Gentleman-Thief*, by Maurice Leblanc. New York: Penguin Classics, 2007. See introduction.

———. Introduction to *The Leavenworth Case*, by Anna Katharine Green. New York: Penguin Classics, 2010.

———, ed. *The Penguin Book of Gaslight Crime: Con Artists, Burglars, Rogues, and Scoundrels from the Time of Sherlock Holmes*. New York: Penguin Classics, 2009. See introduction and story introductions.

———, ed. *The Penguin Book of Victorian Women in Crime: Forgotten Cops and Private Eyes from the Time of Sherlock Holmes*. New York: Penguin Classics, 2011.

Slung, Michele B., ed. *Crime on Her Mind: Fifteen Stories of Female Sleuths from the Victorian Era to the Forties*. New York: Pantheon, 1975. See Slung's introduction.

Stashower, Daniel. *The Beautiful Cigar Girl: Mary Rogers, Edgar Allan Poe, and the Invention of Murder*. New York: Dutton, 2006.

Steinbrunner, Chris, and Otto Penzler. *Encyclopedia of Mystery and Detection*. New York: McGraw-Hill, 1976. Indexed under both author's name and detective's name.

Summerscale, Kate. *The Suspicions of Mr. Whicher: A Shocking Murder and the Undoing of a Great Victorian Detective*. New York: Walker, 2008.

Van Dover, J. K., and John F. Webb. *Isn't Justice Always Unfair? The Detective in Southern Literature*. Bowling Green, OH: Bowling Green State University Popular Press, 1996. This volume covers many detectives; those relevant to *The Dead Witness* include Pudd'nhead Wilson and Uncle Abner.

Watson, Colin. *Snobbery with Violence: English Crime Stories and Their Audience*. Rev. ed. London: Macmillan, 1979.

Winn, Dilys. *Murderess Ink: The Better Half of the Mystery.* New York: Workman, 1979.

———. *Murder Ink: The Mystery Reader's Companion.* New York: Workman, 1977.

Young, Arlene. " 'Petticoated Police': Propriety and the Lady Detective in Victorian Fiction." *Clues: A Journal of Detection* 26:3.

Web Sites

classiccrimefiction.com/history-articles.htm

gadetection.pbwiki.com

motherofmystery.com/articles/plots

mysterylist.com

philsp.com/homeville/fmi/ostart.htm#TOC

wilkiecollins.com